TOO DAMN RICH

JUDITH GOULD

TOO DAMN RICH

A DUTTON BOOK

DUTTON

Published by the Penguin Group
Penguin Books USA Inc., 375 Hudson Street, New York, New York 10014, U.S.A.
Penguin Books Ltd, 27 Wrights Lane, London, W8 5TZ, England
Penguin Books Australia Ltd, Ringwood, Victoria, Australia
Penguin Books Canada Ltd, 10 Alcorn Avenue, Toronto, Ontario, Canada M4V 3B2
Penguin Books (N. Z.) Ltd, 182–190 Wairau Road, Auckland 10, New Zealand

Penguin Books Ltd, Registered Offices:
Harmondsworth, Middlesex, England

First published by Dutton, an imprint of Dutton Signet,
a division of Penguin Books USA Inc.
Distributed in Canada by McClelland & Stewart Inc.

First Printing, August, 1995
1   3   5   7   9   10   8   6   4   2

 REGISTERED TRADEMARK—MARCA REGISTRADA

LIBRARY OF CONGRESS CATALOGING-IN-PUBLICATION DATA

Gould, Judith.
Too damn rich / Judith Gould.
p.   cm.
ISBN 0-525-93665-3
I. Title.
PS3557.0867T66   1995
813'.54—dc20   95-9852
                                                        CIP

Printed in the United States of America
Set in Sabon and Shelley Allegro

Designed by Steven N. Stathakis

*This book is dedicated to
Phil and Louise ("Mama Mac") Henderson,
the ever assertive Nancy Austin,
and to the memories of
Kathryn Wheeler Gallaher
and
Gladys Allison*

"It is better to live rich,
than to die rich."

—BOSWELL, *Life of Johnson*

"No one should come to
New York unless he is
willing to be lucky."

—E. B. WHITE (1899–1985)

Once Upon a Time, In the City of London...

A man by the name of Charles Burghley established an auction business. The year was 1719 and His Majesty, King George I, was on the throne. Burghley dealt in silver and porcelains.

His company flourished.

In 1744, a bookseller named Samuel Baker decided to expand *his* business by turning to auctioneering. His enterprise, too, proved successful, although it was his nephew and successor, John Sotheby, who gave the company its legendary name.

In 1766, James Christie opened the doors to yet another auction house. Since he concentrated on selling pictures and furniture, and did not infringe upon Burghley's area of silver and porcelains, or Sotheby's of books, his venture also thrived.

For nearly two centuries, the three auction houses coexisted happily. When the contents of a major country house were sold, Christie's would send the libraries to Sotheby's, and relegate the silver and ceramics to Burghley's. And although nothing became of it, Christie's and Sotheby's actually considered merging, first in 1934, then in 1940, and again in 1947.

But by 1964 such harmony was a thing of the past. It began with Sotheby's acquisition of the Parke-Bernet Galleries in New York, which in a single stroke established it as the first truly international auction firm. In no time, Christie's and Burghley's had gained Manhattan footholds of their own and, like Sotheby's, began to expand operations to dozens of other cities around the globe.

Now, with the entire world's treasures as possible merchandise, competition between the three houses grew fierce. Each expanded voluminously and added departments and experts to handle furniture, art, rugs, books and manuscripts, wine, photographs, musical instruments, coins, arms and armor, and jewelry.

The age-old tradition of sharing the spoils became a relic of the past.

In the heyday of the eighties, with art prices skyrocketing, Burghley's, Christie's, and Sotheby's was each seeing between two and three billion dollars in annual sales—and reaping a hefty twenty percent profit in double-ended commissions from both sellers and buyers. Even with the softening of the art market in the recessionary nineties, when annual sales plunged a billion dollars or so, the profit at all three auction houses was still enormous.

Naturally, with such vast sums involved, the dowdy, genteel auction house went the way of the Edsel.

Auctioneering had entered the era of Big Business.

And that is where this story begins. , , ,

PROLOGUE

*T*he meeting took place in a remote seaside villa far from the outskirts of this teeming city of gamblers, prostitutes, thieves, and adventurers.

One person arrived by stolen car and used the front entrance.

The other came by sea and docked a stolen speedboat at the jetty out back.

Each was dressed in black, and wore a bulky jumpsuit, gloves, and shapeless hood. Thus, neither would recognize the other if they happened to run into each other by accident.

The same held true of their voices. For added protection, electronic distorters were strapped around their mouths, reducing their words to deep, robotic monotones.

There was safety in stealth, protection in remaining but a code-named entity.

As planned, their paths converged in a windowless marble ante-room, where the rheostat on the crystal chandelier was turned down to a weak glow. Even in the dimness of that shadow-strewn light, their eyes were invisible. For added anonymity, both wore black sunglasses under their hoods.

For a moment they stared at each other with wary respect. Each knew that the other was one of the two most dangerous individuals alive.

The taller one spoke first. "I shall require the ten best specialists in their field," the electronically distorted voice squawked monosyllabically. "I have a list here. Six are laying low. They will have to be found. Four that I know of are serving life sentences. They will need to be sprung. Do you think you can do it?"

"What is the timetable?" the other's identically distorted voice asked.

"There is none yet."

"Good." The hooded head nodded once, the gloved hand took the list, shone a penlight down it, and memorized the names. After a moment, a lighter flared and the list burned and was dropped, the charred remains shredded under a crepe heel. "I will need four months."

"You have it. The job could be soon after, or it might be a year or more from then. Our people will need safe houses and patience."

"And their incentives?"

"Ten million dollars each. After the job is completed."

There was a pause. "And mine?"

"One half share of the remainder."

"Which will be?"

"The same as I get. Approximately half a billion dollars. I take it you find that acceptable?"

The other hooded figure nodded.

"Good. We will meet again in exactly two months' time. I will get in touch by the usual method."

Before the first light of dawn, two "accidents" occurred at opposite ends of the island.

One involved a car which went out of control, hit a stone wall, and exploded upon impact. By the time the fire department arrived, it was but a furiously burning shell.

The other occurred almost simultaneously and involved a speedboat that rammed one of the docked hydrofoils which made the Macao–Hong Kong run. Again, a massive explosion and an enormous fireball rent the night.

Zhang Gu, the island's fire chief, was baffled after he visited the scene of each fire. His investigators and scuba divers had combed every square inch of both accident scenes, and had only come up with wreckage.

"It's impossible," Zhang Gu told Lin Zhu, the assistant fire chief.

"What is, sir?" Zhu asked.

"We have two major accidents, and yet not a shred of human bone or tissue."

"It could have been vandalism, sir."

"I suppose so," Gu sighed. "But I do not like it. Something smells of three-day-old fish."

"So do we continue our investigation?"

Zhang Gu thought for a minute and then shook his head. "No," he decided wearily. "Call the men off. We will not find anything. It would only be a waste of time."

Zhang Gu didn't know how right he was. Both perpetrators had long since vanished.

One of them was already a thousand miles away, on board a Qantas flight bound for Sydney, Australia.

The other was on the first leg of a Northwest flight putting down in Tokyo. Headed for Honolulu and the warm waters of Waikiki.

Book One

"CLUB MET"

GoldMart Chairman Wins Bid for Auction House

Special to the New York *Times*

NEW YORK, Oct. 12—Robert A. Goldsmith, the chairman of GoldMart, Inc., has invested nearly a billion dollars in Burghley's, Inc., in exchange for a major stake in the corporation, Wall Street sources said yesterday.

In the transaction, Mr. Goldsmith has obtained over 50 percent of the company's stock, or about 32.5 million shares in the venerable auction house, which was founded in 1719 and is the world's oldest. This deal represents a financial coup on the part of Mr. Goldsmith, who obtained the stock at what analysts consider a bargain-basement price in the current recessionary climate . . .

1

MacKenzie Turner awakened wanting to take a bite out of the Big Apple.

It was one of those clear, brisk mornings in Manhattan. Even the sky was polished, and not a wisp of cloud or so much as a tinge of smog marred its perfection. But the weather had nothing to do with the way she felt.

That was entirely due to the method by which she was being awakened, surfacing from sweet dreams to an even sweeter reality by the delicious nibbles of her delicious lover, who had his mouth on one of her breasts and a hand down between her soft thighs.

"Mmmmm . . ." Moaning dreamily and half smiling, she changed position without opening her eyes, her body, like a sunflower turning toward the sun, instinctively seeking the radiating warmth of his.

Between her legs, he gently worked two fingers up inside her.

"*Mmmmm!*" Her luminous amber eyes snapped open.

"Thought that might wake you up." He grinned raffishly.

"Never start a job you can't finish!" she said, narrowing her bright eyes challengingly. "So what are you going to do about it, buster?"

"How about this?" Even as his lips closed around her nipple once again, bringing it to its fullest and hardest, his eyes were upon her. Eating her up.

Although their on-again, off-again, no-strings-attached relationship had been sailing along for over a year now, he still couldn't help but feel slightly dazed whenever he was confronted by her mesmerizing, energy-packed reality. Everything about Kenzie Turner seemed to charge the very air around her.

Physical beauty had nothing to do with it. Kenzie would never grace a pinup calendar or *Sports Illustrated*'s swimsuit edition—not with her sable hair, worn in a Louise Brooks cut, framing a mischievous elfin face with high cheekbones, winged brows, and small pointy chin. It gave her a vulnerable and gamine, somehow waiflike, rather than sexually smoldering, look.

But there was something definitely disturbing and at odds about that small, fine-boned face resting atop the ripe female phenomenon that was her body. For from the neck down, everything added up to just the right figures.

It was the sum of these disparate, individual parts which made men want to ravish her and yet at the same time protect her.

Her blissful smile widened as she lazily watched his tongue flick a moist, ticklish path over her sumptuous, blue-veined breasts, and down her latticed rib cage and softly muscled hollow of belly to the generous thatch of her sable-furred mound. A shudder rippled through her as his face disappeared between her legs to plunder her sweetness.

Her wetness spoke for itself, and it was all she could do to keep from going crazy. She absolutely *loved* his tongue—no one, but no one, could feast on female flesh quite like Charley Ferraro!

"Not now, Charley," she begged weakly, trying halfheartedly to push him from between her splayed thighs. "You know I've got to go to work . . ."

His head popped up, black eyes shining. "Sure you do." Then, balancing himself on his forearms, he raised his hips high off the mattress and slowly lowered them, entering her just the way she liked—face-to-face and hip-to-hip.

She let out a whinny of triumph and wonder. Then, as he began to thrust with a very slow, very deliberate rhythm, she let herself go, giving in to glorious depravity as his tempo and breathing intensified.

"Faster!" she whispered eagerly, raising and lowering her pelvis to match his rhythm. Her eyes glowed like an animal's caught in the wash of sudden headlights, and she dug fierce fingers into his buttocks.

"Faster!" she demanded.

"Hey, take it slow, babe," he said softly. "We're not in a race, you know. Take it slow . . ." he repeated. "Just lie back and enjoy the ride . . ."

"Yes!" She inhaled deeply the heightened muskiness of his fragrant male flesh; shivered deliciously at each exhalation of his warm breath against the sensitive heated skin of her breasts. Slowly, the rhythm of his thrusts increased, and she matched them by thrusting her body savagely up to meet him. Greedily she contracted her muscles around him, grinding a circular motion before lowering herself again. Concentrating fully, she kept repeating the maneuver, gasping each time she held him captive. Filling her completely.

Possessing her.

Faster and faster they moved in perfect harmony, as if each of them were an intrinsic, indispensable part of the other.

"Oh, God," she moaned. "Oh, it's so good! So good, Charley, so—"

Abruptly his hands gripped her buttocks brutally, and he half lifted her off the bed. She gasped in surprise. He was jackhammering now, relentlessly speeding up his pounding.

Faster, *faster!* His tempo was increasing, his testicles slapping against her.

Harder, *harder!* Her every nerve ending sang hosannas until, suddenly, the world tilted and went topsy-turvy and she was flying off over the edge—cartwheeling out into a whole new dimension, where up was down and down was up and inside was out and outside in and—

Her face contorted in agony and her scream was primordial as the first spinning wave of orgasm came rushing.

"Oh, God! I'm coming!"

Suddenly she tensed and arched herself half off the bed.

And then he, too, was unable to hold back any longer. Tightening his arms around her, he reared up and drove himself into her as deeply as he could.

Sensing his climax, she clamped herself even tighter around him. Inside her, she could feel him twitch as his own circuits blew, and the orgasm burst out of him in an explosion as they came together in a mind-blowing, body-wrenching, thundering climax of magnificent release.

Her fading scream became a long, drawn-out sigh of marveling wonder. "Oh, Charley!" she whispered breathlessly. "Charley . . ."

He shuddered once more as the last of his juices drained into her, and then, together, they collapsed on the bed. Between drawing deep, ragged lungfuls of air, he managed a lopsided grin. "Good morning," he croaked.

Her eyes were wide. "I'll say it is!" She kissed him and ran her hands through his rumpled thick tangly black hair which, despite his droopy Sam Elliott of a mustache, gave him a sheepish, almost boyish look.

For a while they lay quietly, still joined. Then suddenly her eyes widened in horror. She had spied the alarm clock.

"Shit!" she exclaimed, and shoved him away. He rolled off her, his limp penis slipping out.

"Now what the hell's the matter?" he demanded.

"The damn alarm didn't go off!" she shouted, yanking fistfuls of her hair in frustration.

"I know." Stretching out, he laced his hands behind his head and smiled smugly. "I shut it off."

"You—you . . . what?" She stared at him.

"I told you. I shut it off so it wouldn't disturb us."

"You shithead! You pig! You . . . you . . ." She grabbed a pillow and began beating him over the head with it.

He raised his arms to protect himself. "Hey!" he shouted. "Hey, relax! I've got the day off."

"Well, I haven't! God, now I'm going to be late."

The worst of her fury vented, she tossed the pillow aside, launched herself out of bed, and made a mad dash for the bathroom.

"What are you so worried about, anyway?" he called after her. "Can't you phone in sick?"

Her head popped around from behind the bathroom door. "Have you forgotten, or is your brain between your legs? This morning marks the first official day under new management!"

He looked at her dumbly.

"Gawd!" She rolled her eyes in exasperation. "The corporate take-over I told you about? With the new major shareholder? Well, today's the day the SEC granted approval for it to take effect, you *Dummkopf!*"

She glared at him.

"*Well?* Don't just lie there like God's gift to women! Get *moving,* man! Put on some caffeine! And hurry!" She clapped her hands briskly.

Crossing his arms behind his head, he stretched out lazily and wiggled his toes. "Aw, come on, Kenz. You know I'm no good in the kitchen."

"Well, ex-cuuuuuse me!" She rolled her eyes again, growling, "*Cops!*" in disgust. "Guess I'm doomed to grab a cup on the run. Why, oh *why,*" she demanded beseechingly of the world in general, "did I have to fall for a too-macho-to-even-make-a-cup-of-coffee Italian cop? Would someone please give me the answer to that?"

"Maybe because I'm so good in bed?" he suggested with a leer.

"Too bad you aren't as useful around the house." She eyed him suspiciously. "Say, don't you have somewhere you've got to be? Work you've got to catch up on or something?"

"Naw. No work until tomorrow, sweetums, when I hitch up with my counterpart from Interpol. I told you how I'll be working with him in the art theft squad—"

But she didn't hear. She'd already slammed the door and started the shower, and water was crashing down full blast.

2

*H*igh above Fifth Avenue, Dina Goldsmith awoke with the feeling that something had changed overnight, and momentarily wondered what it might be. Lying in her extravagantly draped fantasy of a Venetian bed, she frowned up at the Fortuny canopy while trying to shake off the foggy remnants of sleep. What had changed? she wondered.

Then it hit her.

Sitting bolt upright, she stretched luxuriously. What a beautiful day this was! How could she have forgotten? Overnight, she had become the Queen of Manhattan Island! *That's* what had changed!

Was it really, truly possible? Perhaps if she pinched herself . . .

She *would* have tweaked her arm were it not for the thick, cumbersome mittens she wore to bed—to protect the antique lace sheets *and* keep her hands slathered with moisturizing lotion.

Amazingly, last night she had gone to bed the same Dina Goldsmith as usual—the beautiful, Dutch-born wife of Robert A. Goldsmith, billionaire owner of GoldMart, Inc., the second-largest chain of (loathesome to her) discount department stores in the nation.

But now, eight short hours later, she had awakened a different Dina Goldsmith—the glorious wife of the *new owner* (or, at least, the single-largest shareholder and chairman) of Burghley's, Inc., the world's oldest, greatest, and undeniably most important purveyor of world-class art, furnishings, jewelry, postage stamps, porcelains, carpets—not to mention God only knows what other staggering treasures.

Burghley's! The very name galvanized, imbued every item that passed through its venerated doors with instant value, provenance, and prestige.

Burghley's! Where every auction during the late great eighties had broken one world record after another—whether for the most expensive Picasso or van Gogh ever sold, to the highest-priced Meissen dinner service or Ansel Adams photograph.

Burghley's! With its three-hundred-year-old headquarters in Bond Street in London, its own block-long palace right here on Madison Avenue, plus twenty-three smaller satellite galleries scattered throughout the world.

Burghley's! Which ranked right up there alongside Christie's and Sotheby's, and whose board of directors and advisory board read like a veritable *Who's Who* of the filthy rich and the titled, many of whom had, until now, looked down their patrician noses at *her*, Dina Goldsmith, dismissing her out-of-hand as the wife of a mere five-and-dime peddler!

Well . . .

Her lips curved into a scimitar of a steel-bladed smile. Things had *certainly* changed—and overnight at that!

Now it was time to act the part.

"Darlene!" she screamed.

Her flustered maid, who had been waiting right outside her bedroom, came rushing in at once. One look at the trembling woman, and Dina could tell that even the servants had gotten the news.

"Run my bath," she ordered imperiously. "And see that the water's precisely twenty-six degrees. That's *Celsius,*" she ordered.

"Yes, ma'am!" Chin down, Darlene scuttled off to the ensuite marble bathroom.

"But before you do that, get a bowl of hot water, untie my mitts, and wash this goddamn goop off my hands!"

"Yes, ma'am!" Darlene was back in a jiffy, with soap, a steaming bowl of water, a box of Kleenex, and stacks of washcloths.

Dina held out both hands, arms extended, like a surgeon. She waited impatiently while Darlene untied the thick terry-cloth mittens and used Kleenex, soap, and water. When her hands were finally clean, Dina said, *"Now* go run my bath."

"Yes, ma'am!" Darlene vanished, along with the debris of Kleenex, water, and washcloths.

Dina activated her bedside speakerphone—not the one with the eight outside lines, but the intra-apartment model. Hearing the dial tone, she stabbed one of the twenty-four preprogrammed numbers.

The majordomo answered on the first ring. "Yes, madame?" His amplified voice came out hollow and tinny-sounding.

"Tell Cook I'll be breakfasting in exactly one hour," she commanded. "I want *hot* fresh decaf. *Half* a cup of plain, no-fat yogurt. And a single slice of low-cal toast. On the light side. *No* butter."

"I'll relay your instruc—"

"Is my husband still here?" she interrupted.

"I regret that he—"

She broke the connection, then immediately reactivated the speaker and called her private secretary down the hall.

One ring . . . two . . . three . . .

"Yeah, yeah?" rasped a gravelly female voice.

"Gaby, have my car and driver waiting downstairs in exactly an hour and a half. And call Burghley's. I want the three highest ranking executives waiting at the front entrance to give us the grand tour."

"Guess that means I'm coming along," came the sour reply.

"You guess correctly."

"I'll get on it." Gabriella Morton's voice echoed weary resignation. "By the way. Don't forget you have a two o'clock appointment at Kenneth's."

"Not anymore I don't," Dina said grandly. "Call Kenneth. Tell him that from now on he can come here if he wants to do *my* hair." Then, severing the connection, she flung aside the covers and popped out of bed.

Stretching luxuriously, she took a few moments to savor her new position. Then, humming cheerfully to herself, she slipped into a salmon pink silk robe trimmed with ostrich feathers and wiggled her feet into fuzzy little salmon pink heels. Thus clad, she swept imperiously off to the bathroom.

For once, she did not dally to admire the van Gogh portrait above the marble mantel, the Degas *Racehorses* over the gilt console, or her treasured trio of sweet little Renoirs. This was one morning that Dina Goldsmith did not need the tangibles of priceless art and antiques to validate her position. Today she knew exactly who she was—and where she stood in this town.

All in all, she had to admit that little Dina Van Vliet of Gouda, the cheese capital of Holland, had not done so badly for herself. She had come a long way in her twenty-nine years—a long, *long* way.

Further than anyone imagined . . .

Dina Goldsmith's earliest memories were of cheese, which was why she refused to touch it now—and woe be to anyone who put so much as an ounce of it in the refrigerator!

Like Proust's petite madeleine, the very smell, indeed the mere *thought* of cheese, was enough to set off remembrances of things past. Which wasn't surprising, considering the fact that her father had worked in one of Gouda's famed cheese factories.

Trouble was, that's what she remembered best about him. The smell of cheese which surrounded him like a miasma. Clinging to his clothes. His hair. His skin. Somehow, no matter how much he bathed, the stench never quite washed out. Even now, after all these years, she still couldn't seem to get it out of her nostrils.

But life, always rich in ironies, had used cheese to provide her the ticket out of Gouda.

Dina Van Vliet was a classic Nordic golden girl. Five feet, nine inches tall, she had hair like cornsilk, sharply etched cheekbones, and wide-set aquamarine eyes. Besides her looks and a knockout body, she possessed legs that made her a showstopper—enough so that she won the title of Miss Gouda.

From there, it was a hop to Amsterdam, where she garnered the crown of Miss Netherlands, and then a skip and a jump to the Miss Universe pageant in Caracas, Venezuela.

Alas, Miss Netherlands never made it to the semifinals. But no matter. Dina Van Vliet was a realist. No one needed to tell *her* what her most valuable assets were. She knew that better than anyone.

She also knew she wasn't about to return to the land of windmills, wooden shoes, and cheese. So she packed up her consolation prizes, took the nine thousand dollars her maternal grandmother had left her, and moved to the mogul-rich canyons of New York City, where she shared a rent-controlled apartment on the fashionable Upper East Side.

More important, she invested in one very good, very expensive, and very revealing multifunctional black evening dress and a passable string of cultured pearls.

Thus armed, and shamelessly using her pageant title to gain entrée, she plunged into the Manhattan social circuit like a cruising shark. Cocktail parties, dinners, opening nights, and charity benefits—Dina worked them all, in the process turning down countless offers for hops in the sack, and just as many marriage proposals, all from some of Manhattan's dreamiest and most handsome young men.

But Dina had no use for trust-fund babies. She knew what she wanted, and was determined to get it.

And lo and behold! Before you could say "Cheese!", she had found her Moneybags in Robert A. Goldsmith, the recently widowed founder and chairman of GoldMart, Inc.

So it wasn't exactly love at first sight.

So he was overweight, unattractive, balding, and fiftysomething.

So he was a little rough and rusty around the edges.

So he wore the same abominable, off-the-rack polyester suits he sold in his nationwide discount department store chain.

And so his West Side penthouse was furnished with cut-rate furniture, orange wall-to-wall shag, artificial plants, and framed prints of clowns, cats, and children with big eyes—GoldMart products all.

So *what?*

He was ripe for the picking, and that was all that mattered. That, plus the fact that he had moolah coming out of his ears.

Equally as important, Robert A. Goldsmith had no ex-wives or children to dispute his estate if and when the time came—she'd checked that out discreetly but thoroughly.

As far as his shortcomings went, Dina was convinced that none were unconquerable. After all, manners could be taught. A strict diet prescribed. His abominable wardrobe changed. And the hideous penthouse on Central Park West redecorated.

Marriage soon followed, and Dina Van Vliet no longer existed. Dina Goldsmith did—and with a vengeance.

Now that she had become an official member of that most elite of all clubs—the wives of the one hundred richest men in the world—she threw herself into the social arena with the same calculation and cold-bloodedness with which she'd set out to capture herself a husband of incalculable wealth.

Her life suddenly became a whirlwind of activity.

There were the daily lunches with fellow socialites at La Grenouille and Le Cirque, where the court bouillon with lobster paled beside the real entrées—juicy gossip and whispered scandals.

The evenings of cocktail parties followed by formal dinners. The opening nights on Broadway. Plus the traditional Monday "dress" nights at the Metropolitan Opera, the requisite charity balls, and the weekend commutes to the Hamptons in the summer and Palm Beach or the Caribbean in the winter.

Anyone would have thought that Dina Goldsmith had it made.

But soon she discovered the truth.

While socializing with certain people was a matter of course, Mr. and Mrs. Goldsmith *weren't* accepted everywhere. At least, not where it really counted. The old guard in New York, Newport, the Hamptons, and Palm Beach snubbed them, and all because Robert was a self-made man, and as such, his money was new money and hadn't gained the patina of respectability which can only be acquired over several generations.

Except when it came to charity fund-raisers, at which any donors were welcome, Old Money locked its doors to them.

Once again, just as she had done at Caracas, Dina took stock of the situation and decided that some major changes were due. First, she and Robert would have to move: to the East Side, no less, and Fifth Avenue at that. She was determined that only a palatial Wasp stronghold along Central Park would do.

Money being no object, she soon found the perfect thirty-four-room duplex, complete with sweeping marble staircase, greenhouse, and no less than two wraparound terraces. She hired the socially correct decorator, a seventy-two-year-old dragon of impeccable Wasp pedigree.

But if Dina thought moving to the right Fifth Avenue address and having the right decorator would magically open all the closed doors, she was dead wrong. And the continued ostracism was driving her crazy.

And now, eight long years later—*Hallelujah!* Her prayers had been answered! Her husband's successful takeover of Burghley's would succeed where all else had failed—for no one needed to tell Dina that his majority stake in Burghley's had suddenly made her the hottest social item in town. And overnight, yet!

After all this time, she had been catapulted to the top! To the very, very pinnacle of Manhattan society!

And now . . .

Ah! Now there were debts to be repaid in kind . . . snobs *she* would snub . . . an entire vanquished society just waiting to lick the soles of her Maud Frizons!

Oh, yes! She would revel in every last minute of it! For was there anything, anything on earth quite as deliciously satisfying as giving tit for tat?

The scented water in the marble Jacuzzi bubbled and boiled as Dina slid down into the huge pink oval tub. Closing her eyes, she rested her head on a pink scallop-shell cushion, her fertile mind doing quantum leaps.

A knock on the door intruded on her pleasant thoughts, and her eyes snapped open as Gaby marched right in. Dina scowled up at her, but Gaby couldn't care less. She was a bossy squirt of a tweedy woman, with gray iron wires for hair, glasses hanging from a chain around her neck, and a voice like James Earl Jones's. Approaching the tub, she smacked the button and shut off the noisy whirlpool mechanism. "There's a call for you," she announced gruffly. "Wanna take it?"

Dina slapped the button to turn the whirlpool back on. "That all depends on who it is," she sniffed.

"Someone named Berg. Sandra Berg." Gaby shrugged.

Frowning to herself, Dina reached for a giant loofah. Sandra Berg? Was she supposed to *know* whoever that might—? And then a lightbulb glowed. Of course! Gaby must mean *Zandra!*

Zandra, who she hadn't heard from in *ages!*

"Hand me the telephone," Dina commanded loftily.

"Pick it up yourself," Gaby snapped, and marched right back out, shutting the door behind her.

Bitch! Dina wanted to shout, but settled for throwing the loofah at the closing door. Then she reached for the remote phone on the tub-side table.

"Zandra?" she squealed happily, sliding back down into the gurgling cauldron.

"Dina?" The British-accented voice came faintly across the wires amid a cacophony of background noises.

Dina could barely hear and shut off the Jacuzzi. "Zandra? Where in heaven *are* you?"

"Thank *God,* Dina! Darling, if I couldn't have reached you, I don't know *who* I would have called!" Zandra's voice—equal measures of clipped upper-class boarding school, Belgravia slur, and Oxfordshire country-house throwaways—for once sounded uncharacteristically panicked.

Alarmed, Dina sat up straight, water sluicing down her bony clavicles. "Zandra! What on earth *is* it?"

"Oh, there isn't time to go into all the *sordid* details now, Dina. I mean, I've had an absolutely *beastly* time. Would it . . ." Her voice turned hesitant. ". . . would it be all right if I came and stayed with you for a few days?"

"Why, you know you're always welcome. And I long to see you."
Dina paused, a frown flitting across her smooth features. "Zandra, are
you in any sort of . . . difficulties?"

"Gosh, Dina, that would take the whole of forever to explain . . . I'm
in a pay phone and—well, I fear it'll just *have* to wait. I've just put down
at Kennedy, you see, and if the traffic's horrendous it might take me a
while to get into the city . . . anyway, you're positive it's all right? I mean,
I know it's awfully short notice and the most horrible breach of etiquette to blatantly invite oneself . . . besides which, I *really* wouldn't want
to impose—"

"Oh, but you're not imposing!" Dina assured her. "I'm delighted,
sweetie! Really I am! Tell you what. Come straight to the apartment. I'll
probably be out until sometime after lunch, but I'll get back as quickly as
I can. Meanwhile, I shall inform the staff to expect you. Feel free to make
yourself at home."

"Oh, you are a darling—you've positively saved my life! And I can't
wait to see you!"

Frowning, Dina looked at the receiver in her hand and then reached
out and replaced it. As she slid back into the now-tepid water, worries nibbled at her. She had definitely detected a disturbing note in Zandra's voice,
almost an undercurrent of . . . yes . . . *hysteria*.

Dina's frown deepened. Indomitable, sparkly, but always level-headed
Zandra panicking? That was most unlike the Zandra she knew. Yet she
was certain she hadn't imagined it.

What on earth, she wondered, *could be the matter?*

3

andra von Hohenburg-Willemlohe, Countess of Grafburg, had no intention of reliving the past twenty-four hours—at least, not if she had anything to say in the matter. She didn't think her nerves could stand it. Now that she was out of imminent danger, she allowed herself to feel a little safer. She was, after all, in America—and three thousand miles of ocean separated her from England and Big Trouble.

"I think I'm in lust," a junior executive keeping pace with her said in a voice just loud enough for her to hear.

When ignoring him didn't thwart his ardor, she iced him with her eyes. "I make it a point never to rob the cradle," she retorted so loudly that passersby smirked, and that having done the trick she hurried on, her outsize shoulder bag bouncing.

Zandra von Hohenburg-Willemlohe had long become an expert at rebuffing the advances of strangers. She'd had to. Without meaning to, she attracted men the same way pollen attracts bees.

Zandra was twenty-eight years old and had the face of the beauty queen she'd once been, and the body of a whore, which she most definitely was not. Her wide-spaced eyes were bright, pranksterish, and mermaid green, and her mouth was wide and full and sensuously pouty.

She was five feet, ten inches tall before she put on her shoes, and her skin, that celebrated Limoges complexion for which the English are so famed, was, in her case, made all the more delightful by the triangle of irrepressible freckles on the tip of her nose. She weighed one hundred and eighteen pounds, and her hair, the precise color of Wilkin and Sons' Tiptree orange marmalade, billowed around her head in a soft, cloudy aura.

On anyone else, the baggy cable-knit sweater, second-hand motorcycle jacket, and tight faded jeans tucked into a pair of crimson, flame-stitched, secondhand Tony Lama cowboy boots would have looked decidedly downscale. But on her the outfit looked absolutely smashing, for she belonged to that tiniest percentage of women who could carry off anything, even rags, and still look the height of chic.

Oddly enough, while men were naturally drawn to her, women never seemed to resent her, for Zandra was altogether too vivacious and down to earth, too fun-loving and crazily uncomplicated for anyone to take offense to her beauty. If anything, her mischievous *joie de vivre* and high-pitched giggles rubbed off on others, and made anything she did—no matter how outrageous—seem blithefully innocent and done without wishing the least bit of offense or ill will.

Twenty-four hours earlier, however, that bouncy spark had deserted her, and was yet to be fully regained.

Now, carried along by the surging horde of passengers following the signs marked TO BUSES AND TAXIS, she silently blessed Dina Goldsmith. Without her old friend, she would have had nowhere to hide out—and then what?

Then I would have been at the mercy of those goons, she thought grimly.

The memory made her shudder, caused the bandaged wound on her forearm to throb and sting anew.

Once outside, on the lower level of the international arrivals terminal, she hesitated, momentarily wondering whether to wait for a bus or to splurge frivolously on a cab. She knew she had less than a hundred dollars to her name, but right now that was the very least of her worries. What mattered was that she was safe and sound and that, except for the blistering wound on her forearm, her body was in one piece.

How easily it could have been the other way around. How all too easily . . .

The birth of Anna Zandra Elisabeth Theresia Charlotte von Hohenburg-Willemlohe, Countess of Grafburg, in London—followed two years later by the birth of her brother, Rudolph—was little cause for celebration.

Delivering Zandra was almost more than her delicate mother could bear, but the strain of Rudolph's birth proved to be too much. Lavinia von Hohenburg-Willemlohe died in the midst of delivery, and only the valiant efforts of a highly skilled team of surgeons had managed to save the child.

Zandra's father, Stefan, was at a complete loss as to what to do. The death of his beloved Lavinia had left him dazed and confused. When he had married her, his fortune, in Czechoslovakia, had been one of the greatest in all Europe, but the Soviets had confiscated everything. His wife's untimely death, like his own decline into poverty, was something with which he could simply not cope. Under the circumstances, a two-year-old daughter and an infant son, possessors of a series of cumbersome and useless titles, presented a serious problem.

Not surprisingly, he took solace in the bottle.

Fortunately, there was no end of rich and titled relatives whose fortunes, based in the West, were not only intact but thriving; European nobility being the incestuous soup that it is, Zandra could count most of the dukes and duchesses of England, as well as the *comtes* and *comtesses* of France, as her various relatives. But thanks to her paternal grandfather, she was linked to the princely house of von und zu Engelwiesen, which meant that Zandra was also a descendant, however convoluted the bloodline, of the princes of the Holy Roman Empire.

Subsequently, the relatives rallied 'round. Zandra's godmother, an English duchess, provided the children with a nanny, while Aunt Josephine, whose husband owned a private London bank, employed the increasingly alcoholic Stefan with a make-work job, and Cousin Colin provided a small but rent-free apartment in fashionable Mayfair. But it was Aunt Josephine who took it upon herself to take charge.

When Zandra turned six, Lady Josephine told Stefan in no uncertain terms precisely to which frightfully costly school his daughter must be sent—the expense being borne by the family, of course. And so began Zandra's education at the most exclusive school of its kind in England. The same held true for Rudolph. Two years later, her brother was sent to the boys' counterpart of the exclusive girls' school Zandra attended.

As Zandra grew older, she came to understand that she was different, and fit neither into the simple world of the commoner nor the Byzantinely formal world of the rich and titled. She and Rudolph belonged somewhere in between, in some kind of society holding pen, their futures to be decided upon once they were of age. "Much like souls in purgatory," Zandra would often tell herself with a sigh, for along with her title and noble blood came a strong core of Roman Catholicism.

When she turned eighteen, she was taken to Buckingham Palace and presented at court. Then came her equally important coming out. Having one's season was, after all, an ages-old ritual which was tried and true, and it was precisely in this very fashion that Aunt Josephine herself had met her husband.

But if Aunt Josephine thought that finding a suitable husband for Zandra would be easy, she was to be severely disappointed. The season came and went, and all Zandra had to show for it were hordes of eligible young men who, for one reason or another, she found fault with. Aunt Josephine finally threw up her hands in frustration. "Beggars cannot afford to be choosers!" she lamented to her sisters, Lady Cressida and Lady Alexandra, "and our Zandra is being altogether too choosy for her own good. Especially," she added ominously, "for someone in 'her position.' "

The sisters commiserated with Aunt Josephine and one of them patted her hand. "You've done your best, Josie, dear," Cressida said. "No one can fault you for not trying."

"Be that as it may," Josephine went on, "Zandra shall either have to continue her education or go to work—although only heaven knows what she's cut out for." She sighed deeply. "I suppose she'll have to decide that for herself."

Zandra decided upon university. And two years later, so did Rudolph, who went off to Oxford.

From that point on, Zandra saw little of her younger brother. Unlike the years he had spent at boarding school, when she could look forward to the summer months as theirs to spend together, he now made plans of his own which, often as not, did not include her.

The reason for this change in sibling relationships was because Rudolph von Hohenburg-Willemlohe had discovered that most enticing of all heterosexual pleasures—women. Before long, his name was linked to a succession of beauties, and his charm and charisma were such that he had members of the opposite sex literally eating out of his hand. Zandra, in the meantime, majored in art history, although she wasn't at all sure where those studies would take her.

And then along came the Miss Great Britain beauty pageant. She wouldn't have dreamed of participating, had it not been for the urging of one of her girlfriends.

"Come *on,* Zandra!" her friend had pleaded. "What have you got to lose? Besides, *I'm* not afraid to enter, so why should you? Really! We'll have *tons* of fun! Do be a sport!"

And so Zandra became a contestant. It was purely a lark, of course. Winning the title was the furthest thing from her mind.

She couldn't believe it when the crown was hers.

Neither could Aunt Josephine, who hadn't been consulted about Zandra's entering the pageant, and who did not think it appropriate for a descendant of the princes of the Holy Roman Empire to be making so public, so common, a spectacle of herself.

Nonetheless, a flurry of brief fame followed, and then came Caracas and the Miss Universe pageant. Regrettably, Zandra didn't even make runner-up; however, she *did* make some new friends—most notably Miss Netherlands, Dina Van Vliet—and then she returned to England to resume her life where she'd left off.

But Aunt Josephine refused to continue financing her education. "I am washing my hands of you," the old lady told Zandra succinctly. "I've tried to help find you a husband, which you've failed to do. I've seen to your education, which you saw fit to interrupt. From this point on, you are on your own."

Being left with no other option, Zandra went out job hunting. She pounded the pavement. Haunted the employment agencies. Tried some modeling, but discovered everyone wanted her to take off her clothes and not put other garments back on. Nor had studying art history, or her reign as Miss Great Britain, given her any particular marketable skills. As far as her noble pedigree was concerned, that didn't buy her so much as a cup of tea. Things got to the point where she didn't know what she was going to do.

Enter a young businessman by the name of Mark Brandon, vice

president of a firm which specialized in handling special tour groups from overseas.

"We've put together a new 'Regal Holidays' package," he told Zandra when he'd looked her up. "It's limited to groups of twenty-four tourists at a time, and they'll stay in various castle-hotels, tour country houses and gardens, be taken to Ascot, and generally be made to feel they're living the kind of rich, titled life they only dreamed about at home."

He went on to explain that what he needed to complete the Regal Holidays atmosphere was a genuinely titled lady to greet the tourists in a beautifully furnished townhouse apartment in Wilton Crescent, off Knightsbridge.

"All it will entail is an hour or so twice a week, sipping champagne, chatting, and posing for photographs with our clientele," he concluded. "After that, they can go back home and show pictures of themselves with a real aristocrat."

Meanwhile, the lavish accommodations would be hers to live in for as long as the arrangement stood; a gown, jewels, and part-time butler would be provided. "We'll pay you two hundred pounds a week." Brandon smiled ingenuously. "What do you say?"

Zandra's frown deepened as she'd listened to his pitch. "I'll have to sleep on it," she told him.

The next day, Rudolph unknowingly made up her mind for her. He had come to borrow money.

"I'm in a bit of a pinch," he said, trying to act nonchalant as he shakily fixed himself a drink.

"All right," she sighed. "How much do you need this time?"

He studied his feet and cleared his throat, the ice cubes in his glass rattling. "How . . . how much have you got?"

"Rudolph!" She stared at him.

"It's . . . it's a gambling debt, you see." He was careful to avoid her eyes. "I've got to pay up, or else those chaps can get quite nasty, you know. Wouldn't want that, now would we?" He looked at her and tried to smile, but it was a ghastly attempt at bravado.

And so she called up Mark Brandon. Accepted Regal Holidays' offer. Moved into the grandly furnished apartment on Wilton Crescent. And met the tourist groups twice a week.

She was very regal. Every inch the countess.

The tourists ate it up.

Aunt Josephine didn't. When the old lady heard about it, she was aghast. So aghast, in fact, that she did a complete turnaround and actually begged Zandra to go back to university.

But Zandra wouldn't hear of it. "I like what I'm doing," she told her aunt stubbornly.

And it was true. She enjoyed her newfound independence, and had no desire to put herself under Aunt Josephine's thumb, or accept family handouts, ever again.

And then her father died. Predictably, of cirrhosis of the liver.

The real trouble started right after.

Stefan von Hohenburg-Willemlohe was barely interred before Rudolph went around to all the gambling clubs, lying through his teeth about the millions he was going to inherit after the will was probated. The club owners' ears perked up; credit and all courtesies were extended to him.

Rudolph lost hundreds of pounds the first night alone; more credit was extended. Over the weeks, his losses accumulated into the thousands, and during the next few months, those thousands multiplied into the tens of thousands. Before he knew it, his debts, combined with the usurious interest rates, had skyrocketed into several hundred thousand pounds.

The club owners discreetly took him aside.

"The solicitors say it'll be any day now," he lied glibly. "The will's still in probate, but it's only a formality. Meanwhile, how about extending me just a few thousand quid more . . ."

Credit was extended. And extended.

And then, inevitably, it was shut off. Rudolph was given seven days to come up with what he owed—or else.

Of course he didn't pay—how could he? And after his week had run out, he came home in the wee hours to find three burly men detaching themselves from the shadows around his front door.

In the glow of the lamplight, Rudolph caught the glint of brass knuckles. Reacting without thinking, he threw himself to the ground, rolled across a bed of ivy, and lunged to his feet. He sensed, rather than saw, a fourth man blocking the open gate to the street, tire iron in hand.

With an almost superhuman strength, he jumped at the high wall that enclosed the front garden, scrabbled up it, and dropped down to the other side. Only his quick reflexes—and sheer luck—had saved him. But it had been a close call. Far, far too close for comfort.

Zandra found out about it when the telephone shrilled her awake at half past four in the morning.

"Just listen," Rudolph's ragged voice babbled from a phone booth somewhere, "and for God's sake, don't interrupt!"

And he told her everything.

"Rudolph, you've got to go to the police," she told him, the level rationality in her voice surprising even herself.

"The police can't help me." He gave a short, derisive bark of a laugh. "That would only make matters worse!"

"Rudolph, where *are* you?" When he didn't reply, she repeated, "Where . . . are . . . you . . . calling . . . from?"

"It's safer for you not to know. Zands . . ." She could hear him swallow. "I-I've got to make myself scarce, so don't worry if you don't hear from me for a while." There was a pause. "I-I've got to dash," he added quickly, and the line went dead.

He had hung up.

Thirteen hours later, a busload of Regal Holidays tourists arrived. Zandra didn't know how she functioned. She went through the ritual on automatic pilot, welcoming them and chatting by rote, somehow managing a bright false smile while having her picture taken with the housewives from Brentwood, the retirees from Jacksonville, and the grain merchants and their wives from Topeka.

But it was as if they weren't really there. *Rudolph.* All she could think about was her brother. *Where is he now?* she worried as her body went through the social motions. *Is he safe? And if so, how can he ever extricate himself from this mess?*

Before the tourists were scheduled to depart, the doorbell rang and the part-time butler—a seldom-employed character actor—went to answer it. He stood by helplessly as three uncouth men in loud suits barged past him and invaded the drawing room.

One, swooping a flute of champagne out of a tourist's hand, drained it in one swallow, then flung it into the fireplace, the Waterford crystal shattering.

Another, plopping himself sideways down on a sofa, rudely propped his shoes up on an incensed matron's lap.

The third, lit cigar in his mouth and hands clasped behind his back, walked slowly around, as though taking inventory. Finally, he took the cigar and deliberately tapped a length of ash onto the Wilton carpet, grinding it in with his heel. "You the countess?" he asked Zandra, an ugly smirk on his pockmarked face.

"I am Zandra von Hohenburg-Willemlohe, Countess of Grafburg, yes." Her voice was calm but her eyes flashed angrily. "If you'll wait out in the foyer, I'll be with you in a moment—whoever you are."

He didn't move. "You know good an' well who we are. We've come to find yer bleedin' brother." Crossing over to her, he lifted the cigar, puffed on it, and regarded her with stony gray eyes. "We think you might know where 'e is." He blew a cloud of smoke directly in her face.

Crimson spots burned on Zandra's cheeks, but she refused to be cowered. Turning to the tourists with born and bred dignity, she said, "I apologize for this rude intrusion. It really was lovely meeting all of you."

Avoiding her eyes, they quietly set down their drinks, gathered up coats and purses, and exodused *en masse.*

"Right cozy, this place is," said the cigar-smoking tough once the tourists and butler were gone. His grin was a rictus. "Wouldn't mind stayin' 'ere meself fer a while. Now . . . whyn't you make it easy on yerself? Just tell us w'ere the bloke calls 'imself yer brother's 'idin'."

Zandra stared at him. "How can I, if I don't know?"

"Pity."

He seemed suddenly absorbed in his cigar, rolling it back and forth between his thumb and forefinger while blowing gently on the glowing tip. Finally he glanced up at her.

"But you 'eard from 'im, din't ya?" His voice was softly menacing.

"Yes, he called me this morning," Zandra admitted. She couldn't take her eyes off the cigar. Fear, like a suffocating wall, was closing in on her from all sides. "But he wouldn't tell me his whereabouts. I really *don't* know where he is!"

"Yeah? Hope you ain't expectin' us to swallow that."

"Believe what you will." Her eyes rose to meet his. "To tell you the truth," she added with contempt, "I wouldn't help you even if I could."

Swift as a cobra, he clamped one steely hand around her left wrist and jerked her toward him. "We'll see about that," he said into her up-turned face, "won't we?"

Slowly, deliberately, he brought the glowing cigar end to within an inch of her bare forearm. Heat radiated from its ashy tip, causing her arm muscles to twitch involuntarily.

"Now, why make it so 'ard on yerself?" he asked, looking at her with eyes as cold as ball bearings. "All you hav'ta' do is tell us where 'e is."

"But I already have!"

Clucking his tongue chidingly, he moved the cigar half an inch closer to her flesh. Her pupils dilated wildly as the radiating heat intensified, and she stared down at herself in horrified fascination.

"Goddammit!" she whispered. "What will it take to convince you I'm telling the truth?"

"How about this?"

And grinning, he ground the cigar out on her forearm.

Excruciating pain seared her flesh, bolted through her like white-hot lightning. Tears sprang to her eyes, and it was all she could do not to scream.

He did it twice more, relighting the cigar each time, and burning her in that exact same spot so that a huge, blistering wound immediately swelled up. Yet somehow, she found the strength to refuse him the satis-faction of crying out.

When it became obvious that she really had nothing to tell, one of the men went around the apartment, methodically tearing out all the tele-phone wires except for the extension in the drawing room. Then Zandra's torturer took her upstairs to her bedroom.

"If yer brother 'ad 'alf the balls you've got," he said, "we wouldn't 'ave 'ad to 'urt you."

She shot him a withering look. "If *you* had half the balls I've got," she retorted, "you wouldn't get your kicks torturing women!"

That said, she stepped voluntarily into the bedroom—and slammed the door on *him*.

She heard him lock it from the outside. Then, pressing her ear against it, she listened to his receding footsteps.

Not wasting a moment, she sprang into action. First, she stripped off her "countess" gown, applied rudimentary first aid to her arm, and pulled on jeans, cable-knit sweater, and scuffed leather motorcycle jacket.

Second, she rummaged in her dresser, where she kept her passport and a stash of nearly three hundred pounds hidden beneath her underwear.

Third, she stuffed the barest essentials in her giant shoulder bag.

And fourth, she quietly raised the window, where a thick branch of the ancient elm in the backyard was obligingly within reach.

Heaving out her bag and boots, she waited a few minutes to see if the men had heard them drop. When she was convinced they hadn't, she climbed over the sill, took a deep breath, and leapt to the branch.

The climb down was swift; her disappearance stealthy.

By the time they discovered she'd escaped, she was already at Heathrow, boarding pass in hand.

Still, it wasn't until the British Airways jet was well over the Atlantic that she finally began to relax.

Now, taking a seat on the Manhattan-bound bus, she silently cursed the cause of her predicament.

Rudolph von Hohenburg-Willemlohe. Her brother the count.

Some count.

First-class *shit* was more like it!

4

MacKenzie Turner, fleet of foot in her pink, white, and blue leather Reeboks (she kept a pair of low-heeled black dress pumps in the bottom drawer of her desk), tried to make up for lost time by speed-walking to work. A stickler for punctuality, she would have double-timed it, but running would have meant working up an unpardonable and most unladylike sweat—hardly appropriate for the hushed old-world atmosphere of Burghley's.

"Damn and blast Charley Ferraro all to hell!" she growled furiously under her breath as her cassis-colored leather shoulder bag bounced against her lats with every hurried stride. She was never late for anything—*never!*

Catching the DON'T WALK light at Madison and Seventy-fifth, Kenzie saw, a block away, her place of employment. Burghley's, the self-proclaimed museum where the art was for sale. Eyeing the regal edifice, a sudden feeling of apprehension fluttered inside her, like a trapped bird desperately seeking escape. For the first time she wondered what the workday would bring.

A change in ownership.

What did that mean? Were cutbacks to be effected? Pink slips being readied? A tighter ship to be run?

Squaring her shoulders, she reminded herself that nothing could be gained through speculation.

She would find out soon enough.

Burghley's occupied the length and breadth of an entire city block, and was located at the sumptuous heart of one of the western world's prime luxury shopping districts, the eastern side of Madison Avenue between Seventy-third and Seventy-fourth Streets. The building was a six-story, neo-Renaissance palazzo of white marble, and worthy of Commodore Vanderbilt himself.

But with one major difference.

At Burghley's, even the air rights brought in big moolah. Rising from the steeply angled verdigris roofs were twin campaniles—two thirty-four story residential high-rises named, appropriately enough, Auction Towers—built and managed by Burghley's International Luxury Realty Division, and advertised as the address, "Where Life Imitates Art."

The Towers had its own separate entrance on Seventy-third Street, and boasted a private security staff, attended underground garage, and around-the-clock white-glove service.

The entrance to the auction galleries proper, however, was appropriately located directly on Madison Avenue, where a pair of baronially scaled, etched-glass doors almost, but not quite, reached the second floor, which sported a continuous carved fretwork frieze—a blatant copy from the Doge's Palace in Venice.

BURGHLEY'S
FOUNDED 1719

The plaque was brass, discreet, and polished; no giant letters were needed to trumpet *this* institution of the art world. But along the sidewalk, recessed eye-level windows held back-lit, blown-up slides of items in upcoming auctions—a *Beykoz* rosewater sprinkler, a Renoir, a gilt samovar, a Tiffany dragonfly lamp.

Today, since time was of the essence, Kenzie didn't so much as glance at the photographs. Even the uniformed doorman, all spit and polish, whom she normally engaged in a few pleasantries, was taken aback by the speed with which she tore past him, yanking open the heavy glass door herself before he could jump to.

Once inside, she sketched a wave at the armed security guards manning the vast lobby and strode rapidly toward the sweeping staircase, virtually flying up it to the second-floor galleries, where she made a shortcut through the carefully lit collection of Highly Important French and Continental Furniture, Decorations, and Clocks, which was slated to go on the auction block the following day.

It was an eye-popping, mind-boggling assortment of opulent treasures, including marble cassolettes, ormolu chenets, mahogany gueridons, gilded console tables, regal bureaus, desks, and commodes, and more chairs than you could shake a leg at—all the more amazing, since auctions of one kind or another at this, the world's ultimate recycling center, were a bi-weekly event, which proved that, with enough money to blow, a palace could indeed be furnished with one-stop shopping.

Pushing open a metal door marked FOR EMPLOYEES ONLY, Kenzie plunged "backstage"—the staff's euphemism for the whole of Burghley's to which the general public was not admitted. She took the flight of concrete fire stairs two at a time and rushed down a narrow carpeted corridor to her tiny office, located in the rear of the building.

Glancing at her watch as she ran, she whispered, "Eek! Gadzooks!"

She was late! To be exact, *forty-two* hair-raising minutes late on this, of all days, when Burghley's new majority shareholder was likely to drop by!

She burst breathlessly into her office, a windowless, fourteen-by-fourteen-foot cube of a cell which she shared with two other members of the Old Masters Paintings and Drawings staff. There was just room enough for the three gunmetal gray desks, all groaning under piles of reference tomes and catalogues, and each facing the kind of wall-mounted lightboard doctors used for viewing X rays—used, in this case, to peruse oversized slides of items whose provenances or values needed to be established.

The first thing Kenzie noted was that while her friend, Arnold Li, was at his desk, her nemesis, Bambi Parker, was absent from hers.

"Ah so!" greeted Arnold in his best Chinese takeout voice. Grinning up at her, he spun around on his swivel chair. "The prodigar daughter arrive at wrong rast."

"And late, too, dammit!" Kenzie cried, lunging for the bottom drawer of her desk to fish out the leather pumps she kept there. "Late!"

"Rate?" Arnold was slim, handsome, and Eurasian: Chinese father, Caucasian mother. Gay, too, and very sharp. He grinned slyly, one eyebrow arched. "Too much ruvemaking, eh?"

"Oh, do stop with that incessant routine!" she snapped in annoyance. "Oh, shit!" she moaned, plopping into her chair and gazing at one of her pumps in dismay. She repeated a string of curses, slamming the shoe on her desk to emphasize each word. "Shit." *Bang.* "Shit." *Bang.*

"Whoa!" said Arnold, reverting to perfect English. "What's the crisis?"

"This." She brandished one shoe malevolently. "I forgot that the heel of this damn thing broke off yesterday! *Now* what do I do?" she wailed.

"Tear off the other one," Arnold said calmly. "Then they'll match. Flats are all the rage, or haven't you heard?"

"D-do you have any idea what these . . . these things cost?" she sputtered in outrage.

He eyed her feet. "Well, then wear your ghetto flyers."

"You know I can't. 'Ms. Turner, have you forgotten?' " She mimicked Sheldon D. Fairey's secretary, Miss Botkin, to perfection. " 'Sneakers may be appropriate attire out on the playing field, but here at Burghley's, they are highly inappropriate—not to mention offensive!' "

That cracked Arnold up, but Kenzie just stared mournfully at her one good pump. After a moment's hesitation, and purposely averting her head, she held out the shoe. "Here," she said, looking away. "You break it off. I can't bring myself to do it."

Arnold took it and she busied herself attacking the laces of her Reeboks, cringing painfully when she heard the sharp snap of the heel.

"All done." Arnold cheerfully got up and with a flourish placed the pump on her desk. "If the shoe fits, wear it."

"Veeeeery funny." Scowling, she wriggled her feet into what, until now, had been her best pair of shoes, and upon which she had recklessly splurged a full week's salary. "And what have you got to be so cheerful about, anyway?" she growled.

"Why shouldn't I be cheerful?" Arnold asked.

"Well, because . . . aren't we supposed to line up outside and greet the new owner, or something?"

"Not that I heard." He sat back down and calmly unwrapped his breakfast bagel. "Relax." He took a bite and chewed. "The only person I know of who's coming to visit is Her Royal Highness."

"Her Royal Highness!" Kenzie snapped her head around. "*Which* Royal Highness? Queen Elizabeth? Queen Sirikit? Queen Beatrix? Queen Noor?"

He cast her a sidelong look. "Try Princess Goldsmith on for size."

"Oh, ho!" Abruptly frowning, she poked a thumb at the third desk in the cramped office. "And where, if I may be so bold, is Miss Locust Valley Lockjaw?"

"How should I know?" Arnold shrugged dismissively. "And anyway, why should you care? I'd have thought you'd be rejoicing that Bambi's not here."

"That's beside the point." Kenzie pursed her lips, momentarily lost in thought. Then she looked over at him and said, slowly, "I just find it highly peculiar that she's not in . . . especially today of all days. I mean, you *know* how she likes to suck up to the powers that be."

"No!" Arnold feigned shock and sat forward in his chair. Its vinyl upholstery squeaked. "You don't mean it! *Our* Bambi Parker?"

Kenzie turned to stare at the unoccupied desk some more. "Not that I really care," she remarked, "but it does make me wonder . . . where *is* Miss Perfect Parker?"

"My!" Bambi Parker marveled in a soft whisper. "*Oh, my!* You're hard already!"

Her fingers deftly unzipped the fly of Robert A. Goldsmith's king-size trousers, felt around for the opening in his baggy silk boxer shorts, and then unsnapped the two gussets.

The better to be eaten, the porcine man slid farther down in the mouse-colored velour seat. They were in the back of his black stretch Caddy, the one-way windows, prudently drawn curtains, and hermetically sealed silence cutting off the raucous, hard-edged world outside.

"Just drive," Goldsmith had growled to his chauffeur/bodyguard after Bambi had climbed inside at the prearranged corner. "I don't care if we just keep circling the goddamn block."

Which was exactly what they were doing now—going around and around Burghley's, catching the red light at every corner.

Slithering between his splayed legs, Bambi sank to her knees on the velour carpeting, barely conscious of the fact that the vehicle was moving, so smooth was the ride.

With clever fingers she dug his phallus out of his pants. By now she was familiar with every last vein, curve, and contour. It was very thick. Very red. And, alas, very stubby, with a big mushroom of a skin-ruffed knob, which never failed to remind her of one of those Dutch portraits with necks swathed in layers of lace. Long ago someone had botched his circumcision—but royally.

"Yummy!" she murmured, licking her lips and pretending greedy passion.

He grunted. "Just don't get any goddamn lipstick on my pants!"

"Don't worry." Bambi was way ahead of him, already wiping Estée Lauder's Knowing Red from her mouth with a handy Kleenex. Shoving the rumpled tissue under the seat, she got busy. Dexterously undid the belt from around his forty-seven-inch waist. Loosened his pin-striped, pleated gray wool trousers. Pulled them and the ultimate turn-off—cerulean blue silk boxer shorts sporting a pattern of hot air balloons—down around his knees. Then lowered her head into his lap.

Like a supplicant.

Or a skilled whore.

As her educated mouth closed around his penis, the new owner of Burghley's shut his eyes and remained perfectly still, content to do nothing but sprawl back and enjoy the ride.

Bambi Parker knew exactly which buttons to push. Three weeks of almost daily assignations had made her an expert on the sexual proclivities of one Robert A. Goldsmith.

They had met while he'd been negotiating to buy the venerable auction house and Sheldon D. Fairey, Burghley's chairman, CEO, and chief auctioneer, had rolled out the red carpet for the potential new owner. During the VIP tour, the two men had stopped in the main exhibition galleries to watch the mounting of an Old Masters Paintings exhibit, which Bambi Parker had helped oversee.

Blessed with a peripheral vision second to none, Bambi instantly recognized the billionaire out of the corner of an eye. And knowing the opportunity of a lifetime when she saw one, Bambi instantly seized the moment. With seeming spontaneity—pretending to ascertain that a Romney portrait (which was hanging perfectly straight), was indeed hanging perfectly straight—she took one step backward and then another and another until—presto!—she'd "accidentally" bumped smack dab into her prey.

"Oooooh!" she'd squealed, eyes widening in counterfeit horror while one hand flew up to her mouth. And turning around, she gushed in her best, whispery little girl's voice: "Gosh, I'm sooooo sorry!"

Robert A. Goldsmith wasn't blind—with his twenty-twenty vision, what he saw was a twenty-four-year-old genuine Barbie doll come to life. Tall, gorgeous, and perfectly groomed, everything about Bambi Parker was so flawless as to seem plasticized: skin, face, body—you name it— including Mykonos-white teeth, courtesy of lamination, and that special way she had of fluttering her long golden lashes before lowering her eyes demurely.

She was Robert A. Goldsmith's wet dream-come-true: a blonde, blue-eyed, hard-bodied *shiksa.*

Their gaze held for a full fifteen seconds.

Whereas Robert A. Goldsmith saw a living Barbie doll, Bambi Parker saw a big galoof with a shambling gait, size twelve feet, and a body that was best not described. But no matter. He possessed something all the male models in the world couldn't compete with—sheer power.

A silent communication passed between them, and Robert A. Goldsmith, who couldn't tell a Leroy Nieman from a Nattier—or care less— suddenly developed a keen interest in Old Masters. He'd diplomatically dismissed Sheldon D. Fairey by suggesting that, "as a departmental expert," Bambi ("Ms. Parker" at the time) act as his personal guide for this particular exhibit.

Sheldon D. Fairey, not about to get on the wrong side of the man he guessed, correctly, would soon become his boss, had wisely made himself scarce.

As soon as he'd gone, Robert A. Goldsmith smiled lecherously at Bambi and said, "I've got a feeling you've got a lot to teach me, l'il lady."

And Bambi, giggling and wiggling and batting her lashes, cooed, "And *I've* got the feeling you'd make a *great* pupil!"

In three shakes of a doe's tail, they'd ended up in the back of his limousine, where she proved her credentials—a Ph.D. in Deep Throat—for the first time.

Now, holding his penis in one hand, she flicked her tongue playfully around its bulbous head before sucking him all the way in. Then her lips closed around the base and her head bobbed up and down, up and down, until he tensed, uttered a slight groan, and his penis twitched as he shot his load.

Right into her mouth.

It wasn't exactly an earth-shaking event. In fact, if it hadn't been for the thick spurts of sticky goo, she'd hardly have known he'd ejaculated at all.

Averting her head and hiding her grimace, she whisked the wad of Kleenex back out from under the seat and spat discreetly into it.

For a while he just sprawled there, breathing heavily, his hooded eyes still closed. She used the time to advantage, scrambling back into her seat and swiftly repairing her makeup. Soon her face glowed in a palette of burnt oranges, spicy paprikas, and Knowing Red.

Then she pulled up his boxer shorts and trousers, nimbly snapped the gussets, zipped him up, and buckled his belt. "Now remember, Robert," she told him, "I'm always at your beck and call. *Always,*" she repeated, giving him a significant look.

When she got out of the car, she leaned down through the open door, smiled in at him, and furled and unfurled her fingertips childishly.

"Bye-bye!" she whispered in that breathy little girl's voice of hers.

He nodded absently, his fingers already pushing the buttons which drew aside the curtains and activated the opaque partition which slid down into the back of the driver's seat.

"Office," he tersely told his chauffeur/bodyguard, an ex-boxer with the flattened nose to prove it.

During the ride down to Wall Street, Robert A. Goldsmith unsnapped his briefcase, took out a draft of GoldMart's third-quarter report, and before tackling it, briefly reflected on Bambi Parker.

Maybe he wasn't one to show his emotions, but truth be told, he needed sex as much as the next guy—hey, maybe even more. And, in his book, there was nothing, nothing on earth quite like a blow job to start the day off on the right foot—especially when it was a blonde Locust Valley/Piping Rock Country Club ex-debutante *shiksa* of a blow job.

But out of sight, out of mind.

His reflection over, he tackled the report.

"Miss Turner?"

The voice was thin, but the ancient gentleman who pecked his head in through the partially open door was even thinner. "If it's not inconvenient, I shall be requiring your expertise this afternoon."

"Mr. Spotts!" Kenzie and Arnold chorused in unison, their chairs shooting away from their desks as they launched themselves to their feet.

"You're back!" Kenzie exclaimed, her heart leaping in delight as Arnold threw the door wide, and the threesome embraced in a warm but gentle hug.

Mr. Spotts kissed Kenzie on the forehead and tousled Arnold's hair with a palsied, paternal hand. Then, regarding them both from over the tops of his half lenses, which were perched at the very tip of his nose, he said: "Yes, I'm back. At least for now, my dears, for now . . ." He cupped a hand to his mouth and cleared his wattled throat. "But that's something we can get into later."

Kenzie had to tilt her head way back to look up at him—A. Dietrich Spotts was that tall. He was also very brittle and, due to severe osteoporosis, very stooped. His eyes were moist topaz, his head bald save for some thin, longish strands of white hair he wore combed back, and his skin was translucent from age. As always, he was immaculately dressed. Today he had on a hand-tailored dark gray wool suit, white shirt with pale gray stripes running through the cotton fabric, a beautifully knotted bordeaux silk tie patterned with tiny rooks, and a matching pocket square.

For the moment the three of them stood there, contently soaking up one another's company. Despite more than a half century's difference in their ages, they got along famously.

"At least now that you're back, things will finally return to normal!" Kenzie said happily, giving the old man another tender hug.

"Well?" Arnold inquired. "What's the prognosis?"

Mr. Spotts clicked his tongue against his teeth. "The good news, according to the quacks, is that I'll live."

"Then why the long face?" Kenzie asked. "What's the bad news?"

"Bad," said Mr. Spotts, giving a feeble sigh. "Very bad."

"Well, just *how* bad?" Kenzie, exchanging glances with Arnold, inquired anxiously.

Mr. Spotts sighed, flicked a speck of lint from his sleeve, and pinched the bridge of his nose with his thumb and forefinger, as though to stem the flow of pain. "Bad enough that I can no longer work," he warbled softly.

Kenzie and Arnold stared at him speechlessly.

"What do you mean, you can't work?" Arnold finally asked, once he found his voice.

"Those damn quacks insist that I take it easy. Told me I must retire and enjoy myself. Humph!" He shook his head, his wattle and dewlaps quivering with indignant outrage. "How can I enjoy retirement when *art* is my life's blood? Can you tell me that?"

"Oh, Mr. Spotts!" Kenzie moaned, looking crestfallen.

Mr. Spotts lifted a gnarled pale hand. "Enough of that. The last thing I want to discuss right now are my cardiovascular problems. In the meantime, Miss Turner, I've been invited to a party tonight by Prince Karl-Heinz von und zu Engelwiesen, one of our most valued clients. I always saw to him personally in the past, so I don't believe you ever had the opportunity of meeting him."

Kenzie shook her head. "I've seen pictures of him in the columns, but that's about it."

"Then all the more reason for me to introduce you. If you're free this evening, I'd be delighted if you would accompany me."

"You're asking me out on a date? Oh, Mr. Spotts! How sweet!"

"Not a date," he corrected, giving her a censorious look over his half glasses. "It's one of those loathsome high society events I usually go out of my way to avoid. However, in this case—" Mr. Spotts shrugged eloquently.

"I'd love to go," Kenzie assured him warmly.

"Good. Oh, and do dress up. It's black tie. Anyway, we'll talk more later. If you're both amenable, perhaps the three of us can have lunch together?" He looked inquiringly from Kenzie to Arnold.

"Sure!" Kenzie enthused.

"That'd be great!" Arnold added.

"Splendid. Lunch will be my treat." Then, lifting a trembly hand in a half wave, Mr. Spotts ducked back out. From the way he shuffled along to his office, it was obvious he was on his way to clean out his desk.

"Poor Mr. Spotts," Kenzie empathized as she slowly sank into her chair and swiveled around to face Arnold. "Retirement will kill him," she said quietly. "You know that."

"Only too well," he answered. "For him, Burghley's has always been home. If they'd have let him, he'd have eaten and slept here."

"You know, it's weird. But I really can't imagine this place without him."

"You're not the only one."

It was true. A. Dietrich Spotts was an institution—the only person left at the New York branch who had been there from the very day when it had first opened its doors, nearly forty-two years earlier. For over three decades now, he had headed the Old Masters Paintings and Drawings department, and neither Kenzie nor Arnold needed to be told that without him, things would never again be the same.

"Hi, guys!" intruded the bright, itty-bitty little chirp that set their teeth on edge as Bambi Parker breezed in, hoisting her Bottega Veneta bag onto her desk.

Mumbling desultory "Hi's," Arnold and Kenzie quickly buried their noses in work.

"Am I late?" Bambi asked, all wide-eyed innocence. "I think my watch has stopped." She made a production of shaking her wrist, frowning at the thin gold timepiece, tapping its face with a fingernail, and then holding it against her ear.

Arnold rolled his eyes; Kenzie, unable to help herself, glanced down at her nemesis's elegantly shod feet. Bambi's Roberto Vianni grosgrain pumps were perfectly intact, just as she'd known they would be. But then, Bambi's heels *never* broke, just as her palomino pantyhose *never* ran, split ends were unknown to her, and her fingernails *never, ever* chipped or broke.

5

*D*ina Goldsmith was on her way, and as the new "owner's" wife, was getting Burghley's red carpet treatment.

Outside, under the scalloped, dove gray awning with its trademark oxblood lettering, waited no less a personage than Sheldon D. Fairey, who held a total of three distinct job titles: chief auctioneer; Chairman of the Board of Directors, Burghley's North America; and President and Chief Operating Officer of Burghley's Holdings, Inc.

He was flanked on his right by Allison Steele, president of Burghley's North America, a deceptively feminine creature who never hesitated to go for the jugular, and on his left by David W. Bunker, Jr., the most senior of the New York branch's nine senior vice presidents.

This bland-faced triumvirate, whose patience had been worn extremely thin after standing there for nearly thirty minutes already, were careful not to show their irritation at the power behind the throne, who had yet to make her appearance.

Dina Goldsmith was—what else?—ultrafashionably late.

Outward appearances to the contrary, inwardly, each of them seethed. Especially Sheldon D. Fairey.

A busy man, he had far more pressing things with which to occupy his time. Every so often, he shot up the cuff of his bespoke suit to consult his gold wristwatch, a rare antique made by the very hands of Louis Elisee Piguet himself, and for none other than the wrist of the late John D. Rockefeller.

But Sheldon D. Fairey kept the true extent of his indignation in check. Aside from periodically glancing at the time, he managed to look outwardly serene.

He also looked to pinstripes born.

Tall, well-built, and perfectly turned out, he was not only imposing—his head could have been a prototype for the Antiquities department's very best Roman busts—but he proved that the looks of a certain few men, like the flavor of a handful of Grand Cru wines, only improved with age. He had thick silver hair combed back from a noble brow, an aquiline nose, solid cleft jaw, and jade marbles for eyes. Somewhere in the neighborhood of sixty, his aura exuded equal amounts of power, polish, and aristocracy.

But looks alone did not the man make. Sheldon D. Fairey was a powerhouse in the art world. He had worked wonders during his ten years at the helm of Burghley's North American operations. For it had been *he* who had guided the auction house to its present number-one position in New York.

Too, it had been at *his* instigation that Burghley's had moved from its pricey, limited rental space on Park Avenue to its current, outrightly owned square block—including not only the spacious palazzo housing the auction house proper, but conceiving and then overseeing the construction of Auction Towers, that prime residential complex which out-Trumped Trump Tower itself.

And finally, *he,* and he alone, had initiated the highly controversial but financially lucrative practice of helping finance multimillion-dollar art for potential bidders.

Now, just as he shot back his cuff to check his watch for the nth time, a block-long white stretch limo with DINA G vanity plates and gold electroplate trim pulled up to the curb.

A full thirty-three minutes late, he noted sourly as he adjusted his cuffs and yellow silk Hermès tie, simultaneously wondering why anyone with Dina Goldsmith's wherewithal would choose such a vulgar, outlandish mode of transportation instead of something tasteful like a dark Rolls-Royce or, even better yet, a discreet Town Car?

New money! he thought in disgust. New money always had to trumpet its bourgeois insecurity!

But his face did not betray so much as a flicker of emotion. Nor did he wait for Dina's chauffeur to come around and open her door. Turning up his famous charm, Sheldon D. Fairey took matters into his own manicured hands and helped the new Queen of Manhattan alight with the same gallant demeanor he would have reserved for the Queen Mother herself.

Dina Goldsmith emerged from the Cadillac looking fashion-runway perfect. Having kept the more subtle light of autumn in mind, she had used restraint on her makeup, with just a touch of amethyst shadowing her eyes and a hint of bronze gloss highlighting her rusty red lipstick. She wore a micro-length, black wool tunic-dress with big gilt buttons. A high-necked black lace blouse. Diamond-patterned black leggings. And her hair pulled back and secured with a gold barrette which did double duty by anchoring the silky, shoulder-length blonde hairpiece that matched her hair color precisely.

But she hadn't been as discreet about wearing daytime jewelry as she'd been about her makeup, because no matter what the etiquette experts pontificated, she, Mrs. Robert A. Goldsmith, fully subscribed to the belief that diamonds *were* appropriate for daytime wear, a fact to which every gemstone expert, diamond cutter, and *cognoscente* could universally attest, for it is only in bright *daylight*—especially dazzlingly bright *north-*

ern light—that diamonds truly came into their own, reflecting and refracting their brilliance the way their cut intended.

Also a firm believer that *bigger* is *always* better, each of Dina's earlobes was weighed down with great twenty-five-carat square-cut diamond solitaires.

"Ah . . . my dear Mrs. Goldsmith!" Sheldon D. Fairey greeted in his plummiest voice.

"Sheldon," Dina acknowledged.

He bent deferentially over her hand and kissed a mere breath on Dina's fingertips. "May I compliment you on how marvelous you look?"

Dina preened visibly, eating up the attentive homage—and for good reason. She had a memory like an elephant, and today was the day she would get back at him for a whole slew of past slights.

Having greeted Dina, Fairey first introduced Allison Steele and then it was her turn to bring the triumvirate's attention to her sidekick—Gabriella Morton. "My secretary." Dina gestured to the tweedy, bossy squirt of a woman. "Miss Morton."

"How do you do, Ms. Morton?" Fairey greeted in his fruity tones.

"That's '*Miss*' Morton, if you please," Gaby sniffed, pumping his arm energetically up and down. "I remember when it was perfectly acceptable to be a 'Miss'—and in my book, it *still* is."

He looked somewhat taken aback. "Er, of course, Ms. . . . er, *Miss* Morton . . ."

Dina felt like hugging Gaby on the spot; instead, she made a mental note to give her a well-deserved bonus.

Well-deserved because, several years earlier, it had been this self-same Sheldon D. Fairey who, at one of the Goldsmiths' parties, had dismissed Dina's prized trio of Renoirs as "minor," and had hinted that her treasured Degas *Racehorses* from Christie's was *possibly* second-rate and had dared—actually *dared!*—to question the authenticity of her Toulouse-Lautrec, the very Toulouse-Lautrec she had successfully bid for at Burghley's while no less an auctioneer's mallet than Sheldon D. Fairey's own had sealed the sale! Then, as if *that* hadn't been provocation enough, she had actually overheard him adding insult to injury by snidely referring to her ornate French furniture as "Louis Cohen" behind her back!

So wasn't it delicious that the tables should suddenly have turned? And that *he*—Sheldon D. Fairey, of all people!—should now be forced to eat humble pie and have to kowtow to *her?*

"Louis Cohen" indeed!

Fairey was smiling ingratiatingly at her.

"I cannot tell you how pleased I am to have this opportunity to show you around," he was saying, placing a solicitous hand under Dina's elbow to steer her inside.

But Dina, pumped up with adrenaline, was not quite ready to move.

"Sheldon, sweetie . . ." She frowned at the uniformed doorman who was holding open one of the thick plate glass doors for them.

"Yes?" he asked.

She gestured. "That—uniform!"

Sheldon D. Fairey inspected the doorman, who was fastidiously groomed and spit-shined as always. "What about it, Mrs. Goldsmith?" he asked cautiously.

Dina turned to him, piercing him with a drill-bit gaze. "Those breeches . . ." she observed frostily, pointing and making a little production of shivering. "And those . . . well, those storm trooper boots! They're too neo . . . you know . . . *Gestapo?*"

Sheldon D. Fairey coughed into a cupped hand. "Actually, it's a faithful copy of an English chauffeur's uniform," he informed her.

"Nonetheless." Dina smiled saccharinely, reveling in his discomfiture. "Those uniforms have got to go. Blazers and ties will do nicely . . . *and* they'll be far less intimidating as far as Burghley's customers are concerned. Don't you agree?"

"Hmmm," he said noncommittally.

"Of course you do," Dina purred before turning to Gaby, who was right behind her, steno pad and pen at the ready. "Make a note of that, Gaby, will you?"

Gaby smirked. "Okie dokie, Mrs. Goldsmith."

"Now then, Sheldon." Dina slid her arm through Fairey's. "Shall we get on with the tour? I want to see everything. Absolutely *evvvverything!*"

And so Dina set about having the time of her life. Busting Sheldon D. Fairey's chops was an eminently satisfying experience.

Once inside the spacious lobby, Dina paused as though to soak in the surroundings, her laser-eyed gaze jumping from one uniformed security guard to the next.

"Really, Sheldon," she said with a frown. "I do believe those guards are half-asleep. Why, look at that one over there!"

She pointed an accusatory finger.

"He's actually sitting down on the job! *Sitting down,* Sheldon!"

Fairey followed the direction of her quivering finger with unease. Just his bad luck for a guard to be caught having his morning coffee and Danish on one of the customers' benches. Gnashing his teeth, he wondered how word of Dina's arrival had not gotten around to everyone, dammit!

"Hmmm," he said, looking concerned.

"Well? Do they, or do they not, seem far less than alert?"

"Less," Fairey was forced to admit, but quickly assured her: "I'll see to it that their boss is informed. That should shake them up."

"I'm afraid talking about it won't be enough. It's action that counts, Sheldon. *Action!* I suggest you fire the entire lot and hire new ones."

"Fire the—" he stammered, looking stricken.

"The entire lot." Dina was unrelenting.

"Very well," he sighed.

Dina turned around to Gaby, who was standing right behind her. "You *are* making a note of that, Gaby?"

"Sure am!" Gaby assured her, not quite able to hide her smirk.

It was all Sheldon D. Fairey could do to grit his teeth and bear it. From his expression, it was clear he'd rather be anywhere but here. In Timbuktu—or, better yet, lost on an ice floe somewhere. Anywhere would have been preferable, so long as thousands of miles separated him from Dina Goldsmith.

In Burghley's Basement, the low-ceilinged, downstairs arcade where a gamut of items ranging from silver to paintings to furnishings were auctioned off every Sunday for customers requiring quick cash, Dina's head swiveled slowly in all directions.

"Sheldon, dear? Don't you agree that the lighting down here is . . . well . . . a bit too garish? I mean, how on earth can we expect people to place respectable bids on items when every chip and crack practically *screams* at them? Just look at this piece of Export porcelain!"

She glared at the offending item.

"It looks like junk under these lights! Would *you* want to buy it?" And before he could utter a reply, she turned to her secretary. "Are you getting it down, Gaby?"

"Word for word!" came the cheerful reply.

As they continued their tour, Dina didn't let up for an instant. She was making up for every slight she had ever suffered from Sheldon D. Fairey—and then some.

At the sales counter upstairs, where books and catalogues from each of the various Burghley's branches were on sale, Dina said, "Sheldon? Are *three* girls behind that one small counter really necessary? I'd prune them down to two at the most! Staff is our biggest overhead, and cost effectiveness means extra profits, you know. And while you're at it, you might see to it that the staff smiles and welcomes potential customers. If you ask me, those young ladies are altogether too snooty and arrogant. Burghley's must be made to seem less imposing and intimidating—and that starts with the staff!"

"I'm getting it down," came Gaby's voice from behind.

In the soaring auditorium that was the main auction gallery proper, Dina's fluid sweep of a hand encompassed the rows of chairs lined up to either side of the wide center aisle.

"*Me . . . tal* folding chairs?" she intoned, a mere arching of an eyebrow emphasizing her distaste. "Really, Sheldon. It's obvious *you've* never had to sit on one of those for two or three hours. Believe me, I have. Clients who sit here for the privilege of bidding thousands, even millions, of dollars on furniture and works of art deserve chairs more appropri- ate to their station." She gave him a saccharine smile. "You do agree, don't you?"

"We haven't had any complaints thus far," Fairey ventured stiffly.

"Be that as it may," she said airily, "the more comfortable the seat, the longer a client is apt to stay. And the longer he or she stays, the more likely they are to bid on items they hadn't even considered!"

Dina turned to Gaby, who, suppressing a snide grin, was scratching away in her notepad.

Next, Sheldon D. Fairey escorted Dina to the conference room, which was sheathed in seventeenth-century, Louis XIV boiserie. Sure- ly, he thought, this was the one place where she couldn't find fault with anything.

How wrong he was.

Dina, after doing an eyesweep of the room in general, advanced on the nearest of the twenty-four identical giltwood armchairs which sur- rounded the twenty-foot-long conference table, and inspected the chair closely. It was splendidly symmetrical and voluptuously wide and deep, with a cartouche-formed backrest, serpentine-fronted seat, and ancient, rust-colored velvet upholstery.

"Why, my goodness!" she gasped. "Unless my eyes deceive me, and I don't believe they do, I could swear these are all authentic Chippendale!"

"Actually, they're not," sniffed Sheldon D. Fairey, immensely pleased to be able to show off his superior knowledge. "They are George III, circa . . . oh, 1770 or thereabouts."

"Hmm. George III . . ." Dina ran an admiring hand along one of the smooth, richly carved backs. "That should make them exceeding- ly valuable."

"Oh, I'd appraise their market value at somewhere in the neighbor- hood of twenty-five and thirty-five thousand dollars per pair," he said offhandedly. "You must agree they really are quite, quite exceptional. Mu- seum quality, to say the least."

Dina did some instant mental computations and gasped. "Why, that means the entire set is worth anywhere between six hundred to eight hun- dred and forty thousand dollars!"

Fairey nodded. "Somewhere in that vicinity, yes," he murmured.

Knitting her brows together, she cocked her head sideways and frowned. "Are they here on consignment?"

"Consignment!" He allowed himself a soft chuckle. "Good heav- ens, no! As a matter of public trust and honor, consigned items are never lent, borrowed, or in any way used while in our temporary custody. No, Burghley's happens to own these outright. Has, for well over a century, I believe."

A cloud flitted across Dina's picture-perfect features. "Correct me if

I'm wrong, Sheldon, but what you're telling me is that they're a corporate asset. No?"

"Oh, indeed they are!"

Her features hardened. "Well, not anymore, they aren't, at least not if *I* have any say in the matter. I suggest they're sold and replaced with copies at once! *Really!* Employees have absolutely no business sitting on such priceless treasures!"

"B-but they've been in Burghley's possession since eighteen—"

"So?" Dina widened her aquamarine eyes. "They also happen to be among Burghley's assets, and as such are, in your very own words, very, very valuable. *Too* valuable, I should think, to just sit here gathering dust. I see that I shall have to bring this matter up with Mr. Goldsmith at once."

Fairey, his face reddening and puffing, looked as though he was on the verge of spontaneous human combustion.

"Gaby?"

"It's down," cackled Gaby, happily scribbling away.

Fairey eyed the twenty-four precious chairs morosely; then, since Dina had him over a barrel, he expelled a noisy breath. "They'll be in the next Fine English Furniture auction," he decreed.

Dina smiled brilliantly and hooked a chumlike arm through his.

"I knew you'd see it my way, Sheldon, dear!" she cooed. "Didn't I tell you we'd get along famously? It's so simple. I tell you what to do, you agree with me, and there's no problem. Right?"

And turning, she winked at Gaby, whose face wore a malicious crocodilelike smile.

Finally, back out on the sidewalk beside her waiting limousine, Dina turned to Fairey and said, "Oh, and one more thing, Sheldon, dear." She wasn't about to ride off into the exhaust fumes without giving his balls one final, departing squeeze.

"You do remember my Toulouse-Lautrec? The very one you sold me right here at Burghley's, and whose authenticity you afterward questioned at my home?"

Sheldon D. Fairey went red as a beet. Swallowing miserably, he cursed himself for ever having opened his mouth.

"Well, to ensure that nothing like that every occurs again—at least not here at Burghley's—I want you to consider the matter of vetting every single item this establishment sells. You *will* bring that to the attention of the executive staff. Won't you?"

He murmured that he would.

"You do that," she said. And giving him a long, hard look, she started to duck into the white stretch limo before changing her mind, stepping back out, and turning to him once again. "Oh, and one last thing," she said in treacly tones, as though it had just occurred to her.

He raised his eyebrows dutifully. "Yes, Mrs. Goldsmith?"

"Doesn't Prince Karl-Heinz von und zu Engelwiesen sit on Burghley's advisory board?"

"Actually, he is on the board of directors."

"Which one? Burghley's North America? Or Burghley's Holdings?"

"Burghley's Holdings," he replied, referring to the auction house's worldwide operations.

Looking thoughtful, she tapped her lips and said, "I see. I shall want to meet him sometime."

"I shall pass along the message," Fairey promised her. "In fact, I'll do so at his birthday party this very evening."

Dina felt her stomach contract. The Sheldon D. Faireys had been invited to the prince's birthday party! *And Robert and I haven't?* She decided to remedy this oversight at once. She was, after all, the new Queen of Manhattan. As such, it was time to wield her power and make her presence felt.

"Sheldon, dear," she said in a voice as smooth as velvet, "the moment you get back to your office, I just know you'll pick up the telephone, talk to Prince Karl-Heinz, and secure an invitation for Robert and myself. Isn't that right?"

He looked positively apoplectic. "I . . . er . . . I'll see what I can do," he murmured, fidgeting uncomfortably with his collar, which suddenly felt exceedingly tight.

She smiled sweetly. "Oh, I know you will, Sheldon! I just know you will! I'll expect invitations for Robert and myself to be messengered to our apartment within the—no. On second thought . . ." Once again, she tapped a perfectly manicured fingernail against her perfectly glowing lips. "We have a houseguest, so you'd better make that an invitation for three . . . no, *four,* since our guest is a lady who will require an escort."

"I . . . I'll get on it right away," he sputtered.

"Of course you will, sweetie!" And with that, she threw him a kiss before ducking into her limousine, secure in the knowledge that he would move heaven and earth to accommodate her.

Taking a cue from her boss, Gaby eyeballed him with a long hard look of her own before piling in after her.

"Home," Dina gaily instructed her chauffeur, and within moments the limousine eased smoothly away from the curb and merged into the dense uptown traffic.

✺ 6 ✺

*L*unch was Mr. Spotts's treat. He insisted upon La Caravelle.
    "My last cholesterol splurge," he sighed sadly as the captain led them past the murals and seated them at a red velvet banquette along the wall of mirrors. "Today, I say the hell with those doctors! I am going to have my usual *terrine de foie gras* followed by *poularde rôtie à l'ail doux,* and top it all off with a frozen cassis mousse in a ring of apple slivers, not to mention a nice vintage bottle of Château Margaux. If my heart gives out from all that pleasure, then so be it. At least I shall have had the satisfaction of dying quite contentedly."

When the appetizers came, Kenzie pushed her *chair de crabe Caravelle* desultorily around on her plate. That the mass of fresh crab meat with cognac dressing, caviar, and lobster roe was a symphony for the taste buds made absolutely no difference to her. She had simply lost her appetite at the news of Mr. Spotts's forced retirement—all the more so, since on the way over to the restaurant, he had dropped the bombshell that today would be his very last day at Burghley's.

She was still in a state of shock.

Mr. Spotts frowned at Arnold Li, who was picking at his truffle-studded *foie gras* with an equal lack of enthusiasm.

"Young man, the way you are eating that is really quite, quite unforgivable," said Mr. Spotts with a gesture of his fork. "Unless, of course, it is inedible, in which case I shall have to summon the waiter and register a complaint."

Arnold shook his head. "You know that's not it," he said tightly, putting down his fork, the tines resting, inverted, on the edge of his plate. He leaned across the table. "It's just that we can't imagine the department getting along without you!"

"Well, you two had better get along without me, Mr. Li." Mr. Spotts paused, smiling acidly, and righteously lifted a stern, crooked pinkie finger in that learned way of his. "Otherwise, that blonde nincompoop named for a Disney cartoon will see to it that our department's most precious asset, its reputation—in short, *everything*—will go right down the drain."

Kenzie took a sip of her Margaux. "What I want to know," she asked listlessly, setting down the wineglass and running her moist finger around its rim, but too lethargically to make it chime even feebly, "is now that you can't work, what are you going to do?"

"Do?" Mr. Spotts looked slightly taken aback. "Why, I'm not supposed to do anything!" He sighed deeply. "Unless you call retiring to the Sunshine State *doing* something?"

His perfectionist eyes consulted theirs and saw no reaction. He smiled grimly.

"My widowed sister, Cosima . . ." he murmured, "has . . . umn . . . what I believe in Fort Lauderdale is referred to as an . . . umn . . . 'Waterfront French Renaissance Estate' . . . if you can imagine such a contradiction in terms?" One eyebrow, the precise color of silverplate, rose in distaste and he tutted his tongue.

"An abomination. Spun-sugar Tara meets Beaux Arts on the Intracoastal, as only a native Floridian could design. But such is life. It could be worse, you know. I have a generous pension and my not inconsiderable collection of Old Masters, which, though second rate, are nonetheless still quite superb. So you see, at least I'm not destitute." His lips broadened into a smile. "However, enough of this depressing subject! The reason I invited you both to lunch is not to talk about me, but to discuss *your* futures."

"*Our* futures?" Kenzie and Arnold chorused as one.

Mr. Spotts tucked his chin, tortoiselike, down into his chest and gave them a severe look from over his half glasses. "As of tomorrow, one of you shall have to take over the reins as head of the department."

Pausing again, he looked from one of them to the other.

"Well? Which of you shall it be?"

Kenzie didn't hesitate. "Arnold," she said.

"Kenzie," Arnold said simultaneously.

All three of them sat there in stunned silence before bursting into spontaneous laughter.

"In all seriousness," Kenzie insisted solemnly once they'd stopped laughing, "Arnold's far more knowledgeable about the seventeenth century than I am."

"Yes, but you're the expert when it comes to the eighteenth," Arnold told her. "And, you display far better leadership abilities, and are by leaps and bounds more diplomatic than I could ever be."

"My God!" Mr. Spotts could only shake his head in exasperated wonder. "Other people would be tearing each other's eyeballs out for such an opportunity! But you? The two of you just sit there, insisting that the other is the better qualified! I must say, never in my entire life have I ever run across anything quite like this. No, never." Then he frowned thoughtfully. "Still, we don't have much time in which to decide this. I have a meeting scheduled with Mr. Fairey for this afternoon. He shall want my recommendation by then. So?" His eyes flicked back and forth between them. "Which of you wants to be in charge?"

Kenzie and Arnold sat there, silently digesting what he had just said. In truth, while neither of them was loath to get promoted, both of them were dedicated professionals for whom quality was not negotiable—both only wanted what was best for the art form to which they had dedicated their lives.

"If it's all right with you, Kenz," Arnold said slowly, "I'd rather not be saddled with all the politics. Besides, you really are the best as far as diplomacy's concerned."

"Well, if you're certain," she said dubiously.

"Of course I am. You know I'm happiest when I'm left alone to either pore over art, or thumb through volumes of dusty reference books. If I'd wanted to deal with management, I would have joined IBM or AT&T."

"Well, then." Mr. Spotts sat forward. "Now that we have that . . . umn . . . little matter out of the way, there is one last thing."

Kenzie looked at him questioningly, but instead of replying, he reached for the battered old leather satchel he always lugged around with him, and which was on the banquette beside him. Unclasping it, he opened it and lifted out two small, flat packages wrapped in plain brown paper and secured with Scotch tape. Looking slightly embarrassed, he handed one across the table to Kenzie, and the other to Arnold.

"What's this?" Kenzie asked.

"Oh . . . umn . . . just a little . . . you know . . ." The old man waved a hand dismissively. "Something to remember me by."

"Oh, Mr. Spotts!" Kenzie chided. "You shouldn't have!"

"But I did, and that is my prerogative. Well?" He gestured impatiently. "Don't just sit there looking stupefied. Open them!"

Kenzie and Arnold tore away the wrapping papers. Then they sat there, staring at a small framed picture in stunned silence.

"Why it's . . . it's . . ."

Kenzie's voice deserted her while her eyes followed every line of the exquisite study of a baby rendered in pen, brown ink, and a purple wash on blue paper, its effect heightened here and there with traces of black and white chalk.

"A Zuccaro!" she finally managed in a breathy whisper. "The one re-touched by Rubens himself!"

Slowly she raised her eyes and stared across the table.

"My God, Mr. Spotts! You know I couldn't possibly—"

"Now, now. You not only can, my dear, but you must. Really, I find this *most* embarrassing . . ." Mr. Spotts glanced around, visibly distressed. "Yes, yes, *most* embarrassing indeed . . ."

"And *this!*" Arnold said shakily.

Kenzie balanced her weight on the back of Arnold's chair as she half stood, looking over his shoulder at the picture in his hands.

"Tiepolo," she murmured automatically, needing but one glance at the buff paper with its red chalk and highlights of black and white. "To be precise," she added, "Giovanni Battista Tiepolo's *Bishop Saint Healing a Young Woman.*"

"All I ask is that you enjoy them," Mr. Spotts said. "Hang them on your walls and derive pleasure from them. Think of them as part of your nest eggs."

"Oh, Mr. Spotts!" Kenzie whispered, tears coming into her eyes. "You know we can't possibly—"

"In that case," the old man said cryptically, "perhaps it will make you feel better to know that these are not . . . umn . . . exactly outright gifts?"

"Oh? Then what are they?"

"They're conditional. You know . . . they come with strings attached?" Mr. Spotts made marionette-controlling motions with his gnarled fingers.

"Strings?" Arnold asked, his interest piqued. He sat forward. "What kinds of strings?"

Mr. Spotts eyed them both solemnly over the rims of his half lenses. "What I need," he sighed quietly, "is to extract one promise from each of you."

"We'd gladly do that anyway," Kenzie assured him. "There's no need to give us presents!"

"I know." Mr. Spotts nodded. "But this particular favor . . . well, it's a rather large one." He stared intently from one of them to the other.

"Just name it," said Kenzie.

The old man was silent.

"Yes, just say the word," pressed Arnold.

"Save the department!" Mr. Spotts's voice was soft but harshly bitter, like a brittle, arctic wind. "That's the one thing I ask!"

Every Tuesday and Thursday Bambi Parker spent her lunchtime at the Vertical Club on East Sixty-first Street. The way she figured it, she was twenty-four, going on twenty-five, and not getting any younger. Besides, at Burghley's you never knew who you were apt to run into. It behooved a single young woman to always be in shape and look her absolute best.

After thirty minutes of concentrated workout, she peeled off her lime green and shocking pink Spandex exercise outfit, showered, dressed, repaired her makeup, and moseyed on back to Burghley's, eating a container of non-fat, lemon-flavored yogurt while checking out the windows of the clothing boutiques along the way. When she finally returned to the auction house, she headed straight for one of the second-floor employees' powder rooms.

This particular one, which she frequented, was known as "The Club," since it unofficially doubled as sorority house for the most popular among Burghley's army of Seven Sisters–educated arts majors—trust-fund babies all—every one of whom was biding her time working in an appropriately genteel job until Prince Charming came along.

Then, once they were swept off to the grand townhouses and penthouses of the upper East Side of Manhattan, plus oceanfront weekend "cottages" out in the Hamptons, or bucolic country estates in the rolling hills of northwestern Connecticut, the roles they now played would be reversed, and the self-perpetuating cycle become evident: Burghley's ex-employees would trade the expertise gained working at the auction house by becoming its most knowledgeable clientele.

Even before opening the door of "The Club," Bambi could already hear the noise coming from within. It sounded like an aviary—albeit, judging from the chatter and coos, trills and squeaks, and more than a few Locust Valley lockjaws, a highly elite aviary consisting of only the most carefully select and singularly bred of all species.

Bambi felt right at home as she squeezed between two girls to get at the long stretch of mirror above the sinks; sometime back, the more enterprising among them had taken up a collection, so that a row of frosted makeup bulbs was installed all the way across the top. A fiercely unflattering light, it was perfect for its purposes.

"Hiya Bambs!" greeted the reflection of the preening blonde leaning into the mirror on her right. "Howareya?"

Bambi smiled into the mirror at Elissa Huffington, who could have been a model if the *Social Register* Huffingtons hadn't instantly put the skids on *that* particular line of work. But Elissa didn't rate much of a reply from Bambi—she was one of Bambi's major competitors in the Great Manhunt for Mr. Right.

"Well?" Elissa asked through a barely moving mouth as she slid Perfect Pumpkin lipstick across her lips. "Aren't ya gonna share the news?"

"News? What news?" Bambi leaned into the mirror, thickening her lashes with lightning strokes of an eyelash brush.

"*What* news! About your boss—what else!"

"Well? What about him?"

"You mean . . . oh, Christ! You *would* be the last to know!"

"Know what?" Bambi's eyelash brush was a blur.

"That 'The Translucent' is finally retiring—*that's* what!"

Bambi's eyelash brush stopped moving. "Say that again?" She stared at Elissa's reflection.

"Gawd!" Elissa rolled her eyes. "It's about time, isn't it? I mean, if anyone's an antiquity, it's gotta be him . . ." Elissa kept her voice deliberately light and chiding, but her sharp eyes, catching Bambi's reflection, gratified her to no end: the tidbit had elicited the hoped-for reaction.

But after a moment, Bambi sloughed off the news with a shrug, leaned back into the mirror, and resumed brushing her lashes. "There've been rumors about Mr. Spotts's retirement since the very first day I started working here," she said dismissively.

"Yes, but this time it isn't a rumor. This is on the up-and-up."

"Oh?" Bambi's eyes flicked suspiciously sideways at Elissa. "Says who?"

"Says Sheldon D. Fairey's assistant secretary. She overheard the whole thing. You might as well face it, Bambs. Today's your boss's last day on the job. So. Who d'you think'll get promoted? You? Kenzie? Arnold? Or d'you think they might bring in an outsider?"

Bambi abruptly felt physically ill. *Why haven't I been informed?* she railed silently, wanting to clutch the sink and retch. *Was that the reason those three traipsed off together? Purposely leaving me behind because they decided to discuss succession?*

She could practically see them, thick as thieves. Hunched over a dim table like a cabal. Whispering. Scheming. Hatching their plot . . .

Her chest suddenly felt as if a boa constrictor had coiled itself around her, and was relentlessly tightening its grip.

Suddenly her heart skipped a beat and something hard and steely gleamed in her eyes. The corners of her lips curved into a bladelike smile. *Well! If* the matter of succession *was* being discussed over lunch without her, then *fine! She* had a trick or two up her own beautifully tailored sleeve, and a better one than that kissy-kissy little triumvirate could ever come up with!

"Anyway, I'd check it out if I were you," Elissa was saying, giving Bambi a pointed look. "Catch my drift?"

"I do, and thanks, 'Liss." Bambi hurriedly stuffed her makeup back into her purse. "See you later."

"If ya hear anything new, you'll let me know? Us debs have got to stick together, right?"

"Uh, right," Bambi said. "I'd better run along now. 'Bye!"

She backed out from the row of chattering girls who, with her departure, immediately spread out further, sensing, more than seeing, additional precious inches of elbow room becoming available.

In the vestibule outside the powder room, Bambi squeezed into one of the phone booths, shut the door, and deposited a quarter. She didn't want to use her office phone—not if she wanted to make certain she wouldn't be overheard should the trio return early from lunch. This was one call which required the utmost privacy—and urgency.

Punching the highly secret number of Robert A. Goldsmith's highly private line down on Wall Street—the one telephone which bypassed his platoon of secretaries—she waited through one ring, two, three—

Then:

"Robert?"

Bambi used her best itty-bitty wittle girl's voice.

"It's me—Bambs. Listen, I'm in a phone booth, so I've got to make it real short."

She cupped her hands around the receiver and glanced quickly over both shoulders, making certain no one was standing within earshot.

"I just heard that the head of my department's retiring," she whispered into the phone. "I want that job, Robert. I want it so badly I can taste it!" She took a deep breath. "I'll do *anything* to get it. And by anything, I mean *anything.*"

Bambi was alone in the office and considering cutting out early when the telephone chirruped. She stared reproachfully at her extension, wondering whether or not to answer it. She knew that she *should,* but that was beside the point.

Why *not* skip out early? Why even answer that damned insistently chirruping phone?

Suddenly it occurred to her that it might be Robert, and she lunged for the receiver. "Old Masters!" she breathed perkily. "Ms. Parker speaking!"

A voice which definitely did *not* belong to Robert A. Goldsmith said, "Hello? This is Zachary Bavosa of the legal firm Calvert, Barkhorn, Waldburger, and Slocum. I'm calling on behalf of a client of ours."

Bambi suppressed a sigh. "And how may I help you?"

"A client of ours who . . . er . . . wishes to remain anonymous . . . has inherited a painting. A Holbein, to be exact."

"Yes . . . ?"

"Both Christie's and Sotheby's, as well as several private dealers, have determined it to be genuine, and have appraised its value at somewhere between twenty and thirty million dollars."

Suddenly Bambi was all ears. "And you wish a third opinion, I take it?"

He chuckled. "Oh, no, Ms. Parker. We're quite convinced it's genuine. Our client wishes to sell it."

Then what's the catch? she wondered. *If it's the real McCoy, both Christie's and Sotheby's must be chomping at the bit to handle the sale. Why call us, also, unless there's a problem?* "We'd be glad to take a look at it," she said carefully. And then, in a reflex action, Bambi threw caution to the four winds and plunged right on it. "I'm sure we'd be delighted to handle it!"

He was silent for a moment. "I could bring it by tomorrow, along with the pertinent documentation of its provenance. Would eleven a.m. be convenient for you?"

Her heart skipped a beat. "Eleven a.m. will be fine," she assured him. "Just ask for me. Bambi Parker."

Well, well, well! she thought as she hung up the phone. *What a coup! From the sound of things, the Holbein will be the star of the next Old Masters auction!* She could see it already. *We'll put it on the cover of the catalogue. Send out press releases and watch a bidding war break out. Chances are, it might even set a world record for the artist.* Bambi could barely contain her excitement. *I can't wait to see Kenzie and Arnold's expressions. They'll be so envious they'll want to tear my eyes out!*

7

832 FIFTH AVENUE

The elegant white letters, outlined in black, graced the creamy whipcord canopy that extended from the building to the street like a convex lozenge.

Engraved plaques, shiny as new money, repeated the three-digit number on either side of the brass and etched-glass Art Deco doors.

The Robert A. Goldsmiths occupied two full penthouse floors in this, one of the most expensive residential addresses in the world. From outside, the pristine prewar apartment house looked like a sand-blasted armory. Inside, a small army *was* on duty around the clock. In addition to the uniformed doorman, two armed security guards were stationed in the marble lobby, and a third guard, a state-of-the-art alarm system, *and* closed-circuit television protected the delivery entrance on East Eighty-first Street.

The security measures were well founded, considering that the tenants had an aggregate worth of between eighteen and twenty billion dollars.

Zandra von Hohenburg-Willemlohe, who had been the Goldsmiths' houseguest before, appreciated the Elysian edifice, and not for its white-glove service, either. For her, it was the ideal hideout. If the London goons somehow managed to tail her here, they would never be able to get past the lobby, since even known visitors were as carefully screened as guests at the gates of the White House.

"You may go on up, madam," the doorman intoned gravely after having conferred over the house phone with someone at the Goldsmiths'. "It's the fourteenth floor."

When Zandra got off the elevator, the pedimented double doors to the Goldsmith apartment were open wide and an impeccably dressed man stood waiting in the luxuriously furnished vestibule.

"I am Julio," he sniffed, "the majordomo. Madame has informed me that you are to be shown every courtesy."

Without turning his head, he raised one hand and snapped his fingers. Instantly, and seemingly out of nowhere, scurried a uniformed maid with downcast eyes and a flustered manner.

Julio cocked one disapproving eyebrow at Zandra's disreputable-looking shoulder bag and the maid instantly jumped to and snatched it.

"If you will follow me, please?" Julio announced loftily, "I shall show you to your guest suite."

They passed an opulent marble staircase with an ornate wrought-iron and ormolu balustrade which swept gracefully up to the second floor of the duplex, the curved, yellow-marbled wall alongside it hung with a succession of eye-popping Old Masters.

Wherever Zandra looked, she noticed that things were totally different and far, far more luxurious than the last time she'd visited, nearly two years previously.

Through one open doorway, she caught a tantalizing glimpse of ancient tooled leather walls and elegant, full-length portraits by Tissot, Boldini, and Sargent, not to mention eighteen-foot-tall silver Regency palms reminiscent of the Brighton Pavilion, whose curvacious fronds nearly scraped the ceiling.

And everywhere the eye wandered, it met priceless luxury: rich, overlapping seas of mysterious, intricate carpets, firelit mantels. Green and scarlet silk lampshades. Brocade banquettes, voluptuous cushions, gleaming rare woods, and elaborate mirrors.

A completely new stage set, she thought to herself. *Dina's been at it again. "When in doubt, redecorate—that's* my *motto!"* her friend had once laughingly confided.

Zandra smiled at the memory. If one thing could be said about Dina, it was that she practiced what she preached. But unfortunately, along with the decor, she apparently replaced the entire staff as well. Zandra saw not a single familiar, welcoming old face.

"Madame said to inform you that she would return as soon as possible," Julio sniffed frostily as he opened a mahogany door and stepped aside.

Zandra entered the guest suite, and he followed her in, going purposefully around the sitting room, switching on all the lamps, and twitching aside the heavily lined and interlined seventeenth-century silk brocade draperies while the maid did likewise in the bedroom.

"If you wish to summon me or any of the staff," Julio said, "use one of the ivory telephones. You will notice it has the numbers of everyone from the cook to myself listed on both sides of the push buttons."

"Like in an hotel!" Zandra said brightly.

"Yes." He was not amused. "For outside calls, this suite has two separate private lines, but you must use one of the brass telephones. Both numbers are listed on each telephone. Now, if there is nothing else . . ."

"Not at the moment, thank you."

After he was gone, Zandra could have sworn the room temperature shot up by a good twenty degrees.

The maid appeared in the doorway of the adjoining bedroom. Smiling shyly, she asked, "Would you like me to unpack your things, madam?"

Zandra shook her head. "No," she smiled, "thanks."

"Then is there anything I can get you?"

"If it's not too much bother, I would appreciate a cup of tea."

"Oh, it's no bother at all, madam!" the maid assured her. "What kind would you prefer?"

"You wouldn't, by any chance, have Lapsang Souchong?"

"But of course we do!"

"Then that is what I'll have."

"Coming right up, madam! By the way, my name's Lisa." The maid bobbed a little curtsey and disappeared without a sound.

Zandra took the opportunity to investigate the suite.

The luxurious sitting room was sheathed in green boiserie highlighted with gilt from which hung several small Fantin-Latour oil paintings of flowers. Four sets of French doors led out onto a planted, wraparound terrace, and the giltwood Louis XVI *bergères à la reine* and settee were upholstered in salmon mohair cut velvet. *Tables en chiffonnière* held ceramic bibelots and vases of fresh flowers.

The adjoining bedroom was very feminine, with a magnificent Aubusson, pale, faded rose silk damask on the walls, marbelized green moldings, and lavish, raspberry silk brocade curtains and bedhangings. A television was concealed in a demi-lune Boulle commode. By any standards, a palatial suite.

Zandra tried the leftmost of two perfectly scaled, artfully symmetrical doors. It opened into an enormous *en suite* bath the size of a studio apartment: all brocatelle marble, with mirrors reflecting everything—herself included—to infinity.

Leaving the bathroom, Zandra shut the door and tried the one on the right. Opening it, cove lighting and indirect tracks automatically clicked on, illuminating a boutique-size, walk-in closet. All empty and awaiting steamer trunks of clothes.

There were Lucite drawers for folded garments, slanting racks for shoes, stands for hats, angled mirrors, and no end of clear plastic garment bags, with sachets of cedar chips attached to every pink silk-padded hanger.

Zandra smiled sardonically and thought, *Everything I brought along could probably fit into a single drawer.*

Hearing a discreet knock, she went back out into the sitting room. Lisa had returned, bearing a damask-draped wooden tray. Zandra smiled and said, "It looks lovely. That will be all, Lisa. Thank you."

Now that she was alone at long last, she poured herself a cup, added a mere drop of cream and a single lump of sugar, and stirred it while carrying it by the saucer into the bedroom. Setting it down, she unpacked the meager contents of her shoulder bag. Hung her motorcycle jacket on a padded hanger. Folded what few rumpled belongings she'd brought along and placed them inside a single Lucite drawer.

Done, she gloomily surveyed the king-size closet. Her wardrobe looked—indeed was—lamentably wanting in even the most trivial, basic essentials.

Wisely, she quickly shut the door against it, and as she sipped her tea, reminded herself that her lack of clothing was the very least of her problems. Thanks to Dina, she had a roof over her head, and a splendid one at that. In fact, she should be thankfully counting her blessings. Considering the circumstances and haste with which she'd successfully eluded her captors and escaped London, it was gratitude—and not self-pity—which was warranted. *Really!* She *must* stop moping, Zandra scolded herself, and start looking on the bright side. Things could be worse.

Thoughts of Rudolph filled her mind.

Rudolph . . . Rudolph . . .

She sighed loudly, as if exhaling a buildup of poisonous gasses. The unvarnished truth was, her brother's uncertain fate cast a dark shadow across her own.

Eyelids twitching, she collapsed, marionettelike, into a chair. Of course her own problems were reduced to insignificance! *She* was safe, if not indefinitely, then at least for the time being. But Rudolph . . .

Tears prickled her mermaid green eyes.

Oh, *God!* What would those animals *do* to Rudolph when . . .

No! she corrected herself, and clenched her teeth. Not *when,* if . . . *if* they caught up with him?

Her hands shook, causing the cup to rattle in its saucer. Setting it down, she got up and paced the bedroom with restless agitation, raking a hand through her billowing haze of hair.

Lunging to the bed, she snatched up her ostrich-skin address book and tapped it against her hand, her marmalade-colored brows drawn together in crooked furrows.

I have to do something, she told herself over and over. *Something . . . anything . . . I'll never be able to live with myself if I don't.*

Her eyes seemed lost and unfocused, but her expression was dogged, her lips compressed in a tight thin line of determination.

But first things first. And her first priority must be to track Rudolph down.

By calling around and telephoning every friend and acquaintance Rudolph had in the British Isles, and that included Ireland, Scotland, and Wales.

Yes! she thought, galvanized into action. She would leave messages all over the place! That way, if he was laying low at a friend's, or happened to run into someone he knew, at least he would receive word to get in touch with her at Dina's.

Zandra could only hope to God her stubborn brother would do so. Because only together—*united*—could they sit down and sort things out. Surely two heads could come up with a viable solution better than one.

Feeling calmer now that she had some sort of plan, Zandra picked up her empty cup, went out into the sitting room, and poured herself another cupful of tea. Taking a sip, she sat on a delicately carved chair with an oval backrest, placed the cup and saucer on the bouilotte table beside it, and reached for the brass telephone.

Now.

Now to get busy.

Placing the telephone on her lap, she opened her address book to the first page. She would start with A and, if necessary, work her way through the entire alphabet, all the way to Z.

"Shit!" Zandra swore furiously as she slammed down the phone. Tossing aside her address book, she flung herself facedown on the lavishly draped bed, bounced on the raspberry silk coverlet, and then just lay there, propped up on her elbows.

She blew a stray corkscrew of marmalade hair out of her eyes. She was frothing mad and disgusted—hardly surprising, considering that she had spent the last two hours on the telephone, methodically working her way from A through C in her address book, and had nothing to show for her efforts. No one had seen hide nor hair of Rudolph.

And, as if that hadn't been bad enough, seven different acquaintances of her brother's—*seven!*—had told her that *they* were looking for him too, and would she be so kind as to pass along a message once she found him? Seems he'd borrowed heavily, and . . . well, not to be pushy, but they'd really appreciate being repaid . . .

Two bright crimson spots burned on her cheeks. "Blast that Rudolph to bloody hell!" she sighed, rolling wearily over on her back.

Blankly she stared up at the shirred underside of the swagged brocade canopy, a muscle twitch tugging at the outside corner of her left eyelid. She knew she should pick up the phone and continue, starting with the Ds and trying the A, B, and Cs which hadn't answered before, but she felt too low. The notion that her calls would only flush out scores of creditors was too depressing to face at the moment.

"*Boo!*" a voice shouted, causing Zandra to jump up as though she'd been goosed.

"Dina!" she gasped, placing a hand over her wildly palpitating heart. "God!" She stared at her friend through saucer-size eyes. "You gave me such a scare! I didn't hear you come in—"

"I *know* I should have knocked!" Dina squealed, abandoning her usual silky voice in her excitement, "but we see so little of each other and—*anyway!*" She flung her arms wide. "Oooooh, but it's so *good* to see you again, sweetie!"

Bearing down on Zandra, she gave her a fierce hug, though not fierce enough to brush cheeks and thereby spoil carefully applied makeup. Then she made Zandra sit on the bed, sat down beside her, and held her at arms' length.

"You look absolutely smashing, sweetie. Yes, simply smashing." Dina's eyes sparkled. "I don't know how you do it; perhaps it has something to do with that moist English climate? Yes. That must be it. Oh, but it's so wonderful to see you!"

"And you too, Dina." Zandra attempted a semblance of cheer. "How's Robert?"

"Robert? Eh, forget Robert." Dina flapped a hand dismissively and gave a girlish little giggle. "There's all the time in the world to talk about *him.* What I want to know right now is, how *you* are!" She was so bright and chipper she positively glowed.

"Oh . . ." Zandra shrugged, one hand oscillating back and forth. *"Comme-ci, comme-ça,"* she sighed. "Alive, at any rate."

Dina was instantly concerned. It wasn't like Zandra to be in low spirits; but then, it wasn't like her to volunteer her personal problems, either—a fact which Dina had long attributed to Zandra's repressive von Hohenburg-Willemlohe genes.

Taking both of her friend's hands in her own, Dina said gently, "Something's wrong, sweetie. It's written all over you. Just remember, I have huge shoulders, a sympathetic ear, and find nothing more delicious than keeping deep, dark secrets."

"Well . . . things *could* be better," Zandra said evasively. "But there's really no need to go into all that right now. It's such a dreadfully long and dreary story we'd still be at it when the sun comes up tomorrow."

"Well, if you're sure it can wait," Dina said dubiously.

"I'm positive."

"If you say so." A frown momentarily marred Dina's features; then she brightened. "I know! Tomorrow night we'll have one of our famous, all-night girl talk gabfests—the kind that drive Robert up the wall!" She clasped her hands to her bosom. "Now then, sweetie. First things first. How long can you stay?"

"Oh . . ." Zandra suddenly seemed preoccupied with inspecting her fingernails. "It . . . it could well turn out to be a rather lengthy visit."

"Wonderful! You're welcome to be our guest for as long as you like. Days. Weeks. Months, even! You know that."

Zandra looked at Dina, reached out, and gave her friend's fingertips a tight squeeze. "I know," she said huskily, "and thanks. But every little bird needs its nest. I'm going to have to start looking around for an apartment." She frowned. "First, though, I suppose I've got to find a job, which means getting a green card—"

"You're planning to stay *that* long?" Dina was positively delighted.

Zandra nodded glumly. "I'm afraid so," she sighed.

"Well, I'm not! This is only the best news since . . . well, since they invented hair extensions!" bubbled Dina. "It'll be just like old times!"

She put her arm around Zandra's shoulders and gave her a sisterly, sideways hug. Then, letting go of her, she tapped her lips thoughtfully.

"Job . . . job . . . jo—" Dina's eyes widened. "But of *course!*"

"What is it?"

"Abracadabra!" Dina clicked her fingers. "Consider yourself employed."

"Dina, really I—"

"Hush, sweetie, and *listen* to me a moment. Robert just bought Burghley's. Or rather, I should say, he bought controlling *interest* in Burghley's, which amounts to practically the same thing. Right?"

"Burghley's? You mean . . . the auction house?"

"Good lord, yes," Dina said happily. "Maybe now I'll be known as something other than Mrs. GoldMart. Anyway, do you realize how *huge* Burghley's is? I just had the grand tour this morning, and the New York branch alone employs several hundred people!"

"Dina . . ." Zandra began skeptically, but was waved to silence.

"Whatever you're going to say, I don't want to hear it. With a staff that large, they must have an opening you can fill. Now then, let me see. What's your greatest area of expertise?"

"You mean . . . as far as a Burghley's department is concerned?"

"Sweetie! What else could I pos-sib-ly mean? Of *course* I'm talking department!"

"Well . . . I did study art," Zandra said rather uncomfortably. "And from all those vacations spent at various relatives' castles and country houses, I suppose I'm most familiar with Old Masters."

"There you have it! Look no further, sweetie: you're now employed. Robert's lawyers can speed up all that green card nonsense so that you can start immediately, and, in the meantime, if you need money you can borrow some from me, or else get an advance on your paycheck from Burghley's, whichever you find most comfortable." The new Queen of Manhattan smiled magnanimously. "Consider it a fait accompli!"

Zandra could only stare incredulously. Everything was happening so fast it made her head spin.

"Now, then." The new Queen of Manhattan rose to her feet, took Zandra by the hand, and pulled her up. "Next, we need to take inventory. Show me the clothes you've brought along," she demanded.

Zandra blinked. "Clothes . . . ?" she repeated blankly. She cast an anxious glance toward the door of the walk-in closet; from the way Dina was talking, she had an absurd mental picture of having packed formal gowns and cocktail dresses on the run. The image was so powerful and ridiculous she didn't know whether to burst into laughter or tears.

"Sweetie?" A troubled shadow flitted across Dina's features. "Is something the matter? Did I say the wrong thing?"

"No, of course you didn't. It's just that I left so suddenly I didn't have a chance to pack a thing. In other words . . ." Zandra gestured at herself. ". . . what you see is what you get."

"Oh, dear," Dina said, without looking in the least bit perturbed. "Well, I'm sure we can find something for you to wear." She stood back and gave Zandra a critical once-over, her skilled eyes measuring her as accurately as the most experienced, sharp-eyed couturiere. "Would you believe, we're still the same size?"

"But why the big worry about clothes? Dina, what in the world is up?"

"What's up? Ah, I'll tell you what's up. I," Dina purred, producing two thick vellum invitations seemingly out of nowhere and waving them in a manner so giddily rhapsodic that they could well have announced the Second Coming, "have just been messengered invitations for the party of the season. Yes, the season! And, would you believe, it's being thrown by none other than—guess who? *Ta da!*"

With a flourish, she held the invitations right under Zandra's nose.

"Yes, sweetie, your very own cousin, Prince Karl-Heinz von und zu. And, as you can see, there are two invitations. One for Robert and me, and another for you and your escort." Dina all but swooned with excitement. "Well, sweetie? Are you surprised, or what?"

"Oh, Dina," Zandra tried to beg off. "Not tonight. Please? I'm frightfully tired. I've hardly slept for the past two days and—"

"And nothing. I shall not, I repeat *not*, take no for an answer. Since the festivities do not begin until seven-thirty, there is plenty of time for you to take a nap and wake up totally rejuvenated."

And taking Zandra by the arm, Dina guided her gently but firmly out of the guest suite, down the grandiose hall, and up the sweeping staircase to her own sprawling suite, chattering like a happy magpie the entire way.

"Thank God my closets are bursting at the seams with clothes I could never begin to wear . . . so, first we'll pick out that appropriate little something, then we'll go through my jewelry to match it with a bauble or two—no, I will not let you utter one word of protest—and after that, I'll give you one of my magic sleeping pills and tuck you in myself. You might not believe it, sweetie, but I assure you: when party time rolls around, you'll look and feel fresh as a daisy!"

8

*W*hat a difference a day makes.

The man who sat down to lunch yesterday in his grand, book-lined study in the Auction Towers penthouse was the world's most eligible thirty-nine-year-old bachelor. The man who was served lunch at the same library table today had turned forty.

It was Prince Karl-Heinz von und zu Engelwiesen's Big Four-O, and the fact that he had turned forty made him aware of more than just his own mortality. The responsibilities his fabulous wealth and title engendered, as well as the peculiar laws of inheritance which had governed his family for nearly three-quarters of a millennium, weighed heavily on his mind.

That he should concern himself with these matters now was in itself disconcerting—especially considering the past two decades of lusty, care-free living.

For Prince Karl-Heinz, indisputably one of the savviest businessmen in the world, was also acknowledged to be one of the most notorious playboys of all time. An exciting, passionate, and well-endowed lover, his life was a chronicle of liaisons and affairs. Movie stars, showgirls, supermodels, and other beauty queens—his amorous adventures did not stop there. An inspired lover of women—all women—his conquests had included the happily married wives and even daughters of friends, business associates, celebrities, and politicians.

Now, hearing a light tap on the study door of his condominium high above Burghley's, he called out in German, *"Herrein!"*

The door opened and in came Josef, his thin, precise secretary-cum-valet, who had been with him since his youth, and who knew his every quirk and peccadillo.

"Guten Tag, Your Highness," Josef greeted formally in German. "And may I take the liberty of wishing Your Highness a very happy birthday and many happy returns?"

"Guten Tag, Josef, and thank you," returned His Serene Highness, Prince Karl-Heinz von und zu Engelwiesen.

Josef hovered. "Would Your Highness like your lunch now or a little later?"

"Later, Josef."

"Very well, Your Highness."

After Josef left, Karl-Heinz became lost in his reverie once again. On this, his fortieth birthday, his stomach felt hollow as he reluctantly faced the harsh realities of his personal life. It was time he settled down, mended his licentious ways, and secured his future—no easy task for a man in his shoes . . .

His Serene Highness, Prince Karl-Heinz Fernando de Carlos Jean Joachim Alejandor Ignacio Hieronymous Eustace von und zu Engelwiesen was blessed with an overabundance of everything. Besides his fortune, which was larger than most; his title, which was older and bluer than most; his aristocratic good looks, which were more handsome than most; he also possessed a libido which—what else?—was more overactively demanding than most. He looked younger than his forty recorded years—recorded, because for the past seven centuries not a single legitimate von und zu Engelwiesen had been born without a trio of lawyers present, whose duty it was to duly witness and certify in an ancient book of bloodstock that the newborn infant was indeed the product of the rightful von und zu Engelwiesen womb, the double loophole in this archaic tradition being, of course, that as many lawyers as not are unscrupulous, and even a triumvirate of them have been known to be bribable. And besides—how could there be irrefutable proof of the paternal sperm serene if lawyers were not present during insemination?

But be that as it may, there was no mistaking Prince Karl-Heinz for anything but the genuine article. The result of a carefully distilled pedigree, he exuded nobility from every pore, not only carrying himself like a prince, but speaking and looking like one, too. His nose was imperial, a true Roman nose: narrow, long, and slightly irregular, with the same central bump which all the ancestral portraits at *Schloss* Engelwiesen bore as proudly as their dueling scars. His ears, small and flat and nearly lobeless, were obviously a throwback to another of the many royal houses of Europe, with whom von und zu Engelwiesens had intermarried over the centuries. However, his eyes, slightly oval, bright blue, and crinkled at the corners, had a whimsical and definitely unprincely, mischievous cast.

Since the age of fifteen, Prince Karl-Heinz had bedded, but not wedded, the most beautiful women on five continents. Yet his highly publicized playboy exploits were but a small part of his character. Behind the libidinous facade there was a core of diamond-hard toughness, ruthless business acumen, and the kind of confidence that only absolute power and a serene birthright can bestow.

Ironically, that very same birthright was now the root of his greatest problem—and *that* could be traced all the way back to the year 1290, when his illustrious ancestor, Eustace, had been rewarded by Charlemagne for services rendered, and made a prince of the Holy Roman Empire.

Deeded vast tracts of lands in what is now Germany, Eustace was also awarded that plum of all plums—exclusive rights to the papal mail routes for the entire western Mediterranean.

And it was that very same Eustace, the first in a long, unbroken line of princes of the Holy Roman Empire, who had laid down the von und zu Engelwiesen family laws governing inheritance for future generations; strict, binding laws which remained in effect to this very day, and to which Prince Karl-Heinz was required to adhere, and to which, therefore, he owed his current predicament.

At the heart of it was primogeniture, not so unusual in itself, since many of the noble houses of Europe still practice the ancient tradition of passing titles and inheritances down through their eldest sons. And as Karl-Heinz was his ailing father's only male offspring, primogeniture should normally have guaranteed his inheritance, and precluded his sister, Princess Sofia, from the running.

However, that was where the distinctive von und zu Engelwiesen complication arose, a problem little appreciated by Karl-Heinz. Thanks to Prince Eustace, the family's particular law of primogeniture clearly spelled out that no less than two prerequisites had to be fulfilled before the eldest son could attain his rightful inheritance.

The first, a precaution to ensure a pure bloodline, was that Karl-Heinz must marry a female who was also a descendant of the Holy Roman Emperors—an obstacle which winnowed the playing field down to a tiny handful of eligible women.

The second was that his wife had to give birth to a male heir *before* the death of Karl-Heinz's own father, the old prince.

If both these criteria could not be met, the inheritance would then automatically pass on to the eldest son of the next closest relative. As luck would have it, Karl-Heinz's sister, Sofia, and her husband, Count Erwein, had managed to produce a virtual army of strapping and exceedingly handsome if featherbrained princelings.

Meanwhile, time was running out for Karl-Heinz. His father, the old prince, was in such deteriorating health that it was doubtful whether he would even live to see his next birthday . . .

Now, with the noonday sun streaming through the windows, Karl-Heinz considered his options, or rather the lack thereof. It occurred to him that if he wanted to secure his rightful inheritance, forty carefree years of bachelorhood had better come to a screeching halt. He would have to dig up an appropriate, blue-blooded wife fast, and hope to God she was a childbearer who could produce a son in record time.

The specter of Leopold, Princess Sofia's lamentably sulky eldest son inheriting the estate which, by all rights should be Karl-Heinz's, loomed ominously in his mind. It didn't take much imagination to see Leopold, a hopelessly provincial spendthrift with harebrained schemes and no business sense whatsoever, run through the entire fortune and undo the work of seven centuries in a single generation. Karl-Heinz had seen it happen to other great and powerful families, and had no desire to see it occur to his.

He felt every one of his forty years weigh heavily today, and sighed gloomily. His thoughts of Sofia and Leopold had definitely taken the shine off his day; they made his entire life's work seem pointless.

Yes, he mused, *if I know what's good for me—and I do!—my playboy days are over. Definitely over . . .*

And with that depressing thought, he could only wonder at his own stupidity in waiting so long . . . perhaps *too* long . . . to secure his birthright.

He was still wondering about it during lunch, oblivious to Cesar, his Spanish majordomo who, hovering discreetly, sniffily orchestrated the perfect serving of everything from the lobster salad to the freshly ground, scalding hot coffee.

But the lobster went uneaten; the coffee was half drunk.

His Serene Highness, Prince Karl-Heinz von und zu Engelwiesen had lost his appetite. How, how on God's earth, he asked himself, could he of all people have been so cretinously stupid, so unforgivably asinine as to wait until today, his fortieth birthday, to see the light? *Truly, such imbecility is unworthy of me!* he thought with the bitter recriminations of someone who has won the lottery, but has forgotten to cash in the ticket.

He needed to make up for lost time—and lose no time doing it.

Yes, Karl-Heinz thought, *uneasy rests the head, even if it wears no crown . . .*

TARGET: BURGHLEY'S COUNTDOWN TO TERROR

The man climbed the shallow marble steps to the head of the grand staircase. To the left was the entrance to the auction auditorium proper; to the right, Burghley's carpeted showroom galleries, a succession of wide open spaces which could be divided or opened up, whichever the occasion required, via instantly movable walls on tracks.

"May I heeeeelp you?" drawled the bored Locust Valley lockjaw behind the sales counter.

He looked at her. She was one of three exceptionally thin, uniquely chic, and peculiarly interchangeable ex-debutantes who sold Burghley's books, catalogues, magazines, and pricey, specially printed books.

"Yes," he told her. "I would like a copy of *Attractions.*"

"The November–December issue?" She raised perfectly plucked eyebrows. "Or the current one covering September–October?"

"The November–December. Also, if you have it, the January–February."

"I'm teeeeeribly sorry, but those won't be in for another month and a half yet."

"Then the November–December issue will be fine."

She turned to the magazine rack behind her, and reached for a copy of *Attractions,* the oversize glossy magazine which was Burghley's preview of upcoming worldwide events.

"Would you like any catalogues while you're at it?" she asked. "We've just unpacked a new shipment, and they cover the whooooole rest of the year."

"No, thank you," he said.

"That'll be twenty dollars, then."

He pulled out his wallet, fished out a crisp twenty, and handed it over. She rang up the sale, stuffed two sheets of oxblood tissue paper into a small silver-gray buff shopping bag with string handles and BURGHLEY'S FOUNDED 1719 printed in oxblood on both sides of the heavy buff paper, and slid the magazine inside it.

"There you are." Handing it across the counter, she smiled automatically, already tuning him out.

Back outside on Madison Avenue, the man took the magazine out of the bag, rolled it up tightly, and stuck it in his coat pocket. As for the shopping bag, he crumpled that and the tissue paper into a ball and tossed it into the trash can on the corner. He didn't even want to be seen carrying around a Burghley's bag—it was too noticeably chic and memorable, and in his line of work drawing attention to himself was not only bad for business, it was a risk he could not afford to take.

He was the most successful career criminal in the world, only nobody knew it.

Which was exactly the way he intended it to remain.

A grand strategist at heart, he hadn't gotten to where he was by sticking out in a crowd. Or trusting anything to luck.

On the contrary. Caution was his middle name, and keeping a low profile his tried-and-true game. Too smart to openly consort with others of his kind, he was not, however, above using highly skilled criminal personnel when needed.

In those cases, he did as he'd done in Macao—delegating the details to an associate who would see to everything while he himself wisely kept his distance and stayed safely, invisibly, far in the background. The melodramatic black disguises he donned on the rare occasions he met with his go-between were no affectation; they were a necessity.

The secret to his success had always been that no one—not even his own second-in-command—could identify him as the mastermind should a job ever go wrong.

To date, this recipe of one part anonymity to one part caution had served him well. Neither Interpol, the FBI, the Sureté, Scotland Yard, nor a single police department on earth had him in their criminal files, not even for so minor an infraction as a parking violation.

Blessed with a photographic memory, he never left a paper trail, was a virtuoso at laundering money, and was worth a hundred million dollars of cunningly concealed assets in gold, diamonds, and cash stashed safely in—and invested cleverly from—an untraceable maze of dummy corporations and numbered bank accounts in Liechtenstein, Grand Cayman, and the Isle of Jersey.

Needless to say, he could long ago have retired in supreme luxury. The only reason he still worked was because he truly *liked* crime.

Now in the midst of planning his curtain call—his biggest and most daring caper ever—his foremost concern was to ensure that it would not go down in the annals of history as merely the crime of the year. Nor the crime of the decade.

No, nothing short of the crime of the century would do.

This was to be the crowning achievement of his criminal career; his glorious swan song before retiring to join the world's law-abiding citizens.

But best of all, he would be able to sit back, far above suspicion, and watch as the authorities ran around in useless circles, trying to hunt down the elusive mastermind.

Because it went without saying that they would never find him, for the simple reason that as far as they, or anyone else was concerned, he did not exist, at least not as a criminal.

And that, he thought with the satisfaction of someone whose life is devoted to matching wits with the guys in the white hats, is nothing if not truly elegant.

9

For Kenzie, home was a walk-up on East Eighty-first Street, where she had the third floor rear of a five-story, one-family brownstone which had long since been carved up into ten rental units.

The circa-1920s kitchen was tiny, and had a minuscule gas range, a countertop oven barely big enough for roasting two tiny game hens, plus an ancient refrigerator/freezer of roughly the same vintage, which required weekly defrosting. But never mind.

The living room had a working fireplace from whose mantel she'd painstakingly stripped and sanded a century's worth of paint, two windows overlooking the garden out back, and relatively high ceilings. Better yet, the walls were thick, the neighbors quiet, and there were two small-ish bedrooms, a steal in Manhattan for a mere rent-stabilized $823.28 a month.

It was also the perfect apartment to share, one reason why she had been attracted to it in the first place. Alas, three months earlier her roommate had discarded a series of boy toys for a dentist with a thriving practice, and had moved on to the greener pastures of matrimony and Westchester County. Without someone trustworthy with whom to share the rent, gas, electric, and cable TV bills, Kenzie had had to apply the brakes on her greatest passion—buying at auction.

She possessed an uncanny knack for ferreting out "sleepers"—those lots at auction which were either misattributed or completely overlooked by other buyers. Thus she managed to purchase treasures for a proverbial song before attributing them correctly, and turning around and either re-selling them for a hefty profit or keeping them to enjoy.

In this way, she had made ends meet while furnishing her apartment with a collection of surpassingly fine if eclectic art and antiques, a luxury which would have been dauntingly prohibitive to anyone but the rich, let alone a young Manhattanite restricted by Burghley's bare-bones subsistence wages—the consensus of management being, the honor of working at Burghley's more than made up for in cachet what was lacking in salaries.

As if cachet put food on the table, Kenzie mused with grim humor, the carefully rewrapped Zuccaro propped between her legs as she struggled with the five heavy-duty Fichet locks on her front door—the wisest investment of any lone female city dweller.

Once inside her apartment, she snapped the door shut with a well-practiced bump of her buttocks and had barely finished latching the fifth and last lock when the back of her neck began prickling.

I'm not alone! a keen sixth sense informed her.

Suddenly she could feel her stomach crawl; rancid bile rose swiftly in her throat. Slowly and cautiously, she turned around, a bass drum pounding in her ears.

"Hel-looooo, beautiful!"

Flashing his blinding whites, Charley Ferraro blew her a kiss from across the room.

"Charley!" she gasped reproachfully. "God! You sure know how to give a girl a scare!" Now that she was in no danger, she didn't know whether to be relieved or angry.

Anger won out, especially since he'd made himself right at home.

With his muscular arms crossed casually behind his head, he was comfortably, if incongruently, sprawled on the voluptuous, cut-velvet Napoleon III sofa with its exuberance of fringes and tassels—an item of furnishing more suitable for an odalisque than a man whose firm, NYPD-trained body was clad in nothing more than skimpy snow white briefs.

"And just what the hell do you think you're doing here?" she demanded in outrage. "Other than trying to scare me to death, that is?"

"As a matter of fact," he said jovially, wiggling his toes, "I never left. I told you I had the day off. Remember?"

Seeing her infuriated expression, he sat abruptly forward, his face registering solicitude. "Hey, what's the matter, babe? You don't seem exactly overjoyed to see me. Have a rough day, or something?"

Letting her shoulder bag drop to the floor, Kenzie slumped against the door in weary resignation. Drawing a deep, ragged breath, she held it in for a full ten seconds before expelling it, the force of her breath lifting the sable bangs from her forehead.

Dammit! Tonight she neither wanted nor needed Charley's company. She'd been looking forward to spending a visually gluttonous hour feasting her eyes on her Zuccaro—not Charley Ferraro's otherwise delicious and wiry free weights-sculpted body—before getting ready for her first-ever, high-society shindig at the Met.

Placing the Zuccaro on the demi-lune table by the door, she put her keys into the glazed green ceramic Han dynasty bowl and then turned to face him, her hands on her hips, her feet planted in a wide, aggressive stance.

"Get out, Charley," she said quietly.

"Excuse me?" He made a production of using an index finger to clear nonexistent wax from his ear. "Babe, did I hear—"

"Charley," she interrupted, unruffled, "are you deaf? I said out! *Out!*" She clapped her hands sharply twice. *"Vámanos!"*

He looked appropriately taken aback as he tried to gauge the seriousness of her tone. "Aw, come on, babe," he cajoled.

Propping himself up on one elbow, he looked at her with a trace of perturbation, but seemed otherwise unconcerned, counting on his cocky charm and far from unattractive looks to win her over. "You don't really mean that," he added, mildly aggrieved.

"Oh yeah?" she retorted. "Try me."

Picking up the Zuccaro, she tore off the wrapping, stalked over to the fireplace, and propped the picture atop the mantel, adjusting it until it was just so. When she finally turned back around, she caught Charley eyeing her buns with unabashed connoisseurship.

"Guess what Super Dick's been thinking about all day?" he asked, waggling his eyebrows like Groucho Marx.

"Super Dick!" Kenzie rolled her eyes. "You've got to be kidding!"

Plopping herself down on a Louis Philippe chair, she untied her laces; by the time she'd kicked off her Reeboks and was standing up, Charley was on his feet too, engulfing her in his strong, bulging arms.

She pushed him away. "Get your paws off me, Charley," she said wearily. "And while you're at it, why don't you collect your clothes, get dressed, and go on home? Hmm?"

Worry lines creased his handsome features; Charley Ferraro was unused to rejection from members of the opposite sex.

"Well?" She stared mercilessly at him.

His frown deepened. "That the thanks I get for saving you from KP?" he asked.

"KP?" She blinked her eyes rapidly. "What is this? Are we suddenly in the armed services?"

"Well, you *are* an army brat, right? And you don't want to cook, do you?" When she didn't reply, he added smugly, "Didn't think so, which is why yours truly called out for grub. It should be here any minute now. Your favorite—Burmese." He took the opportunity to flash her a thousand-watt smile. "Still find me resistible?"

"As a matter of fact," she said inexorably, "yes. Eminently so."

That wiped the grin off his face. "You aren't," he said slowly, "by any chance telling me to get lost . . . are you?"

"Why, that's exactly what I'm doing," she said, pouring on the molasses.

What the hell! Now this was a first! She'd never treated him like *this* before! "Don't you think you owe me an explanation?" he demanded huffily.

She placed both hands on her hips. "Charley," she sighed, "has it ever occurred to you that I might have made other plans?"

He blinked, clearly taken aback. "In that case, may I inquire as to what those plans are? Or is that asking for too much?"

"Not at all," she said magnanimously. "I've been invited to a society party at the Met. The museum, not the opera."

"Well, ex-*cuuuuse* me! And here I was, harboring the distinct impression that you weren't into all that society shit."

She shrugged. "Maybe I've changed my mind."

He glared belligerently. "And who, may I ask, is taking you?"

Her eyes could have drilled holes through his. "That," she snapped coldly, "is none of your business."

And that said, she went around the living room, picking up his clothes and tossing them, item by item, right at him. He snatched them expertly out of the air.

Looking nonplussed, he clutched the bundle against his chest with one arm. "Christ," he muttered. "What's gotten into you?"

"Me?" she said. "Why, nothing."

"Nothing?" He reached out, caught her by the arm, and pulled her close. Thrusting his pelvis against her, he looked down into her eyes and asked, "What do you mean, nothing?" A playful smile touched the corners of his lips.

She'd have had to be comatose to be unaware of the stiff, throbbing glans barely contained within his briefs. For whatever other failings and bullshit Charley Ferraro could be accused of, impotence was not among them.

"See what you do to me?" he now whispered huskily, pressing himself even closer against her.

Kenzie's face was expressionless, but her amber eyes glowed like a cat's. Ever ready though *he* might be, this was one time she wasn't. "Charley, Charley, Charley," she sighed, her soft, nimble fingers venturing down. She slipped them inside his briefs and ignored his tumescence to cup a hand around any male's single most vulnerable spot, his scrotum. "What does it take to make you learn?"

"Learn what?"

"Why, this," she said. And smiling sweetly, she gave his *cojones* a good, viselike squeeze.

His reaction was predictable. "Je-*sus!*" he yelped, letting go of his clothes and very nearly levitating.

She eased the pressure, withdrew her hand, and stepped back, crossing her arms in front of her to watch while he cupped both hands protectively over his crotch and danced a little jig.

He slid her a mean glare. "Now, what did you go and do that for? Are you fuckin' nuts?"

Still smiling sweetly, Kenzie said, "Now then, let's say that was just foreplay, hmm?" She tilted her head to one side. "Think 'Super Dick' would care to experience an entire gamut of new sensations?"

Angrily he snatched his clothes up off the floor and hurriedly started getting dressed. "That does it!" he huffed. "I'm outta here!"

Even as he was still buttoning up his fly, he tucked his shoes under one arm, lunged for the door, and unlatched the five locks, fleeing barefoot down the stairs in record time.

"And good riddance!" Kenzie yelled after him. Slamming the door with all her might, she locked it and clapped her hands, as though ridding them of dirt, or congratulating herself on a job well done. She thought: *Just goes to show there's more than one way to skin a cat!*

Men! She snorted. *Why is it they never seemed to learn?*

She jerked as the downstairs buzzer abruptly blared. Savagely, she whirled around and stabbed the TALK button of the intercom. *"Damn you, Charley!"* she yelled into it. *"What the hell does it take before you get the message?"*

There was a pause. Then a calm Asian voice, sounding like Arnold Li doing one of his routines, said, "Derivery."

Kenzie slapped the palm of a hand against her forehead. *Damn!* she swore under her breath. She'd completely forgotten about Charley's Burmese takeout. Now *she* was stuck with the bill!

Pressing the buzzer which released the downstairs door, she projected, *Gee thanks, Super Dick! Thanks a whole fucking lot!* Then she went to dig through her shoulder bag for her wallet. Being between paydays, it was depressingly thin. In cash, she had three tens, three fives, and three singles to her name.

There was a soft, cautious rap on the door. Composing herself, she once again unlatched all the locks and opened it.

A polite Asian youth, holding a large, neatly stapled brown paper bag in front of him, was standing in the stairwell. "Herro," he said, giving a polite little bow.

"How much?" she sighed.

"Fawty-faw, ninety-three." With a friendly smile, he indicated the bill stapled to the top of the bag, then ceremoniously handed it over. In return, she gave him the entire contents of her wallet.

"Keep the change," she said. "And thanks."

He bowed politely. "Thank you."

Shutting the door, she locked herself in for the third time, her nose wrinkling as she caught a whiff of Burmese food. For once, instead of making her mouth water, it caused her stomach to do flip-flops—not surprising, considering that her food budget for the entire rest of the week was shot. She'd be forced to eat Burmese for days, *after* dumping the beef satay and chayote pork. No way was red meat going to touch *her* lips.

Stomping to the kitchen, she shoved the bag into the fridge and slammed the door shut. "Gee, thanks, Super Dick!" she muttered, adding: "Super Dick, my *ass!*"

❧ *10* ❧

*B*edroom his, bedroom hers.

The Goldsmiths had separate connecting suites, a reciprocal convenience in more ways than one.

Robert tended to stink up the room with his cigars while reading business reports late into the night, and then snored like a bull with defective adenoids. Dina couldn't live with cigar smoke, or without nine undisturbed hours of beauty sleep.

He invariably woke up after four hours, horny as all hell. She was not crazy about being jerked from the midst of sweet dreams, especially not by a hirsute, two-hundred-sixty-pound sex maniac on whom everything drooped but the flagpole.

Consequently, they had long since arrived at a mutually acceptable arrangement: they slept in separate bedrooms and had set aside specified times for conjugal sex. Between those occasions, each had other outlets to satisfy the most imminent urges.

Robert had his Blow Job (as he thought of Bambi Parker and her long list of predecessors), as well as his trusty right hand and a stash of oral porn videos. Dina had her ivory-colored vibrator and her own hidden stash of videos, starring—what else?—hard-bodied, *muscular* young males with hair in the only two places she found acceptable.

Of course, when Dina wanted something badly enough, she wasn't above bending the conjugal rules. With Robert, she knew exactly which buttons to push.

At six-fifteen that evening, Robert turned off the multiple jets in his white marble shower and grumpily wrapped a white cotton bath sheet, like a giant sarong, around his substantial middle. He looked like one of the Aga Khans of yore—or, more recently, the average state-run Black Sea resort-goer somewhere in the former Soviet Union.

Not that he had a personal beef about the way he looked—if he had, he'd have done something about it. The truth was, he'd long ago come to terms with his body. If other people found him offensive and pear-shaped, then so be it. That was their problem. Corpulence had never interfered with his sex life, especially since it was a given that so long as you were rich enough, you could look like the Elephant Man and still get your pick of the litter.

Selecting a cigar from the bathroom humidor, he sniffed it, rattled it next to his ear, then snipped off the end with a silver cutter and lit it. Once he got it going to his satisfaction, he clamped it between his teeth and puffed away, diddling with the sink's dinky gold and rock crystal faucets Dina had insisted upon installing, and which he loathed.

Damned Frenchified things! Each time he used them, he hankered for his plain, old-fashioned chrome fixtures, the honest kind of plumbing stocked and sold in the discount hardware department of every GoldMart store across the country. The kind he'd grown up with, and you could repair with a standard lug wrench instead of a bunch of special-gauge, la-di-da jeweler's tools.

The kind I want back! he thought crankily, the unusually large mound of shaving cream he squirted into his hand, as well as the noisy vigor with which he slapped lather onto his face, attesting to the irritation he felt at having to shave for the second time that day. And all because of a damned last-minute invitation to the Met!

Robert puffed angrily on his cigar, the blue smoke mixing with the rising steam, creating a dense, pungent cloud which the bathroom's one useful item, the giant distortion- and fog-free mirror, kept magically clear.

Parties, how he detested them! And God, how Dina thrived on them! But why she couldn't do like other socialites and get herself one of those *faygeleh* walkers to squire her around, he'd never know—just as he'd never understand how anyone could devote her entire life to crashing society and sucking up to a bunch of hypocritical snobs who didn't give a rat's ass about her.

Well, he'd do what he always did at these kinds of functions. Wait until dinner was over and then wander off to some quiet place where he'd be joined by five or six like-minded cronies—all self-made billionaires who, like himself, had been dragged along by their younger trophy wives. While everyone else danced and air-kissed and stabbed each other in the backs, they'd light up cigars and tell each other off-color jokes. And inevitably get around to reminiscing about the "good old days," back when they'd been hungry young *machers* with nothing more than a few cents and a dream, and times had been rough, but life—ah life!—that incredible journey ever full of surprises had been infinitely more challenging, more exciting, and most of all, more satisfying than it had been ever since!

Lost in thought, Robert was oblivious to the fact that his bathroom door had inched open a crack.

And that a slitted aquamarine eye was peering in at him.

Out in his mirrored dressing room, Dina quickly stepped back from the door. Her lips were compressed in a grim line. She had seen quite enough. Too much, as a matter of fact.

Dressed, her husband was hardly a pretty sight. But undressed . . .

She instantly slammed a mental door on that train of thought. Continuing along it was entirely the wrong approach. She knew from experience that the anticipation was always worse than the act itself. Her lips abruptly turned down at the corners. No, that wasn't quite true. The act was worse. Far worse . . .

Putting off the inevitable, she looked at her infinite reflections in the mirrored closet doors.

The sight which greeted her made her cringe.

She was wearing a pink baby doll top with thin halter straps and white lace trim over matching crotchless white lace panties. There was a white lace collar around her throat and a big white maribou pom-pom pinned to her hair. To top it all off, looped around one index finger was a red ribbon. And dangling from it was the huge, stuffed red satin heart emblazoned "Daddy."

Dina could only shake her head in baffled wonderment, her multiple reflections mimicking her every move. Really, it was too, too bizarre. A woman her age dressing up like a baby doll! How any grown man could get sexually aroused from this was entirely beyond her.

However, if this was what it took, then so be it.

Clenching her jaw determinedly, she adjusted the low-cut bodice so that her breasts swelled voluptuously and left her strawberry nipples strategically exposed. She ran her tongue across her lips to moisten them. Then, swallowing all remnants of pride, she grasped the gilded doorknob and slipped into her husband's jungle-humid steambath.

He was so immersed in shaving, the cigar clenched between his teeth, his head wreathed in a smog of smoke and steam, that he didn't even notice her—at least, not until she opened her mouth.

"Daddy," Dina crooned softly in her very best baby voice.

She had it all down pat. The pout. The starry false eyelashes. Even the penciled-on nose freckles.

"Ba-by's horny!"

Dina's entrance had its desired effect. Robert's head swiveled, then turned back to face his own fog-free reflection before he did a classic double take. He nearly choked on his cigar.

Dina was standing in the doorway, splayed legs planted wide. Sucking on a thumb while twisting her torso childishly from side to side like a six-year-old.

Robert knew his priorities. Tossing his cigar and razor into the jasper sink, and happily oblivious to having nicked his chin, he gave her his full and undivided attention, unconsciously licking his lips while eating her up with lust-filled eyes.

If his face hadn't been such a dead giveaway, Charlie raising the front of the bath sheet in an immediate salute certainly dispelled any remaining doubts.

"Hey, l'il girl!" he rasped, loosening the towel from around his porcine waist and letting it drop. Without even touching it, his erect penis twitched and bobbed—a little muscle control trick he was particularly proud of.

He held out his arms. "Come on over to Daddy, baby."

Dina took her thumb out of her mouth and stuck out her bottom lip petulantly, swinging the red satin heart back and forth, back and forth, the twenty-nine-year-old regressing to six trying to make up her mind.

Finally, she looked up from under demurely lowered lashes. "Daddy's little girl needs to give some *head!*"

"Well then, *I'd* say this is his l'il girl's lucky day!" Robert looked down at himself. "See? Lookit the treat Daddy's got for his l'il baby!"

Dina glanced, with pretended interest, at the thick circumcised penis with its curiously asymmetrical ruff and wondered, as always, who had botched his circumcision.

Licking her lips with feigned hunger, Dina approached her husband. "Daddy, may I?" She looked up at him with huge pleading eyes. "Please?"

The words were barely out of her mouth before he grabbed hold of her head and shoved her face down into his crotch. No foreplay for Robert A. Goldsmith. No, siree! One moment his wife was standing, and the next he had her—*slam bam!*—down on her knees.

Already wheezing heavily, he spread his legs wide. Leaning back against the scalloped edge of the sink, he thrust his ample hips forward, and uttered two words:

"Start eatin'."

Dina, swallowing her revulsion as she'd swallowed her pride, opened her mouth and closed her lips around him, devoting considerable energy and talent to his penis and, by obvious extension, to his dangling, hairy testicles as well. But she was careful not to touch, nor so much as graze, any other part of his body.

Oh no; she wanted every bit of his vast powers of concentration to be centered right there in his crotch—for Dina Goldsmith, like all women (and certain men), knew that when a man was aroused, his brain was no longer in his head but between his legs.

But first she had to bring him closer to orgasm. Tightening her mouth around him, she set seriously to work. Sucked in and out. In and out.

Strangely, she herself felt absolutely no arousal whatsoever. No wetness flooding her loins. No trickles running down the insides of her thighs. No swelling of her nipples.

She was dry and closed. Not that there was anything wrong with her, or that she couldn't get turned on. She just couldn't get turned on to her husband. Sex with Robert was, alternately, a duty, a weapon, or a method by which to extract favors.

Her cheeks drew in as her mouth sucked furiously with pretend hunger, and inflated as she withdrew.

God! Tears were beginning to form in her eyes and her lips were becoming so numb she could barely feel them. How much longer was this going to last? She needed to give her mouth a break! But his wheezes were speeding up; she *almost* had him where she wanted him.

Soon, she consoled herself. *If I don't stop now, it'll be any moment . . .*

She sucked like a maniac. Faster, faster. And then she could sense a convulsive shudder starting to pass through him, felt his engorged penis straining, readying itself for imminent explosion.

And it was at that very instant, a mere fraction of a split second before he could reach orgasm, that she stopped and—*plop!*—let his penis slide out of her mouth.

The engorged organ strained and jerked in midair, like a confused, heat-seeking missile searching for a target which had suddenly disappeared.

"You fuckin' stopped!" he growled accusingly.

Dina raised her head and looked up at her husband with her best Daddy's Little Girl eyes. This was the precise moment she had been waiting for.

"Baby needs a fa-vor from her Daddy."

She batted her starry lashes, the skillful tip of her tongue diddling just enough with his penis to keep it straining on this side of orgasm, like a dog pulling on its leash.

"Yeah?" he rasped, all rational thought replaced by the urgency of dire physical need. "What kinda favor we talkin'?"

Feminine intuition served Dina well, and she fondled his testicles cunningly while artfully giving his twitching penis some cautiously resourceful sucks. Then she stopped again, keeping him poised on the maddening, excruciating brink of exquisite orgasm.

She hung her head and twisted her shoulders childishly. "Baby's best friend needs *help!*"

"Baby's best friend is her Daddy's *dick!*"

Robert guffawed raunchy laughter.

"Baby means her other fwend. Zandra."

Raising her eyes, she fluttered her lashes, her tongue darting out and thrumming his penis just enough to keep him right up there on the wall.

"Please, Daddy?" *Thrum.* "Pretty please? All she needs is a job."

"A job?" he rasped blankly. "Uh, what kinda job?"

"One at Daddy's new company," Dina said, expertly drilling the tip of her tongue into the one-eyed snake's cyclopic eye. "Zandra knows *all* about Old Masters!"

Old Masters! Warning bells jangled and a cold sweat suddenly sleeked his entire body. *Aw, shit,* he thought, *anything but that! Anything!*

Robert A. Goldsmith might have been thinking with his penis, but that didn't mean his mental faculties were entirely shot. Christ Jesus! He'd have to be certifiable to stick his wife's best friend into the very same department at Burghley's of which his current Blow Job, Bambi Parker, was about to be put in charge! All it would take was for the two of them to hit it off and—*yap! yap! yap!*—his ass would be grass.

For, Baby Doll routines aside, he knew that if Dina so much as suspected he was playing around, she'd have his balls on a platter. Sliced, chopped, diced, *and* fried.

"Daddy'll think about it," he grunted, trying to postpone the inevitable. "Now, shut up and be a good l'il girl. Finish off what you've started!"

Dina's lips closed around the bulbous knob some more, her tongue making slow, deliberate revolutions, bringing him even closer to the very precipice of orgasm.

She stopped again.

"Please, Daddy?" she begged. "Pretty please?" His penis twitched and bobbed desperately, meeting only air.

She gave it a mere whisper of a lick.

Her husband cracked. She could tell from the agonized wheeze he emitted.

"Oh, all *right,*" he gasped, making the decision with his penis and suspecting, but momentarily not caring, that he might live to regret it.

"Oh, thank you, Daddy!" Dina squealed. And her mouth pounced and gave his hot pulsing phallus her all.

His semen was boiling, and not ten seconds passed before he tensed. For one tiny instant he was absolutely still, and then a convulsive shudder passed through him and he exploded in a protracted, overwhelming, if one-sided, flood of magnificent release.

Dina struggled to her feet as Robert dizzily staggered, gasping for air, and reeled from wall to wall before collapsing heavily on the toilet. Body limp, and penis getting there fast, too.

Well, there's one thing that can be said for my husband, Dina thought smugly as she fled to her own suite, where she quickly rinsed out her mouth with handfuls of water before gargling with mouthwash. *Once he gives his word on something, it's as good as gold! Robert never, ever reneges, no matter under what circumstances a promise might have been extracted. His peculiar sense of honor would not permit it.*

She was dying to share the good news with Zandra, but a quick glance at the nephrite and pale pink enamel bathroom clock showed that, even with the unromantic but necessary sexual interlude, she had less than forty-five minutes to get ready.

Not a whole lot of time for most women to cleanse off smeared makeup, step under the shower, dry off, paint on her public face, and get dressed from scratch.

But Dina Goldsmith wasn't most women. She was one of a kind, and gifted with considerable foresight.

First, she'd had the sense to lay out tonight's entire wardrobe on her bed, right down to her shoes, pantyhose, silky blonde hair extension, diamond barrette, and every last carat of jewelry.

Second, as far as makeup went, well, she had that down to a science, too.

And third, Dina's personal fashion philosophy was nothing if not pragmatic: No woman should ever wear anything she couldn't put on in five minutes flat, and the same went for makeup.

Forty-five minutes later Dina was ready. She wore Damin Industries' patented Stay-Put Backless, Strapless Push-Up bra inserts that came in a blue aluminum can and a plain, deceptively simple white silk gown from Louis Féraud—the better to set off the long-sleeved killer jacket from Yves St. Laurent, sumptuously trimmed with gold laurel leaves at the neckline and waist, and entirely encrusted with twenty pounds of faceted cut glass.

She looked like a million, but wore at least ten. Who said diamonds weren't a girl's best friend?

There was her diamond solitaire ring, a flawless D in a pear cut, which weighed sixty-six and a half carats.

There was the choker of eight strands of giant round pearls (*real* pearls, not cultured), the kind Queen Alexandra used to wear in the Edwardian era, which had a clasp of—you guessed it—more diamonds.

And finally there were the earrings, huge pearls dangling from great sweeps of four-carat flawless D diamonds, which were pear-shaped like the pearls.

Or my husband, she thought with wry irony.

The Countess wore red. And white. And black.

The red was a flaring silk satin microskirt, Dina's of course. The white was a corset top and a silky crinoline, a lingerie-inspired Lacroix overdress, also Dina's. And the black were the lacy pantyhose, spike heels, and elbow-length gloves she'd borrowed from—who else?—Dina. But the scruffy motorcycle jacket Zandra wore atop it all was her own prized possession, as was her beautifully boned body and thick cascade of marmalade-colored hair.

She was a knockout and knew it. Half Frederick's of Hollywood and half downtown club habitué-turned-couture model, she was that most elusive of creatures which only the true British aristocracy seem able to turn out—every inch a lady, but hip, fun, and thoroughly with-it.

The telephone rang, sending a jolt through her. She knew better than to entertain hopes that it could be her brother, but still . . .

She seized the receiver. "Hello?"

It was Julio. "There is a gentleman here to see you," he announced sniffily.

"I'll be right out," Zandra said, wondering, as she hung up, who her date for the evening was going to be.

Earlier, Dina had told her: "Darling, you know you cannot go alone. An unescorted woman is absolute anathema! You *must* have a walker, and I know just the one. Leave everything to me!"

Taking one last glimpse at herself in the mirror, Zandra left the suite. Julio intercepted her and led her stiffly down the corridor to the library. He opened the door and stood aside so she could enter.

Inside the book-lined room waited her date.

"Hi!" he beamed, striding, hand extended, across the palace-size Savonnerie. "I'm Lex Bugg."

Although Zandra had been a mere child at the height of his fame in the sixties, his name nevertheless rang a bell; even she was acquainted with his psychedelic, Yellow Submarine–style art.

No spring chicken, he possessed undeniably virile good looks and was all duded up in swallow-tailed, Byronesque formal wear. He was six feet tall with a deep, out-of-season tan and a blinding mouthful of expensive teeth. Graying blond hair pulled back in a ponytail, eyes obscured by tinted lenses, and a classic swimmer's build. He was forty-nine years old and fighting every passing day.

From the looks of it, Lex Bugg seemed to be holding his own.

Then, catching sight of the long sliver of rock crystal dangling from a thong around his neck, Zandra gave an involuntary groan. Hoping discussions of pyramids, crystals, and psychics were not in her immediate future, she smiled brightly. Said, "Hello. I'm Zandra."

His handshake was firm, but didn't crush bones. Ever observant, she couldn't help noticing his fingers.

Incredibly, not so much as a smudge of paint showed from beneath a single manicured nail. How he managed to paint *and* do that was entirely beyond her.

Twenty minutes later, after drinks in the library, Dina, Robert, Zandra, and Lex Bugg sallied forth in Dina's white stretch limo, which transported them in garish luxury the few short blocks to the Met.

11

*K*enzie wore a gently used Salvation Army thrift shop find.

She didn't know what had possessed her to drop by the warehouse the day she had, but she blessed her lucky stars, not to mention her sharp eye which was always on the lookout for anything of exceptional quality. That was how she had spotted the sleeveless yellow silk sheath with its rhinestone-studded bodice and matching crusader scarf-cum-cape to begin with.

Unbelievably, it still had its Givenchy couture label intact, and other than a small stain on the bodice (a mere wee stain which could be cleverly hidden with some artful draping of the capelike scarf), it was in mint condition.

Givenchy! From the Salvation Army yet! Who'd ever believe it?

Kenzie hadn't, at least not at first. And when she'd glanced at the price tag, her disbelief had only increased. Not daring to trust her own eyes, she'd hesitantly brought the gown to the cashier's counter, where she'd asked how much it cost. The sales clerk had taken it, not with the reverence it was due, but as though it was just a bundle of worthless rags, and with a disinterested glance at the tag, had drawled, "Thirty-five."

And Mrs. Turner's daughter, who hadn't been raised a fool, had taken the extravagant bounty. Not ready-to-wear, but a donated, honest-to-goodness *couture* gown which had certainly been overlooked during the sorting, and which originally must have set some fashion-conscious worshipper of Monsieur de Givenchy back, *what? Thirty-five thousand? Forty?*

Now, eyeing herself from all angles in front of the full-length mirror inside her closet door, Kenzie thanked whichever gods were responsible for having dropped such unbelievable beneficence into her lap, not forgetting to mention her local seamstress, whose stitches had made it fit to perfection.

Oh, yes. Tonight's was one party where she'd be able to hold her own and fit in with the best-dressed, rich thin women of Manhattan. Neither Nancy Kissinger, Lee Radziwill Ross, Nan Kempner, nor the rest of the usual horde of undernourished social skeletons would be better dressed. The only thing lacking was jewels, but so what? Who needed bijoux with an outfit so glowingly scrumptious, so extravagantly mind-boggling, and so wantonly frivolous that any trinket would only be gilding the lily?

Kenzie, an army brat, was born and raised on military bases. Childhood, or at least the first fifteen years of it, was spent at a succession of Forts—Ord, Dix, Bragg, Bliss, Jackson, and Leonard Wood—not to mention two different bases in Germany, and one in the Philippines.

Despite the turmoil which resulted each time Colonel Turner was transferred to a new post, Kenzie didn't mind all the moving around. Her mother, Rosemary, was one of those gifted military wives who could spruce up even the dullest assigned quarters and turn them into home sweet home. Subsequently, Kenzie was raised in a happy and loving atmosphere. The youngest of a brood of four, she had three doting older brothers, each of whom had been named after a noted military leader, Dwight D., George S., and Ulysses S.

Despite the military blood coursing through the Turners' veins, Kenzie somehow veered sharply off course. *She* gravitated toward art—why, it was never ascertained, since military bases are not exactly known to be bastions of cultural creativity. But there was no denying her talent, which surfaced at an early age.

At first she entertained notions of becoming an artist. When she wasn't drawing or painting, which was how she spent most of her free time, she would haunt the post libraries and pore over whatever art books were available.

And then, when she turned sixteen, her fate was sealed—by the U.S. Army, no less. That was when her father was assigned to the plum of all military assignments, the Presidio in San Francisco.

As far as Kenzie was concerned, she'd died and gone to heaven. For the Presidio, that huge tract of prime wooded real estate overlooking the Golden Gate, suddenly gave her access to no less than *two* nearby museums—the de Young *and* the Palace of the Legion of Honor. Now, no longer having to settle for studying reproductions of paintings in books or magazines, she could finally feast her eyes on the real McCoys.

And she was blown away. Nothing had prepared her for the vivid mastery bursting from the splendid canvases. It was all there. Strength and color, fire and ice, and iridescent brushstrokes ranging from boldly assertive swipes to the most subtle and delicate of shadings.

It was then that she fell madly in love with Old Masters. And it was then, too, that she was forced to face her own shortcomings, realizing just how limited and meager her own talent really was. After much soul searching, she decided that if she couldn't be an artist she would become the next best thing—an art historian.

In her senior year of high school, she informed her parents that she wanted to apply to Columbia University. "It's got one of the best art history departments in the country."

Her father, seeing the fervent fire burning in his daughter's eyes, said, "Honey, you know that no matter what you decide to do, your mother and I will always stand behind you."

So Kenzie applied to Columbia and was duly accepted.

The morning she arrived in the Big Apple was the single most exciting day of her entire life. She didn't even stop to unpack her things at the dorm before setting out to explore Manhattan on foot.

Uptown, downtown, all around the town; New York was so much *more* of everything. Bigger, brasher, and the most electrifying place on earth. It literally hummed and thrummed with excess energy.

And she thought excitedly: *This is where I belong. Here is where I'll make my mark. Right here, at the very center of the universe . . .*

Here is where I'll make my mark . . .

Those seven simple words became Kenzie's motto. They were her creed, her anchor, her bulwark.

Sheepskin in hand, she moved out of the dorm and into a shared studio apartment in Chelsea. However, finding a job in her chosen field was easier said than done. A literal army of other graduates—arts majors all, and many with formidable family and social credentials—were snapping up what scarce but choice positions were available at the various galleries, museums, and auction houses.

But Kenzie was undaunted. She figured that by Christmas, Easter at the very latest, the ranks of the newly employed ex-debutantes would be considerably thinned by marriage, ineptitude, and a craving for leisure. In the meantime, she supported herself with a variety of odd jobs, none of them memorable.

And then, what should jump off the page of the Help Wanted section of the Sunday *Times* but an ad which was right up her alley? The owner of a gallery specializing in Old Master paintings was seeking a qualified assistant.

With alacrity, Kenzie wrote a cover letter, and along with a copy of her résumé, sent it to the appropriate box number.

Two weeks later, a message was left on her answering machine. The caller identified himself as Mr. Pickel Wugsby, "That's Pickel spelled 'el,' " and would she be so kind as to come to his gallery for an interview at eleven o'clock the following morning?

She arrived at the address he gave her ten minutes before the appropriate time. The narrow storefront on Lexington Avenue in the low Seventies did not look promising. It had iron gates and door bars which had long since rusted into place, blacked-out grimy windows, and not so much as a shop sign to indicate that an art gallery—or anything else—could possibly lie within. There was, however, the requisite door buzzer.

Kenzie rang it and waited.

Presently the lock tumblers clicked, the door opened as far as the short security chain would permit, and a suspicious eye peered out at her.

"Yes?" inquired a resonant male voice.

"I'm MacKenzie Turner," she said. "I have an appointment with Mr. Wugsby?"

The man shut the door, undid the chain, then reopened the door just wide enough to let Kenzie squeeze inside before quickly locking it again. "I," he said, "am Mr. Wugsby."

She shook his dry paw briskly but firmly, in the process giving him a swift but thorough once-over.

He was a dead ringer for Mr. Pickwick—a portly, old-fashioned gentleman of indeterminate age. He had very pink skin, beaming blue eyes behind thick little glasses, and mutton chop whiskers edged in pure white, like superior ermine. All that was missing were the tights, gaiters, and black swallow-tailed silk waistcoat, and instead of a white cravat, his capacious chin encroached upon an askew bow tie. But despite the baggy old trousers, mousey, moth-eaten sweater, and ratty old kilim mules he wore in lieu of shoes, he *did* sport a Dickensian gold watch chain and fob.

Her inspection of him over, Kenzie suddenly became aware of all the paintings.

They were everywhere.

Stored sideways in deep, shoulder-high shelves.

Stacked ten deep around the double-height room.

Hung wall-to-wall, from floor to ceiling, frame against frame in apparently happy, if discordant, clutter.

Even the garish light thrown by the bare lightbulbs could not detract from the sheer mesmerizing energy produced by the stock of masterpieces cluttering those decrepit walls.

"My God!" she managed, her voice whispery and reverent. "A genuine Rubens! And a Pompeo Batoni . . . Hans Memling . . . Ghirlandaio . . . Dürer . . . Matthias Grünewald!"

She was overwhelmed, her eyes feasting on treasures ranging from German Gothic to Italian Renaissance; seventeenth-century Dutch to eighteenth-century French. And there wasn't a one the curators of the Louvre, the Met, or the Getty wouldn't have killed for.

Stunned, she slowly turned to Mr. Wugsby. "Why, from outside one would never begin to suspect—"

"Which is the idea," Mr. Wugsby replied with a gentle little smile and sly twinkle in his eyes. "But come."

Gesturing for her to follow, he led the way up a wide, graceful spiral of mahogany stairs to a wraparound mezzanine. Midpoint along it, he stopped and pointed over the balustrade at a gigantic, gilt-framed canvas hanging on the opposite wall.

"Since you obviously know your artists, tell me . . . to whom would you attribute that?" he asked. "Remember, there is absolutely no need to hurry. Please feel free to take all the time you need."

"Mmm." Kenzie, well aware that she was being tested, folded her arms in front of her and first studied the painting from across the room.

It was a curious hybrid of Italian influence, and showed an Arcadian clearing in which frolicking nymphs and neoclassically draped women danced attendance upon an almost girlishly pretty nude Apollo. And it could, at first glance, be easily attributed to either Raphael or Poussin. But that, she knew, was an easy trap to fall into.

After a minute or so, she walked around the perimeter of the mezzanine and examined the artist's technique from close up. Studied the cracked, varnished canvas intently. Ran her fingertips lightly across the dusty surface to get a feel of the brushstrokes.

Looking for clues.

Finally, after five minutes, she went back over to where Mr. Wugsby was waiting. From there, she contemplated the composition a while longer.

At last she cleared her throat. "Anton Raphael Mengs," she said authoritatively.

"Well, goodness gracious!" he said, beaming. "You're hired. Now, when can you start?"

Thus began a three-year-long relationship which turned out to be a better training ground than all the graduate schools combined. They became like family, the short, portly old gentleman and the eager, sparkly young woman who was his willing apprentice.

During her first day on the job, Mr. Wugsby explained why he had hired her. "You are to be my eyes," was the way he put it, and without a trace of rancor or self-pity, told her of the degenerative retinal disease from which he was suffering, and for which there was no cure.

She was so distressed that he ended up comforting her.

"I do wish you'd stop acting as if it's the end of the world," he said, "because it is not. Besides, even if it were, being upset would not solve a thing. Think about it. If you were in my shoes, wouldn't you be annoyed by having someone melancholy moping around?"

She nodded.

"Anyway, when a situation is such that it cannot be changed," he added, "one might as well adapt, and try to make the best of it. In other words, the least I shall expect from you is an attempt at some semblance of good cheer."

From that moment on, Kenzie adored him.

He proved an inspiration in countless ways. His knowledge was ency-

clopedic, and never ceased to amaze her. The first time they previewed an
Old Masters auction together was a case in point:

"What idiots some of these departmental 'experts' are!" he snapped
testily. "That still life is no Chardin! It is too filled with bravura.
Chardin's touch is much more analytical and poetic. Nor is this painting
modest enough: notice how the objects are far too grand . . ."

And ". . . *this* is supposed to be a Stubbs? *Bah!* That horse is much
too sentimental, and not nearly haunting enough. Nor does it have the an-
atomical details reminiscent of Leonardo. Stubbs knew his musculature
backward and forward, since he spent years dissecting animals . . ."

And ". . . Now, *this* Delacroix is sublime and obviously genuine, but
you mark my words: the price will go through the roof . . ."

Kenzie looked and listened and learned.

Before long, she discovered just how truly select and wealthy Mr.
Wugsby's clientele was. Agnellis and Rothschilds, Niarchoses and von
Thurn und Taxis, Thyssen-Bornemiszmas and von und zu Engelwiesens—
like worshippers on a pilgrimage, a steady trickle of them came and
looked and bought.

Nor was he stingy. After the first six months, he gave Kenzie a substantial raise, which she used to move into the rent-stabilized walk-up she
still inhabited. But what she treasured above all was the priceless knowledge Mr. Wugsby handed down to her. All the little tricks of the trade he'd
picked up during nearly half a century of dealing in fine art. She learned
how to spot forgeries by knowing which pigments were discovered when.
How to distinguish genuine patinas acquired over the centuries from those
which had recently been produced with phenoformaldehyde dissolved in
benzine or turpentine. Plus, the various technical techniques, like using
ultraviolet light, having paintings x-rayed, and scraping a microscopic
flake of pigment from a canvas and having a lab technician analyze it
through the use of spectrography.

But perhaps the greatest gift Mr. Wugsby bestowed upon her was his
passion. He had that rare gift of being able to bring a work of art to life,
so that she saw it not merely in decorative or historical terms, but as a living, breathing entity with a pedigree as real, and as vital, as that of any
human being.

In the end, it wasn't the blindness that did him in. It was cancer, and
it was terminal. The doctors gave him six months to live.

Kenzie helped him close up shop and liquidate his stock. Unknown to
her, he called in a favor from an old colleague of his at Burghley's, Mr.
A. Dietrich Spotts, thus securing her a position in the auction house's Old
Masters department.

Kenzie was with Mr. Wugsby at the end.

On his deathbed, he confessed that before she had come along, he
had interviewed twenty-eight other applicants for her job.

"Do you realize," he warbled, his voice painfully thin and weak, "that of all of them, *you* were the only one who attributed the Mengs correctly?"

She hugged his frail, emaciated body to hers.

"But I'd have hired you even if you hadn't," he admitted, a bit of irrepressible slyness shining through. "When you first walked in, I could tell from the way you looked around that art was in your blood . . . that it was your *life!*"

They both smiled at the memory, and then his eyelids fluttered and he was gone. She kissed his forehead solemnly, laid his head gently down on the pillow, and smoothed her fingers over his eyes to close them.

And that was how one chapter of her life ended, and another began.

Admiring her reflection, Kenzie struck a dramatic tango pose when the downstairs buzzer interrupted her fashion high. The tango forgotten, she quickly smoothed the gown, flung the long scarf around her throat, and hurried out through the living room and into the small foyer.

"Who is it?" she asked cautiously through the intercom.

"It's Mr. Spotts," replied a static-filled squawk.

"Come on up." Kenzie hit the buzzer which released the locked door downstairs; a few minutes later, when she let him in, Mr. Spotts inspected her in one sweeping head-to-toe-and-back-up stare. "Good heavens, Miss Turner!" he said.

"What's the matter?" she asked.

"Why, just look at you! I have never seen you quite so beautiful."

She was touched. "Nor have I seen you looking quite so handsome or debonair, Mr. Spotts. Black tie suits you. May I fix you a drink?"

"Goodness, no, my dear. There will be more than enough spirits to imbibe at the party. Besides, I have a cab waiting downstairs."

"Then we'd better not keep the meter running."

She grabbed her coat, he helped her slip into it, and she linked her arm through his.

"Cinderella's all set!" she said brightly. "Let's go have a ball!"

12

At the Met, the cocktail party in the Blumenthal Patio was in full swing, the sea of rising voices drowning out the strains of the valiant Mozart ensemble. Hundreds of mingling guests created a perpetually shifting mosaic, birds of a feather flocking together.

Prince Karl-Heinz von und zu Engelwiesen was stationed at the entrance, where he greeted the constant stream of new arrivals, all of whom were announced by the master of ceremonies.

". . . Her Royal Highness, the Infanta Doña Pilar, Duchess of Badajoz, and His Royal Highness, the Duke of Badajoz . . . Mr. and Mrs. Carter Burden . . . Mr. and Mrs. William F. Buckley, Jr. . . . Lady Dudley and the Earl of Warwick . . . Governor and Mrs.—"

Prince Karl-Heinz acknowledged the women with a kiss on the hand, and the men with firm handshakes and a slight bow.

". . . Mr. and Mrs. Sheldon D. Fairey," announced the master of ceremonies with stentorian gravity.

Sheldon D. Fairey came forward, squiring Nina, his ageless socialite wife who wore an artfully painted palette of a face and a voluminous cloud of emerald silk Oscar de la Renta.

"Heinzie, *darling!*" she dramatized as he kissed her hand, her smile as blinding as it was patently false. "I cannot *believe* you are already celebrating another birthday! To think that a year has passed since . . . well, you are beginning to make me feel positively ancient!"

Karl-Heinz summoned the requisite laugh. "Then rest assured, my dear Nina, I am your very own picture of Dorian Gray. As I become older and more dissipated, you grow younger and lovelier with every passing year."

Expertly, he eased her past to make way for new arrivals.

"Liar!" And tinkling laughter over her shoulder, off Nina swept in a rustle of silk, her left arm linked through her husband's, and her right already waggling her fingers here, there, everywhere.

"I do hope I won't disgrace you," Kenzie fretted. She and Mr. Spotts were climbing out of the cab on Fifth Avenue, thus avoiding the traffic jam of limousines waiting to deposit their passengers at the red-carpeted stairs.

"But why in all heaven should you disgrace me?" Mr. Spotts, placing a hand under her elbow, inquired in a kindly voice.

"Well, in case you haven't noticed," she said nervously, "I'm not exactly society material."

"And what, pray tell," he asked, *"is* 'society material'?"

"Oh, you know . . . private schools, dance and deportment lessons, Swiss finishing schools, being an expert at clever repartee, knowing the right time to hoist the mainsail as opposed to the spinnaker, how much to tip the croupier . . ."

"Ah." He nodded sagely. "In other words, Miss Turner, you are assuming that an upbringing like, er, Miss Parker's, for instance, would have given you all the requisite social skills and polish for an evening like tonight's? Is that not so?"

"Well, something like that," Kenzie admitted uneasily, "yes."

"Well then, I advise you to get that nonsense out of your head at once! I, personally, would not be caught dead with the likes of Miss Parker hanging onto my arm!" His voice gentled. "Look at it this way, my dear. If you're good enough for me, then I daresay you're good enough for anyone else who may be here. Now, I decree that we enjoy ourselves, and enjoy ourselves we shall!"

"Yes . . . but . . . but Mr. Spotts! A Serene Highness? What do I do? Kiss his ring?"

"That, Miss Turner, is reserved for the pope, a cardinal, or an archbishop, and then usually only if one is a practicing Roman Catholic."

He steered her unerringly through limousine row and flashed his invitation to a guard, who unhooked the velvet rope from its portable stanchion.

Climbing the red-carpeted steps, Kenzie stared up with growing trepidation. The Metropolitan Museum of Art hadn't earned its monikers, "Club Met," "The Party Palace," or "Rent-a-Palace," for nothing. She knew that it was the single most prestigious, if not the most expensive, location at which to throw a party—and that in a city chock full of prestigious and expensive places to choose from.

But despite the butterflies in her stomach, she couldn't help but admire the awesome facade, palatial in the wash of silver-green floodlights, the banners snapping briskly in the wind, the crashing fountains sending up plumes of cool white spray which almost, but not quite, masked the ever-present sounds of traffic whizzing by down Fifth Avenue.

It was, she thought, impossible not to imagine this floodlit temple of the arts as anything but the *son-et-lumière* show of a three-dimensional architectural capriccio—huge, Corinthian-columned, and imposing—as if some giant had scooped it up from one of the capitals of Europe and set it down, intact, right here on the edge of Central Park in the very middle of the greatest, noisiest, and most electrifying city on earth.

At last they reached the top, where one of a pair of doormen in eighteenth-century livery, complete with powdered wig and silk breeches, inspected Mr. Spotts's invitation yet a second time before bowing and gracefully gesturing them inside.

Kenzie couldn't believe her eyes. The resplendent lobby with its grand main staircase had been transformed, for this single night, into a latter-day Versailles, right down to the planters of full-grown citrus trees and massive torchères lit with hundreds of flickering beeswax tapers.

A liveried footman directed them to coat check; from a passing couple, Kenzie heard a silvery tinkle of laughter and the rustle of silk, caught, from around a thin patrician throat, the cold flash of diamonds and the rich, blood-red glow of rubies.

Heaven help me, she thought with a sinking feeling as the reality of the soiree sank in. *I'm just a plain working girl. A simple office drone. What on God's earth ever possessed me to come here?*

Well, here goes the lamb to the slaughter, Kenzie thought as Mr. Spotts gave their names to the master of ceremonies. Her palms were moist and slippery and she was terrified of making some terrible social gaffe. Squaring her shoulders, she glanced out at the roomful of guests in an effort to shore up her eroding self-confidence.

A major mistake.

The extravaganza of beautifully gowned and bejeweled socialites only reinforced her feelings of inadequacy. How foolish, the notion that a thrift shop find was all it took to compete with these beings of the upper stratum!

"Mr. A. Dietrich Spotts and Ms. MacKenzie Turner," the master of ceremonies called out.

Stifling a little cry, Kenzie glanced anxiously at Mr. Spotts.

You'll do fine, his smile reassured, and before she knew what was happening, she found herself face-to-face with His Serene Highness.

To her amazement, before she could betray so much as the slightest awkwardness, Prince Karl-Heinz took her hand and raised it to his lips, his breath barely grazing her fingertips. "Ms. Turner . . ." he said, his blue oval eyes meeting hers. He smiled charmingly. "A pleasure . . ."

Then, letting go of her hand, he greeted Mr. Spotts. The two men exchanged pleasantries and then Mr. Spotts shepherded Kenzie on.

"I can't believe—you mean . . . that's *all* there is to it?" Kenzie asked incredulously.

Mr. Spotts smiled. "I'm afraid so. You see, my dear, what did I tell you? There really was nothing to get all worked up about, was there?"

He stopped, expertly canvasing the crush of guests, and Kenzie did the same. Everyone seemed to be acquainted with one another, and social choreography was in high gear, the $942-a-case vintage Cristal priming sharp tongues and furtive whispers. Everywhere, false smiles worthy of Oscar nominations lit up perfect maquillage.

Now that the worst of her fears had proved groundless, Kenzie found herself mesmerized. The sheer profusion of so much haute couture under a single roof boggled the mind. It was, she thought, an opiate dream, an ever-changing kaleidoscope of felicitous grace, mesmeric colors, and intermingling textures which had to be of some other, more prodigal world. Ravenously, her eye for quality ate up the seemingly effortless, flawless tailoring; soaked up, above all, the infinitely prolific and bewildering flights of fancy which were the hallmarks of the couturier's art.

For that was what these garments were. Art. Art to wear. To flaunt. To frivol the night away in.

There were column gowns in Fortuny pleats; waltzing dresses embroidered with iridescent silk roses; rhinestone-encrusted crêpe hourglass dresses; swirling tartan ballgowns; patchwork Gypsy ensembles no Romany tribe could ever have conceived, and more. Much, much more.

"Why don't we find ourselves a drink," Mr. Spotts suggested peremptorily. He smiled out at the crowd with knowing satisfaction. "After that, we can stand back and amuse ourselves ... perhaps watch the social climbers digging in their cleats and pitons?"

Kenzie raised her eyebrows. "Do I detect a note of cynicism?"

"Cynicism! From *me?*" Mr. Spotts pretended appropriate shock, but his eyes danced merrily. "Really, Miss Turner ... !"

"Mr. and Mrs. Robert A. Goldsmith," the master of ceremonies announced stentoriously.

On that cue, Dina swept grandly forward, her extended arm dangling a delicately limp wrist *and* her new diamond bracelet.

Karl-Heinz took her fingertips and raised them to his lips. "Exquisite," he murmured, whether to her sixty-six and a half carat solitaire, her twenty-eight carat bracelet, or to her—Dina couldn't quite ascertain which. Nevertheless, she preened visibly.

Letting go of her hand, Karl-Heinz turned to Robert. "My most sincere congratulations," he said, exchanging firm handshakes.

Robert A. Goldsmith blinked like a sleepy lizard. "Congratulations?" he repeated blankly.

Prince Karl-Heinz smiled. "For buying Burghley's, of course! I must admit I feel a twinge of jealousy. A company of that caliber is, how does one say it?" Karl-Heinz turned to Dina, a slight lift of his left eyebrow chiding her for having wangled a last-minute invitation. "A feather in one's cap?"

But Dina, now that she had become the Queen of Manhattan Island, accepted the gentle rebuke with regal graciousness.

"To show our appreciation for your kind invitation," she purred silkily, "we have brought Your Serene Highness a little surprise."

"Indeed?" The prince looked amused. "And what might that be?"

Dina smiled mysteriously and wagged an admonishing finger. "You'll see momentarily," she promised, and knowing an exit line when it presented itself, off she glided, her husband in tow.

Behind them, the master of ceremonies announced, "Her Grace, Zandra von Hohenburg-Willemlohe, Countess of Grafburg, and Mr. Lex Bugg."

Dina glanced over her shoulder to catch Karl-Heinz's reaction—which, like the proverbial picture worth a thousand words, turned out to be supremely gratifying.

"Zandra . . . ? *Zandra!* It *is* you!" Karl-Heinz quickly got over his tongue-tied surprise. "But this is *unbelievable!*" he exclaimed, greeting her with a long warm hug and a kiss and then another hug.

Finally, holding her at arms' length, he studied her from head to toe. "Is it possible? Can you have become more beautiful than ever?"

"Still the flatterer, I see," she laughed, unable to hide her delight at his delight to see her.

"That is because flattery gets me everywhere." He smiled and shook his head in wonder. "My God! How long *has* it been?"

"Too long, cousin. At least two years. No. Longer. The last time was . . . let me see . . . yes, that dreadful party at Aunt Annabel's."

He made a face. "Ah, yes. An excruciating occasion best left forgotten." Still holding her hands, he said, "I had no idea you were in town!"

"Flying over was a—a spur-of-the-moment lark," she improvised quickly. "Except for Dina, I don't believe anyone even knows I'm in town."

He smiled. "Well, now the entire city does." He gave her another hug. "I hate reception lines, but alas, they are an evil I must contend with. We will talk later?"

She nodded brightly. "I'll be on the lookout for you."

"And *I* shall be on the lookout for *you.* In fact, I shall have the place cards rearranged so we can sit together during dinner. That way we can catch up on all the latest."

"I'd like that," she said, flushed with pleasure.

"Me, too." He smiled and kissed her cheek. "Would you believe, your unexpected presence has made a dreadfully dull party totally worthwhile?"

13

"Look, Robert!" Dina squealed, hopping on tiptoe and waving excitedly. "There's Sheldon D. Fairey!"

"So?" grunted Robert, who since that morning had relegated Burghley's chairman to his multitudinous ranks of minions.

Dina turned to Zandra and Lex. "You two go circulate!" she stage-whispered, making shooing motions. "We'll meet up later."

Once she had Robert to herself, she said, "I think it would only be courteous if we went and said hello to Mr. Fairey."

Prudently, she neglected to mention her ulterior motive. The very least she owed Sheldon was a quick hello and a whispered thank-you—he had, after all, been instrumental in getting them the invitations for this party.

To her surprise, Robert put up no resistance whatsoever. "All right," he shrugged. "If that's what you want, why not?"

Prudently, he neglected to mention *his* ulterior motive. Namely, that this was the very opportunity he'd been waiting for—but who'd have thought that his wife, of all people, would drop it so fortuitously into his lap? For it was his express intention to take Sheldon D. Fairey aside and finalize Bambi Parker's promotion.

Dina, happily oblivious to that fact, clung to his arm and unerringly navigated him over to where Sheldon D. Fairey and two *Social Register* couples were standing around chatting.

"Now remember, Robert," she reminded him sternly, "you promised to find Zandra a job in the Old Masters department. This is the perfect opportunity to bring it up."

"Yeah, yeah, yeah," he scowled, once again cursing his idiocy in acquiescing to what amounted to playing Russian roulette. God, but how could he have been so *stupid?* Tossing Bambi and Zandra together was like lighting a stick of dynamite and waiting around for the explosion. Sooner or later, it was bound to come.

"Sweeties!" Dina, having descended upon their quarry, let go of Robert's arm.

There was a flurry of handshakes and cheek kisses, followed by another round of the same when Nina Fairey—possessed of a social antennae second to none—seemingly materialized out of nowhere.

"*Wonderful* jacket!" Nina cooed. "Yves St. Laurent?"

"The one and only." Dina, for the first time finding herself at the very epicenter of attention, took to the kowtowing like a duck to water.

"My God, that *ring!*" one of the *Social Register* wives exclaimed in shock. "I've never *seen* a rock that huge!"

"This?" Dina purred, sighing happily. "It's new. My sweetie is so generous."

Isn't he just? Robert thought darkly, unwrapping a genuine Havana—a Flor de F. Farach Extra—which he rattled next to his ear, then held under his nose for a whiff. Satisfied, he chomped off the puffing tip. Sucked on it to get it nice and moist. Hoped the ritual would help tune out all that female jabber.

No such luck.

"Now, darling," Nina was gushing, "you really must tell us! How does it feel to own Burghley's?"

Robert heard his wife's glissant scale of light laughter. "Ask me again once it's sunk in," Dina lied, eating up every last bit of fuss, flattery, and deference. "Right now it all seems so, well, so *unreal.*"

"Like hell it does!" grumped Robert around his cigar. Glaring at his wife's gaggle of newfound sycophants, he had a good mind to tell them exactly where they could go—and why Dina didn't was entirely beyond him. Christ, those ass-kissers hadn't given her the time of day before; why should she bother with their brownnosing now?

As these thoughts crossed his mind, he sensed Dina giving him The Look—clearly a signal that he and Sheldon have their little powwow.

He shrugged to himself. Why not? It was as good a time as any, and would provide escape from the hens.

Tapping Sheldon to get his attention, Robert beckoned him aside with a nod. Sheldon dutifully accommodated, and Robert draped a comradely arm around his shoulders and edged him away. "There's a couple a things we need to discuss," he said in a buddy-buddy locker-room kind of voice. "Whyn't we take a stroll. I'm dyin' to light up this here cigar . . ."

Sheldon D. Fairey winced. If there was one thing in the world he hated, it was cigar smoke.

Not that he dared mention it. Who was he to argue with his new boss?

Mr. Spotts scooped two champagne glasses off a waiter's tray and handed one to Kenzie. "Here you go," he said, clinking his glass against hers. "A toast. To your brilliant future."

"Thank you, Mr. Spotts. And may I be worthy of living up to your expectations."

"Come, come, my dear. Now that I've officially been put to pasture, I think we can dispense with the formality, don't you? So let's do drop this

Mr. Spotts and Miss Turner business. Friends should be on a first-name basis." He raised his eyebrows. "That is, of course, if you don't mind . . . Kenzie?" He used her first name tentatively.

She smiled. "On the contrary . . . Dietrich," she replied softly. "I'm honored."

He returned her smile. "I am glad. Now, if you will be so kind as to excuse me, I'm off to hunt down Mr. Fairey. I just want to make certain all the details of your promotion have been ironed out. In the meantime . . ." Mr. Spotts lowered his voice conspiratorially. "Don't look now, but there's a young man standing over there, off to your right . . ."

Kenzie's curiosity was piqued, but trying not to be too obvious, she waited a moment. Then she looked casually all around before finally glancing in the direction he'd indicated.

She drew a sharp breath.

The man in question—*if* he was the one Mr. Spotts had mentioned, and surely he must be—had to qualify as the most handsome male specimen on this side of the Atlantic!

Her voice quavered. "You . . . you can't mean that Nordic god in his mid-thirties? The Viking with the whitish-blond hair?"

Mr. Spotts smiled. "Indeed I do."

"What about him?"

"Oh, only that he hasn't been able to take his eyes off you ever since we entered."

"What! He's been eyeing . . . *me?*" she gasped in disbelief. "Oh really, Dietrich! What makes you so sure he's not waiting for someone else?"

"Because, Kenzie, my dear," said Mr. Spotts in that precise and patient manner of his, "many things may have changed since my remote youth, but there *are,* happily, a very few that have not. And a handsome young man trying to catch the eye of a pretty young lady, I am glad to say, is still one of them. Now, I suggest that while I go scare up Mr. Fairey, you drop your handkerchief or use some other such feminine wile, which, I suspect, is all your young man is waiting for."

"Drop my *handkerchief?*" she said in disbelief.

But Mr. Spotts didn't respond. He was already gone.

Kenzie searched in vain for his tall figure among the crowd, and was startled when a stranger's voice said, "Hullo!"

Looking around, she almost choked. Dear God, *him!* The splendid, beautiful hunk with the whitish-blond hair!

She stood there staring, legs trembling, aware of his great shining greenish-blue eyes. Yes, large and wonderful eyes, like warm, sun-dappled swimming pools in August, the kind you wanted to drown in forever.

And, from close up, she realized something else. He was a man gifted with more than mere masculine beauty; he was, without doubt, the most beautiful man she had ever laid eyes upon.

She lost all concept of time, and had no idea how long they stood there staring at one another. Suddenly she felt like an adolescent again. All arms and legs and no tongue.

He took the initiative, gave her the subtlest of bows with his head. "Since we have not been introduced, allow me to do the honors. My name is Hannes Hockert, but my friends call me Hans. You know . . ." His smile was devastating. ". . . as in Hans Christian Andersen?"

She shook his hand, finding it strong and hard, but with a surprisingly gentle touch. Much like his voice, which was quiet and gentle, yet had a resonant, distinctly masculine timbre.

"MacKenzie Turner," she managed in a daze, her throat so constricted she had to clear it. "My friends either call me Kenzie or Kenz."

"Kenzie . . . Kenzie . . ." he repeated to himself, as though tasting her name on his palate. "Mmm. Rather unusual, but somehow it seems to suit you. Yes. Ah." He indicated her glass. "I see you have finished your champagne."

Champagne . . . ? She looked at him blankly.

Deftly he plucked the empty glass from between her willing fingers, threw back his head, gulped down the contents of his own, and then held it up and grinned disarmingly.

"If you'll notice," he said, winking as irresistibly as he smiled, "it just so happens that I could use a refill, also. I shall return momentarily." He paused. "You won't play Cinderella and disappear on me, I hope?"

Me? Disappear! Kenzie thought, giving a start. *Good God, why should I want to do that?*

"No," she whispered, her eyes dreamily following him as he moved fluidly away with the lean, unconscious grace of a dancer, or some sensuously sleek jungle cat, until he was swallowed up in the crowd.

Only then, once she could no longer see him, did she wonder how she had ever attracted the attention of such a splendidly gorgeous specimen of a man, and without even trying!

Oh my, she thought. Hannes Hockert, a.k.a. Hans, was right up her alley and *exactly* her type. Strikingly handsome. Compellingly masculine. And chivalrous to a fault.

She had to smile. It didn't take much stretch of the imagination to fancy him as some throwback to Leif Eriksson—a proud sea-roving warrior standing at the bow of a marauding, double-prowed Viking longboat, the silk of his white-blond hair whipped by the wind . . .

Mmm, she thought with the secretive delight of a miser hoarding his treasure, no doubt about it. Hannes truly was her beau ideal—and as far as her own taste went, no one else could come a close second. No one on God's earth.

* * *

Lex Bugg hopped, skipped, and jumped—a frog on speed.

At first, Zandra was amused by his frenetic energy as he charged from one circle of acquaintances to the next. Barely able to keep up with him, she shook countless hands, dutifully smiled and laughed, and did her best to put names to faces.

A futile exercise.

Lex introduced her to too many people in too rapid a succession for anyone to make an impact. Everything was a blur.

"Is there anyone you *don't* know?" she quipped good-naturedly.

"Only those who don't count," he responded in total seriousness, his head slowly swiveling as he scanned the sea of faces for any important new arrivals.

It was then, at that precise moment, that Zandra realized to what extent he was using her. Not surprisingly, her initial amusement turned to outrage. It was one thing to be introduced to people, but it was another to be toted around like some prize trophy, having her name and title dropped for no other reason than his trying to impress people.

Well, that was where *she* drew the line.

Spying a world-famous photographer, Lex took her by the arm. "C'mon," he said excitedly, "there's Francesco Scavullo!" He started to make a beeline, but Zandra refused to budge. She was fed up and royally pissed.

"Hey, c'mon!" he urged. "What's keeping you?"

Turning on him in a blaze of hair, teeth, and eyes, she snapped, "Goddammit, Lex! You really are a first-class shit! You know that?"

He looked taken aback. "Is something wrong?" he asked, genuinely perplexed.

"Is something wrong!" she echoed, dripping contempt. *"I'll* tell you what's wrong! For your information, I take exception to the brazen way you're using me as a carrot! I'm not just some kind of social bait you can dangle in front of whomever you please! You're using me."

He pretended shocked innocence. *"Moi?"*

"Yes, *vous."* Anger blazed from her eyes.

His brow furrowed at her sudden transformation. Like he needed this scene! Who'd have thought she'd turn into a complete minus?

"Is that how you really feel?" he asked, trying to keep his cool.

"That's exactly the way I feel!" Her voice was husky, quiet but strong, and something about her face reminded him of tempered steel.

He took a deep breath, inflated his cheeks, then slowly exhaled, deciding to placate her and avert a public spectacle for now.

He said, "Okay, okay. You've got every right to be angry with me, all right?"

Her eyes narrowed appraisingly, her fingers blurring as she tapped the elbows of her crossed arms. Hardly naive, she briefly contemplated his spiel.

He had all the right answers.

And showed the appropriate remorse.

Why, then, couldn't she shake the suspicion that he was only humoring her? Or that his sincerity went about as deep as the laminate on his porcelain teeth?

Correctly reading her skepticism, Lex decided it behooved him to turn up the charm. "You're right," he said earnestly, holding her gaze. "I've been selfish and owe you an apology. What do you say we kiss and make up?"

Zandra, doubts unvanquished, let her silence speak for itself.

Stuck-up bitch, Lex wanted to say, but curbed the impulse. Instead, he gave her his most appealing little-lost-boy expression.

"Look," he reiterated, "I said I was sorry. And I am."

Zandra sighed to herself. So what if his amends didn't ring true? That was beside the point, wasn't it? For an apology, whether heartfelt or not, was an apology—and as such, required a gracious response.

Etiquette came first. Personal feelings last.

"All right, all right. Apology accepted." She raised her hands and waved them, as if partaking in some arcane sorcery designed to clear the air while, all around, glittering as though in reproof, *tout* New York crowded her peripheral vision, a constantly shifting, prismatic explosion of sequins, rainbows, and jewels.

They wandered into the otherwise-deserted Egyptian Wing. Lit glass showcases lined both walls, displaying the plunder of ancient tombs: fragments of textiles and shrouds, Ptolemaic bronzes and limestone steles, quartz heads of kings and painted mummy masks, sacred cat-headed goddesses and canopic jar lids in the form of divinities.

All once-holy icons of a long-lost culture, now reduced to curiosities for the shuffling, daytime masses.

Robert A. Goldsmith rested his elbow, as though to stake claim to its ownership, on the great central sarcophagus. The cigar between his clenched teeth churned up great indulgent clouds of smoke which gradually dissipated into a low blue haze hovering overhead.

Sheldon D. Fairey, intending to avoid the worst of the smoke, stood a few steps back. He found the eerie, tomblike silence of this particular gallery claustrophobically oppressive and disquieting. He was, above all, too aware of the dozens of pairs of mysterious blank eyes which he felt kept watch from behind the walls of their fragile glass prisons.

"The reason I brought ya in here," Robert growled, "is for some goddamn privacy. What I wanna discuss is completely off the record. In other words . . ." He thrust his head forward, a pugnacious, ferociously glaring pitbull, ". . . we never had this conversation. Ya read me?"

Loud and clear, Sheldon thought, masking his alarm behind a carefully composed countenance. Phrases such as "off the record" and "never had this conversation" invariably set off warning bells—and with good reason. Having spent his entire career above reproach, he had adroitly avoided underhanded dealings like the plague. At least, he thought miserably, until now. But in the meantime, what choice did he have but to acquiesce?

"If that is the way you wish it," he murmured tactfully, "yes. Of course this will remain entirely off the record."

"Good. 'Cause if this goes any further'n you an' me, I'll have your ass."

"You can count on my discretion," Sheldon, ever the gentleman, sniffed with dignity.

Robert, luxuriating in confidence, leaned back against the ancient tomb, churned up even greater and more humongous clouds of smoke. Then, taking the cigar out of his mouth, he regarded the hand-wrapped tobacco leaves with something akin to admiration.

"My wife's best friend happens to be in town for an unspecified period of time," he said conversationally. "She's lookin' for a job."

He raised his eyes, pointedly met Sheldon's, and held his gaze. "She needs a green card, too."

Sheldon felt an ominous pluck of foreboding. "Y-yes?" he ventured guardedly.

Robert's plump ruddy features expressed a world of disdain. "For Christ's sake, man, you're in charge of Burghley's! Surely clinching something as simple as this is within your capacity?"

Sheldon, attempting to deflect Robert's stinging barb, coughed discreetly into a cupped hand. "Well, I'll . . . I'll certainly look into it and give it my best shot," he said with an almost maidenly primness.

"You'll look into it?" Robert mimicked, setting Sheldon's teeth on edge. *"You'll give it your best shot?"*

Now Sheldon's blood pounded in his ears and the suffocating anger he felt burned like vicious indigestion. Resolving to remain as outwardly calm and dignified as circumstances would permit, he drew himself up and said, "As I assured you, I'll—"

"Unh-unh." Robert's eyes flashed like multiple razor blades. "I think you've got your wires crossed. See, I'm not *askin'* ya to do it. I'm *tellin'* ya to!"

His voice stung, and with an inward smile, he observed that he'd hit right on target. Sheldon's hands had clenched into fists and he quivered from head to toe with speechless indignation.

"In other words, Fairey, what you're gonna do," Robert continued smoothly, "is tell me what I wanna hear. An' what I wanna hear is that you've already taken care of everything. That the damn woman's already got her job—in Old Masters—and the green card to go along with it."

Robert cupped a hand around his ear.

"Well? Are you *deaf?* Speak up, man!"

Sheldon's lower mandible dropped a good two inches before clicking audibly shut. His cheeks were flaming, and the heat of his humiliation seemed to radiate outward, causing the cool glass cases and the blank-eyed, silent stone heads to ripple as in a Saharan mirage. Never before in his professional career had he ever been treated with anything but deference—never!

Sheldon, in an attempt to recoup some of his lost composure, swallowed hard. What he *wanted* to say was, "I tender my resignation. You may find yourself another flunky," and stalk off, dignity intact. Instead, prudence dictated he do no such thing.

Clearing his throat, he said, "Well, as a matter of fact there . . . there just so happens to be an . . . er . . . opening in that depar—"

"Good!" Robert boomed, his ebullient voice an echo overlapping from the hard surfaces all around. Marble, metal, glass, stone. "That's what I like to hear!" There was about him a presumptuous, ruthless triumph. "Now then, since we've gotten that out of the way, there's one more thing."

Sheldon, feeling everything inside him go on full alert, mentally braced himself. What more could that uncouth fiend want? *No, not want,* he quickly corrected himself, *demand.*

Robert puffed away with deceptive serenity, freshly shaven cheeks a bellows. Then, as a conversational aside: "I heard the head of Old Masters has retired."

"Mr. Spotts, yes," Sheldon sighed, lugubrious as an undertaker. "I'm afraid it's quite unfortunate, losing one of the world's top—"

"I do not concern myself with day-to-day details." Robert brushed aside air with an arrogant wave of his cigar. "Presumably, that's what you get paid to do?"

Despite Sheldon's clenched jaw, the scathing sarcasm easily breached his defenses. And once again, he felt his body betray him. His face stinging with the guilt and repressed outrage of a child trapped by the playground bully.

"Old Masters . . . isn't that the department where . . . now what *is* her name . . . ?" Robert, back still turned, was pressing the thumb and index finger of his cigar hand to his forehead, pretending it necessary to search his memory. "Ah, of course!" His voice was ebullient again, almost a croon. He whirled to face Sheldon. "Now I remember—Ms. Parker! A certain Ms. Parker's employed in that department. Am I right?"

For a moment, Sheldon was stumped. Then the name hit him with full force. *Good grief!* he thought. *Don't tell me he means Bambi Parker! What on earth could he possibly want with her?*

"Y-yes?" he ventured.

"I want her promoted," Robert decreed, once again puffing luxuriantly. He added, "To head of Old Masters."

"What!" Sheldon exclaimed, the words blurting from his mouth before he could stop them. "Good God! You can't be serious!"

"And why not?"

"B-because ..." Sheldon sputtered, crimson cheeks deepening to bruised purple, "... b-because ... well, replacing Mr. Spotts with M-Ms. Parker is ..." He swallowed hard. "... is simply out of the question!"

"Sez who?" Robert's eyes had become flat as a reptile's. *"You?"*

Inwardly, Sheldon quailed. He found it all he could do to suppress the impulse to admit defeat and surrender; even harder, to squelch a far greater urge—to prostrate himself and become obsequiously oily. Instead, he summoned the mustered remnants of his dignity and made one valiant last stand.

"This ... this is extremely awkward, Mr. Goldsmith," he said, the strength of his voice surprising even himself, "but you must ... *we* must ... bear in mind the, er, the experience and knowledge, the ... the *expertise,* as it were, which that position requires."

The reptilian eyes blinked sleepily.

"Not that I have anything personal against Ms. Parker," he was hasty to add. "She simply does not possess the necessary qualifications. In fact, it pains me to have to say this, but ... well, on several occasions, we ... we very nearly had to—"

"Are you quite finished?" Robert interrupted testily. "I thought I made myself perfectly clear. I only concern myself with the big picture. To put it bluntly, Fairey, I don't give a rat's ass about in-house politics or day-to-day minutiae."

"You ... you can't do this!" Sheldon whispered, raking a manicured hand through his perfect silver coif, the sum of all his frustration and fears transparent in that one childlike gesture of mussing his hair. "Don't you realize Ms. Parker might well *ruin* the department ... possibly sully Burghley's reputa—"

Robert, leaning in close, gestured at his own mouth with the wet end of his cigar. "Read ... my ... lips. As of immediately, Ms. Parker becomes head of Old Masters, my wife's friend gets the position she vacates, an' that's that. Now, will you, or will you not, execute my order?" His bushy brows contracted. "A simple 'yes' or 'no' will suffice."

Sheldon gave a shuddering sigh. It was useless to resist, that much was clear. If Goldsmith was hell-bent upon promoting Bambi Parker, then by God, promote her he would, everything else—Burghley's included—be damned!

"If you insist, sir," Sheldon managed, stilling his tremor by clenching his teeth.

Robert accepted the acquiescence with a magnanimous nod. "Well, then, since everything's settled, what do you say we get back to the party? Perhaps cement our new relationship with a toast, eh?"

Numbly Sheldon nodded, his self-loathing having rendered him speechless, his feet virtually immobile. He let himself be guided out, his mind a maelstrom of self-incriminations. For the first time in his career he had knowingly done the unthinkable—the unimaginable!—had, after all these irreproachable years, consciously compromised and betrayed the venerable institution which had been placed in his trust.

Was this to be his epitaph after leading Burghley's with formidable rectitude through a veritable jungle of economic climes—wild fluctuations he alone had uncannily, almost psychically, foreseen? Impossible to think that his dozens of proudly incorruptible triumphs were suddenly reduced to, *what?*

Betrayal? Treason? *Whoredom?*

He felt like a Judas.

No, he told himself, that wasn't quite right. He felt like—a *gelded* Judas.

And the man who'd chopped off his balls had the nerve to drape his arm, buddy-buddy style, around his shoulders.

Not as an act of friendship. Oh, no. Robert A. Goldsmith, he was all too aware, had a far more immediate and transparent motive: to convey one last mocking and not-so-subliminal message:

Making it crystal clear which of them was the puppet.

And which controlled the strings.

14

*I*n the Blumenthal Patio, Prince Karl-Heinz had finally left his post by the entrance. He was circulating, chatting attentively with his guests when a sudden murmur, like a tidal wave gathering momentum, swelled through the crowd. Then, as if a switch had been thrown, all conversation abruptly ceased and the room fell silent. Except for the elegant strains of Mozart's Quartet in G Minor, one could have heard a pin drop.

The focus of attention was the arrival of two fashionably late guests.

He was a bicontinental investment banker of colossal proportions, exophthalmic eyes, and an air of old-fashioned grandeur—and was instantly dismissed.

She was another story. After Princess Di and Queen Elizabeth, inarguably the third most famous woman alive; this rare descent from the heights of Mount Olympus, was greeted with the awe and reverence due a living legend.

For Rebecca Cornille Wakefield Lantzouni de la Vila was precisely that, plus a whole lot more.

A blue-blooded Daughter of the American Revolution, she and her rival twin sister, now the *Vicomtesse* Suzy de Saint-Mallet, had been born into genteel poverty in the beautiful hunt country of rural New Jersey. Luckily, the Cornille Twins, as they were to become known in society circles, were two of the great beauties of the world. More important, both were blessed with that most practical of all gifts—an exceptional ability for choosing brilliant husbands, a brilliant talent in and of itself.

Suzy, the elder by six minutes, married and buried the exceedingly wealthy French *vicomte* before latching onto the richest of all Hollywood producers, a wedding which ended in divorce and a huge financial settlement, after which she continued using her first husband's title.

Rebecca, the greater of the two beauties, married and buried *three* husbands and, like her sister, remained childless, as is often the case with fraternal twins. But if Suzy's marital matches were brilliant, Rebecca's verged on pure genius.

Husband number one was William Winterton Wakefield, III, that most stolidly Republican of all United States Presidents, who left his widow a social position second to none, and a fortune estimated at between twenty-five and thirty million dollars.

Husband number two, Leonidas Danaus Lantzouni, a rich Greek bearing gifts, left her sole heiress to a self-perpetuating empire so vast it reduced the Wakefield millions to a bagatelle.

And Husband number three, the *Duque* Joaquín de la Vila, a sixty-year-young Spanish nobleman with a lethal penchant for fast cars, left Becky with more titles than she could keep track of, and an embarrassment of riches which verged on the obscene.

Subsequently, Rebecca Cornille Wakefield Lantzouni de la Vila, or Becky V, as the press had taken to dubbing her, a sobriquet which had stuck, and by which she was known throughout the world, suddenly found herself *beyond* money; beyond, even, the stratospheric limits of high society itself and occupied that most exalted of all positions—the sun around which all lesser planets gravitate. At once the brightest, most photogenic, and yet pathologically private of all the celestial bodies in the social firmament, it was her air of mystery, remoteness, and unapproachability which had been the final catalyst in catapulting her to near-goddess stature.

Physically she was beguiling, a high-fashion wraith with a clothes-hanger figure. Sable hair worn in the same signature cut as Gloria Vanderbilt, tucked behind the ears and curving forward, commalike, beneath the delicate lobes; taut, surgically stretched skin; a proud Nefertiti-like profile; and eyes of the most incredibly intense violet hue.

But even more compelling than her beauty was her actual physical presence, for Becky V seemed to float regally through life in an otherworldly aura all her own.

Tonight, as always, she was trailed by two suits, obviously Secret Service agents, a courtesy extended to all former U.S. Presidents and their wives for security purposes. And also as always, she was dressed to kill, all in heavenly sapphire blue: A billowing, silk taffeta confection by Carolina Herrera, with a snug bodice cut on the bias, so that one shoulder was left bare while an extravagant silk bow blossomed from atop the other. On her feet, custom-made, pointy-toed heels of the exact same fabric, with ballerina ribbons crisscrossing the ankles, frivolous fantasies whipped up by a Florentine master whose identity Becky V guarded as jealously as her privacy.

And finally, there were drop-dead sapphires. The fabled Kashmir stones known in the trade, and among true cognoscenti, as "The Shah Jahan Suite." Just one of the many gifts from her second husband, the Greek.

Karl-Heinz crossed the enormous room, the guests parting soundlessly for him like the Red Sea for Moses. "Becky!" he greeted with delight, taking both her hands in his and kissing each of her cheeks without actually touching skin. "You honor me with your presence."

She favored him with the elusive smile Leonardo had made famous, but which she had appropriated. *Her famous Mona Lisa smile,* the press called it.

"How could I not be here for your birthday, Heinzie, *chéri?*" she said, her cornhusk voice a complete surprise to those who heard it for the very first time. "But your *fortieth?*" she continued. "I said to myself, *'Pas possible!'* "

Ironically, it was she, who had married a Spaniard, and not her sister, Suzy, who had wed the French *vicomte,* who was the unabashed Francophile, constantly sprinkling her English with enough French to qualify it as Franglaise.

"To me, you do not look a day over twenty-nine," she said. *"Non, non, non,* not one single day!"

"Always the diplomat," Karl-Heinz noted with a chuckle, "and as always, lovelier than ever. You never seem to age. How *do* you do it, Becky? You must tell me your secret!"

That mystifying, unfathomable smile remained. "If I ever divulge that, *je tu le promets, mon chéri,* you, and you alone, shall be the only person I shall tell!"

Karl-Heinz, who knew she would do no such thing, cocked one eyebrow in amusement before politely turning his attention upon her escort.

"Lord Rosenkrantz," he acknowledged with a slight bow, gripping the firm hand of the bristly browed gentleman. "A pleasure to meet again."

"On the contrary!" boomed the British-born financier. "The pleasure is entirely mine. May I wish you all the best, and many happy returns."

While the men talked, Becky V slowly, majestically, surveyed the room, her gaze purposely high so that she saw over the guests' heads and thus avoided catching anyone's eye, a technique she'd perfected for dealing with crowds during Bill Wakefield's presidential campaign.

"Mon Dieu!" she exclaimed softly, a little bewildered. "Is it my imagination, or is *le tout* New York out in full force?"

"You need not worry," Karl-Heinz, well aware of her aversion to throngs, however choice its denizens, was quick to assure. "Your timing is perfect. We are about to dine, and since only half these guests are invited to the dinner itself, the crowd will thin out perceptibly. But first, just to be polite, we really ought to circulate for a minute or so. That is," he added solicitously in light of her privileged status, "if you do not mind?"

Becky V gamely slipped an arm through his. *"Il le faut,"* she pronounced imperiously. "Today is your birthday, so just this once I must do as you command. *Tu marcher en tête!"*

"Leapin' lizards!" gasped Kenzie in a voice of reverence. "Did you get a load of who just arrived?"

Her new-found Adonis, returning with their drinks to find her all agog, smiled tolerantly and pressed a glass of champagne into her hand. "Rest assured," he said, "your eyes did not deceive you."

"Then you saw her, too?"

Hannes smiled. "How could I have missed her? She only caused this entire crowd to fall silent."

"Yes," Kenzie said solemnly, "that she did. And here I was, always under the impression that in these circles, people were immune to such star-struck behavior."

"Yes, but Becky V is notorious for never appearing in public," he said.

"So is Michael Jackson," she pointed out.

He smiled. "Why? Do you miss him?"

"Truthfully, no. But enough about that." She held out her glass and proposed a toast. "Here's to—"

"—us?" he interjected softly, staring intently into the glowing depths of her eyes.

Thrown completely off guard, Kenzie was deaf to the clink of their glasses and the surrounding swirl of chatter and laughter, was aware only of her own heightened sense of visual perception. Acutely conscious of nothing but the indecently superb male specimen she had attracted.

Us! she thought jubilantly, wanting to burst from exultation. *He said, "us!"*

Taking another sip, she waited to swallow, savoring the tingly burst of bubbles in her mouth. Privately celebrated his male proximity by imagining him a bee and her own nude body a blossom ripe with promising, fragrant pollen. Wondered, among other things, whether meetings such as theirs were accidental or predestined, and if he could hear her heart thumping wildly against her rib cage.

"You've suddenly become very quiet," he observed. "Is that because silence is golden?"

She did not speak.

"Ah. Then perhaps the proverbial cat has your tongue?"

"Perhaps," she admitted with a hint of a yawn, deliberately trying for disinterested cool, but not quite pulling it off and not really caring one way or the other if she did. "Are you here with someone?"

"You mean . . . a lady?"

She let her silence speak for itself.

"To answer your question," he replied, obvious amusement playing on his face, "yes, I came with a lady. But have no fear. It seems that I have been deserted."

"Dumped!" Kenzie exclaimed, her surprise genuine. "You! For another man?"

He grinned. "Thank God. She was quite tedious."

"But beautiful?"

"If you consider artifice beauty, then I suppose so." Hannes swallowed some champagne, all the while holding her gaze. "And you? I gather you did not arrive here alone, either?"

"Nooooo," she said slowly. "Does that make a difference?"

"Only sometimes. Now let me see ... is he tall, dark, and handsome?"

Kenzie did a moue and pretended to consider. "Well, he *is* tall," she allowed flirtatiously, enjoying the sexually charged banter immensely.

"And handsome?"

She had to subdue a smile. Mr. Spotts was hardly bad-looking—especially considering his age—but no one could ever accuse him of being handsome. "Well, I ... I suppose you could say he ... he looks ... mmm ... distinguished," she ended cagily.

"But he's not your husband?" Hannes glanced at her unadorned ring finger.

Kenzie was pleased. It seemed ages since someone other than Charley had come on to her. In fact, she had almost forgotten what such attention was like, or how deliciously it stroked the feminine ego.

"Whatever gave you the idea I was married?" she wanted to know.

"Just asking."

She smiled. "Well, since you want to know, I'm still single. There." Without waiting for a reaction, she sipped another milliliter of champagne. "And the lady you accompanied here? Is she your wife?"

"God forbid!" he laughed.

"Mistress, then?"

"She'd better not be, or else her husband might well take a shotgun to me!"

"Ouch!" She made a face. "I take it he's the jealous type?"

"Oh, yes," he said, "very. As well as a splendid marksman."

"Sounds awfully romantic," Kenzie said, meaning it.

"I suppose that's one way of looking at it."

"But isn't he afraid of entrusting his wife to your ... care?"

"Why? Should he?"

Kenzie found herself blushing. Lowering her eyes, she looked down into her glass, slowly twirling it back and forth by the stem. "Well ... what I mean is ... you're ... well, you're not exactly ..."

"Exactly what?"

"Well, not the Elephant Man, that's for sure."

Hannes threw back his head and laughed. It was a spontaneous, open-mouthed laugh which reached his eyes and crinkled their corners, a laugh which instantly disarmed, contradicting the strength of his too-handsome features, bringing his chiseled perfection down a notch and proving that he was, after all, a lusty, flesh-and-blood human instead of some narcissistic marble deity.

Pretending a calm disinterest she did not feel, she tore her eyes away from his and abruptly changed the subject. "What . . . what kind of a name is Hannes?" she asked, apropos of nothing.

His voice was a seductive whisper. "It is Scandinavian, Kenzie. I was born in Porkkala. That is a town on the Finnish Riviera, slightly to the west of Helsinki."

"I can't believe you're from Finland!" she exclaimed.

"And why is that, Kenzie?"

"Because . . . well, your English! It's flawless. You don't have the least trace of any accent."

"That," he explained, "is because my father was a career diplomat. His work took us to every conceivable corner of the world, and I attended English boarding schools, as well as American embassy schools in . . . oh, it must have been a dozen different countries."

She stared at him, half paralyzed, her heart knocking ever harder, and she had the sensation of the room receding and growing silent until it seemed they were the only two people there.

"And you're the first Hannes I've ever met," she whispered huskily. "Or, for that matter, the first Hans . . ."

Once again they were captured by each other's gaze, his so hypnotic that Kenzie's breath left her altogether, and she knew with a certainty, with an absolute dead certainly, that she was gone. There was no use fighting it; resisting him would only fuel the flames of her own desires, a point proven when he caught her arm and drew her swiftly to him as if he meant to kiss her. When she realized, after a moment, that it was only so a waiter with a champagne-laden tray could pass unhindered, she felt the dull, empty ache of disappointment.

He sensed it, and instead of letting her go, held her all the more tightly against him, his lips curved in a mischievous little smile.

Her lips went suddenly dry and she could feel a fever raging in her loins; a kind of fire leaping between him and herself.

Oh, how alive and vital and lustful he was! And ah, how wondrously spellbinding, this silent communication!

Why on God's earth, she asked herself, *would I* want *to resist him?*

And yet, her better judgment hadn't entirely deserted her—from somewhere far within the recesses of her mind, some dormant wisdom told her to take it slower, cautioned that things were proceeding too fast.

A stranger as handsome as Hannes has got to spell trouble, the voice in her head warned. *If you know what's good for you—and you do— you'll quickly make your exit. At least give yourself time for a breather. Why not repair to the ladies' room? Who knows? You might even avoid a ton of potential heartache . . .*

Extricating herself from his arms, she murmured vague excuses about visiting the powder room, and backed away on unsteady legs. Then, turning swiftly, she fled, plunging through an opening in the dense crowd while repeating, "S'cuse me ... s'cuse me ... s'cuse me ...," giving strangers she bumped apologetic little smiles to show she'd meant no offense.

Too late, Kenzie saw the tall figure hurtling toward her on a collision course, an orange-tressed figure wearing red, white, and black who, like she herself, was hurrying too fast to be able to stop.

For an instant, time seemed suspended, then sped up as the inevitable occurred. The two young women collided—*slam-bam!*—breaths exploding before each bounced backward a step, the champagne glasses flying out of their hands.

Liquid sloshed, drenching their bosoms before two distinct crashes, one right after the other, signaled glass shattering on the floor.

Kenzie and Zandra both let out simultaneous moans of horror. Pinched their skirts and held them out, looking down at themselves to assess the damage. Then, slowly raising their heads, each glared accusingly at the other.

The crowd, which only moments earlier had wisely jumped back, now pressed eagerly forward, soles and heels crunching on broken glass.

"Oh, God!" Kenzie whispered, appalled. She half shut her eyes, wishing the floor would open up and swallow her whole. "I could die!"

"You could die!" wailed Zandra. "This outfit isn't even mine! It's borrowed!"

For one drawn-out, eternal moment they eyed one another like vipers, faces blazing with mutual reproach. And then, inexplicably, they both pointed at one another and burst into rich peals of helpless laughter.

"God!" Kenzie giggled. "Are you ever a sight!"

"Me!" Zandra hooted. "You should see yourself!"

"Oh, Jesus!" Kenzie looked at her for guidance. "What are we going to do?"

"Do?" asked Zandra, immediately taking charge. "What do you think we're going to do? Come on."

Taking Kenzie by the arm, she unerringly turned her in the direction of the powder room.

"Let them gawk," she said grandly, giving the bystanders a dismissive wave. "*We'll* show them what one ingenious Yank and one brilliant Brit can come up with, right?"

"We will?" Kenzie sounded dubious.

"Of course we will!" Zandra beamed. "I just came from the loo, and guess what?"

"It's disgustingly filthy?"

Zandra burst out in a fresh round of laughter. "In *this* place? For heaven's sake, no! But someone's conveniently provided blow driers at every sink, bless their little hearts, so we'll be dry and look presentable in no time. Now, chin up! The very least we can do is depart the scene of this mishap with dignity!"

Which is exactly what they did, heaping on the hauteur while they were at it.

15

$\mathscr{S}$heldon D. Fairey was no longer up to snuff. Valiantly as he tried, he simply could not convey his customary aura of superior power and masculine command. Bilious anger and rancor twisted his insides, burned ulcerously in his gut, thanks to Robert A. Goldsmith—*may the bastard rot in hell!* And now, that bitterness was compounded by humiliation as he found himself cornered by Mr. Spotts. *Will tonight never end?*

"Yes, Dietrich," he murmured, "I'm fully aware of Burghley's traditions."

There was a plummy false richness to his voice, the kind of timbre a second-rate actor playing a chairman of the board affects, but is unable to quite pull off.

"Of course the departing head of a department gets to recommend his choice of a replacement—which, as is customary, is a prerogative you have already exercised. Also, as we both well know, with the exception of a very few isolated cases, such recommendations are usually granted."

"Then does this mean," asked Mr. Spotts, his forthright eyes drilling into Fairey's, "that I can inform Ms. Turner that her promotion has been officially confirmed?"

"Hmm, er . . ." Fairey, avoiding the direct gaze, started to raise his glass to his lips, seemed startled to find it empty, frowned, and slowly lowered it. "Well, under normal circumstances I would, er . . . I would not hesitate to say yes . . ."

It was as if a harsh inner light suddenly illuminated Fairey's insides, exposing some cancerous character flaw. But Mr. Spotts, a veteran when it came to displaying patience and hiding his emotions, effectively masked his alarm behind a countenance of outward serenity.

Clearing his throat uncomfortably, Fairey added: "Your recommendation has, of course, been duly noted." He smiled acidly, the bile inside him shaping his lips. "However, in this particular instance there . . . there seem to be . . . er . . . extenuating circumstances."

What the devil? Mr. Spotts could not believe he'd heard correctly. Refusing to back down, he said, "Sheldon, what is all this nonsense? *What* extenuating circumstances? I do believe you'll have to be a bit more specific."

Putting off the inevitable, Fairey looked around, spied a cruising waiter, and signaled for a refill. Glasses exchanged hands and he took a shaky gulp.

"Sheldon?" Mr. Spotts reminded him quietly.

"Look, Dietrich!" Fairey snapped. His impatience ricocheted accusingly back at him. Then, endeavoring to temper his irritation: "As you are surely aware, times . . . well, times change." He attempted a ghastly, twisted approximation of a smile. "Granted, it's difficult for us old-timers to adapt with changing climes, but that's life, eh?"

Having delivered that circumventive little gem, Fairey quickly poked his nose back into his glass, willing Mr. Spotts to disappear.

But Mr. Spotts had no intention of letting Sheldon D. Fairey off the hook—certainly not that easily—nor until he got to the bottom of all this evasive hemming and hawing.

"Goodness gracious, Sheldon," he said, "just listen to yourself. Why, you're as agitated as a nest of hornets. Now do stop giving me the runaround. Out with it, man—out with it!"

Fairey gave a febrile, shuddering sigh. "Believe me, it is—no one of my choosing."

"Ah." Mr. Spotts nodded. "By that, I presume it must be the choice of either Mr. or Mrs. Goldsmith?"

"Bingo," Fairey grouched. "Advance to Go and collect two hundred dollars."

"So? Who *is* it?"

"It is—*she* is—a calamity, disaster, the plague of the Israelites, all rolled into one. She is the . . . *the decline of Empire,* Dietrich, as far as Burghley's is concerned!" Fairey raised his glass, as if to fling it against something and watch it smash.

"Sheldon, must I *squeeze* the name out of you?"

Fairey eyed the glass he'd raised, then slowly lowered it as his body visibly deflated. "It's Ms. Barbara Parker, if the name rings a bell." Appraisingly, he hefted the glass once more, as if again considering its demise. His voice hissed. "*Now* do you understand?"

Mr. Spotts jerked involuntarily backward, as though sustaining a fatal blow, before, head reeling, he leaned toward Fairey and squinted narrowly.

"Ms. Parker?" he croaked in throaty disbelief. "Please, Sheldon. *Please,* tell me we are not talking about *Bambi Parker!*"

Fairey, again averting his gaze, wished Mr. Spotts would go away, now that he'd learned the identity of his replacement.

But Mr. Spotts did no such thing. Tall, gnarled, and stubborn as the proverbial Monterey pine, he just stood there staring. "Sheldon . . ." His voice had a razor edge to it. "I asked you if you meant *that* Bambi Parker!"

"Of course I meant her, goddammit!" Fairey half shouted. Then he checked himself, raked an unsteady hand through his hair, and forced his voice lower. "I'm sorry to have to break it to you, Dietrich, but *she,* and not Ms. Turner, is your replacement."

Mr. Spotts had lost enough of his famous composure and imperturbability that Fairey could see his subtle facial muscles contort and tic. Meanwhile, he himself felt like a villanous actor holding his audience in thrall. Which was, he thought grimly, exactly what he was doing—even if he played to but an audience of one, and the script . . . well, the script was certainly one he'd just as soon not star in.

"There, now the cat's out of the bag, Dietrich." Something ugly had come into Fairey's voice. "Well? Did forcing the answer out of me make you any happier? Are you content now?"

Mr. Spotts, disgusted by the unfolding drama, its message, and its actor, turned away.

"Well, my friend," he observed heavily, his smile thin and humorless, "there's only one thing I can say."

"And what is that?"

"If Mr. Goldsmith was stupid enough to have made his bed—" *And for obvious reasons,* Mr. Spotts thought, *it has to have been his doing and not the missus's; no way would Mrs. Goldsmith ever permit an estrogen-suffused fox like Bambi Parker into* her *henhouse.* "—then it's a bed he's going to have to lie in. Not that I envy him in the short run." A sour kind of humor came into Mr. Spotts's voice. "And even less so in the long haul."

"I'm sorry, Dietrich," Fairey said hoarsely, fidgeting with fussy little movements. "I tried. Believe me, I tried. But that infernal man—"

"I know." Mr. Spotts patted his arm in understanding, then nodded and tucked his head, tortoiselike, into his stooped shoulders. Starting to walk away, he stopped in midstep, slowly turned back around, and craned his neck so that the wattle stretched tautly.

"Seems my health bailed me out just in the nick of time, eh, Sheldon?" The words tasted of bitter irony. "Well, best of luck with the philistines, my friend. At least fate intervened and my hands remain clean."

"Dietrich! Surely you don't believe I *wanted* to dirty mine!"

Mr. Spotts shook his head. "No, no," he assured him quietly, "of course not." Then, a firm believer in dispensing with bad news quickly, he sketched a wave and wandered off in search of Kenzie—who, as it turned out, had seemingly vanished into thin air.

In the ladies' room, like space-age pistolleras armed with two blow driers apiece, Zandra and Kenzie were aiming whirring blasts of heated forced air at one another's bodices and skirts.

"Well?" Zandra demanded gaily above the racket of multiple blow-ers. "What did I tell you? Somebody who knows women had a hand in *this* party! Why else would these obliging gadgets have been put here?"

"I'm just glad someone provided them," Kenzie shouted back, "and that you knew about them. Otherwise, we'd have been up . . . well, up the proverbial creek without a paddle."

"Oh, for heaven's sake!" Zandra scolded cheerfully. "Feel free to use all the four-letter words you want. I doubt there's a one *I* haven't heard."

"You know," Kenzie confessed, "I'm awfully relieved it's you I ran into, instead of some shrill old battle-ax."

"You can say that again!" Zandra enthused. "But wasn't it *dee-voon,* the dramatic splash we made? Anyway, I just know we'll become the best of friends!" Now she had both blow dryers aimed at Kenzie's waist, and moved them around in slow circular motions. Glancing up, she added: "I've always been inclined to believe that the best friendships are those made under adverse circumstances. Don't you agree?"

"Mm. I've never really given it much—" Suddenly Kenzie remembered something. "Oh, God!"

"What's the matter?"

"Didn't you . . . didn't you say your outfit was borrowed?"

"Yes, but don't worry. Knowing my friend, since it's been worn once it'll never see the light of day again." Zandra switched off a dryer, shelved it above the sink, and kept the one in her left hand blasting. "Now then. We haven't been properly introduced yet." She held out her right hand.

Kenzie also put one dryer away and gave Zandra's hand a firm shake. "MacKenzie Turner's the name, but to my friends I'm plain Kenzie. Also, you should be forewarned. I'm not really what I appear to be."

Zandra raised her eyebrows. "How so?"

"Well, I'm a fish out of water. I mean, *I* wasn't invited; I'm only accompanying my retiring boss. Otherwise, Cinderella here's just your average nine-to-five working girl."

"So? What difference does that make?"

"I don't know. I just didn't want you to get the wrong impression. I'm hardly a socialite, and this Givenchy you're aiming hot air at?" In the reduced noise resulting from only two blow dryers running, Kenzie heard a toilet flush in one of the cubicles and glanced around for eavesdroppers. "It's second-hand," she confided in a near-whisper. "Would you believe—a thirty-five-dollar thrift shop find?"

"That's *all?*" Zandra looked at her in amazement. "Brilliant! You *must* take me shopping with you!"

Kenzie stared at her. "Don't tell me you're on a stringent budget, too?"

"Stringent?" Zandra gave a self-deprecating laugh. "Nonexistent's more like it!" Then, more cheerfully: "I'm as penniless as they come. See? We've more in common than you thought. Plus, the only reason *I'm* here is because the friends I'm staying with were invited."

"How long are you planning to be in New York?"

"Who can tell?" Zandra thought of her hurried departure from London and knew the time to share *those* kinds of sordid details wasn't now—if ever. "All I know," she murmured, "is that I'll be here long enough to become a working girl like you."

"Really! Have you been out pounding the pavement yet?"

"No, but I don't need to worry about that, thank God, even though I just flew in from London today. I *think* I've already found a position . . . or, rather, one's been found, if not created—" A grimace expressed her distaste at the word. "—especially for me."

"But you still haven't told me your name," Kenzie pointed out.

"That," Zandra gloomed, "is because it's a cross my ancestry forces me to bear."

A cubicle door opened and a sinewy woman in fluid, amaryllis-red Scassi swept to the farthest sink, well out of earshot. "Surely your name can't be all that bad," Kenzie said encouragingly, adding: "Can it?"

"Oh, no?" Zandra sighed, while down by the last sink, the woman in red was leaning into the mirror touching up Russet Moon lips. "Then why don't you try this mouthful on for size: Anna Zandra Elisabeth Theresia Charlotte von Hohenburg-Willemlohe."

Kenzie stared. "You've got to be kidding!"

"I assure you, I'm not." There was a peculiar touch of exasperation, wistfulness, and irritation in Zandra's tone which Kenzie found oddly touching. It was as if she were suddenly privy to the reality behind a lifetime's notion of romantic fairy tales—a rare insight she'd never before had cause to consider. "Do you have any *idea,*" Zandra went on, "how many times I've wished I'd been named something normal? Something like . . . oh, Jane Smith, for example?"

"Anyway." Kenzie gestured with the blow dryer. "With all those Hapsburg-sounding names of yours, I'm at a loss as to what to call you."

"Oh, but I'm not a Hapsburg, even if my name does rather sound like one," Zandra explained, keeping her convoluted lineage to a minimum in order to avoid confusion. "I mean, here and there I must have a sprinkling of distant Hapsburg relations, true, but that's only because all the ancient families of Europe are one big incestuous soup pot. But as far as my first name is concerned, I go by Zandra. It's unique, you see, and seems to best suit my personality."

"*Zahn*-drah," Kenzie repeated slowly, pronouncing it the way Zandra had. "Mm. Yes, I do believe it rather suits you."

Zandra gave a secretive little smile. "Promise you won't laugh, but the real reason I like it is because ever since childhood, I've always had the most maddening crush on any word beginning with the letter Z. Bizarre, don't you think? But then, what's life but a string of bizarre coincidences? I mean, look at the way we met. Or how I landed the job I've been offered—"

"Which," Kenzie reminded her, "you've neglected to specify."

"Sorry! I wasn't trying to be mysterious." She waited until the woman in red, touch-up complete, swept regally past and went out. "It's just that during the past twenty-four hours, my entire life's been turned topsy-turvy. Everything's happened so fast! But as far as I can tell, I'm going to be working at Burghley's—"

"Burghley's!" Kenzie squeaked incredulously. "You don't mean the auction house?"

"The one and only. Yes." Zandra looked concerned. "Why? Is something wrong there that I should know about?"

"Wrong?" Kenzie exclaimed, grinning. "Things couldn't be more *right*! Zandra, I work at Burghley's, too!"

"You don't!" Zandra's jaw dropped.

"I *do!*" Kenzie squealed. "Isn't this *great?*"

"I'll say! We'll have a grand time!"

"The best!"

"See what I mean? This proves it. Our meeting *has* to have been preordained." Zandra switched off the second dryer. "There," she said, shelving it alongside the other. "I think that about does you."

Kenzie felt herself with one hand. "Dry as a bone," she announced. "And you've only got this one teensy-weensy spot left." She diverted the blow dryer to the last damp stain on Zandra's overskirt. "So what's your area?" she asked, glancing up.

"My what?"

"You know—your area of expertise. Chinese ceramics? Islamic art? Mughal paintings?"

"Oh, nothing that exotic. The only thing I'm familiar with are gloomy old paintings. You know. Ancestral portraits . . . landscapes with ruins . . . any such cracked, varnished, gilt-framed monstrosities with impeccable provenances—"

"You mean Old Masters?" asked Kenzie faintly, not daring to believe her ears.

"Yes, I believe that's what they're officially called. Why?"

"Because," Kenzie blurted in a headlong rush, "that's *my* department, too! Oh, this is too much! Now I know you were right. Our running into each other—"

"—quite literally," interjected Zandra with a giggle.

"—must have been divine providence!" Kenzie finished. "There! This last spot's dry now." She unbent herself and switched off the blow dryer. The sudden silence in the powder room was almost unearthly. Pinching the skirt of her own dress, she lifted it up for inspection. "Well?" she asked. "What do you think? Am I presentable?"

"Under these unflattering fluorescents," Zandra observed, "some faint stains are bound to show. But once we're back outside, I guarantee you no one will be the wiser."

"Perhaps we can sit together during dinner?" Kenzie tossed over her shoulder at Zandra, who was right behind her.

"I'd love nothing more, but at this late point," Zandra said delicately, remembering Karl-Heinz's invitation to sit at his table—a spur-of-the-moment change which had, no doubt, played havoc with the seating arrangements, "that would probably present a social dilemma."

Kenzie shrugged philosophically. "Oh well," she said, pulling open the ladies' room door, "that's hardly a tragedy. We can catch each other afterwards."

"Yes! We'll do that!"

And off they sailed, side by side, both beaming with delight at their newly forged friendship.

But their smiles faded the instant they returned to the Blumenthal Patio.

"What the—" Kenzie began, staring around in disbelief.

For the huge room, which had been a veritable beehive of social activity when they had left for the powder room, now stood silently, accusingly empty. Only the Mozart ensemble, busily packing up sheet music and instruments, a few waiters sweeping up debris, and three men waiting in the center of the now otherwise unpopulated expanse, attested to a party ever having taken place. During their absence, everyone had evidently migrated to the Engelhard Court for dinner, everyone, that is, except for Prince Karl-Heinz, Mr. Spotts, and Hannes Hockert.

"I could die!" Kenzie murmured uneasily. "Looks like we're *awfully* late!"

"Better late than never," Zandra quoted blithely, and calmly taking Kenzie by the arm, propelled her forward.

Karl-Heinz was the first to see them coming. "There you are!" he called to Zandra, rapidly outstriding Mr. Spotts and Hannes, both of whom followed close behind.

"I hope I didn't make us terribly late for dinner. Heinzie—our drinks had a slight altercation!" Zandra looked around. "Where's Lex?" she inquired, her lips turning down in a frown.

"Lex?" Karl-Heinz repeated blankly, before making the connection. "Ah, you must mean the gentleman with whom you arrived?"

"Lex Bugg. Yes," she nodded.

"The last I saw of him," Karl-Heinz told her, "was when he accompanied some older woman in to dinner."

Zandra's eyes narrowed. *Why, the little shit!* she thought. *He would desert me!*

As if reading her mind, Karl-Heinz chased away her momentary flash of anger with a smile. "I do believe it's for the best," he soothed, "don't you? Now I will not have to share you with anyone, and can have you all to myself."

And with that, he placed a proprietary hand under one of her elbows, the other in the small of her spine, and swooped her away, leaving Kenzie, Hannes, and Mr. Spotts behind.

Zandra turned her head to give Kenzie a quick, helpless glance over her shoulder. *We'll talk later!* she mouthed.

Okay! Kenzie mouthed in return as she slipped one arm through each of those proffered by the men flanking her. "I'm sorry I disappeared like that," she apologized, the three of them following in Zandra and Karl-Heinz's wake. "There was a slight . . . accident."

"Nothing serious, I hope?" Mr. Spotts asked, giving no hint of his inner turmoil, which was considerable.

"Not serious in the least," Kenzie assured him lightly. "I only hope I didn't inconvenience the two of you."

"No, no," Mr. Spotts was quick to respond. But inwardly he groaned. He *had* hoped to have a moment alone with her, in order to break the bad news about her being passed over for promotion. *Better she hears it from me instead of from somebody else,* he thought. Now, unfortunately, he'd have to wait until after they were seated for dinner.

This is not auspicious timing, he thought glumly as they entered the Engelhard Court. *No, not auspicious in the least . . .*

But Kenzie, still happily unshadowed by the drama in which she'd featured so prominently, was too intoxicated with the effect her dramatic entrance was having to notice that anything was amiss in her world.

All in all, she asked herself euphorically, basking in the knowledge that her physical presence was magnified by two gallant gentlemen—one on each arm—*was* there any other way to arrive anywhere? Because, no matter which way one looked at it, two escorts not only doubled the pleasure, but *multiplied* it, and were infinitely, irrefutably, better than one!

☜ *16* ☞

For the time being, reality was suspended.

In the Engelhard Court, the flickering tapers, the gold-dipped floral centerpieces, the necklaces of twinkle lights strung along arched trellises, the glow and sparkle of gold and gemstones—all conspired to gild the guests and food alike.

Everything seemed to have been conjured up by some magic-imbued genie. The swagged canopies with their elaborate jabots and bursts of ostrich plumes which hovered in midair above each round table. The army of white-gloved waiters who glided about like so many silent ghosts. The smoothness with which everything hummed along. Even the vibrato of buzzing conversations, punctuated by fanciful flights of musical laughter, seemed somehow to have been expressly orchestrated for this event by benevolent higher beings.

It was perfection—everyone said so.

No one more so than Dina Goldsmith, who was in the fast lane and loving every minute of it!

Now, surveying Karl-Heinz's immediate social fiefdom—his own table at the very epicenter of the Engelhard Court at which, thanks to Zandra, she and Robert found themselves seated—Dina regarded her A-list dinner companions with a pleasure so intense it nearly verged on physical pain. On her immediate left sat Lord Rosenkrantz, then Nina Fairey, then Robert; directly opposite her were Becky V and His Serene Highness, their host; then Zandra; and on Dina's immediate right, an unusually reticent Sheldon D. Fairey.

Predictably, the conversation at the prince's table centered around him, whose birthday was being celebrated.

"You cannot be serious!" Nina Fairey was in the midst of exclaiming. Like every woman at that table with the exception of Zandra, she only made a pretense of eating the appetizer of hot oysters with endives in a fragrant lemon-cream sauce, thus ensuring her skeletal figure perpetual clothes-hanger status. "*I think it's monstrous!*"

"Perhaps so," replied Karl-Heinz with a shrug of his princely shoulders, "but it is the tradition in my family. Also, such by-laws are not at all uncommon, you know. Many of the titled old families of Europe still ob-serve the custom of primogeniture. For example, the Thurn und Taxis still do, and I could name many, many others."

That said, he began to turn toward Zandra, but Dina quickly picked up the conversational thread. "I've never heard of anything so unfair," she declared.

Karl-Heinz turned to her and smiled. "My dear Dina, as you probably well know life seldom *is* fair."

"Perhaps, but this virtually blackmails you into marriage!"

"Yes," Karl-Heinz agreed calmly, "it does. But don't forget, that was the original intention: to ensure a continuing dynasty of the right bloodstock."

"Still, you *haven't* married," she pointed out.

"No," he replied, "I haven't."

"And doesn't that worry you, now that you've turned . . . well, whatever?" Diamonds flashed as she waved away his age.

"Of course it has crossed my mind," he said. "No one with a shred of sanity would jeopardize a fortune of that size."

Her voice was quiet. "But you have," she pointed out.

"Yes," he sighed, "I have."

She held his gaze. "And if your father dies? And you haven't produced an heir by that time? What happens then?"

"Then," he said simply, "I lose everything."

"Good heavens!"

"Of course, that does not mean I would be destitute. I do have a fortune of my own, and even if I didn't, the same family by-laws which kept me from inheriting would also ensure that I would be well provided for."

"But the bulk of the fortune?" Dina asked. "The *power*. To whom would that pass?"

"Regrettably to Prince Leopold, my sister's eldest son." *Who is a drug addict and a delinquent,* he thought grimly as he reached for his wineglass. "At any rate, let us hope my father lives a while longer, shall we?"

"And how is *le vieil Prince?*" Becky V inquired. "In good health, *j'espére bien?*"

"I'm afraid not," Karl-Heinz confessed. "His health has been deteriorating quite rapidly."

Silk rustled as Becky V went rigid. "*À dieu ne plaise!*" she exclaimed. "*Cher ami!* Surely that must alarm you!"

Karl-Heinz lifted the wine to his nose to assay its bouquet. "Naturally his health causes concern," he admitted. "Just as Damocles never forgot the sword hanging over his head, so too, I never forget the one hanging over mine. But what can one do?" He shrugged. "Life goes on."

"How old is your father?" Dina inquired.

He sipped the wine, which went dusky and mellow on his palate. "Nearly eighty."

Becky, quick to pat the princely hand, added: "*Naturellement,* it goes without saying that Heinzie was a change-of-life baby!"

There was dutiful laughter, but not from Dina. Having tasted first-hand of the bitter cup of poverty, she had, if nothing else, gained a healthy respect for all matters financial.

Now she leaned across the table toward Karl-Heinz. "Sweetie! Think of all the billions of dollars at stake! Why *not* get married? Why *not* have an heir, secure your inheritance, and be done with it? It can't be all that difficult . . . can it?"

Karl-Heinz half smiled. "In some ways, my dear Dina, yes. It can be."

"But . . . *why?*"

"Because I am a romantic and have yet to find the right woman. Or at least, one I would care to spend the rest of my life with."

"*Voyez-vous,*" Becky explained for Dina's benefit, "wife-hunting is not as simple for Heinzie as it is for most men. Besides producing a male heir *before* the death of his father, *le vieil Prince,* Heinzie's wife must, like he himself, be a direct descendant of the Holy Roman Emperors."

"And you should see what most of those descendants look like!" Karl-Heinz gave a theatrical shiver. "With the exception of Zandra here, they all have any number of ghastly, but highly prized royal or serene deformities. You know . . . the most horrid bulbous noses, or no chins to speak of, or jaws full of crooked tusks . . ."

At the mention of Zandra's name, a calculating glint had come into Dina's eyes. "You mean . . ." she asked slowly, furrowing her brow, ". . . *Zandra* would be considered appropriate?"

"She is a distant cousin, but yes." Karl-Heinz nodded. "Zandra would be highly appropriate. In fact, if I wish to inherit, it is impossible for me *not* to marry a relative. The Hapsburgs . . . the Hohenzollern-Sigmaringen . . . the Borbón dos Sicilias . . . however distantly, somewhere along the line, everyone appropriate is related to everyone else . . ."

Dina tuned out, her mind a million light years away.

She knew precisely what needed to be done, and exactly how to go about it. Best of all, it would kill two birds with one stone: provide Zandra a marriage of discriminating quality and incalculable wealth, and, the old prince's health and Zandra's womb permitting, ensure Karl-Heinz his imperiled inheritance.

What could be more perfect, or obvious?

It's a wonder Karl-Heinz and Zandra haven't thought of it yet. Clearly, they're meant for one another. They make the perfect couple. Anyone with half a brain can see that just by looking at them. Besides, what are best friends for, if not to help steer two emotionally repressed souls toward a match made in heaven—not to mention on earth?

Dina smiled to herself. *What indeed . . .*

* * *

Kenzie couldn't remember a time she'd enjoyed herself more. It wasn't just Hannes's presence and the sexual heat he generated. Nor was it entirely due to her delightful encounter with Zandra who, she now saw, was seated beside none other than their host at his table.

No. What beguiled her was no single person or thing in and of itself, but the whole dreamlike fantasy, the entire tapestry of this fairy-tale event.

As the appetizer plates were whisked away, Mr. Spotts cleared his warbly throat. "Kenzie, my dear?"

Eyes alight, Kenzie turned to him, the smoked oysters in lemon-cream sauce still lingering symphonically on her palate. "Yes, Mr. Spotts, I mean, Dietrich—?" Her hands fluttered self-consciously. "Sorry. I'm still not used to our being on a first-name basis."

"That's quite all right, my dear," he said, taking a fortifying breath. "There is something . . . well, rather unpleasant . . . which I feel I must get off my chest."

Kenzie's brow furrowed. "What's wrong?"

"Everything," he sighed, "absolutely everything." Nodding abstractedly, he looked down at the tablecloth, and with a long gnarled finger traced the circular impression left by the appetizer plate. "I do wish I could spare you this, my dear." He raised sorrowful eyes to hers. "Especially tonight."

"Don't worry. If it's bad news, you might as well get it over and done with."

He nodded. "But I'd like you to know that I had no idea these machinations were taking place behind my back. In fact, I only learned of them myself while you were in the powder room."

"Y-yes . . . ?" The furrows in Kenzie's brow deepened.

"It concerns your promotion. I'm terribly sorry, Kenzie. I'm afraid . . . well, according to Mr. Fairey, it's . . . it's not in the bag after all." His pink-rimmed eyelids blinked rapidly. "Can you believe it? My recommendation was tossed aside. Just like that!" His quivering voice rose an octave in outrage.

"It's all right," Kenzie said quietly.

"No, it is *not* all right!" Mr. Spotts whispered intensely. Trembling with barely contained indignation, he drew himself up. "*You* are the most qualified person to head the department! *You,* also, are my chosen successor. And now . . . well, everything I've worked for . . . everything I've striven to build up—"

Suddenly his voice cracked, and his fingers clutched the edge of the table as though to keep himself from being swept off into the farthest reaches of outer space.

Kenzie placed a hand over his. "You needn't worry," she said softly. "Arnold and I will still be there. We'll keep things on track."

He shook his head. "You don't understand. It's not just your being passed over that's so abhorrent. That too, but . . . well, worse still is the new head of the department."

"Who's it going to be? Do you know?"

He exhaled heavily. "Yes," he said tightly. "And we can thank Mr. Robert A. Goldsmith for that choice!"

At the mention of his name, Kenzie's eyes strayed across the room to where Burghley's new owner was seated at the prince's table. She caught sight of Zandra and Dina touching glasses in a toast. Slowly she drew her gaze back in.

"Well?" she asked again. "Who is it?"

It was all he could do not to choke on the name. "Bambi Parker," he whispered hoarsely.

It went like a stab through her heart.

Bambi? In charge?

Sick with shock, Kenzie sat there in bewilderment, disbelief robbing her facial planes of vitality, her chin of its strength. In her stomach, oysters and champagne roiled violently.

I've been cheated.

The realization detonated like mental sticks of dynamite.

Bambi robbed me of my promotion.

Mr. Spotts inspected his fingernails. "At any rate, I no longer hold you to your earlier promise. Saving the department from Ms. Parker is too much to ask of anyone." He smiled bleakly. "What I said about the gift coming with strings attached—"

"It's not the Zuccaro I'm—"

"I know," he commiserated gently, "I know."

Two waiters glided toward their table, smoothly setting down plates of roast duck with brandied fruit compote.

The rich aromas of fowl and liquor were too much. Kenzie found herself engulfed in a sudden swirl of heat and nausea.

Abruptly she pushed back her chair and staggered to her feet. "I—I'm sorry," she gasped. "I'll be right back. I—I've got to— to—"

Clapping a hand over her mouth, she stumbled through the maze of tables, making it to the ladies' room just in time. Lunging for the nearest sink, she bent over it and threw up oysters, lemon sauce, and champagne.

After the worst of her wretching had subsided, she raised her head to the mirror. Her face was drawn, her complexion sallow. Loosening her grip from the counter, she fumbled with the cold water tap, grabbed a handful of paper towels, and soaked them. With her left hand, she pressed them to her forehead; cupping her right, she scooped handfuls of water into her mouth and rinsed, spat out, rinsed again.

Tears stung her eyes; from time to time, great convulsing dry heaves continued to wrack her body.

Passed over in lieu of Bambi Parker!
The injustice churned sickeningly.
How in God's name can I endure working under that bimbo?
How many times have I had to rectify her asinine mistakes?
She thought: *So this is what it tastes like, the bitter cup of defeat!*

It had begun to drizzle as Bambi Parker and Garth Wheeler Stewart II hurried up the carpeted steps to the Met. Garth, the blandly handsome young heir to a multimillion-dollar toilet paper fortune, carried an outsized umbrella which sheltered them both.

"It would have been nice if you'd rated an invitation for the dinner," Bambi reproached in her breathy little girl's voice, "instead of just the dance. If you ask me, *I* think it's insulting."

"If it bothers you, we can go on," Garth said. "There are at least four other parties tonight that I know of. Bet this place is full of geriatric cases anyway."

"No," Bambi said quickly. "We've come this far, we might as well stay for one little drinkipoo. Besides, this is supposed to be a real bash, and I want to see for myself what the hullabaloo's all about."

Wisely, she neglected to mention her real intention for coming—expressly, to see whether or not Robert A. Goldsmith was here, and if so, to "accidentally" bump into him and make certain he'd pulled the necessary strings for her promotion.

Once inside the museum, Garth handed over his invitation and went to check their coats and umbrella. Bambi smoothed her revealing, beaded blue minidress trimmed with blue ostrich feathers at the hem and got out her compact. A swift inspection assured her that her face was perfect. She looked young and bright and *au courant.*

Just the way Robert liked.

In the Temple of Dendur, the Peter Duchin Orchestra segued smoothly from "Fascination" into "Moon River."

On the dance floor, the couples slowed their pace accordingly. Above their heads, the minor Egyptian temple, a gift to the United States for saving Abu Simbel from the Aswan Dam, glowed as though the sandstone was washed by mysterious moonlight. Outside, Central Park was dark, and the towering gridwork wall of rain-streaked slanted glass reflected, like a tilted mirror, the glitter from the floating, flickering candles and lotus blossoms in the temple's reflecting pool.

"Isn't this romantic?" Dina sighed as Lord Rosenkrantz, despite his size, proved himself an exceptionally adept dancer. "I had no idea you danced so well!"

His chest swelled with pride. "That comes from being paired with such a beautiful young lady," he said staunchly, lifting her hand and kissing the tips of her fingers.

Dina positively preened. She was floating on cloud nine and wished this party would never have to end. "Isn't this music divine?" she crooned. "Really, I do believe I could dance all night. Tell me, Lord Rosenkrantz. Does every dance partner of yours feel as if she's wearing the Red Shoes?"

"Alas, madam, never one as beautiful as you. Ah, isn't that your husband?"

"Where?"

"Over . . . there." He turned Dina around in a slow, fluidly sweeping 180-degree turn.

Over Lord Rosenkrantz's shoulder, she caught sight of Robert scowling at her from the sidelines, unlit cigar clenched between his teeth.

Serves him right, she thought happily, pretending not to see him. "Please, Lord Rosenkrantz," she whispered, "you must hold me closer! I don't know why, but I'm suddenly possessed of the most *fiendish* urge to make my husband jealous! He doesn't appreciate me all he should, you know. *I* think it's time he's taught a little lesson."

Lord Rosenkrantz obliged by pressing her more tightly against him. "Is this better?"

"Oh, yes!" Dina smiled. "This is purrrrr-fect!"

And she thought: *Maybe* this *will teach Robert to dance with me!*

At the edge of the dance floor, Robert A. Goldsmith nearly bit his cigar in two.

What in damnation's come over that fool woman? he growled to himself. *Does she* have *to make such a public spectacle of herself?*

Chewing on the Havana like a riled-up pit bull, he surveyed the immediate area to see if anyone else noticed the way his wife and Lord What's-His-Name were carrying on.

Naturally, no one paid them the least bit of attention.

Goddamn bunch of hypocrites!

From behind, he suddenly felt a firm tap on his shoulder.

He turned around, coming face-to-face with the last person he expected to see—Bambi Parker. His immediate reaction was to flash a quick guilty look in his wife's direction.

Christ, he thought. *What the hell's Bambi doing here?*

"C'mon, Garth, give me some space, will ya?" Bambi told her date. "I won't be but a few minutes."

She shooed Garth off with peremptory flicks of a wrist. Then, taking both of Robert's hands in hers, she gave him the full impact of her fluttering baby blues.

"Robert," she breathed in that teensy-weensy voice, "why don't we go dance, huh? That way, we can talk without arousing any suspicion."

Like hell we won't! he thought, his eyes darting furtively toward Dina.

Fortunately, she and Lord Rosenkrantz had disappeared from sight, swallowed up by the sea of dancing couples.

Bambi tugged on his hand. "Robert!" She sounded exasperated and accusing, and he half-expected to see her stamp her foot petulantly.

"Okay, okay," he muttered grouchily. "One dance."

He tossed his cigar in the reflecting pool and Bambi let go of his hand, leading the way out onto the dance floor. Once there, she stopped and looked back at him.

Robert hesitated for all of three seconds. *Oh, what the hell,* he thought, throwing caution to the winds. Quickly he followed her. *What harm can one dance do?*

This gorgeous hunk certainly has all the right moves, Kenzie thought pleasurably as Hannes danced her fluidly along the edge of the pool, his searching fingers moving slowly down along her back. After a half hour in the ladies' room, she had decided to march back in and have a good time. The hell with Bambi Parker.

"Mmmm," she murmured dreamily. She had her eyes closed, her cheek resting against his warm broad chest, and her arms looped loosely around his neck. "I love these slow dances . . ."

"So do I," he said softly and cupped her buttocks, pressing her pelvis tightly to his.

Her eyes flicked open and the breath caught in her throat. It was impossible not to feel the tumescent jolt of his manhood straining against his trousers.

Raising her head, she tilted it back and stared up at him, her eyes bright, luminous pools.

"Just making sure you are still awake." He smiled, moist teeth flickering in the light from all the floating candles.

Again she laid her cheek back against his chest, listening to the comforting strong beats of his heart. "You smell like fresh apples," she murmured.

He had his nose in her hair. "And you of wildflowers."

Again she raised her head. "You aren't, by any chance, trying to seduce me?" she asked huskily.

He held her gaze. "And if I am?"

Her voice was hushed. "Then I'd say you're already halfway there."

The smile on his lips reached his eyes. "Only halfway?"

The air crackled with sexual currents flowing back and forth between them.

"Well . . . perhaps a little more than halfway," she allowed.

"Would you like to have another drink first ... perhaps find a nice quiet spot in the halls and look at some quartzite heads from the twelfth dynasty?"

Her arms tightened around him. "And if I don't care for the twelfth dynasty? If I prefer the classical Greeks, and Priapus in particular?"

He smiled again. "Then I can only hope that a priapic surrogate shall suffice."

Unbidden, an image of his taut, thrusting body leapt into her mind. "Yes!" she replied throatily, feeling a raw scorching heat rise up within her. "That ... that would suffice quite nicely."

"Good. Because what I want to do is hold you and make love to you forever."

As though in a daze, she drew his head down to hers. There was a rapturous kind of intensity in her face which he had not seen before.

"Well?" he asked softly. "Are you ready to go?"

Her knees were curiously weak and she felt as if she were drowning in the bottomless pools of those great greenish-blue eyes.

"Yes!" she replied in a fierce, urgent whisper. "Let's get out of here! Let's leave now!"

$\mathscr{A7}$

*B*eing a host has its drawbacks.

Being a Serene Highness on top of it—especially as eligible a bachelor as Prince Karl-Heinz—makes for even further encumbrances. The flurry of interest in him, which naturally had to be returned in kind, presented more than its share of social difficulties.

It made it impossible, for instance, to bestow his undivided attention upon the one person he was delighted to see—Zandra. However, now that he had obligingly danced with a half dozen very select partners, he intended to remedy that. He'd kept one eye peeled for her, so that as he came off the dance floor with Nina Fairey, he politely excused himself and made a beeline toward her.

"Quickly!" he said, his voice registering urgency. "Follow me."

Before Zandra could ask why, he was already propelling her through the throng, his brisk pace and friendly nods at friends and acquaintances indicating that he was pleased to see them, but momentarily too indisposed to stop and chat. Out of the Temple of Dendur he rushed her, through glass-lined exhibition rooms to the front entrance.

"Fetch your coat," he told her, pulling a folded, wafer-thin cellular phone from inside his breast pocket and flipping it open.

Zandra stared at him. "You mean, you're leaving your own party!"

"Yes, I'm calling my driver to bring the car around—the demands of those social vampires grate." He punched a memorized number. "Now hurry," he urged, "before some attention-starved vulture detains us!"

"Well, if you're sure," Zandra said, giving him an oblique look.

"I'm positive." Phone to his ear, he turned his back to keep new arrivals and early departees at bay.

Getting her scuffed motorcycle jacket from coat check, Zandra wondered whether Dina would be annoyed by her disappearance. Somehow she doubted it. *She's having too good a time to miss me. As for Kenzie, I'll see her at work tomorrow . . .*

Pulling on her jacket, she joined Karl-Heinz, who was already at the entry doors, folding the phone shut and pocketing it. "My driver should pull up momentarily," he said.

And out he hustled her; down the massive flight of stone steps they dashed. The drizzle had turned into a deluge, and they both held their jackets over their heads.

Moments later, laughing like truant schoolchildren, they ducked into the back of his Bentley Turbo.

"Did you find out about the latest club?" Karl-Heinz asked his chauffeur.

The driver glanced into the rearview mirror. "Yes, Your Highness. After you called, I checked with some of the other drivers. They say a place called Dante's Inferno is all the rage. It's down in the East Village."

"Good. Then that is where we shall go."

Now that he had Zandra to himself, Karl-Heinz settled back in the rich glove leather, the luxury of which never failed to bring a stir of ambrosial well-being.

"At last!" he said as the car merged smoothly with the Fifth Avenue traffic, the arcing flicks of the windshield wipers and the reflections of taillights on wet asphalt giving the impression they were drifting down a wide, rubied river. "For a while, I was afraid we would never have an opportunity to be by ourselves. Would you like a drink? There is a minibar—"

"Not right now, thanks." Zandra's smile was radiant. "Oh, Heinzie! This is *so* fabulous!" She reached for his hand and gave it a squeeze. "I swear, it seems like *ages* since we saw each other last!"

"That," he smiled, "is because it has been. You cannot imagine my delight when you walked in tonight. You really were the last person on earth I expected to see."

"I'm glad you're pleased," she said. Then her smile abruptly faded and she fell silent.

"Zandra?" He looked concerned. "What is it?"

"About your father's health. Is it true what you said during dinner?"

He nodded soberly. "Yes," he sighed, "I'm afraid so. The doctors don't give him long."

"Damn!"

He shrugged philosophically. "It isn't as though it's unexpected, you know. Father is, after all, quite old."

"Yes, but still . . ." Her voice trailed off, supple leather creaking as she changed position on the seat. She sensed that despite his acceptance of the situation, it weighed far heavier on his mind than he cared to let on.

How like him to neither complain nor indulge in self-pity, she thought. *Publicly, at least, he's ever the Serene Highness, graciously bowing to the inevitable—*

—to death.

With a chill shiver, she stared past the chauffeur and out the cleared arcs of windshield. She saw, but didn't absorb, the dark expanse of Central Park giving way to the whorishly lit Plaza Hotel, and then the enticing luxury emporiums below Fifty-ninth Street—*Bergdorf Goodman . . . Van Cleef and Arpel . . . Tiffany . . . Bendel's.* The soft squish of tires on wet pavement was more imagined than heard, such was the soundproof cocoon of this stately car.

Karl-Heinz's voice was soft. "Zandra?"

She turned to him, both their faces flickering from the swiftly moving shop windows which flashed past on either side, like passenger trains speeding in the opposite direction.

"Let's forget my father for tonight. All the worrying in the world is not going to help."

She drew a deep breath, held it inside her, and let it out slowly. "No, I suppose it won't." She stared intently over at him. "But Dina did hit the nail right on the head, didn't she?"

He did not reply.

She reached out and touched him on the arm. "Heinzie, you really must start thinking about securing your inheritance. Before it's too late!"

He smiled at her earnestness. "I appreciate your concern, but that, too, is a problem which shall keep until morning. Now, then." He clapped his hands together briskly. "Enough about me. I want to hear all about *you*—are you still breaking hearts, raising hell, and causing Aunt Josephine apoplexy?"

"Oh, I think Aunt Josie gave up on me years ago—'Washed her hands' of me, as she rather succinctly put it." Zandra laughed. "Not that I really blame her. In retrospect, I suppose I have been rather a handful. But let me see . . . *something* must be new besides my embarrassing the family in one way or another, or my unexpected arrival here this morn—"

"Unexpected?" he asked. "Why? Is something wrong in England?"

Damn! she thought, subconsciously placing a hand over the sleeve of her forearm, under which the burn wound throbbed anew. *How like him to pick up on that. I'm going to have to watch my every word.*

"Who said anything was wrong?" She forced her voice to sound light.

But she thought: *What isn't wrong? Only Rudolph and his gambling debts . . . the toughs who frightened me so badly I fled the country . . .*

But those particulars, she knew, were only the tip of the iceberg, the symptoms of a much larger and far more ominously looming problem— specifically, how to raise the cash Rudolph owed, and, even more precisely and to the point, how to repay it *before* the interest kept doubling, tripling, or quadrupling the principal.

Paying off that debt is the only way Rudolph and I can ever feel safe.

Money. She needed to get hold of Big Money, and fast.

And who, an opportunistic voice piped up in her head, *has more money than Karl-Heinz?*

She instantly put the skids on that train of thought. She would never, could never, appeal to Karl-Heinz for help. Pride precluded it.

Bad enough I'm a poor relation, she thought. *I'm not about to compound that by going begging. Even asking for a loan is moot, since I haven't a hope in hell of ever repaying such an astronomical sum . . .*

"Something is troubling you," Karl-Heinz said with uncanny acuity. "Why don't you tell me what it is. Perhaps I could be of assistance."

Tempting as his offer was, she quickly shook her head. "It's nothing," she lied. "But thanks all the same."

On impulse, she scooted across the seat and pecked him lightly on the cheek.

He looked both surprised and pleased. "What was that for?"

Her voice was soft and throaty. "For caring. For being you. For your birthday. For making this my lucky night."

"No," he said quietly, "you are wrong. It is you who have made this my lucky night."

Even in the dimness of the car, Zandra could feel the gentle force of his gaze.

She thought: *He really is a prince, and in more ways than one. I only hope to God he gets married in time . . . and that whoever she is, the lucky lady will deserve and appreciate him . . .*

Dancing.

Robert A. Goldsmith wasn't very good at it. What he *was* extremely good at, however, was playing grab-ass. Now, as the orchestra played "Someone to Watch Over Me," his hands were all over Bambi Parker's aerobics-firm buttocks: feeling, kneading, groping, *squeezing.*

"You mean you've arranged it?" Bambi batted seductive lashes. *"Already?"*

"Yeah," he grunted, more intent upon her perky derrière than on his dancing. "Not that this promotion's makin' either of us very popular."

"So?" Bambi tossed her head, baby blues hard and challenging. "Why should we care what other people think?"

"Why?" he repeated in disbelief, realizing just how uncomfortably big she was getting for her britches. "You wanna know why? 'Cause the consensus is, you're not up to the job."

She froze in mid-step. "Would you care to repeat that?" she said in a Freon voice.

He continued to fondle her buttocks. "I heard you nearly got yourself fired a few times."

She pulled away from him and stepped back, standing just out of reach. "You've been talking to that decrepit old Mr. Spotts, haven't you?" she accused. "That sounds like something he'd come up with!"

"Actually, it was Sheldon D. Fairey who brought it up."

"That son of a bitch! I think you should fire him."

Placing her hands on her hips, her frontal equipment rose and fell within the snug, low-cut armor of glittering blue beads.

Pouting, she added: "You would, you know, if you really cared about me."

Robert went ballistic. Seizing her bare arm, he yanked her roughly against him. "What kinda games d'you think you're playin'?" he snapped into her upturned face. "And whaddya think I am—*stoopid?* Maybe you'd kill the goose that lays the golden eggs, but I sure the hell won't. Who do you think made Burghley's the leading auction house in this country? Huh?"

Bambi made a face against the spray of spittle.

"Well, I'll tell ya who," he went on grimly. "Sheldon D. Fairey. And since I've invested a hell of a lot of money in that company, my first priority ain't a piece of ass—it's protectin' my investment."

"Are you trying to tell me that I'm expendable and Fairey isn't?"

"What do you think?"

"I think you are a real bastard!"

He jerked her even closer, plastering her breasts so tightly against him that he could feel her wildly beating heart. "You can think what you like. I'm just giving you some friendly advice."

"Oooooh," she said sarcastically. "I'm shaking!" With a faint wicked smile, she thrust her hips right up against his, slid her free hand deftly between him and herself, and felt his phallus through his trousers.

His erection was immediate.

"Always hard, aren't you, Robert?" she taunted.

"Christ Jesus!" he whispered fiercely. "Are you nuts! God alone knows how many people are watching!"

"Will you chill out? In this crowd no one will notice a thing. At least," she laughed, "not so long as we continue dancing—and you keep old J.P. tucked inside your pants!"

As they moved to the music, her hand tightened over his phallus and he drew a deep shuddering breath. There was something about playing with fire that ignited some base sense of urgency within him. He could feel his blood speeding in his veins, his pulse racing, and his heart pounding away like kettle drums. Trapped inside boxer shorts and trousers, his penis strained and reared, craving to release the juices of life itself. If only she would undo his fly and take it out! Hold his cock in her hands and bring him to orgasm right here amidst this crowd!

After a minute, she looked up at him. "Well, Robert?" Her voice was softly mocking. "Still want to throw me to the wolves?"

Silently he cursed his cock. Ever since he could remember, he'd had to guard against it being his downfall—and if he wasn't careful, he knew that one of these days it would be.

He was breathing heavily. "All I was . . . saying," he managed, disgusted with his ill-timed physical reaction, "is you . . . you better not blow your promotion. I can only . . . go to bat for you . . . so often . . ."

It was as if he'd struck her. Her body suddenly tensed and she iced him with her eyes. "If you intend to leave me in the lurch, then be man enough and say so now." Her breathy little girl's voice had gone cold and bitter. "But remember, Robert. If you don't scratch my back, don't expect me to be around to scratch yours."

To make her point, she let go of his crotch and pulled away again.

He still had her by the arm and tightened his grip. "Listen, you little prick tease." His voice was soft but had a harsh, savage edge. "You wanna join the big league and play hardball? That it?"

She did not reply.

"Then how about we start by taking this promotion of yours one day at a time? Huh?"

Suddenly she felt unsure of herself, as though the pond she was skating upon had inexplicably turned to very thin ice. Her voice almost trembled. "What's that supposed to mean?"

"Exactly what I said. You displease me once and you're out on your ass." His fingers dug into her flesh. "Still like the big league?" he taunted.

"Ro-*bert!* You're hurting me!"

His eyes drilled right into her. "I wonder if you know what pain really is."

She remained silent.

"But just so we're on the same wavelength, I'll give you one last piece of advice." He drew his lips back across his teeth. "Never forget that you're expendable. Blow jobs come a dime a dozen in this town!"

Angrily she tried to wrench herself free, but he was too strong. Her eyes flashed with spite and her bosom heaved with every quickened breath.

"Well? Still wanna threaten to withhold your cunt?"

She seemed on the verge of hissing a reply, but then thought better of it. Her lips tightened into a thin line. "No, Robert," she said almost meekly. "But I want to be more than just another blow job."

"Smart girl." He loosened his grip and grinned. "Maybe now that we understand each other, you'll stop bitching. You got what you wanted, didn't ya?"

She was no longer certain of anything. "If you say so," she said guardedly.

"Just don't let me down," he warned. The orchestra was segueing into "Smoke Gets in Your Eyes." He looked at her questioningly. "Well? What're you waitin' for?"

Bambi looked puzzled. "What do you mean?"

Pulling her close, he guided her hand back down to his groin. "Aren't you going to show your appreciation?"

"But I thought it was time I made myself scarce."

"Why? Is there a fire?"

"You said one dance," she reminded him.

"So I changed my mind." He gave her a lewd wink. "Seems to me, there's a lot more to dancing than I previously thought."

Dina was enjoying herself immensely. Lord Rosenkrantz was such an unbelievably good dancer that even the most intricate, out-of-date steps were a breeze to pick up. Despite his beer-barrel physique, he was so light and agile on his feet that it was easy to fancy herself as Ginger Rogers to his (well, *his rather plump,* she allowed herself charitably) Fred Astaire, so smoothly and effortlessly did he lead her, and . . .

. . . and unless her sharp eyes were deceiving her, wasn't that her husband, Robert—the very *same* Robert who always refused to set foot on a dance floor, and claimed to absolutely *loathe* dancing!—doing exactly that with a peach-complexioned blonde plastered right up against him?

The momentary glimpse she'd caught became a dark, ominous cloud hovering on her social horizon. Strangely enough, what she found most troubling of all was not Robert's weakness for PYTs—Pretty Young Things. Nor was she particularly disturbed by possible philandering on his part, at least not for the time being. No; that could wait. What evoked her wrath was his sense of timing.

Why *now?* Why did he have to overstep the bounds of propriety on this, the night of her single greatest social triumph when everyone all but salaamed obsequiously before her?

Well, he'll soon be sorry! Dina vowed darkly, and immediately detached herself from her dance partner.

Lord Rosenkrantz looked concerned. "Is something the matter?"

She summoned her best false smile. "Only my feet, Lord Rosenkrantz," she lied. "I'm afraid it's these new shoes. I should have known better than to wear them tonight."

Lord Rosenkrantz looked as sorrowful as if she had announced a death in his immediate family. "More's the pity, madam," he murmured, and then his voice regained its ebulliency. "However, your comfort and well-being must take priority!"

He cocked his arm, she hooked hers through it, and he gallantly escorted her off the dance floor.

"Alas," he told her when they reached the sidelines. "I am bereft. Having once experienced feet lighter than air, I cannot conceive of dancing with anyone else."

"You, Lord Rosenkrantz," she laughed, "are the most incorrigible flatterer!"

"And you, madam, flatter me with your very presence." He took her hand and raised it to his lips.

She felt the merest whisper of breath on her fingertips.

"May I get you a libation?"

"Please." Dina decided some serious fortification was in order. "I'll have a double vodka," she decided. "Straight." Then, remembering her calories, she quickly changed her mind. "On second thought, make that a club soda. No ice."

"At once, madam," he said with a courtly bow, every inch the Continental gentleman.

She waited until he was gone, then hopped on tiptoe and craned her neck, her slitted eyes sweeping the area of the dance floor where she had last caught sight of her husband.

Where *had* he disappeared to . . . ? She knew she had seen him, he must be—

—*there!* A sudden opening in the cluster of dancers momentarily revealed him before obscuring him once again.

She felt her cheeks draw in; her stomach shift poisonously. The glimpse she'd caught was only fleeting, but she had seen enough to sense—to *know!*—that something untoward was going on.

Because Robert and the blonde were not so much dancing or flirting as they were positively *glued* to one another, joined as though in sexual embrace!

Dina felt the jolt of physical agony. Suddenly she had a dissonant sense of confinement in this vast, jam-packed space. Makeup-laminated faces took on a menacing, Daliesque surreality; ordinary laughter curdled into the screeches of the deranged.

How could Robert! she quailed. *How* could *he? He's my* husband!

Through sheer willpower, Dina forced away the hallucinatory edge of panic; fought to bring reality back into focus.

Slowly her breathing calmed and anger replaced shock.

She thought: *I could always pretend I didn't see anything and confront Robert later, after we get home. The only trouble is, by then he'll have thought up any number of excuses, and even try to convince me I was imagining things. No, best to nip things in the bud* now—*before they get out of hand* . . .

Having decided upon a strategy, Dina was ready to slay dragons. She marched onto the dance floor and expertly navigated her way through the slow-dancing crowd.

Homing in on her target, her raptorial eyes didn't miss a trick.

Not Bambi's aerobics-toned body or sensuous movements, nor the way Robert's hands were all over her, and especially not the way the girl's arm was—*good heavens!*—covertly doing the hokey pokey!

Robert, Robert, Robert, Dina chided wordlessly, shaking her head and clucking her tongue against the roof of her mouth. *What am I going to do with you?*

But she already knew.

Stealing up on him from behind, she gave his buttocks a sharp tweak and exclaimed: "Sweetie! Why didn't you *tell* me you have a girlfriend?"

For once Robert A. Goldsmith was caught completely off guard. He and Bambi leapt apart like scalded cats.

"D-D-Dina!" he blustered. "What a pleasant—"

Dina cut him off with a merciless glare. Then, turning to Bambi, she snapped, *"Adiós,* Cinderella!"

Bambi wisely made tracks.

Dina watched her departure through slitted eyes. Knowing trouble when she saw it, she filed away a mental mugshot; chances were, this girl might pop up again sometime in the future. Of course, it behooved Robert to make certain she wouldn't.

Still, I've been forewarned. It won't hurt to monitor him more closely from now on.

With Bambi gone, Dina turned her full attention upon her husband.

". . . goddamn hot in here," he mumbled, mopping sweat from his forehead with a white handkerchief.

"Well, you know what they say, Robert. If you can't take the heat, stay out of the fire."

"What's that supposed to mean?"

"Sweetie, you know exactly what it means." She smiled saccharinely. "Crossing the line with your little Junior Miss, what else?"

"Crossing the line?" he said indignantly. "What line? We were only dancing. Anyway, if you hadn't been so busy with Lord What's-His-Name, I'd have asked you."

"Oh, *really?*" Dina's voice dripped sarcasm. "Well, never mind. You were looking to dance with me, so how about it?" She extended bracelet-laden arms and awaited his embrace. "Shall we?"

Robert had no choice but to comply. He held her clumsily, dancing with stiff, awkward movements.

Dina burst out laughing. "My God, Robert, you dance as if you're constipated! You certainly weren't this uptight with your little Junior Miss. Now relax—" She enjoyed his discomfiture immensely. "—all you have to do is follow my lead. But first, you might want to hold me a little closer . . . you know . . . like you held *her?*"

Robert, loosening up a little, stole a longing glance in the direction in which Bambi had fled.

A major mistake.

Dina's spiky heel came down on his toes. *Hard.*

Letting out a yelp, he hopped comically up and down on one foot. "Now what did you do that for?" he accused, looking aggrieved.

"Why, to get your attention," Dina cooed, "what else? And while we're on that subject, I strongly suggest you forget her."

He played dumb. "Forget who?"

"Your little Cinderella. Really, Robert. Need I remind you that we're married? Or reel off the names of men who were toppled from the *Forbes* Four Hundred, and all because of divorce settlements?"

She was pleased to see him blanch.

"I didn't think so," she purred, smugly secure in the knowledge that she had scored her point and hit where it hurt most.

Not below the belt, but in his most painful spot of all.

His wallet.

18

*A*s soon as they stepped outside, Hannes's features knotted into an expression of disgust. The night was wet and shiny: what had begun as a drizzle had turned into a full-fledged cloudburst. Sheets of silvery rain, hard as a heavyweight's fists, thrashed the city with a vengeance.

To his surprise, Kenzie uttered a cry of sheer joy and turned a bright face to his. "Isn't it *glorious?*" she breathed.

And before he could reply that no, this abominable weather was definitely *not* glorious, she waved away the footman who came rushing with an oversized umbrella, left Hannes standing in the shelter between two massive columns, and darted out into the downpour.

Tilting her head heavenward, she spread her arms wide and twirled, reveling in the pounding, cleansing rain.

"You are mad!" Hannes shouted from under the sanctuary of the overhanging cornice. "Do you know that? Utterly, depravedly *mad!*"

"Wonderfully mad!" she enthused, her hair already plastered to her skull like a sleek dark helmet. Running back to him, she grabbed both his hands and tugged him, protesting, out into the rain. Then, clinging tightly to his arm, she tromped happily beside him down the sodden, red-carpeted steps.

"Now admit it," she said. "Doesn't this feel great?"

"Being with *you* feels great," he offered with meaningful emphasis.

"Oh, yeah?" She stopped and tipped her head to one side in order to favor him with a pleased look.

"Yeah." He pulled her into an embrace.

Agile as a Fagin urchin, she squirmed out of his arms and laughed, playfully skipping the rest of the way down with him in hot pursuit.

Reaching the bottom, she found herself facing limousine row. From left to right, slant-parked as far as the eye could see was a veritable armada of dark limousines and Lincoln Town Cars—plus a single white superstretch Caddy with blacked-out windows and DINA G vanity plates, whose chauffeur was leaning against the driver's door under an umbrella. He had observed Kenzie's descent with interest. Now that she was within ten feet, he pushed his peaked, visored cap back on his head and gave her an appreciative once-over.

Kenzie, aware of his gaze, saw a whippet-thin guy who smoked from a cupped hand while simultaneously chewing on a wad of gum *and* a toothpick. Caught him flashing her a knowing grin and a wink, both of which she ignored.

She turned to Hannes as he caught up with her. He was laughing and lifted her easily off her feet and gently twirled her around and around in a circle.

"Why do I feel as though I'm fifteen again?" he asked once he set her back down.

"Because you are." Her voice was a whisper amid the crashing of the rain. She reached up and touched his cheek tenderly with her fingertips. "Because tonight we *both* are."

He looked at her. A streetlamp threw its harsh glare around them, but she had her back to it. Her face was in shadows. Only her eyes shone with a peculiar light all their own. Despite the cold lashing of the rain he could feel the fires within her reach out toward him.

Then she lowered her hand and turned away. Abruptly the spell was broken. She gestured in front of her.

He stood beside her; then followed her sweeping hand as it encompassed all of limousine row.

"Am I correct in assuming that none of these vehicles is yours?"

He could detect a note of humor in her voice and smiled. "You are, so it's good you like the rain. Come. Let's find a taxi."

He took her by the hand and pulled her in single-file between the white superstretch and a midnight-blue Town Car.

Dina's chauffeur made himself thinner so they could squeeze past. Recognizing pocket change when he saw it, he quickly drew on his cigarette and flipped it into the gutter.

"Yo!" he called. Kenzie and Hannes stopped and turned around.

He sidled over and included them under his umbrella. It muted the roar of the downpour to a steady, muffled drumbeat. "I take it you folks're lookin' for a cab?"

Hannes nodded. "Yes."

The driver's toothpick waggled. His face was expressionless as he squinted slowly over at Fifth Avenue to gauge the downtown traffic. He looked back at Hannes. "Fifth's usually crawlin' with so many cabs, you stick your arm out, a whole fleet of 'em'll aim right at you like a school o' hungry sharks. But that's when it's nice out. Right now, Fifth looks like it's filled with nothin' but off-duties and occupieds, but what can you expect in this kinda weather? 'Fraid you'll have a tough time findin' one tonight."

"He's right, you know," Kenzie murmured from long experience.

The driver waggled his toothpick some more. "Where you folks headed?"

"First Avenue and Thirty-seventh," Hannes answered.

The man nodded. "Tell you what. My boss won't be ready to leave for a while yet. Fifteen bucks'll get you home in style."

Hannes didn't hesitate. Reaching for his wallet, he forked over a twenty. "Keep the change," he said.

"Hey, mister, you're all right! Thanks!"

The driver palmed the bill as deftly as a seasoned maître d'. He popped open the rear door and held it.

"Hop on in, folks," he invited. "Enjoy the ride."

Kenzie crawled in first, sinking into a deep, L-shaped leather banquette. A moment later, Hannes plopped himself down beside her.

"Nice, huh?" she said, glancing around the interior.

It was decorated like a yacht. All buttery leather and burled elm, with gold accents, mood lighting, and dual everything—TVs, VCRs, cellular phones, faxes.

Kenzie stretched her legs straight out in front of her. "Can you *believe* this? There's enough legroom to do sit-ups!" Sighing blissfully, she crossed her arms behind her head. "Ah, for the lifestyle of the rich and famous!" she murmured. "A girl could get used to this. Yes, indeed . . ."

The partition separating passengers from driver slid soundlessly down.

"You'll find a built-in bar between the TVs," the chauffeur called out. He was backing the big car slowly out of its berth and expertly swinging it around in a tight reverse turn. "There's booze, ice, the works. Help yourselves. Drinks're on the house."

The partition slid back up.

Hannes looked at Kenzie. "Would you care for something?"

She hesitated, then shook her head. "I'd better not. I already drank more than my limit."

Hannes decided to check out the bar anyway. Sure enough, the cabinet was custom fitted with padded, molded slots containing cut-crystal glasses and matching decanters topped with silver pouring spouts. A compartment below it held a mini-refrigerator and a freezer filled with cubed ice.

Kenzie watched as he fixed himself a Scotch rocks.

"Oh, hell's bells!" she declared, deciding there was nothing to be gained from abstinence. "I'll have a vodka and tonic—but I suggest you go real light on the booze. One drink too many, and everything starts spinning." With a sly little smile, she added, "The last thing I want is to spend the night with my arms wrapped around a toilet."

He laughed. "Yes, I'd much rather they were wrapped around me—so I think you'd best prepare yourself for the weakest drink in the world."

She watched as he tonged ice cubes into a glass, added a splash of vodka, a precut sliver of lime, and a heavy dose of Schweppes. Finally he gave the drink a brisk stir with a glass swizzle stick.

"For you."

He proffered the Baccarat highball with both hands, like a priest-ly offering.

She accepted it in the same solemn, ritualistic manner, holding it in both hands, and took a tentative sip, all the while looking at him over the rim with wide amber eyes.

"Yummy," she murmured, giving a deep, pleasurable sigh. "Sheer perfection."

Slowly she ran the moist pink tip of her tongue across her upper lip, her face taking on an unmistakably playful cast.

"Tell me, Hans. Are you as good at everything as you are at mixing drinks?"

He stared intently at her. "What do you think?"

She looked thoughtful and took another sip of her drink and swal-lowed, all the while holding his gaze.

"I think I'll have to reserve judgment until after the experience."

"A consummation devoutly seeking to be fulfilled," he murmured, scooting closer against her and making soft caresses.

Even as the limousine pulled out onto Fifth Avenue, merging smoothly with the swift downtown traffic as though with a school of vermillion-tailed fish, Kenzie and Hannes were already at it, letting their hands and lips do the talking as hidden stereo speakers emitted soft, early Streisand—just what the doctor ordered to enhance the strong sexual chemistry crackling in the air.

Their departure had not gone unnoticed.

Behind the unmarked police car's arthritic, ineffectual wipers, Charley Ferraro sat rigidly erect, clammy, shivering hands gripping the steering wheel with such ferocity that his knuckles shone white. He felt wounded, stung, *betrayed*. Like the child who'd been warned about never hear-ing good things said behind its back, but who'd gone ahead and eaves-dropped anyway.

He supposed the same went for spying on people.

Only it hadn't been his intention to spy upon Kenzie. The sole reason he'd come and suffered more than a half hour of the stifling, humid con-fines of this car had been to offer her a lift home, prove he bore no grudge for having been eighty-sixed from her apartment earlier in the evening.

He laughed mirthlessly, a harsh, grating rasp like that of sandpaper on iron.

And how had the Good Samaritan been rewarded? Why, by getting to witness her departure—her umbrella-less dash down the steps while pursued by—well, whoever the guy was! And watching him twirling her around in the rain—the two of them acting like lovers in a goddamn Broadway musical!—before climbing into the back of that garish white superstretch.

His chest felt tight, ready to explode.

"Shit!" He clenched his right hand in a fist and slammed it down on the steering wheel. Too late, he wished he'd stayed the hell home. He sure could have saved himself a ton of heartache if he had.

But the fact of the matter was, he *hadn't* stayed home! Like an idiot, he'd had to come and try to patch things up.

Despite himself, Charley leaned in close to the fogged windshield and wiped a spot clear with his cuff. He stared, as though narcotized, through the streaks and runnels left by the wipers as the limousine, emitting a burst of warning beeps and red taillight flashes, backed out of its slot. He watched as all but the tip of its low-slung hood swerved slowly out of sight. Then the alarm and flashes ceased.

A moment later, the big car rolled majestically forward, the driver having to cramp the wheel hard to the left before reversing again in another tight arc, the automatic *son-et-lumière* shrilling and flashing.

Finally the noise and flashes abated.

The limo, now undocked, came gliding forward; approached head-on.

Charley threw up an arm to shield his eyes against multiple headlamps. For an instant, the wide grille seemed to line him up in its sights, like some deadly, interstellar gunship assessing whether or not to beam him to oblivion.

Then, as though scorning his vehicle as beneath contempt, the hood turned disdainfully to the left and the blinding wash of headlights swung away, followed by the long white one hundred thirteen-inch ghost of a body, the whole skimming serenely across wet pavement like an enormous cruise ship: haughty, insolent, *scornful.*

Charley let his arm drop.

"Let the bad times roll," he muttered, and turned the ignition. He waited until the limo had a twenty-yard head start. Then he tailed it—a piece of cake.

On Seventy-second, it hung a left and continued on east until Second Avenue, where it did a slow, tight right before accelerating and racing downtown. At Thirty-fourth, it slowed again, swung another left, then yet another, and for three blocks cruised sedately up First Avenue in the left lane.

Between Thirty-seventh and Thirty-eighth streets, it pulled over in front of a monstrosity of a high rise.

Charley cut the ignition, killed the headlights, and let the battered old maroon Plymouth coast to a halt. Steeling himself for the inevitable, his grip on the wheel tightened.

Everything before him seemed to unfold in exaggerated slow motion: the chauffeur's door creeping open; the building's doorman, gradually mushrooming umbrella in hand, forsaking the bright dry comfort of the lobby and heading sluggishly, as if struggling through invisible molasses, to the dripping end of the awning; the slow-gaited chauffeur reaching for the rear doorhandle—

Charley moaned aloud, realizing, belatedly, that he *hadn't* steeled himself for the inevitable. Hadn't watching their departure from the Met been trauma enough?

Once they were inside, Charley drew in his breath as he watched them, hands held, hurriedly crossing the gleaming marble on their way to the elevators—

—like lovers unable to wait to get upstairs!

Suddenly the scene sped up. Ferocious storms, full of sound and fury, shrieked and raged within him.

They're behaving like goddamn newlyweds!

Then, mercifully, they finally disappeared from view.

Charley drew an anguished breath and slumped back in his seat. At least now that he no longer had to see those two lovebirds, the sharpest jolts of pain subsided, became a constant, dull, but almost tolerable ache.

He knew there was nothing to be gained by waiting around. He'd seen plenty. Pulling himself together, he fired the ignition, threw the car in gear, and savagely floored the accelerator—taking off like a squealing, rubber-burning rocket.

He knew what he would do. Head uptown and wait in front of her place. He'd confront Kenzie there.

Becky V's departure created as much of a sensation as her arrival. This was entirely due to her pathological obsession for privacy. She never over-exposed herself, and thus kept the hungry multitudes—even the highest and the mightiest—yearning to see more.

A case in point: this party.

Except for the scant minutes she'd spent circulating with Karl-Heinz during cocktails, smile frozen in place, and then the dinner itself, during which she'd erected invisible walls around Karl-Heinz's table, she'd honored her host with the first dance and thereafter had immediately seques-tered herself in the seclusion of the Patrons' Lounge on the top floor of the Wallace Wing.

There, in one of the plush, Regency-furnished sitting rooms, she had held court for the duration of the evening, but only to a handful of highly select close friends.

Now, at eleven o'clock, she was ready to return to the Olympian heights of her penthouse across Fifth Avenue. Lord Rosenkrantz, sum-moned from downstairs, jumped to with alacrity and took the elevator straight up.

Five minutes later, flanked by Becky's ever-vigilant Secret Service detail, they made a single circumference of the Temple of Dendur where, without breaking her regal pace, Becky nevertheless slowed to bid good night to certain friends and acquaintances.

Dina was overcome to find herself singled out for one of these queenly farewells.

"It was a pleasure to meet you," Becky told her.

"Oh, no, the pleasure was all *mine!*" returned Dina with star-struck effusiveness.

Becky smiled her enigmatic smile and, as she moved on, suddenly remembered that Robert A. Goldsmith had just purchased the controlling interest in Burghley's, and since she herself sat on the advisory board of the parent company, Burghley's Holdings, Inc., future interaction with the Goldsmiths would be inevitable.

Moreover, Rebecca Cornille Wakefield Lantzouni de la Vila was nothing if not practical. Sole mistress of an empire worth in excess of six and a half billion dollars—an otherwise daunting responsibility which, thanks to Lord Rosenkrantz, who was to high finance what Picasso was to art, virtually ran itself—she could devote her entire energies to cultivating the world's very, very rich and truly famous for one express purpose: to pick their pockets for the scores of charitable causes she championed.

Thus, it was with this ulterior motive that she stopped, turned back to Dina, and graciously said, "Perhaps we can meet for lunch one of these days?"

Dina was so overcome that, for the first time in her life, she was rendered absolutely speechless.

"Also," Becky continued smoothly, "I'd love to invite you and your husband to my house in the country for a weekend. That is, of course, if you're interested."

If we're *interested?* Dina wore the bleary expression of a woman who was holding a winning lottery ticket but was still finding it difficult to believe her eyes—or in this particular case, her ears.

"I . . . we . . . we'd *love* to come!" she blurted as soon as she found her voice.

"Good! You shall be hearing from me."

And with that, Becky and her retinue moved on.

Dina stood there, transfixed in ecstasy. Then, elbowing her husband sharply in the ribs, she gloated: "Did you *hear* that, Robert? Imagine! *Us* invited to Becky V's!"

Robert breathed an imperceptible sigh of relief. His wife was so agog and sparkly eyed that—God willing—she might forget his minor transgression on the dance floor.

He needn't have worried.

Bambi Parker was the last thing on Dina's mind, for what could compare with one of the single most exclusive social doors on earth opening to her?

Why, nothing under the sun!

Oh, yes. Little Dina Van Vliet, late of Gouda, was in like Flynn—and higher than a junkie on speed!

19

Dante's Inferno was jammed. The orgiastic pounding of techno-rock blasted the eardrums. Yellow and red streamers, powered by fans set beneath grilles around the perimeter of the dance floor, leapt and shimmered and licked the air like devouring flames.

Karl-Heinz looked around him as strobes freeze-framed the dancers like flashes of a stop-motion camera. There were girls who looked like boys, boys who looked like girls, curiously androgynous creatures who looked like neither, and some who even looked like what they really were.

Zandra, for instance. In a place chock full of fashion statements, she more than held her own and caught every eye, blooming like that rarest and most fragile of orchids, but for a single night.

Karl-Heinz could swear that his younger cousin, whose vibrating physical presence he had never noticed before, was more than a little enchanting. There was, in fact, no way he could ignore her impact, or keep from feasting his eyes upon her.

She didn't rave or vogue or indulge in trendy, unstructured aerobics like everyone else on the dance floor. On the contrary: she moved with a felicitously natural, unstudied, and entirely fluid grace all her own, half the time with her eyes shut, as if she were cloistered in some world only she could see.

Forget it! he told himself. *She's too young for me. She must think I'm an old man.*

As if to prove the point, he abruptly stumbled, elbow colliding with another dancer's. He felt a threatening grip on his arm, heard a post-adolescent challenge: "Yo! You dissin' me, Pops?"

His head snapped sideways, resenting the implication of infirmity, his awareness of the generation gap—*of all this youth!*—heightened by the hardness of the kid's pimply young face.

Karl-Heinz responded by staring him down.

As if threatened by superior powers, the acned youth backed off. But Karl-Heinz felt no triumph. Irrationally, he chafed at this crowd of grunge chameleons and banjee kids with their multiple-piercings and boundless energy. For the most part, they were years younger even than Zandra.

Yet somehow she seemed to belong, managing to slip into a downtown persona with the effortless ease with which she'd change clothes, something he would forever be incapable of doing.

For God's sake, he wondered, *what in the hell am I doing in this punked-out kindergarten? I don't belong here. I should be uptown, foxtrotting with blue-rinsed heiresses in some stodgy, socially acceptable establishment!*

"Heinzie!" Zandra yelled to make herself heard over the amplified techno-rock. Then she moved fluidly over to him and grabbed his arm, rescuing him from his grim self-absorption. "Let's cut a rug, cousin!"

Karl-Heinz was hesitant at first, but ultimately Zandra could not be ignored. He heard the urging in her voice and saw the gleeful smile in her eyes. She was irresistible, and despite his concerns about not fitting in, he found himself being led farther onto the crushing dance floor. With Zandra's coaxing, he finally overcame his inhibitions and gave himself up to the music, swinging, swaying, stamping, and jerking orgiastically, as if in pagan worship, all in time with his seductive cousin. Together they writhed to the bludgeoning beat, watching each other in the painfully flashing strobes and synchronizing their movements to the concussive noise. Together they laughed at their blatantly sexual movements, first Zandra's, then his, one trying to outdo the other, dancing with the indefatigable youths packed sardinelike around them.

Finally, they'd both had enough and collapsed, hot and sweaty, onto each other.

"It is getting late," Karl-Heinz mouthed.

"Yes." She nodded vigorously.

Karl-Heinz reached out and took her arm, and they cleaved their way through the sea of dancers to the coat check.

Outside, the rain was blasting down with renewed fury, and flotsam rode the swift currents, bypassing overflowing storm drains. But they were oblivious to it, laughing as they dashed arm and arm to the waiting Bentley.

Sitting side by side on the drive uptown, Zandra recalled how charming Karl-Heinz had been all evening, and began to see him in a new, beguiling light. He no longer seemed just an older, far-removed cousin . . . but something more, something much more indeed.

The bedchamber was dark.

Hallowed silence here, high above the city where time itself seemed suspended and of no consequence. Through the vertical blinds of the curving bay window, the indigo night was suffused with shimmering, rain-blurred lights from the millions of windows glittering in the darkness.

Bending forward, Hannes deposited her gently on the bed, on sheets soft and white and inviting as flesh itself; pale shadows thrown by the blinds rippled snakelike across both of them.

Kenzie let her arms slip from around his neck and stared up at him, her eyes wide and luminous.

Did he seem to tower above her because she was prone and he was standing? Or had she already forgotten how incredibly tall he was? And what about the chiseled masculine beauty of his face, the marblelike lucency of his skin, the shimmer of his whitish-blond hair?

As her eyes adjusted to the dim nocturnal glow emitted by the city that never sleeps, she was struck by how his lashes were the exact same whitish blond. And those eyes, those *eyes!* How easy it was to lose herself in the bottomless depths of those great shining pale pools!

Feeling the mattress shift as he lay down beside her, she turned her head and looked at him. He was half-propped on an elbow, staring so intently as though to commit her every feature to memory.

She found herself paralyzed with longing, hypnotized by his intensity. Everything about him added up to just the right kind of chemistry.

"Ah, Kenzie," he murmured, reaching out and caressing the soft creamy taut skin of her face with feathery fingertips. "Beautiful, beautiful Kenzie . . ."

Deliberately, teasingly, Hannes traced first the ridge of one cheekbone, then the other; slowly felt the curvature of her forehead, the pert sweep of her nose. So ethereally did his fingers drift, so languid and controlled was his touch, that a warbled sigh, composed of equal parts anguish and delight, involuntarily escaped her. Already, she could feel the torrent of moistness welling up between her thighs.

When his fingertips grazed her lips, the agony of protracted foreplay grew unbearable. Greedily she opened her mouth, closed her lips around his fingertips, and sucked them in.

Swearing softly, he pulled his hand free, seized her by the wrists in an iron grip, and forced her arms apart, splaying them across the bed as though in crucifixion.

Her pupils dilated wildly and she lifted her head. Fighting to free herself, she writhed, arched her spine, and jackknifed—all to no avail. She was no match for his strength. Beneath his dress shirt, his arms were corded sinews.

"Relax, Kenzie," he soothed. "There is no need to fear me. None at all . . ."

Something about his voice did it. Abruptly the fight left her and her body went slack. She let her head drop back on the pillow.

"There," he said. "That's better . . ."

Instead of fear, she was suddenly filled with a peculiar kind of excitement. "Oh, God!" she whispered. "Undress me, Hans!" Her eyes were rapt. "If I can't have you inside me, I'm going to go crazy!"

"Patience, Kenzie," he said softly. Releasing her wrists, he took her face in his hands and locked eyes with her. "You are very beautiful and passionate. Yes, very much so," he nodded, stroking the hollows of her cheeks with the soft pads of his thumbs. "But there is still one thing you must learn."

Her voice was soft and throaty. "And what is that?"

He began to unwrap the capelike scarf from around her throat. "That love is an art. And true art can never be rushed."

The fires in his eyes seemed to reach out and go right into hers. "Then teach me!" she said in a raspy whisper. "Let me be your willing pupil!"

Arousal, raw and primitive, made further words unnecessary. He lowered his head and covered her soft, full lips with his, plundering their pliant sweetness.

Kenzie gasped. His mouth seemed to scorch, and she thrilled to the intoxicating maleness of his scent, the heady rapture of his touch. His tongue stroked her lips lightly, then demanded entrance and explored deeper; darted about like fiery quicksilver.

Clutching hold of his arms, she met his tongue with her own, and they danced an oral duet to music only they could hear.

She wanted it to go on forever.

"Don't stop!" she whispered, pressing herself tightly against him when he came up for air. "Hans—"

"Sssh." He placed a finger across her lips. "Do you know what it is I want, Kenzie?" His eyes seemed to glow in the dark.

She stared up at him and slowly shook her head. "What do you want, Hans?"

"You," he said simply, reaching down and deftly loosening her rhinestone-studded bodice.

Each touch of his fingers sent electric currents, like tingling shock waves, rushing up and down her spine. Enthralled, she leaned forward on her elbows and watched as he eased the damp, heavily encrusted silk down over her shoulders.

The sudden rush of cool air pebbled her flesh and her breasts leapt free. They were full and strong, with erect nipples jutting proudly forth like the stems of luscious fruits.

He skimmed them with his fingertips and lifted them admiringly, running his tongue across their silken flesh. Then, when he captured her left nipple in his mouth, the pleasure was almost too much for her to bear.

Shivering violently, she fell back and clutched his head to her bosom as he sucked, fluttering his tongue as delicately as hovering hummingbirds' wings. Suddenly she was aware of myriad sensations: the cool eddies of air circulating about the room, the heat emanating from both their bodies, the thrumming of his tongue—even the tickling sensations from his hair, which descended over his face like cornsilk and swept her flesh with his every movement.

"Oh, Hans!" she breathed, pressing his head even closer into her bosom. "Hans—"

He rolled the nipple between his teeth and glanced up at her. She was flinging her head from side to side on the pillow, her eyes wide and moist.

He suckled and nipped and she cried out, but now her eyes were closed. Tears seeped from their corners. Her lips were parted and she was breathing heavily, as though intent upon emptying the room of its oxygen.

Letting go of her right teat, he teased it with his fingers, tongued a moist trail to the left nipple, and bit down on it, cruelly giving the right one a squeeze.

Her spine arched, her eyes snapped open, and she screamed, her voice reverberating from the walls. She leaned abruptly forward.

"Hans!"

He raised his head, the nipple still clenched between his teeth.

She stared at him, her eyes luminous. "I never want tonight to end!"

He laughed softly, the nipple slipping from between his lips. "We have yet to begin and already you are insatiable!"

Her eyes continued to gleam. "And is that so bad?"

He held her gaze. "It could be . . . for a lesser man."

Her expression did not change. "But you're not a lesser man," she said huskily.

He smiled. "No, I'm not."

And with that, he rolled her over and undid the entire back of her gown, peeling aside the yellow silk like a husk. He kissed the nape of her neck, then traced his tongue down the bumpy ridge of her spine. He kissed her once on each buttock and gently turned her around.

Completely naked now, she watched him shed the restricting carapace of his clothes. Her eyes widened. Perfection he was: the sculpted beauty of a Greek masterpiece in the flesh. Imperial perfection marred only by the large deep scar running diagonally down the right side of his chest. Then her eyes fell, inexorably drawn to his manhood. A sound of disbelief rose from her throat.

"My God!" she whispered, unable to believe her eyes. "Take me!" Kenzie whispered hoarsely. "For the love of God, Hans! What are you waiting for? Take me before I can no longer stand it!"

Poised above the beckoning dark arrowhead of her pubis, Hannes looked down at her.

Her response was instinctual. Parting her legs in invitation, she rocked herself backward, bringing her knees to the sides of her head and holding them there.

Slowly he lowered himself, penetrating the petals of her sable-furred mound.

For a split second, Kenzie saw the cosmos explode. Then he was inside her. She jackknifed her legs and clamped them fiercely around his torso and held tight.

He began slowly, all the while kissing her sweetly on the lips, ears, eyes, neck, chin, breasts: anywhere his hungry mouth could reach while he thrust steadily in and out, in and out.

Beneath him, she writhed and lifted her hips to meet him, and so harmoniously were they fused that they achieved that perfect syncopation in which two entities thought, acted, and functioned as one.

Dazzling sensations washed over her, made her buoyant, sent her rising and dipping in the troughs of great oceanic swells.

"Oh, God!" she moaned, feeling the stirrings of orgasmic pleasure building up strength. "Oh, Hans! *Hans!*"

His tempo increased and she kept up the rhythm, thrashing and flopping wildly beneath him. Her head was whipping from side to side on the pillow, her hair in constant, frenzied motion.

"Faster!" she cried. "Oh, Hans! Hans, I'm going to come! I can't help it! I'm— I'm—"

Harder and faster, he now jammed into her, his hips bucking furiously.

"Here comes!" she cried. "Oh, Hans! *Hans—!*" And her cries and moans became screams of ecstasy.

Suddenly her entire body spasmed, worlds collided, and her final orgasm flung her out, out, out beyond the farthest constellations, drowning him in the flood of her juices.

The frenzy of her climax proved too much. Hannes's face contorted in agony as an exquisite pain rushed from the base of his spine. Rearing like a bull, he threw back his head and bellowed, simultaneously jettisoning his seed inside her.

Then his strength drained, the agony passed, and his eyes glazed. Together they collapsed, panting and still joined, into each other's arms, wracked by ever-decreasing seismic aftershocks.

They lay there quietly, eyes unfocused, waiting for their thundering hearts, runaway pulses, and rapid breaths to return to normal.

"Wow!" Kenzie finally whispered. "Now *that* was awesome!"

"Yes," he smiled, "that it was."

She snuggled closer, inhaling the heady, musky maleness of his sweat. With the tip of her tongue, she licked one of the sinewy, down-covered forearms which cradled her.

His skin was warm, and tasted tart and salty.

"Uh-oh," he said after a moment.

"What is it?"

He didn't need to reply. Her eyes widened as she felt the slumbering giant inside her once again beginning to stir.

"But you just *came!*" she exclaimed. "Hans! Don't tell me you're horny already?"

He laughed quietly. "It would appear so."

"Mmm," she murmured happily. "Then we'd best do something about it, don't you think?"

20

Chatter. Laughter.

For block after block, Zandra and Karl-Heinz dissected the evening—first the party, then the crowd at the club. But, finally, they could hardly contain their curiosity about one another.

At Fourteenth Street, the traffic light changed from green to yellow. The chauffeur gave a burst of speed and the Bentley surged through the swamped intersection, grandly parting water like the prow of a high-speed yacht. Then the big car slowed again, nosing sedately on up First Avenue, catching green lights all the way to Twenty-third.

"Zan—"

"Hei—"

They spoke at the same time, then simultaneously fell silent. Looking at each other, they burst into spontaneous laughter.

"Go on, Heinzie. You first!"

"No, you. Please."

"Oh, gosh. Well . . . I hope you enjoyed tonight. I mean . . ."

Karl-Heinz wished he could tell her how he really felt, how he was seeing her in a completely new light, how he felt drawn to her, compelled to get to know her better, but he thought the best course of action would be to keep it light. The last thing he wanted to do was scare her off.

"Zandra. Of course I had a good time. I had a wonderful time." He took one of her hands in his. "We'll have to do this again soon."

"Oh, Heinzie," she said, "I think . . . I think that would be fabulous. We've got so much to catch up on."

Her face, flickering in the passing lights, looked so innocent—so vulnerable and beautiful—that he felt the urge to put his arms around her. Instead, he asked, "And you, Zandra? Did you really enjoy tonight as much as I did? Dancing with your long-lost old cousin?"

"Oh, Heinzie, honestly," she laughed, "you're hardly *old*. And yes, I told you I enjoyed it. It was super." She thought, in fact, that she had not had so much fun for a very long time. That Heinzie was more than a little attractive, that he had qualities that she found . . . well, immensely seductive.

The Bentley pulled up in front of the Goldsmiths' pre-war, and the chauffeur came around and opened Zandra's door.

She reached over and placed a hand on Karl-Heinz's. "Don't get out, darling. I'll run for it. Can't wait to see you again." Then she gave him a quick chaste kiss on the cheek.

Karl-Heinz returned the kiss, also chaste. "Call you soon."

"Toodle-oo!" she called, and she was gone.

"Your Highness?"

"Yes . . . ?"

It was his chauffeur, awaiting instructions. "Where to now?"

"Where?" Karl-Heinz laughed. "Home, I guess."

When he let himself into his Auction Towers penthouse high above Burghley's, the telephone was chirruping.

Quickly locking the front door, he hurried through the foyer to answer it, knowing from experience that his valet would have retired for the night. For Josef was a manservant steeped in the grand old European tradition, and prided himself upon discretion and that uncanny knack of sensing exactly when to be around and when to make himself scarce.

Karl-Heinz's mouth twisted with irony. For once, Josef had seriously miscalculated. Tonight there would be no wine, no women, no song.

Reaching the nearest extension phone, he found a thick vellum card propped against it. Recognizing Josef's precise, old-fashioned script, he picked it up and scanned the message:

Your Highness,
   Princess Sofia has been calling repeatedly from Augsburg. She says an emergency has arisen.

Respectfully,

J.

Frowning, Karl-Heinz shot back his cuff. According to his gold Vacheron Constantin wristwatch, it would be eight a.m. in Germany, not too early to call his sister.

Although, he thought, listening to the relentless chirrups, *that's probably her calling right now.*

He picked up the receiver. "Yes?"

There was silence, then a hostile blurt of German: "Well! *Finally!*"

He sighed to himself. He had guessed correctly. It was his sister.

"*Ja,* Sofia?" he said wearily, automatically switching to the same language.

"I've been trying to get hold of you for hours," she complained. "*Hours!*" she repeated, as though he had not heard.

"I just walked in and was about to call you," he said calmly. "What is the emergency?"

But she wasn't through conveying her martyrdom. "Really, Heinzie," she sniffed. "As if I didn't have enough to contend with, I had to spend the entire night trying to track you down! In future, you might tell that abominable servant of yours—"

"Sofia . . ." His voice was low, but had a menacing edge to it.

She backed down. "It's Father," she said tersely. "He's had another stroke."

Everything inside Karl-Heinz came to a dead stop. It was a moment before he could speak. "How bad is it?"

"Bad enough for you to fly home."

And with that, Sofia hung up.

The LED numbers on the nightstand Westclox glowed 2:49 A.M.

Kenzie was back in her damp yellow Givenchy sheath. She was sitting on the edge of the bed, bending forward and stifling a yawn while slipping a foot first into her left shoe, then the right. Finally she stood up and wiggled both heels all the way in.

Hannes came out of the adjacent dressing room. He was a walking advertisement for Timberland: moleskin slacks, jacquard knit sweater, water-resistant leather field coat, and Gore-Tex-and-leather two-tone moccasins. He was holding a Burberry raincoat.

"It is still raining hard," he told her. "You had better wear this, or else you will catch cold."

He draped the raincoat around her shoulders with a flourish.

Kenzie smiled. "Thanks. I'll gladly borrow this, but really, Hans. You don't have to see me home. I'm perfectly capable—"

He placed a silencing finger against her lips. "No argument, Kenzie. I was taught one must see a lady home, and so I shall."

"My, a real gentleman," she mocked gently, basking in the warmth of old-fashioned chivalry. Then, catching sight of her reflection in a mirror, she fluffed her hair with her fingers. Turning back to him, she smiled brightly. "Well? Ready when you are!"

Armed with a furled umbrella, he cocked his elbow. "Shall we go?"

She slipped her arm through his. "You know something?" She gazed up at him, giving his arm an affectionate squeeze. "You really *are* the last of an endangered species!"

"A hopeless romantic," he agreed, nodding.

They took the elevator down, crossed the lobby, and stepped outside.

Reality hit—literally, in the form of buckets. It had gotten considerably colder, and a powerful wind was driving the downpour sideways, drenching them with a chill wet blast which flapped the overhead canopy like a sail and turned Hannes's umbrella inside out the moment he had it open.

"*Brrr!*" Kenzie said, clutching the lapels of the raincoat together. Not wasting a moment, she left Hannes to struggle with the umbrella, hurried to the curb, and scouted the sparse but swift oncoming traffic.

Lo and behold! There it was—that rarest of all Manhattan miracles—an unoccupied taxi on a rainy night.

Flapping out one arm, she jammed two fingers in her mouth and rent the night with a traffic-stopping whistle. Brakes screeching, the cab slammed to a halt. Leaping forward, she chucked open the rear door and dove inside. Hannes, tossing his useless umbrella into the gutter, dove in right after her.

"Eighty-first between First and Second," Kenzie said breathlessly.

The words were barely out of her mouth before the turbaned Sikh floored the accelerator.

The force of the takeoff pushed Kenzie and Hannes back in the seat—and they remained that way for the entire fourteen-minute ride—a hair-raising experience.

"Who's he think he is?" she moaned. "Aire Luyendyk at the Indy 100?"

But she had to hand it to him. Despite a dozen near misses, the Sikh swung them into Eighty-first Street in record time, in one piece—and in a hard, broadside skid.

"There, on the right!" Kenzie yelled. "By the—"

She braced herself as the cabbie stomped on the brakes, bringing the cab to a screeching, whiplash halt.

He turned around and beamed proudly. "Better than the Coney Island ride? Yes?"

"All I know is, somebody upstairs must be, ah, looking out for you," Kenzie said weakly.

Hannes struggled out of his field coat. "Keep the meter running," he told the cabbie, and tented the coat over his head. He opened his door, jumped out into the downpour, and dashed around the cab to Kenzie's side. Then, sheltering her under the water-resistant leather, he ran her to the front gate and up the steps of her brownstone, where the recessed entry with its twin carriage lights offered protection from the elements.

Hannes lowered his coat and shook off the water while Kenzie rummaged inside her little evening bag. Before she could produce her keys, he had his arms around her and was pulling her close.

She looked up at him in surprise, the Burberry sliding off her shoulders, the better for him to grab a handful of buttocks.

"Hannes!" she laughed, pretending shock. "Stop that!"

He pressed his lips to her neck.

She made a halfhearted attempt to push him away. "The cabbie's probably watching!"

"So?" He raised his head and grinned. "Why deprive the poor man the pleasure?"

"You *are* incorrigible!"

"Am I?"

And before she could respond, he covered her mouth with his. Greedily now, she pressed herself against him and slipped her arms around his neck, their tongues dancing an impromptu dervish.

Ah, she thought, how pliant she was in the arms of this beautiful man she knew so very intimately, and yet not at all!

When their lips parted, he raised his head slowly, pale eyes searching her upturned face.

"Before we part here on your doorstep, tell me something, Kenzie."

She stared up at him. He had fallen momentarily silent, then stroked her cheek gracefully with his fingertips.

That simple touch set off a chain reaction of sensations, sudden delicious thrills rippling down her spine and along her extremities. But the playfulness was gone from his eyes and lips; he was regarding her with a calm solemnity, with a gaze so intent it was as if he were reaching deep inside her.

"Is tonight only the beginning?" he asked softly. "Or is it the end?"

She caught her breath, unable to tear her eyes off that masterfully sculpted face. Bathed as it was in the brightness of the carriage lights, it seemed to glow with an inner radiance all its own.

A tightness came up in her throat. Damn. Not only did he have all the right moves, but he had all the right words, too.

"Well, Kenzie? Which is it to be?"

She continued to stare at him.

Noises. She was aware of the turbulent rushing of her bloodstream. The hammering of her pulse. A mad thundering she knew to be her heart.

And Hannes, motionless, the cause of all these amped-up emotions, was still staring at her. Irresistibly. Hypnotically.

And lowering his head, he rewarded her with another kiss.

Forgotten now was the waiting taxicab and its running meter, the diagonal sheets of wind-driven rain behind them, the key ring in her open evening bag. So lost was she in him, and he in her, that nothing else on earth either mattered or existed—not the slam of a nearby car door, nor the approaching sound of footsteps on pavement, nor even the squeaking of the front gate as it was being pushed open.

"Aw right, ya lovebirds! Knock it off—"

The male voice, cutting sharply through the rain, sent Kenzie jumping back from Hannes. She whipped around—only to be blinded by a high-powered flashlight.

Squinting, she raised an arm to shield her eyes. "Ch-Charley . . . ?" she called out into the brilliant, colorless void. "That you?"

"Sorry to break up the party, folks."

Now there was no doubt in her mind. It *was* him—Charley Ferraro, her on-again/off-again, self-proclaimed "no-strings-attached" lover!

Right, she thought wryly. *No strings attached. So what the hell's he doing here?*

Well, we'll know soon enough, she muttered darkly to herself.

Stepping in front of Hannes, she placed her hands on her hips and waited, face averted, until Charley had climbed the front steps. Only after he lowered the flashlight did she turn to him. Coronas of light, like double-exposed film, still swam in her vision.

"And what are *you* doing here?" She quivered in outrage while her eyes, seething with indignation, raked him from head to toe.

Instead of replying, he flipped out his badge.

For a moment, Kenzie's jaw actually dropped. "Would you kindly," she snapped, glaring at him with righteous fury, "explain what the *hell* you think you're up to?"

It was as if he hadn't heard. "Who's this?" Charley played the beam on Hannes's face. "C'mon, buddy." He held out his other hand. "Let's see ya cough up some ID."

"Now just wait a goddamn minute!" Kenzie objected, bristling. "Charley, you've got absolutely no right rousting innocent people. So why don't you switch off that obnoxious flashlight, put that badge back in your pocket, and go fuck off!"

"Ma'am?" Once again, he directed the beam of light into her eyes. She averted her face, but not quickly enough. "You lookin' for a disorderly conduct summons?"

"A *what* . . . ?"

She suddenly felt as if all the oxygen had been sucked out of her and the heat of a terrible anger, like some overpoweringly combustible gas, was filling her to bursting. It was all she could do not to explode.

Breathe deeply, she advised herself. *Keep your cool . . .* She reminded herself that he was jealous and on a power trip. *And hiding behind his badge, the goddamn creep!*

"Get that light out of my eyes," she demanded quietly. *"Now."*

The authority in her voice surprised even herself. It must have surprised Charley too, for he instantly complied.

"Kenzie?" Hannes's voice came from right behind her. "I assume you know this gentleman?"

"*Gentleman!*" She snorted her contempt. "That's certainly elevating him! But to answer your question," she sighed, "yes, I know him." And flashing Charley a look of sheer disgust, she added, "Or rather, I should say I *used* to know him—but that was before he signed up for the Gestapo."

Charley ignored her jibe. Hand still extended, he said, "Hey, buddy.

Thought I asked to see some ID." Furling and unfurling his fingers to show he was serious. "C'mon. Make it snappy."

Hannes stared at him coldly.

Charley stared right back.

The air crackled with bad vibrations.

"Oh, Christ!" stewed Kenzie. "Just what I need—a pissing contest in the middle of the night!" Moving away from both of them, she slumped wearily against the wall. "Hans," she said tiredly, "would you please show Dirty Harry here some identification? Maybe then, God willing, he'll be satisfied, and hopefully get lost?"

In short order, Hannes produced his wallet and handed over his international driver's license. Observed Charley running his flashlight over it. Couldn't miss the way he looked suddenly taken aback, as if acting out the word *Whoa!* "You Hannes Hockert?" he asked.

Hannes nodded. "Yes," he said.

"*The* Hannes Hockert?"

Kenzie frowned. *Now what can Charley have meant by that?* she wondered, staring over at Hannes. *Have I found myself a tennis champ? Or maybe even some European racecar driver?*

"Would somebody," she spoke up in exasperation, "please fill me in on what, exactly, is going on here?"

Hannes was sliding something else out of his wallet, so she pushed herself away from the wall to have a look.

As it turned out, he was neither a Grand Prix driver nor a tennis champ, at least not according to his identification.

Interpol! Kenzie thought with a sinking heart. *Wouldn't you know it—a cop! As if one in my life isn't enough, I have to go out and find myself another!*

"Well, what a coincidence," Charley was saying in amazement, his voice real nice and warm now. He promptly switched off the flashlight and handed Hannes both his IDs. "I'm Charles Ferraro."

Now it was Hannes's turn to stare. "*You* are the policeman from the New York art theft squad?" he asked in disbelief. "The one I am assigned to work with over the next year?"

Charley grinned. "The one and only," he said, holding out his hand.

And Kenzie, suddenly relegated to the sidelines, gnashed her teeth in frustration. Having witnessed their turf war, she wasn't about to stick around for the sole purpose of being excluded from the only thing on earth more powerful, and infinitely more exclusive, than male bonding: *cop bonding.*

Kicking aside Hannes's Burberry, she snatched her keys out of her bag, unlocked the front door, and flounced inside. Peeved, she slammed it shut and tromped heavily up the stairs.

Briefly she wondered whether either of them had noticed her departure.

Not that it mattered. *They* could play all the macho games they wanted.

Tomorrow was a workday. *She* was going to bed!

21

The following morning, the prevailing westerly had scrubbed the sky clean. At nine past six, the sun rose gloriously over Manhattan, anointing the glass ziggurats, apartment châteaux, and cat's cradle bridges with undiluted sunshine. The puddles dried up and there was a brisk autumnal nip in the air.

Kenzie's alarm clock jarred her awake after five and a half hours of sleep.

On her way to work, she darted into a coffee shop for a cup of regular and a bagel to go. Belatedly remembered she didn't have a dime, thanks to Charley's stiffing her for order-out Burmese. Cursing him under her breath, she headed on to work, resigned to drinking the vile brew from the communal coffee urn.

Fortunately, Arnold Li took pity on her. He insisted she borrow forty dollars until payday. She gave him her equivalent of a papal blessing, but he shrugged off her thanks.

"It's the reast I can do," he quipped, launching into his routine. "Must prease new boss. Right, missy? Chop-chop!"

"I'm not the new boss," she gloomed, proceeding to impart the news of Bambi Parker's promotion.

If she expected shock and outrage, it wasn't forthcoming. Arnold took the disclosure remarkably well.

"Look on the bright side," he smiled, reverting to his perfect English. "At least it gets you off the hook."

"Hook? What hook?"

"You just wait and see," Arnold predicted cheerfully. "She'll nuke herself in no time. I give her six months, max. Sooner or later, the position's yours anyway. And in the meantime, since you're *not* the boss, you're saved the aggravation of having to give her the ax. See? You'll have your cake and be able to eat it, too."

Popping out for a container of decent coffee and a bagel, Kenzie pondered Arnold's wisdom.

He could be right, she thought. *Then again . . .*

Trouble was, she had no way of telling.

Least not yet.

* * *

Bambi Parker drifted into Burghley's at half past ten. The first thing she did was head to The Club. She silenced the powder room and announced her promotion.

Squeals of congratulations followed.

Twenty minutes later, she moseyed along to Mr. Spotts's vacated office.

At eleven, Zachary Bavosa, the attorney from Calvert, Barkhorn, Waldburger, and Slocum, arrived on behalf of his anonymous client. In tow were two armed security guards, one of whom carried a slim, briefcaselike crate containing the Holbein.

Bambi perused the painting. Small but magnificent, it depicted a girl with flowers and a spaniel. Moreover, it seemed genuine, and the sales receipt from 1946 looked in order.

What more could she ask for?

A second opinion.

However, she wasn't about to summon Kenzie or Arnold. *They'd only waste days, even weeks, trying to find fault with the picture or its provenance,* she thought. *Who needs that? Besides,* I'm *in charge now.* I'm *calling the shots.*

Right then and there, Bambi came to a decision.

"We'll be happy to handle the sale," she assured the attorney with her best smile, and called down to Consignments.

A few minutes later, one of the girls from The Club came up to usher Zachary Bavosa, the security guards, and the Holbein downstairs, where the appropriate paperwork would be filled out, and the painting locked in one of the walk-in vaults.

Twice that morning, Charley Ferraro called Kenzie at work.

And twice she hung up on him.

Keeping his cool, he decided to wait a few days before trying her again. Given time, he was certain she would come around.

At noon, he met Hannes Hockert for lunch at Wollensky's Grill, where they dug into the prime ribs with the same gusto as they discussed international transportation of stolen art, and the increasingly wily methods used by smugglers. In passing, he happened to mention that Kenzie was employed at Burghley's.

After lunch, Hannes decided to give her a call.

His greeting, also, was met with chill silence and a click.

She'd hung up on him, too.

Four thousand miles away, Karl-Heinz's jet landed at Munich airport and taxied to a remote apron, where an executive helicopter awaited. Also on hand were officials from customs and immigration, who waived the usual formalities.

Twenty minutes later, the helicopter put down on the grounds of an exclusive private hospital in the picturesque foothills of the Bavarian Alps.

The director of the facility personally escorted Karl-Heinz to Intensive Care. There, he found his sister, Princess Sofia, keeping vigil at their comatose father's bedside.

"How is he?" Karl-Heinz asked, coming into the room and bending down to kiss her on the cheek.

His lips met air; Sofia was already on her feet, snatching up her things. She was a study in protected and endangered species: leopard (hat and coat), black alligator (oversized handbag and shoes), and ivory (necklace, ear clips, and bracelet).

"It's about time you arrived!" she snapped. "I've been alone with him for twelve hours straight. I suppose I should *thank* you for relieving me?"

Heels clacking, she marched to the door, swung it open, and then paused and turned to him. "Welcome home," she said bitterly.

And the door closed behind her.

Karl-Heinz felt drained. Two minutes with Sofia was a lifetime of torture. Small wonder her husband had developed a knack for disappearing at just the right moment. *Marriage to her must be a fate worse than death.*

Slowly, heavily, he lowered himself into the chair she had vacated and focused his attention upon the patient.

Who . . . ?

There was a momentary sense of disorientation, of having wandered into the wrong door, which only added to his confusion. He blinked his eyes rapidly, then hunched forward and stared anew at the shrunken, unmoving stranger on life support.

Either I'm in the wrong room, or someone's made a terrible mistake, he thought . . .

. . . for what other explanation could there be since this curiously sexless, translucent-skinned creature was not his father? No. This was not the once-vital man from whose loins he had sprung. *It cannot be. I must summon the doctors, tell them there has been a mix-up . . .*

But of course, there hadn't been. It *was* him. His father. The old prince. *The merest ghost of him, perhaps, but him nonetheless . . .*

Wrapping his arms around his chest, Karl-Heinz closed his eyes. *How wretchedly cruel life can be!* he kept thinking.

The hours crept by. Periodically, doctors and nurses came and went on soundless crepe soles, checking the tubes and monitors, moving the comatose body to avoid its getting bed sores, holding whispered conferences while consulting charts. Last night's glittering soiree at the Met seemed a million light years in the past, his only memory of it reduced to but a single powerful thought: *If only Zandra were here beside me . . .*

* * *

Zandra, unaware of Karl-Heinz's departure and the crisis which precipitated it, reported to Burghley's at precisely ten o'clock in the morning. She spent an hour being processed by personnel, filled out an application for a green card, and received a two-week advance on her paycheck, as well as a check-cashing card for use at the nearest Citibank.

Then Kenzie, only too happy to get off the phone—she was hanging up on Charley for the second time that day and had already hung up on Hannes once—showed her to their shared office, where she introduced Arnold Li.

He rose politely from behind his desk. "Herro," he said solemnly, shaking Zandra's hand and giving his best Asian bow. "Prease caw me Arnod. Rov'ry to meet you."

For a moment he had Zandra fooled.

"Don't be taken in by that routine," Kenzie said with a touch of exasperation. "He speaks perfect American English. If you want my advice, don't even hesitate—whenever he starts, just tell him to shut up."

"I will do." And Zandra turned to Arnold and said, "Shut up."

They all three burst into laughter, and their friendship was cemented right then and there.

For Zandra, that first day at Burghley's flew by in a blur. This was what she had always wanted. A real job, where she would be earning her keep while doing something constructive. No other employment ever after could compare, of that she was certain.

And how amazing that it should be in a field so familiar to her, as if her entire life, spent among the masterpieces in her various relatives' stately homes, had been in preparation for this very position!

Any self-doubts concerning her abilities disappeared on that first day. At last, she had found her niche in the working world. And how familiar, this singular atmosphere of riches and breeding! And yet how unstuffy and wonderfully casual, especially compared to that stiff-upper-lip world she had left behind. She felt like a caged bird must after it had been set free and allowed to soar.

She loved it here. She adored it. In fact, she couldn't imagine working anywhere else. Even the most mundane of tasks seemed novel and exciting.

Kenzie and Arnold introduced her to employees of various other sections, and explained the fundamentals of how the Old Masters department operated. They gave her stacks of past auction catalogues and sale results lists, so that she might compare estimates versus actual prices. Finally, they took her down to the vast, climate-controlled, subterranean vaults to view the three hundred twelve lots which would comprise the next Old Masters auction.

And it was there, surrounded by the staggering profusion of paintings, that Zandra surprised Kenzie and Arnold—and most of all herself—

with knowledge she was not even aware she possessed: "Oh. Gosh. An *Oudry*. He was *terribly* good at these sweet little animals, wasn't he?"

And: "Definitely French School. Eighteenth century. Her dress is the clue. I'd say the sitter was definitely English."

And: "Oh, *bugger* it! Why *ever* did they restore this? Makes it much less desirable, don't you think?"

And: "What an absolutely *marvelous* still life. Cristofaro Munari, unless my eyes deceive me . . . should fetch a *fortune.*"

And: "My *goodness!* However did *that* slip in? Patent fake, I'm afraid. Best check the provenance thoroughly. Someone's *bound* to have cooked it up."

She caught Arnold and Kenzie staring at her with open mouths.

"Oh. Sorry! I must be *barmy*. I didn't mean to be presumptuous or try to show off. Gosh no. It's just that my dreary relatives all have such *frightfully* huge collections—"

"It's not that," Arnold explained gently. "It's just that after Bambi Parker, we didn't expect someone this fired-up, let alone knowledgeable."

He was so sweet that Zandra was thoroughly charmed, and a faint blush colored her cheeks. "Bambi Parker?" She frowned. "Should I know her?"

"You will," Kenzie assured her dryly, "you will. God! I don't know how that painting got past us," she fretted anxiously. "But now that you mentioned it—"

"Don't *worry*, darling," Zandra said. "I'll get on it first thing. Oh. And what's the best newspaper for flat listings?"

"You mean apartments?"

Zandra nodded. "I'll be needing my own place."

"Well, unless you're independently wealthy, good luck," Kenzie said. "For all the prestige, working here doesn't exactly buy you champagne and caviar." She added dryly, "Rice and beans is more like it."

"So what do you suggest? I'll be needing a place to live."

"How fussy are you?"

"On my budget? A room with kitchen and bath privileges will suit me fine. So long as it's on the cheap."

"Well . . . I'm looking for a roommate," Kenzie said slowly.

"Brilliant!"

"Not so fast. Before you take the plunge, I think you'd better drop by and check it out for yourself."

"May I? After work all right?"

"After work's fine. But I've got to warn you. You're going to be awfully disappointed."

Zandra smiled. "Somehow I seriously doubt that."

At noon, Zandra dashed to Citibank, where she cashed her advance on her paycheck and opened a checking account. Lunch was a deli sandwich grabbed on the run, and the rest of the afternoon was spent examining the suspect painting and investigating its provenance, a painstaking process of tracing its ownership backward through time.

Zandra found it exhilarating, more like playing detective than working.

At quitting time, she walked home with Kenzie to check out her apartment.

"I'm afraid you're used to a lot better," Kenzie murmured as she tackled the last of the five locks. The tumbler clicked, she pushed on the door, reached around the jamb, and hit the lights. "After you."

Once inside, Zandra craned her neck this way and that.

"*Kenzie!* It's *terrif!* So grand, and yet almost *English* in comfort. Gosh. However did you do it?"

Flipping on lights as she went, Kenzie showed her around: ". . . Here's your basic, out-of-date Manhattan kitchen . . . circa 1920s bathroom . . . *my* bedroom—"

Zandra peeked inside. "Oh, but it's positively *dee-voon*. And so wonderfully welcoming. I *do* love cozy rooms. They're *so* intimate."

"Small, you mean." Kenzie smiled, shrugging. "But what can I say? The price is right." She opened the door across the hall and stepped aside. "And this," she said, "ta-*da!*—is the spare bedroom. It would be yours. Hopefully, you won't mind its being furnished."

Zandra went inside and looked around. It was, she thought, surely the most delightfully eclectic room she had ever seen.

"All auction sleepers I picked up for a song," Kenzie explained with a sheepish grin. "As you can see, I'm a sucker for bargains."

"Oh, but it's absolutely *marvelous*. I'd love to take it. Gosh, there I go again—being *awfully* presumptuous . . . I should say, I'll take it if *you're* willing to have *me*."

"Have you!" Kenzie looked taken aback. "Of course I'll have you," she said staunchly. "Why wouldn't I?"

TARGET: BURGHLEY'S COUNTDOWN TO TERROR

Nowhere, Nevada, November 22

It was not the name of the place; there was simply nothing else for miles around.

The old Texaco filling station on this lonely, mountainous stretch of U.S. Highway 95, halfway between Vegas and Reno, had stood derelict for close to a decade now.

But tonight, two different vehicles, each arriving separately, had pulled into the overgrown island where gas pumps had once ruled proud. After dousing their headlamps, they drove stealthily on around back, where they were hidden from view of any motorists who happened by.

The Jeep Cherokee had been driven up from Vegas.

The four-by-four pickup had come down from Reno.

Here, in the middle of nowhere, they parked side by side, but facing in opposite directions so the drivers had only to roll down their windows with leather-seamed hands.

Both were alone. And both looked as they had in Macao, human only in form. Jumpsuited and hooded, faces rendered insectile by convex black lenses and strapped-on electronic voice distorters—like Saturday matinee aliens, but lethal as all hell.

The man in the Cherokee was the first to speak. "What have you to report?" His altered monosyllabic words had a metallic, robotic edge.

"Of the ten specialists you requested," came the equally synthesized reply, "all have been contacted. Five have already arrived at the safe house. That includes the first of the four prison inmates. We sprang him just last week."

"The helicopter escape from the Mexican prison yard?"

"That is the one. Ortez. We smuggled him across the Texas border that very same day."

Laughter rasped like a scythe on rusty metal.

"Damn fools are still turning Mexico upside down looking for him!"

"And the three still in prison?"

"We are working on that. The one in Colombia and the one in Turkey are as good as sprung. But the IRA explosives expert is another story. That British prison is like a fortress. I take it there is still no timetable?"

"Not yet, but there will be as soon as our friend in England is freed. Everything hinges upon him."

"Can no one else do it?"

"No!" The man in the Cherokee shook his head adamantly. Explosives experts were a dime a dozen, but the Irishman was the only one he could trust to do this particular job. Donough Kildare was an artist in his trade, and could detonate entire buildings using a few ordinary household materials.

Materials so innocuous that they would pass unnoticed before even the most suspicious and skillful team of arson investigators in the world.

An accident! he would instruct the Irishman. That is what it must look like! That is the conclusion the investigators and analysts and adjusters who will sift through the rubble have to come to! A verdict of accidental death—

—accidental! Nothing less would do, for this explosion was the foundation—the very cornerstone!—of the entire operation. The "accident" had to occur for the timetable to begin!

One fiery chance. That was all the Irishman would be permitted, or else all the intricate plotting and planning would have been a waste, the entire operation aborted.

"It has to be Kildare!" the Cherokee driver reiterated harshly. "There can be no substitute! You must get him!"

The other nodded. "And the target?"

"You do not want to know!" reverberated the reply. "Advance knowledge of that carries an automatic sentence of death!"

Strident amplified breaths punctuated the warning, rasped distortedly. Then: "And the Irishman?" the driver of the pickup asked. "He will be privy to that information. After he has served his purpose, what is to become of him?"

"What do you think? Dead men tell no tales."

The one in the pickup nodded approvingly. "And the ten million he has coming? What happens to that?"

"That is a little bonus we shall split between us two. But remember! You must deliver the goods! The Irishman is the key! Unless you can spring him, the entire operation will be cancelled." There was a pause. "Is that understood?"

"Roger."

"Good. Then we are in agreement. Now, if there is nothing else, we can leave. I will keep in touch by the usual method."

Taking that as his cue, the driver of the pickup started his engine and put the vehicle into gear. Slowly, without lights, he drove around to the front of the filling station. Looked both ways.

Highway 95 stretched empty in either direction.

Cramping the steering column hard to the right, he stepped on the gas. Only after the pickup jumped onto the asphalt did he switch on his brights. Then, chasing the swath of his headlights, he listened to Tammy Wynette stand by her man as he sped north through the night.

North, back to Reno. Back to "The Biggest Little City in the World."

The driver of the Cherokee waited a few minutes before starting his engine. Pocketing his dark shades, he used his night vision and four-wheel drive to bounce around to the side of the old Texaco station. There, he stopped, looked, and listened.

He could see the lights of a northward-bound car approaching from far off to the south, and waited patiently until it had whooshed past. Then, swinging a hard left, he hit the halogens and floored the accelerator.

The Cherokee gobbled up the miles as he headed south.

South, back to Vegas. Back to that garish, neon-painted whore in the middle of the Mojave.

A hundred-and-fifty-odd miles and he would be there.

Book Two

STATES OF THE ART

Dispute Surrounds Planned
Sale of a Holbein

NEW YORK, Jan. 9 (AP)—Burghley's yesterday maintained that it would proceed with the sale this month of a painting whose provenance has come under fire from dealers and auction house experts on both sides of the Atlantic.

The painting, Hans Holbein the Younger's *Girl With Flowers and a Spaniel* is an 18¼ by 12½-inch portrait painted during the artist's second stay in England, after 1532.

While many experts say the work was stolen from a castle near Darmstadt after World War II, Burghley's maintains it has sworn evidence that the painting had actually been sold to an American military officer, who has since died, and whose heirs have put it up for sale.

Allison Steele, Burghley's chief operating officer for North America, said that under the law, the seller and not the auction house guarantees the title of a work of art. Sheldon D. Fairey, Burghley's chairman, president, and chief auctioneer, was traveling yesterday, and could not be reached for comment. . . .

22

"*G*oddammit! Surely *somebody* in this room is responsible for this disaster!"

The thundering from inside the conference room burst through the closed door like a warning. Kenzie, hand on the knob, fortified herself with a deep breath. Then, willing herself small, unimportant, *invisible,* she turned the knob and slipped inside.

The mahogany blinds were angled against the wintry sun, and seated at the head of the long table, Sheldon D. Fairey was a commanding silhouette against the cold slats of horizontal light.

"How the hell a mess of this . . . this *stupefying* magnitude could occur to begin with is entirely beyond me . . ."

Kenzie soundlessly shut the door and tiptoed to the far end of the conference table, where he and his small, captive audience were clustered.

". . . but occur it has, and we are faced not only with a legal and public relations debacle, but an incident which has sparked a diplomatic crisis between the United States and Germany! I find this situation quite intolerable."

His audience flinched, but whether or not he even noticed was impossible to tell. For, like a beast catching a whiff of fresh prey, he slowly swiveled around on the ergonomic armchair from which, thanks to Dina Goldsmith, he was now forced to preside, and turned his flinty eyes in Kenzie's direction.

"Ah, the prodigal Ms. Turner, unless my eyes deceive me."

Kenzie froze, one tiptoeing foot ridiculously poised in midair.

"How kind of you to honor us with your presence," he said mockingly. "I haven't, by any chance, *inconvenienced* you by calling this meeting?"

Kenzie flushed brightly. "No, sir. Sorry I'm late."

He waited, but no excuse was forthcoming, which seemed to pacify him. "Please sit down, Ms. Turner."

"Yes, sir." Kenzie lowered her foot and darted the last few steps to the table, where she pulled out the empty chair beside Zandra's and quickly sat down. One look around confirmed her worst suspicions.

This was definitely a power meet. All the big wheels were out in full force.

Allison Steele, Burghley's chief operating officer. David W. Bunker, Jr., senior vice president. Ileane K. Ochsenberg, senior in-house counsel. Eunice Ffolkes, head of public relations. Fred Cummings, the chief comptroller. Plus the crew from Old Masters: Bambi Parker, Arnold Li, Zandra, and now Kenzie.

Sheldon D. Fairey was looking down the table at her. "As I was telling your colleagues, Ms. Turner, I received a call from the secretary of state. You wouldn't, by any chance, be able to venture a guess as to what we discussed?"

"Yes, sir. It's got to concern the Holbein."

"Very good." Fairey smiled a little, or rather, bared some teeth. "I was informed," he sighed, "that the German ambassador has lodged an official complaint over the sale of a stolen national treasure. Also, that at the general prosecutor's office in Frankfurt, the German Cultural Institute has filed a criminal charge of theft against person or persons unknown."

"Ouch." Kenzie winced.

"Ouch, indeed." Resting his manicured hands on the tabletop, Fairey laced his fingers and looked down, ostensibly inspecting his knuckles. "Tell me something, Ms. Turner. You were one of Mr. Spotts's bright young protégées." Raising his head, he once again glanced at her and made eye contact. "Would you be so kind as to tell us how you, personally, would rectify this appalling situation?"

Kenzie didn't hesitate. "Well, that's easy enough," she said. "We don't really have a choice, do we? I mean, that painting should never have been accepted for consignment in the first place. If you'll recall, I circulated a memo last November in which I detailed its shaky provenance, and argued that we either do not proceed with the sale, or at least hold off on it until the provenance could be established beyond all doubt. The memo was cosigned by both Mr. Li and Ms. von Hohenburg-Willemlohe."

"Yes, yes, yes," Fairey said testily. "But that's all water under the bridge. What I want to know is, what course of action would you take *now?*"

"The way I see it, we are faced with two unalterable facts. One: the painting was accepted for consignment. And two: it's featured right on the catalogue cover." Kenzie picked up a copy from in front of her and held it up. "There's no escaping this. The harm's already been done." She tossed the catalogue back down. "In my opinion, the most we can hope for is to contain the fallout."

"You mean, by withdrawing it from the auction."

"Yes, sir. And publicizing our intent to pursue a further investigation of its provenance. I'm afraid anything less would ... well, to put it bluntly, sir, would give the impression that we deal in stolen plunder."

Fairey grimaced at the last two words. "Well?" he asked, glancing around the table. "Would anyone like to comment on Ms. Turner's evaluation?"

"Yes," Allison Steele said. "Ms. Turner, isn't it possible that you might be reacting with undue haste and alarm?"

Kenzie shook her head. "On the contrary, Ms. Steele. In this particular case, I don't believe we can act hastily enough. And as far as alarm is concerned, I wasn't the one who called this emergency meeting."

There was no refuting that, and an uncomfortable silence hung in the room.

"We have a lot riding on that painting," Fred Cummings, the comptroller, spoke up. "First and foremost, there's the presale estimate of twenty-five million. If the painting's withdrawn from the auction, we lose two-and-a-half million in buyer's commission, and the same amount in seller's." He tapped the notepad with the end of the pen. "That's an outright loss of five million dollars. More, if it would sell above the estimate."

"With all due respect, Mr. Cummings," Kenzie countered, "but I have to disagree."

"Oh?"

"Yes," Kenzie nodded. "You're calculating on the assumption that the painting *will* reach its reserve price and sell. However, we all know that lots in every auction, even important lots, often go unsold. In other words, you're not talking about a bird in the hand, but about two in the bush. According to my calculations, Burghley's won't suffer any loss if we withdraw the Holbein, for the simple reason that we have no guarantee it will sell."

"True," Cummings conceded. He put down his pen, carefully aligned it with the edge of the notepad, and frowned. "But we must also remember that the Holbein is the star of this sale. Without it, a lot of important buyers are going to stay away."

"Yes," Kenzie agreed, "they might. But I feel that's a risk we're going to have to take."

"Even if it means shrinking the presale estimate from a hundred and twenty million down to ninety-five?"

"Yes."

"Ms. Turner," David Bunker, the senior vice president, said in a plummy voice. "Is it not true that without the Holbein, if other items in the sale go for below their estimates, or some do not sell at all, our actual sales figures could be much *lower* than the revised estimate of ninety-five million?"

She was beginning to feel like a witness undergoing interrogation. "That could very well be the case. Yes, sir."

"And you are resigned to the fact that, next to Christie's and Sotheby's, our Old Masters totals for the season might . . . er . . . turn out to be spectacularly awful?"

"That's right."

"The shareholders won't be pleased," he murmured with a vinegary expression.

"No," Kenzie agreed, "I expect they won't."

It was like hearing the voice of doom. In the ensuing silence, there was no sound other than the ominous ticking of the longcase Dutch staartklok between the windows. Then, as if someone was slowly turning up the volume, the harsh sounds of the city filtered through the double-glazed windows: the honks of perpetually gridlocked traffic, the wails of converging sirens, the high-pitched screams of a car alarm, a jet scratching its way across the sky.

Finally, Sheldon D. Fairey cleared his throat, and the noises of the city once again receded. "David's brought up a valid point," he said. "Ms. Turner, indulge me, if you will. What would *you* tell a roomful of angry shareholders?"

Kenzie locked eyes with him. "Why not the truth?" she said bluntly.

"The truth!" There was chiding mockery in the rich fruity tones, in the strained, unpleasant little smile. "Surely, Ms. Turner, you are not as naive as all that! Unless, of course, shareholders suddenly care more about 'the truth,' as you call it, than about their quarterly dividends?"

"They might care," Kenzie declared, "if somebody told them how our coming out of this crisis—reputation intact—is directly linked to their profits!"

Her face was obstinate, passionate, almost childlike in its shining intensity.

"Pray do continue," he murmured, steepling his fingers and tapping them against his lips.

Kenzie raked a hand through her hair. "I mean, my God, sir!" she burst out, rolling back her chair and jumping to her feet. "Think about it! What's the financial loss from *one* item compared to Burghley's single most precious asset, its reputation? That—nearly three hundred years of unblighted consumer confidence—is the thing we must protect at all costs, everything else be damned!"

To make her point, she brought her fist crashing down on the table. Then, suddenly aware of how carried away she'd gotten, she blushed and quickly sat back down.

"Sorry," she said in a tiny voice.

"A moment or two longer, Ms. Turner, and I do believe you would have had me bidding for the Brooklyn Bridge."

Fairey no longer sounded angry, and his altered mood seemed to soften the hard, wintry light bounced back by the table's mirrorlike, calamander veneer.

"Perhaps you should address the next shareholders meeting for me?"

"Thank you, but I'd rather not, sir," she murmured.

Fairey permitted himself a faint smile. "I cannot say I blame you," he said. "At any rate, your impassioned plea has been duly noted. Keeping Burghley's reputation untarnished *should* be our first priority. Well, then." He looked at the others. "Anyone have anything to add? Eunice?"

"From the standpoint of public relations, I'd have to side with Ms. Turner," said the director of public relations. "Taking the Holbein off the market is certainly in our best interests."

Fairey looked at Ileane Ochsenberg. "What about the legal ramifications? Say the painting's withdrawn from the sale, but further investigation proves it to be plunder. Could we, in any way, be held liable for trafficking in stolen goods?"

"Not at all." Ileane shook her head. "As you know, under the law the seller, and not his agent, guarantees the title to the work. Therefore, under normal circumstances the seller would be held liable. However, in this instance the painting was inherited, and since the person who originally acquired it is dead, there is no culprit to convict. An heir cannot be held culpable."

"Good, good." Sheldon D. Fairey tossed his splendid silver-coiffed head. "Then that lets us all off the hook." Fairey was silent for a moment, then leaned back in his chair and frowned. "Which leaves us with one last dilemma. Our ethical duty to our client." He pursed his lips. "After all, it was one of our employees who accepted the painting for consignment."

"And?" Ileane looked at him questioningly.

"Well, what worries me is, won't withdrawing it from the auction be construed as deserting our client in order to save our own skins?"

"I don't see why it should," Ileane said. "We accepted the painting in good faith, and had every reason to believe that our client had free and clear title to it. It's not our fault that he didn't. Nor is this the first time something like this has ever happened."

"And it won't be the last," gloomed David Bunker, the senior vice president. "But at least we're not alone."

"Indeed not." Ileane pushed her glasses farther up her nose. "There are countless legal precedents . . . that Joachim Wtewael, which Sotheby's had to withdraw from their London sale . . . the ongoing dispute over the Sevso silver, which both the former Yugoslavia and Hungary are claiming as theirs."

"Not to mention our own problems over the Kálimnos Kouros, back in 1982," Fairey murmured.

Ileane smiled. "I purposely left that one out," she confessed. "But to continue. Our first indication that the Holbein may have been illegally procured was a result of Ms. von Hohenburg-Willemlohe's research. We then immediately corresponded with our client's legal representative, stating that we couldn't go ahead with the sale unless it was cleared by the proper German authorities."

"Which," Fairey muttered, "it subsequently was. Only now they've obviously had second thoughts."

"I'm afraid so," Ileane said. "But we have copies of every piece of correspondence, all of which prove that we are above reproach."

"Also," David Bunker interjected, "don't forget that we—on our client's behalf—were the ones who initially contacted the Cultural Institute about it. We brought the Holbein to their attention, not vice versa."

Ileane nodded. "Of course, that's standard operating procedure in such cases. It gives the original owner the opportunity to purchase the work at a special price before it goes on the auction block. However, the reply we received from the Cultural Institute was that the museum could not afford to buy it, and that we should proceed with the sale."

"Famous last words," Fairey growled.

"Indeed. Still, there's a bright side," Ileane pointed out. "Aside from the unprofessional manner in which the consignment was initially accepted, our subsequent dealings in this matter will hold up to the closest scrutiny . . . and that includes any and all legal and ethical questions which may arise."

"You're certain?" Fairey asked sharply.

"Oh, absolutely." Ileane nodded definitely.

"Still, taking it on in the first place was skating on very thin ice," Fairey said. "This would never have occurred under Mr. Spotts."

Everyone was silent.

He raised his head magisterially. "In order to avoid such future fiascos, until further notice, any major work accepted for auction by the Old Masters department must be agreed upon by committee. Specifically, that means *three* out of the department's four employees must approve any work of art valued in excess of one hundred thousand dollars." His eyes roved from Kenzie to Zandra, and then from Arnold to Bambi, on whom they rested accusingly. "Have I made myself clear?"

They all nodded and murmured their agreement.

"Good." He sat back. "Then I would like to take this opportunity to commend Ms. Turner, Ms. von Hohenburg-Willemlohe, and Mr. Li on a job well done."

Kenzie had to hand it to him. His solution for diluting Bambi's power was brilliant. If he'd insisted upon their unanimous agreement, Bambi would be able to sabotage their every decision.

But a vote of three out of four makes that impossible, she thought. *Arnold, Zandra, and I can override her every time.* Bambi was still head of the department, but a lame duck.

Fairey assumed an air of brusqueness. "I believe it's time we took a vote on the Holbein," he said. "The Old Masters department will kindly abstain. Now then, those in favor of withdrawing the painting from the auction, please raise your hands." He held up his own.

Kenzie glanced around; one by one, the others' hands crept up also, until each person's was raised.

"It's unanimous then. The painting shall be withdrawn and we'll publicize an in-depth investigation. Eunice, prepare a statement for Allison, will you? But I want to go over it with Ileane before you schedule a press conference."

"Will do," Eunice Ffolkes said.

Fairey looked around. "Any questions?" he asked.

There were none.

"In that case," he said in his best Chairman of the Universe voice, "this meeting is adjourned."

Chairs were scooted back and everyone began to file quietly out of the room. Bambi, shouldering her way past Kenzie, shot her a glare of pure venom.

Kenzie was nearly out the door when Sheldon D. Fairey's voice stopped her.

"Oh, Ms. Turner?" he called out.

Kenzie turned around. "Sir?"

"Could you please stay for a few minutes? There's something I'd like to discuss with you."

"Please sit, Ms. Turner."

The last person out had shut the conference room door. Kenzie, slipping into the seat next to his, waited for him to speak.

He was sitting erect, frowning at the far wall, apparently deep in thought. Kenzie's gaze wandered briefly in that direction. A van Gogh print of Provençal blooms hung there, gilt-framed and smug, a relic of the shop-till-you-drop eighties, when Burghley's had sold it for the world's auction record, an amount still unequaled.

When he spoke, his voice was quiet. "Do you know what Burghley's main function is, Ms. Turner?" he asked.

"Of course, Mr. Fairey. To sell art and decorative objects."

He drew his eyes back in. "Is it?" He gave a bitter little smile. "I used to think so. Now I'm beginning to wonder." He heaved a weary sigh. "More and more, it seems that the treasures we deal in are secondary to the commissions they generate."

She nodded. "That is true also."

Slowly he rose to his feet and switched chairs, seating himself directly opposite her. She gazed unblinkingly across the table at him.

"You look people straight in the eye," he observed.

Her expression did not change. "And so do you, Mr. Fairey."

Leaning forward, he eyed her thoughtfully. "Tell me something, Ms. Turner. This is completely off the record. What is your opinion of this . . . this Holbein debacle?"

Kenzie shrugged, carefully keeping her face impassive, her voice neutral. "I suppose it's par for the course," she said noncommittally.

"Par for the course!" he exclaimed.

She nodded again. "Considering our volume of business, incidents like this are bound to occur every now and then."

"Indeed!" He raised frosty eyebrows. "Then are you saying this *fiasco* was unavoidable? Are you suggesting it was *not* the fault of that . . . that *dim-witted, empty-headed dummy* who was foisted upon us?"

She stared at him levelly. "Mr. Fairey," she said softly. "My job is to best serve the department. And I like to believe I do. However, what I don't like is to speculate or point fingers of blame. Especially after the fact. Art—not in-house politics—is what interests me."

"A devoutly noble sentiment," he murmured.

She was silent.

He held her gaze. "Does this mean you have *no* comment about this incident? None whatsoever?"

"Only that I'm glad it's under control, and that the worst damage can be contained."

She stared into his face, daring him to challenge her.

"I see . . ." His breath sighed out. Then, bending his head over the table, he furled the fingers of both hands, as though intent upon inspecting his manicure. "Earlier, you suggested that we publicize further investigation into the Holbein's provenance."

"I did. Yes, sir."

"And you realize what this means, don't you?"

"That our efforts will be closely monitored by the press in general, and the art world in particular," she said, nodding.

"Good. Then you will undoubtedly understand why I'm putting you in charge of this investigation."

"Me! But . . . but Ms. von Hohenburg-Willemlohe is more than capab—"

"Yes, yes, yes," he interrupted irritably, waving her to silence. "I'm quite aware of her proficiency. However, she's only been with us for three months, and we need an expert—*an old hand,* if you will—to surpervise this investigation. Ms. von Hohenburg-Willemlohe can do the actual research, but you shall be in charge. And you will report directly to me."

He paused.

"I *can* count on you, Ms. Turner?"

"Yes, sir." Kenzie nodded.

"Thank you, Ms. Turner." He rubbed his chin. "I seem to recall that on several occasions you've worked closely with an officer of the art theft squad . . . what *is* his name . . . ?"

"Charles Ferraro," she supplied automatically, before the name even registered in her brain. When it did, it pierced her like a poison arrow.

"Ah, yes," Fairey nodded. "Officer Ferraro. Well, then, I suggest you contact him immediately and work together on this. He will have resources available to him that we do not."

Kenzie's mind was reeling. *Oh, God! He can't expect me to work with Charley,* she thought with a sinking feeling. *He can't!*

It had been three months now since the party at the Met, and in all that time, she had refused to see either Charley or Hannes. She'd hung up on their phone calls. Had even had her locks changed, since she'd once given Charley a set of keys to her apartment.

And now, just when she thought she'd gotten rid of him once and for all, what had to happen? She was stuck with him again!

"Ms. Turner? Ms. Turner!"

The voice cut sharply through her turmoil, brought her to with a start.

"Is something *wrong,* Ms. Turner?"

"Only that . . ." She swallowed to lubricate her throat. ". . . that I'd prefer not to deal with Officer Ferraro again."

"Oh?" His eyebrows shot up. "And why not, pray tell?"

"I'd rather not get into that, sir."

"I'm afraid that's not good enough, Ms. Turner. Too much is at stake here—to paraphrase your own words, nearly three hundred years of sterling reputation! Burghley's 'single most precious asset' is the way I believe you put it?"

She sighed miserably. *Damn.* She'd really painted herself into a corner this time! *Why, oh why did I let myself get so carried away?*

He was leaning forward. "Do you *still* have a problem with this simple request, Ms. Turner? Am I asking too *much* of you?"

"No, sir," she said in a weary voice.

"Good. Then I expect to be kept informed of any developments. That will be all, Ms. Turner."

And the discussion was over.

Kenzie returned to her office, sank into her chair, and just sat there looking dazed.

"Kenzie?" Zandra was eyeing her with speculative concern. "My goodness, darling, you look absolutely pale. Whatever's the matter?"

Kenzie didn't reply. She was staring balefully at the telephone in front of her.

Charley, she thought miserably. *I've got to call Charley—*

—and I'd rather walk on hot coals!

But what choice did she have?

Resigning herself to the inevitable, she lifted the receiver and punched his work number, wondering how long it would take before her memory erased it.

"NYPD," a female voice answered. "Art theft squad."

She shut her eyes. "Officer Ferraro, please."

"Who's calling?"

"Ms. Turner."

"One moment, please."

Kenzie heard the woman calling out, *"Ferraro! Line two."*

And in the background, Charley's all-too-familiar voice: *"Who is it?"*

"A Ms. Turner. Should I put her through?"

Silence. Then: *"Naw. She's waited this long. Let her stew awhile. Might do her some good."*

Kenzie slammed down the receiver. *Fucking bastard!* Christ, he was unbearable!

She clenched her jaw determinedly. *But he hasn't heard the last of me,* she vowed grimly. *Unh-unh. Not by a long shot!*

Snatching the receiver back up, she hit redial.

Same female voice: "NYPD. Art theft squad."

"I would like to speak to Officer Ferraro," Kenzie said through clenched teeth. "This is official business."

A pause. Then: "I'm sorry, but Officer Ferraro just stepped out. Would you like to leave a mes—"

Kenzie slammed down the receiver.

She was seething.

⚜ *23* ⚜

*B*usy, busy, busy!

These were busy days for one Dina Goldsmith.

Now that she'd reached the Everest of society, she wasn't about to sit back and rest on her laurels. Far from it; she had as clear a sense of direction as a homing pigeon, and had mapped out a social strategy worthy of the joint chiefs of staff.

A case in point: Today.

According to her Filofax, she had a grueling schedule ahead of her:

7:00 A.M. Meet with Julio—instruct staff
7:15 A.M. Personal trainer
8:00 A.M. Bath
8:45 A.M. Correspondence, phone calls
9:30 A.M. Masseuse
10:00 A.M. Hairdresser and manicurist
          Cream Chanel Suit & Verdura Pieces-of-Eight:
10:30 A.M. Interview new chef
11:00 A.M. Sotheby's lecture—Portraits in 18th Century England
12:30 P.M. Fitting—Oscar de la Renta
1:30 P.M. Lunch—Becky V
2:45 P.M. French Lesson—*Irregular Verbs!!!*
3:45 P.M. *Everyone Must Eat* committee
          Meeting—re: Spring Gala
5:00 P.M. Wildenstein Galleries re: *Gainsboroughs*
5:30 P.M. Quality downtime
Black Herrera Evening Suit & Cartier "Gatsby" Pearls w/ Emeralds:
6:45 P.M. Knoedler Gallery—Donald Sultan opening
7:30 P.M. "Puccini and Champagne"—
          Met. Opera Guild—Hunter College
9:00 P.M. Met. Benefit Dinner—Colony Club

It was like living in a constant hurricane, but Dina wouldn't have had it any other way. She thrived on the social whirl. And to think it had all begun at Karl-Heinz's party, when Becky V had singled her out!

Ever since, all doors hitherto closed to the Goldsmiths had magically opened. The invitations poured in. And the Goldsmiths went out. To Brooke Astor's. To Oscar and Annette's (town *and* country). To the Buckleys'. To the Kissingers'.

Everywhere, New York's prime welcome mats were spread.

For about two months, Dina had felt she was living a fairy tale. And then, she awoke one morning to discover she was still not quite satisfied.

So she'd reached the top. So she and Robert had been accepted by the highest ranks of society. So *what?*

She was determined to go even farther. Yes. Little Dina Van Vliet of Gouda, the Netherlands, had decided to be more than just your run-of-the-mill socialite, and had set her covetous sights on the greenest pasture of them all.

In short, she was obsessed with nothing less than becoming a *legend.* A true social star.

She had already made strides.

Taking a cue from Becky V, she had traded in her garish white superstretch Caddy for a discreet Lincoln Town Car, and was working on Robert to do likewise.

Knowingly or unknowingly, a virtual horde of socialites, past and present, had a hand in educating Dina.

Daily lessons in French soon resulted in a vocabulary peppered with *"voulez-vous"* and *"n'est-ce pas"* and *"chérie,"* just like the multinational lingo of Becky V and Susan Gutfreund.

Inspired by Jayne Wrightsman, that authority on eighteenth-century French furniture, Dina decided it might behoove *her* to become master of one subject, too. And so began her thrice-weekly tutoring in Renaissance paintings.

Tales of Oscar and the first Mrs. de la Renta's informal Sunday evenings—when everyone popped in after returning from the country—prompted Dina to throw open her own doors for come-as-you-are, open-house Sunday evening buffets.

They were an instant hit. To paraphrase the late Kitty Miller, who contended that all you had to do was hang out a ham and people would beat a path to your door, Dina did exactly that.

But with one important difference. She was learning that discretion is the better part of good taste, and that the smaller and more exquisite the ham, the better. Which was why, where once she would have overdone it by throwing huge formal banquets, she now concentrated upon *under-doing* it, and soon mastered the fine art of giving the kind of perfect, intimate little dinners everyone started talking about.

Instead of sending a hostess an embarrassingly expensive thank you gift, she began searching high and low for the unique, the tasteful, the inexpensive, and occasionally, the hilariously vulgar.

She kept a notebook in which she jotted down everyone's likes and dislikes—be it food, wine, flowers, dinner partners, friends, and, above all, enemies, so that no two foes got invited to the same party.

And always, she was refining, honing, *perfecting*. Learning to do all the right things.

At 6:45, dressed in her exercise outfit (fluorescent pink, yellow, and Kermit green Spandex), she rang her majordomo.

"Yes, madame?" Julio's voice over the in-house phone sounded sleepy.

"I'm running a bit ahead of schedule." Dina wasn't in the least apologetic. "We'll take our meeting *now.*" She paused for two seconds. "In here."

"At once, madame."

When he arrived, she was seated on the sofa in her adjoining sitting room, sipping coffee Darlene had just poured from the silver pot.

Julio hovered. "Madame?"

"Thank you, Darlene," Dina said crisply. "That will be all."

"Yes, ma'am." Her maid half curtsied and fled.

Julio, sniffing disdainfully, eyed the departing figure with disapproval.

Dina's knowledge of fine things might have needed honing, but her claws did not. Fixing him with a sharp gaze, she said, "Julio. Sit." Sounding like a dog trainer. "No, no, not in that chair." She pointed. "In *that* one. There."

Meekly he obeyed.

"*Architectural Digest* is coming to photograph this apartment next week," she said, coming right to the point. "They will be here on Wednesday, Thursday, and Friday. I expect you to extend them every courtesy." She paused. "In fact, you are going to bend over *backward* for them."

"Yes, madame." He got out his pocket-size notebook and Cartier pen and scribbled away.

"On Tuesday, Renny is coming to do the floral arrangements. He or one of his assistants will also be on hand each of the following three days to freshen up the bouquets. I expect you to bend over backward for him, also."

"Of course, madame." He made a note of it.

Dina took another sip of coffee. "Now, concerning last Sunday's buffet. *Must* I reiterate that it is casual *for guests only?* Last week, I distinctly detected *shoddiness* on the part of the staff. You will not permit this to happen again."

"No, madame."

"You were not here last Sunday," she pointed out.

"I was visiting a sick relative and—"

"You will call on your friends and relatives on your own time. Is that clear?"

"Perfectly, madame. I'm sorry—"

"See that it doesn't happen again."

They discussed general household matters, during which Dina consulted a little gold notepad and rattled off a litany of complaints: Dust here ... smudged marble there ... a cobweb in a chandelier—a *cobweb!*

He made a note of everything.

Darlene knocked, announcing that the personal trainer had arrived.

Dina glanced at the tiny Fabergé clock on the end table. It was seven o'clock; he was fifteen minutes early. *Good.*

Dina spent the next twenty-five minutes in her mirrored, Nautilus-equipped gym, where Scott, her merciless trainer, put her through rigorous paces.

A soothing bath followed, after which she met with Gaby.

Personal telephone calls ate up another half hour.

At nine-thirty, Dina submitted to a robust massage, and at ten, to her thrice-weekly ministrations from her hairdresser and manicurist.

Later, dressed in cream Chanel with black frogging and heavy Verdura pieces-of-eight (necklace, bracelets, ear clips, and brooch), she interviewed the Pritikin chef (Becky V had one, why shouldn't she?) and hired him on a trial basis.

Then she sallied forth.

Morning and noon flew by in a blur. One Sotheby's lecture and a de la Renta fitting later, Dina arrived at Becky V's.

It was one-thirty, and despite her grueling schedule, she wasn't the least bit exhausted.

Far from it. Dina Goldsmith had energy to burn. She was in the fast lane—and loving every damn minute of it!

"Merci, Uriah. That shall be all," Becky V told the shaky, beaky-nosed old retainer who set down the tray laden with sterling: teapot, coffeepot, sugar urn, and creamer.

"Yes, Madame!" shouted the ancient Uriah, who, like so many hearing-impaired people, yelled rather than spoke.

Becky caught Dina's disapproving glance at the departing servant; reaching for the Limoges cups, she explained: "Uriah and I have grown quite fond of each other. Did you know he was with my last husband, poor dear Joaquín, for over fifteen years? And for thirty years with his father before him? *Oui.* Uriah is of the old school. His pride precludes him from considering retirement. Personally, I think it would kill him."

Tilting her head, she regarded Dina with that famous, unfathomable smile.

"Alors. Uriah and I have an understanding. He puts up with my eccentricities, and I ignore his little infirmities. It is as my grandmother

taught us: 'First our servants take care of us, and then we must take care of them.' It is a sacred obligation. *Oui.* Look at Uriah. It is a small price to pay for nearly fifty years of devoted service, *n'est-ce pas?*"

Dina nodded.

Becky gestured to the tray. *"Alors.* Would you prefer coffee or tea?"

"Coffee, please."

Becky picked up the coffeepot, fashioned one hundred ninety-four years earlier by Joseph Richardson, Jr., of Philadelphia, and tipped the spout delicately toward the cups. She pressed on the lid with the forefinger of her left hand and kept the pinkie of the right extended. She poured a thin steaming arc for each of them and set the pot back down.

"Au lait?"

Dina shook her head. "I always take mine black."

"Moi aussi." Becky nodded approvingly, handed Dina a cup and saucer, and sipped her own strong French roast as delicately as she had poured it, again with the pinkie extended.

They were enjoying these *après*-lunch coffees in the shadowy *cabinet d'amateur* of Becky V's penthouse, a mysteriously seductive cocoon created by the maestro of the world's most sumptuous interiors, Renzo Mongiardino.

The room, which Becky called her *"cabinet,"* was like the inside of a precious Renaissance jewel casket—an effect conjured through masterful tromp l'oeil on all four walls and coved ceiling, every square inch of which had been painstakingly painted, then poetically mellowed.

A plethora of simulated, "aged," surfaces abounded. Ebony, tulipwood, porphyry, agate, scagiola, gilt.

But this shimmering, spectacularly rich background was not merely decorative. Indeed, a single calculated purpose lay behind the profligate opulence: to enhance, without bringing immediate attention to, the sixteen superb miniature Goyas embedded in the walls like half-hidden gems.

Unable to help herself, Dina found her eyes constantly roving, enviously eating up the details of this glorious room in this glorious apartment, which could have come from a *hôtel particulier* on the Quai d'Anjou, and reassembled here, in the heart of Manhattan.

Drunk on this intoxicating atmosphere, Dina also realized with a pang, that her own nearby duplex, of which she had been so proud, was nothing if not woefully, hopelessly, unforgivably *nouveau riche* and just . . . well, just too everything.

But this—Becky V's premeditatedly aged château-in-the-sky, redolent with an air of history, lineage, titles, and breeding—*this* was what Dina truly hungered for.

Yes! It was high time to redecorate, and with the help of a master! Renzo Whatever-His-Name was, who else? Indeed! Before departing, she would ask Becky for an introduction.

After all, Dina asked herself, *hasn't my motto always been, "When in doubt, redecorate"?* And didn't everyone know it?

"*Alors.*" Becky set down her cup and saucer.

"Wha—" Dina gave a start. "Oh, dear. I *am* sorry. My mind was—"

Becky gestured with a languid hand. "*Point du tout.* There is no need to apologize. I was only saying that I have a small confession to make."

"Really!" Dina looked at her raptly, all thoughts of decor forgotten. "*Do* tell!"

"I had an *arrière-pensée . . .*" Becky smiled. "What you would call an ulterior motive . . . for inviting you here. However, I believe you will find it most amusing and intriguing . . ."

"Oh, but I do!" Dina, all ears, was breathlessly perched at the edge of her seat. "I already do!"

Becky lifted a cautionary finger. "But first, a warning. Utter discretion is *impératif.* This cannot go further than this room." She raised her chin, her eyes suddenly hardening. "This must remain our little secret. *D'accord?*"

Dina stared at her. Sharing a secret with Becky V! Good heavens. Would miracles *never* cease? She tried to reply, but to her chagrin discovered she was hopelessly tongue-tied.

Becky picked up her cup, took another sip of coffee, and set it back down. "I *can* rely on your *discrétion,* then?"

"Er, uh, uhm," stuttered Dina, still at an utter loss for words. And then, before she could help herself, she blurted the first thing which popped into her head: "*Oui!*"

As soon as it was out, she placed her fingers against her lips. *Oh, God,* she thought, appalled. *I've really blundered now!*

But Becky merely smiled. "As this concerns one of my best friends and one of yours, it is only natural that we join forces. *N'est-ce pas?* Especially since we are both in such a unique position to help."

Join forces? With Becky? Dina immediately warmed to the idea. *How extraordinary!* she thought. *What on earth can Becky have in mind?*

"I see I must explain." Folding her hands in her lap, Becky gazed contemplatively up at the faux rosettes of the coffered ceiling. "Prince Karl-Heinz is arriving back in town tomorrow."

"Is he? I had no idea . . ."

"I believe I am the only person who knows." Lowering her eyes, Becky met Dina's gaze directly. "I shall be frank, *oui?*"

Dina, still overwhelmed at being taken into Becky's confidence, didn't trust herself to speak, and merely nodded.

"Apparently, *le vieil Prince*'s condition has stabilized. That is not to mean Heinzie's father is healthy; far from it. He is in a coma which is believed to be irreversible. However, he *is* out of immediate danger. And, more *importantly*—"

Pausing, Becky sat forward and exhaled an explosion of breath: *"He
. . . is . . . legally . . . alive!"*

Her eyes had widened, the unsurpassed violet pupils floating in a sea
of white.

Dina stared at her with dawning understanding. So *this* was it! she
thought, feeling something twitching to life deep inside her. She took a
quick gulp of coffee. Now she had a good idea of exactly why Becky had
invited her, and where this conversation was headed. Together—

—the two of them could bring Karl-Heinz and Zandra together!

Becky's face shone with an inner light. "Ah!" She nodded slowly. "So
you *do* know of what I speak, *chère amie."*

Dina was silent.

"Of course you do."

"Yes," Dina managed, and then, finding her voice, said in hushed
tones: "The prince is your best friend, and Zandra is mine."

The intensity of her own face seemed to mirror Becky's.

"Apparently we have both come to the same conclusion. He needs an
heir before his father dies—and Zandra is the obvious candidate."

"Exactement!"

Becky's perfect teeth gleamed moistly, and for a fleeting instant Dina
glimpsed the steel behind the fathomless da Vinci smile.

"But neither of us can bring this about alone. *Alors.* We must
work together."

"Like two puppeteers?"

"S'il vous plaît! I prefer to think of us as . . . as wise and well-
intentioned friends . . . fairy godmothers, if you will. Would you like some
more coffee?"

"Well . . ."

"Un peu?"

"A little, perhaps. Yes. Please." Dina held out her cup for a refill.

Becky continued talking as she poured, delicate pinkie extended: "After all, there is no denying that Heinzie and Zandra are perfectly suited for
one another."

"Yes," said Dina, who'd mulled this over ever since the night of the
party at the Met. "But there might be one or two, er, stumbling blocks."

"Oh?" Becky frowned. "And what might those be?"

Dina sighed. "Love, for one thing."

"Love!" Becky sat there, unfazed. "What's love got to do with it?"
She laughed softly, chidingly. "Really, *chère amie.* We are speaking of
fortunes, birthrights, bloodlines. We are speaking of *one of the largest em-
pires on earth!* And you speak of *love?"*

"Plus there's their age difference," Dina pointed out.

"Age!" Becky waved a hand, as at an irritating fly. "In light of every-

thing Zandra and Heinzie have in common, that is *insignificant. Dit moi:* Have not you yourself . . . and I on one occasion . . . married older men?"

Dina nodded.

"And are not Zandra and Heinzie both blessed with that aura of multiplying the other's allure?"

Dina nodded again.

"And would they not make an exceedingly splendid and dashing couple?"

"Yes," agreed Dina, "that they would."

"*Alors.* There you have it." Becky regarded her unblinkingly for a moment. "I *can* count on you, then? You *will* help?"

Dina met her questioning gaze. *Of course I will,* she thought. *Isn't this exactly what I wanted?* She pictured Karl-Heinz and Zandra together, then unconsciously sighed with pleasure. *They really are the perfect match,* she decided. *As perfect as they come . . .*

"Oh, yes," she said. "You can count on me."

Becky smiled warmly. "*D'accord.* You don't know how delighted that makes me!"

Dina basked in the narcotic of Becky's approval. It made her feel all warm and glowing and tingly inside, like a good belt of brandy in midwinter. Already, she could see her powerbase expanding. But best of all, she was being courted by none other than Becky V!

Who needed caffeine on top of *that?*

Becky was saying, her voice thoughtful: "What we shall do is the following. This Saturday, there is an auction of Fabergé and *objets de vertu* at Christie's. Heinzie collects such things, you know. I shall be viewing the exhibit with him the day after tomorrow. Afterwards, I shall suggest we lunch at Mortimer's—"

"Where," said Dina, picking up the conversational thread and running with it, "I'll be lunching with Zandra."

"*Exactement!*" Becky smiled with feigned languor, but her violet eyes were alert, the sharp angles of her cheekbones creating rakish shadows. "However, our meeting must appear accidental . . . totally without premeditation."

Dina shrugged. "I don't see why that should present any problem. People run into each other at Mortimer's all the time. We'll simply act appropriately surprised."

Becky nodded. "*Bon.* Now then. The Sheldon D. Faireys. How well do you know them?"

"Not very," Dina admitted. "Why?"

"They own the estate next to mine in New Jersey. Did you know that? It was left to Nina by her maternal grandmother, I believe."

Dina waited.

"We shall be requiring the Faireys' help," Becky said slowly. Tapping her lip with a clear-lacquered talon, she gave Dina a significant look. "However, they must under no circumstances suspect what we are plotting. Nina is the most terrible chatterbox, and secrecy—"

"—must be maintained at all costs." Dina bobbed her head up and down. "Yes, yes. I quite understand."

Becky tapped her lips some more. "If only you were closer to the Faireys. Extracting an invitation to their estate would definitely make our little intrigue less obvious."

Dina smiled. "Just leave that to me. Don't forget, Sheldon is head of Burghley's, and my husband is the majority shareholder. If I say, 'Jump,' Sheldon will ask, 'How high?' You'll see. The instant I suggest it, an invitation shall be forthcoming."

"Ah!" Becky's face betrayed a piquant trace of amusement, a dash of zesty evil. "I must compliment you. Your deviousness is almost French." She laughed throatily. *"Oui.* Together we are *très formidable!"*

"Yes. But as far as the Faireys are concerned, the sooner you give me a firm date, the better."

"À coup sûr. But first, I must find out what Heinzie's plans are. I should know more the day after tomorrow. *Alors.* I believe the time has come to toast our little endeavor, *non?"*

And Becky pressed a button affixed to the underside of the gueridon.

A minute later, a wide, vertical band of golden light streamed in as Uriah opened the door and shuffled into the room. "You rang, Madame?!"

"Yes, Uriah. Iced Dom Pérignon and two glasses, please."

"Coming right up, Madame!"

And so shouting, he shuffled back out.

Dina once again glanced around, feasting her eyes on the intricately stenciled paneling, the complex patterns of the shimmering silk Heraz, the voluptuous luxury of this most magnificent of rooms.

Uriah returned with an ornate ice-filled silver bucket. After much fumbling, he managed to wrest the cork from the chilled bottle. He poured some shakily into two dazzling cobalt flutes, shuffled back out, and shut the door behind him.

Becky plucked up one glass and raised it in a toast. "To their Serene Highnesses, the Prince *and* future Princess von und zu Engelwiesen!"

Dina lifted her own fragile, gold-banded glass. "May they live happily ever after!" she added in a whisper.

Then, exchanging smiles, they clinked their glasses and sipped. The champagne was very, very good. But the intrigue was even better.

24

"*S*elf-centered bastard, spiteful chauvinist *pig!*" steamed Kenzie as she and Zandra sat in the huge subterranean vault, Kenzie's refuge in times of crises. All around, hundreds of priceless, tagged paintings and drawings were stored sideways on metal shelving, like books. "I have a good mind to take a cleaver to his you-know-what!"

"Oh, gosh," Zandra said. "How perfectly awful. D'you think he's just having a beastly day? You know men—striking out at you could be a matter of . . . of transference!"

Kenzie looked stupefied. "Transference?" she repeated blankly. "What the hell's transference got to do with this?"

"Oh, Kenzie, you know. Men are *so* moody—comes from repressing their emotions . . . all that macho posturing has got to get to them sometime! I mean, you could simply be the handiest surrogate for whatever's really bothering him. Right? Just don't take it personally."

"Don't take it personally? For God's sake, what other way *can* I take it?"

Zandra exhaled a sigh. She was utterly at a loss. Making commiserating noises and providing a shoulder to cry on was one thing; rallying her out of a bottomless funk was quite another. Kenzie needed help, that much was clear. The only question was . . . how to proceed?

"A knife," Kenzie murmured dreamily, her eyes glittering with fantasized revenge. "Yes, one of those superbly balanced Hoffritz chopping blades would do nicely."

"Kenzie . . ."

"Or better yet, one of their *cleavers. There's* a prime example of what good old Solingen steel will do! Now, if only I were a trained Benihana chef—"

"Kenzie, *stop* it," cried Zandra. "You're being perfectly horrid. For God's sake, you're a vegetarian."

Kenzie slumped in defeat and looked imploringly at her friend. "So what should I do?"

"*Forget* it for now. That's the clue."

"Forget it?" Kenzie squeaked. "Zandra, how *can* I?"

"Then at least keep in mind what my Aunt Josephine always used to say: '*Diem adimere aegritudinem hominibus.*'"

"Zandra! *Will* you speak English?"

"I *am* speaking English, luv." Zandra addressed her as she would a younger sister, lovingly but with the slightest hint of exasperation. "I only quoted the Latin to make it . . . well, to tell the truth, sound less *trite.*"

"But I don't speak Latin!"

"So? I'll happily translate. Literally, it means 'Time removes distress.' "

"Aha!" Kenzie slid her a gimlet glare. " 'Time heals all wounds.' Why is it," she muttered sourly, "that whenever certain situations arise, people unfailingly fall back on clichés?"

Zandra suddenly perked up. "Latin. Oh, Kenzie, I just got an idea." Zandra sat there with a blissful smile, because inspiration had finally dawned.

What, she asked herself triumphantly, *were the ancient Romans but Italians by any other name? And who, with the possible exception of Jewish mothers, knew how to nurture damaged souls better than Italians? Indeed. Everyone with the slightest trace of Latin blood understood that the absolutely swiftest remedy for any ailment, like the quickest way to a man's heart, was* undeniably *through his stomach.*

Popping to her feet, Zandra announced: "Darling, I know exactly what you need!"

"You do?" Kenzie's voice was laced with skepticism.

"Yes, luv, I do." Zandra paused for a beat. "Food."

"Food!"

"Oh, Kenzie. I mean, honestly. Don't you know anything at all? Food's the antidote. *Real* food. Italian *comfort* food. You'll see. Now, let me think . . ." Her voice took on a dreamy tone. "We'll start with a heavenly tartine con il gorgonzola . . . follow it up with some frivolous tagliatelle alla romagnola, or perhaps you'd prefer risotto coi carciofi?— whichever. And, Kenzie, *while* we're making such *absolute* pigs of ourselves, we might as well go *whole* hog and splurge on the most *divine* bottle of really good Chianti, after which we'll top it *all* off with espresso, amaretto, *and* the most sinfully rich gelato di cioccolato in town."

She paused, eyes aglow.

"Well, darling? What do *you* say? *Shall* we? Oh, Kenzie, *let's!* You'll see. Nothing's *ever* so bad on a full stomach!"

"What you're proposing," said Kenzie inexorably, "is removing the symptom but not the cause."

"Well, at least it works. I mean, if you had a headache, you'd *want* to get rid of it. Wouldn't you?"

"Yes, but my headache happens to be one Officer Fer-fucking-raro," Kenzie sighed. "It's not lunch I need, but some way to kick his ass in gear, and *without* leading the horny bastard on!" She gnashed her teeth in frustration. "Where, oh *where*," she demanded plaintively, "are the police when you need them?"

"Oh, Kenzie, will you stop? Now, do you want to go and have lunch, or don't you?"

"Lunch?" sniffed Kenzie, wounded. "I think I'll pass."

Zandra threw up her hands in despair. "Have it your way, then. Really!" She eyed Kenzie with disgust.

And whirling around, she left the vault.

Watching her depart, Kenzie snorted under her breath, hit the lights, and pushed the armored door shut. She punched the electronic lock code, from force of habit testing the door to make certain it was secure. Already, she could hear the nearby slam of the service elevator; the unmistakable whir of hydraulics.

It was Zandra, ascending.

Kenzie didn't bother waiting for the elevator to return. Nor did she head for the nearest stairwell. For some unfathomable reason, perhaps because it had been awhile, she was possessed of a sudden urge to cut diagonally through the building via the convoluted, subterranean labyrinth.

Most people avoided venturing far into the bowels of Burghley's, and not without just cause. Even the newer engineers were constantly getting lost down here, and anyone unfamiliar with the layout would have required a ball of string to find their way back.

Not Kenzie. Long ago, her spirit of adventure and fascination with all things Burghley's had compelled her to explore every last nook and cranny of this neo-Renaissance palazzo, and she'd committed to memory all six above-ground floors and both subterranean levels.

The uppermost, B1, was equally divided between "Burghley's Basement" galleries and Auction Towers's underground parking garage.

The subbasement, B2, through which she now unerringly picked her way, was where the various departments had their storage vaults.

Here, in this maze of tunnels making up ninety-six thousand square feet, could be found the expected—all the unsightly machinery necessary to keep a building this size humming: malevolent furnaces and boilers, noisy pumps and silent backup generators, Baby Bell terminals and Con Ed conduits, garbage rooms, and machine shops.

And here, too, could be found the unexpected—a cavernlike area for a vast collection of garden statuary, small temples, fountains, and pergolas, at once mysterious and enchanting in a menacing kind of way.

And farther on was another, even more dreamlike space where chunks of antiquities too big for the vaults—a pair of secretive sphinxes, fragments of columns and carved friezes, statues in Parian marble, larger-than-life bronzes, and a gargantuan head of Medusa positively writhing with stone snakes, even a giant Roman foot broken off at the ankle—had found a temporary sepulchre.

There was something appropriate about the tomblike atmosphere, about the relics of past millennia reposing underground. The sight never failed to quicken Kenzie's heart, as though she were the first to stumble upon some hitherto inviolate temple, such was the power of the illusion emerging from ruin.

Everything conspired to trick the eye. The outsized proportions of the artifacts, their haphazard arrangement, the way they seemed to give a deep, false perspective, a perfect symmetry disappearing into gloom. That was what she loved down here. That haunted secretiveness; the feeling, however ridiculous, that there were many more such wonders waiting to be discovered.

On she walked, her clicking footsteps echoing, gradually fading like phantoms as she made her way along the shadowy concrete corridors. Wall-mounted bulbs, protected by wire mesh, punctuated the dark at regular intervals, made dusty white pools of light.

Overhead, the ceilings were a hodgepodge of tortured pipes and conduits and stealthy ducts which branched off into tributaries at each bisecting corridor.

Yet despite the overwhelming ominousness, Kenzie felt no fear. Nor was she the least bit claustrophobic. Her explorations had familiarized her with every square foot, and she was certain she could have found her way around even in a blackout.

As she continued, she alternately shivered or perspired, for unlike the interiors of the room-size vaults, climate and humidity control did not extend to the rest of the subbasement. The air was perpetually dank, always stuffy or chilly, depending upon the vicinity of the heating ducts and hot water pipes.

Not once did she run across a soul, but she knew she was never entirely alone, either. Video cameras were everywhere—mute, ever-vigilant sentinels panning each corridor with Cyclopean eyes and sending her image back to the control room of security, where walls of television monitors were manned 'round the clock.

Pulling open a gray steel door with a glass-and-mesh inset, she stepped into a cinderblock stairwell. Behind her, the door closed automatically; B2 was painted on it in huge red letters.

She started up. On the next floor, she passed an identical door labeled B1. Above that, another marked G. Two landings later, and she was on 2.

She pushed that door open.

After the dimness of the subbasement and stairwell, the carpeted hallway seemed bright to the point of blinding. Recessed fluorescents cast diffused, shadow-free light, and warm air circulated from vents along the baseboards. Cream-painted doors punctuated both walls at regular intervals.

Each was identified by a Lucite plaque with burnished gold letters. The third one down was it: OLD MASTERS

Underneath, a smaller plaque with slide-in slots held three nameplates:

A. LI

M. TURNER

Z.V. HOHENBURG-WILLEMLOHE

Opening the door, Kenzie announced, "I'm ba-*ack!*"

No one greeted her. No one was here. A quick glance at the coathook confirmed that both Zandra and Arnold had gone to lunch.

Which is just as well, she thought. *Some things are best done in private . . . especially things like stretching the truth . . .*

Shutting the door, she sat down at her desk and eyed the phone accusingly. It seemed to sit there, taunting her with smug superiority.

"Well," she sighed, "might as well get it over with." And grabbing the receiver, she jabbed redial.

One ring . . . two . . . three—

"NYPD," the female voice answered. "Art theft squad."

"Yes. This is Ms. Turner again. It's imperative that I speak with Officer Ferraro."

"I'm sorry, but Officer Ferraro is in the field."

"The field? What field?" Kenzie demanded in outrage. "I'm calling from Burghley's on official business. Now, why don't you be nice and go scare him up?"

"Because he's not in the office, ma'am. If you'll kindly leave a number where—"

"Oh, for crying out loud! Look, this is a bona fide emergency, okay? Now, will you, or will you not, patch me through to wherever Officer Ferraro might be? Otherwise, I can save myself a lot of trouble by going directly over his head." Kenzie paused. "Which'll it be? The choice is yours."

There was a moment's hesitation. "What did you say the emergency was?"

"I didn't. It's a stolen work of art with an estimated value of twenty-five million dollars."

No argument now. "Please hold," the voice said briskly. "I'll transfer you."

Within fifteen seconds, Kenzie was patched through.

"This'd *better* be an emergency," Charley snapped, with irritation. "The shit's been hitting the fan. Or haven't you heard?"

"Heard what?"

"I'm at the Artisteria Gallery. Bunch of perps tied up the staff and made off with art to the tune of half a mil. Can you believe it? Right in broad daylight."

"Some thieves." Kenzie had to laugh. "What did they steal? Ertés?"

"That's not funny."

"No, I guess it isn't."

"So . . . what's your reason for calling?"

"Mainly," she said stiffly, "because Sheldon D. Fairey ordered me to."

"And?"

"And nothing. I just didn't want you to get the wrong idea. It wasn't my choice."

"Kenzie, I really am pressed for time. Now, either cut to the chase, or I'm hanging up. You've got one minute."

"Jesus, will you *cool* it? For your information, this painting happens to be worth a fortune."

"This concerns that Holbein, right?"

Her eyes narrowed with unease. "What makes you say that?" she murmured cautiously.

"Because I read the papers, Sherlock. Shit, Hans is gesturing. Gotta go. I'll be in touch once the mess down here's—"

"Don't you dare hang up! Charley, if you refuse to work with us on this, so help me God I'll . . . I'll . . ."

"You'll what?" he asked calmly, yawning with bored amusement.

"I'll call 'Page Six.' Yes! And *New York* magazine! And the *News* and *Newsday* and . . ." Kenzie smiled dreamily, wondering what other threats she could possibly pull out of her improvised grab bag.

"Kenzie?" he drawled.

"What?"

"Blow it out your—"

"No, *you* blow it out *yours*, Charles Gabriel Ferraro! Either we meet to discuss this *today*, or your public affairs officer'll be working overtime. In fact, I wouldn't rule out a special mayoral investigation. Who knows? With the stink this has already raised between D.C. and Bonn, maybe the secretary of state will personally give the police commissioner a call. So do yourself a favor and wear your Cerruti suit. You'll want to look your best for TV."

"Why, you . . . you *bitch!*" he whispered with a kind of grudging awe. "You do know how to fight dirty, don't you?"

"I'll take that as a compliment," she said loftily. "And one more thing, Charley," she added inexorably. *"Do* try to avoid wearing one of those awful garish ties which are all the rage? I think your red Hermès will look best on camera."

He threw in the towel. "All right, all *right!*" he snapped, in disgust. "You win. But I'm running late. It'll have to be sometime after seven."

"Sometime after seven's fine. But don't come here; I'll be at home. You *do* remember the address?" she asked, heaping on the syrup.

He replied by slamming down the phone.

Smiling, Kenzie replaced the receiver. *There! That wasn't so difficult!*

No, indeed. She had Officer Ferraro over a barrel, all right, she thought smugly. *She* knew it. And more important, *he* knew it, too. But the one thing he *didn't* know was that she now had a roommate. And with Zandra present, there'd be no danger of his libido acting up.

Not that any amount of sex appeal was going to help Charley this time. Because, whether he knew it or not, she, MacKenzie Turner, was totally immune to his charms. In fact, she felt absolutely nothing for him.

Nothing at *all!*

Theater, *real* theater, Zandra had discovered during the past three months, was not found On or Off or even Off-off Broadway so much as it was on the teeming streets and sidewalks of Manhattan.

This held true even on the posh Upper East Side, where despite the prevalence of vast wealth the cast was likely to comprise an egalitarian mixture: the sable-coated socialite hurrying past a ragged panhandler, the daredevil bicyclist in neon Spandex narrowly missing the custom-suited banker, the leggy supermodel giving the obscenity-screaming maniac a wide berth, and, oblivious to it all, the unflappable black nurse's aide pushing a wheelchair-bound elderly.

Zandra, whose experience on stage had been limited to beauty contests, always felt as if she'd blundered onto the set of the *real* greatest show on earth: the constantly running theater that was Manhattan, a directorless hodgepodge of *Marat Sade, Barefoot in the Park, Private Lives,* and *The Three-Penny Opera,* the exact allotment of each play depending upon such vagaries as the weather, the economy, the time of day, and even the phases of the moon.

However, this thousand-ring circus was not on her mind as she now drifted, content and purposeless, along Madison Avenue in her new black cashmere-blend coat, an after-Christmas markdown which she'd enlivened with a crinkle-pleated Issey Miyake tricolor scarf, to indulge in a lunch hour of window-shopping, that spectator sport necessitated by the most stringent of budgets.

As always, the unabashedly rich store windows drew attention and enticed. Not that Zandra envied the flush shopper darting out of Gianni Versace, or the collector frowning at a Francesco Clemente in the window of the Gagosian Gallery, or the tourists poring over frivolous bric-a-brac at Mabel's. Having been raised virtually penniless, she had early on learned the value of a farthing and to pinch it till it bled while simultaneously observing from her vastly rich, spoiled cousinage that happiness was the one thing no amount of wealth could buy.

Thus, confronted with temptations ranging from a floral springtime confection at Givenchy to a dazzling Art Deco suite of bijoux at Fred Leighton, she felt quite content merely to browse and . . . well, to be honest, perhaps indulge in just a wee bit of dreaming. Otherwise, she was quite satisfied.

And why shouldn't she be? New York had been exceptionally good to her. What more could she possibly want?

Well, two things actually, the only two things missing from her life. One was a steady boyfriend. The other—far more important and disturbing—was the fact that Rudolph, her brother, had yet to surface.

Zandra sighed. His absence had the habit of stealing up on her, like a guilt, at the most inopportune moments.

Every call she had made to England—by her last reckoning, nearly two thousand dollars' worth—had proved a dead end. Either her brother had gone to ground so successfully that he couldn't be found, or else he—

He—*what?* Occupied a shallow, unmarked grave somewhere? Lay, weighed down with lead, at the bottom of some obscure body of water? Was part of some unspecified landfill?

Sighing more loudly, she slammed a mental door. She wouldn't allow herself to contemplate his fate. To do so would drive her stark, raving mad.

Pulling the lapels of her coat tighter around her throat, she moved on, until a female's fluty Oxbridge tones called out:

"Zandra? Zandra von Hohenburg-Willemlohe?"

Startled, Zandra whirled around. Her brows knitted as she frowned, trying to place a familiar face in unfamiliar surroundings. Then her mental circuits connected; memory cells clicked.

"Oh, gosh. Penelope. Penelope Gainsborourg! Is that you?"

"In the flesh!" giggled the lanky, carrot-curled thing in the humongous bag lady coat by Fendi, all strips and balls of various pelts, leathers and suedes in every conceivable shade of brown.

The requisite hug, and kisses strategically aimed past each other's cheeks, followed.

Then, holding each other at arm's length: "My goodness, Penelope. Darling, you *are* looking well. And how's Dicky?"

"Gone," came the cheerful reply.

"Gone!" Zandra's eyes widened, became dramatic saucers. "What ever do you mean?"

"The name's not Gainsborourg any longer, darling—that's the clue. It's Troughton now. Mrs. Alex Troughton." Penelope affected the same disjointed, fractured speech patterns as Zandra. "*And . . .* here's twenty-two *flawless* carats to prove it. See?" She extended a limp hand.

Zandra stared at the giant diamond. "Why, it's . . . it's huge."

"Grotesquely huge and absolutely bourgeois!" Penelope giggled happily. "Still, diamonds *are* a girl's best friend. Never return one, that's my motto . . . make a scalp bracelet—*necklace* is more like it the way I'm going. I mean, third divorce *and* fourth marriage? All Mexican quickies and me only twenty-six? Can you imagine? Anyway, you should have *seen* the scandal. Everybody boffing everybody else! First Lucinda Troughton running off—God only knows where—with another woman, then Dicky with Alex's *butler* . . . can you imagine anything more awful . . . I mean, running off with someone's *butler,* of all people! And finally me with poor sweet Alex, well—"

"Goodness, Penelope. How absolutely frightful. I must say, I don't know *when* I've heard anything quite as convoluted."

"What?" Penelope stared with open-mouthed astonishment. "You mean . . . you hadn't heard?"

"Oh, Penelope, I'm afraid not. I'm terribly out of touch, you know."

"You must be! God. Last time we talked . . . I remember! You rang to ask about Rudolph . . . yes . . . hear he owes Dicky *tons,* not that I give a *fart.* Fact is, I hope Dicky never sees a *shilling*—*that's* just deserts for running off with Alex's butler, wouldn't you say? Especially with decent butlers heading the endangered species list . . . or are they extinct already? Anyway! Imagine. Bumping into you *here,* of all places. Darling, what on earth are you doing in New York?"

Zandra, trying to keep abreast of the loquacious twists, turns, and detours, said, "Oh, gosh. Well, that's a terribly long story. I live here now." At a loss for a more detailed explanation, she deftly turned the conversational tables. "But, darling, what about you? What brings you here? Still hiding from Fleet Street, are you?"

"Hiding? Good heavens, no!" came the bright reply. "Honeymooning with Alex—what else?"

"But darling, that's marv. Happy, are you?"

"Lord, yes."

"Congrats. Doesn't this call for a drink or something?" Zandra glanced around. "Wherever *is* the lucky man?"

Penelope's face fell. "Would you believe, came down with the flu, of all things? Really. I *warned* him: 'Get inoculated, darling.' Well, men bloody well never listen, do they? *And,* would you believe, we have front-row seats for *Sunset Boulevard* tonight? Hate to waste the tickets, but that's out now . . . I mean, who wants to go alone?"

Abruptly Penelope brightened.

"Of course! How utterly silly of me! Zandra! Why don't *you* come? We'll have dinner before . . . the Russian Tea Room's my absolute *fave.* Oh, do say yes. It'll be divine."

"Why . . . I . . . *yes.* Why not?"

"Zandra, that's super! You're a darling. I mean, you've only positively saved my entire evening. We've *tons* to catch up on . . . oops! Better run! Playing Florence Nightingale between shopping. You know. Anyway, we'll meet at six?"

"The Russian Tea Room. Yes."

"I can't wait! We'll look positively *glam*. Remember, reservations are for Troughton. Mrs. Alex Troughton." Penelope giggled. "Off I go!"

Swift kisses punctuated air; fingers waggled blurrily.

"Toodle-oo!"

And the bundle of couture rags dashed off.

Zandra stood there, staring. She felt as if a minitornado had swept her up and then left her, whirling on to wreak havoc upon whoever—or whatever—lay in its path.

Moseying on along Madison, she thought about the evening ahead. The Russian Tea Room and a Broadway show.

Why not? It wasn't as if she had anything better to do.

25

"*Will* you stop pacing and settle down?" Charley snapped irritably. "Christ, Kenzie. You're as nervous as a cat in heat. What d'you think I'm gonna do? *Bite?*"

"Nervous? Who's nervous?" challenged Kenzie, lowering herself onto a slipper chair with lofty affront—no way was *she* going to sit beside him on the couch. Unh-huh. Hell would have to freeze over first!

Too, she wisely sat on her hands in order to make it impossible to fidget, for, words to the contrary, her body was a veritable human tuning fork of nervous energy. If she'd known that Zandra—some friend!—was going to desert her in this, her greatest hour of need, she would never have agreed to meet Charley here, alone in her apartment.

No. She would have been careful to choose neutral turf. After all, it only made sense to confront a lecherous deviant in a crowd, and not in private quarters.

But now here she was: *alone* with the world's number one bastard— that incomparably egotistical sex maniac who thought he was God's gift to women.

"Look, Charley," she said in a brisk, businesslike tone, "let's keep this discussion on a purely professional keel, shall we? The only reason we're both sitting here is because we have a mutual problem to solve."

"Oh?" he said, fingering one end of his droopy, Sam Elliott of a mustache. "Is that so?"

"It is," she replied crisply.

"Unh-unh. No, Kenzie." Abruptly he stopped worrying his mustache. "No. It is not so. You see, you are looking at this from a fundamentally wrong angle." Charley flicked an index finger between himself and her. "*We* do not have a problem. Granted, *Burghley's* may well have a problem, ergo—" He leveled the index finger at her, "—*you* have a problem. But neither the NYPD art theft squad nor I has one."

Lounging back on the sofa, he crossed his arms behind his head and made himself comfortable. "Now, the sooner you digest that minor fact," he said smugly, "the better off we'll both be."

Kenzie's face stung. *How dare he lecture me!* she thought, with rising fury. *Who the* hell *does he think he is?*

And, more to the point, had he forgotten that the police department was—in theory at least—an organization comprised of public servants? And that Burghley's, as a tax-paying institution, had as much a right to its services as the Artisteria Gallery, that second-rate peddler of dubious prints by Leroy Neiman, Erté, and Dali?

Damn right it did! However, she knew that this was neither the time nor the place to let the fur fly.

Let Charley be smug, she told herself. He can act as immaturely as he wished; she, Burghley's appointed representative in this matter, would remain outwardly calm, businesslike, aloof, and entirely above reproach—so unflappably above reproach that it would drive him clear up the wall.

"Sorry, Charley," she said. "Like it or not, you're on this case. And, if it turns out that the Holbein was *indeed* stolen—"

"Aha. Hold it right there." Charley held up a hand, palm facing out: a cop stopping traffic. "You're saying it had to have been smuggled into this country. Am I right or am I *right?*"

"*If* it was stolen, yes." She nodded.

"Then it's a matter for Interpol and the FBI. Or need I remind you that international trafficking in stolen art is way beyond NYPD jurisdiction?"

"You do not. And you're wrong. Granted, it's a matter for Interpol and the FBI. But it also concerns the NYPD. That painting's in our Madison Avenue vaults, Charley. On New York City soil. Moreover, it was brought in to our New York galleries by a Manhattan attorney representing the seller who, for reason or reasons unknown, prefers to remain anonymous."

"A dead giveaway that something's not kosher, hmm?"

"Charley," she said, as patiently as she could, "I didn't take that painting on, okay? Also, I don't need to tell you that we deal with intermediaries all the time. Lawyers, art consultants, private dealers . . . we both know why sellers use them."

"In order to remain anonymous."

"Right. Whether for fear of thieves or kidnappers, or because the owner's fallen on hard times and doesn't want to broadcast that fact, or because he's some mad recluse who'll go to any lengths to maintain his priva—"

"Aw right, aw *right!*" Charley said testily. "Just tell me what you want me to do. Arrest someone we don't even know exists?"

"On the contrary. For now, your job is to help expedite our own investigation. In short, you have access to information we may be unable to obtain. Also, we might need you to liaise—"

" 'Liaise'?" He gave a mock start; made a little pretense of looking impressed. "That the word of the day now?"

"Ha ha, the smartass surfaces. Now then. I take it we can count on your, uh, expertise?"

"Why not just hire a detective?"

"Because you *are* one," she pointed out inexorably.

"Yeah, but I meant a private dick."

"Is *that* why we're taxed out the whazoo?" she asked indignantly. "To pay the private sector for the same services for which we already pay the city?"

"Shoulda known you'd have an answer handy," he muttered darkly. Tilting her head, she smiled with great sweetness.

"Okay," he sighed. "Would you mind telling me exactly *what* information I'm supposed to procure, and *who* I might need to, er, *liaise* with?"

"I was hoping you could tell me." She was all smiles. "You're the cop."

He mashed a hand into his face. "Christ. Walked right into that one, didn't I?" He gnashed his teeth in frustration. Of all the creatures vile and evil, this she-devil really, truly took the cake! How like her to use his own words against him. And how incredibly phenomenal that so much ruthless calculation—so much devious selfishness!—could be contained in such a deceptively cute and petite package. There really ought to be a law about people's outsides matching their insides, not that it mattered much anymore. She'd fooled him once, and he'd learned his lesson the hard way. Still, in retrospect, it was difficult to imagine he'd once been so gullible as to have granted this cunning bitch the all-encompassing warmth of his body and soul. Well, at least there was no danger of *that* ever happening again!

"Aw right," he sighed, reluctantly firing up his gray cells. The quicker he got this over with, the sooner he'd be gone. "Who's the intermediary?"

"An attorney named Zachary Bavosa."

"Shit."

"Why 'shit'?" Kenzie asked, giving him a strange look. "I take it this means you know something about him?"

"Yeah. Matter a fact, I do."

"Like?"

He showed some teeth. "Like you're dealing with a real scumbag."

Takes one to know one, she thought, but didn't articulate.

"A true, world-class lowlife," he reiterated. And frowning thoughtfully, added: "Better count me out."

"Whoa!" Kenzie said heatedly, feeling warmth prickling her cheeks. "Back up there." Her hands were itching to crawl out from under her buttocks, and it was all she could do to keep sitting on them. But sit on them she must: the urge to grab him and shake information from him was altogether too great.

"Look, Kenzie." He rested his forearms on his thighs and leaned across the kilim-draped coffee table. "Bavosa might be a lowlife, okay? But he's strictly small time. The Artisteria robbery . . . yeah. I could see him acting as an intermediary for their kinda stuff. But a Holbein?" He shook his head. "No way."

"Ah! So you admit to putting a penny-ante heist above what's possibly a major theft!"

"Like hell I am! A robbery's a robbery. People were bound and gagged at the Artisteria Gallery. For your information, they coulda easily been killed."

"Yeah," she smirked. "And for Lex Buggs or Ertés. God. Imagine the *insult.*"

He wasn't amused. "You realize how many people a day are killed for less?"

"Lots, I'm sure. But how," she demanded, "do you know someone wasn't killed acquiring the Holbein?"

"I don't, but that's a lifetime and four thousand miles ago. Meanwhile, the Artisteria robbery's here and now."

"So's the Holbein," she snapped, not in anger, but with conviction. "At least, according to Washington and Bonn it is. And, penny-ante or not, Bavosa's the intermediary."

"Probably through sheer luck, and because there's no conspiracy involved."

"How can you be so sure?"

"Because anyone with half a brain would steer clear of him, that's why. Tell you what—I'll inform Officer Kopensky that you'll be in touch. She's eminently capable, and you can work with her. Now, I've got more pressing things to do, so unless there's something else, I'm outta here."

He rose to his feet.

She jumped to hers. "Oh no you don't!" she huffed. "You're not going *anywhere,* Charles Gabriel Ferraro. Not if *I* can help it."

He snatched his overcoat from the sofa and started past her. "Then you just watch me," he said grimly, striding to the front door.

"Like hell I will!"

With the speed of lightning, she darted unerringly in front of him, reached the door first, and stood there, splay-legged, barring his way. Her arms were crossed in front of her, and she stared up at him, amber eyes shining like coals.

"Kenzie," Charley sighed wearily, "when are you gonna stop playing games? Will you *please* step aside?"

Her nostrils flared as she tossed her head. "Not if my life depended upon it." Her feet were firmly planted and she stood there, resolute as a rock.

He stared down into her upturned face. "Does this mean I must *physically* remove you from my path?"

"Oooooh!" she taunted, her eyes growing wide. "So now you're into police brutality." She barked humorless laughter. "Why am I not surprised?"

"Kenzie," he sighed, "c'mon. You're leaving me no choice."

"Charley, if you so much as lay a . . . a goddamn *finger* on me, so help me God I'll . . . I'll . . ."

"You'll what?"

Her pupils dilated. "I'll physically restrain you!"

"*You?* Restrain *me?*" He laughed. "Don't tell me. You into jujitsu now?"

"Go ahead." She sniffed loftily. "Make fun of me if you want."

"I'm not making fun," he said quietly. "I'm asking you nicely. Now, for the last time, will you *please step aside?*"

She kept her chin raised. "No fucking way."

"Then you leave me no other option." He reached out for her, but again, she was quicker.

Unthinkingly, and totally without premeditation or warning, she launched herself directly at him, grabbing him around the neck with her arms while jackknifing her legs and scissoring them tightly around his waist.

She caught him so utterly unaware, so entirely by surprise, and impaired his vision so completely, that he staggered backward and dropped his coat.

"Are . . . you . . . *mad?*" he gasped, pulling at her thighs with both hands in an attempt to wrench her loose.

Instead of replying, she clung to him like a monkey, but with one vast difference. No simian on earth had so unyielding a grip, or was so smooth-skinned, so ripely, voluptuously, and undeniably feminine. Under the circumstances, there wasn't a red-blooded, heterosexual male on earth who stood a chance, especially not with the crotch of her red jersey sweats pressed right up against the crotch of his twills. Despite his angry curses, he could already feel something stir beneath the layers of fabric, and so could she.

He was definitely getting hard.

"Get . . . the hell . . . *off* me!" he gasped hoarsely. In vain, he tore at the drawstring waist of her sweatpants. "Let . . . *go!*"

"Never!" she panted. Her hold around his neck and middle tightened.

"You . . . fuckin' . . . *bitch!*" Even as his penis swelled, he made one last ditch attempt to free himself. Grabbing the back of her sweats with both hands, he yanked the waist apart with all his might. A sudden ripping noise ensued as fabric rent; seams and drawstring gave way, ragged cotton drooped. Instantly Kenzie felt the rush of cool air as all that stood between her and bottomless nudity were the briefest of red briefs.

"You . . . you barbaric *Neanderthal!*" she huffed, shaking with rage.

Unable to see past her, he staggered around blindly.

Savagely she pummeled his buttocks with both feet and beat his back with her free fist. "Defiler!" she ranted, biting his ear with knife-sharp teeth for good measure.

He yelped in agony. "Lunatic!"

"Pervert!" she screamed. *"Rapist!"*

And then his foot caught on the edge of the carpet. Letting out a yell, he teetered dangerously, lost his balance and toppled over backward, landing heavily on the floor. Air whooshed out of his lungs.

Fortunately for her, he'd landed on his back, so *she* wasn't squashed. However, she *had* rolled off him. Now, being the first to recover, she scrambled right back atop him, in her haste not noticing that she was straddling him *upside down,* in the classic position universally known as the sixty-nine. *Damn!* Talk about facing in the wrong direction!

She tried to scoot around, but it was already too late. Charley was coming to, his hands pushing on her buttocks and trying to lift her, while his face, pressed against that most glorious of all obstructions, the mound of her barely covered pubis, exhaled radiant warmth right into the core of her being.

Kenzie's entire torso arched, and she went momentarily stone cold. Then something inside her—the icy resolution she'd believed impervious to combustibility—ignited and melted away in a blaze.

And still the internal explosions continued, on and on, as if fed from a bottomless source. Violent shudders, fierce and deeply sexual, wracked her body from head to toe, and the feeling of physical urgency was curiously liberating, as though shackles were cracking apart and setting her free. Suddenly, it seemed only natural to focus all her attention upon the groin of Charley's gray twill trousers.

For, unlike Oakland, there was a *there* there. And, from the way the fabric twitched and strained, there was a *lot* of there there. A whole lot.

A killer erection, if she gauged it correctly.

Reaching out, she firmly took hold of his cloth-enshrouded penis.

He nearly levitated.

She sighed aloud with pleasure. How had she done without for so long? And whatever could have possessed her to lead these last few months of mean, self-induced celibacy in the first place? A lively sex life, like a fine wine, was to be enjoyed.

"Kenzie . . ." Charley's voice was muffled, but the vibrations it sent coursing through her were electric. ". . . we're both . . . gonna regret . . ."

But she wasn't listening. An intense heat, like from a furnace, radiated from deep within her, and a warm sticky moisture dampened her panties and wet her thighs.

"Please . . ." she heard Charley gasp. "This . . . isn't . . . fair . . ."

"Charley," she chided, bowing her head into his groin, "haven't you heard? All's fair in sex and war."

Gently she took the zipper pull between her teeth and slowly unzipped his trousers.

His fly opened like a husk, and when she loosened his trapped phallus and scrotum, his penis twitched the air, a heat-seeking missile in search of its target. With its enormous swollen head and prominent veins bulging in deep relief, it rose stalwartly from its thicket of pubic hair, looking like nothing so much as a delicious sculpture fashioned of the finest, surpassingly pink nephrite.

"I . . . I'm . . . not responsible," Charley managed, his voice, like his warm breath, lost in her moist, private-most regions.

"Oh, do shut up, Charley," she said, without rancor. "Didn't anybody ever tell you you talk too much?"

And gripping the stem of his manhood with one hand, she loosened his belt and trouser button with the other, all the while leisurely pressing her groin into his face.

His pleasurable groans were a dead giveaway, as was his tongue working its way beneath her panty line.

She knew now that he was lost; they'd reached the point of no return. Good.

Taking a long, deep breath of delight, she lowered her mouth and trailed the feathery tip of her tongue teasingly along the length of the engorged shaft and then reverentially across the succulent globes of scrotal fruit.

With her every lick, Charley gasped and pushed his pelvis upward.

Well, he can shake, rattle, and roll all he wants, she thought, with a smile. *Not that it'll do him much good.*

On the contrary. She had done without for too long to rush things along now, and was resolutely—obstinately and inexorably—determined to savor every last delectable millimeter of him, and for as long and leisurely as was humanly possible.

Under her ministrations, his phallus impatiently jerked and thrummed and leapt.

"Cool it, Charley," she murmured, treating the slit of his penis to a swirl of her questing tongue. "What's the hurry? Can't you just lie back and enjoy the ride?"

And opening her mouth wide, she closed it solemnly around the head of his penis and held it there, waiting until he was absolutely still. Then, and only then, did she yield, her lips and tongue working in tandem to treat him to the strong and unfaltering suction of her mouth.

He responded in kind, pulling down her briefs and drilling his tongue past her glorious dark pubic nest, and through the fleshy outer lips of her pouting clitoris.

She shut her eyes, happily refamiliarizing herself with every last vein and curve of his phallus.

This—this sex act—was no mere lust, she knew. There was pent-up passion here; the perfume of bodies driven by desire; the sensation of time stopping so that this moment, and this alone, comprised the reality of living.

Now she was no longer able to control the wild thrusts of her hips, and she sucked ravenously. Taking his cue from her, he lathed her vigorously, his own pelvis bucking upward in demanding, jackhammer movements.

Oh, how right this felt! she thought. How blessedly, wonderfully *right!* And ah, how the remembrances of tangy smells and familiar tastes helped fuel the fires of carnality!

Garments were deemed too constricting. These were mutually, wordlessly, speedily disposed of: some easily shed, others torn off in the throes of passion.

Now they were naked. Regal. Gleaming.

She could feel her heart pounding fiercely, the blood racing madly through her veins, the juices of life starting to build up inside her.

Unbidden, tears sprang into her eyes. What *was* she feeling for him? *Love,* that woefully inadequate four letter word? Or mere *lust,* that craving so potent and possessive that beside it, all else in the universe paled?

But these answers, she knew, must wait. Later, there would be time for introspection. Here and now, words were redundant; nothing existed except for flesh against flesh.

Still gripping his penis by the base, she slid around to face him. Her eyes had a wild kind of look as she straddled his pelvis and raised her buttocks high.

For a moment she seemed perfectly still, as though suspended in midair. Then, with a smooth, graceful elegance, she slowly lowered herself down upon him.

Her eyes widened as she impaled her moist female warmth upon his tumescence. There was a jolt of pain, and then he was in, sliding all the way up inside her.

Slowly, deliberately, she rose back up, as if to expell him, then lowered herself completely again. Beneath her, she could see him grit his teeth; heard him grunt involuntarily as slowly, rhythmically, she lifted and lowered her pelvis: up and down, up and down, up and down . . .

Suddenly he was no longer content to just lie there. Greedily, his pelvis rose to meet hers, and together, their movements quickened, their hips moving in a blurry, sensuous dance as old as time itself.

Faster, faster, faster! Ever more furiously they took their pleasure, twisting their hips in delirium, consumed with but one purpose—to satiate unquenchable passions.

More, more, more! It was as if neither of them could seem to get enough. Ravenousness begot more ravenousness; hips, hands, legs, breasts: all worked in feverish tandem.

And then her eyes glazed over, her mouth opened in ecstasy, and a guttural cry issued forth from her throat. Locking him tightly to her, she felt the torrent rise inside her; the universe explode into dazzling pyrotechnics.

It was but the first of multiple orgasms. With each she screamed in agony, yet each was like a regeneration.

Still she proved insatiable.

Never before had it been like this. But then, never before had she been celibate for so long. Every orgasm came as a thundering upheaval, each gaining in strength.

And then it was he who could hold back no longer.

It seemed the earth shook and the very heavens split asunder. With a primordial howl, he clamped his hips to hers, and his testes exploded, spilling forth his seed.

And contracting her vaginal muscles, she orgasmed one last time, her screams merging with his as together they burst across the finish line in an apocalypse which seemed to have no beginning and no end.

Thus spent, lungs bursting and breaths rasping, they clung to one another.

Long minutes passed.

Finally Charley stirred. As he let go of her, he felt his phallus slide out of a vagina. Then, recognizing its proprietor, he looked away before doing a classic double take.

And very nearly choked.

Kenzie!

What the devil?

Abruptly sitting up, he shook his head to clear it while trying to figure out what, exactly, had hit him.

Only one answer was possible.

"And with what," he demanded hoarsely, "did you spike my drink?"

"Don't be silly," she said calmly. She lay there, the very picture of a nubile, blissfully satiated Venus. "I didn't even *offer* you a drink. Remember?"

He scratched his touseled head and frowned. "Right. So what exactly did happen?"

She smiled. "Why, I like to think *I* happened."

"Jeez!" he exclaimed. "You know what's wrong with you?"

"What?" She positively purred.

"You've got an ego the size of Mont-fucking-Blanc!"

"Aw," she said sweetly. "I ever tell you how cute you look when you get angry?"

His scowl deepened.

Kenzie wondered why that particular remark always got a man's goat, but it did. She'd never once known it to fail.

Pretending to ignore him, she stretched luxuriantly, laced her hands behind her head, and wiggled her toes.

"My God!" Charley, who recognized a direct lift from his own repertoire when he saw one, croaked hoarsely. *She's imitating me!* he realized. *Fuckin' mimicking me!*

"Is nothing sacred?" he asked coldly.

"Yep!" she replied, happily wiggling her toes. "Cows."

Cows? He wasn't even going to ask what she meant by *that.*

"You know," he said, "at times you can be a real pain in the ass."

"Yep!" she repeated brightly. "But momentarily a very, *very* sexually appeased pain!" She blew him an extravagant air kiss. "Thanks, lover boy."

Clenching his jaw to keep from exchanging another word with this vilest of creatures, he rose to his feet. Scanned the floor. Snarled: "Socks."

Retrieved one. Savagely pulled it on his left foot as he hopped around on his right.

Leaning up on her elbows, she watched with growing amusement as he stomped around—here, there, everywhere—plucking items of discarded clothing from wherever they had landed.

Aware of her watchful gaze, he prudishly turned his back on her and set about getting dressed.

Oh, great! she thought. *Now the big stud needs privacy!* She rolled her eyes and let her head drop down to the carpet. *As if there's any part of his anatomy I haven't seen!*

She sighed to herself. Men. They really could be such assholes at times.

Finally he was ready. Properly buttoned, zipped, tucked, and laced.

Adjusting his tie, he marched stiffly past her, scooping his overcoat up off the floor on the way. Reaching the front door, he lost no time unbolting the topmost of the five Fichet locks.

"Oh, Charley," Kenzie called out in a lazy drawl.

She waited, but he was too intent upon unlocking the door to pay her any heed.

Damn him, she thought with mild vexation. *He's deliberately ignoring me.*

She sat up and placed her hands on her hips. "Aren't you forgetting something?" she asked, raising her voice slightly.

He flicked her a sideways glance. "Like what?"

"Like this." And jumping up, she snatched a thick Jiffy bag off the coffee table and flung it across the room at him.

He was left with two choices—either to get coldcocked, or to reach out and catch it. Wisely he chose to do the latter.

"Jesus," he glowered. "What are you trying to kill me with? Lead?"

Kenzie crossed the room. She was moving with an agile, unselfconscious grace, her breasts riding high and proud.

Charley felt the blood ascend into his face. Quickly he averted his gaze. *Christ!* She had him so befuddled, he actually had to *concentrate* just to work his way down the row of locks! Why couldn't she keep her distance? Her physical proximity engulfed him like a palpable caress.

"That package," she informed him, "contains the Holbein file."

Now he had four locks open. He thought: *One more and I'm outta here!*

"You should find everything you need in there," she continued. "Catalogue, appraisals, color transparencies, sales receipts, transfers of ownership, copies of correspondence . . . you name it."

The last lock cylinder clicked.

"If there's anything else you need," she added softly, "don't hesitate to whistle."

Like hell! he thought, and yanked the door wide. He tromped quickly down the stairs, the package under one arm.

Kenzie poked her face around the door. "I'll phone you tomorrow?" she called after him.

His head disappeared down the stairwell.

Smiling to herself, she shut the door and locked it.

This has certainly been an interesting evening, she decided. *Yes. Most interesting indeed . . .*

For not only had she corraled Charley into working with her, but she'd even been brought to multiple orgasm in the process!

Which just goes to prove one thing, she thought. *If you play your cards right, you* can *have your cake and eat it, too!*

And smiling with smug contentedness, she stretched luxuriantly. Why was it, she wondered, giving a mighty yawn, that making love always made her so sleepy? Really, if someone could bottle post-coital bliss, they'd be rolling in dough. Put sleeping pills totally out of business . . .

Crossing the room, her bare toes poked something silky. She stopped to investigate. Good Lord. Her red panties.

She perused the rest of the floor. Oh, my. The carpet was littered with evidence of gratified debauchery, including her ripped, red jersey sweatpants. Oh my, oh my.

She knew she ought to pick up her things now . . . fluff the sofa cushions . . . do what had to be done to straighten the room up.

She yawned blearily. Bah! What was the rush? Zandra wouldn't be home until—when? A couple of hours from now? There would be plenty of time to clean up . . . oodles and oodles of it. And curling up on the sofa, she tucked a cushion under her head, and practically purred. Ah, this felt sooooo nice . . .

Her eyelids drifted shut.

Sweet dreams soon followed.

Such sweet dreams that she slept until Zandra returned.

Then she awoke with a start.

There was Zandra. *Playbill* in hand. Gazing about the living room floor with a mixture of curiosity and amusement.

"*Whaa-!*" Kenzie, momentarily disoriented, sat up suddenly. Realized she was buff naked. Grabbed the cushion and hugged it against her.

"Ssssh!" Zandra put a finger to slyly smiling lips. "Go back to sleep!" she stage-whispered, making a production of tiptoeing past. "*I* won't natter." And with a knowing wink, she sang, "Mum's the word!"

"It isn't what you think!" Kenzie growled, knowing full well that it was.

Zandra pointedly detoured around the ripped sweats. She did not speak. But then, she didn't have to. The evidence spoke for itself, as did her raised eyebrows.

Kenzie slumped. "Oh, God," she groaned. "I'll never live this down!"

"*Never* say never," Zandra advised. "But, darling, you mustn't *fret!* Honestly, it's not as though you're underage. Gosh. I mean, long as it was good—it was, wasn't it? No, don't tell me . . . right to privacy and all. 'Never complain, never explain.' That's the creed. So you see, darling? You don't have to explain a *thing*"—Zandra couldn't quite help herself—"though personally, I think it's awfully *sweet*. I mean, you and Charley actually *kissing* and making up." She gave a great sigh. "God, how marvelously romantic!"

"Arrrgh!" Kenzie gnashed her teeth, flopped back down, and covered her face with the cushion.

Zandra feigned a yawn. "Darling, the sandman calls. Isn't it simply awful, shows always putting me to *sleep?*" She drifted past, headed for her own room. "Want me to switch off the lights?"

Kenzie was silent.

Zandra interpreted that to mean yes. "Well, night-night!" she chirped, hitting the lights.

The living room was plunged into darkness.

"Shit!" Kenzie whispered vehemently. And curling up in the fetal position, she promptly fell back asleep.

26

*L*ate the following morning, at Park Avenue and Fifty-ninth Street, the smell of money was heady on the second floor of Christie's.

On this particular exhibition day, less than twenty-four hours before the scheduled auction of *Fabergé, Russian Works of Art, Objects of Vertu, and English, Continental, and American Silver and Gold,* the scent of wealth seeped from the silver-gilt and enamel tea sets, and emanated from the voluptuously gilded pairs of eighteenth-century royal doors, one of which depicted a full-length St. John Chrysostom, and the other, St. Basil. It wafted, like elusive perfume, from the sets of hand-painted Imperial Factory porcelains, and rose, like a provocative whiff, from the glass showcases containing intricate Caucasian daggers and centuries-old snuff boxes.

Among objects of this quality, one was compelled to whisper—even a connoisseur as discerning as Becky V. Despite the decades she'd spent roaming the world's finest auction galleries, private collections, and museums, she never failed to thrill to the wonder of treasures whose provenances read like a distillation of *Burke's Peerage, Debrett's,* the *Almanach de Gotha,* blue-book society, and *Who's Who*—mere *things* which by virtue of certain temporary custodianships, had been imbued with historical or social significance and, in a very few, very special cases, truly magical auras.

For what could compare to a silver goblet from which Marie Antoinette had once sipped?

Or an enameled egg touched by a doomed czarina?

Becky slowed in front of a glass display case. Prince Karl-Heinz, who only the previous day had returned from Germany, was following her around, coinhabiting her bubble of insular remoteness while contemplating samovars, Augsburg silver, and gold demitasse cups. From a discreet distance, Becky's Secret Service detail hard-eyed everyone else in sight.

"So . . . *le vieil Prince?*" Becky whispered in her mellow, whiskey-toned voice. She had temporarily lowered her guard and raised her mask: her ubiquitous, huge dark glasses rested atop her sable-haired head. "Your father's condition is at least stable?"

"For the time being," Karl-Heinz replied in an equally soft voice, "yes. But it was a very close call." With a wry smile, he added: "I suspect my sister, Sofia, was devastated when he pulled through."

"*Naturellement!*" Becky slid him a significant sidelong look. "Think of the *billions* she and that husband of hers . . . what *is* his name—*je oublier*—Egbert? . . . would have held in trust for their eldest son!"

Karl-Heinz smiled. "Not Egbert. Erwein."

"Erwein!" She pronounced the two short syllables as if with a surprised little cry. "Now why did I think his name was Egbert? *Comment se fait-il que?*"

"Perhaps because it suits him?" he suggested.

"*Oui*. It does." She smiled, without humor. "I met him once or twice, *le malheureux*. Dreary, dreary little man!"

"Worse than you can imagine," Karl-Heinz agreed. "And he's so *boring*, which is perhaps the gravest sin of all."

Becky stopped to study an exuberantly carved, eighteenth-century silver wine cooler. Then, frowning slightly, she shook her head and slowly moved on.

She was wearing a short-skirted Chanel suit in sapphire blue with emerald trim, a perfect foil for her Nefertiti-like profile, and size-four body. Her earrings, bracelet, and necklace matched the trim on her suit. They were emeralds: carved antiques with cameo faces.

"And you?" Karl-Heinz inquired politely, walking in the Germanic fashion with his hands clasped behind his back. "You are well?"

"You should know that life always agrees with me. Hmmmmm . . ."

Becky stopped at a table, where she covetously eyed an exceptionally splendid, two-foot-tall silver and enamel tabernacle. It was shaped like a Russian church, and had one central turquoise onion dome surrounded by four smaller, turreted ones at the corners. On three of its four sides was a hinged door with an embossed, chased figure of Christ.

Peering at the lot number, she leafed through her catalogue.

"*Fine silver and enamel Darokhranilnitza, Nicolai Tarabrov, Moscow, circa 1910*," she read aloud. She glanced at Karl-Heinz for his opinion.

He was smiling. "Here at Christie's, it's a '*darokhranilnitza.*' Anywhere else, it's a mere tabernacle."

"*Finaud.*" Smart-aleck. Becky pinched his arm affectionately. "With your twelve billion, you can afford to lack *snobisme. C'est vrai?*"

So talking, she circled around the table, bending down to study the tabernacle closely from all sides. She fiddled with one of the tiny doorpulls, opened it, and peered inside. Then she closed it just as carefully and stood up straight.

"*Alors,*" she decided. "I am going to bid on it. *Qu'en pensez-tu?*"

"It is very beautiful," he agreed. "A masterpiece in miniature."

"*Oui.* One thing about *Les Russes.* They always were so very good at these kinds of things." She frowned slightly at the catalogue. "The estimate says six to eight thousand. I believe that's on the low side." She glanced at him. "Hmmmmm . . . ?"

"Definitely." He nodded.

She slid an arm through his and led him to a wall of icons.

"Now then," she said, pulling him into the privacy of a corner. "While we're on the subject of money . . ." She let go of him and suddenly whirled around. "Heinzie! We must talk finances!"

"Oh? Are you short? How much do you need?"

"Finaud!" Her whisper was like a whiplash. "This is no laughing matter!"

"Why, Becky." He looked both surprised and amused. "You sound so serious."

"That's because I am serious." She sighed, placed her gloved hand on his chest, and for a moment lowered her head, as if to contemplate her gracefully poised fingers. Then, gathering her thoughts, she stared back up at him. "Heinzie, for your own good, listen to me! *Please!*"

He was silent.

Her voice was hushed. "I beseech you. Once and for all—*get married!*"

He laughed almost silently. "So this is why you were so anxious to see me today?" It was more a statement than a question.

"Oui," she admitted. "It is time you secured your inheritance." She took hold of his lapels. "And before it is too late!"

Nearby, two celebrity watchers were huddled in whispered conversation, obviously undecided about whether or not to approach Becky, while her Secret Service detail, always ten steps ahead, already prepared an intercept.

"You know I'm right, Heinzie!" she whispered.

She let go of his lapels and instinctively smoothed them. The celebrity-watchers hurried forward, and were expertly rebuffed.

Not that Becky or Karl-Heinz noticed. Unaware of anything happening outside their insular bubble, they were holding each other's gaze.

"You cannot put it off any longer!" she warned. *"Dieu sait!* Hasn't this close call with your father been lesson enough? *Mon ange,* be sensible."

Karl-Heinz sighed. He rubbed his forehead and turned toward the wall.

Faces and eyes of stylized icons, like mute witnesses, stared at him from within the intricate armor of their silvered *okhlads*. The Virgin of Vladimir holding her child; St. Nicholas of Moshaisk; the Centurian Longinus. St. George with his lance. And the archangels, St. Michael and St. Gabriel, swords in hand. They seemed out of place in these bright, modern surroundings: plundered treasures from a strange and distant shore.

"Heinzie," Becky implored softly. "Why . . . why must you, of all people, be so disinterested in your fate?"

"Why?" He turned to her with a wry smile. "Perhaps because I have you, my dear Becky, to worry about it."

"*Cela suffit!*" Her eyes flashed angrily. "I won't have you uttering such nonsense. *Non.* The only reason I worry is because I am genuinely fond of you."

"I know that," he said gently.

"I cannot bear to see you lose your inheritance," she continued. "But you must face the facts, *chéri.* One of these days, *le vieil Prince* will not pull through." She took a deep breath. "And then what?"

Not for the first time, Karl-Heinz felt the force of her will, was aware of the iron hand under the kidskin glove.

"You know the answer to that as well as I do," he replied softly.

"*Oui,*" she sighed. "But it does not have to happen that way. It cannot! *Mon Dieu!* Did you multiply the family fortune only to relinquish it to your sister's *imbécile?* And for what? Mere want of a male heir?"

He did not speak.

"Listen to me, Heinzie. You know what will happen if that *imbécile* takes over. The empire will lose direction. Its momentum will slow. It will rot and crumble from within!"

His gaze had not changed.

"*Alors.* You are your family's captain. So please, Heinzie. For everyone's sake—especially your own—don't give up the ship!"

He gave a bitter laugh. "You make it sound so easy!"

"That's because it *is* easy!"

"Oh?" He raised one cynical eyebrow. "Keeping a dying old man alive? Getting appropriately married? And siring a male heir in time?"

"*Oui.*"

"Becky, I am not God!"

She stared at him. "No one expects you to be," she said, undeterred. "But did you build that empire into what it is only to see it torn apart? *Non.* You love the businesses, Heinzie. Admit it. They are your life's blood. As are your social positions. The various *Schösser.* The art collections. The power. You love everything that comes with being head of the family, *except for settling down!*"

"My one true duty?" he mocked. Again, the raised eyebrow, this time accompanied by a sardonic little smile.

"Dammit, Heinzie!" she breathed through clenched teeth. "Must you be so stubborn? Marry, for God's sake! Produce a male heir! Ensure that what is yours shall continue to be yours!"

"Why is it," he sighed, "that I can sense my carefree bachelorhood coming to an end?"

"Because it's time!" she said sharply. "You have had a reprieve—now use it to your advantage!"

"And marry."

"*Oui.*"

He turned away, as if to study the wall of icons. After a moment's silence, he said, cynically: "Let me guess. You have already picked out the appropriate bride?"

"Of course, *chéri*. And just think. She's been right under our noses all this time!"

He shut his eyes. "Zandra," he said painfully.

"Of course, Zandra!" she said, her eyebrows drawing together. "Why *not* Zandra?"

Karl-Heinz opened his eyes and stared at the icons a while longer. Then, putting his hands in his pant pockets, he turned to her and said: "You don't understand. I have known her since she was born."

"*Alors?*"

"She still has her entire life ahead of her. My God, Becky! Marriage to me, with all its responsibilities, could destroy her!"

Becky's eyes narrowed. "Are you certain about that?"

He shrugged. "Sometimes," he sighed, pinching the bridge of his nose, "I'm not certain about anything anymore."

His passionate tone alerted her. "*Dit moi,*" she said slowly, in the tones of a woman who trusts her intuition. "How do you really feel about Zandra?"

"How—" An anguished look came into his face. "*Verdammt noch einmal!* How could *any* man feel about her? She's enchanting, dammit! There is something magical about her!" He added, savagely: "Is that what you wanted to hear?"

"Why, Heinzie!" Eyes aglow, Becky clasped her hands against her bosom. "How wonderful! I do believe you are in love with her!"

He flinched at the word *love*.

"Now then," she asked. "Have you made your feelings for Zandra known?"

"To her?"

"Of course to her!" she said impatiently.

He shook his head. "No," he whispered hoarsely.

"And why not?"

"For one thing," he said with stiff dignity, "I do not relish rejection. For another, I am neither a lecher nor a pederast."

"You! A pederast!" Becky laughed. "Don't be ridiculous. Zandra is not a child. She is a mature woman. Far more worldly and mature than you give her credit for."

"Perhaps," he admitted grudgingly.

"Heinzie." Becky's voice was quiet. "Don't you see? You really have no choice. You must marry her!"

"That," he said a little tartly, "is easier said than done."

"*Au contraire, chéri.* It really is quite simple."

"Oh?"

"*Oui.* I will play fairy godmother to you both!"

"I see," he said, rubbing his chin. Then, with dawning suspicion, he added: "You wouldn't, by any chance, have already begun planning this without me, now would you?"

"*Mais oui!*" she admitted brightly. "After all, there is no time to lose! Now, the plan is this . . ." Placing her gloved hand on his arm, she lowered her voice and guided him slowly around the perimeter of the gallery. ". . . I shall invite you for a weekend to my house in the country. Zandra—and her friends, the Goldsmiths—shall be invited by my neighbors, the Faireys. That way, your . . . *ahem!* . . . chance meeting will appear less obvious."

"Always the soul of discretion," he commented dryly.

She gestured. "All I ask is that you trust me. You will see. Two days around you, and Zandra shall be unable to resist."

"Oh? Is that a guarantee?"

"I don't see why not. *Oui. Oui.*" Becky nodded to herself. "With your charm, you should be married within the month."

"All right," he sighed. "Since you seem to have all the answers, perhaps you can tell me something."

"*Alors?*" She looked at him questioningly.

His voice was quiet. "What does Zandra get out of this?"

Becky stopped walking and faced him squarely. "Why, that's obvious, isn't it? She gets *you*—one of the world's most eligible bachelors! She becomes the chateleine of one of the world's greatest and richest families! Plus, she is elevated from a mere countess to a princess! *Mon Dieu!*" She stared at him. "What more could a young woman want?"

"Someone her own age, perhaps?"

"*Bêta.*" She reached up and touched his cheek affectionately. "Can it be that you men really know so little?"

He did not reply.

She smiled. "Remember, Heinzie. Don't ever underestimate me. I always accomplish what I set out to do."

"Even this."

"Especially this," she said definitely.

He was silent for a moment. "Then what I always thought about you really is true. You are the most determined woman in New York."

Becky flexed her fingers, adjusting the fit of her glove. "*Alors,*" she said, changing the subject. "It's lunchtime. Do let's pop over to Mortimer's for a bite to eat."

She hooked an arm through his.

"Shall we, *chéri?*"

"K enz," Arnold Li called from out in the hall, "gentleman here to see you."

Kenzie, on an overseas call, put a hand over the receiver. "Oh, tell Charley to cool his heels!" she snapped, not bothering to turn around. "You know how long it took me to get through to Miskolctapolca, Hungary?"

Then, uncovering the receiver, she segued right back into the conversation, her voice bright, smooth, professional. As if the interruption had never occurred.

"I really appreciate you taking the time for this, Professor Tindemans. I hate bothering you during your cure ... I'm so glad you understand, sir ... Yes, I'll keep an eye peeled for your fax ... Of course I'll convey your regards to Mr. Spotts the next time I speak to him! I know he'll be delighted ... You've been *most* helpful, Professor ... I hope you enjoy the cure, and please accept my apologies for the intrusion ... Thank *you*, Professor Tindemans!"

She hung up the phone with a flourish. Rolled back her chair. Flung both fists triumphantly into the air and crowed: "Yes!"

" 'Yes'?" Zandra inquired in puzzlement. "Darling, what is it? I mean, one would think your team had won the World Cup."

"Naw. Only the next best thing." Kenzie sighed happily, folded her arms behind her head, and smiled at the precarious skyscrapers of books and catalogues on her desk. "What a lovely, lovely gentleman. So gallant. And Zandra?"

"Yes?"

"You can stop researching the Holbein."

"Stop? What do you mean, *stop?*" Zandra objected, more puzzled than ever. "You know we can't. This has priority."

"Not anymore. I followed a hunch and hit paydirt. You see, Mr. Spotts once told me that Professor Tindemans is to Holbein what E. K. Waterhouse is to Reynolds. Well, not only was he right, but—would you *believe*—Professor Tindemans actually studied our very painting back in 1939?"

"He did? Oh, Kenzie, *super!*"

"Mmm-hmmm. All I had to do was track him down from Brussels to

Hungary, where he's at some remote spa which has—now get this—naturally radioactive grottos."

"Radioactive!" Zandra gave a shudder. "But how awful. What is it—an underground Chernobyl?"

"Sounds it, but it's supposed to have curative powers for asthma or something. At any rate, he's calling his assistant in Belgium, who'll fax us the pertinent pages of his new treatise. It's scheduled for publication this fall, and is on German artists in the fifteenth and sixteenth centuries. *And*—are you ready for this?—it includes our Holbein's provenance from A to Z! So *voilà!* Current ownership and smuggling issues aside, our part of the work's complete."

"Gosh, Kenzie. Well done. You *are* the miracle worker, and all in one morning!"

"Mmm-hmmm. All we have to do now is sit back and wait for the fax. *Then,* keeping Bambi out of the loop, we'll distribute copies of it to Mr. Fairey and our legal department, and drop the entire case into the laps of those—" Her voice turned smugly sarcastic "—super pricks of detection, Charles Ferraro and Hannes Hockert."

"Kenzie!" Zandra hissed in a whispered attempt to shush her. "Your visitor!"

Kenzie blinked. *My visitor? Who—?* She had already forgotten. Then a mental lightbulb clicked on and shone brightly. She thought, *Oh, shit. Charley. Well, so what if he overheard me? He is a bastard, and if the shoe fits . . .*

She spun her chair around.

But it wasn't Charley—

Everything inside her came to a dead stop, then slowly rearranged itself. She drew a sharp breath and swallowed.

—it was Hannes Hockert.

Kenzie's scrutiny started with the soles of his brown Bruno Magli boots and traveled ever-so-slowly up his silk and wool trousers, cut full and loose to accentuate his slim waist and narrow hips. Ditto the double-breasted jacket of matching lignite brown with its subtle, almost iridescent weave of taupe, which he wore open and to great effect.

No constricting nine-to-five uniform this. No, siree. And definitely not cheap. Kenzie knew an Armani suit when she saw one.

Kenzie's heartbeat kept increasing as she stared at him, at the masculine beauty of his face. Dear God. How could she possibly have forgotten his drop-dead good looks? He really was so beautiful, this bright blond Viking of a man, that it was impossible to tear her eyes away from him, just as it was impossible to retract her stinging barb.

Not that it had made any difference. That much was clear from the intensity of his gaze.

She stared at him.

He stared at her.

Time itself was suddenly meaningless. Both of them were in a world of their own.

Zandra, attuned to the sexually charged chemistry, looked on with growing interest, as did Arnold, who hovered just outside the door. Grinning, he gave Kenzie a thumbs-up.

But the signal didn't register; neither she nor Hannes were aware of their audience. All they had eyes for was each other.

"Good morning, Kenzie," he greeted softly, finally breaking the silence.

Kenzie forced herself to speak. "Hans," she acknowledged, her voice trembly and barely audible.

"It has been a long time, Kenzie."

"Yes," she whispered, still holding his gaze, "it has."

Three months, she thought. *That's how long it's been since I told him—him!—to take a hike! Christ, I need to get my head examined! What single girl in her right mind would chase away a hunk like him?*

"Then you don't mind my dropping by like this?" he asked. "Unannounced? Without an appointment?" The smile emanating from his lips and eyes was warm and embracing, so utterly enveloping that it made her go weak all over.

"So . . . what brings you to . . . to my neck of the woods?" she murmured, thinking: *I* must *pull myself together. For Chrissake, I'm an adult—not some young twit with a schoolgirl crush!*

He drew a few steps closer. "There are several reasons, Kenzie," he said quietly.

She was silent, unable to wrest her eyes from his.

"Business," he murmured. "And pleasure."

He leaned casually against her desk and folded his arms.

"You see, Kenzie, I'm a great believer in combining the two."

Kenzie, conscious of her hands fidgeting in her lap like some trapped, high-strung animal, forced herself to still them, and struggled to regain at least a semblance of professional decorum.

"Why . . ." She had to clear her throat. "Why don't we stick to business?" she suggested in a tightly gartered voice.

"If you like. Yes." He inclined his head in acquiescence. "Why not? That sounds reasonable enough. And we *are* both reasonable people, are we not, Kenzie? Reasonable and . . . well, perhaps a bit impulsive?"

She remained silent, not trusting herself to speak.

And then he smiled again.

To the casual observer it was a public smile, the crowning touch of Continental politeness and old-world charm, while to its recipient it sent a different and altogether very private message.

For Kenzie, it spelled memories, promises, passion, *bed.*

And, under the bright wash of the overhead fluorescents, she became aware of something else. His pale bluish eyes weren't really a matched set. Rather, each was a slightly different shade, the right iris a hint bluer, and the left a tad greener, an irregularity which she found compellingly intriguing and—banish the thought!—terribly sexy.

"Now then." He rubbed his chin. "To get business out of the way . . ."

She waited.

"What can I tell you besides what you've already probably guessed? That yes, this is an official call on behalf of Interpol regarding the Holbein. And yes, it's at the specific request of the Federal Republic of Germany and the U.S. Department of State. As to whether I'm empowered to use all necessary resources to help the courts resolve the issue of ownership—yes again."

He spread his hands, palms outward, and grinned.

"And there you have it," he said. "In a nutshell, of course."

Kenzie's expression had not changed. The soughing of hot air from the heating duct was the only sound in the room at the moment, other than the rustling of paper coming from Zandra's desk.

"That's not to mean that you need any assistance," Hannes added. He turned up his smile to its most devastating wattage. "From overhearing you, it seems you have everything well under control. However, I'd be delighted if you'd drop this case—"

He leaned over her gently in order to whisper in her ear.

"—*and anything else you'd like*—into my lap."

The come-on was unmistakable, and Kenzie's face colored with the heat blooming under her skin. With a massive effort, she tore her eyes from his, made a quarter-turn on the swivel of her chair, and pretended to busy herself at her desk.

Her emotions were in turmoil.

Why was it that men were suddenly dropping into her lap? For three long months she had been celibate; had not even *dated* anyone. Now all of a sudden, her cup runneth over.

Last night had brought Charley.

Today—Hannes.

And she *wanted* him, dammit! That was the worst part.

Only one snag. His temporary partner—*Charley.*

She sighed to herself. The last thing she needed was having the two of them fighting over her. Or—God forbid!—exchanging bedtime stories and locker-room jokes about her behind her back.

So . . .

To rebuff or not to rebuff? That was the question. And the time to decide was now. *Before* things got out of hand.

"Here is my work number, Kenzie," Hannes said. "You can reach me there during the day. If I'm not in, just leave a message."

She turned her face a little, watching him slip a hand inside his suit jacket, watching him extract one of those wafer-thin, black calf business card holders. The expensive kind, with a rounded gold corner set with a teeny sapphire cabochon.

Kenzie felt a surge of irrational jealousy.

Obviously an overpriced gift from some girlfriend, she thought bitingly. _Men never buy those kinds of things for themselves._

And that decided her. The hell with prudence. She had as much a right to life, liberty, and the pursuit of pleasure as the next person.

So Hannes and Charley were working together. So _what?_

Last night had been a moment of weakness, a mere hormonal accident. It wasn't as if she _intended_ to take up with Charley again. Nor did she owe him her fidelity. In fact, she didn't owe him a goddamn thing!

She looked on as Hannes performed that one-handed trick of flipping out a business card and holding it between the middle and index fingers— the while-collar version of striking a match with one hand.

"I wrote my home phone number on the back, Kenzie," he said softly.

She reached out to take it, but was unprepared for what happened next.

The card was like an extension of his body. The instant she touched it, a powerful electric current jolted through her.

Unbidden, her mind flashed back to that rain-slashed night last October, when his tongue had fluttered delicately against her naked flesh and she had offered him her treasure, that soft, moist sanctum between her thighs.

He held onto the card a moment before letting go.

And that was when she realized it.

I've missed him, she thought in amazement. _Goddammit! I've really missed him!_

She swallowed to lubricate her throat. "You . . . you said there were several reasons you dropped by," she reminded him softly.

He smiled. "Well, one other."

She raised her winged brows.

"I would like to take you to dinner this evening. If you are free, that is?"

Dinner, she thought to herself. _That's harmless enough. It isn't as though I'm committing myself to anything._

"Yes," she whispered. "I . . . I think I'd like that. Only I don't eat red meat, so—"

"No problem," he assured her. "I know just the place. I'll pick you up at seven?"

She nodded hypnotically. "Seven's fine," she said thickly.

"And if the fax arrives in time, you'll bring me a copy?"

She nodded dreamily.

"Well, I'd better fly." His teeth flashed brilliantly again. "I'll see you this evening," he said.

And he was gone.

"Well, well, well," observed Zandra archly. "Darling, he's divine. When it rains it certainly pours—seems your dry spell's over and a monsoon's begun. How *ever* do you do it? Well, never mind. I'm off to lunch—"

But Kenzie didn't hear a word. She was smiling drowsily into space, anticipating the pleasant evening ahead.

Hannes, she thought. *Hot damn!*

28

$\mathcal{M}$ortimer's, on the corner of Lexington Avenue and East Seventy-fifth Street, is the kind of neighborhood restaurant which wouldn't normally elicit a second glance. The main dining room has café-curtained windows, bare brick walls, a long bar to the left, and tables with white cloths to the right. Above the bar hangs a drawing of the restaurant's namesake—the fictional Mortimer—rendered as a romantic young man.

Inevitably, great potted palms (or, as on this day, giant arrangements of blossoming dogwood branches) sit atop the bar, leftovers from the previous night's private party.

That there is never a shortage of these horticultural extravaganzas attests to private parties being not the exception, but the norm: for nearly two decades, the city's rich and famous have adopted Mortimer's as their unofficial but highly exclusive club.

Now, at lunchtime, the main dining room was buzzing as the new arrival breezed in. She carried herself with a kind of breathless theatricality, and posed by the door for a long moment, her eyes spinning about to see who was already here.

Obviously, the usual battalion of ladies who lunch but do not eat.

Holding court at the preferred window tables were the likes of Gloria Vanderbilt, Annette de la Renta, Nancy Kissinger, Pat Buckley, Joan Rivers, Nan Kempner, and a Rothschild or two. Plus their pet escorts—Bill Blass, Jerry Zipkin, Johnny Galliher, and Kenny Jay Lane.

Even as the new arrival eyed them, so too did this cliquish audience eye her right back.

Dina Goldsmith did not disappoint. Her face was immaculate, tweezered, *defined*. Subdued makeup glowed in a palette of warm almond, creams, and rose. Her blonde hair was pulled tightly back and held in place with a gold barrette and fell loosely down her back like shimmering cornsilk. She was wearing a sable coat over a turquoise Chanel minisuit with orange and lilac braid trim. There were long ropes of tiny, carved, green onyx leaves around her neck, and matching earrings, bracelet, and brooch. Her purse and shoes were black crocodile, and she was carrying a shiny little string-handled red shopping bag.

Her entrance had the desired effect; it set off waves of sibilant whispers.

She savored the talking heads and appreciative looks. They were proof positive that she had *Arrived*—and with a capital A!

The proprietor, horn rims perched on the tip of his nose, scurried over to welcome her. "Mrs. Goldsmith!" he greeted warmly. "Ms. von Hohenburg-Willemlohe is already here."

Dina smiled brilliantly and, taking little high-heeled running steps, followed him past table 1B—the one just to the right of the door, and which was still unoccupied—to the second one down, where Zandra was seated by the window, facing away from the door.

"Hello, sweetie!" Dina sang.

Zandra, who hadn't noticed her entrance, gave a start. "Dina! Gosh! Darling, how are you? Hullo!"

"Sorry I'm fashionably late, and I did *so* try to be punctual!" Dina leaned down and put her arm around Zandra and almost, but not quite, touched cheeks. "Mwah!" she air-kissed. "Mwah!"

The proprietor pulled out the chair facing the door, and Dina hopped around the table and sat down opposite Zandra and got settled. She put her bags down and pulled off her gloves and shrugged off her sable. Finally, placing her elbows on the table, she leaned forward. "There!" She smiled brightly.

"Gosh, Dina. But darling, you look *smashing*—it's so great to see you . . . seems like it's been yonks! Life treating you well?"

"Oh, you know me, sweetie," Dina said, with a negligible wave. "Life always treats me well. Oh, I *am* glad you could make it—especially on such short notice!"

Dina's aquamarine eyes couldn't stay still but kept snapping here, there, everywhere. She was like a feverish bidder at auction, except that she exchanged little finger waggles and long-range air kisses with half the lunchers.

"Haven't you heard?" Zandra grinned. "Us working girls will go anywhere for a free meal."

"Pshaw! As if you eat much more than a bird!"

A young waiter appeared. "Would you like something from the bar?" he asked.

"Mineral water." Dina looked at Zandra. "And you?"

"I already have mine."

Dina smiled dazzlingly at the waiter. He was back in no time and poured from a little green bottle. Dina ordered salmon with ginger, and Zandra chose the chicken paillard.

"So what brought you out today?" Zandra asked when the waiter had gone.

Dina took a tiny sip of water. "Shopping, sweetie," she said cheerfully. *"Tons* of shopping. You wouldn't *believe* how exhausting it is!"

One certainly couldn't tell by looking at her. Besides, as Zandra well knew, Dina positively thrived on shopping marathons.

"Yes, tons of shopping. Thank God for the car. It's packed full, and there's still the whole afternoon left! Oh. Speaking of which . . . here. I got you this." She passed Zandra the little red shopping bag.

"Cartier! What's this?"

"Oh, just a little something. Take it! When I saw them, I knew they had your name written all over them."

Zandra gave her one of those I-wish-you-wouldn't-have looks and accepted the bag and peeked inside it. She took out three boxes wrapped in white paper with red ribbon.

"Well? Open them!" Dina, finished scanning the restaurant, placed her chin on her hands and smiled with anticipation.

Carefully Zandra undid the ribbon of the smallest box and pulled away the wrapping paper. She eyed the tiny padded red box.

"Dina," she protested again.

Dina rolled her eyes in mock exasperation.

Slowly Zandra lifted the lid. She let out a little gasp. Nestled in a bed of white silk was an exquisite gold ladybug minibrooch in red and black enamel.

"Likee?"

"Yes, but—"

"No buts. I saw it when I got these. See?" Dina extended a limp wrist to show off her carved onyx bracelet, then fingered her matching necklace. "Now, do go on." She gestured with barely suppressed excitement. "Open the rest!"

Zandra dutifully unwrapped another box. It contained ladybug earrings.

"Di-*na!*"

"Hush, sweetie. One more to go."

With a sigh, Zandra opened the longest of the three boxes. The breath caught in her throat. The bracelet, consisting of delicate gold links interspersed with enameled ladybugs, was the most exquisite piece of all.

"Gosh. I—I don't know what to say . . . they're . . . *fab!* Dina, you are a darling, but I couldn't possibly—I mean . . . it's not even my birthday!"

"They're yours, and that's the end of it," Dina said with finality. "The subject is closed." Her voice dropped to a whisper. "Look! There she goes already."

Zandra frowned. "There goes who?"

Dina tilted her head toward a bone-thin socialite who was leaving the room. She leaned across the table. "Haven't you ever noticed?" she

whispered. "Really, sweetie! The way *she* runs back and forth to the ladies' room, I'd say it's time she stops taking laxatives!"

Zandra giggled. "Goodness, Dina . . . is there anything you *don't*
know about these people?" The salads arrived. "Oh, super. Thanks."

Dina continued to dispense gossip until the entrées arrived. The noise
level had swelled by decibels; table-hopping had begun in earnest.

Suddenly, without warning, the dining room fell completely silent.

Dina, glancing beyond Zandra toward the door, murmured: "Goodness!" Her eyes had widened. "So *that's* who's getting the A table!"

Who . . . ?

Zandra twisted around in her chair.

Karl-Heinz had just entered with Becky V, two members of a superior
species seemingly indifferent to the sensation they created.

Zandra, mouth falling slightly open, felt a disturbing collision of emotions, and stared at him in surprise, her ears tuning out Dina's running,
whispered commentary:

". . . well, he *would* be accompanying her, wouldn't he . . . I mean,
considering all *her* titles *and* his . . ."

Zandra's fingers tightened around her fork; brandished it in the air as
if the piece of chicken were some freshly speared trophy. Curiously, time
did the impossible: *contracted*—compacting the past three months, during
which she'd neither seen nor heard from him, into a split millisecond.

Oh, dear God—Heinzie! What was it about him that made her go
all weak—

The room blurred, as with fog, everything going shapeless and out
of focus. In the silence, Zandra could hear her heart thundering like
a piledriver.

And then the roar and clatter of the diners resumed. Her vision sharpened.

Oh, Lord, it can't be happening! she thought, guilt closing around her
like a trap. *I can't be falling for him. Christ, he's my bloody cousin—!*

Her breast heaved, as if her lungs were struggling for air, and her
heart continued to pound deafeningly, arrhythmically.

*What is wrong with me? Why am I acting like some silly, infatu-
ated schoolgirl?*

"Zandra?"

His voice startled her, jerked her like the strings of a marionette.

"Zandra! Why don't you and your friend join us? Look, the table's
laid for four. *Zandra?*"

She stared at him.

He stared at her.

Neither of them noticed Dina and Becky exchanging barely percepti-
ble, knowing looks.

All they had eyes for was each other.

* * *

"Ms. Turner?" said Sheldon D. Fairey, popping his head in the door. "Emergency. A client's asked for an appraisal. Afraid she wants it done yesterday, which means this afternoon. Could you be so good . . . ?"

Kenzie pulled a face. "It has to be today?"

"Afraid so. It's a special VIP case."

"All right." She nodded. "I'll take care of it personally."

"Good. I really appreciate it." He handed her a slip of paper. "Don't want to lose this one," he said. "Well, I have to dash. Lunch with a potential client. Huge collection."

And he was gone.

Kenzie stared at the slip of paper he had given her. Then slowly she unfolded it.

Suddenly she sat up straight, eyes bulging.

Certain she was imagining things, she shut her eyes, counted to ten, and looked at the note again.

Kenzie's years in New York might have jaded her, turning her into a cynic and a skeptic whom nothing, and no one, could impress. However, just when she had developed the blasé indifference of the true cosmopolite, what should pop up but an exception.

She was floored—who wouldn't have been by the name Mr. Fairey had jotted above the address and the appointed time?

> *Lila Pons*
> *447 E. 52nd St.*
> *4:00 p.m.*

Fabled legend of the silver screen, Lila Pons had been right up there alongside Dietrich and Garbo—and had become, if such a thing is indeed possible—even more reclusive than that most famous of all recluses, Garbo herself.

Lila Pons.

Kenzie sat there in stunned disbelief. Somehow, it felt unreal. Was it truly possible that she, of all the world's experts, should be chosen to appraise the Great Hermit's collection, perhaps even meeting the legend in person?

But there was the proof, right in her hand. In black and white. *Lila Pons.* "Jesus Christ," she whispered.

Zandra gulped the last of her coffee. "Sorry, darlings," she announced, putting down the cup. "Hate to eat and run, but I really have *got* to dash."

"Leaving already?" Karl-Heinz sounded disappointed.

"Afraid so, darling. Duty calls." Zandra scooted back her chair.

"Auction's next week, means work galore. And, with this Holbein fiasco, I'll be backlogged until God only knows when ... I mean, everybody, but simply everybody's, breathing down everybody else's neck. You wouldn't believe the stink. Honestly, you'd think they'd announced World War Three."

"Well," Dina murmured, "if you really have to be getting back, I suppose we can't keep you."

"I'm afraid there's no choice, darling. Things are in a bit of an uproar. You know how it goes. Starts at the top of the food chain and works its way down." Zandra smiled good-humoredly. "Look at it this way. At least it's not *dull.*" She stood up and pulled her coat from the back of her chair.

Karl-Heinz rose also. "Perhaps you'll permit me to escort you?" he asked softly, taking her coat and helping her into it.

"Oh, gosh. Heinzie, shouldn't you stay and have a cordial or something?" she asked. "Really. It isn't necessary to escort me."

"I know, but I would like to." He glanced at Becky. "You do not mind?"

"*Juste ciel, chéri.*" Becky gestured elegantly. "Don't be ridiculous. Off you go."

"I'll call you later," he told her. Then he took Dina's hand and raised it to his lips. "It has been a pleasure."

Dina preened. "The pleasure was all mine."

"Becky." Karl-Heinz gave a slight Prussian bow.

Becky's sculpted features did not alter as she blew him an almost imperceptible kiss. "*À bientôt, chéri.*"

Zandra leaned down and embraced Dina. "Marvelous lunch," she said. And, more softly: "But, darling, honestly ... you've simply got to stop with the gifts! *Really.* Not that they're unappreciated, but you're going to spoil me absolutely rotten. You know I'll love you forever anyway."

"Oh do stop, sweetie," Dina begged, although she looked pleased.

Zandra, smiling radiantly, turned to Becky. "It's been fab seeing you again!"

Becky smiled that famous Mona Lisa smile. "And you also, *chérie.*"

Zandra tossed her scarf around her neck and shouldered her leather bag. "Well, toodle-oo you two!" She waggled her fingers and Karl-Heinz took her arm and guided her to the door.

Then they were gone.

"*Alors.*" Becky, lifting her espresso, looked over the rim of the tiny cup with hooded eyes. "That went rather swimmingly, *n'est-ce pas?*"

"Yes," Dina agreed softly, "it did." She peered through the café curtains in time to catch Zandra and Karl-Heinz hurriedly jaywalking across Seventy-fifth Street. "You were right," she told Becky quietly. "They do make the most attractive couple."

"*Oui.*" Becky sipped her espresso and put down the cup. "*Alors.* I believe the time has come for your little *tête-à-tête* with Monsieur Fairey."

Dina smiled. "About the weekend in the country."

"*Oui.* A week from this Friday would be perfect." Becky looked thoughtful and nodded slowly. "Quite perfect indeed . . ."

Emotions collided inside her like a raging firestorm. Zandra couldn't remember when she'd felt so utterly powerless or vulnerable. She hated the sensation of helplessness, the inability to dominate her passions. Her reaction to Karl-Heinz had caught her completely off-guard.

On one level, the physical attraction he provoked was intoxicating, uncontrollable, energizing. That was the plus side.

On the negative, she found herself feeling tainted, shamed, *repulsed*.

He's my relative! she told herself grimly. *Good Lord, what I'm fantasizing most likely amounts to incest—*

Of course he was a distant enough relation for that not to be an issue. But, appalling as some people might find the notion, Zandra couldn't help wondering what an intimate relationship with him entailed.

Sliding him a brief, contemplative sideways glance, she thought: *Sheer bliss, no doubt. Yes, sheer unadulterated bliss . . .*

Because Karl-Heinz was everything a woman could possibly want. Sleekly handsome, charismatic, holder of one of the world's oldest titles, and possessed of that aura of casual confidence which is the by-product of great wealth and power. He also looked younger than his forty years, and was thoughtful, amusing, and strong as the proverbial rock.

Heaven help me! she quailed inwardly. *Why can't he have stayed at Mortimer's with Becky and Dina? Why did he have to insist upon coming along with me?*

She was not aware of the traffic lights, or the clusters of lunchtime shoppers, or even the perilous fleets of speeding vehicles. The only thing of which she was conscious was Karl-Heinz's disturbing proximity.

Which explained why, at Seventy-third Street, she stepped off the curb without looking.

"Watch it!" Karl-Heinz yelled.

Grabbing her arm, he yanked her back to safety just as a taxi, horn blaring, went barreling past her.

"My God!" he gasped. "You were nearly run over! Zandra, you really must look where you are going!"

She raised her face and gave a jerky little nod. "Yes," she said hoarsely, obviously shaken by the close call.

"You *are* all right?" he asked, solicitously holding her by both arms and looking deep into her eyes. His touch was so electric, and his distress—instantly followed by immeasurable relief—so genuine, that she felt herself drowning in the depths of his eyes.

And it was then that she understood the true extent of what was happening.

There are men who are boy toys, men who are providers, still others who are protectors, and one in many millions who is the sum of them all. And he was one of the latter—she knew that in an unsettling flash of absolute, crystalline clarity.

His blue eyes, the color of gas flames, burned with a fierce intensity, and the wind lifted his thinning hair, which, Zandra noted with appreciation, he didn't try to comb over his receding hairline. Though handsome, slender, and perfectly groomed, he was no youthful Apollo, which was precisely the point. It was his very maturity which appealed. She'd had her share of vain young Adonises in her past.

The problem was pedigree.

Centuries of inbreeding had related her family and his. In the long-ago past, the adverse effects of genetics had been pretty much of a mystery, and the only requirements for noble marriages and propagation had been to forge political alliances, broaden sovereign powers, fortify and raise social positions, and multiply lands and immense fortunes. Among the ruling classes, marital matches had always boiled down to keeping power in the family.

Naturally, the by-product of all this inbreeding—hereditary disorders such as hemophilia, dementia, and birth defects, to name but a few—had cursed all the great ruling families of Europe.

In the last decade of the Second Millennium, though, the inherent problems of marrying one's kin were common knowledge. She had absolutely no desire to play procreative roulette. The very notion was unsavory, and fraught with potential disaster.

I'm not about to play with lives. Every child deserves a fighting chance.

The traffic lights changed, but she and Karl-Heinz remained immobile, an obstacle for the pedestrians surging in both directions. Despite the jostlings and occasional curses, neither of them moved.

He was still holding onto her arms. "We can cross now—*safely,*" he said with a gentle smile.

Then he let go of her.

She nearly gasped, so unprepared was she for the sudden deprivation of his touch.

It was time to will herself to move. She knew that. Yet still she continued to stare at him, and despite January's freeze, a wave of incapacitating heat hit her like an accusation. She could feel the beads of moisture breaking out on her forehead. Leaving a glistening, telltale sheen, no doubt.

What is it with me? she wondered. *Why am I staring at him so long? And how much more of a spectacle can I make of myself?*

With a supreme effort, she managed to tear her eyes from his. Then, before her resolve could weaken, she got her feet working and mobilized herself, fleeing across the street—

—as if escape from one's emotions were that easy.

Karl-Heinz caught up with her and matched her brisk clacking stride. He hoped her need for silence was the result of introspection rather than a symptom of anger.

His breath sighed noisily. Whichever the reason, he wasn't exactly left with many choices. Two, to be exact. He could either drop behind and let her go on alone, or keep up, contenting himself with sliding furtive, inquisitive glances in her direction.

He chose the latter—not through arrogant confidence, but because her mere presence, however moody, put a shine on his day. His perseverance was rewarded by treasured little glimpses.

A burst of radiant sunshine lighting her head and illuminating her haze of billowing orange hair like that of some glorious pre-Raphaelite—a Rossetti maiden sprang to mind.

A gust of wind causing a streamer of corkscrew curls to flutter across her face, and the casual, automatic way she flicked them aside with her fingers—a simple reflex—somehow seemed special and appealed mightily; made him feel the overwhelming need to possess this astounding creature of thoroughbred lineage, devil-may-care elegance, and innate, unstudied sophistication. Most of all, he wished it were *he* who could reach out and gently, intimately, stroke aside the hair which the wind kept blowing in front of her face.

Why was it, he wondered, that she, of all women, should be the one to make him realize what he'd missed out on during decades of cutting a swath through life as a playboy? Good God, but she even made the prospect of domestication seem a *pleasure* to look forward to, rather than the tedious duty he'd always believed it to be!

Even so, the merciless disregard she showed him, dismissing his presence as if he didn't exist, lancinated his heart. He felt the sting of rejection as he hurried, in enforced, unnatural silence, alongside her. They might as well have been strangers, coincidental pedestrians sharing the same sidewalk, her proximity a mockery.

Finally, after they'd gone an entire block without speaking, he could take it no more. He *had* to shatter the invisible barrier separating them. If he didn't, he thought he would go mad.

His hand sought hers and, holding it tightly lest she escape, he stopped walking. She turned to him with huge reluctance.

"For God's sake, Zandra! What *is* the matter?"

She would not look at him. "What should be the matter?" she murmured, shrugging. Then she pried her hand loose and turned away, studiously perusing the hardware in the dusty window of a locksmith.

Standing beside her, Karl-Heinz thrust his hands into the pockets of his cashmere overcoat and studied her while she, as if with utter fascination, leaned into the flyblown glass and pretended to study the assortment of locks, doorknobs, window gates, and keys. They might have been a display of new spring dresses for all the attention she gave them.

He drew a deep breath. "Zandra," he pleaded. "Why won't you speak to me? Or is it too difficult to tell me what's wrong?"

"Wrong? What should be wrong?"

"I don't know," he said. "Why don't you tell me?"

"Maybe there's nothing to tell."

And abandoning her examination of the hardware, she hurried on, staring purposefully straight ahead. Her face closed. Making it clear the discussion was over.

On they rushed, her silence enforcing his, until they reached the faux-Renaissance palazzo where she worked, and high above which he lived.

Zandra felt a curious mixture of relief and heartache. Relief because she could finally flee Karl-Heinz's unsettling presence; heartache because, much as she longed for it, things *could* never—*must never!*—progress naturally between them as a man and a woman.

The awkward, oppressive sense of silence continued as they stood, buffeted by gusts of wind, under the flapping dove gray awning in front of the entrance. Neither of them seemed to know what to say. Zandra glanced longingly, almost edgily, toward the doorman and the giant etched-glass portals through which she'd make her escape.

But ingrained manners and protocol required that she bid Karl-Heinz farewell. And that meant looking him in the face.

She raised her eyes slowly.

Damn. She should have known. Those intense blue eyes of his were altogether too mesmeric, and conveyed entire unspoken words—desire, love, loyalty, need—all evident for her to see. She could feel her resolve weakening, her knees trembling and threatening to buckle. A lump rose in her throat.

You don't mess around with Mother Nature.

The silence grew. And grew.

It was Karl-Heinz who finally broke it. "I'm going to be in town for the next three or four weeks," he said.

She glanced desperately at the heroically scaled doors.

He took her hand in his. "I know you have to get back to work," he said. "But don't be a stranger. Okay?"

Zandra's nod was ambiguous, its two meanings cancelling each other: the first that his words registered, the second that she agreed. It was all a matter of interpretation.

But she knew she had to *say* something. They couldn't just part in silence.

She thought: *He reaches too deep inside me. For both our sakes, I have to keep my distance. Somehow I must make certain we'll never see each other again.*

Aloud, she said, "I'll be in touch."

The fiction was convenient and harmless; a necessary white lie. But her smile would have left Troy up ship's creek.

"See you," she added.

And she was like quicksilver. Here one moment and gone the next.

29

*L*ila Pons owned an apartment in River House, arguably the single snootiest and most exclusive address in New York, if not the entire world.

She'd moved in during the summer of 1954, thirteen years after the FDR Drive had been built, and until then, the sedate dowager of a building had fronted directly on the East River, where it had even boasted its own yacht mooring. That, like so many other things, had changed as time had passed, but River House itself had not.

Built on the heels of the 1929 Crash, it had symbolized optimism and confidence in both the city and the country's economy, and from the beginning, had been home to many of the city's—and indeed the world's—richest, most prominent, and most socially acceptable residents. It still was, and being accepted by the co-op board was something akin to passing the scrutiny of the CIA, the Stalinist-era KGB, J. Edgar Hoover's FBI, MI5, the Morgan Bank, and the *Social Register.*

To the casual observer, the towering brick and stone edifice gave off an aura of pre-war stability and solidity, and looked as if it had always been there and would remain there forever.

Like some legendary memorial. Or a monument to its most famous and reclusive resident, Lila Pons.

Before reaching East Fifty-second Street, Kenzie ducked into a doorway on First Avenue, untied her Reeboks, stuffed them into her shoulder bag, and wiggled her feet into her best shoes.

She checked her watch. She still had six minutes to go. Good. Time enough to reach the building right on the button.

River House was the very last building at the cobbled end of East Fifty-second Street. Its U-shaped façade had a canvas awning, and on the ground level, wall-mounted stone faces stared at each other across the recessed entrance, the mouths of which, in warmer weather, streamed water into scallop-shell basins, and which now gaped dryly, like idiots. The doorman was outside, enjoying what weather he could in the deep, lengthening shadows of the afternoon. He wore the requisite uniform and peaked cap and looked as though he'd been there since the creation.

"May I help you, ma'am?" His reedy voice was extremely polite.

"Yes. I have an appointment to see Ms. Pons."

She could have sworn his face—eyes, mouth, even nose and ears—went totally blank. "There's no one here by that name, I'm afraid."

Kenzie wasn't deterred. She said, "I'm from Burghley's, the auction house, and Ms. Pons called us to appraise her art. Here's my card." She unbuckled her bag and passed him one.

He took it and held it mere inches from his eyes. It was European style, larger than the standard American size, and thick as fiberboard:

BURGHLEY'S
FOUNDED 1719

721 Madison Avenue
New York, New York 10021

MacKenzie Turner
Expert-in-Charge
Old Master Paintings and Drawings

(212) JL5-5000   (212) JL5-5121

He scratched the engraved letters with a thumbnail, sighed, and said, "If you'll wait here, ma'am, I'll be with you shortly."

Kenzie smiled. "Thank you."

She watched him shuffle inside to use the house phone and took the opportunity to look around at the too-tall buildings lining this short narrow block. Glancing out over the FDR Drive, she saw a tug nosing a barge upstream against the swift current of the East River. Then, turning in the opposite direction, she had to squint and hold up a hand to shield her eyes from the grit-filled blast of wind shooting through the vertical canyon from across the Hudson in New Jersey.

Hearing the doorman's discreet cough, Kenzie faced him with a smile. He looked sincerely apologetic. "I've spoken to the housekeeper, ma'am," he said with gravity as he handed Kenzie back her card. "She asked me to tell you that Miss P. is currently in Japan."

"Japan!" Kenzie frowned. "That's rather peculiar, isn't it? I mean, if she's overseas, why should she have called us?"

"I'm sorry, ma'am," he said ever-so-politely, something in his manner conveying that they were both merely the victims of some higher power's whim. "I am only conveying what I was told."

Kenzie hesitated before shrugging philosophically. "Well, it's not your fault." She took several backward steps and raised a hand to sketch a friendly wave. "Thanks all the same."

He seemed grateful that she didn't pry any further. "Anytime, ma'am," he said, doffing his cap.

She started retracing her way back toward First Avenue when something . . . a sudden premonition, perhaps? A kind of sixth sense? . . .

caused her to slow down and glance up at the building's blank windows. Abruptly she stopped walking.

Was it her imagination?

Or had her eye caught—*what?*

She wouldn't swear to it in a court of law. Nor even to herself. But by some keen intuition she had glimpsed—was it an hallucination? just wishful thinking on her account?—a curtain behind a closed fifth-floor window twitching furtively aside, and a ghostly face materializing before darting, swift as quicksilver, back into the shadows?

Kenzie, a shiver rippling up her spine, stood rooted to the spot, unable to keep herself from staring up at that window. It was dark and mysterious; the curtains still. Nothing moved. Nothing stirred.

Chiding herself for letting her imagination run amok, she walked reluctantly on, but not without giving that casement window one last upward glance over her shoulder.

It was just another blank window among countless multitudes, she told herself. So what if a curtain had moved? It could have been anyone's apartment; God alone knew how many tenants occupied a building of that size.

Fleetingly, she wondered whether this errand had been someone's idea of a bad joke.

Or had Lila Pons really wanted her collection appraised . . . but then changed her mind at the very last minute?

Perhaps time would tell. And then again, perhaps it would not.

Either way, Kenzie knew she would not easily forget this particular wild-goose chase.

The very idea of calling upon one of the greatest screen legends of all time—especially one who had become a mysterious aged recluse living behind locked doors—only made this errand, in vain though it might have been, that much more fascinating.

Under her breath, Kenzie said softly, "I vant to be alone."

God, she thought in self-disgust. *How unoriginal can I get?*

"Tell whoever it is that I'm in . . . Japan!"

Now, that was original, all right!

Especially when you wished upon a star.

And the most nebulous star, at that . . .

30

The instant Dina Goldsmith hit home, she let Julio know that she was not—repeat, not!—under any circumstances to be disturbed. With that decree, she repaired to her silk-walled boudoir, secure in the knowledge that she could spin her web in absolute privacy.

There, presided over by Sargent's elegant *Countess of Essex* and no less than *two* languid Boldini beauties, Dina slipped off her crocodile pumps and made herself comfortable on the plump-cushioned, Louis XV *duchesse brisée,* once the property of none other than that most celebrated connoisseur of French eighteenth-century furniture, Mrs. Charles (Jayne) Wrightsman. The very same Mrs. Wrightsman whose bequest of a series of Versailles-like rooms formed the nucleus of one of the Metropolitan Museum's major collections, the Wrightsman Rooms.

Humming softly to herself, Dina lifted the brass telephone off the table beside her and placed it on her lap.

There. Now she was all set.

But before getting on the horn, she permitted herself a moment's reflection.

The pair of full-length Boldinis, time-frozen survivors of an extinct, pre-war species, drew her eye. Tilting her head slightly, she perused them as fondly as she had on a thousand other such occasions.

Whenever her self-assurance faltered, she had only to come in here to draw strength from them, so powerful were their auras of complacent confidence, of leisured tranquility. She often wondered what kind of alchemy empowered them to reach out to her from within the gilded frames, what sort of magical osmosis took place that enabled them to give her self-esteem the necessary, vicarious boost.

Dina's thoughts turned to the task—the intrigue she and Becky V had so carefully and brilliantly devised.

Mentally reviewing each step of the process, she allowed herself the pleasure of self-congratulatory excitement.

Three months. Three *long* months. That was how long it had been since the party at the Met, when the idea of a match between Zandra and Karl-Heinz had first struck her. But it had remained exactly that, a mere idea. It had taken Becky V to help crystallize it into a tangible reality.

Now, with Becky having successfully completed Phase One, corraling

Karl-Heinz into the scheme, Phase Two was at hand—literally *in* Dina's hands!—and she savored the triumph to come.

Because it will come! she reiterated to herself. *It must!*

Not only was the timing right, but Dina knew it could never be *more* right.

It's now or never, she told herself.

If there was anything as heady or intoxicating as playing matchmaker for a real-life prince and his future princess, she had yet to run across it.

After all, a marriage between Prince Karl-Heinz von und zu Engelwiesen and Zandra, Countess of Grafburg, would hit countless birds with a single stone. Not only would it validate and consolidate Dina's own importance and power; it would, in one fell swoop, *cap off* her dizzying winning streak of social triumphs *and* put Karl-Heinz and Zandra firmly into her debt.

Careful, she cautioned herself. *It's dangerous to celebrate prematurely.*

Without changing position, she moved her gaze from the Boldinis and rested a hand lightly atop the telephone. She had procrastinated long enough. It was time to stop daydreaming. Time to get *busy.* Time her fingers did some *walking!*

And lifting the receiver, she punched Sheldon D. Fairey's private number at Burghley's.

Lunch had left a warm, convivial glow as Sheldon D. Fairey returned to work, the savory, full-bodied smugness of having pulled off a major coup. Eyes beaming like headlights, he bestowed a sunny smile upon his secretary, the sharp-featured, formidable Miss Botkin.

Without hesitation she rose from behind her desk to take his coat, scarf, and gloves.

He basked in her fussy, wifelike ministrations. No feminist, she. Not by a long shot.

Miss Botkin—*she* insisted upon being addressed as Miss, not Ms.— was one of the last of the old-fashioned holdouts. Not only did she pride herself upon bringing her boss a cup of coffee, but trusted no one but herself to grind the beans, brew it just so, and then serve it, using the big formal silver set and creased linen napkins and fine china.

Elsewhere standards might have slipped, but not in this office. Nor would they while *she* was alive. Miss Botkin clung to her inflexible, Victorian values with a rectitude that was as amazing as it was outdated.

Fairey patted the sides of his silver hair, straightened his tie, and then strode victoriously into his inner office, shutting the door so he might savor his triumph in private.

He had gone to lunch anticipating the very worst.

He had returned feeling downright euphoric.

And with good reason. Leonard Sokoloff, producer of mind-numbing,

tooth-grating television sitcoms, it turned out, was not your stereotypi-
cal Hollywood ego who collected art as an investment or because it
was fashionable.

Shrewd, articulate, and sharp as a tack, Sokoloff had one finger on
the pulse of the nation's couch potatoes, and the others on a whole variety
of subjects ranging from politics and philosophy to business and art. Particularly modern art.

Thus, courting the producer—or rather, wooing his collection of con-
temporary art, which was soon to go under the hammer—had turned out
to be a highly agreeable experience for Fairey. But what had astonished
him the most was Sokoloff himself; the man showed a genuine passion for
his Mondrians, Klines, Lichtensteins, and Klees. He'd talked about them
as affectionately as if they were his children.

Unfortunately, he'd have been better off showing the same kind of
passion to his wife. If he had, the collection might have stayed intact. As
things were, it had fallen victim to one of the "Three Big D's" of auctions—death, debt, and divorce—and was going on the block because of
the last.

Fairey shook his head in commiseration. Just as there were two sides
to every coin, so too was one man's misery another one's gain. The ultimate loser in this case was Sokoloff. The big winners would be the divorce
lawyers, who'd haul in outrageous fees; Sokoloff's soon-to-be ex, who was
raking him over the coals; and Burghley's, which would earn a hefty commission on the sale of his art.

Because Burghley's—not Christie's or Sotheby's, but *Burghley's!*—
would be conducting *this* sale! That had been agreed to over lunch.

That was why Sheldon D. Fairey was so bloated with triumph.

The abrupt bleating of his private line pricked his pleasure's balloon.
Certain it was his wife calling, he picked up on the second ring. "Yes?"

"Sheldon! *Sweetie!*"

The voice at the other end was all purrs and bright tinkles and most
definitely not his wife's.

"It's *Dina!*"

Oh, Christ, he thought, feeling his testicles shrivel. *And to what,* he
wondered, *do I owe the displeasure of* this *call?*

"Mrs. Goldsmith," he acknowledged warily.

"I'm not disturbing you, Sheldon? Am I?"

Damn right you're disturbing me! he wanted to snarl. Naturally, he
voiced nothing of the sort.

"Because if you *are* in the middle of something," Dina went on magnanimously, "we can talk later."

Dina showing concern? His internal alarms went on full alert. This
kinder, gentler Dina was way out of character.

"Of course you're not disturbing me," he lied smoothly. "Not a'tall."

"I'm *so* glad! You are well, I take it?"

"Fine, thank you," he said. Now flashing red lights had joined the klaxons screeching inside his head. "And you?"

"Oh, you know . . . *comme ci, comme ça.* But overall quite well, I suppose." Dina cut right to the chase. "Sweetie, the reason I'm calling is—I need your *help!*"

"Y-yes . . . ?" he said cautiously, wishing he were still lunching with Leonard Sokoloff or . . .

. . . or better yet, that he was halfway around the world somewhere, on a desert island, perhaps, or in the Himalayas—any place, so long as it was out of reach of the long arm of Dina Goldsmith.

"The problem," Dina explained, "is this. You see, Robert and I are looking for a house in the country. He's set his sights on Connecticut, while I prefer the Hamptons. I'm not sure he realizes how boring the country can be."

"Oh, very boring," Fairey assured her, feeling a terrible premonition coming on.

"Well, then I spoke to Becky V . . ." Dina paused, obviously to make certain the exalted name sank in. ". . . and you'll never guess what *she* said."

He shuddered to think. "No . . ." he said softly.

"*She* suggested I take Robert to New Jersey. Somewhere in the hunt country. She assured me it's so quiet there that one weekend will cure him of the country once and for all."

"Hmmm," he murmured noncommittally.

"Becky also told me you have neighboring estates."

Fairey put a hand over his face and shut his eyes. *Dear God,* he thought. *What hath Thou wrought?*

"Yes," he admitted in a whisper, "we do."

"Anyway," Dina continued, "I was wondering if we might impose upon you one of these weekends. Just to get a feel for the area. You know . . . so we can drive around? Look at places? So Robert can see for himself just how boring it is?"

His mind was racing. *Imposing! For a weekend!* Good Lord, he had to head her off—and now, *before* she got any more ideas.

"I'm afraid our place is . . . well, quite shabby, Mrs. Goldsmith," he said quickly. "My wife rides, and the stables are in better condition than the house." He forced a jovial laugh. "I'm afraid you'd absolutely hate it."

"Never mind me," Dina said inexorably. "So long as *Robert* hates it, that's all that matters."

He couldn't believe this! Bad enough that he had to put up with the Goldsmiths in New York. But in the country? In his very own house?

"You *do* see, sweetie?" she went on. "Unless my Robert finds it horribly dull and horrendously boring—and he must!—I'll end up somewhere in Litchfield County instead of Southampton. And the moment I saw the house I found there, I *knew* it had my name on it. You see? Sweetie, my *happiness* is in your hands! You *must* help me make Robert see reason!"

He gulped, visions of Dina's bullying and Robert's uncouth manners and smelly cigars tainting the purity of his weekend sanctum.

"I-I'm really not sure my wife and I can be of much help," he murmured stiffly.

"Oh, but you *can*, sweetie! You *can*! Now, what do you say to . . . the weekend after next?"

The what—! His mouth gaped at her audacity. "I . . . I'll have to check with my wife," he said.

"*Naturellement!* That goes without saying."

"I'll let you know what she says."

"You do that." Dina paused. "And Sheldon?"

"Yes, Mrs. Goldsmith?"

"Just remember, sweetie," she trilled. "One hand washes the other!"

And with that, Dina rang off.

One hand washes the other . . . The phrase echoed endlessly in the chambers of his ears. *One hand washes the other* . . .

Its meaning was crystal clear.

"Damn that woman!" he screamed, beating on his desk with his fists. "Damn her to eternal hell!"

Then, regaining his self-control, he jabbed the automatic dial button of his home.

His wife did not pick up; the answering machine did.

Swiftly he broke the connection and stabbed the next button down, the number of her cellular phone.

A swift series of electronic tones. Silence. Then one ring . . . two . . .

He could hear his breath ricocheting off the mouthpiece, feel his fingers gripping the receiver as though to break it.

Come on, come on . . . answer it, dammit!

He had to talk to Nina. She always knew the most plausible excuses. Maybe *she'd* be able to extricate them from a weekend with the Goldsmiths . . .

. . . from a weekend in *hell!*

While her husband was suffering testicular trauma, Nina Fairey was ordering an entire new riding habit at Hermès. Cap, blouse, jacket, jodhpurs, *boots*—beaucoup bucks at any equestrian supplier's. But at Hermès, a major investment.

Nina Fairey preferred to think of it as a capital improvement.

Her order was being written up when the cellular phone in her Kelly bag cheeped. "Excuse me," she told the saleslady, taking out her Microtac and flipping it open. She unclipped a heavy bas-relief earring before lifting it and saying: "Hel-lo-oh."

"Thank God! *Nina*. Where are you?" She could hear the relief quavering in her husband's voice.

"At Hermès," she replied. "I told you I had an appoint—"

"Yes, yes, yes," he hissed, cutting her off in midsentence. "Listen, something's come up which can't wait. Can you talk freely?"

Nina glanced around at hovering salespeople and browsing shoppers. "N . . . no," she told him, "not exactly. But wait a moment." She pressed the hold button and looked at the saleslady. "Is it possible for me to take this call in private?"

"But of course! If madame would please follow me?"

Nina was led past glass counters filled with a display of bone china with toucan motifs, another with trellises, pagodas, and butterflies, then riding tack and wood-and-leather campaign furniture before being shown into a private office in the back.

As soon as the door shut behind her, Nina punched the hold button and lifted the phone. "Sheldon? You there?"

An explosion of breath: "Yes!"

"We can talk freely now," she said. "Darling, what happened? You sound beside yourself."

"What happened?" His laughter was ragged and high-pitched, as if he was on the verge of hysteria. "Genghis Khan happened, that's what!"

She rolled the gold earring between her fingers. "I'm afraid I don't follow."

"Nina, for God's sake—the *Goldsmiths have happened!*"

"Darling, what do you mean?"

"Didn't you hear what I said?"

"Sheldon, I'm not psychic. Will you stop talking in riddles and be more forthcoming?"

"Okay. Okay! But you're not going to believe this!"

She took a seat in a campaign chair. "Why don't you try me."

"All right." She could hear the soughing of his breath. "I come back from lunch, and what do you think greets me?"

She was silent.

"—ringing phone. My private line, dammit! You know how I guard this number, it's not even listed!"

Nina made commiserating noises.

"Anyway, who should it be but Dina Goldsmith? God alone knows *how* she got hold of this number, though I'm not surprised that she did— that ballbuster's capable of anything!"

Nina pressed two fingers against her brow to forestall an oncoming headache. "Slow down, darling. Please. I don't have the foggiest notion as to what's going on. Now then: Dina called."

"Yes!" he shouted.

"Well, what did she want?"

"Would you believe, she invited herself to . . . to our house in the country? *Our house,* goddammit!" he sputtered, his voice rising feverishly in outrage. "Christ, is nothing sacred anymore? Whatever happened to a man's home being his castle?"

Nina remained calm. "And what did you tell her?"

"What do you think? God knows, I *tried* to turn her down graciously, not that *that* did any good."

Again a burst of mirthless laughter; she recognized the telltale, strung-out vibrato of nerves stretched to the breaking point.

"That woman doesn't know the meaning of the word *no!*"

"Sheldon, cool your heels. Let me think, darling—"

"Well, you'd better think fast!" he snapped. "Otherwise, we'll be stuck with her and that slob of a husband the weekend after next!"

"Did she happen to mention *why* she wanted to come?"

He filled her in on what Dina had told him. "Not that her song and dance fools me," he said. "She's got some other, more devious motive up her sleeve, though what it is I can't begin to guess."

"Hmmm." Nina tapped her lips thoughtfully. "The weekend after next . . ."

"Yes! Nina, you've got to do something! Find a way to wheedle out of this—"

"Sheldon! For God's sake, *will* you calm down? This isn't the end of the world. In fact . . ." She admired the wood and leather campaign chair and smiled to herself. ". . . it could very well be a new beginning. And definitely work to our advantage."

"Nina! What are you *saying?*"

His voice had once again taken on that tremolo of panic. She felt mildly irritated at having to dispense the necessary antidote, but forced herself to be forebearing.

"Darling, I'm only saying that I have our best interests in mind. Your career . . . our social position. Really. When you think about it, having the Goldsmiths out to Somerset might not be such a bad idea—"

"Nina!"

"Darling, trust me. Now forget all this nonsense and get on with your work. I'll take care of everything."

"Nina—Nina! You *are* going to head them off! Aren't you?"

"Sheldon, will you stop?" God, she hated it when men whined! "I know what I'm doing."

"Oh, Christ . . . !"

"Hush, darling. Need I remind you that despite being neighbors, we never got past square one with Becky V?"

"So?"

"So—" She crossed shapely, mocha-stockinged legs. "—rumor has it that Becky V and Dina Goldsmith have become thick as thieves, or at least allies of some sort. Therefore, it stands to reason that the easiest way to enhance our own social stature is by hitching our star to Dina's."

"Hitching our—Nina! Have you gone mad?"

"Not at all, darling, not at all." Smiling to herself, Nina regarded her crossed leg and curled the pointy toe of her caramel-colored high heel. "Opportunistic, perhaps. But crazy? Definitely not. Now, I have *got* to get busy. Darling, I'll talk to you later—"

"But—"

"*Later,* Sheldon," she said firmly. "Right now I've got my work cut out for me. Just give me Dina's telephone number so I can get back to her right away."

When Dina hung up, she felt the gratifying afterglow of having wielded a small fraction of her considerable power.

Ah, power. Can anything else compare?

Dina didn't think so.

But there'd be plenty of time to reflect on her triumph. Right now she had more pressing matters on her agenda. Calling Zandra, for one. Nina Fairey had, of course, extended an invitation to the three of them—Robert, herself, and Zandra.

And, if everything went according to plan, Zandra would be the next Princess von und zu Engelwiesen!

Not wasting another second, Dina dabbed out the number of Burghley's Old Masters department. "Sweetie! It's me!"

"Gosh, Dina," Zandra said lazily into the phone. "Hullo!"

She was sitting behind her desk watching the fax machine extrude a length of thermal paper into Kenzie's waiting hands.

"I didn't forget my purse or something at the restaurant, did I? I mean, I can be so horridly scatterbrained at times . . ."

"No, no," Dina assured her quickly. "Sweetie, you didn't forget a thing."

"Oh, good. Sometimes, I believe I'd leave my head somewhere if it weren't attached to the rest of me."

Dina laughed dutifully. "Sweetie, the reason I'm calling is to invite you to the country the weekend after next."

"The country! But, Dina, this comes as a *total* surprise."

"I *can* count on you, sweetie, can't I?"

"I . . . uh . . ." Zandra tried to think. The invitation was so unexpected that she was momentarily thrown. *Did* she have any plans for that weekend? "Who else is going to be there?" she asked, flipping the calendar on her desk.

"Oh, nobody of any consequence," Dina said dismissively. "It's at the

Faireys, and it'll only be them, Robert, and the two of us. You know. Just an informal, *intime* little weekend."

"I . . . I don't know what to say!"

"Sweetie! You must say yes! If you don't, I . . . I'll *die* of boredom and never, ever, forgive you!"

"Oh, Dina. Darling, I really need a minute to—"

"Did I catch you at an inopportune moment?"

"No, that's not it at all. It's just so sudden, and—well, I hadn't exactly planned—"

"But you *must* come!" Dina wailed. "Sweetie, I insist! I command you! In fact, your presence is required!"

Zandra frowned and thought: *Required? Of course my presence isn't required. Why should it be? And why's Dina making such a big deal of it?*

"Dina—" she began, and then halted: from across the room came a sudden whoop of triumph as Kenzie raised one fist and shouted, "Yes!" Obviously, Professor Tindemans's fax was everything he said it would be, and the Holbein fiasco could now be dumped into the laps of the authorities and the courts.

"Zandra?" Dina's voice squawked from the receiver. "Sweetie, what *is* going on?"

"Gosh. Dina, I've simply got to hang up."

"But what about next weekend?"

"Darling, I'll be there," Zandra promised, just to get her off the phone. "Count me in. And, it'll be fab. Just like old times . . . we'll talk later—this evening. That's a darling. *Ta!*"

Hanging up the phone, Zandra looked thoughtful.

A weekend in the country. At least it would get her out of town. In three months she hadn't set foot off Manhattan.

A change of scenery was definitely overdue.

The *cabinet d'amateur* of Becky V's penthouse.

Like a precious jewelbox, the mellow, Goya-studded walls paid homage to its single most priceless treasure.

There she was, seated in a thronelike, flame-stitched chair. The former First Lady. Studying a gilt-framed painting on a strategically placed easel. Glowing in a shaft of dim, dust-mote sprinkled light was a Corot, *Bathing Venus,* which a Madison Avenue gallery had sent over on approval.

To buy or not to buy . . . That was the three-and-a-half-million-dollar question.

And overriding that, since money was no object, loomed an even larger and more important issue: Was the quality of the painting superb enough for her collection?

She sat there, frowning, trying to decide.

A loud knock on the door interrupted her thoughts. *"Oui?"* she called out.

Uriah, her ancient servant, shuffled in and cleared his throat. "Madame!" he shouted. "Mrs. Goldsmith is on the telephone!"

"Merci, Uriah." Still studying the Corot, Becky felt for the extension phone beside her and picked up the receiver. *"Allô?"*

"Sweetie! It's Dina!"

"Chérie!"

"Everything is fixed. Fait accompli!"

"And Zandra?" Becky's eyes never strayed from the painting.

"She's agreed to join us."

"Bon. You have done well, *chérie.* I shall call Karl-Heinz at once."

31

*L*ater that evening, Manhattan glittered frostily. Seen from above, it looked like that famous black-and-white aerial photograph by Berenice Abbott, a signed, platinum-processed copy of which hung in Karl-Heinz's corridor.

But there was one unique difference between image and reality: *color.*

The millions upon millions of incandesced windows glowed yellow instead of white. Down at street level, the traffic lights winked in constant repetition: red, yellow, green . . . yellow, red, green . . . Blinking, multicolored neons abounded. And the streets and avenues were rivers of white headlights and ruby taillights.

Other than that, little had changed since Ms. Abbott had taken her bird's-eye view. Oh, the buildings were taller. The traffic denser. The lights more profuse. But overall, it still looked as it had back in 1932.

Seen from way, way up, Manhattan was instantly recognizable.

Even if you were Berenice Abbott.

It was seven-thirty when Hannes and Kenzie arrived at Luma, a storefront restaurant on Ninth Avenue in Chelsea, where he had reserved a window table.

"You told me you don't eat red meat," he said as he held Kenzie's chair.

She smiled, touched that he remembered, and glanced around the soothing peach and celadon interior. Frosted triangular sconces spilled serene pools of nile green on the walls.

Kenzie placed her elbows on the round table, laced her fingers, and rested her chin on her hands, watching Hannes as he seated himself opposite her. Again, she was struck by his physical beauty and commanding presence. It occurred to her that she'd never known a man who was so . . . so *complete.*

Nor was she alone in that opinion. A casual sweep of the dining room confirmed it. Every female eye was aimed in his direction.

An odd mixture of pride and jealousy welled up inside her. She thought: *Sorry, gals, but he's spoken for.*

Hannes shot back his cuffs and smiled. "I hear this restaurant serves the best organic food in the city."

Kenzie, not wanting to rain on his parade, didn't let on that she'd been here several times in the past. And then she remembered with whom. A spasm of guilt stabbed her. *Do I have no shame? The other times I was here, I was with Charley!*

Dear God, she thought queasily, feeling the jaws of guilt snapping with renewed force. *Only twenty-four hours ago I was with Charley! Maybe we hadn't planned on having sex, but one thing had led to another. And now, here I am—with his partner of all people!*

She quashed the feeling of shame. Muddled emotions would lead her nowhere. *I have no reason to be penitent. Charley's in my past. I can't let him dictate my future.*

Hannes was saying, "I don't believe they serve hard liquor here. What do you say we start with wine?"

Kenzie gave a start. "I'm sorry." She lowered her hands and smoothed the indentations of her elbows from the white tablecloth. "My mind was wandering."

He eyed her with concern. "Are you all right?"

"Yes, of course." She smiled. "Wine would be perfect."

He ordered a 1982 Château Lynch-Bages Pauillac, then said, "I meant to ask you. Did you receive Professor Tindemans's fax?"

Kenzie slapped her forehead. "What is it with me? I must be losing my mind."

She slung her shoulder bag from the back of her chair, took out a manila envelope, and passed it across the table. "Here. I Xeroxed you a copy."

As though considering its immediate importance, he regarded the envelope a moment, and then put it aside. "You will forgive me if I don't get to it until tomorrow morning? I much prefer to devote this evening to present company."

His voice was so quiet, so intimate, and so undeniably warm and promising, that Kenzie felt a warm tremor firing up her flesh.

She was saved from replying by the arrival of the waiter, who with some ceremony displayed the label on the wine bottle. Kenzie watched while the cork was expertly extracted, and a splash of wine poured into Hannes's glass, the bottle smartly turned so that any stray droplets spun back inside it.

Hannes picked up his glass. Swirled it. Inhaled the bouquet. Took a sip. Put it back down and nodded. "Very nice," he said approvingly. The waiter topped off both glasses and discreetly withdrew.

Hannes lifted his glass by the stem. "A toast," he said.

Kenzie raised her glass and looked at him.

"To us," he said softly.

She could feel the rush of his warmth reaching out to her. It was as if a flurry of sparks had burst inside her, and was flash-dancing up through her arms and down her legs.

"To . . . us," she whispered, carefully tipping the rim of her glass against his.

They held each other's gaze as they sipped. The atmosphere was so supercharged with sexual energy that she half-expected to see electrical currents ricocheting between them.

Lowering her eyes, she set down her glass. Her voice was husky. "The wine's very good."

He was looking at her intently. "Yes," he said. "But the company's superior. In my estimation, definitely *grand cru.*"

She had to laugh. "Bet you say that to all the girls."

With thumb and forefinger, he turned his wineglass around and around on the tablecloth.

"I wouldn't wager too much on that," he cautioned. "You're liable to lose."

She smiled. "Does this mean you invited me this evening just to seduce me?"

"That, and to get better acquainted, yes." He nodded. "Last time we never had the opportunity to really talk."

His honesty was disarming and unsettling. She emptied half her glass in one swallow.

"Well." She gestured. "Talk away."

"I was hoping you'd do most of the talking. You see, Kenzie, I'd like to learn more about you."

She laughed. "But I'd rather hear about *you!* Your background sounds fascinating. I believe you told me your father was in the diplomatic corps?"

He nodded.

"So how did you end up at Interpol?"

"I'm afraid it is a long story, Kenzie."

"So?" Her eyes didn't waver. "I have all night."

He took a deep breath and let it out slowly. "All right. But I must warn you, it is not one of those 'happily ever after' stories."

She stared at him. "Most of real life isn't."

"No, I suppose it is not."

He kept turning his glass around and around. "I'm wondering where I should begin," he said after a moment.

"Why not at the beginning?" she suggested gently.

"Yes," he said. "Why not?"

As he began to talk, she listened raptly. The life which he described was so much like hers that she found it uncanny. There were only two major differences. The first was that she'd had three brothers, while he'd been an only child. And the second was that instead of being shuttled from one military base to another, as she had, he and his family had hopscotched from one capital city to another.

"It sounds more glamorous than it actually was," he confided. "Granted, living in all those exotic countries *was* fascinating. I saw a lot of the world early on. Bangkok, Nairobi, Washington, London, Moscow, Mexico City . . ."

He drank some of his wine.

"The problem with embassy life is its insularity. It is such a closed society. One doesn't get to mix much with the local people, only embassy personnel and their families, and officials of the host country. Also, it seemed that each time I made friends, my father would be assigned to another part of the world, and off we went."

He smiled wistfully at the memory.

"But do you know the one thing I missed most . . . *truly* missed above all else?"

Kenzie shook her head.

"Never having had a real home—a *permanent* home—to return to."

Kenzie could commiserate with that. *Sounds just like my childhood,* she thought. *We never had a permanent home, either. And we'd barely get settled on one army base before Daddy'd get orders and be assigned to another.* She could also relate to the havoc such constant moves played with young friendships. *Forging long-lasting relationships was impossible.*

Hannes was saying, ". . . coming from a diplomatic family, it was only natural for my parents to hope that I would follow in my father's footsteps." He laughed quietly. His eyes had become distant, focused on some point in his past. "They had my future in the foreign service all planned."

"But here you are," Kenzie said.

"Yes," he said, "here I am."

He drained the rest of his wine and set the glass down. The waiter caught his eye and he nodded. They didn't speak until both their glasses were topped and they were each handed a menu.

When the waiter withdrew, Hannes continued. "Strange, isn't it," he mused, putting his menu aside, "how we expect to do certain things in life, and then end up doing something completely different?"

She nodded.

"Consider my real ambition. Not my parents', but my own." He paused. "Would you believe, I've always wanted to become an artist?"

"Really!" she exclaimed, delighted that yet another part of his background paralleled hers.

He smiled. "Yes, really. Ever since I was old enough to hold a pencil, I was always either drawing or painting. Everyone said I had a talent. And to me, the future was self-evident."

She smiled. "Let me guess. You were planning on living in a garret in Paris . . . painting your heart out . . . arguing about art late into the night in smoky cafés . . . having exhibitions . . ."

". . . waiting to be discovered," he completed, his voice turning wry.

"Were you good?"

"I believed I was."

He raised his glass in a self-mocking toast and then put it down and continued to turn it around and around by its stem.

"And then I woke up one morning and realized the truth. You see, I *was* good, Kenzie. Damn good." He paused. "But I wasn't good enough."

"So you joined Interpol?"

"No." He smiled. "Not then. First, I studied political science."

"Ah. The dutiful son following in his father's footsteps."

He nodded. "Exactly."

"But you didn't," she pointed out. "Follow in his footsteps, I mean."

"No," he whispered, "I did not."

She could see the light in his eyes go dim as a cloud of unhappiness blotted out the pleasant memories.

"Kenzie, listen to me!" There was an urgency in his voice.

Abruptly he reached across the table and took her hand. He pressed her fingers so hard that they hurt.

"This world is a terrible place! No matter how insulated a life one leads, or how safe one may feel, it is an illusion. Violence is never far away. It can strike anywhere, at any time. You must never forget that!"

She shivered, an uncontrollable reflex to the chill of sudden fear. Her coat of well-being, in which she'd luxuriated warmly, was now gone. Yet she found this melodramatic turn in conversation intriguing as well as frightening.

I wish I knew the specifics of what he's trying to say, she thought. But she didn't want to pry. *I must be patient. He'll tell me about it when he's ready.*

Sensing her fear, he let go of her hand. "I'm sorry, Kenzie. I do not mean to be an alarmist."

She nodded.

"I will explain, and then you shall understand. I think I owe you that much."

He paused, forehead creased, and pinched the bridge of his nose.

"You realize, of course, that I was not always as cynical and cautious as I am now. There was a time I was carefree. When, with all the fervor of youth, I truly believed we can master our own destinies."

As she listened, Kenzie picked up her glass and sipped a little wine. The sounds of the restaurant made a comforting, privacy-veiling murmur in the background.

"I studied political science at Oxford," he told her, "and then at Yale. Upon my graduation, my father called in favors, and I was assigned to the Finnish embassy in Paris. Not in an entry-level position, mind you—I worked closely with our ambassador. Soon I was on intimate terms with his family. Under those circumstances, I suppose falling in love with his daughter was inevitable. Her name was Helena. After a brief courtship, we were engaged to be married."

An irrational tweak of jealousy plucked at Kenzie. "Was she beautiful?"

"Helena?" He shut his eyes, and sighing, he nodded slowly. "Oh yes. She was . . . extraordinarily beautiful."

"Then what—?"

"Destiny!" he said bitterly.

His eyes snapped open and the curtain of his guard lifted. On the table, his fingers curled, closing into such a tight, trembling fist that the knuckles turned white.

"God, how I—" He stopped in midsentence and bit his lip, momentarily incapable of continuing.

There was no mistaking his misery. For all his self-assurance and manly strength, he could no longer hide the deep and suppurating wound at the core of his being. A moistness came into his eyes, and Kenzie knew he was on the verge of tears. Then he quickly looked away, but not before she recognized something else in his face—

—something besides pain.

With a shock, she realized what it was: a simmering, dangerously subdued menace which emanated from the furnace of a potent and unassuaged rage.

What kind of trauma could he have suffered to cause a reaction like this?

Reaching across the table, she gently, soothingly, cupped both hands around his twitching fist. Under her ministrations, the trembling lessened, then eventually stilled.

"Hans," she said huskily, "please. Don't torture yourself like this. It's really not necessary."

He turned his face to her, his features grim. "It is—it *is* necessary," he said tightly. "You have a right to know!"

She held his gaze. "I'll leave that up to you. But I don't want to pry—"

He nodded and cleared his throat, a splintery, cracking sound like that of a sailboat's hull strained by enormous pressure.

"It was violence—stupid random violence!" he said bitterly. "Seven years, three months, and twelve days ago. The day of our *wedding!* And all because Helena and my parents were in the wrong place, at the wrong time!"

"Oh, Hans!" Kenzie whispered.

"It happened, as if things like this just *happen*—"

His voice cracked, and he shook his head savagely, a wet sob bursting forth, jolting Kenzie. Hannes pushed a hand through his hair, then hunched over the table and lowered his head, as if inspecting the white service plate for flaws.

"They—Christ, they were on their way to the *church* ... only stopped at the bank for an heirloom we kept in the vault, a necklace which brides in my family traditionally wore—"

A muscular tic made his cheeks flutter, and he swallowed noisily.

"A necklace, Kenzie! Can you imagine? They died because of a ... a trinket!"

"My God! But how—?"

Hannes's murmur was so soft as to be barely audible.

"Robbers—*gunmen* ..."

She had to lean forward and strain to hear.

"... returning from the vault. Father, Mother, and Helena stumbled upon the thieves, *surprised* them—"

Kenzie's horror grew as the story unfolded.

"All three of them, shot dead in cold blood. Father ... Mother ... Helena—"

Their names exploded from his lips, and he gripped the edge of the table with both slender, knobby-knuckled hands.

"What kind of sentences—"

"None!" he whispered. "It remains unsolved to this day."

Kenzie shuddered in disbelief. The notion that people could murder one's nearest and dearest, and get away with it, was beyond her comprehension.

She thought: *From childhood, we're programmed to believe that criminals are caught and punished, just like in the movies or on television. But real life isn't like that. Real life is ugly and brutal and unfair.*

Hannes raised his eyes slowly, and she could see the held-back tears glittering in the corners.

He said, "It is worse, Kenzie ... far worse than anything you can imagine."

"But how ... how did you ever cope ... ?"

"The only way possible," he sighed, shrugging his shoulders. "I became obsessed with finding the killers. Bringing them to justice kept me going."

And he added softly, "It still does."

"Even after all these years."

"Yes," he nodded. "Especially after all these years."

Then his gaze cleared, became focused.

"And there you have it, Kenzie. The reason I devoted my life to law enforcement. Though admittedly—" He smiled wryly. "—I imagined myself tracking down killers, not specializing in art theft."

"So how did that come about?"

"My superiors decided it for me. At any rate, it turned out for the best. I seem to have a special aptitude for it."

A mask seemed to drop over his features, obliterating them of emotion.

"But enough of this," he said gruffly, waving the subject aside. "I didn't invite you to dinner to burden you with my demons. Now then. Shall we order?"

Kenzie picked up her menu and scanned it.

It was useless. The words blurred. Food was the last thing on her mind. All her powers of concentration were centered upon Hannes.

If he hadn't told me, I'd never have known the suffering he's gone through, she thought soberly. Too, she knew it couldn't have been easy for him to share his misery. *He's the type who normally keeps his emotions bottled up.*

Not surprisingly, the knowledge that beneath his charming, secure exterior lay a core of sensitive vulnerability made him more attractive than ever.

"Do you know what you want to eat?" he asked.

Kenzie smiled vaguely; she chose the easy way out.

"Why don't you choose for both of us?" she suggested, putting her menu aside.

She eyed him appraisingly as he ordered Luma verde salads and grilled and roasted vegetable platters.

A man both macho *and* sensitive. Now there was a rarity.

She felt a rush of warm satisfaction. She knew exactly how she wanted this evening to end.

And, judging from his sudden grin, so did he.

Finally, the Wall Street warrior was home. Late, lumbering, wheezy, and crabby.

Dina wasn't fazed. She accorded him a hero's welcome right inside the front door. Pressed herself tightly against him. Nibbled on his ear. Purred, "Sweetie, I thought you'd never get home!"

Her affection was instantly suspect. "Awright, Dina," Robert rasped. "Whaddya want now?"

Dina pulled back and batted pale, innocent lashes. "Why, nothing, sweetie!" She had lying through her teeth down to a science.

"Ha!" He didn't believe a word and treaded heavily on down the hall.

"Rooooo-beeeeert . . ."

Now what? he grouched. Heaving a sigh, he stopped, turned around, and did a double take.

Small wonder.

Dina, who suffered his cigars in aggrieved silence, had produced one of his Flor de F. Farach Extras and was slowly, deliberately, passing it under her nose and rattling it against her ear before snipping off one end.

As he watched, she sucked obscenely on the other end, all the while salaciously closing the distance between them.

Her efforts had the desired effect. Robert A. Goldsmith sported an instant boner.

God*damn!* he thought. *What is it about a woman with a cigar?* There was definitely something priapic about it. *Yes, indeed.* Still . . .

"Dina? You flippin' out, or what? I thought ya hated—"

She popped the cigar in his mouth.

That silenced him, and she struck a wooden match and held it to the cigar end.

Saurian eyes squinting with suspicion, and knowing full well he was being manipulated, Robert nevertheless puffed away like a gulping fish. Soon he was churning up affluent clouds of expensive blue smoke.

The hand-rolled tobacco went smoothly on the palate. Lulled him into a deceptive sense of well-being.

Her hands were clasped girlishly behind her back and she was twisting her torso from left to right and right to left.

"Daddy!" she squealed. "Baby's got a surprise for you! A big surprise!"

Wincing, he glanced furtively around.

It was all Dina could do to keep from bursting out laughing. Really! Did Robert think she was brainless enough to perform in front of the help?

Give me a break! she thought, and said: "Don't worry, Daddy. Baby gave everyone the night off!"

"Oh yeah?" he growled. "Then what're we gonna eat? Huh? I'm starved."

"Baby's gonna bring Daddy food in bed. Just go upstairs, Daddy. Please?"

He hesitated. Gave her an unblinking, appraising stare. Wished, not for the first time, that he could read her mind. At least that way he'd know what she was after.

Whatever it was, it had to be something major. She wouldn't have gone through the trouble of banishing the staff otherwise.

"Please, Daddy?" Dina tilted her head and pouted. "Pretty please? Baby'll be right up. I promise."

Robert puffed away with deceptive nonchalance. Then he gave an inward shrug and thought: *Why the hell not?* It wasn't as if it *had* to cost him anything. He turned and lumbered down the corridor; trudged slowly up the curved marble staircase.

Dina waited until he got upstairs, listening to his heavy echoing gait and wheezy expelled breaths. Only once she heard his bedroom door shut did she go on up, glancing at the giant Old Masters hanging on the yellow marble stairwell as she passed them—lusciously clothed Renaissance princelings and elegant noblewomen. Yet further validation of her own power, position, and taste.

On the second floor, she stopped in the service kitchenette. Took a precooked platter out of the refrigerator. Popped it in the microwave.

Then, repairing to her suite, she headed straight for her dressing room, where she opened the closet in which she kept her stash of erotic costumes.

No teddies, girdles, garters, micro nighties, or crotchless panties were on the agenda tonight. No, sir. Nothing that ordinary would do. With a clenched face, she contemplated the outfit she'd selected. *If this is what it takes,* she told herself grimly, *so be it.*

Without further ado, she shed her designer clothes, left them scattered on the floor for Darlene to pick up in the morning, and squeezed into the teensy costume.

Two minutes at her vanity table and one wig later, she inspected herself in the floor-length mirrors.

"Heidi Heidi Heidi ho," she said.

At which point she went to fetch Robert's nuked dinner.

It went without saying who would be dessert.

Outside Luma, Hannes flagged down a cruising cab. Without consulting Kenzie he gave the driver his address.

Kenzie didn't object, just made happy little noises and snuggled against him on the backseat.

In short order they were in his high-rise bedroom, bodies locked in carnal passion.

Hannes was nothing if not inventive. Besides being a skilled lover, he enjoyed giving pleasure as much as taking it, something Kenzie could appreciate. Able to count her sexual partners (including Charley and Hannes) on two hands, she had learned the hard way how truly special such attentiveness was. All too often, men were only after one thing. Their own gratification.

This did not apply to Hannes. He knew it took two to tango, and went out of his way to accommodate a lady.

Tonight he was in exceptional form.

Laid out on the bed, she felt him surrounding her completely, a great masculine force, arms and legs slithering, intertwining hers like serpents: powerful, sinuous, sensuous. His fingers fluttered along her naked flesh and his tongue flicked, snakelike, into every crevasse, and over each curvaceous mound and hollow, causing her skin to ripple with delicious shivers.

It was like being caught up in a riptide, in the throes of forces beyond her control, forces she felt absolutely no *desire* to control, so great was the rush of exhilaration.

He lifted his eyes and gazed at her, his breaths warm puffs against her fiery flesh.

"Are you familiar with the *Kama Sutra,* Kenzie?" he whispered.

She shook her head. "No," she whispered.

He said: " 'Kama' is what one learns from the *Kama Sutra,* which literally means 'Science of Love.' It is a love manual written by the Hindu sage, Vatsyayana, some two thousand years ago.

"The word 'kama' means to enjoy oneself using all five senses. Seeing. Hearing. Smelling." He put his nose in the cleft of her breasts and inhaled deeply. "Feeling." He smoothed clever fingers along her inner thighs.

She raised herself on her elbows and gazed raptly down at him.

"Tasting." Looking solemnly at her, he fastened his lips around one erect nipple.

She arched her spine and uttered a little cry.

"According to the *Kama Sutra,* Kenzie, there are many places one may kiss." Knees on either side of her, he leaned forward, then slid down along her body, tenderly kissing each spot as he named it.

"Forehead." *Kiss.* "Eyes." *Kiss.* "Cheeks." *Kiss.* "Lips, throat, bosom, breasts."

Paralyzing, these kisses; this magical, ritual lovemaking. Kenzie lay back and shut her eyes. Body and soul, she surrendered. She was his, and he hers, and nothing outside these four walls seemed to exist.

Sliding yet farther down her body, he gently parted her thighs and lifted her bare buttocks. "The jewel of your secret place ... that, too, Kenzie, is to be kissed," he murmured, and pressed his lips against her vagina.

She nearly wept with joy, and whimpered with anxiety when he lifted his head and lowered her thighs.

"Also, Kenzie," he said, "everything in the *Kama Sutra* has a special name," he continued, moving his body up along hers until he was once again face to face with her. "For instance, should either of our tongues touch the other's ... that is called 'The Fighting of the Tongue.' "

He covered her mouth with his, and their needs were such that it seemed they would devour each other in a feeding frenzy.

Finally he tore his lips from hers. "And, if I were to capture you in my arms, place my legs outside yours, and enter you while I squat, pressing your knees against my sides, that is the position called *Dadhyataka.*"

Her fingernails dug into his arms. "And if we were to ... to lie side by side ... or atop each other ..." She stared at him. "If I were to take you in my mouth, and you used your tongue on me ... ?"

He laughed softly. "That, Kenzie, is called *Kakila.*"

"*Kakila,*" she repeated.

"It means 'The Crow.' It is an act supposedly performed by slaves ... and other lowly persons."

Her eyes were wide and shiny. "Then let us revel in lowly pleasures! Hannes! Let's be base and coarse!"

Her voice dropped to a trembling whisper as she added: "Let me be your slave!"

"Papilein!" Dina crooned.

She skipped into Robert's bedroom looking like she was struggling with the big serving tray. Which, in truth, she was. The steaming platters of sauerkraut, knockwursts, potato salad, and four chilled steins of beer weighed a ton.

Robert's eyes all but popped. Beached on his California king-size bed like some great pink cigar-puffing whale, he endeavored to sit up.

Dina glanced at his already-hard pecker. She ascertained that it was responding nicely, as evidenced by its sudden twitching.

As well it should.

Papi's little girl was wearing a blonde wig with two long fat braids, a minute Bavarian-style minidirndl which left her breasts entirely exposed, and a smile that went from ear to ear. Plus a variation on the usual makeup—giant starry lashes and oversize, penciled-on freckles.

Heidi Does Manhattan, she thought grimly, and quickly suppressed the image. She had no room for negative thoughts. A positive frame of mind was essential, especially since she intended to hit him with a double whammy.

"See, *Papilein?*" She glanced at him shyly from where she'd stopped just inside the door. "Baby's brought you dinner! Just like I promised!"

"Well? Don't just stand there, l'il girl!" Robert patted the mattress. "Bring it 'ere!"

"Ja, Papilein?" Dina feigned wide-eyed, childish pleasure. "May I really?"

"Yeah," he rasped with a lecherous leer. "L'il girl's Daddy's *real* hungry. So c'mon. What're ya waitin' for—Christmas?"

"Oh, *danke, Papilein!*" she squealed.

And braids, hooters, and tushie bouncing, Dina bounded across the room. Deposited the tray on the bed. Leaped up beside him. Acted as frisky as any six-year-old with energy to burn.

The fact that Dina had turned thirty a month earlier made absolutely no difference. She gave the performance her all. And Robert loved every minute of it.

She began by finger-feeding him, as if he were one of those corpulent, licentious Roman emperors.

A prolonged game of "hide the knockwurst" followed.

Robert couldn't get enough, and Dina worked her oral magic.

Soon his brain was where she wanted it to be—in his cock. His resolve not to promise her anything had evaporated.

For nearly half an hour, Dina kept him on the very brink of orgasm. Then, and only then, did she make her move.

Deciding to start off small, she sprang the weekend at the Faireys on him. Believing he was getting off cheaply, Robert committed himself with alacrity. Hell, it wasn't as if it was going to cost him anything.

However, Dina wasn't quite finished with him yet. She continued honking his horn and stopping moments before he could climax.

From his wheezy groans, she finally judged his faculties to be sufficiently impaired. If she dragged it out much longer, he'd start getting crabby. Or worse, he might surprise her and shoot his load.

She decided it was time to go for the jackpot.

"Papilein?" she ventured, alternately tonguing his penis and giving its ruffled head little tugs with her lips.

He grunted unintelligibly.

"Baby needs something real badly!"

Robert snickered. "All baby needs is Daddy's *dick!*"

Very funny, she thought, not in the least bit amused. Nevertheless, she batted starry lashes. "Baby needs to redecorate!"

He rolled his eyes. "Should'a known there'd be a payoff!" he growled.

"Is *not!*" she countered, with a pout.

"Then what would *you* call it?"

She tossed her head indignantly. "Baby calls it a present!"

"Yeah," he guffawed. "So does every hooker in town."

Shit! He obviously wasn't incapacitated enough.

Dina quickly fixed that by showing him what her mouth was *really* capable of.

"Oh, Baby," he moaned. "Oh, yeah. Yeah! *That's* the spirit—"

She gave it her all, head bobbing furiously, mouth working triple-time.

"Oh, Baby," he gasped. *"Baby—"*

Then she felt the telltale tremor shuddering through him, knew he was reaching the point of no return—

—and stopped.

Right in the nick of time, too. A few more tugs of her lips and he'd have exploded.

"Goddammit, Dina!" he howled, aggrieved.

She puckered her lips. Blew teasing puffs of air at his penis. Tickled its swollen red head with the tip of her tongue.

"Please, *Papilein?* Can Baby have her present?" She kissed the tip of his penis. "Pretty please?"

He drew a deep, resigned breath—and knew she had him.

"Oh, aw right!" he croaked grumpily. "You win. *Now* will ya finish what ya started?"

Bingo! She'd hit the jackpot!

Dina deemed it time to show her gratitude. The way he liked best. By bending her head and setting seriously to work.

Robert climaxed half a minute later, unaware what those thirty short seconds would cost him.

Well, he'll discover that soon enough, Dina decided. *Why ruin his pleasure by telling him he'd just had a multimillion-dollar blow job?*

The sandman wouldn't come.

Hours had crept by, and still Zandra lay awake in the dark, alone with her thoughts.

Even though her room faced on the back, she could hear the songs of the city. Distant wails of sirens and the screams of car alarms; the bass beat of a stereo seeping out of a neighboring building, the billow of laughter and raised voices in the stairwell, the thunder of rap music blasting from a passing vehicle.

But she'd become inured to these sounds, and knew they weren't the reason sleep kept eluding her.

The real reason was because her mind, like an endless loop, kept replaying every detail from lunch—or rather, from that instant when Karl-Heinz first entered Mortimer's to the moment she had made her escape from him in front of Burghley's.

She simply couldn't get him out of her mind. Karl-Heinz. Her cousin. Her—

—obsession?

No. Never. Not in a million years.

Zandra heard Kenzie return and tiptoe past her door. She glanced at the alarm clock. It was going on one-thirty.

How she yearned for sleep.

Trouble was, it wouldn't come.

Karl-Heinz couldn't sleep, either. He prowled restlessly from window to window in his sky-high penthouse. Earlier, the view had resembled the platinum-processed Berenice Abbott photograph hanging in his hallway. But that had been hours ago.

Now the cleaning crews had departed from the office towers, and most of the windows had gone dark. So had many in the high-rise apartment buildings.

But he didn't notice. Even as he stared out at it, the cityscape was the furthest thing from Karl-Heinz's mind.

His thoughts were consumed by Zandra. By the myriad questions he had concerning her. The mental list he'd compiled was endless: *What goes on inside that beautiful head of hers? How does she feel about me? Is there someone else in her life? Will Becky's scheme work?*

For one of the few times in his life, His Serene Highness, Prince Karl-

Heinz von und zu Engelwiesen, was at a total loss. He knew that he loved Zandra. He'd known that since the night of his birthday party last October.

However, what he *didn't* know was the extent of—or the lack of—Zandra's feelings toward him.

If only I had an inkling, he thought.

But he didn't. Nor would he, until the weekend after next.

He stared out one of the north-facing windows. At this very moment, she was out there somewhere, in one of the countless thousands of buildings of this great metropolis.

Zandra. No doubt sleeping the deep, contented sleep of the innocent.

Suddenly he was tired. For a moment he shut his eyes.

Please, God, don't let me corrupt her.

TARGET: BURGHLEY'S COUNTDOWN TO TERROR

Long Island City, January 14

"How much longer are we to remain here? Or have we exchanged one prison for another?"

The outburst was uncalled for, the lack of respect shown, unforgivable. The hooded figure, rendered inhuman by the black convex lenses, electronic voice distorter, jumpsuit, and gloves, was tempted to lash out and make an example of the belligerent Libyan.

But for now, he decided to let him off with a warning. The Arab possessed skills which would prove essential.

The eerily distorted voice barked: "Would you rather stand trial for that skyjacking? Your return to prison can always be arranged!"

His words had the desired effect: the swarthy Libyan backed down. Cast desultory eyes upon the concrete-slab floor, studiously avoiding the hatred emanating from his eight teammates.

So, the hooded man thought to himself. *There's no love lost between them. Good.*

They were in the safe house, a former die-cutting factory set amid the industrial wastelands on the Queens side of the East River. All the equipment had long been torn out and hauled off. Vast cold, empty space surrounded them.

As did darkness.

He had ordered the fluorescents switched off before his arrival. Now the only sources of light were the haze of Manhattan glittering across the watery divide and the moonlight leaking in from the overhead skylights.

Even in daylight, it was a grim and forbidding place.

At night it was downright hostile.

Thick concrete supporting columns, rising like squat sentinels, stretched into stygian blackness. Gusts of blustery wind shrieked through broken panes. And foraging rats, like evil whispers, scuttled in the unseen perimeters.

But worst of all was the noise. It came from directly above—the constant, maddening din of traffic buzzing across the Fifty-ninth Street Bridge—and sounded like the amplified whirring of angry hordes of bees.

From between a thin slit in his black lenses, the man studied his hand-picked crew. There were nine—eight men and one woman. Disenfranchised terrorists all:

The former Israeli commando. Fearless and inventive, he was a veritable one-man army.

The German. A master electrician, he didn't need a circuit chart to shut down a building, or an entire city.

The Libyan, whose forte was hijackings. He was an expert at having ransom demands met.

The ex-navy SEAL. Master of the big bang, he could single-handedly bring down a wall, a bridge, or an entire building.

The Frenchman. A daredevil who could drive a Formula One, pilot an F-15 or a 747, and sail or steer anything afloat.

The Colombian brothers. Finesse was neither's strong point, but if it had a trigger, they could shoot it, with deadly results.

The Japanese. Yoshi Mori was his name and electronics were his game. Specialty: computer hacking. Given time, he could break into most any system, civilian or military.

The Italian woman. Formerly of the Red Brigades, she was chic, slim, and beautiful—and deadlier than any male.

With one exception, thought the hooded man. *Me. I'm the deadliest of the lot.*

He tossed a long cardboard tube at the nearest of them. "Here."

The German snatched it neatly from the air.

"Inside are blueprints. Study them until you can remember every detail in your sleep. That goes for all of you."

"Then-a this-a is our target?" The harsh, accented voice belonged to the woman.

"Yes. But all identifying words have been censored. You will know the exact address when the time comes."

"And-a when-a is that?"

He thought: *When the Irishman is free.*

"Soon," his robotic voice rasped. "In the meantime—" He jabbed a finger in the Libyan's chest. "—you can teach our friend here the art of patience. Remember. All your lives depend on it."

Then he turned and moved soundlessly on rubber-soled feet, a swift shadow sliding around the structural columns and down two flights of steel steps. In the loading bay below, his van door slammed, the engine caught, and tires screeched.

Then he was gone.

He left the stolen van in the Queens Plaza parking lot. Quickly, he got out and carried the gym bag containing his disguise to the far end, where his rental car awaited.

A panhandler bundled in filthy blankets detached himself from a doorway. "Please, mister? Spare some loose change?"

He paused, tempted to reach into his pocket. Then he remembered what Benjamin Franklin had once written: "A fool and his money are soon parted."

He almost laughed aloud. *A fool.* Well, that was the last thing anyone could accuse him of being.

Why break a perfect record now?

"Get lost!" he snarled, and continued walking.

Fifteen minutes later, he was speeding across the Fifty-ninth Street Bridge on his way back into Manhattan, the tires of his car adding yet another buzz to that crazed, constant din which, from below, sounded like swarms of attacking killer bees.

He glanced down as he passed above the safe house.

Sleep tight, my friends, he thought sardonically. And added aloud: "If you can."

He was smiling coldly.

Book Three

"LET'S MAKE A DEAL"

Special to the New York *Times*

NEW YORK, Jan. 19—Robert A. Goldsmith is riding high these days. The slack sale Tuesday of Old Masters at Sotheby's, the auction house, has not dampened his spirits. Shrugging aside worries over tomorrow's Old Masters sale at Burghley's, Inc., the 61-year-old retail and investment billionaire said yesterday that he plans to form a new global company by merging four diverse companies.

The new company, GoldGlobe International Holdings, Inc., would be formed by combining four companies in which Mr. Goldsmith holds controlling stakes—GoldMart, Inc., Burghley's Holdings, Inc., the Home-on-the-Range restaurant chain, and Mystique Cosmetics.

"Today's market is definitely global, whether you're selling dungarees, million-dollar art, or fast food," Mr. Goldsmith said in yesterday's news conference in Manhattan, citing planned expansion to new overseas markets, including former Soviet republics and South American and Eastern European countries.

"This merger will enable us to put four different companies into each new market we enter."

Shares in GoldMart, Inc., rose nearly 4 percent yesterday to $25.85. Burghley's stock was up 40.5 cents to $18.25, and Home-on-the-Range closed at $12.20.

Mystique Cosmetics is privately owned. Plans for offering equity in the company were suspended last year because of investor resistance . . .

❦ *32* ❧

"*I*'m moving tomorrow," Bambi Parker announced breathily as she repaired her makeup. "No more roommates. I've sublet a studio." She moved her gold compact this way and that to inspect her reflection: up, down, left, right.

Robert A. Goldsmith, half-sprawled in the backseat of his stretch limo, lifted his massive buttocks a few inches and pulled up his giant trousers. "This mean your phone number's gonna change?" His fly went *ziiiiip!*, and he tackled his belt.

"Uh-huh." Bambi finished applying lip gloss, then snapped the compact shut and handed him a folded slip of paper. "My new address and phone number," she said.

Without glancing at it, he took the paper and pocketed it.

Bambi had expected him to show at least some interest, and the fact that he didn't made her feel downright peeved. "R*obert!*" she reproached. "Don't you want to know why I'm moving?"

He looked at her and blinked. "Why? You're stayin' in town, aren't ya?"

"Well, I'll tell you why. Because I moved for both of us, dammit! So we don't always have to make it in this . . ." She gestured around. ". . . this damn fuckmobile!"

Her vehemence took him by surprise. "What've you got against the car? It's big, private, comfortable, an' convenient."

"Maybe for *you* it is, but every once in a while, I'd like to do it in bed. Besides, my new digs are just as convenient."

Women, he thought, giving an inward groan. *Why is it they're always hell-bent to complicate the simplest thing?*

For his own part, he couldn't imagine anything more convenient than this car. All he had to do was open the door and in she'd hop.

What the hell do we need a bed for?

"Anyway, I want you to come and see it," she was saying. "Why don't you drop by tomorrow? And plan on staying an hour or so?"

She showed the pink triangular tip of her tongue.

"You won't be sorry, Robert. I guarantee it."

"Okay," he grumbled, hoping he wouldn't live to regret it. Lately, it seemed that no matter which way he turned, women were putting the screws to him. "But I better not have to go out of my way to get there," he growled.

"You won't," she assured him quickly. "I already told you that."

"So where is it?"

"Right up there." She pointed at the roof of the limo.

"Huh?"

"Auction Towers," she said, casually dropping the bombshell.

"Where?" he exploded, going purple with rage. "Are you fuckin' nuts? You think I'd be caught *dead* visitin' you in that building? We might as well take an ad out in the *Times!*"

"Calm down," Bambi said, unperturbed. "Don't you see, Robert? You *own* that building, or at least the unsold apartments. Plus, one of your companies manages it. If anyone has a right to be seen coming and going from there, it's you."

"The missus ever found out, my goose'd be cooked." He made up his mind. "No way am I gonna set foot up there. And that's *that!*"

Bambi sighed to herself. She'd had an inkling that he might take it badly at first. But *this* badly? She hadn't counted on that, and wondered if she mightn't have seriously miscalculated.

Not that it mattered. She was determined to put her foot down.

He punched the button in the door panel to signal his chauffeur to pull over.

Within moments, the limo had coasted to a halt in the no-standing zone of a bus stop. Without another word, Robert chucked open his door.

Bambi hesitated, then climbed over his splayed legs. Once outside, she ducked down and stuck her head back inside. "The apartment number's on the note," she said, striving to sound firm. "We'll meet there, or not at all."

"You're really tryin' my patience," he warned in a dangerously quiet voice. "You might as well get it into your head. I'm not settin' foot up there. Ever."

"And *I'm* not setting foot in this car until you do!"

They glared stubbornly at one another, each refusing to back down. Bad vibes ricocheted like bullets.

"In that case," he said quietly, "it's over." He started to close the door, but she grabbed hold of the handle.

"I'll pretend I didn't hear that, Robert," she said stiffly. "If you change your mind, call me."

"Better not hold your breath," he advised.

"I won't. But at least there's one silver lining to *this* cloud! The carpeting in this car's been hell on my pantyhose!"

And with that, she slammed the door, tossed her head, and marched off to work.

* * *

"If madame will permit a suggestion?" murmured Sergei, Becky V's hairdresser, to whom Dina had recently defected.

"By all means, sweetie," Dina said magnanimously. "Suggest away!"

They were in Dina's in-home beauty parlor, a mirror-sheathed room replete with adjustable chair and chock full of professional equipment. Dina, submitting to her daily coif and manicure, was, at this very moment, receiving a silk wrap from May, the pretty Asian manicurist.

"I was thinking, madame would perhaps like to update her look?"

Dina frowned at her multiple reflections. "Update? In what way?"

Sergei gathered her hair in both hands, pulled it up, and held it in place atop her head. "*Very* Claudia Schiffer," he raved.

Dina studied herself critically. It made her look, she thought, as if she was sprouting a fountain of blond hair. "I don't think so, Sergei. It's . . . too Ivana."

"But youthful, no?"

"Perhaps, but it's not *me*. The usual will do just fine."

"As madame wishes," he murmured, acknowledging her superior taste.

Dina settled back in the chair. Being a slave to couture was one thing, but following the latest trends? No way. Let ordinary women copy Claudia Schiffer and Ivana and Princess Di; she, Dina Goldsmith, had her own signature look down pat, a look from which she never deviated, and which was instantly recognizable, not to mention highly photogenic.

Brisk knocks presaged Dina's secretary, who came charging in. "You've got a long-distance call," Gaby announced, in that James Earl Jones voice of hers. "From It'ly." She lifted her eyeglasses, which dangled from around her neck, and used them to consult her spiral notepad. "Mon . . . gar . . . dini? Some name like that. You in or not?"

"Of course I'm in," Dina snapped. "You know very well I was waiting for this call. Gaby, quick! Hand me the phone!"

"Who do I look like?" her secretary groused. "Step n' Fetchit?"

Sergei diplomatically intervened. Reaching for the phone, he handed it to Dina with a flourish.

"Why, thank you, sweetie!" she purred.

And, flashing Gaby an acid look, she added: "At least *someone* around here's versed in the social graces!"

Gaby smirked. "Yeah, and he even looks every inch the gentleman, too," she said snidely, referring to his curly, waist-length mane, yellow-tinted glasses, and white snakeskin cowboy boots.

Dina had better things to do than listen to petty squabbles. Pressing the talk button, she crooned, "Hel . . . lo . . . oh? . . . *Signor* Mongiardino? . . . Mrs. Goldsmith here . . . You spoke to Becky V? . . . Yes, she did mention something about your not working overseas anymore . . . I was positively *heartbroken* . . . You'll *what!* . . . Make an exception? . . . I can't thank you enough! . . . This coming Monday's purrrrrfect . . . Naturally, there are no budgetary constraints . . . Cost is no object . . . I'm looking forward to meeting you also . . . Thank you, *Signor!*"

Sighing with pleasure, Dina handed Sergei the phone, leaned her head back against the padded headrest, and let her eyelids flutter shut.

Ah! she thought dreamily, as May got busy silk-wrapping her right hand. *How simply marvelous!*

She could see it already! A Mongiardino interior to rival Becky V's! *No wonder I'm feeling so heavenly!*

In that case, it's over . . . Robert's words left Bambi badly shaken. So much so, that she deviated from her morning ritual and foresook popping into The Club. The last thing she needed on this, of all days, was powder room gossip, especially since she herself might soon be the subject of it.

All Robert has to do, she thought, *is pick up his cellular phone and call personnel. That's all that stands between my job and a pink slip.*

She couldn't imagine the humiliation. Just thinking about it was enough to give her chills.

I'd rather die.

Instructing her secretary to deflect all calls, Bambi holed up in her office, where she sniffed sachets of apple-spice herb tea (to reduce stress), while agonizing over her spat with Robert.

How could I have been so stupid as to give him an ultimatum? That's the province of wives, not mistresses!

Nor was it like her to lose her cool. What in hell could have possessed her?

When she finally began to calm down, she wracked her brains over how to go about exercising damage control.

Should I swallow my pride, call Robert, and apologize? she wondered. *Should I wait for* him *to call* me? *Or should I let sleeping dogs lie—and see what develops?*

Trouble was, she had no idea. This was unexplored territory. In the past, *she* had always been the center of attention, and it had been the boys—and then the men—who'd danced attendance, and who'd had to kiss *her* and make up.

Yes, but would Robert?

She really didn't know. He was in a different league from most men, and aside from sex, remained an enigma. She had yet to discover what made him tick.

Several times, she found herself reaching for the phone and punching his number—only to realize what she was doing—and quickly slamming the receiver back down.

If only she could confide in someone, ask their advice! But who?

Certainly not any of the girls from The Club. Divulging a secret to one was like telling them all, and speculation about the man in her life would spread like wildfire. Sooner or later, they'd put two and two together.

After much soul-searching, Bambi finally made up her mind. *It's up to Robert to call me,* she decided.

And if he didn't?

Then screw him, too.

Robert's motto was this. *If you can't fuck it or eat it, then piss on it.*

Which, figuratively speaking, was what he'd done to Bambi. He had no intention of ever seeing her again.

That was in the morning.

By the time noon rolled around, he found it difficult to concentrate on work. Visions of Bambi doing what she did best kept intruding.

Before long, he was wondering if maybe, just this once, he hadn't been . . . well, perhaps a little *too* hasty in severing relations . . .

At one-thirty, he was so horny smoke was practically pouring from his ears. And before two, he caved in and called her at Burghley's.

Bambi picked up on the very first ring, hesitantly saying, "Robert?" Sounding real nice and sexy.

Every shred of common sense told Robert to slam down the receiver—*now.* Before it was too late.

Instead, he found himself saying: "How'd you know it was me?"

"Because you're the only one who has this number."

He grunted approval. "Good. You know, I been thinkin'. Maybe I will come over an' see your new place. But it's gotta be today."

"Robert! The movers aren't coming till tomorrow. The apartment's totally bare and—"

"So? Who needs furniture? You got a key, don'tcha?"

There was a pause. "When do you want to drop by?" she asked softly.

"How's about right now?"

"I'll be waiting."

Hot damn!

Five minutes later, he was in the back of his limo. Libido in overdrive.

Headed uptown.

To the very place he swore he wouldn't be caught dead.

❧ *33* ❧

The Old Masters auctions were all held during the same week. Sotheby's had been on Tuesday. The art world—and Christie's and Burghley's in particular—had watched closely and held its collective breath.

Zandra and Kenzie had attended.

"This should give us an indication of how we'll fare on Thursday," Kenzie had whispered as they took their seats.

Zandra looked around doubtfully. "It seems frightfully empty. Darling, where on earth do you suppose everyone is?"

"Let's just hope the bidders who are here are in an upbeat mood," Kenzie said grimly.

They hadn't been; nearly half the one hundred eighty-four lots went unsold.

Christie's held its auction on Wednesday. Again Kenzie and Zandra attended. And again, little more than half the two hundred eleven lots sold.

Afterward, they trudged back to Burghley's on foot, their moods as dark and gloomy as the weather. When they'd arrived before ten, the sun had shone weakly; now, at two-thirty, the wind had picked up and the sky was a uniform, oppressive blanket of gray.

"It's this damned economic slump," Kenzie said dispiritedly, wrapping her scarf tighter around her. "Top of the market always sells, but no one else is buying."

"Bugger it!" Zandra muttered darkly. "We could certainly have used that bloody Holbein."

"Tell me about it," Kenzie sighed. "But that's water under the bridge. Meanwhile, the only activity there *is* going on is bottom fishing, and not enough of that. Trouble is, people won't open their wallets. Damn, but it's a good time to snap up bargains!"

At Sixtieth and Madison, they waited for the pedestrian light to change.

"I'm definitely not looking forward to tomorrow," she added unnecessarily.

Zandra pulled a face. "It's going to be *extremely* uncomfortable and humiliating sitting up there on that damn podium taking telephone bids and not receiving any and trying to look busy, whatever the hell that is, while the people who will show up and don't give a fart are all bloody staring at us, as if we're animals in a zoo *and* somehow to blame."

"C'mon!" Kenzie grabbed her by the arm. "While we're standing here gabbing, the light's turned green. Let's *go!*"

They started hurrying across.

"Shit!" Abruptly Kenzie stopped dead in her tracks and stared upward.

"Kenz, what *is* it?"

"It's starting to snow!" Kenzie wailed. "If this keeps up, tomorrow's turnout will be worse than godawful!" She looked imploringly at Zandra. "Why, oh why, can't we just call in sick in the morning?"

"You know why, Kenz. Professionalism. Esprit. Pride. Must keep the department safe from our Great Beloved Leader!"

North Korea's late Kim Il Sung had provided the inspiration for Arnold's most recent nickname for Bambi Parker.

"Right."

The light changed, and drivers began honking their horns.

"Come on, Kenz! Don't just stand there! Darling, we're *both* liable to get run over!"

Kenzie smiled wryly. "Sounds pretty tempting, doesn't it?"

"No, it bloody well does not!" Zandra snapped, and yanked her across.

By the time they reached Burghley's, the snow was coming down steadily.

"I've listened to the weather reports," Arnold Li said. "They now predict six to eight inches."

It was almost seven o'clock and they were still hard at work, par for the course on the eve of an auction.

"Now tell me some good news," Kenzie pleaded, *"please."*

"Thirty more absentee bids have come in by fax. I'm entering them in the computer now."

"Any more . . . bad news?"

He nodded. "Four lots have been withdrawn."

Shit. "Which ones?" she asked wearily.

"Lots 64, 113, 161, and 201."

Kenzie knew them by heart. The Jacob Jordaens, estimated at $200,000 to $300,000; the Lorenzo di Niccolo, estimated at $100,000 to $150,000; the Hendrik Terbrugghen, estimated at $300,000 to $500,000; and the Veronese, also estimated at $300,000 to $500,000.

Four of the best paintings in the sale.

Kenzie shut her eyes. *There goes tomorrow,* she thought.

By six-thirty the following morning, five inches of snow had accumulated, and it was still coming down in a white, opaque blanket. Radio broadcasts reported that schools were closed, all three airports had shut down, and alternate-side-of-the-street parking was suspended.

If only auctions could be cancelled as easily, Kenzie thought.

Turning up the newscast, she headed into the kitchen, put her favorite mix of coffee beans, half Colombia excelso and half Brazil Bourbon Santos, through the electric grinder, filled the coffeemaker, and switched it on. Soon it was gurgling and hissing and steaming up a storm.

Zandra, sleepy-eyed and barefoot, padded from her bedroom clad in an oversize white bathrobe. Her nose twitched, rabbitlike, as she sniffed the air.

"Fresh coffee? You're a saint. Shan't ever be able to go back to tea again. Nothing like a good jolt of caffeine to jump-start one awake. Have a good sleep?"

"I was dead to the world," Kenzie said. "And you?"

"Slept like a baby." Zandra yawned and stretched, went over to the living room window, and peered out from behind the curtains.

It was still night out, but not dark: the back garden was peculiarly and faintly luminescent from the reflection of the snow, and the air was alive, swirling with millions upon millions of fat, seemingly weightless flakes.

"Gosh, Kenzie. Snow's still coming down!"

"Tell me about it. Airports and schools are shut."

Zandra let go of the curtain and turned to her. "What about the auction?"

"Oh, I suspect it'll be business as usual," Kenzie sighed.

"What!" Zandra stared at her.

"You know the saying," Kenzie said wryly. " 'The show must go on.' "

"Yes, but ... Jesus, Kenzie." Zandra gestured at the window. "In *that?*"

"Presumably so. In all my time at Burghley's, I can't recall one auction ever having been postponed."

In the kitchen, the coffeemaker had quieted down.

"Aha. Our fix is ready." Kenzie went and returned with two steaming mugs and handed one to Zandra. "Here."

Zandra took it in both hands, blew softly on the surface, and lowered her head to take tiny birdlike sips. When she looked up, she was frowning.

"Honestly, darling, if they had *any* sense at all they'd bloody well postpone the sale. Just getting across town must be hell. I mean, how's anyone supposed to get there—"

The telephone chirruped.

Kenzie glanced at the mantel clock. It was only quarter till seven.

"How very odd," Zandra murmured. "Who could be calling this early?"

"Only one way to find out." Kenzie strode to the nearest extension. "Hello?"

"Kenz?"

"Arnold! Don't tell me you're stuck and—"

"No, I'm at work," he said. "I camped out here rather than risk a morning commute. Listen, you and Zandra had better get in here. Fast."

"Now? But why?"

"All hell's breaking loose."

And he hung up.

Frowning, Kenzie replaced the receiver. She didn't know what was going on, but she knew that whatever it was had to be serious. Arnold was not one to raise false alarms.

"Throw on your clothes," she told Zandra. "No time for hair or makeup. We can do that on the train."

Five minutes later, they were flying out the door.

"I say!" Zandra exclaimed, and stopped short.

A frazzled Arnold, collar open and shirt sleeves rolled up, was frantically punching lit and flashing buttons on his phone. "Please keep holding, ma'am. Someone will be right with you—" He glanced up, saw Kenzie and Zandra, and with circular motions of his arm gestured them hastily to their desks.

"What's going on?" Kenzie mouthed silently as she slipped out of her coat.

With an index finger he signaled that he'd be right with her.

"Yes, ma'am," he said into the receiver. "Uh-huh. Uh-huh." He rolled his eyes in exasperation. "Just half a minute longer, ma'am, no more. I pro—"

Another line rang.

He stabbed the flashing button. Said, "Burghley's Old Masters please hold," like one word.

Then, dropping the receiver, he made bug eyes, inflated his cheeks, and slumped back in his chair.

"Whew!" He expelled a noisy breath. "Am I ever glad to see *you* guys!"

Kenzie said: "I think you'd better fill us in on what's happening, and fast."

"It's the phones. They're ringing off the hook! Everybody and his brother's calling in absentee bids, and that doesn't take into account the ones being faxed. God alone knows how many of them have piled up."

Kenzie glanced over at the fax machine. The tray was overflowing, and copies of completed bid forms were scattered all over the floor.

She turned back to Arnold. "So by 'all hell breaking loose,' you meant we're getting swamped with *bids?*"

"That's right."

Good God, she thought. *Talk about things coming out of the blue!*

Kenzie was suddenly so excited she could barely breathe. It was truly staggering. The phones overloaded, the faxes accumulating.

I've never seen anything like it, she thought jubilantly.

"But why?" she asked Arnold. "I don't understand."

"Neither do I. My best guess is, people who're trapped at home or in hotels or only God knows where are leafing through our catalogue and calling in bids. You know, sort of a cross between shopping and laying bets."

Kenzie shook her head. "Puts a whole new spin on 'home shopping,' doesn't it?"

Another line rang.

"Shit." Arnold started to reach for it, then flapped a hand. "Whoever it is can leave voice mail."

"Not for long." Kenzie, having sized up the situation, now took charge. "Listen up, you guys. Arnold, your voice sounds like you've been talking yourself hoarse. It could use a break."

"You can say that again!"

"Then give the phones a break and cover the fax. All those bids have to be entered into the computer, and the sooner you get started, the better. But first call out for some coffee."

"Will do."

"Zandra, you and I'll work the phones till nine-thirty. Then we'll recruit the first three people who show up for work, and I don't *care* which department they belong to!"

"Take the call on line three first," Arnold advised. "Poor woman's been holding forever."

"Right." Zandra punched line three. "Hallo? I'm very sorry to have kept you waiting. Thanks so much for your patience . . ."

And Kenzie, punching line six: "Old Masters, may I help you . . ."

For nearly two hours it was as if they'd been swept up in a whirlwind. It was all they could do to keep up with the deluge of calls. But despite the awesome volume, Kenzie, Zandra, and Arnold worked together like a well-oiled piece of machinery.

Each kept the others up to date by shooting voice bullets in code:

"Lot 21, de Hamilton. Nine thou! Within est."

And "160, Guardi, four point nine mil. Within est."

And "208, Hendrik Meyer, twenty thou. Just under."

And "74, Rynacker, quarter mil. *Over* est."

It was dizzying. Kenzie had never experienced anything like it. For the first time in three days, she permitted herself to feel hopeful, and then euphoric.

Please God, she prayed. *Let this continue.*

Her prayers were answered until nine o'clock. That was when a curveball was thrown from way out in left field.

Zandra said: "*Kenzie.* Major trouble, I'm afraid. Could you pick up line seven?"

Kenzie covered the receiver with her hand. "Who is it?"

"Bambi."

"From whom," said Kenzie grimly, "no news is good news. All right." She sighed with resignation. "I'll take it. *After* I'm done with this client."

Bambi stared impatiently out the glass wall at the billions of flakes swirling in the turbulence. They blotted out the entire city except for the two nearest high-rises, which had taken on a kind of half-glimpsed, spectral magic. Under other circumstances, she might have fantasized herself a storybook princess high in a castle tower.

This morning, however, reality in the shape of a slender naked man obviated the need for fairy tales. All she wanted was to resume snuggling and screwing, hence her itchiness to get off the phone.

What is taking Kenzie so long? I don't have all day!

"Come *on,*" she muttered testily, pink fingernails like teaspoons scratching the rumpled sheet. "Come *on . . .*"

"Yeah, babe. Can't *wait* to come!" The mattress shifted and last night's pickup pressed himself against her back, his head coming down so he could suck on her shoulder.

She shivered, a rush of delicious desire thrumming from her head right down to her toes.

They'd connected at a party yesterday evening, where they'd discovered they had crystals, New Age, and Gregorian chants in common, and had come back here to her new apartment. She and Lex Bugg, Mr. Psychedelic Pop. On whom she'd harbored a crush since childhood, a direct result of those cute stylized rainbows, moons, stars, and clouds he painted.

Now here he was—sharing her bed!—naked but for the sliver of crystal hanging from the thong around his neck. Pressing his warm chest against her back, arms holding her, tongue trolling the fragile contours and shoals of her shoulder.

And meanwhile, I have to waste time holding for Kenzie!

Finally she heard a click and Kenzie's voice, crisp and impersonal, came on the line: "Bambi? Kenzie here. What's the matter?"

Lex's fingertips played itsy-bitsy spider.

"Hiya, Kenzie. Nasty day, isn't it?"

"Oh, I don't know. I suppose that depends upon the way you look at it."

"Well, from here it looks pretty bad," Bambi said, lying down and coiling the telephone cord around her finger. "And Mr. Fairey agrees. I just got off the phone with him. We decided to postpone today's sale."

"You what!" Kenzie's voice blared so loud that Bambi cringed and held the receiver away from her ear. "Are you crazy?"

Bambi took offense. "I won't have you talking to me like that!" she snapped. "You are not in charge. *I* am!"

"In which case I strongly suggest you reconsider. I take it Zandra's filled you in on what's going on here?"

"Yes, and it proves my point. The sale will go even better once it's rescheduled."

"Bambi, do you have any idea how *badly* Christie's and Sotheby's fared this week?"

Bambi caught Lex's gaze and made yak-yak motions with her hand.

"Look, Kenzie. I don't see what Christie's or Sotheby's has to do with it. It's not *our* fault if they got stuck with works of lesser quality."

"Bambi?" Kenzie's voice was soft. "Did you actually go and *see* those paintings? Or, for that matter, did you even bother to look through their catalogues?"

Bambi sniffed loftily. "I don't have to answer to you. And I won't argue about it, either. The sale's off, and that's *that.*"

"You're making a big mistake," Kenzie warned.

Bambi slammed the phone down.

"That's telling it like it is, babe!" Lex flashed her a blinding white grin. "Don't take shit from nobody."

Kenzie glared at the receiver. "And a nice day to you, too!" she told it, before hanging up.

"Kenzie," Zandra called out. "What do I tell people?"

"Keep taking bids. To the best of your knowledge, the auction's still on."

"You're sure?"

"Absolutely." Kenzie wasn't about to let Bambi KO the sale, not while they were on a winning streak. Snatching up the phone, she called Sheldon D. Fairey's office.

As expected, there was no answer. Just a recording to leave voice mail. Which she did. Tried Allison Steele next. Same thing. Left another message.

There. That took care of protocol.

Next, she got busy tapping computer keys. Brought up the Faireys' unlisted home number on the telephone directory file. Punched touch-tone digits.

"Hello?" a woman answered on the third ring.

"Mr. Fairey, please. This is MacKenzie Turner from Burghley's."

"I'm afraid he's in the shower right now. This is Mrs. Fairey. Perhaps I can be of some help?"

"Yes. Could you please tell him that it's extremely urgent? I'll hold."

"Certainly."

Kenzie pulled her lips back across her teeth. The art world—some glamour industry! A place where back rubbing and back stabbing went hand in hand was more like it! If you were at the top of the food chain, it was a constant battle to stay there. If you weren't, you battled to get there, or at least to paddle in place.

The art world. If anyone doubted Darwin's theories, they need look no further. Here was irrefutable proof. Day in and day out.

A familiar plummy voice boomed: "Sheldon D. Fairey."

"Mr. Fairey? MacKenzie Turner. I apologize for disturbing you at home, sir, but we seem to have a problem."

"Fire away, Ms. Turner."

Kenzie proceeded to fill him in on the bids which were pouring in. She finished by saying: "You do see, sir, don't you? This is a once-in-a-lifetime opportunity! If we postpone the auction, we run the danger of bids being withdrawn. We *have* to run with it!"

There was a pause. "You're certain, Ms. Turner?" he asked quietly.

"Certain enough to stake my job on it!" she declared, in a blaze of bold conviction.

Zandra, waving frantically at her, silently mouthed: "No! Are you crazy?"

He cleared his throat. "In that case, I shall call Ms. Parker and rescind the order."

The reprieve made Kenzie go weak with relief. "Thank you, sir."

"And Ms. Turner?"

"Sir?"

"Good luck," he added dryly.

As Kenzie hung up, she noticed that her palms were sweating. And her hands shaking.

The auction was scheduled for ten o'clock sharp.

At 9:55, Bambi led Arnold, Kenzie, and Zandra across the dais, where they took their seats behind a table on which multiline telephones and four computers had been set up.

Kenzie felt exultant. Soon she would be vindicated. Reveling in triumph.

Zandra took her hand and pressed it encouragingly. Arnold leaned forward, held up both hands, and showed crossed fingers. Only Bambi, thin-lipped and silent, ignored her completely.

At 9:56, the first potential bidder arrived. At 9:57, a couple strolled in. A minute later, a well-known dealer.

Kenzie suddenly felt a terrible sense of foreboding.

By 9:59, of the two hundred seats, one hundred ninety-six were still vacant.

Only four people had shown up.

It was then that the enormity of her decision hit her. *I've really done it this time,* she thought bleakly. *If there aren't enough absentee bids, I can kiss my job good-bye.*

She watched Sheldon D. Fairey, immaculately groomed as always, approach the lectern. He moved gracefully, as though it was a packed house, and members of the media were recording his every move. His chiseled face was expressionless as his eyes scanned the empty seats.

He's going to go ahead with the sale, Kenzie realized, feeling the horrified fascination of a spectator watching an accident occur. *We're headed straight for disaster. And all because of me. I'm never going to get another job after this. Heaven help me. Why did I have to go out on a limb?*

And now—too late!—she suddenly realized something else. For five minutes now, the telephones had been silent. Ominously silent.

Oh, God, she beseeched. *Why couldn't I keep my trap shut?*

"Lot number one," Sheldon D. Fairey announced. *"Portrait of Lady Digby* from the studio of Sir Anthony Van Dyck."

Two green-aproned young men carried the gilt-framed painting onstage and placed it on an easel. Simultaneously, a slide of the picture was projected onto an overhead screen.

"Bidding shall start at one thousand dollars."

Arnold, glancing at his computer screen, lifted his pencil.

"We have a bid for one thousand dollars—"

On the back wall, the currency conversion board's bright LED numbers converted the dollars into six exchange rates—Japanese yen, Deutsche marks, English pounds, Italian lira, and both French and Swiss francs.

"Do we have a bid for one thousand one hundred?"

Kenzie and Zandra, on the phone to clients, raised their pencils, as did Arnold.

"Do we have a bid for one thousand two hundred . . . one thousand five hundred . . . two thousand . . . three thousand . . . four thousand . . ."

The dollars spiraled, as though conjured up by the effortless swirl of a magician's wand, and seemed to take on a life of their own.

". . . Ten thousand . . . ten thousand five hundred . . . eleven thousand . . . twelve . . ."

A dizzying half minute later, the gavel banged down. "Sold. To a telephone bidder for eighteen thousand dollars."

Four and a half times the high estimate.

Kenzie, weak with relief, exhaled a deep, shaky breath. *So far, so good,* she told herself. *Now, if this only keeps up . . .*

The green-aproned porters carried the painting offstage as two other porters lugged out the next one.

"Lot number two."

Behind his lectern, Sheldon D. Fairey exuded confidence, authority, and a quiet, reassuring assertiveness.

"*Portrait of an Italian Nobleman,* also from the studio of Sir Anthony Van Dyck. Bidding shall begin at one thousand dollars . . ."

Zandra and Kenzie were already on the phone with long-distance clients; Arnold, with his eye on his computer screen, was again executing bids on behalf of absentee buyers.

And again, like an enchanted thread snatched out of thin air and woven into a dazzling fabric, the dollars spun and soared, as though wrought by some sorcerer's arcane spell.

"Do we have a bid for six thousand . . . six thousand five hundred . . . seven thousand . . . seven thousand five hundred . . . ?"

The numbers billowed, swarmed, multiplied.

"Fifteen thousand . . . fifteen thousand five hundred . . . going once, going twice—"

The hammer fell.

"Sold. To an absentee bidder for fifteen thousand, five hundred dollars."

Nearly four times the high estimate.

Kenzie felt the narcotic of relief, like a tranquilizer, anesthetizing her jumpy nerves. Dared she nurture the sputtering flame of hope?

It was too early to tell. Still, the sale was off to a better start than she had dared anticipate.

Who knows? she thought optimistically. *Maybe, just maybe, we can pull this off. We might even come out of it smelling like roses.*

But then the tide turned.

Neither Lot 3, a crucifixion by a follower of Van Cleve, nor Lot 4, a tiny Barent Graat of sheep and goats, nor Lot 5, *Portrait of a Lady as Venus* by van der Helst, found a single bidder. Sheldon D. Fairey hammered down each of them with one expressionless but ominous word: "Passed."

Kenzie felt each accompanying bang of the gavel like a physical blow. *We're in trouble,* she thought. And instantly revised that opinion. *Nope. I might as well call a spade a spade. We're in deep shit. Real deep shit.*

But the gods of fortune laughed, and once again teased her by spinning in her favor.

Lot 6, *Adoration of the Magi* by Jan van Scorel, estimated at $10,000 to $20,000, sold for $21,000.

And Lot 7, a madonna and child by Raffaelino del Garbo, went for $36,500—$16,500 over the high estimate.

Kenzie did not permit her hopes to surge, which was just as well. The next six lots failed to reach their reserve price. Each pound of the gavel was accompanied by two inexorable words: "Bought in."

Kenzie, feeling a headache coming on, rubbed her forehead. From experience, she knew what lay ahead and dreaded it.

We're going to have a lot of unhappy consignors, she thought. And some would inevitably blame Burghley's for their paintings not selling, which meant *she* would be fielding a flurry of angry calls.

Sheldon D. Fairey was saying: "Lot number fourteen, *Still Life* by Pieter Claesz. Oil on copper. Signed in monogram and dated 1630."

At a presale estimate of $500,000 to $700,000, it was the first of the sale's truly spectacular and expensive works.

"Bidding shall begin at $250,000."

Kenzie, knowing what was riding on it, literally held her breath.

A brief but intense battle between Zandra's telephone bidder and one of Arnold's absentee bids resulted in a hammer price of $1.25 million.

It took Kenzie a moment for the success to register. When it did, she was so sick with relief that it was all she could do not to throw up.

And that was the pattern the rest of the sale followed—a constant roller coaster of exhilarating crests and bleak descents.

By ten-thirty, eleven more seats had filled as veteran bidders, timing their arrivals to coincide with the lots which interested them, arrived to bid in person.

By eleven o'clock, that number had grown to a total of thirty-three, including a reporter from the New York *Times*.

Despite the small turnout, there was electricity in the air, as well as a tiny clutch of bargain hunters.

A little over two hours after the auction began, Sheldon D. Fairey's gavel fell for the last time. "Ladies and gentlemen," he announced, "that is the end of the sale. Thank you."

The auction was over.

Kenzie collapsed limply in her chair. The sale had taken its toll. She felt completely wiped out, and just sat there in a daze while Arnold finished his computerized tally.

"Hmmm," he murmured. "Take a look at this."

"Thanks, but I'd rather wait," Kenzie murmured, thinking: *If no news is bad news, then what's the big rush? We'll learn the extent of the damage soon enough. Besides, the auction's over. It's too late to do anything about it now.*

Zandra was more upbeat. She had kept an approximate mental count, and peered eagerly at Arnold's screen. His numbers confirmed hers.

Of the two hundred twenty-eight lots, nearly two-thirds—one hundred thirty-nine to be exact—had sold, and the auction had generated a grand total of $56,609,112.00.

Four paintings alone accounted for nearly a quarter of that grand total:

Lot 160, the Francesco Guardi, which had gone for $6.75 million.

A small Titian, which had brought in $2.64 million.

A Géricault, which had commanded $2.42 million.

And a Joachim Wtewael, which went for $1.8 million.

"Goodness, Arnold!" Zandra said. "How *ever* did we do it? Kenzie, you really must look!"

"No, thanks," Kenzie said weakly. "I don't think I can bear it."

"Balls! Course you can!" Zandra declared stoutly. "In all, we've totaled fifty-six-point-six million dollars. Can you believe it? Fifty-six million, Kenzie! Darling, you should be thrilled!"

"Fifty-six . . . ?" Kenzie repeated dully.

"Darling, do snap out of it. I mean, honestly. I know it's somewhat below the presale estimate, but you have to admit the estimates *were* on the steep side . . . Darling? Did you hear me? We fared tons better than Christie's or Sotheby's. See? You were absolutely right about the show going on."

Kenzie blinked. "I . . . was?" she said in a tiny, hesitant voice.

"I'll say. You're vindicated—to the tune of fifty-six million. Arnold—shouldn't we drink to this, or something?"

"Definitely," he agreed, and launched into his Chinese takeout routine. "Come on, radies. We workeee, now starvee. Join me in a rate runch?"

Kenzie shook her head. "Why don't you two go? I couldn't possibly keep any food down."

"So?" Zandra wouldn't take no for an answer. "Have a liquid lunch, darling. That's the antidote. Nothing like a good stiff drink."

She took Kenzie's hands and pulled her to her feet.

"You're coming, and that's that. No argument now. *That's* a good girl!"

When they got outside, a snowplow was scraping noisily past on Madison. Kenzie turned her face up to the sky.

"Wouldn't you know it? Now that the auction's over, the snow's stopped."

※ *34* ❦

ecky V set out for the country at eleven o'clock in the morning. For anonymity's sake, she drove an unassuming, dark gray Chrysler Le Baron hardtop, and wore big round sunglasses and had an Hermès scarf tied around her head. Lord Rosenkrantz, with his pink baby face and Dickensian paunch, sat beside her in the passenger seat. They were followed by a dark blue Ford Taurus, driven by her Secret Service detail, which in turn was followed by a black Chevrolet Astro minivan.

The van was driven by Becky's Pritikin chef, and was loaded down with baskets of fresh black *and* white truffles, cases of 1988 Duque de la Vila Rioja, bottled on Becky V's own Spanish estates, five-kilo tins of Beluga Malossal caviar packed in dry ice, and coolers filled with fresh seafood bought that very morning at the Fulton Street fish market.

With Becky in the lead, the three-car motorcade took the Holland Tunnel under the river and were soon in the famous New Jersey hunt country: unspoiled woods, rolling pastures, and farmland. The winding country roads, though plowed, were treacherous, and the going was slow.

Half an hour later, they turned into a private, unmarked lane which cut through white-fenced, snow-blanketed pastures. This lane, too, had been cleared.

A quarter of a mile later, there it was. Becky V's equestrian estate. A sprawling compound, to say the least.

The main house was a handsome, white, thirty-room mansion said to be one of the finest examples of Greek Revival architecture in America. Then there were the outbuildings. The guest house, which she'd put at Lord Rosenkrantz's disposal. Twin brick stables with cupolas facing each other across a cobbled courtyard—one for horses, the other used as a multicar garage. A blacksmith shop. Glass hothouses. Barns and sheds.

For recreation, there were indoor and outdoor pools. A tennis court. A 40,000-square-foot indoor riding arena. Plus two outdoor arenas.

And, last but not least, a caretaker's house and staff building.

As soon as Becky arrived, she and Mrs. Wheatley, the housekeeper, made the rounds of both the main house and the guest house. Accompanied by Mr. Wheatley, the estate manager, she then inspected the barns, sheds, garages, and indoor riding arena and swimming pool. Next came a tour of the hothouses with the head gardener, where Becky inspected the plants, fingered the moistness of the soil, talked fertilizer, and selected the out-of-season flowers and blooming potted plants she wanted brought into the house and guesthouse.

Horses being her passion, she left the stables for last. There, with the head groom in attendance, she unhurriedly examined her fifteen beloved thoroughbreds and fed them cubes of sugar.

Her inspection over, she decided a ride was in order. She loved the thrill and freedom of a gallop over snow-covered pastures and rolling hills.

"Saddle up Sparky," she said, naming her favorite horse, a nine-year-old gelding. "I'll be taking him out in a few minutes."

Then, secure in the knowledge that everything in the compound met her impeccable standards, Becky returned to the house, where she changed into jodhpurs, boots, down-filled blue ski parka, helmet, shawl, and fleece-lined gloves.

When she returned to the stable, the two Secret Service agents were waiting. Both had changed into jeans and bulky, fleece-lined suede jackets.

"Is this really necessary?" she asked. "I'm only going for a short ride."

"Afraid so, ma'am," the one in charge said politely. "It's for your own protection."

Becky nodded and told the groom to fetch Sparky. "And then saddle up Moonbeam and Firefly for these gentlemen, would you?"

The groom looked at her in surprise. "Ma'am? Are you cer—"

Becky cut him off. "Just do it."

"Ma'am!" He hurried away and returned leading Sparky, who breathed plumes and pranced friskily in place. He was magnificent—big and shiny black, with sculpted muscles and white points, excellent head, long sturdy legs. The groom held the reins and gave Becky a leg-up.

She waited until Moonbeam and Firefly were saddled up and brought around. Moonbeam was a skittish, willful white stallion; Firefly, a recalcitrant, elderly mare.

Becky watched in amusement as the two men struggled to mount. Then, once they were in the saddle, she said, "Giddy-yap!" and shook Sparky's reins.

And she was off.

A glance backward made her burst out laughing. Moonbeam, rearing and bucking, threw his rider, and Firefly refused to move faster than a sedate trot.

Which of course was exactly what she'd been counting on.

The ride through the crusty snow was beautiful; the air, though stingingly cold, was bracing and pure. Sparky jumped fences with ease. Raced gracefully up sloping hillsides. Surprised a family of deer and sent them leaping for the shelter of the nearby woods.

An exhilarating hour later, Becky returned to the stable. The Secret

Service men were waiting. One was obviously angry. The other looked sheepish. She dismounted Sparky, who was lathered with sweat, and tossed the reins to the groom.

"Gentlemen," she told her bodyguards. "I seem to have lost you."

Both their faces turned red.

Returning to the house, Becky had a maid run a hot bath. Then, sliding into a tub for the second time that day, she reflected on the delights of country life.

Afterward, dressed in sweater and slacks, she pondered the weekend ahead.

Zandra and Karl-Heinz. They seemed a match made in heaven. Whether the same held true on earth remained to be seen.

Still, one thing was for certain. It promised to be an interesting weekend . . .

. . . a very interesting weekend indeed.

The Sheldon D. Faireys set out for the country at noon. New England Wasps to the core, they drove an appropriately sensible vehicle—a much-dented, decade-old Country Squire station wagon.

Likewise, they were suitably attired for a commute to the country. Sheldon had on a red and black flannel shirt, olive corduroys, and an old shearling jacket. Nina was in oatmeal (oversize cowl-necked sweater) and tobacco brown (sueded twill pants and lace-up lugger boots). You couldn't tell by looking at them, but they had more money than Ivana Trump—only they knew how to hold onto it.

Offspring of New England bankers (Nina), and New England brokers (Sheldon), both had been raised to believe in God, country, the almighty dollar, and Yankee understatement—not necessarily in that order—and each could recite the Five Wasp Commandments by heart:

> I. Thou shalt never touch the Principal, no matter what Thou might covet.
> II. Thou shalt live off a *portion* of the Principal's interest—the remainder to be automatically reinvested so that the Almighty Principal shall multiply fruitfully.
> III. Thou shalt not display thy wealth for all the world to see.
> IV. Thou shalt practice thrift and be frugal.
> V. Thou shalt under no circumstance touch the Principal.

Which was why the casual observer could be forgiven for not guessing that the Faireys lived on a six-figure salary (his), plus the six-figure interest generated by blue chip investments (hers).

And so off they drove in their rusty, ten-year-old station wagon. The only baggage which did accompany them was in the form of garment bags, and even those were an exception, entirely due to receiving a dinner invitation from Becky V for them and their houseguests.

Taking the Lincoln Tunnel to New Jersey, they hooked up with I-95, then changed to I-78, and got off at North Plainfield. A prudent stop in a nearby shopping center ensued, where they thriftily stocked up on staples and discount liquor (Jersey prices and sales tax being a lot lower than pricey Manhattan's). Afterward, they drove the familiar country roads through snowy woods and pastures. Five miles after Middlebush, they passed the lane leading into Becky V's estate. A quarter of a mile farther, and they made a sharp left onto their own modest but sufficient ten acres, Cedar Hill.

A short gravel drive, recently plowed, led straight up to the house, which had been built atop a cleared incline, so that it seemed to dominate its setting. As always, the sight of it gave the Faireys a warm rush of pleasure. It was red brick, two stories, authentic Federal. Perfectly proportioned and symmetrical. There was a steep, snow-laden roof, a stately two-storied central portico, and tall brick chimneys at either end. On both sides, short one-story wings had been added at a later date.

The one on the left functioned as a one-horse stable and two-car garage. The other had been converted into a small caretakers' apartment.

Halfway to the house, the station wagon was intercepted by two golden retrievers, which barked joyfully while bounding circles around the now-creeping vehicle.

The Faireys drove carefully around to the back, where they parked beside the kitchen. Mrs. Pruitt, the caretaker's wife, opened the door, wiping her hands on her apron, to say she would unload the car.

Nina and Sheldon spent the next few minutes fussing over the dogs. Long slavering pink tongues licked faces; giant paws made snowy prints on clothes.

Looking around, Sheldon sighed wistfully. The sky was a pellucid blue, the sun shone brightly, and the air was crisp and clean. All in all, it promised to be the perfect winter weekend.

Only one dark, ugly cloud smudged his pleasure's horizon. The Goldsmiths.

Prince Karl-Heinz also set out for the country at three-thirty, but he eschewed driving by car. He simply went to the East Side heliport and boarded the lush comfort of a waiting executive helicopter.

It took off at once and the pilot vectored it southwest, heading down over the East River and its quartet of bridges—the Queensboro, Williamsburg, Manhattan, and Brooklyn—past the towers of Wall Street, and zoomed out across the choppy gray waters of Upper New York Bay.

Karl-Heinz gazed out as they flew south along the coastline of Staten Island.

Below, set among trees, were low apartment buildings, stately old Victorians, developments of tract houses. Suburbia-in-the-City, the American Dream alive and well—and within sight of Manhattan.

The juxtaposition was discombobulating. Across the water, the needlepoint skyline. Here, another world entirely.

Neat gridworks of snowy lawns. Curving drives among rows of ranch houses, split levels, Colonials. And residents who sneered at their sophisticated sister borough across the bay, who were middle-class proud, wore their provincialism like a badge, and regularly made noises to secede from New York City.

Next came the familiar, industrial wasteland of New Jersey. Perth Amboy and Metuchen. Docks, refineries, oil storage tanks. And finally, the Raritan River, where once again suburbia flourished before giving way to true countryside. Forests, farmland, rolling hills—

—and the helicopter roared in low over the rooftops of Becky V's compound, hovered in midair above the front lawn of the Greek Revival mansion, and then set down, the wash of its whirling rotors whipping up great blizzardlike flurries of snow.

The hinged door of the main cabin opened, the boarding stairs were lowered, and Karl-Heinz exited, suitcase in hand. From force of habit, he half ran, hunched forward, until he cleared the rotors, to where a Secret Service agent wearing dark aviator shades was waiting.

The agent stared at him for a moment, then raised his arm and murmured, Dick Tracy-like, into his sleeve while covering an ear with his other hand. Only afterward did Karl-Heinz notice the tiny earphone.

"You're expected, sir." The agent had to shout to make himself heard. "If you'll follow me—" He pointed toward the mansion.

Karl-Heinz nodded and followed him, glad to turn his back on the stinging whirlwind of snow. Behind him, the boarding stairs were retracted, the hinged door pulled shut, and the helicopter rose, banked sharply, and climbed, like some giant metallic insect recalled by the now-purpling sky, its roar lessening until it soon faded altogether.

Upon reaching the mansion, the imposing front door was opened from inside.

"Prince Karl-Heinz?" It was a second Secret Service agent.

Karl-Heinz nodded and the agent stepped aside to let them enter the oval, pilastered foyer with its grand sweeping staircase.

"Sorry, sir. A mere formality." The agent waited for Karl-Heinz to put down his suitcase. A swift, professional frisk followed.

"Mon dieu!" rang out Becky's rich, opulent voice from the landing above. "Really!" she said with amusement. "I hardly think that's necessary."

The three men looked up.

Becky, clad in black turtleneck, one hand in the pocket of her loose, pleated tan Garbo pants, the other on the ebonized banister, was coming down the stairs. Making as casual and devastating an entrance as Marlene Dietrich, or Garbo herself.

Upon reaching Karl-Heinz, she placed her hands on his shoulders, hopped on tiptoe, and pecked his lips.

"*Cher ami*. You must forgive my watchdogs their enthusiasm! They do mean well, you know."

She stepped back while the butler relieved him of his cashmere coat and silk, cut-velvet scarf. At a signal from her, both Secret Service agents made themselves scarce.

"They are most remarkable, you know," Becky continued. "The way the Service trains them! Such fierce loyalty. Can you believe, they will fling themselves directly into the line of fire?"

She regarded Karl-Heinz with her incredible violet eyes.

"I think, my dear Becky, that we would all gladly do that, were it your life which was at stake."

"Surely you jest." But she smiled with pleasure. "*D'accord*. Just leave your suitcase there. Someone will see to it. Now come. Let us go into the sitting room. You will have plenty of time to freshen up later."

She slid an arm through his and walked him into the enormous room, where flaming logs fluttered in both marble fireplaces.

Despite its crystal-chandeliered grandeur, the yellow-lacquered room was comfortable with cigar smoke, paintings, bookcases, and rich carpets. One entire wall of latticed windows, framed by garnet velvet, looked out upon the cobalt blue night beginning to fall.

But here inside, everything glowed with warmth.

All around, in pools of soft lamplight, were voluptuous couches upholstered in cognac suede and heaped with petit point cushions. Deep comfortable armchairs of varying styles which invited gossip, just as draped round tables, piled high with books, encouraged reading and contemplation. And here, there, and everywhere, bushes of rare orchids, branches bent under the weight of heavy, brown-speckled blooms, had been placed in giant, turquoise-glazed Sung dynasty bowls and amber Tang vessels.

Lord Rosenkrantz, rimless half glasses perched on the tip of his nose, was ensconced in a scuffed, brown leather club chair. He had a folded newspaper on his lap and a glass of red wine, glowing like rubies, at his elbow. Expensive cigar smoke swirled from a scintillating rectangle of crystal.

"Ah!" he boomed. "The guest of honor!" And with a rye-crisp smile, he quoted: " 'Plots, true or false, are necessary things, to raise up commonwealths—' "

" '—and ruin kings'?" Karl-Heinz finished for him, arching an eyebrow in amusement.

"Let us fervently hope not, dear boy!" Lord Rosenkrantz's cherubic features were rosy with a Boucher-like glow, whether from the reading lamp at his side or the wine he'd consumed, it was difficult to tell.

Becky waved a dismissive hand. "Don't listen to his rubbish, *chéri*. Whatever this weekend portends, one thing is for certain. At least it won't be boring." She slid Karl-Heinz a sly sidelong smile. *"N'est-ce pas?"*

And with a swirl of her wide-legged trousers, she kicked off her gold-buckled slippers, sank into the sofa nearest the fire, and tucked her legs under her.

She gave the spot beside her an imperious pat.

"Alors. You shall sit right here, Heinzie. With me. Now, do you have a *préférence?* Coffee? Tea? Or perhaps something a bit stronger?"

He smiled. "Why? Do you think I shall be needing it?"

"Take my advice, dear boy," Lord Rosenkrantz called out, amid the crackling of newspaper. "Opt for fortification. Remember, 'One can drink too much, but one never drinks enough!' As for this weekend, I believe the latter, rather than the former, shall hold true."

35

The Goldsmiths occupied Cedar Hill's "best guest room"—Nina Fairey's term—a large north-facing room on the second floor. Despite its size and period furnishings, it was by no means luxurious. Rather, Dina thought to herself with mental lip-pursing as Mrs. Pruitt, having lit a fire in the fireplace, now marched briskly back out, heels clacking sharply on bare floorboards, it was decidedly *anti*-luxury: puritanical, prudish, and penitential as only authentic Colonial can be.

Dina, huddled in her ranch mink, glanced around with growing despair. Everywhere, her luxury-seeking eyes met nothing but relentless sobriety.

It was evident in the rectitude of the four-poster, skeletal, without bedhangings, and covered with a patchwork quilt. In the no-nonsense, three-paneled oak chest at the foot of the bed. In the primness of the unadorned, free-standing wardrobe. In the kneehole bureau which, thanks to a plain, mahogany-framed mirror, doubled as a dressing table. Even in the two very early Early American armchairs which flanked a chest of drawers.

The only concession to decoration was on the wall: a dour pair of naive portraits—husband and wife—both of whom projected silent disapproval, she in a stiff lace bonnet and holding a prayer book, he in what appeared to be clerical garb.

Turning her back on them, Dina drew close to the fire and stood, hands extended, soaking up whatever warmth it gave off while waiting—she prayed not in vain!—for the heat to come on, but not daring to go so far as to tempt fate by actually *looking around* for evidence of radiators or heating vents. Since none had caught her eye thus far, she was afraid that—

She squashed the thought.

Surely the Faireys could not be such radical purists that their passion for authenticity precluded them from having installed central heating.

Could it?

Mr. Pruitt trod in and set down the last two of Dina's six Vuitton cases. "That's it, then," he said, leaving before she could pluck up her courage to inquire about the heat.

Crossing her arms, she tucked her hands into the armpits of her fur sleeves and glanced through the arch to the adjoining sitting room.

Robert, who couldn't give a damn about his surroundings so long as he had a roof over his head, was right at home. Seated on a stiff camel-back sofa, cellular phone in hand, the Pembroke table in front of him littered with the usual detritus—ashtray, cigars, pens, calculator, laptop computer, and the inevitable sheafs of reports and printouts. No doubt making money in some far-off time zone where the business day was just beginning.

Dina tightened her lips in annoyance. Obviously, no sympathy would be offered from *that* quarter. Not that she'd expected any. In truth, she had never understood how her husband could go through life oblivious to everything but business and sex. And not necessarily in that order.

Abruptly disgusted with him, she paced the bedroom. She had to find something to do to keep her mind off the cold. If she didn't, she would go stark raving mad.

But what?

She eyed her suitcases malevolently.

No, keeping herself occupied did not extend to unpacking, especially considering that she had brought at least six times as many clothes as that single dreary wardrobe could hold.

"What did I do to deserve this?" she wailed. "Oh, why can't I be back *home?* Or at least *some*place nice and warm?"

But of course, she knew why.

How could she forget how quickly she'd jumped at the chance to play matchmaker. Now here she was, regretting it already!

Talk about learning the hard way, she thought. *This will teach me. From now on, I'll find out exactly* what *I'm getting into before I commit to something!*

She became aware of knuckles rapping on the door.

Now what! she wanted to scream. *I'm miserable enough! Can't I be left in peace?*

The knocks continued.

Narrowing her eyes, she scraped her chair around. "What?" she shouted.

The door opened just enough for an inappropriately cheerful face to peer around the jamb. "Getting settled, are you?" Zandra asked brightly.

And suddenly the door burst wide open. The two huge dogs, tails wagging furiously, forced their way past and headed straight for Dina—nearly knocking her over as they leaped up on her and bestowed ecstatic licks.

"Help! Help! Ugh!" Dina covered her face with mink-sheathed arms to avoid the slobbering tongues. "Sweetie!" she cried desperately. "Get these brutes *off* me! I'm going to get bitten!"

"Oh, honestly," Zandra drawled. "Don't you know anything? They're retrievers. Absolute marvels. Don't make good watchdogs, though . . . would hold a flashlight for a burglar."

"I don't care! They're smelly and disgusting! I hate animals! I—"

"Nonsense. Never met anyone could hate a retriever. They're the absolute greatest. Aw, will you look at that? Darling, they *adore* you!"

As if to prove it, the male tightened his forelegs around Dina's knees and started humping her legs.

"Zandra!" Dina screamed. "Do something! I'm being raped by a dog!"

"But, darling, you really can't blame him. I mean, *look* at yourself. You're one big *frightfully* furry thing. Teach you to stop wearing poor slaughtered little minks!"

"Zandra! If you don't get these monsters off me *right this very minute,* so help me God, I'm . . . I'm going to call the ASPCA!"

"No reason to get your nose out of joint. I'm getting them off you. Might take me a minute."

Zandra grabbed hold of both dogs' collars and tugged.

"George!" She tried for an assertive tone. "Get down. Down, I say. Martha. Sit. Sit!"

"Zandra?" Dina peeked out from between her arms. "Did I hear you call them . . . George? And Martha?"

"As in Washington. Yes. Aren't they splendid, though? How *ever* could you not like them?"

Easily, Dina thought. Now that the dogs were obediently seated, tails thumping on pegged pine, drooly jaws panting like bellows, she cautiously lowered her arms.

"Oh, no!" she wailed in distress.

"Darling, what is it now?"

Dina gestured at herself. "Just look at me! I have dog hair . . . and . . . what's this? Slime! *Slime*—all over me! And this is my very best Maximilian natural Red Glow mink—"

"God's sake, darling. It's hardly the end of the world. Chill out."

"Chill out?" Dina, quivering with rage, stared at Zandra incredulously. "Chill out, did you say? What do you *think* I've been doing? Sitting in a sauna? Enjoying this blistering *heat?*"

"Granted, it's rather on the cool side. So? Doesn't mean you can't wash up and change."

"Wash up?" Dina's voice dripped sarcasm. "Am I being led to understand that there's running water in this house? Hot running water?"

"As a matter of fact, yes."

"Well, forget it. *I'm* not about to get undressed in this cold. Do you have any idea what the temperature must be?"

"Higher, I suspect, than in most stately homes in England. Anyway, why do you think I advised you to buy sweaters?"

"There." Dina pointed an offending finger at the row of Vuittons. "In whichever one Darlene packed them."

"Darling, you mean . . . you haven't even begun to unpack?"

"How could I? There aren't any closets."

Zandra took a quick visual inventory. "There's this chest . . ." She pointed at the foot of the bed. ". . . that dresser . . . and that's surely a wardrobe . . ."

"I *know,*" Dina gloomed. "I just can't bring myself to do it!"

"Tell you what, darling." Zandra grabbed the nearest Vuitton case, swung it effortlessly up on the bed, and sprang the brass latches. "You see about getting cleaned up, and I'll do your unpacking. How's that for a deal."

Dina looked at her blearily. "Sweetie?" she whispered, her voice thick with emotion. "You'd really do that? For me?"

"Especially for you, pain in the arse though you may be!"

"You're too wonderful, sweetie. Too, too!" For the first time since setting foot in the house, Dina glowed with radiance. "Yes. I think I *will* get cleaned up after all. Mmmm . . ."

She tapped her lips with a peppermint-nailed finger.

"But first I have to use the phone." She glanced through the connecting arch. "And Robert's glued to the cellular."

"So? What's wrong with this one?" Zandra gestured at an old black rotary phone on one of the nightstands.

"No," Dina said quickly. She was terrified that Zandra, overhearing the conversation, would put two and two together. And that had to be avoided. *Zandra must never discover the scheme Becky and I hatched,* Dina thought. *If she finds out about it, she might well be furious.*

It could also, she realized, put a severe strain on their friendship, something which hadn't even occurred to her before.

Although it's a little late to get cold feet now. I should have thought of the consequences earlier.

"I'm going downstairs," Dina said. "Perhaps there's a phone in the kitchen. Chances are, it'll be the warmest room in the house."

And she darted guiltily out. Glad to make her escape, however brief it might be.

Suddenly she wished she'd never gotten involved in this plot.

Callas was in rare form. Becky, posing gracefully on the couch, was engaged in deep conversation with Karl-Heinz. From the leather club chair, Lord Rosenkrantz was conducting the La Scala orchestra with the CD remote.

The butler entered and made his way woodenly across the room to

Becky, a cordless phone on his sterling salver. With a flourish of the make-shift baton, Lord Rosenkrantz silenced Verdi.

The butler cleared his throat. "Excuse me, madam."

Becky looked up. "Yes, Mumford?"

"Mrs. Goldsmith is on the telephone."

Lord Rosenkrantz glanced over at Becky, raising his exophthalmic eyes above the level of his reading glasses without actually lifting his head. "Sooooo," he observed deliciously. "The plot thickens!"

"Would you like to take it, madam? Or are you indisposed?"

"*Mais oui,*" Becky said, lifting the phone from the proffered salver. "I will take it. *Merci,* Mumford. That shall be all."

Becky extended the telephone's plastic-coated antenna and dabbed the talk button. "*Allô?* Dina?"

"Yes." Dina's voice was guarded.

"*Alors.* You are well, *j'espère bien?*"

"Not . . . really."

Becky's smile faded. This was hardly the kind of reply she found encouraging. Nor did Dina's reticence bode well, either. She said carefully, "*Chère amie.* You sound distressed. What is the matter?"

There was a silence.

"Ah. *Je comprends:* you cannot speak freely. Someone might overhear."

"Yes."

"I take it you are at the Faireys'." It was a statement, not a question. Dina's sigh spoke volumes. "Am I ever!"

"*Alors.* Let us play a little game. Could you tell me, using one key word, what this problem relates to? That way, I can possibly infer what it might be."

There was a moment's silence, during which Becky could picture Dina glancing over both shoulders. Then Dina whispered: "Cold."

"*Naturellement!*" Becky laughed lightly. "*Chérie,* it is winter."

"Inside?"

"Oh. You mean their furnace or boiler has broken down?"

"Worse."

"*Non!*" A look of utter amazement came into Becky's face. "*Pas possible.* You cannot mean . . . they *still* have no central heating?"

"I don't believe so. No."

"*Incroyable! Ma pauvre petite,* I had no idea. Truly. I see now that we must do something."

"I'd really appreciate it."

"It is nothing. I have plenty of spare rooms with—I assure you—plenty of heat. *Alors.* We shall work things out so that you will stay here. However, we must also be cautious."

Dina waited.

"Have you unpacked your luggage and such?"

"Barely. I can always stop—"

"*Non!* You must do no such thing. It is imperative that neither Zandra nor the Faireys get wind of anything. Simply carry on as usual. As if nothing was out of the ordinary. You can do that?"

"Yes."

"Then have no fear, *chère amie.* I shall take care of everything."

And Becky punched the off button and put the telephone down.

"Did I hear you correctly, or have my ears finally deceived me?" Lord Rosenkrantz asked. "You've invited them here?"

"*Oui.*"

"My dear, do you think that's wise?"

She shrugged. "Perhaps not. But what other choice do I have? *Cher ami,* the poor thing is overwrought. Not that I can blame her. *À vrai dire!* This compulsion the Faireys have for authenticity really has gone too far. Aren't the nineties plagued with enough ills? Or must one experience the genuine *mals* of the eighteenth century as well? *Quelle horreur!*"

"You don't imagine they do without medication or antibiotics, do you?" Karl-Heinz asked.

"Only in the country, and only if Nina Fairey is not having another facelift," Lord Rosenkrantz said archly.

"*Cela suffit,*" Becky said, and rang for the butler.

Mumford appeared forthwith. "Madam?"

"Mumford, could you please see to it that two guest suites are prepared?"

"Of course, madam. Do you have any particular ones in mind?"

"Yes. For the double, the Toile de Jouy suite, I think. It has two bedrooms, a sitting room, and two baths."

And is perfect for the Goldsmiths, she thought, *since it's the farthest from my own.*

"As for the single," she decided, "make it the Tree Poppy suite."

Which is perfect for Zandra, since it's close to Karl-Heinz's, but not so close as to be obvious. Also, it's appropriate for her, being the most English of all the rooms, with its stately four-poster, George II furnishings, British paintings, and Tree Poppy chintz.

Mumford said: "I shall see to it at once, madam."

Dina's chauffeur had long since returned to the city with her Town Car, so there was no choice but to pile into the Faireys' station wagon for the short hop over to Becky V's.

They were all turned out as differently as night and day.

Sheldon in a classic, single-breasted blue blazer with brass buttons, tan flannel trousers, and black wool turtleneck.

Nina Fairey in a high-necked black jacket, tartan kilt, black stockings,

and black ghillies. The jacket was nipped in at the waist and had frog clo-
sures, and the kilt had a big decorative safety pin on the front.

Robert in one of his thousand-and-one identically tailored business
suits, this one in charcoal pinstripe.

Zandra in loose, anthracite tweed slacks, Fair Isle sweater with horizontal zigzags in black, white, and gray, and short black granny boots.
Wearing no jewelry and looking great.

Dina a rhapsody in blue sapphires. The real thing at neck, wrist,
and ears; faux on the sapphire tulle minidress she wore over sapphire velvet stretch pants. She had on a dyed, sheared beaver cape and blue
suede shoes.

The drive took all of eighteen minutes, the night pitch black as only
moonless nights out in the country can be.

But at Becky V's, lights blazed from every window, and Zandra had
the impression of approaching a festively lit cruise ship, with the surrounding hilly terrain its watery troughs.

The moment Sheldon pulled up at the mansion, Dina was out of the
car. Charging up the front steps to the door. It opened before she could
reach it, and bright yellow light, Brahms, and distant laughter tumbled out
into the night.

Dina turned to look down at the car. She waved impatiently, urging
the others to hurry, and started to cross the threshold—

—when a Secret Service agent materialized, blocking her way.

"Oh!" Hand fluttering on her breast, Dina took a startled
step backward.

Then she heard a masculine voice boom: "For God's sake, man! Let
the poor lady in before she freezes to death!"

And Lord Rosenkrantz welcomed her inside.

"Remember." He wagged a finger at the bodyguard. "There's to be
none of that dreadful frisking nonsense."

Not that Dina would have objected. She was too curious, busily cran-
ing her neck and looking around the oval, pilastered foyer with its
portrait-hung staircase and massive tarnished Dutch chandelier directly overhead.

"Madam, can I help you with your coat?" It was the butler.

Dina obliged by gyrating out of her cape. The butler took it, folded
it carefully, and handed it to a petite maid.

Nina, Zandra, Sheldon, and Robert came in. One by one, the butler
helped them out of their wraps, which joined the growing stack in the
maid's arms. She hurried off to hang them up.

"Thank you, Mumford," Lord Rosenkrantz said. "If you don't mind,
I'll personally show our guests into the sitting room."

"Very well, m'lord."

Lord Rosenkrantz spread his arms wide, shepherding them toward the sitting room like a benevolent schoolteacher.

Dina walked in first, her eyes everywhere at once, breathlessly taking inventory.

Candles, music, fires going in both grates: props for the graciousness of rural living. So perfectly composed was the scene, and so cozily comfortable, that Dina had the impression she'd blundered onto a stage set, with the actors frozen in position, waiting for the curtain to rise. Becky, perched sideways on a couch, legs tucked under her. Prince Karl-Heinz standing by the marble fireplace, elbow on the mantel, drink in hand—

—and a curtain must have risen, for the *tableau* suddenly sprang to life.

Karl-Heinz, looking across the room, made eye contact with Dina, and said something to Becky.

Becky, turning around with an expression of astonished delight, quickly uncoiled herself and rose from the couch. Still barefoot and casual in Garbo slacks and turtleneck, she hurried across the room, arms extended in welcome.

"*Chérie!*"

She and Dina almost, but not quite, made contact; blew kisses past each other's cheeks.

"I'm so glad you could come!" Becky said brightly. "*Ça va?*"

But before Dina could reply, Becky looked past her, eyes going round as saucers with surprised artifice.

"Zandra!" she exclaimed. "Don't tell me! *You're* also staying with the Faireys? *Quelle surprise!* But how wonderful!"

And Zandra found herself being pulled into the room, where she was suddenly face-to-face with—

—*him!*

Dear God. Her cousin. Prince Karl-Heinz von und zu Engelwiesen, who was looking at her so intently that a warm flush shot from the very tips of her toes straight to the top of her face.

"Zandra," he said softly. Then he reached out and gave her a warm hug.

It was a chaste greeting, but nonetheless so electric that she felt her nipples beginning to tingle and harden. Swiftly she pulled away and drew a deep breath.

"Heinzie," she whispered, barely trusting herself to speak.

He smiled. "We seem to keep running into each other."

"Yes. It does seem that way. Gosh. *Heinzie.* I had no idea you'd be here." She half turned to Dina, expressly to break his gaze. "Did you, darling?"

But Dina was smiling at Karl-Heinz. "Your Serene Highness," she purred.

With an effort, Karl-Heinz tore his eyes from Zandra, lifted Dina's hand, bowed over it, and gave it a kiss. "Mrs. Goldsmith."

"Why so formal? Please, call me Dina. Everyone else does."

"Only if you," he said gallantly in return, "stop calling me 'Your Serene Highness.' " He smiled. "You don't know how wearisome it can get. Besides, Heinzie is much less of a mouthful."

Dina all but swooned.

"I'll go turn down the music," Lord Rosenkrantz was saying.

The others had come in, and the conversation grew animated.

"Sheldon," Nina Fairey said, "look! A Stubbs. Over there . . . there—"

"Sorry, darling, artist's name's Marshall. Ben Marshall. Did magnificent horses."

"Yes, it's awfully well done."

"Mumford? *Alors.* Why don't you find out what everyone is drinking. *Oui?*"

"Very well, madam."

Robert asked, "Aw right to light up a cigar in here?" already in the process of doing just that.

"Sweetie, isn't it nice and *warm* in here?" Dina said happily, leaving things to gestate between Zandra and Karl-Heinz, and heading for the even toastier environs of the nearest fireplace, where she checked herself out in the elaborate Régence mirror over the mantel.

"There," Lord Rosenkrantz said as the Brahms became muted background music. "That's better, eh?"

Robert rasped: "Bourbon, neat. Older the better. An' make it a double."

"A white wine for me," said Nina, "and a scotch rocks for my husband."

"*Alors.* And Mumford. Don't forget the champagne. There's Veuve Clicquot on ice, *n'est-ce pas?*"

"Of course, madam."

"Hmmm. Exquisite terra cotta," Sheldon said, bending down to admire a small divinity, part of an artfully arranged tablescape. "Syro-Hittite."

"Looks like Marty Feldman, you ask me," Robert guffawed, blowing rich smoke.

"Or Estelle Winwood," Nina Fairey added.

"Huh?" Robert stared at her and blinked. "*Who?*"

"British actress," Lord Rosenkrantz explained. "Did mainly stage, but a few memorable movies as well. Character actress. You know."

"Yeah? Good-lookin' broad?"

"Only if your tastes run to Marty Feldman," chuckled Lord Rosenkrantz, who could run intellectual circles around almost anybody.

There was a burst of laughter.

And all this time, Zandra and Karl-Heinz were silent, inhabiting an isolated little world of their own.

Dammit! Zandra cursed herself silently. *What is it with me? Why am I acting like a teen on a first date?*

"*Alors.* Here comes Mumford with the drinks. Why don't we all sit down and get comfortable?" Becky suggested, gesturing to where she'd been sitting in front of the fire. "Jacinta shall be bringing the hors d'oeuvres shortly."

Everyone began heading to the end of the room she'd indicated— everyone, that is, except Zandra and Karl-Heinz, who seemed not to have heard.

"*Allons!*" Becky said, touching each of them on the arms.

Zandra and Karl-Heinz both gave guilty starts.

Becky smiled. "*Mes chères,* we are going to sit down. You will join us, *j'espère bien?* Come . . ."

And hooking an arm through each of theirs, she led them over to the fireplace.

The formal dining room shimmered. Logs blazed in the fireplace and candles glowed in the gleaming silver candelabra. They brought to life the villages, pagodas, and rocky islands on the eighteenth-century Chinese wallpaper, infused the mahogany breakfront and Federal sideboard with a rich luminescence, and reflected off the Paul Revere silver.

The long Chippendale table was like a dark, reflective lake set with Chinese export porcelain, Federal flatware, linen napery, and bowls of hothouse roses. Rioja glowed, bloodlike, in cut-glass decanters and goblets.

Becky was in her element. The head of the table was just right for her. From it she presided with a quiet, regal presence, and did what she did best—orchestrating the serving and keeping the conversation flowing:

"The secret to this wine—" she lifted her glass of Duque de la Vila 1988— "is we age it entirely in barrels of French oak. That is what gives it its muted, Bordeaux-like flavor."

And: "*Chéri—*" this to Robert— "do tell us how you created all those thousands upon thousands of superstores out of a single *petit* storefront in . . . where was it? . . . St. Louis?"

And: "We have among us a most superb *equestrienne.* Now *chérie,* don't be so *timide—*" she smiled at Nina Fairey— "we are all dying to hear how you became a female jockey."

And finally: "Pity, how little use the facilities here get. Truly, it is almost criminal. When you consider the horses and the indoor everything— pool, tennis courts, riding arena . . . And this white elephant of a house! Imagine rattling around in it. Sometimes I am actually tempted to sell it."

"Sell it!" Nina Fairey exclaimed. "But it's so beautiful!"

"*Peut-être que oui.*" Becky smiled. "Of course, the reason I don't is because I've become so sentimentally attached to it. Every corner is filled with memories. Even so, it does get lonesome at times."

"But, sweetie! I thought you *cultivated* privacy," Dina pointed out.

"*Naturellement!* Sometimes I seek solitude. Who does not? But you must remember: I spent much of my adult life as a married woman."

No one knew what to say; clearly, this conversation was headed toward a patch of delicate ice.

"I suppose everything would be different if I'd had children," Becky mused. "*Oui.* That is what this house needs. Children. Perhaps then it would truly come to life."

Mumford, circumnavigating the table, was discreetly refilling goblets with wine.

"Do you know what else I miss?"

A distant look came into Becky's eyes and she raised her chin, her Nefertiti-like profile flickering in the candlelight as she looked around the table.

"Those old-fashioned weekend house parties," she said. "Zandra. You and Heinzie know the kind I mean."

"Gosh, Becky. But, darling, last real one of those was at Chatsworth. That was yonks ago."

"*Oui. Oui.*" Becky nodded. "I remember: we were invited, but then my poor dear Joaquín died so tragically . . ."

Mumford poured her some more wine.

"*Merci,* Mumford."

Becky lifted the goblet by the stem, and then suddenly her eyes grew huge. She set the goblet back down. "I *know!*" she breathed, as though she'd only thought of it that very instant. She leaned forward in excitement. "*Chéries!* Why don't you all stay *here* this weekend?"

Dina pounced. "Here? You mean . . . in *this* house, sweetie?"

"*Oui.*"

The Faireys exchanged hopeful looks, and Karl-Heinz flicked a glance at Zandra, who looked a bit startled.

Becky was positively radiant. "It shall be like an old-fashioned house party! Why not? This house is certainly large enough. I have lost count of exactly how many rooms there are. Only . . ." She bit her lip.

"Sweetie! What *is* it?"

"*Mon dieu!* In my excitement, I have completely lost my manners. Nina, *chérie.* How thoughtless of me. You will forgive me? I did not mean to steal your guests—"

"No apologies are necessary," Nina assured her.

"Absolutely not!" Sheldon added.

"*Alors.* It goes without saying that the invitation includes the both of you."

"How amusing," Nina cried. "A spur-of-the-moment house party!"

Dina clapped her hands. "It sounds wonderful!"

"But what about our things?" said Zandra, eliciting a kick and a glare from Dina.

"*Rion do plus facile.*" Becky waved a hand dismissively. "Mumford and someone else can go over to pack everything up and bring it back here. Well, *mes amies?*"

She looked around the table.

Robert was frowning, but there were no vocal objections. Lord Rosenkrantz caught her eye and sketched a sardonic toast with his goblet.

"*Alors,*" Becky decreed. "It is settled. A house party it is." She raised her goblet. "Let us salute old friends and new."

Goblets were raised and everyone chorused: "To old friends and new."

"Both of which are very precious," added Lord Rosenkrantz who, arching a bristly eyebrow, smiled thinly. "In the words of Lord Lyttelton: 'Women, like princes, find few real friends.' "

"And was it not Pindar," retorted Becky, no intellectual slouch herself, "who said, 'Often silence is the wisest thing for a man to heed'?"

"Touché, my dear," Lord Rosenkrantz smiled, "touché."

Not, she knew, for the part of the quote she'd spoken aloud, but rather, for the part she'd left unsaid:

"*Not every truth is the better for showing its face.*"

⚜ *36* ⚜

$\mathscr{E}$arly afternoon the following day, Becky held court from a cushioned nineteenth-century wicker chaise in the light-filled garden room, where potted trees and winding lianas thrived.

The three glass walls, an extension added to the back of the mansion, were a delicate gridwork of wrought iron, and had been designed so that each octagonal pane of clear glass had a diamond-shaped cabochon of blue Bohemian cut crystal at its corners. Blinding sunlight, bouncing off the white snow outside, made the blue insets glow like sapphires.

Lord Rosenkrantz occupied the chaise beside Becky's. Between them, an ebonized table with bamboo-turned legs held the accoutrements of the idle rich: a sterling coffee and tea service, champagne in a sweating bucket, antique crystal, and linen napery.

Dina was nearby, on a cushioned wicker armchair and ottoman which had been expressly angled so she could divide her attention equally between indoors and out.

Nina and Sheldon, still dressed in tennis whites, had just returned from the indoor courts, towels around their necks. High on endorphins, sipping San Pellegrino, and asking about Robert.

"He's upstairs, sweetie," Dina sighed, rolling her eyes. "Using his computer to make money."

In a wing chair in the far corner, surrounded on three sides by fragrant orange trees laden with fruit, sat Karl-Heinz. He was flipping through a priceless folio of botanical watercolors by Redoute which he'd found in Becky's library. But he wasn't concentrating on the exquisite renderings. In truth, he was feeling too agitated to concentrate on anything.

He raised his eyes without lifting his head.

Across the room, half-hidden behind Dina, the reason for this rare emotion reclined on a chaise. Zandra, arms raised, was dangling by its stem a huge orange-and-black parrot tulip, so that the ragged, waxy petals brushed lightly against her face.

The glimpse of her, so tantalizingly near, clogged his throat. *Right now I should be over there beside her,* he thought. *Making my moves. Dazzling her with charm.*

One small obstacle. When it came to Zandra, his famous charm deserted him.

Gott im Himmel! he thought. *I'm behaving like a child harboring a secret crush!*

And there was no reason for him to feel that way. No reason at all.

I'm rich, titled, and self-assured. I'm the man who supposedly has it all.

Right.

Then why were butterflies fluttering around inside him, thrumming against the lining of his stomach as though seeking escape?

Zandra was feeling decidedly antsy, this despite the morning walk she'd taken, and the grueling laps she'd swum in the indoor pool before lunch. Trouble was, just lying around doing nothing was an entirely new experience. Ever since she'd arrived in the Big Apple, her every waking minute had been chock-full of frenzied activity. She'd never once taken a moment to decompress.

Now that the opportunity to do so presented itself, what should happen?

Why, irony of ironies! She already missed the never-ending urban fireworks, that constant, energetic rumpus and tumultuous multiring circus she'd grown used to, and come to love.

Next to that, the quiet out here was positively unsettling.

Turning her head sideways, she caught sight of a magnificent fox loping slowly past outside. It stopped, looked in through the glass wall at her, then turned its head and trotted casually on its way.

She stared out at the paw prints it left behind in the snow. *I've got to get out of the house,* she decided.

Yes. Perhaps a horseback ride would perk up her spirits.

Anything's better than just lying around.

Lord Rosenkrantz was saying, "So she bequeathed her entire fortune to this foundation he'd set up, but there *wasn't* any foundation, don't you see? It—"

"Shhhhh." Becky, silencing him, possessed an early warning system that would have done the Pentagon proud. Sitting straight and tall, she glanced out through the octagonal panes.

It was just as she had thought. Zandra, who had left the garden room some minutes earlier, was striding purposefully across the yard to the stables.

Thanking God that the Faireys had auspiciously gone upstairs to shower and change, Becky said, *"Excusez-moi, mon cher.* Duty calls."

"Bubble, bubble, toil and trouble, eh?" said Lord Rosenkrantz.

Ignoring him, she rose from the chaise and crossed over to where Karl-Heinz, still in the wing chair, pretended to be engrossed in an elegant study of *Metrosyderos Lophanta.*

Becky leaned down, her voice almost a whisper. "Heinzie," she said.
Karl-Heinz looked up at her. She gestured toward the wall of glass.

He followed her hand to where Zandra, in borrowed riding togs—
boots, jodhpurs, and a thick brown drover coat with a partial cape—
proved that it was not a case of the clothes making the lady, but the lady
making the clothes.

"Our fair maiden is going for a ride. *Alors.* It is time to get to work."

He nodded, knowing he should already have given chase. So
what was keeping him glued to this chair, hesitant and immobile? Scru-
ples? Morals?

A hint of a frown crossed Becky's face. "What are you waiting for?
Mon Dieu! This is your chance. Heinzie, follow her! *Go!*"

When he still didn't move, she reached down, lifted the folio off his
lap, closed it, and set it aside. Then, taking both his hands in hers, she
helped pull him to his feet.

He sighed to himself. Becky was nothing if not determined.

Whoever coined that phrase about women being the weaker sex, he
thought, *obviously never ran across Becky V.*

"Now off with you," she said. "And try to remember what's at stake.
If all those billions should end up with Sofia and Egbert—"

"Erwein," he corrected her automatically.

"Whichever," she said, without the least concern. "Now go. And
bonne chance!" And with that, she gave him a little prod and sent him on
his way.

When he reached the door, he turned around and looked back into
the garden room.

Becky, one hand on the wing chair, was staring at him. She stood tall
and sure of herself, and there was something about her quiet strength
which reminded him of newly minted steel.

Then, his expression pained but resigned, he went upstairs to change
into his riding habit.

"Horse she took's Amethyst Dream," the stable lad informed Karl-Heinz.
"A chestnut mare. All you gotta do is follow them tracks. Alidad here'll
catch up with her—" he snapped his fingers "—like that."

He was referring to the glossy black stallion he was holding by the
leading rein. A magnificent, high-strung Arabian, Alidad literally danced
in place, neighing and snorting plumes of vapor as he tossed his head
and tail.

The stable lad squinted at Karl-Heinz. "You sure you're up to rid-
in' him?"

"Quite sure," Karl-Heinz smiled. "But thank you for the concern."

"Mrs. V. don't like it, a guest a hers gettin' injured."

"I'll take full responsibility," Karl-Heinz assured him. He took the leading rein, held it tight, and spent a minute stroking the horse's muzzle and talking to him in calm, reassuring tones.

Perhaps it was a case of one thoroughbred recognizing another. Or maybe it was that telepathy peculiar to horses. Whatever the reason, Alidad instantly calmed down and put his muzzle against Karl-Heinz's neck, his nostrils making whiffling movements.

"You sure seem to have a way with him," the stable lad said admiringly. "I'll give you that."

Karl-Heinz smiled and swung himself expertly up into the saddle. One shake of the reins and they were off.

Alidad was in his element. No stable horse, he. His long straight hocks proved themselves with lengthy strides.

Nor did fences stand in his way. He sailed over them superbly, with plenty of room to spare.

It was a perfect day for riding. The sky cloudless, the air frigid but windless, the sun warm. Snowy meadows and fenced paddocks undulated gently toward distant forests.

Cresting a hill, Karl-Heinz abruptly reined Alidad in. There she was, one furlong ahead. Zandra on Amethyst Dream, moving at a sedate trot.

Karl-Heinz stood up on the stirrups. "Zandra!" he called out.

Hearing her name, she turned Amethyst Dream around and halted, shielding her eyes with an arm as she faced into the sun.

Karl-Heinz waved at her. Then, jerking on the reins, he bent low over Alidad's neck and sent him flying.

The distance between himself and Zandra closed rapidly, and he galloped up beside her, stopping in a spray of snow.

She lowered her arm. "Gosh, Heinzie. What an absolutely magnificent horse!"

The cold, he noticed, had turned her face rosy, the sun brought out the highlights of red in her orange marmalade hair, and she literally glowed with a healthy vitality.

He thought, *She looks, if that's possible, more splendid than ever.*

"Mind if I join you?" he asked.

"Oh, not at all. I mean, why should I?" She smiled ravishingly. "But I'm only out for a short ride," she warned. "Temperature's dropping rapidly. Another hour or so, and it'll start getting dark."

She moved the reins and Amethyst Dream obediently began walking at a sedate pace. Karl-Heinz fell in beside her, keeping Alidad, who itched to accelerate, tightly reined in.

"Haven't ridden in eons," she told him. "That's why they gave me Amethyst here. Tamest of the bunch, I gather. But I mean, there *is* something to be said for being *too* tame, isn't there?"

"Definitely," he smiled.

They were climbing up a slight incline through virgin snow. In the stillness, they could hear the crunch as the crusty surface broke under the weight of the hooves. Up ahead, the snow-laden trees thickened into dark, bluish-black pines.

When they reached the edge of the forest, they turned around and looked back the way they had come.

"Oh, Heinzie!" Zandra exclaimed. "Look! Isn't it Christmas-card perfect? And so unspoiled."

"Then why don't we stretch our legs, give the horses a rest, and enjoy the view?" he suggested.

"Splendid!" She dismounted, tethered Amethyst to a branch, and tramped happily through a snowdrift.

"You'll get your feet wet," he warned, tethering Alidad.

She glanced over her shoulder at him. "So?"

"You might get pneumonia."

"Like going outside with wet hair?" she scoffed, laughing. "*That* old wives' tale! Long as I change when we get back, I'll be fine."

She bent down, scooped up a handful of snow, and made a snowball. Then she half turned. "Heinzie?"

"Yes?"

And she flung it at him.

It hit him squarely in the chest. "What the—!" he began angrily, looking down at himself.

She laughed gaily and quickly scooped up more snow.

"Zandra!" he called. "Now stop that!"

"Oh, Heinzie. Must you be such an old fart?"

She pitched the second ball at him, which he deflected with his arm. Nevertheless, sprays of snow flew all over him.

"Zandra, I'm warning you . . ."

She laughed with delight and quickly made another. Started to toss it when—

—a ball hit her hard on the shoulder.

"Shit!" she cried. "Now you're *really* going to get it!"

She flung back her arm and launched her snowy missile. He saw it coming and ducked, and it sailed harmlessly on.

Then another one came hurtling toward her, connecting with her thigh.

"Goddammit! Now stop it, Heinzie. That hurt!"

Seeing him scoop up more snow, she screamed happily and began to run.

Grinning, he flung his ball, but it went wide of its mark. Then he merrily gave chase.

Zandra, glancing over her shoulder, saw him coming, and quickly launched another snowball. It hit, but did not deter.

Pretending terror, she scrambled through the calf-high snow, but he tackled her from behind and down they both went, rolling over and over. Giggling and screeching like five-year-olds.

When they stopped rolling, she found herself pinned underneath him. Staring up into his face, which was but inches from hers.

She caught her breath. Her heart was skipping and her head felt light. And still she stared, unable to take her eyes off him.

Even as she stared at him, so, too, did he stare at her, and with no less intensity. A great heat seemed to engulf him, and he could feel his heart pounding thickly in his chest.

The moment seemed to stretch into eternity.

She was acutely aware of his long, leanly muscled physique, the impertinent azure of his eyes, and above all, his unpardonably alluring and seductive mouth, the lips of which seemed to have been sculpted for one purpose, to invite kisses.

He was acutely aware of the warmth of her body, the crystals of snow, like fragile moist jewels, sparkling on her lashes, the triangle of freckles on her nose, the glowing mermaid green of her irises, and the pre-Raphaelite haze of her bright marmalade hair.

And still the moment stretched elastically, seemingly without beginning or end.

But it did end, for Karl-Heinz gave a start and abruptly came to. Shaking his head as if to clear it, he rolled off her, realizing he still had a snowball clenched in his fist. He tossed it absently backward, into the trees.

It flushed out a brace of birds, which burst, screeching, from between the branches behind them.

They both looked up and watched, as overhead, the winged creatures chased each other, flew elaborate loops, fluttered momentarily in place, and then made a dash downhill, where they did an aerial ballet before streaking off.

"Aren't they darling?" Zandra mused. "I do believe those birds are in love."

Smiling enchantingly, she turned to Karl-Heinz, her elbow in deep snow, her head resting on the palm of her hand.

"What do you think, Heinzie?"

He thought it the perfect opening. "I think I'm in love with you," he said quietly.

It came as such a shock that she couldn't contain herself: she burst out in giggles. How preposterous! she thought. He, who she'd known since early childhood, *he* was professing his love for *her?*

Of course, she thought, *he's only joking.*

But if so, why were his eyes so smolderingly intense? And why had his voice turned so husky with sincerity?

Holy Mother of God! she thought. *He's not joking! He is serious!*

All she could do was stare stupidly at him, like some tongue-tied idiot.

He was saying, "I know this must come as something of a shock to you, but you do things to me, Zandra. You really do. Around you, life seems so . . . different. Rosy and innocent."

Fun and exciting. Worth living. He could have named dozens of such things.

"You're positively certifiable," she said fondly, "you do know that, don't you?"

"Zandra," he said softly, hesitantly. "Darling, I'm *serious.*"

This is crazy! she thought. *We might be distantly related, and I have known him since God only knows when, but in some ways, we really know nothing about each other!*

She wondered if, somewhere along the way, she hadn't somehow led him on? Perhaps given him the wrong impression? She didn't *think* so . . .

She was startled when he took her hand in both of his and lifted it to his lips.

Her throat was suddenly dry. "Heinzie," she protested, but his name seemed to stick in her gullet; came out as a garbled croak. She had to clear her throat.

"Heinzie," she said again, louder, clearer, more assertively.

"Zandra."

He kissed her fingertips, his eyes reaching out and drowning in hers. "Sweet, sweet Zandra. Don't you know what you are to me?"

"Oh, Heinzie, course I do. I'm your cousin."

"No." He shook his head and kissed her fingertips again. "You're much, much more than that."

She stared at him.

"I want to marry you," he said. "I want you to be my wife."

"*You . . . marry . . . me?*" She burst into a fresh round of giggles. "But, darling, honestly! I can't even sew on a button, let alone cook without burning down an entire house."

His eyes never wavered. "Zandra, sweet Zandra, *will* you take me in holy matrimony? *Will* you let me love and cherish and honor you until the day that I die?"

Oh, shit! she thought. *He's serious! He's really dead serious!*

"I . . . I'm sorry, Heinzie," she said shakily, and withdrew her hand from his. "It . . . it just wouldn't . . . I mean, I don't . . . What I'm *trying* to say is . . ."

She was so flustered that she had to take a deep breath.

"I'm just not ready for marriage," she said. "Not to you. Not to *anybody.*"

"Then you don't love me?"

"God, of course I love you. That goes without saying. But I mean, it's beside the point, isn't it? Doesn't mean we have to take the plunge and get married."

"Why not? Because we're cousins?"

"Yes. No. Oh, hell, I don't know." She made fluttering motions with her fingers. *"Honestly,* you caught me totally off guard."

"If it's genetics you're worried about, I had a scientist look over our genealogy. He says there shouldn't be any problem."

She sighed. "Heinzie, even if that's the *case"* —Zandra, having had the unexpected popped upon her, had to think carefully before she spoke— "I need to be certain of *my* emotions and not make a mistake we might both end up regretting."

"I know I wouldn't regret it."

Her face underwent a subtle change, as though a shadow had slipped under her skin. "But I might, Heinzie," she said as gently as possible, praying the words wouldn't wound. "I'm not sure I love you *enough."*

He did not speak.

She compressed her lips and forced herself to go full steam ahead. "You do understand, don't you, darling? I love you as a cousin, and for absolutely ever. You're a perfect marvel, and you'll make some very lucky girl a super husband *and* very, very happy. But I'm just not sure whether *I* can love you that way—"

His eyes had dimmed and gone flat, and he was looking at her with a freeze-dried kind of smile.

She winced inwardly, thinking: *Oh, God. Now I have wounded him! I really didn't mean to.*

"I . . . I think we'd better start heading back," she said, getting to her feet and starting to brush snow off her coat.

He rose also, feeling awkward, standing there like a supplicant, hands at his sides.

"And if love's got nothing to do with it?" he whispered hoarsely, unable to look at her, his thumbs twitching against his thighs.

The hand brushing at her coat sleeve froze, and her eyes slowly came up. "Heinzie," she said. "Whatever are you trying to say?"

He exhaled a strangled breath, an arid, raspy sound like the scraping of rusty metal. "I'm asking if—even though you say you don't love me— whether you could . . . could find it in your heart to marry me anyway?"

"Heinzie, but what utter nonsense! Whatever would we be marrying for?"

"Convenience's sake?" He loathed himself for the taut desperation in his voice.

"But, darling, I don't understand."

He gave a sickly sort of smile. "Surely you know about the von und zu Engelwiesen criteria for inheritance?"

Everything inside Zandra suddenly ground to a dead stop. "My God," she exclaimed softly. "I don't *believe* this."

He tightened his lips miserably.

"You hypocrite! You goddamn *hypocrite!*"

The accusation came now, loosened like a small avalanche.

"You don't really love me at all! The only reason you're proposing to me is to help you secure that damn inheritance! That's all you actually give a fart about, isn't it?"

He flinched, as though from a physical blow.

"Well, isn't it?"

He didn't speak.

"Oh, this is rich!" Her boot blurred as she kicked savagely at snow. "Christ, this is really rich—"

"Zandra, listen to me!"

"What do you think I've been doing? And what did you expect? That I'd drop to my knees in gratitude for being used as any port in a storm?"

With a toss of her head, she stalked angrily over to where the horses were tethered.

"Zandra!" He caught up with her and seized her by the wrist. "For Christ's sake! Won't you please hear me out?"

She whirled around, a blaze of teeth and nails, magnificent in her fury. "Let go of me!" she said coldly, trying, in vain, to wrench her wrist loose. "I have nothing more to say to you."

"Look, I can appreciate your anger—"

"Oh, *can* you, now?"

"If you'll only let me explain! You're taking this entirely the wrong way—"

"Oh, I don't think so." Her eyes drilled right into his. "You're one hell of a cheeky bastard, and you've bloody well proved it."

"I love you, dammit!" The declaration burst from his mouth on its own accord. "Inheritance or not, sooner or later I'd have proposed to you anyway. Can't you see that?"

She laughed bitterly. "And I suppose these woods—" she gestured at the forest behind them "—are inhabited by elves, fairies, and trolls?"

He took a deep breath. "Zandra, whether you choose to believe this or not, you're the only woman I've ever really wanted."

"Oh! You want me, do you? Well, how nice. I gather you're waiting for me to drop on my knees and kiss your bloody feet in gratitude?"

He winced at the contempt in her voice.

"Well, bugger that!" she snapped. "What about *me*, sod it? How about what *I* might want? Or haven't you bothered to give me any thought?"

"I've thought about you constantly," he said truthfully.

"Right. So, about this marriage you've so kindly proposed," she continued remorselessly. "What would *I* get out of it, pray tell?"

He sighed. "You would become one of the richest women in the world. You would have money. Power. Position."

"None of which, truth be told, I find all that appealing."

So it's useless, he thought. *I should have known. But how he could* have made such a mess of it . . . !

He felt wretched, cheap. Appalled with himself.

She used a thumb and index finger to remove his hand from her wrist. He let go willingly, and fully expected her to jump on Amethyst Dream and gallop off.

Instead, she continued to stand there, hugging herself with her arms while frowning down at the snow-carpeted landscape below.

"So *this* was the reason!" she exclaimed softly. "Now it all falls into place!"

He glanced sideways at her. "What does?"

"Why Dina was so insistent about my coming this weekend. Obviously, the two of you were in cahoots, along with Becky, I imagine. Yes. You three had it all figured out. But first, of course, I had to be lured *here.*" She gestured at the rolling countryside and Becky V's mansion in the distance. "Otherwise, how could you spring your proposal on me?"

From his expression, she knew she had guessed correctly.

"Zandra—" he began.

She cut him off. "Heinzie, please," she begged. "Don't."

"But I must. Granted, you were invited under false pretenses. But my feelings for you—"

"Heinzie!" Her eyes filled with tears.

He drew a deep breath and let it out slowly. Christ, but he'd blown it! He couldn't have botched it worse if he'd tried. Hurting her had never been part of the plan.

Do we always wound the ones we love? he wondered.

"Zandra," he pleaded, "try not to judge me too hasti—"

But she had had enough, was running to her horse and, a moment later, had Amethyst Dream galloping downhill. Heading for the Greek Revival mansion in the distance.

Except for Alidad, Karl-Heinz stood alone atop the rise, a solitary figure watching helplessly as Zandra fled—

—putting distance between herself and him . . .

. . . for good.

Lord Rosenkrantz was sipping champagne when a movement outside the wall of windows caught his eye. It was Zandra, astride the chestnut mare, hurtling toward the stables at full speed.

"Oh, my," he said, clucking his tongue. "Oh my, oh my. Do my eyes deceive me, my dear Becky, or does there seem to be a spot of trouble?"

"Trouble?" Becky instantly sat up and followed his gaze. "*Alors.* Not if I have anything to do with it," she said determinedly, rising to her feet.

"Wait," Dina said, getting up. "It may be better if I took care of this."

Becky hesitated, then nodded acquiescence. "*Oui.* Why not? You know her better than anyone."

As Dina hurried out, Lord Rosenkrantz lifted the champagne bottle out of the bucket.

"It looks," he predicted ominously, "as if some fortification might well be in order. More champagne, my dear?"

⚛ *37* ⚛

"*S*weetie?" Dina inquired, voice syrupy with concern. She was speaking to Zandra, who she'd intercepted in the mud room. "Is everything all right?"

Zandra, heel in a boot jack, yanked her leg savagely out of a riding boot. "Why shouldn't it be? I mean, this *is* the perfect country weekend." She glared at Dina. "Isn't it?"

A frown marred Dina's flawless, Buf-Pufed complexion. "I'm not sure I follow you, sweetie."

"You can drop the act. Game's over, *darling.*" Zandra shook her head in disbelief. "Jesus. You had it all figured out, didn't you?"

"Sweetie?"

"My fairy-tale wedding to Heinzie!" Zandra snapped angrily.

"Oh," Dina sighed, "that."

Zandra yanked her leg halfway out of the other boot and kicked it off, sending it flying across the room.

"Tell you what, sweetie," Dina suggested. "Why don't we go into the library and talk this over nice and calmly?"

"We can bloody well talk about it right here!" Zandra stared at her. "How dare you! What the fuck did you think you were up to? Or do you make a *habit* of pimping for Karl-Heinz?"

"Oh, dear." Dina switched into her Injured-Party Mode. "Really, sweetie, I wish you wouldn't be so distressed."

"Do you think I like feeling this way?"

"Of course not. I only wanted what was best for you."

"Right." Zandra's tone made it clear she thought otherwise.

"Plus, you and Heinzie are tailor-made for each other," Dina added.

"Are we?"

"Sweetie, you're the perfect couple. Each of you has something the other needs."

"Do we now?"

"Yes, you do. Heinzie desperately needs an heir. Otherwise he cannot inherit."

"And me? What do I supposedly need?"

"Why money, of course! Sweetie, you'll become one of the richest women in the world!"

"Dina," Zandra said wearily, "has it ever occurred to you that money isn't everything?"

"Of course it has. But believe me, sweetie, it is better to have than to have not. And I speak from experience."

"And does this *experience* of yours extend to the bloody birds and the bloody bees?"

"What do you mean?"

"Dina! Ensuring Heinzie's inheritance involves having *sex*. And bearing a child! More than one, if the firstborn happen to be female. He needs a male heir in order to inherit!"

"Yes, yes. I know."

"And has it also occurred to you that I might not *want* to sleep with Heinzie?"

"Who says you have to?"

Zandra stared at her. "What? You mean, the stork delivers it?"

"In a manner of speaking, yes," Dina smiled. "It could."

Zandra could only shake her head.

"It's simple, sweetie. You see, there's a loophole in the von und zu Engelwiesen law of primogeniture."

Zandra kept staring at her.

"For some reason," Dina explained, "it fails to specify that the prince must be the father. Apparently, back in the olden days, wives didn't dare stray."

Zandra remained silent.

"The only important thing," Dina said, "is that the requisite trio of lawyers witness the birth. But who's to say *how* the child was conceived?"

Zandra was speechless.

"Therefore, if sleeping with Heinzie is not your cup of tea, it can all be done through artificial insemination, so nice and clean, don't you think? Science has made remarkable strides."

"So you've thought of everything," Zandra said quietly.

"Why, yes," Dina said brightly, "I suppose I have."

"Except you overlooked one minor detail."

"And what's that, sweetie?" Dina suddenly looked worried.

"You'll have to find another victim," Zandra said coldly. "It won't be me. Or do you see me wearing a 'Womb to Let' sign?"

It was Dina's turn to stare.

"So forget it. My womb's not for sale. Nor for hire, either!"

And with that, Zandra left the room, slamming the door behind her.

"*Chérie?*" Rap tap tap.

Zandra could hear Becky knocking and calling to her through the door. "*Chérie . . .*"

Can't I even lick my wounds in private? Zandra thought angrily. *Or is being left alone too much to ask for?*

"*Chérie,* please. *Do* open up."

God, how she wished Becky would give up and go away!

No such luck.

Might as well get it over with, Zandra decided. *Maybe then I'll be allowed some peace.* Unfolding herself from the overstuffed chair, she crossed the sitting room of the Tree Poppy suite and opened the door.

"*Mechanceté, mechanceté!*" Becky wagged a playful, reproachful finger. "You had me worried. May I come in?"

It's your house, Zandra wanted to retort, but manners would not permit. She opened the door wider and stepped aside.

Becky sailed in, shut the door, and adroitly steered Zandra over to the green damask sofa facing the pine mantel. They sat side by side, angled slightly toward each other in order to facilitate conversation.

Becky looked around the red and green room, as though its Tree Poppy walls, Tree Poppy chintz curtains, huge dark paintings, brick-red overstuffed chairs, and walnut furnishings were all new to her.

Nodding, as though in approval of the decor, she folded her hands in her lap, saying, "Interesting. So English, this room. *N'est-ce pas?*"

"Yes."

"Personally, in the city I prefer the French style, but it does not translate well to the country. *Non.* But the English! Only they know how to make country houses comfortable. *Oui.*"

Becky tilted her head and gave Zandra the full treatment of her famous violet eyes.

"*Naturellement,* I have not come to discuss decorating."

Zandra met her gaze directly. "I didn't think you did."

Becky nodded. "Dina tells me she and you had *une bisbille* . . . a small tiff?"

"Oh, but that was *nothing!*" Zandra said, with grandiose understatement.

"*Bon.* I am happy to hear it."

First Heinzie approaches me, Zandra thought, *then Dina, and now Becky. What is this? Tag team wrestling?*

"Dina mentioned it had something to do with Heinzie," Becky said. "*C'est vrai?*"

"Yes. He proposed, I turned him down. End of story."

"Pity. You would have made a most attractive couple. And he could use your help, you know."

"My *help.* Yes, I suspect that's why I was lured here."

Becky's violet eyes went opaque. "Sometimes such subterfuges are necessary. I deemed this to be one of those occasions. I did not mean to insult you, *chérie.* If I have, I extend my sincerest apologies."

"Apologies accepted."

"*Alors.* Now there is no more need of subterfuge. May I speak frankly?"

"Please do."

"I am appealing to you on Heinzie's behalf. *Chérie,* won't you reconsider?"

"And marry him, you mean?"

Becky nodded. "*Oui.*"

"I'm sorry, but the answer is still no."

"Even if we make it worth your while?"

"Even then. Yes."

"May I ask why?"

"Because I have my own feelings to consider."

"Feelings," Becky sighed. "*Chérie,* must you be so *obstiné?* Can you think of no one but yourself?"

"If I don't," Zandra said, "who will? Heinzie? Dina? *You?*"

"You are a silly, selfish little ingrate. I see that now."

Zandra flared. "*I'm* selfish? Haven't you got it turned around? It's *you*—you and Dina and Heinzie—who are being selfish. Please, darling, do me a favor. Next time someone needs a descendant of the Holy Roman Emperors, kindly leave me out of it?"

Zandra started to get up, but Becky caught her by the forearm and pulled her back down.

"We're not quite finished, *chérie.*"

Zandra thrust out her chin determinedly. "I'm afraid we are."

"You silly child!" Becky's lacquered talons dug into Zandra's arm. "Why must you be so difficult? Why—?"

Zandra had no desire to argue, and remained silent.

"People get married for convenience all the time," Becky went on. "To get their green cards. To secure tax advantages. To hide unsavory predilections behind respectable facades. The reasons are endless."

Zandra still did not speak.

"All you have to do is marry Heinzie and give him a son. Afterwards, you can do as you wish. Divorce him. Live in luxurious splendor for the rest of your life . . ."

Zandra had had enough. "You might as well save your breath. I'm really not interested."

Becky's eyes narrowed. "Ten million dollars. Is that enough to interest you?"

"You haven't been listening. I said, *no sale!*"

"Twenty million, then?"

"You can make it a hundred million, and you'd still be wasting your breath!"

"*Vraiment!*" Becky scoffed. "*You?* Turn down a hundred million?"

"Yes. *Me.*"

"*Chérie,* please. Don't make me laugh!"

"*Chère amie,* I'm not trying to." Zandra imitated Becky to scathing perfection. "*Alors.* This discussion is *fini.*"

The mimicry was so arch that Becky let go of Zandra's arm and jumped to her feet.

"How *dare* you!" she hissed.

"Perhaps now," Zandra said tightly, "you'll kindly leave. Think it's time I started packing my *things.* Wouldn't want to outstay my welcome."

"That," Becky said icily, "might not be such a bad idea. I shall arrange for a car."

And turning on her heel, she left, shutting the door soundlessly behind her.

Five minutes later, Zandra was on her way back to the city.

At Becky V's, predinner drinks were being served. Nina Fairey, roaming the huge sitting room, nursed a glass of white wine.

"What," she wondered aloud, "is keeping Zandra?"

It was Becky who replied.

"I'm afraid she took ill, *chérie.* But she did ask me to convey her regrets."

"It's nothing serious, is it?"

"*Non. Non.* Probably just a stomach virus. You know. Ah! Here come the hors d'oeuvres. You really *must* try the miniature pizzas. They truly are sublime!"

38

"Dom Pérignon!" Kenzie exclaimed. "Are we trying to make amends?"

"What's with this sudden 'we' shit? You hanging around with nurses now? Anyway . . ."

Charley went over to the gilt-framed mirror with a cocky little strut and craned his neck, adjusting his tie like John Gotti.

"Told you I'm not a Cold Duck kinda guy, didn't I?"

She laughed. "Yes, you did."

"Classy," he said, brushing his lapels with his fingernails. "Yep. That's-a me."

"All right, Narcissus. You've done enough preening for one day. Here. Why don't you make yourself useful and pop the cork? I'll go scare up some champagne glasses."

Kenzie felt a sudden pang of guilt. *Good Lord*, she thought. *I used almost the exact same phrase with Hannes the last time I saw him!*

She went into the kitchenette, rebuking herself for feeling guilt.

It's fine for a man to see more than one woman, she thought. *That's called virility. But if a woman sees more than one man, she's called a whore.* She told herself that worrying about this double standard was worthless. *It won't get me anywhere.*

Charley, peeling the dark green foil from around the neck of the bottle, squeezed past her to toss it into the kitchen trash. An empty bottle of Krug sticking out of it stopped him short.

"Whoa!" he said, reaching down and fishing it out. "You were right."

"About what?"

"Your taste. It's definitely going upscale. But Krug? I'd say that's a little pricey for a working girl to buy for herself, wouldn't you?"

Kenzie turned around, a glass in each hand. It was difficult to tell which flashed more, the cut crystal or her eyes.

"Detective Ferraro," she demanded, "are you on a case, or am *I* going to have to open that damn bottle?"

His grin was mocking her. "Touchy, touchy. Hit a nerve, huh?"

Her eyes narrowed. "You see an engagement ring on my finger?"

"Nope."

"All right, then. Mind your own business."

He tossed the Krug back into the trash. "Stuff's for a guy sorta likes a girl. Now, he's *really* nuts for her? He brings her the real thing." He held up the Dom Pérignon and grinned.

"Oh, give it a break, Charley," she said wearily.

His grin broadened as he popped the cork and filled first one glass, and then the other. He put the bottle down. Took one of the glasses. Clinked it against hers.

"To us," he said. " 'Cause I care enough to give the very best."

"Charley, are you sure you're not Irish?"

"Positive. Neapolitan through and through. Why?"

"Because, the last time I heard this much blarney, I was dating an Irishman!"

She went out into the living room and he followed her.

"We're still going to make your world-famous risotto?" he asked.

"Certainly. But first I'm going to enjoy a glass of the very best," she said, sitting down on the sofa. *"Then* I'll get busy in the kitchen."

"Fair enough." He sat down beside her.

Hearing someone sticking keys in the locks, they both turned toward the front door.

"You expecting company?" Charley asked quietly.

"No."

"Your roomie?"

"I already *told* you," Kenzie whispered. "She's not due back until tomorrow."

"Landlord? Super?"

"Neither one's got keys."

The first lock cylinder clicked.

"Somebody sure the hell does. So. If you're not expecting anybody, and nobody's got keys to this place, and your roommate's out of town. . . . Think it's a burglar?"

Kenzie smiled. "Then I'd say he's in for a big surprise. One of the benefits of entertaining a cop."

The second cylinder clicked.

Charley put down his glass, got up, and made his way quietly over to the door. He looked back at Kenzie and put his finger against his lips.

Three more cylinders clicked and then the door burst open.

Charley, service revolver out, yelled: "Hold it right there!"

Kenzie, seeing who it was, popped up from the couch and cried: "Zandra!"

And Zandra, tossing her overnighter inside, slammed the door. Oblivious to them both, she fumbled to lock the bolts and headed straight for her room, tears streaming down her face.

"Shit!" Charley exclaimed, putting his revolver away. He looked at Kenzie accusingly. "I thought you said—"

"Charley! Something's very wrong. You saw the state she's in."

"Shit," he repeated, but softly.

Kenzie headed for Zandra's door. Knocked, opened it, and slipped inside. A minute passed. Charley gulped his glass of champagne. Then the door opened and Kenzie came out.

"Whasamatter?" Charley asked.

"The poor thing's had a bad shock. Charley, listen . . ."

"Oh, no!" He held up both hands and shook his head. "Unh-unh. Don't tell me. I don't want to hear it!"

"I promise I'll make it up to you," Kenzie said, pushing him toward the front door. "She's beside herself and needs me. Now, *will* you go? It's girl-talk time."

"Guess this means no risotto," he sighed.

"Afraid not." She took his coat out of the cloak closet and shoved it at him.

"You tossing me out among the huddled masses?" he asked.

"That's one way to look at it. Yes. But it's really only a rain check. Now *please,* Charley. Will. You. *Go?* I already told you I'd make it up to you."

"With risotto?"

"Yes!"

"Then hold the mushrooms. Save 'em for the huddled masses."

"I'll make it with radicchio." She had the front door open.

"Yeah? Taste as good as it sounds?"

"Good-bye, Charley."

She literally shoved him out the door.

"A princess, a genuine princess, you could have been a real-life, honest-to-goodness fairy tale princess—"

Kenzie sighed wistfully over her third vodka on the rocks, not her beverage of choice, but all they had on hand since polishing off the Dom Pérignon.

"—just like Di or Caroline or Stephanie," she went on dreamily. "Zandra, you do know how to hurt a girl, telling her she *almost* had a princess for a best friend, you really do."

"It would hurt tons more to find oneself *saddled,"* sniffed Zandra loftily, "with a certain frog for a prince, not to mention two witches instead of fairy godmothers."

"Yeah, I guess you've got a point there."

"Oh, Kenz! How ever could I have been such a fool as to trust my oldest friend in the world, only to discover that all this time she's been scheming behind my back—"

"Forget about it," Kenzie advised.

She lifted the fifth of Smirnoff and refilled both their glasses to the rim.

"These kinds of things happen to the best of us. To err is human, or didn't you know?"

"Yes, but I walked straight into it with both eyes wide open—"

"Hold it, kiddo. Hold it right there."

Kenzie, like a traffic cop, held up a hand, palm facing out.

"You can't keep hitting yourself over the head with this. What's done is done. Take my advice. Chalk it up to experience."

"Yes, that's all fine, well, and dandy to *say*. But Becky and Dina aside, how could someone who is my very own relation—whom I first met when I was still learning to walk, for Christ's sake!—pounce on me just to hit the big jackpot?"

"I dunno," Kenzie sighed. "C'mon. Drink up."

But Zandra wasn't listening.

"What really hurts," she was saying, "is that it should be Karl-Heinz, of all people. Little as I've actually seen him over the years, he's always been my absolute fave when it came to relatives. Of course, that's totally changed, I can tell you that."

"Can't say I blame you," Kenzie commiserated. "I wouldn't have expected it of him, either. Not Prince Karl-Heinz ... so handsome ... so rich ... so ... so *royal.*"

"Serene," Zandra corrected her. "Prince Charles is royal. Karl-Heinz, like Rainier of Monaco, is merely serene."

"Serene ..." Kenzie murmured dreamily. "I do rather like the sound of that."

"You'd like it a lot less if it meant marrying that jackal!" Zandra said darkly.

"Castles in Bavaria ..." Kenzie mused. "Hunting lodges in Schwaben ..."

"Thick dank walls and moldy fabrics ..." Zandra gloomed. "Drafty rooms and endless halls ..."

"Titians and Tintorettos ..." Kenzie went on dreamily. "Banks and breweries ... that ancient lineage ... the *continuity* of all that blue blood ..."

"The inbreeding. Those horrid lobeless ears ..."

"And those wonderful private jets and helicopters and servants galore—"

"*Kenz!*" Zandra cried out in distress.

"Wh-what?" asked Kenzie, jerking out of her boozy reverie.

"You're getting carried away!" Zandra accused. "You've got to stop that! You're beginning to make him sound attractive!"

"What? Oh, shit." Kenzie made herself frown severely. "But don't worry. That wasn't me speaking, that was Mr. Smirnoff. All eighty proof of him."

"Then I suggest you tell all eighty proof of him to shut up, or else he's going to make me very, very angry, and you don't want to see that, believe me."

"*You* . . . angry with me?" Kenzie giggled.

"Yes, and it's no laughing matter, either. The von Hohenburg-Willemlohe temper is legendary, and to be avoided at all costs."

"You mean . . . there's an inherited temper in your family?" Kenzie was fascinated.

"Like Hapsburg jaws or those lobeless von und zu Engelwiesen ears." Zandra nodded. "Yes."

"And?"

"And, I think it goes back to Albrecht von Hohenburg-Willemlohe, who in 1680-something cut off the tip of his nose in a conniption fit." Zandra frowned. "Or was that his brother, Lucus? I keep getting them mixed up."

"Go-o-lly!" Kenzie, despite launching into boozy Gomer Pyleisms, was thoroughly enchanted.

Zandra tossed back half her glass and gave a noisy, satisfying burp.

"It really isn't easy, you know, coming from a family with such a frightfully long and wretchedly convoluted history. *Aside* from struggling to keep track of everybody, you wouldn't believe all the hereditary *traits* one's susceptible to. It's surprising one doesn't turn into the worst hypochondriac. I mean, honestly."

Her eyes suddenly widened.

"Oh, shit!"

"What is it?"

"I just remembered! I've inherited more than just the von Hohenburg-Willemlohe temper!"

"What?" Kenzie asked in horror. "Hemophilia?"

"Worse," Zandra gloomed. "Hedwig of Saxony's inability to hold liquor!"

"Don't be silly. You seem to be holding it quite well. You're only one glass behind me, and—"

"Come to think of it," Zandra said dolefully, "poor luckless Hedwig shares another trait with me."

"Which was—?"

"She was much too trusting as far as men went. God, sounds just like me, doesn't it?"

"Zandra, one rotten apple doesn't mean the whole barrel's spoiled."

"Darling, that's easy for you to say. Maybe . . ." Zandra paused. "Yes! Maybe I should just accept my shortcomings. *And* give up men entirely. What do you think?"

Kenzie guffawed. "I think you'd make one hell of a lousy lesbian!"

"I wasn't thinking lesbian, Kenz," said Zandra severely. "I was thinking more along the lines of something . . . noble. You know. Like joining a religious order?"

"*You*—a nun!"

"Well, Mother Teresa *could* use another devoted sister, couldn't she? Washing beggars, feeding cripples, caring for lepers—"

"Zandra!" Kenzie cried in horror. "You wouldn't!"

"Well, you've got to admit those white habits with blue trim look awfully cute."

"They'd look ghastly on you! Turn you into a walking logo."

"Logo? Logo?" Zandra frowned. "Darling, what ever are you talking about?"

"Well, they're . . . they're Pan Am colors."

"Pan Am? What Pan Am? You mean . . . the airline?"

"The one and only. Yep."

"So?"

"*So* . . . Pan Am went belly up."

"Oh, I remember. But how terribly boring. Well, perhaps the Black Hole of Calcutta isn't exactly me. Now, Kenzie. Let me try this one on you. How about one of those orders that wear those giant, starched winged hats? You know the ones. Very *haute couture*. What do you think?"

"No, Zandra, *no.*"

Zandra sighed. "Well, maybe I won't take up the habit then."

"Come on, drink up," Kenzie said, vastly relieved. "The lay life isn't all that bad, once you accept its ups and downs. And besides, despite their failings, men still are the best thing God has come up with, at least until there's a better alternative."

"Which there isn't."

"That's right. So look on the bright side! Zandra, you're exceedingly attractive. Articulate. Sexy. Young—"

"I'll be twenty-*nine* next month, and my biological clock is ticking."

"So? Karl-Heinz isn't the only eligible bachelor out there. The world is full of them."

Kenzie frowned, and her voice suddenly turned introspective.

"Just listen to me. I'm the *last* person who should talk. Who else would have two affairs going simultaneously, and with cops who're teamed up together?"

"Bad girl!" Zandra wagged a smug finger at her. "Shame on you!"

"It's not funny," Kenzie fretted. "Everyone knows that cops and their partners are closer than husbands and wives. So I ask you. How's *that* for emotional stability?"

"Oh, Kenz. At least you're having fun. You are, aren't you?"

"Yeah, but what happens if Charley and Hans exchange bedtime stories?"

"They wouldn't! Would they?"

"You never know." Kenzie drained her glass, lifted the bottle, and morosely eyed the remaining half inch of vodka. "Cops," she declared, pouring herself the rest, "are worse than teenagers when it comes to locker-room stories."

"Couldn't you just drop one of them—" Zandra hicupped "—and keep the other?"

"That's the trouble. I can't make up my mind. When I'm with Charley, it's as if he's the only guy in the world. And when I'm with Hans, I feel exactly the same way!"

"But, surely there are other things besides just looks and sex? I mean, one of them must have some trait you can't stand."

"That's Charley," Kenzie said. "Egotistical and chauvinistic."

"Then drop *him.*"

"God knows, I've tried. But then, when I see him . . . oh, damn! Why does life have to be so fucked up and complicated?"

"You're asking me?"

"Whoops! Sorry. I forgot. Mr. Smirnoff's fault."

"Speaking of whom," Zandra said queasily, "I think I'm t-t-totally smashed."

And with the extreme concentration and overcautious movements of the truly inebriated, she got slowly to her feet.

It was a mistake. The instant she was standing, the room began to spin around her. She swayed dangerously, regained her equilibrium by windmilling her arms, and then held them straight out from her sides, like a tightrope walker.

"D-d-darling, this isn't a revolving room, is it? Like one of those b-b-beastly rooftop restaurants catering to t-t-tourists?"

"Nope, 'fraid not."

"Didn't think so. Fuck. Must have c-c-consumed more than my limit."

Arms still extended, and brow furrowed with concentration, Zandra applied herself to negotiating a few wary steps.

"Here. Better lemme give you a hand," Kenzie suggested.

She got up, and although she *knew* she wasn't on a boat, the deck abruptly listed beneath her feet.

"Uh-*oh,*" she said. "Seems Mr. Smirnoff snuck up on me, too."

She staggered over to Zandra, who looped both arms around her neck.

"D-d-darling, you've been an absolute *angel,* not to mention one d-d-devil of a b-b-bartender," Zandra said, with pie-eyed love. "D-d-don't know whether to kiss you or c-c-curse you."

Kenzie, the slightly lesser soused, took the initiative. Still, it was almost, but not quite, a case of the blind leading the blind, or to be more precise, the drunk leading the drunk.

Weaving unsteadily toward Zandra's room, she got the door open and managed to drag Zandra inside.

And just in the nick of time.

Zandra's arms went slack, and she toppled over backward, falling diagonally across the bed.

She was out like a light.

Kenzie didn't bother undressing her—it was all she could do to make it to her own room and collapse.

From somewhere far, far away in the land beyond sleep, the telephone was ringing. Zandra moaned and rolled over. She buried her face deep into the pillow and pulled another one over her head and held it there until the ringing ceased.

The next thing she knew, Kenzie was shaking her roughly.

"Yo! Sleeping Beauty! Wake up! You've got a phone call."

"Go 'way."

"Zandra! Yoo-hoo. *Zandra!* Wake up!"

Kenzie clapped her hands, then flickered the lights, turning them on and off, on and off.

"Up, up, *up!*"

"Wha-*wha* . . . ?" Zandra muttered thickly.

"You don't get up, you're going to find yourself in Betty Ford!" Kenzie threatened. "Enrolled in a twelve-step program!"

"What time is it?"

"Six in the morning. Now get on the phone. It's about your brother, Rudolph."

Rudolph! The name pierced Zandra's grogginess. Her eyes snapped open and she sat up, instantly regretting the sudden movement. Splinters of pain shot through her skull.

Kenzie picked up the extension phone and thrust it at her.

Zandra fumbled with the receiver; banged it against the side of her head. More splinters shot through her skull.

"Rudolph!" She could barely contain her excitement.

"Zandra?" It was a female voice.

"Yes. Who is this?"

"Penelope Troughton, darling! You know, *née* Gainsborourg? We met again in New York—"

"Oh . . . Penelope. Gosh. Hello. What's this about Rudolph? Did you *see* him? *Talk* to him? Please, you've got to tell me!"

"Actually, I didn't see him. Alex did."

"Alex?" Zandra repeated blankly.

"Alex Troughton. My new husband."

"And?"

"Rudolph's been taken to hospital."

"Hospital!" *Dear God,* Zandra prayed, *it can't be true. Tell me it isn't true!*

"I do so hate being the messenger who brings bad news."

"Penelope! *Please.* Is he—"

"He's alive, if that's what you want to know. But he's in bad shape, darling. *Very* bad shape. From the way he was worked over, Alex says it's a miracle he's even alive!"

The walls seemed to close in on Zandra from all sides.

The way he was worked over. The words reverberated like thunder in her ears. *A miracle he's even alive ... Rudolph ... bad shape ... worked over ...*

Oh, God, she prayed, *please, let him be all right.*

Three-and-a-half hours later, stomach churning and head still splitting, Zandra was over the Atlantic on a British Airways jet, bound for London.

⚝ 39 ⚟

Weatherwise, that Sunday was a 3-D day: dreary, depressing, and dark.

Prince Karl-Heinz's mood was just as somber. Soon after Zandra's departure from Becky V's, he had left also, returning to Manhattan and his Auction Towers penthouse.

There, he had spent the longest night of his memory.

He had tried sleeping, but all he'd been able to do was lie there, as though marooned on that huge giltwood bed as if on a desert island, his mind full of painful reflections and self-reproaches.

He had tried reading. Listening to music. Watching a movie on video.

Useless. Nothing distracted him. No amount of escapist entertainment could detract him from his pain; even the anesthetic of alcohol was unable to fill, however fleetingly, the empty spot in his soul. Over and over, his mind replayed that appalling scene on the snowy rise, when those lamentable words had burst from his lips:

"And if love's got nothing to do with it . . . surely you know about the von und zu Engelwiesen criteria for inheritance . . . could you find it in your heart to marry me anyway?"

He winced each of the hundreds of times he relived that ghastly moment. *Gott im Himmel!* No wonder she had fled! If their positions had been reversed, he would have done the same.

How he could have been so *stupid* . . . so preoccupied with himself, *his* desires, *his* inheritance . . .

Um Gotteswillen, *but I'm an idiot!* he thought. *No—worse. At least an idiot's blunders can be forgiven. Mine cannot—*

—and so he had forfeited Zandra. Forfeited her forever . . .

With excruciating slowness, the endless night had stretched into morning, and daylight, weak and disspirited, revealed a low, uniformly gray blanket of cloud.

But even this was too much light for the bleakness of his mood, the aching emptiness in his soul. Darkness, he sought, the stygian blackness of night; the welcome amnesia of nothingness.

Pressing the button beside his bed, he rang for Josef.

His valet, who was up before the crack of dawn, answered the summons at once.

"Your Highness?"

Karl-Heinz gestured to the windows. "Close the curtains," he said listlessly.

Kenzie called Charley at noon and spoke to his machine. "I don't suppose you want to take your rain check this soon?" she said. "But if you do, just whistle."

Fifteen minutes later he called back, whistling.

"I think I get the message," she told him.

"What about your roommate?"

"She was on the nine-thirty British Airways flight to London."

"This mean we'll be alone?"

"No, I'm expecting my Aunt Ida from Altoona," she said sarcastically.

"Knowing you, it's not that impossible. Okay. When?"

"Soon as I hop out and get some radicchio."

"Tell you what. You put on the soft music, I'll bring the radicchio."

"How romantic. Are we going to do for radicchio what *Last Tango in Paris* did for butter?"

"I don't suppose," he said, "that you saved any of that champagne?"

"You don't mean *yesterday's* champagne?"

"Yeah, I do."

"All gone."

"Ouch."

"Ouch yourself. Everyone knows champagne doesn't keep."

"Don't you have one o' them special gizmos?"

"Gizmos?"

"You know. Those chrome corks you flip open? Seals it airtight?"

"Oh, one of those," Kenzie said dismissively. "Yeah, but it's still not the same."

"Shit. And today *would* be a Sunday. All the liquor stores are closed."

He paused.

"Lemme see what I can do."

Kenzie hummed as she bathed and put on navy blue leggings and a vintage football jersey which reached to her knees. It was khaki, with navy blue stripes on the sleeves, and sewn-on pads at the elbows. Chopin on the CD player, a spritz of Chanel No. 19 on her person, and she was ready to break hearts.

Charley arrived with another bottle of Dom Pérignon. "And for Pete's sake," he said, "don't ask where it came from."

She pecked him on the lips. "Well? Where did it come from?"

"My favorite restaurant. The liquor authority finds out, it's liable to cost them their license. And speaking of costs, don't ask what I paid for it, either."

"I wouldn't give you the pleasure! Awwwww. Just look at you." She ruffled his hair playfully. "My big spender. Guess I'll have to make it worth your while, huh?"

Why was it, Zandra asked herself as she wandered the bleak Victorian hallways in search of Rudolph's room, that hospitals the world over always had to *smell* like hospitals? And why, more often than not, did they have to be housed in what looked like intimidating old armories?

This one in particular was a direct throwback to Charles Dickens—grimy brick on the outside, grim and institutional on the inside—just what you'd expect from a nineteenth-century lunatic asylum. That this wasn't a mental health facility, and that the sick and the infirm were helped and healed here, rather than imprisoned, was somehow difficult to reconcile.

Room 432 . . . 433 . . .

Zandra's heels clacked on the worn, concave granite, echoed resoundingly from the vaulted ceiling and bare walls. In one hand, she was carrying her weekender, still stuffed with the balled-up clothes she'd never unpacked from the weekend; in the other, she held a drooping, pathetic little bouquet of overpriced chrysanthemums she had bought at the airport.

She felt as wilted as they looked, if not worse. The royal hangover she still nursed, despite having thrown up on the plane, stabbed her head, made it feel as though it were a confection of fragile spun glass and would, at any moment, shatter or splinter, breaking up into tiny, murderous pieces.

Room 447 . . . 448—

There! 449!

Unoiled hinges squeaked in protest as she slowly opened the heavy door.

"Rudolph?" she crooned softly.

One look inside, and she fell silent: it wasn't a room, it was a ward. Metal-framed beds of chipped, yellowed enamel seemed to stretch to infinity, and the buckling linoleum, waxed to a mirror finish, reflected the beds lining both sides, giving the illusion they were stacked bunks. At the far end, rain pelted the Gothic windows with the force of thrown pebbles.

Whatever the sun was, or was not, up to on the other side of the Atlantic, she had landed at Heathrow to fog and rain; had arrived in London to see it at its absolute worst.

Welcome home, she thought grimly, quietly shutting the door and making her way down the aisle.

Her eyes scanned the facing rows of beds—all occupied—her gaze darting constantly from left to right, left to right, in search of her brother's familiar, handsome countenance.

What if I can't recognize him? she fretted. *What if his face was so badly damaged, or is so bandaged, that I won't even know him? What if—*

—her heart gave a symphonic surge. There he was! Sallow and pale, eyes closed. Her brother!

So thin he looked. So gaunt and drawn. So *ill,* hooked up to the IVs.

And what were those machines with LED readouts doing at the foot of his bed? And those tubes snaking *out* of it and *into* those huge black leather and Velcro Robocop-looking things, like fat futuristic legs with calipers at the knee joints, which covered both his legs from crotch to ankle?

Good Lord! What's been done to him?

Her footsteps quickened as she rushed over to his bedside.

"Rudolph!" she whispered, dropping her weekender and tossing the bouquet on the nightstand. "Oh, darling, I was out of my mind with worry—couldn't imagine *what* had happened—"

He slept on, dreaming a deep, painless morphine dream.

Oh, how the sight of him hurt her. How the sight of her dashingly handsome brother reduced to this pierced her heart.

How could I have deserted him when he needed me most? she wondered guiltily. *Why didn't I try to help him?*

Tears flooded her eyes as she bent over the bed and kissed his stubbled cheek.

His eyes opened slowly, but they were remote and unfocused. *Narcotized.*

"Rudolph," she whispered, placing her cheek against his. "Darling, it's *me,* Zandra."

"Zan . . . dra," he murmured, his lids drooping shut again.

She straightened and looked around. *I have to talk to his doctor,* she thought. *Or at the very least his nurse. I must find out what, exactly's, been done to him.*

"Rudolph," she repeated gently. "Darling, can you *hear* me at all—?"

"Doubt it," said a cockney voice from right behind her.

She gave a start, twisted around, and looked up. In the excitement of seeing Rudolph, she hadn't even noticed the thin young man who lounged against the bed opposite Rudolph's. Who was cleaning his clear-lacquered fingernails with a penknife.

Do I know him? she asked herself. *Should I? He looks familiar, but . . .*

Unbending herself, she straightened and frowned, trying to place him.

He was hard-faced and well-built, with a russet complexion and beard-shadowed jaw. His features were almost feral and his eyes looked dead, but his shiny black hair was very much alive. No doubt he thought the retro-fifties pompadour made him look like Elvis.

In truth, it made him look like a two-bit hood.

Everything about him gave Zandra the willies. Even his expensive sharkskin suit and shiny, pointy black shoes.

"Shot 'im up good in the operatin' room, they did," he said, pausing amid his manicure to nod at Rudolph. " 'E ain't feelin' no pain, I can tell you that."

"Who *are* you?" she demanded, her forehead creasing. She tilted her head. "Don't I know you from somewhere?"

"I saw to it that your brother was brought 'ere," he said.

"Well, then you're a friend of his," she assumed. "Why didn't you say so in the first place? It's nice of you to visit him, is all *I* can say. Frightfully dreary, these places. Can use jollying up."

"Well, I wouldn't exactly call meself a friend, old girl," he said.

"Oh?" The "old girl" had done it; her frown was deepening. "What *are* you, then?"

"You know. Acquaintances, like?" he said, with a smirk. "Joe Leach's the name, an' burnin' pretty countesses the game?" He winked lewdly, and the smirk turned into a mirthless, stretched grin. " 'Member me now, *countess?*"

"*You!*" she gasped, the deafening memory shrieking through her mind like a runaway train. Unconsciously, she touched her left arm where, last October, he—*this very monster!*—had burned it with his cigar! Her skin was still paler where the burn had healed; always would be, too.

How could I possibly have forgotten him? she thought. *Did my mind try to bury that incident? No. It must be his hair.* Yes, that was it. He'd worn it much shorter then.

"Gave us the slip last October, you did." He winked again, displaying crooked little National Health teeth. "Din't you?"

"Go away!" she hissed shakily. "Leave this place at once!"

"All in good time, *countess.*"

He grabbed the curtain that was attached to overhead tracks and walked around the bed, screening off the space for privacy.

"First," he said, "we're gonna 'ave us a nice little chat, right?"

"*Wrong,*" she said quietly, something hard and unfamiliar coming into her voice. "We have absolutely nothing to discuss, *Mr.* Leach. Now, if you'll be so kind and just leave—"

He ignored her. "We can either 'ave our chat 'ere, or . . ."

"Or what?"

"Or we can 'ave it nice and civilizedlike, over dinner at the Ritz. Never been there with a real *countess* before."

"Honestly," she declared, "I'd rather go straight to hell before I'd dine with the likes of you."

"Yeah—" he winked again "—but would your brother?"

She stared at him. "You wouldn't dare lay a finger on him!"

" 'Ready did. Why you think 'e's 'ere?"

Joe Leach sauntered deliberately back around the sickbed toward her. When they were face-to-face, he raised his penknife so that the blade caught the light and flashed.

This is a hospital, she told herself, *a place of healing. Keep calm. He won't dare do anything. Not in here.*

She held her breath and waited.

After a moment, he snapped the knife shut and pocketed it. "You got more balls than your brother, I'll give you that."

The relief she felt was almost unbearable.

"Well, *countess?* A spot of dinner?"

Zandra raised her chin stubbornly and shook her head. "Why don't you just say what you must and get it over with?"

"Well, *ain't* we tough? Tryin' to make things 'ard fer us, that it? Well, best not blame me for what I gotta do. It's all your fault, see?"

His gray slippery eyes winked obscenely again, and he reached out and took Rudolph's right hand in his.

"Pinkie's first." He held Zandra's gaze. "But what's another broken bone, right?"

"You're bluffing," she said weakly, feeling all sick inside.

"Try me." He held her gaze. "Well? We goin' to the Ritz?"

She *wouldn't* go with him—*couldn't!*—not after what he'd done to her in October; not after what he'd done to Rudolph!

"No," she whispered.

He did it then, his eyes watching her the whole time. Bent the little finger all the way back until it touched Rudolph's wrist.

Zandra winced when she heard the unmistakable snap of the breaking bone. The sound went right through her, and she had to clap a hand over her mouth to stifle a scream.

On the bed, Rudolph barely moaned.

Thank God he's full of painkillers, she thought. *He probably doesn't feel a thing. At least, not yet, he doesn't . . .*

"His bleedin' index finger's next."

Joe Leach smiled cruelly, like a maladjusted youngster pulling the wings off a fly.

Crepe soles squeaked on the linoleum, and Joe Leach hesitated, then reluctantly let Rudolph's hand drop.

A nurse drew aside the curtain. "Mustn't close these, luvs!" the matronly woman scolded reprovingly.

"Sister," Zandra said anxiously, "how is my brother? Can you tell me anything? I just flew in from New York—"

The nurse clucked her tongue sympathetically. "Poor luv," she said, eyeing Rudolph and shaking her head. " 'Ad two smashed kneecaps, 'e did."

Zandra went weak.

Kneecaps smashed by that smirking monster! And he's just standing there, cool as day!

She glared at Joe Leach, felt revulsion and loathing souring her throat. She wanted to launch herself at him, claw at his eyes, rip out his throat.

" 'E was operated on this morning," the nurse added, fluffing Rudolph's pillows.

A terrible fear twisted Zandra's insides. "Will he . . ." she began, and stopped to take a deep breath. "Sister, he *will* walk again, won't he?"

"With therapy, the surgeons think 'e'll recover quite nicely. Replaced both 'is kneecaps with plastic and titanium, they did. But it'll be a few months before 'e's up and about, luv."

It was all Zandra could do not to scream and scream and never stop screaming.

"You all right, luv? You've suddenly gone all palelike."

Zandra nodded. "Yes, I . . . I'm fine, thanks."

"If you're sure . . ."

"I'm positive."

"Good." The nurse gestured to Joe Leach. "This nice gentleman 'ere 'elped bring 'im in, you know. 'E was there when the accident 'appened, and 'asn't left 'is side since. Renews your faith in the 'uman race, don't it?"

Zandra glanced at Joe Leach, who just stood there, smiling like an altar boy. She felt like vomiting.

"Poor dear," the nurse continued, looking at Rudolph. "Imagine, stepping between a parked car and a lorry, and 'aving the lorry back up on you!" She shook her head. "Gives me the shivers, it do. 'Orrible. 'Orrible!"

It's a lie! Zandra wanted to scream. *A damned lie!*

"Doctor will be making his rounds at half-past six," the nurse said. "You can talk to 'im then, luv. I'm sure 'e'll be able to answer all your questions."

She moved off to attend to other patients.

Joe Leach picked up Rudolph's hand again and gave Zandra another stretched grin.

"Funny, innit? It don't even matter if the curtain's open or drawn. I can break every bleedin' finger of 'is, and 'e won't make a sound."

Zandra watched in horror as he took hold of Rudolph's index finger.

"Well, *countess?* You still turnin' down my dinner invitation?"

And he slowly began to bend Rudolph's finger back.

Suddenly Zandra couldn't stand it any longer. "For God's sake, stop it!" she whispered. "I'll have your bloody dinner!"

Joe Leach let Rudolph's hand drop. "Now, why did I 'ave the feelin' you'd see it my way? Well, come on, then. I'm bleedin' 'ungry!"

Zandra followed him in disbelief.

How can he eat after what he's done? she wondered. *How can I?*

* * *

The dining room of the Ritz is probably London's most beautiful public room. All period armchairs, pink tablecloths, and an abundance of gold leaf and crystal, its soaring windows look out at Green Park.

They had an alcove table under one of the murals of Ionic columns wrapped in garlands. That Joe Leach should be sitting opposite her in this otherwise soothing setting was, to Zandra, both discordant and obscene.

Despite his expensively tailored suit, he did not fit in among this sleek, well-dressed crowd. Everything about him shouted lack of breeding—his garish, purple-and-pumpkin striped tie, his gauche manners, his piercing cockney voice. One look, and it was obvious that eating fish and chips out of greasy newspapers was more his style.

Not that he seems to notice or care, Zandra thought.

"I always assumed reservations were necessary here," she said.

"Sure they are." He grinned. "But not if you go puttin' on the Ritz."

"I beg your pardon?"

"Slippin' the maître d' a hundred quid."

"How much?" She stared across the table at him. *He's got to be crazy!*

The unsettling thought occurred to her that he probably was.

"What I want to know is," he said, "if 'e'll give us a table fer a hundred quid, what d'you think 'ed do for two hundred? Drop his undies in public?"

And he laughed so loud that heads turned.

Zandra wished the floor would open up and swallow her. *Please God,* she prayed, *don't let me run into anyone I know.*

Leach snapped his fingers to get a waiter's attention. " 'Ey, guv! Bring us a good bottle of shampoo, and not tomorrow!"

It was all Zandra could do not to get up and leave.

"Figger out what you want to order?" Leach asked her when a bottle of Taittinger Brut Réserve was popped and poured.

"I'm really not hungry."

He ordered for her anyway. "We'll both 'ave the marinaded salmon on the salad of ginger and lime," he said, reading from the menu. "Then the rib roast with Yorkshire puddin'. And sherry trifle for dessert."

Zandra didn't touch a bite. In fact, she didn't even bother pushing the food around on the pink-and-white plates.

"You're wastin' good money," he reproved, talking with his mouth full.

She couldn't bear to watch him. He ate like a pig, with his napkin appropriately tucked into his shirt collar.

She'd never spent such a miserable dinner in her life.

"Now that's better," Leach said, when he finished both their desserts. He pushed his chair back. "Ain't civilized to discuss business on an empty stomach, right?"

She was silent.

He burped noisily, fished a wooden toothpick out of his pocket, and began to clean his teeth.

"Y'know, your brother's a right card 'e is, owin' money and runnin' off like that. Caused my people a ton o' grief."

"Why don't you just leave him alone?" she said quietly.

"Maybe I'd like to. Maybe I'd like to do lotsa nice things for a pretty bird like you." He winked again and laughed. " 'Course, pity's I can't do that. 'E owes my people too much."

"How much?"

"Let's see . . . countin' interest, I'd say it's up to about a flat million pounds."

Zandra was staring at him in shock. When she spoke her voice was hoarse. "A million! You must be joking!"

He kept picking his teeth while he talked. "Interest 'as a 'bit of pilin' up, you know."

She sat there, trying to digest the enormity of the sum.

"Funny, innit? We'd never 'ave found 'im if 'e wasn't so bleedin' stewpid. 'E 'ad 'imself 'idden away where we couldn't find 'im. But 'e just couldn't stay away from the tables. It's 'is undoin', gamblin' is."

There was a long, drawn-out silence.

"Well, he's no use to you in hospital," Zandra said. "Not if you want the money. Did you give that any thought?"

Leach grinned. "Seems 'e ain't much good outta 'ospital either, eh?"

She didn't reply.

His gray eyes darkened. "Got to make an example of 'im. Ain't got no other choice."

Zandra's face was ashen. "Of course you have a choice."

He burped again. "Your brother's got twenty-four 'ours to pay up. After that, it's 'is elbows. Forty-eight 'ours after *that,* both 'is 'ands. 'Uman bones crunch and snap as easy as chicken wings, but I guess you already learned that, huh?"

"You're barbaric!" she whispered, her eyes drilling into his.

He shrugged. "Don't matter *what* I am. What matters is that 'e pays. Otherwise, when there's nothin' left to break, 'e'll be floatin' in the bloody Thames."

Zandra felt a sudden panic. *Oh, God,* she thought. *This can't be real. It's a nightmare, and I'll wake up at any moment.*

Joe Leach grinned again. "Not a pretty sight, floaters. Just ask any copper."

Zandra's expression hardened. "Speaking of which, you so much as touch Rudolph again, and I'll go straight to Scotland Yard. Do I make myself clear?"

Joe Leach's smile faded. "Coppers can't do nothin'! See, your brother's too bleedin' scared to sing!"

"Maybe he is, but I'm not."

He leaned across the table. "Then go to the bleedin' coppers. See if that'll do 'im any good. But I can tell you this much." He stabbed a finger toward her. "You sing, and your precious brother'll be a floater fer sure. And it'll be on your conscience, birdy."

Zandra's mind was reeling. *There has to be a way to save Rudolph!* she thought desperately. *He's my brother! I can't just stand by and let him be worked over and killed.*

Joe Leach excavated his molars with the pick. "Twenty-four 'ours, that's all 'es got, *luv*. Otherwise, 'e'll never move 'is arms again, least not normally."

"You bastard!" Her voice was a whisper. "You get your bloody *jollies* doing this, don't you? You're hoping he can't pay!"

Joe Leach sat there, grinning broadly. *She's right,* he thought. *But there's one thing I enjoy even more. And that's spunky women, especially beautiful spunky women. Getting my hands on them and slowly but surely killing off that spunk is what I really like doing best.*

Zandra took a deep breath. "And if *I* pay the gambling debt?" she said softly. "Then will you leave Rudolph alone?"

He looked at her narrowly. "You got that kinda money?"

"Not yet. But I can arrange it."

"In twenty-four 'ours?"

She shook her head. "I'll need at least two days. Possibly even three."

He puckered his lips thoughtfully. "Aw right," he said at last. "You got sixty 'ours. Period."

Zandra nodded.

"And if the money's not on time, it's bye-bye elbows—*yer* elbows, not yer brother's. You understand?"

She nodded weakly, but her voice was firm. "Yes," she said.

"And you got to pay the full amount. No partial payments."

She raised her chin. "Did I ask for partial payments?"

He didn't reply. "Mind telling me 'ow you're gonna raise it?" he asked.

"As a matter of fact," Zandra said coldly, "that is none of your damn business."

"Hell do you mean? Now that it's *yer* debt, it's my business aw right. Get a bit worried, people owe me big." He made a pistol with his fingers and pointed it at her. "Get my meanin'?"

"And if I don't tell you," she asked facetiously, "what are you going to do then? Tear out my fingernails?"

"If I was you I'd bloody well take this serious, *luv.*"

"Well, you're not me, are you?" she said wearily. "And, you don't really scare me." It wasn't exactly the truth . . . no, not the truth at all. In fact, she *was* scared—scared stiff. But she wasn't about to give him the pleasure of showing it.

With a squinty look, he reached inside his jacket, took out a business card with nothing but a telephone number printed on it, and used a gold pen to scribble down another number and an amount.

"The bank's Barclay's. I wrote down the number o' the account. The money can be wired directly into it, old luv."

He extended the card across the table, holding it between his index and middle fingers.

Zandra snatched it, looked down at it, did a double take, and then glared at him. Her nostrils flared.

"What the hell is this shit? You said the debt was a flat million. Here you wrote down a million and a quarter!"

"Yeah." He grinned and rocked back in his chair. "That includes additional penalties, interest, and transfer of title."

She blinked her eyelashes rapidly. "Transfer of *what?*"

"You know. Transfer fees. Like vehicular ownership registration."

She stared at him. "You really are the most *amazing* first-class prick."

"Yeah?" He leered. "That's me. First class, an' all prick."

She rolled her eyes. "Oh, give me a break," she said in a bored voice.

He stopped rocking his chair and leaned forward. "I'll give you somethin' if you want it, *luv.* An', you don't pay up, I'll give it to you even if you bloody *don't.* See, I'm really lookin' forward to that."

She gestured for him to lean closer. When he did, she said: "Dream about it, arsehole."

He grinned. "I already am!"

The waiter came with the check.

Leach waved a hand dismissively. "Lady's payin'," he said, the toothpick bobbing up and down from the corner of his mouth.

Zandra accepted the salver with the check on it. As soon as the waiter had gone, she said: "I see that I've been mistaken. You're not only a prick. You're a *cheap* prick."

He took the toothpick out of his mouth, leaned across the table, and before she knew what he was up to, stuck it between her lips.

She spat it out in disgust.

"*Adiós,* countess," he smirked, getting up and sketching her a mock salute. Then, adjusting his lapels, he strutted off.

Zandra watched him leave. She didn't know when she had met a more loathsome creature.

Wearily, she turned the check over and stared. Dinner had cost the equivalent of a week's salary.

Reaching for her purse, she blessed the American Express card Burghley's issued its employees.

Thank God I didn't leave home without it, she thought. *If I had, I'd be in the kitchen washing dishes.*

Unknown to Zandra, Joe Leach had passed the maître d' a business card, along with the extravagant tip.

"*Call this number and tell whoever answers to 'ave Freddie meet me 'ere,*" he'd whispered. "*Got that?*"

The maître d' obviously had.

Now, on his way out, Joe Leach met up with the aforementioned Freddie. A handsome man in his early forties, he could have passed for a respectable banker with his bowler, thick topcoat, and umbrella.

"You get a good look at the bird I was with?" Joe Leach demanded.

"Yeah."

"Follow 'er. Don't let 'er out of yer sight. Call me on the cellular phone. I want to know 'er every move."

"Consider it done, guv."

Zandra took the Piccadilly Line back to Heathrow, where she planned to catnap in the waiting room.

I've got to come up with one and a quarter million pounds, she thought over and over. *Almost two million dollars.*

And she had all of sixty hours in which to raise it.

She glanced at her watch and felt a sudden chill. No, that was wrong. Her calculations were flawed.

I have nearly eleven hours until my flight departs, then six hours of flight time, and a good hour or two more to go through customs and get into Manhattan. That leaves me with only thirty-nine or forty hours—if the flight's not delayed!

Zandra sagged in her seat. She was almost physically ill.

One and a quarter million pounds, she kept thinking. *I have to raise nearly two million dollars—or else.*

Meanwhile, the seconds were ticking rapidly toward countdown—

—like the timer on a bomb.

As the train pulled into stations, stopped for passengers to get on and off, and pulled out again, she wondered: *What is my pain threshold? Will I pass out when it becomes unbearable? Will I die?*

She had no idea.

Joe Leach was in one of the posh London casinos he managed when the cellular phone chirruped. "Yeah?"

"She's at 'eathrow."

"Probably waitin' for a New York flight. Stick around and see which one she's on."

"Should I try to detain her?"

"No. Let her go."

I'll have local talent waiting for her in New York, he decided. *They can trail her and make sure she doesn't take a powder.*

40

*M*onday morning in Manhattan. Clouds again. Plus a few rents of pellucid sky, the weather's way of apologizing for all the gloom.

Dina breakfasted with Robert, going on and on about Becky's this and Becky's that. Robert, reading the *Wall Street Journal,* grunted occasionally and did his best to tune her out. If she wanted to hear herself talk, then that was just fine by him. It wasn't as if he *had* to listen. In fact, he'd become highly adept at turning a deaf ear to her chatter while still making the appropriate noises when called for. However, when he heard her mention Auction Towers, he decided it might behoove him to pay attention.

"Back up there, will ya," he grumped. "You're yakkin' a million miles a minute."

"Sweetie!" she accused, with a little-girl pout. "You haven't been listening to a single word I've said!"

"Oh yeah? Then how come I asked you to back up?"

Dina couldn't argue with that. "I was talking about our move," she said.

"Move? *What* move?"

She rolled her eyes. "That's what I *mean,* sweetie. You haven't been paying attention. I told you we'd have to vacate the apartment while it's being redone. Right?"

"So?"

"*So,* it just occurred to me that you've got—what? Thirty? Or is it forty?—unsold condos in Auction Towers. All empty and going to waste."

"They ain't goin' to waste," he said crabbily, alarmed by the direction the conversation was headed.

Thank God his ears had perked up in time to avert Big Trouble. The last thing he needed was to move into the same building as Bambi Parker. As if things weren't dicey enough as they were!

"If they're sitting there empty, then what *are* all those units doing?" Dina asked.

"They're bein' *shown.* Prospective buyers tromp through 'em all the time."

"Through *all* of them?"

"You never know. Why? You suggestin' we *show* a place we *live* in?"

"Of course not, silly!" she said, with a touch of asperity. "I was only trying to save you money, Robert."

Shit, he thought. *Dina save money?* That was a laugh.

"Sweetie, we have to move *somewhere.*"

He had a good mind to tell her, *No, we don't* have *to move anywhere.* He had a good mind to tell her, *I was just getting used to the current decor as it is.* He had a good mind to tell her, *I liked the place on Central Park West the best.* He had a good mind to tell her, *I still miss my good, serviceable GoldMart furniture.* And he had a good mind to tell her, *Above all, I miss my goddamn recliner!*

"I guess you'll just have to find us a place," he said.

"You know that's easier said than done, sweetie."

"Then what's wrong with stayin' in a hotel?" he suggested.

Dina's eyes lit up. "What a good idea!" she squealed. "Oh, Robert! I just knew you'd think of something!"

"You make the arrangements," he told her, and thought: *How much can a hotel suite run? Not nearly as much as an overstaffed apartment. Besides, with hotel services, we can fire everybody—cook, majordomo, maids . . .*

"I'll get on it first thing," Dina promised.

"You do that," he said, congratulating himself on steering her clear of Auction Towers.

"And you'll have final approval of whatever I find," she told him.

"Unh-unh." He shook his head. "I'm much too busy to waste time lookin' at places," he said, deciding to drop by Bambi Parker's later that day. "It's all in your hands."

"You won't be sorry, Robert," Dina said—key words which should have set off all his internal alarms.

But he wasn't listening. Having decided to visit Bambi, he spent the rest of the meal fantasizing about what the morning might bring. Dina would have his ass in a sling if she guessed what he was planning.

Luckily, her mind was on other matters, notably which hotel she preferred—the Pierre, the Sherry Netherland, or the Carlyle—and how many rooms they would need.

Needless to say, her idea of hotel living was different from Robert's. And, best of all, he'd forgotten to put a cap on expenditure, another major mistake.

Not that she saw any reason to broach that particular subject just yet. He'd find out soon enough, anyway.

By which time it would be too late.

Just as well I don't have a window office, thought Kenzie, schlepping into work with a small paper bag containing two paper cups of takeout coffee and two cheese Danishes.

"Rovery!" Arnold Li cried.

"Please," Kenzie begged. "It's too early for that."

"In that case, thank you kindly. Oh. I checked our voice mail. Here're yours." He handed Kenzie pink *While You Were Out* slips.

Kenzie swiftly scanned them. "Nothing from Zandra?" she asked.

"No. Why?"

Taking off her coat and scarf, she quickly filled him in on Zandra's sudden departure.

"Well, time to hit the grindstone," she said. "I might as well start by getting these calls out of the way."

"Forget the calls," Arnold said. "The only important one's the three-one-three area code."

"Three-one-three . . ." Kenzie frowned.

"Detroit and environs. Specifically, Grosse Pointe."

"Ah."

"And, more importantly, it's where one of the bodies is buried."

"Oh-*ho!*"

"Where the bodies are buried" was art world jargon, and referred to certain treasures whose changes of ownership everyone kept track of.

Kenzie felt a potent surge of excitement. "Don't tell me," she breathed, her eyes sparkling. "Da Vinci's studies for his unfinished *Adoration of the Magi!*"

"Bingo! That's the good news."

"Oh. So there's bad news, too?"

"Yep. The trustees for the heirs are trying to pit us, Christie's, and Sotheby's against one another."

"So what else is new?"

"Apparently, they're demanding special terms, *including* a guaranteed flat amount, whether or not the sketches fetch that much."

"Shit," she said quietly.

"I couldn't have expressed it better myself. Christie's will probably balk, but knowing Sotheby's, they'll jump at it. They've done it often enough in the past."

"Not to mention making preauction loans to buyers," Kenzie gloomed.

"Uh-huh. Anyway, I called Sheldon D. Fairey, and he wants to see you ASAP." Arnold swiveled in his chair and picked up his phone. "Just to be on the safe side, I'd better call the airlines and see about getting you on a flight to Detroi—"

He swiveled back around, but Kenzie was already gone.

For once, the dour Miss Botkin did not solemnly usher Kenzie into Sheldon D. Fairey's office—she practically hustled her inside.

"Ah, Ms. Turner."

Sheldon D. Fairey's voice was at its plummiest, and he looked formidable seated behind his mammoth, ivory-inlaid calamander, thuya, and ebony desk.

"Please." He gestured. "Do sit down."

"Thank you, sir."

Kenzie took a seat on one of a pair of Anglo-Indian, carved ebony armchairs and waited.

Shooting back the cuffs of his gorgeous suit of charcoal wool flannel, Sheldon D. Fairey rested his elbows on the tooled green leather writing surface, steepled his pink-palmed hands, and tapped his index fingers against his lips. "I gather you have a good idea why I wished to see you?"

She met his gaze directly. "Yes, sir. The Leonardo sketches."

"Quite right." He nodded and frowned. "Tell me, Ms. Turner. How much would you estimate they are worth?"

Kenzie stared at him. *Oh, boy,* she thought. *Talk about the sixty-four-million-dollar question!*

"Well, sir," she said slowly, "I really couldn't begin to guess. If they are indeed the real thing, they're . . . well, priceless. There's no way I could put a dollar value on them."

"Of course not." He permitted himself a slight smile. "My answer exactly."

She waited.

"Unfortunately, philistine as it may sound, as auctioneers we are in the business of constantly appraising priceless articles expressly to put a financial price on them. Is that not true?"

"I know that, sir, but as for a Leonardo sketchbook . . . Well, first of all, I've never seen any of these drawings in person, only in photographs, and I don't need to tell you that photographs can lie. Also, a lot depends upon the condition they're in. Are they faded? Smeared? Foxed? Torn? And finally, there's the matter of rarity. Leonardos aren't like Picassos. They hardly ever come on the auction block. The last time I can remember was when Basia Johnson—"

"Yes, yes, I know," he said testily, and sighed. "Please, Ms. Turner," he said in a soft voice, "humor me. *Try.*"

Kenzie held up her hands. "That's just it, sir. I don't know! All I can do is speculate, and even then I'd first have to judge their quality, authenticity, and condition. And to do that, I'd have to see them in person."

"I take it Mr. Li told you about the trustees pitting us against Christie's and Sotheby's?"

"Yes, sir."

"Apparently, they're demanding an instant decision—" He held up both hands, palms facing outward, to fend off her protests. "I know, I know. It's highly irregular. However, in view of the fact that they *are* Leonardos . . . well, we must be flexible."

Kenzie was silent.

"Also, the trustees want us—and the other auction houses—to guarantee a certain minimum price. Needless to say, they'll choose whoever's offer is the highest."

"Correct me if I'm wrong, sir, but . . . aren't there twenty-four sketches in all?" Kenzie asked.

"I believe so." He nodded briefly. "Yes."

"Good lord! That means *each* of them may be worth millions!"

"Which is precisely why I'm counting on you, Ms. Turner. We cannot let this opportunity slide through our fingers. I want you to fly to Detroit at once, and if the sketches are indeed authentic—"

"I'll arrange for hotel reservations," she said. "How long do I have? One week? Two?"

He smiled humorlessly. "Several hours, I'm afraid."

"What!" Kenzie stared at him in disbelief. "You *are* joking, sir?"

"If only I were."

"But this is madness! Merely authenticating—"

"I know, Ms. Turner, believe me, I *know*. However, if we want to handle this sale, we are forced to guarantee a price."

Kenzie stared at him. "By 'we,' " she said carefully, "I gather you mean *me*? That *I'll* have to decide?"

"Yes, Ms. Turner," he said. "You will have the authority to make the decision."

She thought: *And be the sacrificial lamb if anything goes wrong.*

He tapped his steepled fingertips. "Therefore, in case they *are* authentic and in good condition, we need to establish what we would consider to be a fair price guarantee. One that would hopefully top Christie's—and especially Sotheby's—offers."

How am I supposed to guess price guarantees? I haven't even seen the damn things. What if they're clever forgeries?

"Ten million?" he asked. "Twenty million? More?"

I've never seen that much money. How many stacks of twenty dollar bills would that make? Suitcases full. It must weigh a ton.

"Naturally, I'll need to clear this with Mr. Goldsmith," Sheldon D. Fairey said, reaching for his telephone and stabbing the number of Robert A. Goldsmith's cellular phone. "Let's just hope to God I can get hold of him. For all we know, he could be in Timbuktu."

If only he were. I wouldn't care whether he's in deepest, darkest wherever—or on land, air, or sea—just so long as it's someplace where no one can reach him.

Fat chance.

Robert A. Goldsmith was not only very much within reach. Unbeknownst to either Kenzie or Sheldon D. Fairey, he happened to be right above them.

In Bambi Parker's twenty-seventh-floor Auction Towers sublet. Lying naked on a fur spread while Bambi, aerobics-firm and pink as a Georgia peach, knelt penitently between his splayed thighs, expertly giving head.

Bambi kept her eyes and ears conveniently shut—the former, the better not to see his gelatinous bulk; the latter, to drown out his obscene, running litany:

"Yeah, baby . . . uh-huh . . . that's right, *eat* Daddy's dick . . . that's a *goooood* girl . . ."

She performed admirably, especially considering that her mind was on cruise control:

One dick is just like the next. I'll pretend it's Lex Bugg's, and that after he's good and hot he'll fuck the bewaddens out of me.

Robert's short but sturdily built penis twitched and strained and grew thicker.

This afternoon's my appointment at Georgette Klinger's. Maybe I'll treat myself to a massage along with my facial.

His wheezy groans were coming faster and she could feel his thighs quivering.

And then I'll stop at Bendel's and splurge on one of those resin and raffia pendants . . .

At this point, his cock was ready to explode, and she could feel the beginnings of a shudder coursing through him when—

Bleat . . . bleat . . . bleat—

His cellular phone began to ring.

Bambi, hoping to bring him to climax sooner rather than later, treated him to an even stronger suction, but his hands pushed her away.

Shit! she thought. *Now I'll have to start all over from scratch.*

"*Ro*-bert!" She sat back on her heels and pouted. "Can't you just let it fucking ring?"

Her perfect blonde hair was mussed and her face was all red from the blood rushing to her head while bending down to suck him off.

"Business before pleasure," he rasped. "Now bring me the damn phone."

She sulked. "*Ro—*"

"Phone."

"Oh, all right!" she said crossly.

Bambi climbed to her feet, got out of bed, and went to fetch it from his coat pocket. When she tossed it at him, he unflipped it, pressed *send,* and grunted: "Yeah."

"Mr. Goldsmith? Sheldon D. Fairey here."

"Whassamatta?"

"Something urgent has come up, and I need your approval."

"Aw right. Gimme it in a nutshell."

Fairey did, and Robert listened, every now and then giving a noncommittal grunt.

Still pouting, Bambi climbed back up on the bed and settled on her haunches between Robert's splayed legs. She could hear the squawk of the voice on the other end, but couldn't make out any of the words.

"I suppose you need an answer now, huh?" Robert was saying. "Okay. About this Ms.—What's Her Name? Turner—"

Bambi perked up at the mention of Kenzie, and silently started mouthing something.

"—you trust her judgment?"

Robert listened some more, ignoring Bambi's furious sign language.

"Aw right, tell ya what. There's twenty-four of 'em? Okay. *If* she's a hunnert percent sure they're the real McCoy, I'll authorize up to eighteen mil. Yeah, for the whole shebang! I don't give diddly what they're *probably* worth. 'Probably' don't cut no ice with me. She has the least doubt, she's to drop 'em. Like a hot potato, yeah. Lemme know what happens."

Robert pressed the *end* button and tossed the phone aside.

"*Ro*-bert!" Bambi complained. "*I'm* supposed to be the head of that department."

He drilled her with his porcine eyes. "Talkin' about *head,* why don'tcha shut up and *gimme* some?" he growled.

"But—"

"Just do as you're told."

Zandra was on a pay phone at Kennedy Airport.

"Gosh, Arnold, Kenzie's *where?* In Detroit? Oh, *I* see. No, it's nothing important. Thanks, Arnold. See you."

She hung up and sighed.

Damn, she thought. *So much for moral support. Well, might as well roll up my sleeves. The sooner I get this nasty piece of business over with, the better.*

41

$\mathcal{P}$rince Karl-Heinz von und zu Engelwiesen had been up since the crack of dawn. Having spent Saturday night and then all of Sunday locked in his bedroom, he had abruptly snapped out of his funk.

One and a half days of soul searching had paid off. He had come to terms with his father's numbered months—or was it weeks or days?—and had resigned himself to losing his inheritance and seeing it passed on to his sister, Princess Sofia's, eldest ne'er-do-well.

Ironically, from the moment he'd accepted that fate, he'd felt strangely buoyant and unencumbered, as though he'd sloughed off a heavy burden.

And the family empire *was* a burden—any multibillion-dollar enterprise is. *Perhaps it's time for someone else to wrestle that multiheaded hydra,* he thought.

Besides, an early retirement appealed. He had a multimillion-dollar fortune of his very own, so he certainly wouldn't starve. And as for the empire . . . well, did it really matter all that much in the greater scheme of things?

Now, seated behind his purplewood *bureau plat* in his Auction Towers study, he signed the last of the documents which had been brought by special air courier from Germany. He looked up as his valet appeared at the door.

"These need to be faxed back immediately, Josef," he said in German as he carefully blotted his signature. "The originals can go by FedEx."

"Yes, Your Highness."

Josef paused, and cleared his throat discreetly. "There is one other thing, Your Highness."

"And that is?"

Karl-Heinz capped his solid gold fountain pen, gathered up the sheaf of documents, and aligned their edges by tapping them on the desktop.

"Countess von Hohenburg-Willemlohe is in the lobby."

Karl-Heinz stopped what he was doing and drew a deep breath. His lips tightened momentarily, and then a kind of gentle sorrow came into his eyes.

So, he thought. *Zandra has dropped by.* He was surprised and yet not surprised. *I wonder what she wants.*

"Invite her up," he said, handing Josef the documents.

Josef nodded solemnly. "Very well, Your Highness," he said, and withdrew, walking backward and bowing formally once he reached the double doors.

Karl-Heinz pushed back his chair, rose from behind the desk, and walked thoughtfully over to one of the windows. He stared out, hands clasped behind his back.

Uniformly low gray clouds pressed down upon the city, shrouding the tops of the tallest buildings. Already at three o'clock, lights glowed brightly in windows, and from far below, the screams of sirens drifted up, ever so faint but nonetheless persistent.

Sirens, car horns, alarms. Those were the sounds he equated with these hard-edged, vertical canyons. No matter how isolated and cocooned one was, the torment of this writhing megalopolis could never be completely silenced. Reality was just a wall away.

Suddenly he longed for the unearthly solitude of his European castles. *Perhaps,* he thought, *it's time I went back and recharged my batteries.*

His musings were interrupted by Cesar. "Countess von Hohenburg-Willemlohe," he announced.

Karl-Heinz turned around. "Thank you, Cesar."

"Your Highness." The majordomo bowed and shut the double doors quietly.

Zandra stood hesitantly just inside the book-lined room. She knew she looked terrible—drawn and pale, her red eyes rimmed with pink from lack of sleep. Having literally been awake for two entire days, her body was worn down by jet lag and jangled nerves, and she was on the verge of exhaustion. Her glands were swollen, and her throat felt raw.

"Well?" Karl-Heinz smiled. "Are you just going to stand there? I don't bite, you know."

She managed a tiny smile. He was right. She was standing there like an idiot.

She crossed the glowing carpet and raised her cheek for his kiss, a greeting which, in her profound agitation, she was too flustered to reciprocate.

"This won't take long, Heinzie," she said apologetically. Her vocal cords were hoarse from lack of sleep. "I'll get right to the point."

"What's the rush?" he said, his voice pleasantly tolerant.

Her breasts rose as she heaved a sigh, and then she tightened her lips and looked down at the swirling pattern of the Aubusson. After a moment, she raised her eyes and met his.

"About this past weekend, Heinzie—" she began.

Karl-Heinz laughed. "Weekend? What weekend? Some things are best forgotten. Don't you agree?"

She shook her head, her face serious. "Please," she said softly. "You're not making this any easier for me."

He looked at her with concern. "Zandra? Are you al—"

"About the weekend. I . . . well, I won't pretend it didn't take me by complete surprise—I mean, *honestly*, Heinzie, it was so . . . unexpected."

She twisted her hands in front of her.

"And I know the way I reacted was beastly. It's just that I was absolutely thrown."

"I think that's forgivable. As I recall, I made rather a mess of it. Tell you the truth, I was appalled with myself."

"Anyway, you're probably wondering, and quite rightly, what the devil I'm doing here. The truth is, I . . . I've come to see whether you might possibly be interested in a business proposition."

"In that case," he said gently, taking her by the arm and leading her to the nearest sofa, "let's have a seat. I make it a point never to discuss business standing up."

She smiled gratefully and sat.

He sank into the chair opposite her. "Can I offer you something? A drink? Coffee?"

She shook her head. "No. I . . . I'd like to get this over with. *Heinzie.*"

She swallowed nervously. She stilled her hands by clasping them firmly in her lap. She crossed, and then recrossed, her splendid legs.

"I won't blame you if you'll think me frightfully despicable—"

He leaned forward. "I seriously doubt that. I don't believe you're capable of doing anything despicable."

"Please!" She heard her own stridency and quickly dropped her voice. "Let me finish before you judge me too hastily," she whispered, looking away, unable to hold his gaze.

He was silent.

"I understand the circumstances which led up to last weekend. I also realize that it must have been damn hard for you." She took another deep breath. "Just as this is damn hard for me."

For fear of saying the wrong thing, he didn't say anything.

"Your proposal . . . well, I assume it really *was* a business proposition—right?"

Something deep inside him twisted excruciatingly, pierced him with brutal, lancinating pain.

Oh, Lord God—if only she knew the truth! If only he could give it voice. More than anything, he wanted to take her in his arms and sweep her off her feet.

"I mean . . ." Zandra looked down at her fidgeting fingers. ". . . I *was* supposed to marry you and have your billion-dollar baby. Presumably, that was the whole point."

"Yes," he said miserably.

She raised her eyes from her lap and held his gaze. "Well? Still interested?"

He was taken aback.

"I mean, why on earth shouldn't you inherit? All it takes is an heir. I mean, what's the big deal of marriage and giving birth? This *is* the nineties. Over half the marriages end in divorce anyway. *And,* we wouldn't exactly have to stay married forever and ever, right?"

"No," he said tightly, "we wouldn't."

"And, since you'll inherit all those billions because of *me* . . . well, I'm entitled to something, wouldn't you agree? Sort of like a . . . a finder's fee . . . or an agent's commission?"

His eyes were hooded. "So you're here to sell yourself," he said in a raw whisper.

"No, Heinzie," she corrected him firmly, "no. Not sell. Rent. You can rent me, Heinzie. Me and my most precious asset, my legitimate, priceless, Holy Roman Empire womb."

"Zandra—"

"Of course, I can't guarantee the sex of the child we'd have, but I'll do my best to see that you'll inherit. I'll even stick around and have a second child, if the first turns out to be female."

"And this . . . this womb rental," he asked dryly, "how much is that going to cost me?"

"Exactly one and a quarter million pounds sterling, for me and my womb both. Payable immediately and in full."

"Why one and a quarter million?" he asked in surprise. "Aren't you undervaluing yourself? Why not a flat quarter billion? Or half a billion? God knows, you're in a position to name your price."

"I already did."

"But why settle for a paltry one and a quarter million?"

She looked away from him. "That is no concern of yours," she said softly.

He sat forward. "Zandra," he said quietly, "are you in trouble? Is that it? You don't need to sell yourself—"

"I'm not selling myself!" she blurted angrily. "I'm renting myself."

"But you don't have to. I'll gladly help you anyway."

Tears threatened to blur her vision, and it was all she could do to fight them back.

"Look, Heinzie, I don't *want* help. This is strictly business. Now, let's make a deal, or let's not. Just tell me which it'll be."

He sighed and looked at her sadly.

"For Christ's sake!" she said angrily. "You need me to inherit! Fine! Here I am. A bloody marvel. The perfect product, all ready for leasing! Now, *will* you make up your mind?"

"Zandra," he said gently, "you're not a product."

Salty tears stung her eyes. "Oh, cut the shit, Heinzie!"

She got up and looked down at him, her anguish apparent.

"Do you, or do you not, want me?" she said quietly. "It's either now or never. Which will it be?"

He rose to his feet. "All right, Zandra," he sighed.

"What does that mean? Yes? Or no?"

"It means yes."

The relief which flooded through her was almost unbearable.

But not because of my inheritance, he wanted to add. *Because you need my help. Because I'm in love with you.*

She fumbled for the business card Joe Leach had given her, thrust it at him, and looked away.

"Wire one and a quarter million into this account at Barclay's, London. The moment it's transferred, I'm all yours."

"All mine?" he said, thinking: *How can you be all mine? The last I heard, nobody's come up with a way to capture a ray of sunshine and bottle it.*

"Yes, all yours. What you see is what you get. All five feet, ten inches of me. Head to toe, golden womb, and all."

He tapped the business card in his hand. "The money will be wired within the hour."

"And there's one more thing," she said.

"Oh?" He raised his eyebrows.

"I want your lawyers to draw up a prenuptial agreement in which I relinquish any and all claims to alimony, inheritance, child support, and anything else."

"Aren't you being a little harsh on yourself?" he said.

She shook her head vehemently. "It's a condition I insist upon."

"Very well," he said. "Consider it done."

She took a deep breath, turned her back to him, and reached behind her head, holding up her hair.

"Unzip me, Heinzie, will you?" Her voice was suddenly strong and sure.

A painful tightness came into his chest. "The money hasn't been wired yet."

"So? You're a man of your word. Best we get a head start, don't you think? Got to make that billion-dollar baby."

She waited, but he still made no move.

"Heinzie!" she said impatiently. "I can't do this on my own, you know. Takes two to make—"

He grabbed hold of her and turned her roughly around. "Zandra, stop it!"

Her eyes went wide with fear. "Does this mean you don't want me? That the deal's off?"

"Don't be silly. But I'm old-fashioned and want to do this the right way."

She stared at him. "Why, I believe you are serious!"

"Very."

"If that's the way you want it," she said softly.

He nodded. "I do."

She looked at him a moment longer, then her chin came up. "Let me know about the arrangements," she said, thinking: *Why does it sound more like a funeral than a wedding?*

"I will."

Her eyes were still on his. Then she reached up, touched him tentatively on the cheek, and swiftly turned and ran from the room.

Only once she hit the street did she allow the poisonous, suffocating cloud to engulf her. Seeking the refuge of the nearest doorway, she hid in its shadows, her forehead pressed against cold, hard granite. Sobs racked her, and burst from deep within her chest.

In one fell swoop she had bartered the only three things she could ever truly, inviolately, call her own: her name, her body, and her self-respect.

Which left her with nothing. Absolutely nothing.

⟋ 42 ⟍

*T*he senior partner of the law firm of Freiman, Steinberg, Hirst, and Andrews, P.C., looked up as his secretary came into his plush office in Detroit's Renaissance Center. He took the sealed envelope she was carrying and placed it solemnly on his desk.

"Sotheby's guarantee?"

"Yes, sir."

"Who is looking at the drawings now?"

"Mr. Adeane and Ms. Blow. From Christie's."

"What about Burghley's?"

"Their specialist is waiting out in reception."

"Good. I take it you walked the Sotheby's representatives to the elevators?"

"I was going to, but they said there was no need."

"What was their mood?"

"*Very* excited."

"Ah. Most excellent. Now then, why don't you tell the Burghley's specialist it'll be a while. Apologize for any inconvenience we may have caused him—"

"It's not a him, sir. It's a her."

"Whatever. You know the routine, Mrs. Silber."

"Yes, sir." The secretary hurried out to the reception area. "What the—" she began, and looked around.

Kenzie had vanished.

A few minutes earlier, Kenzie had been sitting in the posh reception area, bent over a tome on Leonardo drawings she had brought with her when three people approached and stopped beside her chair.

"The elevators are right this way," she had heard Mrs. Silber say.

"Thank you, but we can see ourselves out," a man's vaguely familiar voice replied. "Our flight isn't until seven-fifteen, and we have a few hours to kill. Could you recommend a bar on the premises?"

"Well, there are quite a few," Mrs. Silber said.

"I suppose the restaurants are already closed?" a woman asked.

Her voice also sounded familiar. Keeping her head down, so that her profile was hidden behind her curtain of Prince Val bangs, Kenzie slid the party a curious upward glance.

Standing right beside her, yuppie-perfect and groomed to the nines, were Robert Sullivan and Gretchen Ng—her counterparts from Sotheby's.

"Just take the elevator down to the ground level," Mrs. Silber directed. "When you get out, turn right. There's a very nice bar there that also serves snacks. You can't miss it."

"It sounds perfect," Robert Sullivan told her warmly. "Thanks ever so much."

They exchanged handshakes. "I hope you were pleased with the drawings," Mrs. Silber said.

"Pleased doesn't begin to describe it!" Gretchen Ng enthused. "I'm sure we'll be in touch."

"You have a good flight back, now," Mrs. Silber said. "It was lovely meeting you."

She left, and Robert Sullivan went to the cloak closet to fetch their coats.

Kenzie continued to keep her head down, hoping she wouldn't be recognized.

"This your coat, Gretchen?"

"That's it. God, Bob! Could you believe those drawings?"

"They're incredible. I've never seen anything like them."

"Think we stand a chance of handling them?"

"I don't see why not."

"Yes, but our guarantee—"

"I've got to wet my whistle. Why don't we discuss it over a drink? Got everything?"

And together they left the reception area, opened the glass doors etched with FREIMAN, STEINBERG, HIRST, AND ANDREWS, P.C., and disappeared down the lushly carpeted corridor.

Let's discuss it in the bar . . . Those six little words had done it.

Slamming the book shut, Kenzie shoved it in her shoulder bag and jumped to get her coat.

"If anybody asks, I'll be back shortly," she told the receptionist. "What's the fax number here?"

The receptionist scribbled it down and handed it to her. "Where can you be reached in—"

But Kenzie wasn't listening. She was already flying out the etched-glass doors and down the corridor to the bank of elevators. Pressing the down button, she waited for the next car and took it to the shopping arcade level.

It was bustling with people, and there were shops galore. *I don't have time to search and browse,* she thought. *There has to be a quicker way.*

There was. A uniformed security guard.

She rushed over to him. "Excuse me. Could you direct me to the nearest hair salon?"

"There's one right down there," he informed her, and pointed. "But I'm afraid it's one of those old-fashioned parlors—"

Her heart beat a little faster. *That's exactly what I'm looking for,* she thought.

"Thanks!" she told him.

It really did turn out to be an old-fashioned beauty parlor. The window was shared by faded blown-up photos of outdated hairstyles and faceless Styrofoam heads modeling dusty wigs.

She opened the door and went inside.

For all the Renaissance Center's futuristic sleekness, it was like stepping backward in time. The air stank of permed hair, and women leafing through glossy magazines were seated under a row of noisy hooded dryers.

"Sorry, hon," a red-haired woman in a blue smock and big pale blue designer frames told Kenzie. "We're all booked up."

"That's okay. I just came to see about buying a wig."

"Wig! You sure got the wrong place, hon. We only do *hair.*"

"But . . . what about those wigs in the window?" Kenzie demanded.

"Oh, them. They're just win'der displays. Been there ferever."

Kenzie reached for her wallet.

How much can one of those wigs possibly be worth? she wondered. *Twenty bucks is pushing it.*

She pulled out a hundred dollar bill. "I'd really like the long blonde one."

The woman fished the money from between Kenzie's fingers. "Then it's all yers, hon. I'll go git it right now."

A minute later, Kenzie left the beauty parlor, sunglasses on her nose and mid-1970s Farrah Fawcett tresses bouncing. Catching sight of her reflection in a store window, she paused and cringed.

My own mother wouldn't recognize me.

But then, that was precisely the point.

The cocktail lounge was dim and mostly empty, and its Gay Nineties decor was a salute to petrochemical byproducts: phony "stained glass," red acrylic carpeting, fake gaslights which flickered, and a tufted, red vinyl, horseshoe-shaped bar. There were red vinyl booths along three of the walls, wood-grained formica tables, and laminated Gibson Girl posters on the red-and-gold flocked wallcovering.

What I won't do for Burghley's, Kenzie sighed, lowering her sunglasses a hair to scan the premises from the doorway.

Not that there was much to see. A bored bartender polishing glasses.

Two businessmen at a table. The mandatory drunk hunched over the bar. A sweet-looking, blue-rinse grandmother tanking up on gin. And, occupying a booth in the far corner, Robert Sullivan and Gretchen Ng.

Bonanza!

Kenzie made her way over to them and took the adjoining booth. They both fell instantly silent. Then, obviously dismissing her, they picked up right where they'd left off.

Sitting back-to-back with Gretchen, Kenzie overheard every word:

"Another Kir Royale to celebrate?" Robert Sullivan. *Smug. Confident.*

"You don't think it's premature?" Gretchen Ng. *Guarded. Prudent.*

"Get real, Gretchen! What's there to worry about?"

"Oh, just minor things. Like what if Christie's or Burghley's—"

"Oh, for crying out loud! You know that Christie's is so snooty they'll refuse, and Burghley's is *famously* cheap."

Oh, we are, are we? Kenzie had a good mind to blurt.

The snap of bubblegum cracked like a gunshot. Startled, Kenzie looked up.

"Get ya somethin'?" It was the waitress.

"Oh." Kenzie was momentarily thrown. Then she remembered that she'd better disguise her voice. "Ah . . . ah thank ah'll have a mint julep," she drawled, saying the first thing which popped into her mind.

"One mint julep comin' right up."

The waitress sashayed off and Kenzie settled back to listen.

. . . inarguably the finest drawings I've ever . . .

. . . market's so tiny . . .

. . . even the Royal Library at Windsor doesn't . . .

. . . the Getty Museum, a handful of collectors . . .

. . . twenty mil's awfully little considering . . .

Bingo!

Having found out exactly what she needed to know, Kenzie was ready to split.

"Here ya go!" The waitress set her drink on the table.

"Wha, thank yewwwww," Kenzie said. "How much do ah owe yew?"

"That'll be three ninety-five."

Kenzie handed her a five. "Thank *yewwwww!*"

And leaving her drink untouched, Kenzie hastily gathered up her bag and coat, scooted out of the booth, and hauled ass.

The waitress stared after her, then shrugged and carried the mint julep back to the bar.

Kenzie was speaking into a pay phone.

"Mr. Fairey? Kenzie Turner."

"Yes, Ms. Turner. Have you had a chance to look at the Leonardos?"

"No, sir, not yet. I'm next in line. However, something interesting has developed. You might wish to call Mr. Goldsmith again."

There was a pause. "And what about, may I ask?"

Kenzie told him, then read off the fax number the receptionist had given her.

"Thank you, Ms. Turner," he said. "I'll let you know one way or the other."

Kenzie pulled off the wig, stuffed it in the nearest trash container, and took the elevator back upstairs.

"Ms. Turner?" the receptionist called out. "A fax just came in for you."

"Thanks." Kenzie took it and read:

01/23/1995 15:47 BURGHLEY'S SINCE 1719 PAGE 01
VIA FAX
TO: FREIMAN, STEINBERG, HIRST, AND ANDREWS, P.C.
ATTN: MacKenzie Turner
FROM: Sheldon D. Fairey
Approval granted.
S. Fairey

Now that, Kenzie thought, *was certainly a fast response.*

Mrs. Silber was reporting to the ancient senior partner.

"The experts from Christie's just left, sir."

"And?"

"They said they would be delighted to handle the sale, but declined to leave a guarantee."

"Hmm. That is not entirely unexpected. And Burghley's?"

"Their legal department sent us a fax of a blank sales guarantee for Ms. Turner to fill in. She is studying the drawings now."

"Excellent."

"Yes, sir. However . . ."

"Yes, Mrs. Silber?"

"I'm not sure, sir. It's Ms. Turner. She strikes me as rather . . . unpredictable."

"Does she now? That should make things interesting."

Two attorneys and a security guard were present in the conference room as Kenzie, armed with thin cotton gloves and large padded tweezers, studied the Leonardo drawings in the unforgiving brightness of halogen floods.

Outwardly calm, she was inwardly intoxicated. Her heart pounded and her pulse was going at breakneck speed. She could barely breathe.

Never—not even at Mr. Wugsby's, nor at Burghley's, not even in any museum!—had she ever encountered anything so exquisite!

Dear God, she thought. *Neither the Uffizi's nor the Royal Library at Windsor's Leonardo drawings are comparable to these! They truly are priceless.*

And that there should be twenty-four of them!

It was astonishing. Beyond comprehension . . .

If only I could share this momentous occasion. If only Arnold were here, or Zandra. Mr. Spotts would be in seventh heaven, and as for Mr. Wugsby—that dear old connoisseur would be beside himself, may he rest in peace!

Overwhelmed, Kenzie put the last of the drawings down and sat back. She put the tweezers aside, and slowly stripped off the gloves. Then she shut her eyes and massaged her eyelids.

The drawings seemed indelibly imprinted upon her retina. *If only they would stay there forever,* she thought.

She opened her eyes. "About the minimum sales guarantee," she said softly.

"Mrs. Silber will help you with that," one of the attorneys told her.

Kenzie nodded and rose. "Gentlemen," she said.

"Ma'am." They both got to their feet.

Mrs. Silber was waiting outside and led Kenzie into a small empty office. It had a desk, a chair, and a small copy machine on a table.

"Here is your sales guarantee form," she said, handing Kenzie a one-page document. "You'll notice it's a fax prepared and sent to us by your own legal department on Burghley's letterhead. All you have to do is fill in the dollar amount in figures and script, just as you would a check. Then sign it, make a copy for your files, and seal the original in this envelope. Oh, and be sure and sign it across the envelope flap. Any questions?"

Kenzie shook her head.

"I'll be waiting right outside." Mrs. Silber walked out of the room and shut the door.

Without sitting down, Kenzie read the document, picked up a pen, and filled in the amount:

Twenty million and one dollars and zero cents
$20,000,001.00.

She signed it, made two copies, and slid the original into the envelope. Then she went back outside.

Mrs. Silber registered surprise. "Goodness! That was certainly quick!"

Kenzie handed her the envelope.

Mrs. Silber checked to make sure that the flap was signed. "Well, what did you think of the drawings?" she asked.

"Oh, they were okay." Kenzie affected a bored yawn. "Sorry. It's been a long day. Anyway, thanks. I can see myself out."

The ancient senior partner aligned Burghley's envelope with Sotheby's.
"That's it, then."
"Yes, sir."
"And this Ms. Turner. What was her mood?"
"Decidedly odd, sir. I was told that in the conference room, she seemed literally awestruck. Yet she gave me the exact opposite impression."
"She seems unpredictable indeed. Fascinating. Well, then . . ."
He cleared his throat.
"Call our clients and inform them that the envelopes are ready."
"At once, sir."

Her business completed, Kenzie still had an hour to kill before she had to leave for the airport. Returning to the cocktail lounge, she decided to celebrate with a split of champagne.

This time, she sat as far across the room from Robert Sullivan and Gretchen Ng as possible.

The popping of bubble gum announced the arrival of the waitress.

"Don't tell me," she said to Kenzie. "A mint julep."

Kenzie stared at her, too stunned to correct the order.

"I never forget a face. Frankly, I liked ya better as a blonde. You sorta looked like Farrah Fawcett."

Farrah who? "Gee," Kenzie said. "I'm flattered."

"I'll go get you that drink."

Kenzie watched her sashay to the bar. *I'll be damned,* she thought. When the mint julep came, she drank it.

01/23/1995 19:34 FREIMAN, STEINBERG,
HIRST, AND ANDREWS, P.C. PAGE 01
VIA FAX
TO: BURGHLEY'S, INC.
ATTN: Mr. Sheldon D. Fairey
FROM: Martin D. Freiman
RE: Leonardo da Vinci drawings

Your sales guarantee has been accepted. Please contact Mrs. Silber for details concerning transfer of monies and shipping.

Sincerely,
Martin Freiman

43

"Poor traumatized thing, you proud old-fashioned fool," Kenzie chided affectionately.

She and Zandra were sprawled on the Anatolian kilim sipping Campari and champagne in front of the blazing log fire.

"You told me Rudolph was ducking creditors, but what you conveniently neglected to mention was that he was hiding out from mobsters."

Zandra sniffled and stared into her glass. "There are some things," she enunciated clearly, despite her distress, "which are difficult enough to cope with by keeping them to oneself, without adding to one's misery and making the whole blasted nightmare seem even more real by giving it spoken credence. God knows, it's not like some treat one wants to share. It's bad enough merely having to think about—and that doesn't hold true in England anymore, where it's fodder for the gossip mill and virtually everybody who's anybody, and a lot of people who aren't, are talking about it already. Well, one could go out of one's mind discussing it. I certainly would. Last thing I needed was constant reminding. Not that I could forget. I couldn't. Not for a minute."

Kenzie reached out and touched Zandra's hand. "Silly fool," she chastised gently. "I would have tried to help."

Zandra sighed and looked up, each of her lower eyelids holding an unspilled reservoir of tears.

"Oh, darling, don't you see? There's nothing you could have done. Not a thing. You're an absolute marvel, and bloody wonderful. My one and only true friend on earth, and I'll love you forever. But this thing is bigger than the both of us."

"But I would have been here for you! If I'd had an inkling, I could at least have given you moral support."

"No, Kenzie, no. If I'd talked it out beforehand, I might actually have lost my nerve. Believe me, darling. It was better this way."

"When I think of what you've been through over the weekend!" Kenzie shook her head in amazement. "The marriage plot—"

"—for which I have *two* honorary stepmothers to thank."

"Your brother—"

"—the *turd.*"

"Going to Prince Karl-Heinz—"

"—to *sell* myself."

"And here it's only Monday night! Makes you wonder what Tuesday will bring."

"It *is* Tuesday, darling," Zandra corrected her. "Two-thirty a.m., or thereabouts."

"My," said Kenzie morosely, "time does fly when you're not having fun."

She had arrived from Detroit three-and-a-half hours earlier, and upon letting herself into the apartment at a quarter to midnight, had fully expected to head straight to bed. Finding the living room dark except for the fire, and Zandra sprawled across an ottoman like a pre-Raphaelite funerary figure draped, elegantly weeping, over a tomb, certainly had put an end to that.

Quick thinking—namely an SOS call to the local liquor store, which was in the process of closing, and promises of a *huge* tip, a *humongous* tip—had resulted in first aid in the form of three chilled bottles of Korbel and a one-liter bottle of Campari to be delivered forthwith.

"Oh, Kenzie," Zandra had wailed. "Honestly, darling, it's a total waste of money."

"Let me be the judge of that, will you?"

"But I can't eat or drink a thing, and nothing on earth will cheer me up. Things are too, too serious. If you care about me at all, you'll just go to bed and leave me be."

"Not before you get your prescribed dose of Dr. Turner's Specially Patented Medicine Show Tonic and Cure-All," said Kenzie staunchly, tossing a few more logs on the fire and getting comfy.

She regarded her friend with concern. Poor sweet Zandra. Whatever was the matter, one thing was for certain—this was no time to desert her. Misery needed company. Clearly, some serious drinking was called for.

After all, Kenzie told herself, it was like lancing a boil. Sometimes the accumulated poisons needed to be punctured and drained, or else they could become septic and prove fatal. Twelve-step programs aside, everyone knew that some emergencies simply *required* a good stiff drink.

"Just one little sip," Kenzie had cajoled, "just one teensy little swallow."

And sure enough, one sip had led to another, and then another, and before long Zandra's tongue had loosened and the poisons came spilling out.

"Well, now that everything's out in the open, it's time to forget the bad," Kenzie advised, refilling their glasses and going extra heavy on the Campari. "That's water under the bridge. It's time to ac-cen-tu-ate the positive. Time to look on the bright side of things."

"The . . . bright side?" Zandra echoed suspiciously. "*What* bright side?"

"Well, there's always your prince."

"Heinzie?" gloomed Zandra, chin cupped in one hand. She tapped her cheeks in quick-time with her fingers.

"Now, now. Don't give me that look. Admit it, Zandra. He's definitely the catch of the year."

"Especially," brooded Zandra, "for someone who's not ready for marriage." She took a long pull on her drink and shuddered. "Goodness. Kenzie, since when are we drinking Campari straight?"

"Here." Kenzie grabbed the neck of the champagne bottle and tilted it over Zandra's glass. "That should do it."

"Now where were we?"

"On the bright side," Kenzie said.

"Right. Is it any wonder, darling, that we haven't made a bit of headway? What in heavens could we have missed?"

"Why, the . . . the bundle of joy, of course! Your own wonderful, precious, darling little precocious Serene Highness of a baby!"

"Please," Zandra begged weakly. "Don't remind me."

"Of what? Motherhood?"

"Darling! Did you have to *say* it?"

"But it's wonderful!"

"No, Kenzie, it's not. Motherhood means morning sickness. Motherhood means stretch marks."

"Both of which go away."

"And, motherhood means diapers. Bottles. Formula and rashes, colic and tantrums—"

"For God's sake, Zandra! You'll have a whole army of trained nannies who'll worry about all that!"

"Oh." Zandra abruptly brightened. "Why, yes. I suppose I will . . ."

"And just think. While the rest of us gals are beating the bushes for husbands, *you'll* be floating down the aisle, without even having had to find a man! Wait till word hits Burghley's about this! The girls in The Club'll be scratching your eyes out!"

"Those twits," Zandra said, with disdain.

"Still, you have to admit you'll make a lovely bride."

"Hmm," Zandra said dreamily. "Yes, I suppose I will. Speaking of which, I shall be able to count on you, shan't I, darling?"

"Of course. I'll be beside you every step of the way."

"Oh, good. Then you will be my maid of honor?"

Kenzie stared at her. "But . . . Zandra! What about Dina?"

"What about her?" said Zandra darkly.

"Well, won't she feel snubbed?"

"Dina deserves to be snubbed," Zandra decided. "She can be an attendant. For that matter, Becky can, too."

Zandra giggled for the first time in days.

"As a matter of fact, between Heinzie's friends and relatives, and mine, I'll have the oldest bunch of bridesmatrons ever *seen* at a wedding. And, if I were truly mean and horrible—"

"Zandra . . ."

"—I'd insist they wear the most ghastly dresses in . . . in something like lime green! Or perhaps puce? Which do you think's worse?"

"You wouldn't!" said Kenzie, awed.

"Don't tempt me, darling. It would serve them right, don't you think?"

"Yes, but . . . wouldn't that be rather like using Christmas as a means of punishment?"

"Darling, where have you been? Christmas *is* punishment. Ask anybody. So are weddings."

"C'mon, Zandra. Don't be such a spoilsport. Weddings are fun. And who knows? *I* might even catch the bridal bouquet."

"Did I hear you say bouquet, *singular?* You, Kenzie? Darling, I'm afraid that at the rate you're going, you'd have to catch *two."*

"Now, now, we'll have none of that. We're ac-cen-tu-at-ing the positive. Remember?"

She smiled at Zandra and sighed blissfully.

"A princess. You'll be a real life, honest-to-goodness fairy-tale princess, after all! A von und zu Engelwiesen."

"Shit," said Zandra softly.

"What now?"

"I just remembered. Along with weddings and births come . . . *funerals."*

"So? Zandra, what have funerals got to do with weddings?"

"For a von und zu Engelwiesen, everything, darling. Everything."

"Such as?"

"Such as, one is buried in three different locations. Did you know that?"

"Three . . . ? I . . . I don't understand. Educate me, please."

"All right. Let me see. One's embalmed body goes into a special mausoleum in the crypt of Augsburg Cathedral."

"And what's so bad about that?"

"But one's heart," Zandra went on, "is pickled in some sort of brine or other, then placed in a sealed vessel of some sort, and entombed in the crypt under the chapel at Schloss Engelwiesen."

"You said there were three locations?"

"I'm getting to that. The liver . . . or is it one's bladder or spleen or appendix?—I forget which—is taken to some remote little Bavarian church to which, if you can believe it, people actually make pilgrimages, since it's supposedly famous for its miraculous cures." Zandra shuddered. "Admit it. It's really the most awfully ghoulish tradition."

"Well, at least you're young. Death is still a long way off. Zandra, you have your whole life ahead of you."

"Life! As a von und zu *Englewiesen?* Don't make me laugh. Kenzie, darling, von und zu Engelwiesens don't have lives."

"Oh? Then what do they have?"

"Duties, darling. Von und zu Engelwiesens have duties."

Becky, seated on a goose-stuffed sofa piled with gaufraged cushions of brown silk velvet luxury, said: "*Chérie,* I thought you should be the first to know. Heinzie and I had *déjeuner* together."

It was early afternoon of the following day, and she and Dina were in the *Salon des Cuirs* of Becky's Fifth Avenue penthouse. The painted Cordovan leather panels which gave the room its name, and which looked like splendid figural tapestries, had been attributed—depending upon which expert's opinion was to be believed—either to Govaert Flinck, a student of Rembrandt's, or else to the great master Van Rijn himself.

"And?" Dina, delicate cup of Calvados-flavored apple tea raised to her lips, looked breathlessly over the gilt rim. "Do tell! What transpired?"

"*Voilà.* It is done," replied Becky, Mona Lisa smile in place. "He and Zandra are engaged to be married."

"No!" Dina put down her cup with a clatter and sat forward. "Truly?"

"*Mais oui.*" Becky nodded serenely and sipped tea. "It is a fact."

"But . . . I don't understand! When did all *this* occur?"

"According to Heinzie, yesterday. Apparently Zandra went to see him."

"Oh?" Dina was smarting. She could hear Becky's voice saying something, but the words flowed past her like a rippling stream, and did not register. All she could think of was how embarrassed and—yes, hurt—she felt.

She thought: *After all I've done for her, Zandra didn't even have the decency to call me. If she didn't want to tell me beforehand, she could at least have told me about it afterward.*

But apparently even that had been too much to expect.

I have to hear it from a third party! God, the humiliation!

Then she became aware of Becky's voice. "*Chérie? Chérie,* are you quite all right?"

Dina pulled herself together and nodded. "Yes," she lied. "Of course."

"I take it you have not yet spoken to Zandra?"

"No, not yet."

"*C'est dommage.* I do hope she doesn't hold our *petite intrigue* against you."

"She won't," Dina said with more certainty than she felt. "She'll come around . . ."

She lifted her teacup with trembling fingers and sipped.

"I just don't understand it. Zandra was so dead set against marrying Heinzie. What could possibly have changed her mind?"

"Je ne sais pas." Becky shrugged eloquently. "But it is done. The banns are in the process of being posted."

"And the wedding? When is it to take place?"

"In six weeks' time."

"Six—"

"I know, I know: time is of the essence. *Alors.* You must understand, *chérie*. That, too, is part of the von und zu Engelwiesen tradition." Becky waved a manicured hand, the square-cut emerald flashing from a finger. *"Naturellement,* it goes back hundreds of years, to when the postal systems took months, and there were no such things as telephones or fax machines."

"I suppose," Dina said slowly, "I should call Zandra when I get home."

"C'est une bonne idea." Becky nodded wisely. *"Oui.* I imagine she shall ask you to be the matron of honor."

Dina blinked, momentarily startled. *She will? Why, of course she will!*

Dina immediately felt a whole lot better. Yes, indeed. She was definitely bouncing back after the initial shock.

"At any rate, *ma chère*, I was thinking . . ."

"Yes?"

"Well, you *are* Zandra's best friend, just as I am Heinzie's. *Alors.* It might be a good idea if the four of us got better acquainted, *n'est-ce pas?"*

"What do you suggest?" Dina asked, bowing to Becky's superior knowledge.

"Oh, an *intime* little dinner to celebrate the engagement might be appropriate."

"How clever of you! Yes. I shall arrange it at once!" Dina said brightly, instantly rising to the occasion.

Miraculously, her spirits were already completely restored.

The marble floor of the picture gallery in Schloss Engelwiesen, on the island of the same name, in the lake of the same name—Lake Engelwiesen, the second-largest lake in Bavaria—shone icily, like the surface of the frozen water outside.

One ninety-foot wall of deeply recessed, evenly spaced French windows sent brilliant dazzles of northern light streaming into the long room; hanging from floor to ceiling on the opposite wall were hundreds of gilt-framed Old Masters—superb, museum-quality Bellinis and Botticellis, Rubenses and Rembrandts, Titians and Tintorettos—only the mere tip of the iceberg as far as the von und zu Engelwiesen art treasures were concerned.

And, overhead, suspended from the barrel-vaulted, twenty-six-foot ceiling which had been painted in the style of Charles Le Brun two hundred years earlier, were two rows of thirty matching, rock-crystal chandeliers.

It was a room for contemplation, for feasting the eye and boggling the mind.

At the moment, Princess Sofia was anything but contemplative or boggled. The majordomo had brought her a cardboard FedEx envelope, sent to her from New York by her brother, Prince Karl-Heinz. Opening it, she had found two smaller sealed envelopes inside.

Having torn open the first, she now stalked furious circles, her mauve, ostrich-trimmed gown stirring up great agitated currents of air.

"*Verdammt noch einmal!*" she screeched, waving the thick, engraved invitation so violently she was losing bits of ostrich feathers in the process. "*Do* something, Erwein! Or are you just going to sit there and let our inheritance walk away?"

"What can *I* do?" her husband, Count Erwein, whined from one of the carved, thronelike Louis XIV armchairs which lined the length of both walls. "You know your family's law of inheritance."

"You useless insect!" Sofia's screech was so strident that Etti, Welfy, Popo, and Luisa, her four King Charles spaniels, leapt from their perches and fled the room, ears flat against their heads. "Sometimes I wonder why I ever married you!"

She whirled around, wild things dancing primitive dervishes in her eyes.

"Coward!" she accused. "*Untermensch!*"

Count Erwein Johannes Emmanuel von der Grimmkau cringed and shuddered and tried to make himself as invisible as possible. His wife was one-third princess, one-third long-suffering martyr, and one-third shrew. She had the most terrible temper he had ever known, and he was completely cowed by her. It did not matter that she was beautiful, for Sofia's was a cold beauty, all sharp planes and shiny angles and razor edges. She was one hundred percent von und zu Engelwiesen, with castles and land, riches and power, and blood so blue it made Erwein's own distinguished bloodline and title seem thinly diluted and third-rate by comparison, facts which she never let him forget.

Everything was hers—including a streak of such greed, possessiveness, and envy that all her waking hours were spent on plotting how to get even more. If someone had something she didn't, she could not sleep until it was hers.

And usually, Princess Sofia slept very well.

For whatever or whomever stood in her path, she ruthlessly cut down to disposable size. And whatever or whomever she couldn't cut down or chop up or easily destroy, she weakened through sheer persistence—and eventually triumphed over by scheming.

Princess Sofia was Lucrezia Borgia incarnate. Erwein knew. How well he knew! Because he had suffered more at the hands of this woman than any man should ever have to endure.

Now, Sofia's wrath was building as she worked herself up into one of her world-class rages.

Erwein sat there, trembling and cowering in the thronelike chair. He couldn't imagine a single worse incident for inflaming his wife's temper than the announcement of Karl-Heinz's impending marriage.

Now Sofia will be truly impossible, Erwein thought with trepidation. *If only I could run away. If only I could take a rocket ship to the stars . . .*

"Erwein."

Sofia's voice sent arrows of dread piercing into his flesh, and he looked up guiltily.

"There is only one thing we can do." She paused and gave him a hard look. "It is all up to you now."

"Me?" he squeaked.

"Yes, you. Or don't you love our children?"

"Of course I love them," he lied miserably.

I hate them! he thought. *They all take after their mother.*

"And you want everything to be theirs, do you not?" Sofia went on. "The businesses and castles? The true power of the von und zu Engelwiesens? You *do* want them to have what should rightfully be theirs?"

"I . . . I don't understand," he stammered, and squirmed nervously in his chair.

Sofia smiled without humor. "Oh, I think you do, Erwein."

But Erwein really didn't understand. His mind was incapable of deviousness. He truly had no idea of what she was getting at.

"My father!" Sofia hissed softly, quickly glancing around to make certain none of the multitude of servants was eavesdropping. "Don't you see? Only life support is keeping him alive!"

Erwein sat there and swallowed, his prominent Adam's apple bobbing.

"If Karl-Heinz and that bitch Zandra have a male heir before he dies, our children will end up with nothing! Do you hear me, Erwein? *Nothing!*"

She paused again, and her voice went colder and harder.

"It's up to you to do something, Erwein. For the first time in your life, be a man and *fix* things!"

Erwein felt a suffocating cloud closing in on him. "But . . . but what can I fix?"

"You have only to go to the clinic and unhook my father's life-support system. That is all you have to do, Erwein."

Erwein's eyes got as big and round as dinner plates, and his mouth fell open in protest. But his vocal cords were frozen. He was too shocked to emit a sound.

"For once, Erwein—just for once—you can do something for us and the children. Is that asking for too much?"

Somehow Erwein managed to find his voice. "W-why don't *you* do it?" he whispered.

Sofia stared at him, the thin lines around her mouth tightening. "Believe me, this is not the first time it has crossed my mind. However, until now there has never been any need to resort to it. Heinzie has always been a confirmed bachelor! Who would have thought he'd have it in him to settle down? But *this*—" Sofia brandished the wedding invitation and shook it wrathfully. "—*this* suddenly changes everything! Now, will you do as I ask?"

"But . . . why me?" Erwein whimpered. "Why don't you do it, Sofia? H-he's your father!"

Sofia looked at him with such fury that he cringed, but suddenly she sighed deeply, and her face grew uncharacteristically gentle and pensive.

"I can't!" she whispered, pacing back and forth in a flurry of agitation. "Much as I'd like to, I simply . . . can't. *Um Gottes willen*, he's my *father!* I *love* him."

"I-I can't do it either," Erwein stuttered.

Sofia stopped in midpace and glared at him. "*Was zum Teufel ist los mit Dir?*" she demanded. "It's not like he's your father."

"I-I can't commit murder, Sofia. *Bitte,*" he begged. "Don't ask me to do this. I-I can't."

She looked at him with disgust. "You wretched, spineless little *Untermensch!* Don't think this subject is closed," she said ominously. "We will discuss it later."

Turning away from him, she tore open the second envelope. *Probably something else to do with plans for that* verfluchtes—

She scarcely read a few lines before she let out an unearthly shriek.

Erwein's blood froze.

She balled up the paper and tossed it as far as she could throw it. "I'll kill him!" she screamed. "*Gott behüte!* As you are my witness, Erwein, with my own two hands I will *kill* that rotten brother of mine!"

This, Erwein knew, was an idle threat, and would never happen. For some reason, Sofia never ranted or raved or threw fits in front of her brother. Somehow, Karl-Heinz was the one man she could neither frighten nor intimidate.

"The nerve!" she seethed. "The *gall!* The humiliation! Oh, how dare he? How dare he!"

"Wh-what did he write?"

"He wrote—" Sofia spat bitterly "—that we have to vacate these premises! He *wrote* that he's exercising his prerogative as first-born son! He *wrote* that he intends to make this *Schloss* his primary residence!"

Erwein didn't have to pretend to be shocked. He was, but for altogether different reasons than his wife.

To Sofia, Schloss Engelwiesen had always served as a personal showcase. It was her pride and joy, and although she and Erwein had lived in it through the good graces of Karl-Heinz, she had come to think of it as her very own.

To Erwein, Schloss Engelwiesen meant a degree—however slight—of safety and freedom. Because of its sheer size, it was the easiest of all the von und zu Engelwiesen castles and hunting lodges in which to hide from Sofia.

He couldn't imagine living anywhere else.

"Do you realize what this means?" Sofia keened. "Erwein. Erwein! We'll have to go and live in . . . in Schloss Schweingau!"

Erwein's mind reeled. Schloss Schweingau, traditionally the residence of the eldest von und zu Engelwiesen daughters, was a dreary castle on the shores of that dreariest of all Bavarian lakes, Starnberger See, the very lake in which Mad Ludwig had chosen to drown himself.

Worse, Schloss Schweingau was small, and because of its compact size, Sofia would always be underfoot.

There would be no escaping her.

As these thoughts rushed through Erwein's mind, Sofia pressed one hand to her forehead and turned her back on him. Slowly she walked over to the nearest window recess and stared out across the frozen lake at the view of the distant snow-covered Alps, a view she had always taken for granted.

Tightening his lips, Erwein slid a glance over at the nearest door.

This is my chance, he thought.

Holding his breath, he slipped out of the chair and began to tiptoe stealthily out.

Sofia's voice stopped him before he was halfway there.

"Errrrrweiiiiin," she cooed in that parody of sexual intonations which always caused his hair to stand on end.

Erwein slowly turned around, his eyes white and frightened. He could feel his testes shriveling, and he began to tremble. He knew only too well what was in store. Sofia intended to take all her anger and frustration out on him.

She came slowly toward him, her fingers already unhooking the back of her ostrich-trimmed gown.

Erwein backed away. "*Bitte,* Sofia," he begged. "Don't hurt me?"

"Hurt you!" She laughed derisively and moved inexorably closer. "What makes you think I would want to hurt you, you miserable, cowardly, flatulent little *Maus!* You are not worth hurting!"

Sofia let the gown slide off her shoulders. Like a diaphanous mauve cloud, it seemed to hover in the air before drifting, crackling with static, down to the marble floor.

Naked, Sofia looked even more powerful and deadly than she did dressed. She was a Valkyrie, Erwein decided, not for the first time.

He swallowed nervously, his giant Adam's apple working overtime. A painful erection was already straining against the rough linen undershorts he wore as a kind of hairshirt to discourage tumescence.

Not that it helped. Nothing would, or could—not once he caught sight of his wife's naked breasts.

Sofia slapped her hands sharply against his face and held it captive. Then, yanking his head down toward a thrusting breast, she looked out over his head.

"I only hope for your sake, Erwein, that it turns out to be one hell of a rotten wedding!"

TARGET: BURGHLEY'S COUNTDOWN TO TERROR

Porston Prison, Great Britain, January 27

The Victorians had not built this desolate, top-security prison for rehabilitation. The thickly walled compound with its watchtowers had been built expressly for punishment. It was said to be escape-proof, this island marooned upon the wintry, mist-shrouded moor.

Inside the cell block, footsteps echoed as Leatham, the uniformed guard, semiautomatic rifle at the ready, led the priest and the nun down a grim institutional corridor.

The nun was sweet-faced, and wore the traditional black-and-white habit, complete with wimple and veil, and seemed to glide rather than walk.

The priest was ruddy-complexioned, and had on a black suit with a black shirt and a white clerical collar. He was carrying an ancient leather satchel, the contents of which had already been searched twice.

Inside it were the portable accoutrements for celebrating Mass: a collapsible crucifix, a container for the Host, a missal, a plastic vial of holy water, and two candles.

They came to a steel-barred gate.

At a signal from Leatham, it rolled noisily aside. A few yards farther on, a second, identical gate remained locked.

The priest and the nun looked at Leatham questioningly.

"Father. Sister." With the rifle, Leatham gestured for them to precede him.

The nun eyed the weapon warily as she passed him.

"Sorry, Sister." He raised the barrel higher. "It's necessary, you know. We keep the most dangerous and violent prisoners 'ere."

Smiling sweetly, she nodded and cast her eyes demurely downward.

Leatham followed them and signaled again.

Behind them, the heavy steel gates clashed shut. The nun flinched.

Then the gate ahead rolled open. Leatham led the way and they continued on; behind them, the gate slammed shut.

Leatham said: "Too bad you can't see 'im in the visitin' room. It was built so's you can't see the walls and watchtowers. Just the moor, properlike."

"Good heavens!" the priest exclaimed as they approached a walk-through metal detector flanked by two more armed guards. "Another one of these gadgets!"

"Security in 'ere's tight, Father. 'As to be."

"That's quite all right, my son."

The priest handed over his satchel and a ring of keys from his pocket. "Sister?"

The nun undid the rosary from her waist and relinquished it.

She walked through the metal detector first, and the priest followed. The detector was silent.

The satchel was thoroughly searched for a third time. Then it was handed back, along with the keys and the rosary.

Now they had to pass through yet another set of heavy barred gates.

The nun gazed around in consternation. This cell block was even more eerie than the one they had just left.

No natural light intruded. No windows punctuated thick stone walls. Only naked high-wattage bulbs, mounted high and covered with mesh, glared and cast long evil shadows.

To the left and right, lining both walls, were rows of thick iron doors inset with peepholes. Near the floor, each had a slot where meal trays could be slid through.

The nun glanced at Leatham.

"Solitary confinement," he explained.

She crossed herself swiftly.

He was waiting. Seated on his narrow cot like a predator, head tilted.

They were coming.

Donough Kildare looked down at his hands. Very slowly, and seemingly on their own accord, his strong callused hands began clenching and unclenching.

Freedom.

It was so close he could almost taste it.

As they passed the steel doors, they could hear sounds. Coming from behind one, hisses; from another, crazed laughter; from yet another, screamed curses. And always, from far away, the eternal echoes of slamming gates.

"God help them," the nun whispered.

Another guard, semiautomatic rifle at the ready, huge ring of keys clipped to his belt, patrolled the corridor.

" 'Ello, Brompton," Leatham greeted. "They're 'ere to say Mass for Kildare."

"Well, you'll 'ave to be present, Keith. You know the rules. 'E can't 'ave no visitors alone. Not even clergy."

"We know that," the priest said quietly.

"Might as well get it over with, eh, Brompton?" Leatham said.

"It's yer funeral, Keith."

"Yeh. I guess it is, mate."

Brompton unclipped his ring of keys, selected one, and approached a steel door. He peered in through the peephole and stuck the key in the lock.

Kildare hung his head, clearing his mind, feeling nothing, fearing nothing, doing nothing, permitting events to unfold by themselves. His forearms rested on his thighs and his hands stilled; he appeared relaxed, yet was as tense as a tightly coiled spring.

Suddenly he heard the key being inserted, and what passed for a smile crossed his lips.

His friends were here.

" 'E looks quiet enough," Brompton told the priest and nun. "But be careful. 'E's already got so much blood on 'is 'ands, 'es got nothin' to lose from spillin' more."

"God will protect us," the priest said with quiet conviction.

"Yeh. But if he don't, just 'oller. I'll be right out 'ere."

And Brompton turned the key and swung the door open.

Leatham went in first, keeping his rifle aimed on Kildare, seated on the cot. The priest and nun followed him inside. There was barely room for one; the four of them comprised a crowd.

The thick iron door slammed shut and the key turned in the lock.

They were alone with the killer.

Donough Kildare slowly raised his head and looked up. He was a handsome man of thirty-eight, hard-faced and lean of body. His eyes were the deep dark blue of bottomless lochs, and he had thick black hair, beetling brows, and a full beard.

"You came, priest."

"A man of God always comes when summoned, my son," said the priest, opening his satchel and emptying its contents on the cot. "Are you ready to hear Mass?"

"I'm ready for everything." Kildare smiled, and a dazzling array of shiny white teeth gleamed moistly.

"Then let us begin." The priest made the sign of the cross. *In nomine Patris et Filii . . .*"

"*. . . et Spiritu Sancti.*"

Leatham was Church of England, and to him Latin was mumbo jumbo, as indecipherable, foreign, and lulling as voodoo or Swahili. Numbing enough to put a man to sleep.

Not that he was about to nod off. The cramped quarters of the tiny cell bothered him; kept him alert and on edge. With three of them standing, and Kildare kneeling, he had to keep his rifle aimed at the ceiling instead of the prisoner.

God help us if Kildare tries anything, he thought. *There isn't enough room in here to aim.*

"Mr. Leatham?" the nun whispered.

He relaxed his guard on the trigger and looked sideways.

She was fingering her rosary. "God will forgive us all," she said.

As she spoke, she unscrewed the top of the small crucifix hanging from her rosary. Then, quick as lightning, she plunged the needle into Leatham's side.

He felt the prick and jerked. "What the—"

"Sssssh . . ." The nun put a finger to her lips. "Mustn't talk during Mass, Mr. Leatham!"

And then he was paralyzed by the poison, his lungs unable to breathe. He dropped to his knees, and the nun gently took his rifle.

The last thing he saw was her sweet, gentle smile.

Outside the cell door, Brompton sensed a change in the rhythm of the Latin coming from behind the iron door. He looked through the peephole, but all he could see was the priest's back. He was holding the Host aloft and invoking prayer.

Christ! he thought in disgust. *Bloody Papists! There ain't enough Masses in the world to help fuckin' Kildare!*

Brompton stepped back and began to pace. He wished the priest would hurry the hell up.

How long does a bleedin' Mass take?

Suddenly three bursts of gunfire thundered from inside the cell.

"What the bloody—"

Brompton lunged for the nearest alarm button, and sirens instantly began wailing. Dashing to the door, he peered through the peephole, then swiftly unlocked it and ran inside the cell. Dropping to his knees, he felt all four bodies for pulses.

The nun—dead.

The priest—dead.

Kildare—dead.

He was afraid to turn over Leatham's body. The guard's uniform was soaked with blood. His face was unrecognizable, grisly with flesh and blood and bits of bone.

Oh, Christ—

Taking a deep breath, he felt the neck for a pulse, then twisted around, and screamed: "Get a bloody chopper! *Now!* Leatham's still alive!"

The helicopter climbed and began to turn, then dove into the twilight, skimming across the dark barren moor.

"How's he doing?" the pilot shouted over his shoulder.

"He may make it," the medic shouted back, unaware that the body on the gurney was unstrapping itself. "I don't bleedin' get it. Blood pressure's fine. Pulse is fine—"

He never finished. Donough Kildare, wearing Leatham's uniform, reached up, twisted the young man's neck, and broke it.

A minute later, the screaming pilot was kicked out in midair.

Kildare climbed over the seat, grabbed the controls, and brought the spinning and yawing chopper under control.

Turning it around, he dropped below radar level and headed for the coast—and a rusty tramp freighter which waited, beacons blinking, out in international waters.

The five crewmen were also his friends.

For now.

Book Four

THE BIG BANG

Terrorist Still At Large

LONDON, Feb. 11 (Reuters)—After two weeks of Britain's most intensive manhunt ever, police here and in Ireland admit they are no closer to capturing Donough Kildare, who escaped from Porston Prison on January 27 by murdering five persons.

"It's as if he disappeared into thin air," a Scotland Yard spokesman said, referring to the Irish Republican Army explosives expert who posed as a wounded guard and hijacked a medical emergency helicopter.

In a bizarre twist, IRA leaders stoutly deny any involvement in aiding and abetting the fugitive.

"We've washed our hands of him long ago," reads a statement signed by the most respected and influential Catholic leaders in Northern Ireland. "Years ago he was perceived as a hero, but that was before he became a common terrorist-for-hire."

The manhunt, consisting of forty thousand troops and fifteen thousand policemen, has been the country's largest.

"Quite frankly, we have no idea," the Scotland Yard spokesman said, when questioned whether Mr. Kildare was still thought to be in the United Kingdom. "We've had roadblocks set up everywhere, and all ports of entry and exit have been under tight security."

He added that the helicopter used in the escape has still not been recovered, and that Interpol, the Sureté, and the FBI have been called upon to assist.

"He could be anywhere," he said, "but one thing is for certain. Wherever he is, he isn't there to promote peace."

44

"It's been gorgeous to see you, too, darlings. Actually, I feel frightfully guilty running off, but there's so much to *do*. Can't wait till all this is over. I'm just dying for some girl talk. *Mwah! Mwah!*"

They exchanged a flurry of air-kisses and then Zandra rushed off in a breathless whirlwind of vigorous navy plaids (diagonally patterned vest, horizontal-and-vertically patterned blazer), black turtleneck, slim-cut black leather mini-skirt, tattoo-patterned tights by Jean-Paul Gaultier, and black paddock boots with stacked heels—proof positive that cast-offs, thrift shop finds, and one pair of frivolously expensive tights could hold its own in a restaurant full of the world's haughtiest and hautest couture.

"A bridesmaid, a mere run-of-the-mill *bridesmaid* . . ."

Dina, unable to vent her steam in public, spoke tightly from between falsely smiling lips as she and Becky sat back down on the banquette and watched Karl-Heinz escort Zandra out of Le Cirque, where the four of them had lunched together.

". . . really, sweetie. I've never felt so . . . so thoroughly humiliated."

Becky, wearing a fitted black-and-white plaid wool dress by Valentino, with white collar, big black floppy velvet bowtie, and diamond and onyx cufflinks on starched white cuffs, paused in the midst of lifting a cup of cappuccino to her lips.

"*Chérie,* please. Listen to me. The slight of which you speak, if indeed it *is* a slight—"

"Of course it's a slight. What else *can* it be?"

"—is unintentional. *Oui.*" Becky set down her cup and nodded.

"Unintentional? How can it be unintentional?"

Dina, wearing a fortune of velvet scraps—a fantasy of hand-sewn, crazy-quilt patchwork, from Christian Lacroix—had felt positively matronly beside Zandra's vibrantly youthful, inexpensive outfit. Just another of the many recent injustices she felt she had been expressly selected to suffer.

"Of course Zandra did not mean any harm!" Becky said.

"No? Sweetie, not only did my *so-called* best friend wait this long to ask me . . . and when she *did* it wasn't even to be the matron of honor but a mere bridesmaid . . . and you don't think I should feel slighted?"

"Of course not! You are her oldest and closest friend."

"Oh, really?"

"Oui. You know you are."

Dina, smile cemented on her face, waggled her fingers, returning a wave from another table. "Then why, pray tell, was she too busy—yes, sweetie, *too busy*—for the dinner *I* planned for her? Why did *I* have to settle for this lunch—what?—two weeks later, instead?"

"Chère amie. You must try to understand. Ever since the wedding was announced, Zandra has been deluged. Overnight, she has had to assume endless obligations. Becoming a princess is not easy, you know. There are serious responsibilities."

"Perhaps," Dina allowed. "But where is she off to now, may I ask? Mmm?"

Becky was silent.

"You heard her, sweetie. Why, to Vera Wang's for her bridal gown fitting! And who is she meeting there? Kenzie Turner!"

Becky sighed. *"Chérie—"*

"Every way I turn, I suddenly hear nothing except Kenzie Turner this and Kenzie Turner that! Kenzie Turner: roommate. Kenzie Turner: maid of honor. Kenzie Turner: new best friend."

Becky blew an obligatory kiss at new arrivals.

"So what am I?" Dina demanded. "A discarded piece of baggage? Why, Zandra would never have *met* Kenzie Turner if it hadn't been for me!"

"Chère amie. I know how you must feel. I want you to listen to me. However, what this calls for first," Becky decided, signaling for a waiter with a mere lift of a finger, "is a *digestif.*"

"What this calls for," Dina murmured darkly, "is a hit man who will gun down Kenzie Turner."

"Quelle horreur," Becky said without much concern, and smiled at the approaching waiter. "Two Drambuies, Julian. Please."

"Yes, *madame.*"

When he was gone, Becky said: "What you must do, *chérie,* is keep everything in perspective."

"Which," brooded Dina, "is easier said than done." Her wide-set, ice-blue eyes had turned even more glacial, as remotely and opaquely blue as frosted glass. She couldn't find it in her heart to let Zandra off easily. No: too many wounds had recently been sustained and rubbed raw.

"Quelle sottise! What utter nonsense," Becky said. "Of course it is easily done. Remember: until the marriage, Zandra will be a working girl."

"So?"

"So, have you forgotten that you lead a privileged life of wealth and power?"

"Of course I haven't. But I don't see what that has to do with anything."

"It has everything to do with it, *chérie*. Absolutely everything. You see, at this moment it is only natural for Zandra to gravitate toward Kenzie Turner. She has more in common with her than with you. However, it is hardly worth getting worked up over."

"Hardly worth—"

Dina fell silent as the waiter set down two cordial glasses of dark amber liqueur.

Becky looked up and smiled. *"Merci,* Julian."

"Mesdames." The waiter departed.

Becky lifted the little glass delicately. "Let us drink to the bride-to-be, shall we? You will see. Once the wedding is *fini,* everything will be back to normal."

"You're sure?"

Becky smiled knowingly. *"Mais oui.* Why should it not be?"

"And Kenzie Turner?"

"Shall no longer be Zandra's roommate, nor her closest *confidante.* She will become . . . irrelevant."

Dina stared at her. "How can you be so sure?"

"Trust me, *chérie,"* Becky said patiently. "In time, everything will sort itself out."

"And when everything's said and done," Dina continued thoughtfully, "and the vows are exchanged and Zandra's married, what happens then?"

"Why, then Zandra will have so many responsibilities within her own circle that she won't have time for Mademoiselle Turner. Bear in mind that these are the last few weeks she and Zandra will enjoy . . . well, if not exactly *equal* social footing, then as equal as they will ever be."

A hint of malice touched Becky's Mona Lisa smile. "You do see my point, *chère amie?"*

Dina returned a broad smile. "Of course," she said.

Becky had not only put things into perspective, she had made everything beautifully crystal clear.

What would I do without her?

Dina really didn't know.

"Bon." Becky nodded with satisfaction. "Soon now, Zandra will truly be part of our circle . . . financially as well as socially. Naturally, for friendship she will gravitate toward the one person she knows best. You."

It was just what Dina needed to hear, and she was thrilled to the very tips of her toes. "Sweetie, you wouldn't believe how much better you've made me feel! I'm *so* glad we could have this little chat!"

"Whatever are friends for?"

"And I treasure our friendship," Dina added warmly.

"*Oui?*" Becky looked pleased. "*Alors.* Then let us be profligate and celebrate with one last Drambuie."

"Now, Kenzie, I want your honest opinion," Zandra warned, sailing resplendently out of the changing room on the second floor at Vera Wang's on Madison Avenue.

Kenzie stared at her in wonder, and the coterie of staff stood back and sighed blissfully in unison.

Zandra was wearing a fairy tale gown with a thirty-foot train, a concoction which, veil included, must have required a good hundred-plus yards of antique, off-white Valenciennes lace, not to mention tens of yards of heavy white silk satin, and several thousand freshwater seed pearls.

"Well, darling?" Zandra demanded, hands clasped around a temporary, silk-flowered bridal bouquet. "I *insist* upon the truth, the whole truth, and nothing but the truth, so help you God."

"You look . . . awesome," Kenzie managed, swallowing. "I . . . I'm speechless."

Zandra eyed herself in the surrounding mirrors and frowned. "Awesome . . . speechless . . . Humph! It's awesomely *frothy*," she murmured. "It's hopelessly romantic and insistently *bridal*. Actually, Kenzie, let's cut the shit. If you ask me, it's awesomely awful."

The staff looked at her sharply.

"Zandra!"

Kenzie jumped up from the little chair and walked agitated half circles around her friend.

"It's mind-blowingly gorgeous! I really can't understand what you're complaining about. Why, it would do Princess Di proud. I mean, even the queen mum, bless her tipsy heart, would be hard-pressed not to approve."

"That's the whole point, darling. Kenzie, I do like it, I really do, otherwise I'd never have chosen it in the first place."

"Then what is it?"

"Well, for some extraordinary reason, now that it's made and *on* me, it . . . it seems so frightfully stuffy, so . . . so positively Elizabethan and un-*me*. And, to wear it just the once *and* hate it, I mean, that defeats the purpose, and doesn't begin to justify the cost, now does it?"

The staff exchanged pained expressions. How, they were wondering, could a wedding gown of such regal and incomparable beauty defeat any purpose? And if, as His Serene Highness Prince Karl-Heinz had assured Ms. Wang, money was no object, how could any bride *not* be nuts about the single most beautiful wedding gown ever created?

But Zandra, unfortunately, was not just any bride. She was a designer's nightmare, a reluctant princess bride—in short, as frustrating a client as ever walked through the door.

"Okay," said Kenzie slowly. "Out with it, kiddo. What don't you like about this gown? And I want specifics, because the longer *you're* going to take, the more miserable *you're* going to feel, and the more miserable *you* feel, the more miserable all of *us* are going to be."

"I know, I *know,*" Zandra said in a meek little voice, worrying her engagement ring, the Pink Lady, 14.42 pear-shaped carats of the finest flawless pink diamond in the world.

"Then I suggest we get on with it. The gown fits, doesn't it?"

"Of course it fits," Zandra replied. "That's not the point I'm trying to make, not at all. Oh, Kenzie. Darling, why do I even need a wedding gown? Why can't Heinzie and I just pop by some justice of the peace and get the damn ceremony over with? Is that really asking for too much?"

"It is and you know it. Remember how you told me that the ceremony has to follow certain family traditions and dictates? That otherwise it wouldn't be considered legal?"

"God, Kenzie. You've a memory like an elephant." Zandra scowled prettily. "I see that in future I'm going to watch every word."

"Plus," Kenzie reminded her, "there's the small matter of publicity to consider."

"Oh, Kenzie," Zandra sighed. "I loathe publicity. I absolutely abhor the idea of being in the public eye."

"Well, you'd better get used to it, or else find yourself a different bridegroom."

"That's easy for you to say."

"Zandra, listen to me. I love and treasure my own privacy, so I have a pretty good idea of what yours must mean to you. But good heavens! Your wedding is only one rung below a royal wedding in social stature! Surely there's no way it *wouldn't* attract attention."

"I know," Zandra said glumly, still worrying the giant, scintillating pink diamond. "How well I know it."

"And, since it will be attracting all that attention, how would it look if you went to the altar inappropriately dressed? Especially having to face photographers, reporters, television crews, guests, and God only knows who else?"

"Kenzie, you're frightening me. Frightening me lots."

"You'd feel silly, that's what!" Kenzie continued inexorably. "People would have a fine old time laughing and picking you apart."

"Stop it."

"Don't you *see?* Zandra, to coast through this ordeal as smoothly and easily as possible, and with the minimum amount of fuss, you *have* to look like a dream bride."

Zandra frowned thoughtfully. *Perhaps Kenzie has a point. I never thought of a bridal gown in these terms before.*

"Anything less," Kenzie added, "would only draw that much more attention to you. Besides—" She smiled smugly, neatly pulling out her ace "—there's nothing quite like a bridal gown when it comes to a disguise."

"Disguise?"

"Yes, disguise. Zandra, don't you see? It can make you virtually invisible! Did you hear me? Invisible! It's the *outfit* everyone will be looking at, not the woman beneath the veil!"

Zandra's ears perked up. *Trust Kenzie,* she thought, *to be so practical and sensible. Yes. I was right in bringing her along instead of Dina, who'd have "oooooh-ed" and "aaaaah-ed" and never scratched the surface of the issue.*

"Now, why don't we start over?" Kenzie suggested in a kindly voice. "Tell us exactly how you feel about this gown."

Zandra turned back to the mirrors and gestured at herself. "Well, for one thing, it's too . . . too everything. You know."

"Pretend that I don't."

"All right." Zandra drew a deep breath. "It's too traditional, too romantic, too regal, and too . . . well, too bloody bridal!"

"I see." Kenzie looked taken aback. "Anything else?" she asked wryly.

"Only that it's depressingly virginal." Zandra caught the expressions on the staff's faces. "Oh, dear, seems I've really put my foot in it now!"

"You haven't put anything anywhere," Kenzie assured her. "You're the bride. If you're not happy, no one else will be, either."

Zandra eyed her multiple reflections some more.

"You do see my point, darling, don't you? I mean, I want this to be *my* wedding—not this bloody gown's, but *mine*. Who wants to be upstaged by a dress?"

"Good." Kenzie smiled encouragement. "Now that you're ventilating, we're getting somewhere. Go on. Suggest away."

"Well, couldn't we . . . you know . . . shorten this gown a wee bit?"

Kenzie eyed the floor-length hem. "Shorten it," she murmured.

Zandra nodded.

"Of course it could be shortened . . . if that's what you want. But you do realize it would no longer be a gown, but a dress?"

"Really, Kenz."

"And that you are going to have an old-fashioned wedding? A sumptuous, old-fashioned cathedral wedding, with a cardinal, a prince of the Church, officiating?"

"Now you're being a prude. Darling, nobody said I can't be a *rebel* princess. Did they?"

Rebel princess? Kenzie looked startled. "What is that supposed to mean?"

"All it means, darling, is that I intend to have some fun. And if having fun means making Stephanie of Monaco look like a tame, trained lapdog, then so be it."

"Then make sure the blame's not laid on me. So what do you think? Midcalf?"

"Kenzie, really!" Zandra scoffed.

"Higher?"

"Higher."

"But below the knee?"

"Above the knee," Zandra said adamantly. "Eight inches above."

"Eight?" Kenzie was so shocked that her voice squeaked. "Eight *inches?* Tell me you're only kidding. Please, Zandra, tell me you're joking."

"I want it eight inches above the knee," Zandra said obstinately. "Above the *top* of the kneecap," she added ominously.

"That's what I thought you said. What are you trying to do? Give the European Old Guard communal coronaries?"

"It's about time someone shook those stodgy old dinosaurs awake!"

"But all that bare leg! And in a cathedral!"

"Whoever said the legs have to be *bare?* What do you say to . . . white fishnet stockings?"

"No. Zandra, I forbid it. What do you want to look like? The hook-er bride?"

"Well, then what about . . . lace," Zandra said dreamily. "Lace stockings? Yes. White lace. I love it. Kenzie, darling, *now* we're cooking!"

"If you say so." Kenzie sounded dubious.

"And, I want to wear high, *very* high white stacked heels," Zandra went on, getting into the spirit of it. "But nothing vulgar, like stilettos. Nor platforms. You know . . . sort of like . . . like Lotte Lenya shoes! Very, very ugly, with lots and lots of across-the-ankle straps? Or maybe laces? At any rate, they must be terribly ugly *and* terribly chic." She giggled. "You know, so they look almost *orthopedic?"*

"Zandra . . ."

"And, darling, we'll puff this skirt out further. Like this." Zandra grabbed handfuls of the gown and demonstrated. "A kind of late 1980s pouf. But short-short. Without a train, and the veil reaching exactly to the hem of the dress."

"You'll . . . Zandra! You'll look like a lace bell with legs!"

"Hmmm. Yes, I rather will, won't I? But it's different, right?"

"Oh, I definitely think so."

"And, most important, it's me! Oh, darling, do you realize, this is the most fun I've gotten out of this whole wedding thing so far . . . Now, Kenzie, I want the truth . . . how far should the skirt pouf out . . . to here . . . or all the way to *here . . . ?"*

TARGET: BURGHLEY'S COUNTDOWN TO TERROR

Off Grand Abaco Island, The Bahamas, February 12

Sunset at the 75th meridian.

After the troughs of the wintery North Atlantic, the six-foot chop in the Caribbean was like a placid pond in midsummer.

The small tramp freighter *Beatriz,* on her nineteenth day out of Marseilles, was one hundred twenty miles northwest of Grand Abaco Island when the captain ordered the engines shut down.

Purples and pinks and great chrysanthemum clouds of orange painted the sky and tinted the water. It was the kind of exuberant sunset which at Key West attracts crowds and applause.

Aboard the *Beatriz,* however, nature's fireworks went unappreciated. Four of the crew were busy on the foredeck, where the cargo boom was lifting a ten-meter sailboat from its cradle in the hold.

Across the boat's stern was the legend: ALOHA LADY HONOLULU.

The captain and his sole passenger watched from the bridge as the boom swung the sailboat overboard and lowered it slowly into the water. Two crewmen scrabbled down a rope ladder, unsnapped the blue canvas cover and raised and bolted the foldaway mast in place.

Aloha Lady was fully provisioned with stores, and its diesel tank had been topped off. All that remained was for the 450-square feet of furled canvas to be hoisted, and the trim little craft could sail off into the sunset.

The captain, a stocky Spaniard with skin as deeply tanned and weathered as the shell of a walnut, turned to his passenger.

"So we part here, *amigo.*"

"That's right, *capitán.*" Donough Kildare looked at him through cold, unsmiling Irish eyes. The minor facial cuts he had inflicted upon himself at Porston had healed, and his hair and eyebrows were dyed a yellow-white. "It was a most interesting journey."

The captain burst into jovial laughter. "Interesting! *Por Diós*, but that's the understatement of the year!"

The captain's eighteen-year-old son scrambled up the rope ladder from the sailboat and waved, signaling that everything was in readiness.

"*Adiós, capitán,*" Kildare said quietly.

"*Adiós, amigo.*"

The mate, a gleaming black man with a shaved head, sidled up to the captain and watched Donough Kildare climb down the companionway and cross the foredeck. "I still say we should kill him, mon," he said softly.

The captain shook his head. "He has done us no harm. And he has made us rich."

"I don't trust him, mon. His eyes are the eyes of death."

"*Silencio!* You and your voodoo rubbish. Eyes of death indeed! See, Marcel? There he goes. Now do you feel better?"

They both heard the steady put-put of the sailboat's inboard diesel, and watched the graceful craft motoring away, a black silhouette against the blazing sunset.

Perhaps, the captain thought, *I'll use my share of the money to retire.* His eyes followed the sailboat. *Maybe I'll buy myself a boat like that one.*

A voice intruded on his thoughts.

"*Capitán?*" It was the fat Greek cook.

"What?"

"All the soap powder in the galley is missing."

"So? Get more out of the stores."

"But there were four full boxes—"

"Don't bother me with it."

"*Papá.*"

"*Sí?*"

"I was just in my cabin. I noticed my alarm clock is gone."

"Don't you have work to do? You can look for it later."

"*Capitán?*" The radio operator.

"Now what?"

"The radios. They are both smashed!"

"Whatever is wrong can be fixed or replaced once we reach Grand Abaco."

"*Capitán!*" The engineer.

"What!"

"The barrel of gasoline for the launch. It is empty."

"Get down to the engine room!" the captain bellowed. "*Now!*"

"*Sí, capitán.*"

The captain felt a strong black hand clamp around his wrist.

"Listen to me, mon!" the mate whispered. "Something is wrong. Can't you feel it?"

The captain shook his arm free, went into the wheelhouse, and picked up a telephone receiver. "Start the engines," he commanded.

Soon he could hear the familiar noise as the big diesels were fired up and the decks began to hum and vibrate.

"See?" the captain said to the mate. "You are worse than an old wo—"

He never finished the sentence. There was a sudden blinding flash, and a tremendous explosion lifted the *Beatriz* clear out of the water and then tore her apart, the homemade napalm raining fiery debris all around.

A quarter of a mile away, Donough Kildare braced himself against the shock waves. One moment the *Beatriz* was there; the next she was gone.

All that was left were furiously burning pieces of flotsam.

"*Bon voyage,*" he said softly, giving a sardonic salute.

Then, adjusting his course for Fort Lauderdale, he sailed off into the sunset.

45

Saturday, March 9, the day of the princely wedding, dawned stormy and gray. Princess Sofia awoke to flashing lightning and booming thunder. A fierce rain lashed Schloss Engelwiesen's hundreds of tall windows, and the waters of the lake seemed aboil with malevolent fury.

"*Wach auf!*" Sofia elbowed her husband awake.

"Ow!" Erwein, tasseled bedcap harking back to an earlier century, let out a startled yelp and sat up straight.

For a moment he didn't know where he was. And then he remembered. They were in the bedroom of a two-room suite on the second floor, to which Karl-Heinz had relegated them, and about which Sofia had complained bitterly.

He looked at her. "*Was gebt's?*" he mumbled sourly.

Her eyes glowed like a cat's in the dark. "Oh, Erwein, listen! Just *listen*—" She gestured to the window.

As if on cue, an ear-shattering crack of thunder shook the *Schloss,* accompanied by particularly impressive flashes of lightning.

Sofia smirked. "You see? What did I tell you, Erwein? It is just as I said. The big day," she announced triumphantly, "is going to be a *disaster!*"

"*Ja, Liebling,*" Erwein sighed, thankful that the storm had put her in a good mood. "You were right, as always."

Yes, Sofia thought smugly, *I was.*

Erwein lay back down and fell fast asleep.

But on this day, Sofia's disposition was dependent upon the vagaries of the weather, and it seemed the weather was out to taunt her.

By nine o'clock, she was back on the warpath.

The thunderstorm had long passed, and the prevailing easterly had swept away every last vestige of cloud. The sun shone brilliantly, the deep blue lake was mirror-smooth, and the distant snowy Alps looked like jagged mounds of whipped cream, the view so razor sharp that she felt she could almost reach out and touch them.

Erwein was in the bathroom shaving when he heard her calling.

"Errrrrweiiiiin . . ." she cooed.

His hand jerked, and the pearl-handled straight razor slipped and cut a gash in his cheek.

"Errrrrweiiiiin . . ."

He looked around wildly, desperately seeking escape. Unfortunately, this particular bathroom had only the one door and a small window.

Scheisse! He was trapped.

"Errrrrweiiiiin . . ."

Shoulders slumping, he dropped the razor in the sink. *Might as well get it over with,* he thought miserably.

"*Ja, ja,*" he said, weary resignation in his voice. "*Ich komme schon . . .*"

The wedding ceremony, with typical Germanic punctuality, had been scheduled for exactly two-thirty in the afternoon.

At one forty-five Zandra was still upstairs in the *Brautkammer* of Das Trauungshaus, the von und zu Engelwiesens' bride-to-be's residence in Augsburg, turning a deaf ear to the anguished cluckings of Gräfin Fuchswalder and Baroness Fröhlichhasen, both of whom insisted it was time to head to the cathedral, and—*Gott im Himmel!*—the bride wasn't even dressed yet! As if they could leave without the limousines having arrived, or the trio of aunts—Lady Josephine, Lady Cressida, and Lady Alexandra—part of Zandra's English contingent, still dawdling in their respective guest rooms, presumably powdering themselves or doing whatever it was old ladies did.

Kenzie, who had also stayed the night in this, the finest Renaissance house on the Maximilianstrasse, the finest Renaissance street in all Germany, doubted that those grand old ladies would permit themselves to be rushed.

She herself, however, was pacing the front parlor, the uniquely chic, Empire-waisted violet silk mousseline gown with its one gold-embroidered sleeve and a single long matching gold glove, at odds with her bourgeois agitation.

Weddings always made her uneasy, but *this*—a princely wedding in a cathedral, with a guest list culled from the oldest, the noblest, and the grandest of all European noble families, as well as a veritable *Who's Who* of international café society—only added to her disquiet.

The doorbells chimed, and from upstairs, the voices of Gräfin Fuchswalder and Baroness Fröhlichhasen rose in feverish pitch.

Not that Kenzie could fault them. The two noblewomen, who made their living by arranging proper comings out, weddings, and funerals, had been put in charge of the wedding—a major feather in their hats if it came off well, the certain road to bankruptcy if it didn't.

A uniformed maid showed two identically dressed arrivals, who wore humongous round yellow hats pinned back at the front, into the paneled parlor.

"So where's the bride?" Dina inquired, swirling out of her yellow bouclé coat and turning around in a diaphanous cloud of pale lemon yellow silk.

Kenzie pointed upstairs.

From the sounds drifting down the stairwell, it was obvious that the well-bred composure of the wedding planners was being severely tested.

Becky said: *"Mon Dieu!* Who is making that wretched noise?"

"The Gräfin and the Baroness," Kenzie sighed. "They're worried that Zandra is going to be late."

"How utterly Germanic," Becky pronounced, discarding her coat on a low-backed chair with stretcher-joined legs and gold-fringed velvet. "In my experience, it is the prerogative of a bride to be late to her own wedding. *Alors."*

She looked around.

"A glass of champagne would be exceedingly welcome, *n'est-ce pas?* Especially in view of the fact that a High Mass precedes the ceremony." Dina beckoned imperiously at the maid who was picking up their coats. "Bring us two champagnes, please."

As an afterthought, she glanced at Kenzie.

"Oh. Would you like one, sweetie?"

"That would be nice. Please."

"Three." Dina held up three fingers and spoke as to a child. *"Drei.* Champagne. Chilled. Er . . . *kalt. Kalt!"*

"Chilled champagne, yes," the maid replied in perfect English. "Would you prefer Dom Pérignon or Cristal?"

"Cristal," Dina said, adding, under her breath: "Show off!"

Becky drifted, slapping long yellow gloves in the palm of her hand as she gazed around.

"Wonderful woodwork!" Dina effused.

"Oui." Becky shrugged. "If you like Renaissance *mit* Hun."

Dina frowned. Then, as if truly registering Kenzie, she glided forward for a closer inspection.

"So," she said, pretending to have to search her memory cells. "Ms. . . . Turner! Is that right?"

"That's-a-me!" Kenzie said, trying for humor.

It was lost on Dina, who seemed momentarily at a loss for words.

But no matter—just then the three aunts, slowly descending the staircase, drew their attention. All three wore flower-heavy hats, and Kenzie calculated, correctly, that the slim, haughty one in the lead, Lady Josephine, was the most formidable.

Lady Alexandra, at near eighty the eldest and frailest, was a sweet-faced, gin-scented darling with yellow seed-pearl teeth and a perpetually startled expression, as if surprised to find herself still alive.

Lady Cressida, moon-faced and largish, had an unsettling mongoloid look, with eerie, wide-set pale, pale eyes, each of which went in a different direction, and a tiny horizontal sliver of a lipless mouth.

All three wore outdated, flower-patterned garden party dresses, strands of exceedingly good and very, very large real pearls, and positively reeked of Old Money.

"Z-Z-Zandra?" Lady Alexandra tottered across the room and peered nearsightedly up at Becky, then Dina, and finally Kenzie.

"Zandra's not here, Alex," Lady Cressida half-shouted.

"*What?*" Lady Alexandra cupped an arthritic hand to her ear. "I can't hear you!" she shouted. "Why don't you speak up?"

Lady Cressida took her by the arm. "Looks like Zandra's still upstairs," she said, having to raise her voice. "Where's your hearing aid, dear?"

The ancient lady's chin went up. "I refuse to be seen with it," she shouted with dignity.

"Where *is* it, Alex?"

Lady Alexandra smiled triumphantly. "I flushed it!"

Cressida rolled her eyes. An unsettling sight.

The maid came with the champagne.

"Ah, *gin!*" Lady Alexandra clasped her hands to her flowery bosom. "Lovely."

"No, Alex, it's champagne."

"Oh."

Cressida patted her on the arm. "Don't worry. We'll get you a gin, dear."

Lady Alexandra looked around. "Where's Rudolph?"

"In hospital, dear. Remember?"

"Hospital?" Lady Alexandra blink-blinked her eyes. "But *someone* must give the bride away! Oh, dear. Who will give Zandra away?"

"I imagine I shall," Aunt Josephine intoned regally.

"Oh," Lady Alexandra fretted. "Oh oh oh! If only poor Stefan were—"

" '*Poor*' Stefan *drank* himself to death," Lady Josephine said ominously. "Thank God he's not here. And as for Rudolph—" She pronounced his name with rolling R's, as if it were a two-syllable song "—he'd probably be passed out by now."

"Josie!" cried Cressida, scandalized.

"Well, he would do. Takes after his father," Josephine sniffed.

Suddenly the sound of horses' hooves could be heard outside the window, and a car horn hooted, followed by a rapid-fire stream of urgent German coming from directly above.

Then Baroness Fröhlichhasen leaned over the landing of the staircase, one hand clutching the banister, the other holding onto her big turquoise picture hat.

"The vehicles are here!" she called down. "Help us, somebody! The bride refuses to come out of the bathroom! She has locked herself inside!"

The aunts looked at one another serenely, as if this were common behavior in the family, and was to be expected.

"Please . . . anybody!"

Becky looked at Dina.

Dina looked at Kenzie.

Becky looked at her, too.

Guess I'm elected, Kenzie thought, and hurried upstairs.

Zandra, wearing her white slip and white lace stockings, was doubled over the sink.

She didn't know what had come over her. She had barely picked up her bridal outfit when a rush of intense heat had engulfed her. Dropping the dress, she'd rushed into the bathroom and locked herself inside.

She barely made it in time.

When there was nothing more to throw up, Zandra ran cold water and splashed handfuls of it up into her face and thought, *Some bride I am.*

She stared at her pallid reflection in the mirror.

It must be my nerves. Just a case of the last-minute jitters.

Suddenly a convulsive sob rose from her chest. The reality of the wedding was more than she had bargained for.

It's too much. It's all too damn much. She felt as if her life had spun crazily out of control. *And it has.*

Zandra remembered the poem, "The Road Not Taken," by Robert Frost. *But when,* she wondered, *did two roads diverge for me?* When *had* she taken that first fateful step which eventually led her *here,* to this particular spot, at this very moment?

Knuckles rapped an urgent staccato on the bathroom door.

"Zandra?" The concerned voice was Kenzie's. "You okay, kiddo?"

No. I'm not okay. What did W. C. Fields say? "I'd rather be in Philadelphia."

"Zandra? Will you let me in?"

"One sec."

Swiftly Zandra rinsed out her mouth with handfuls of water and patted her lips dry on a towel. Then she unlocked the door, opened it just wide enough for Kenzie to slip through, and quickly bolted it again.

Kenzie took one look at Zandra and shook her head. "Lord have mercy."

"Is everything all right in there?" Baroness Fröhlichhasen called from right outside.

"It will be, if you'll leave us alone," Kenzie called back. "This is Zandra's wedding. If she's a little late, it won't make the trains not run on time."

Despite herself, Zandra had to giggle. "Gosh, Kenzie. You darling, darling fool. *Mussolini.* He's the one who made the trains run on time, *Mussolini,* Kenzie. Not Adolf."

"Who cares? They both wore weird pants."

"Awfully baggy, weird pants," Zandra agreed, giggling some more. Then her composure abruptly faltered.

"Oh, darling," she gasped. And holding out her arms, she began to weep.

Kenzie engulfed her in a warm embrace. "That's right. C'mon . . . let it all out . . ."

Zandra buried her face in Kenzie's shoulder. "It's as though—" She was racked with sobs "—as though everything's suddenly so . . . *real.*"

"Shush."

"And I'm frightfully scared and—"

"There's nothing to be scared of." Kenzie patted the stooped, heaving bare back.

"But there is."

"Why? Because you can't go through with the wedding? Is that it?"

"It . . . it's not a matter of *can't.* Darling, I-I've got to."

"You do not! You have a God-given right to pursue your own happiness."

Zandra choked back a sob. "I told you. I made a deal."

"So?"

Kenzie pulled away and held Zandra at arm's length. "You know Heinzie won't hold you to it."

Zandra bit her lower lip.

"Don't you?"

"Yes. That's why it's up to *me* not to put *him* in a compromising position."

"Is that the famous von Hohenburg-Willemlohe pride speaking?"

"Oh, bugger pride! I believe in paying debts of honor."

"Zandra, listen to me! Paying one's debts is one thing. But slavery's been outlawed."

Zandra sniffled and wiped her eyes.

"Now, be honest with me," Kenzie said softly. "This is just between the two of us. Okay?"

Zandra nodded.

"Do you love Heinzie?"

"Jesus, *shit,* Kenzie. Hell kind of question is that?"

"The honest kind that requires an honest answer."

Zandra sighed. "Well, if you must know, at times I actually think I do."

"And at others?"

Zandra pinched her slip here and there and pulled it straight. "At others, I'm not quite sure."

"But he did say he loved you?"

"He told me so." Zandra gave an assessing frown. "Yes."

"But you're still not sure?"

"Kenzie," Zandra said. "Whatever powers do you attribute to me? I'm not clairvoyant, you know."

"I know that. But it's not too late to change your mind."

"Yes, but I won't."

Now that her physical upheaval had lessened, Zandra wiped her eyes and peered around, as if to orient herself. With her fingers, she brushed back a tangle of marmalade hair which had fallen over one eye. Then, seeing her reflection, she braced herself like steel.

"God. *That's* me? How could I ever have made such a mess of my makeup! Hand me a tissue, darling, would you?"

Kenzie pulled out a handful.

"Oh, good. Now, if you'll help me repair the damage, I'd walk through hot coals for you."

"I take this to mean you're going through with it?"

"Of course. Told you. For richer, for poorer; for better, for worse. Yes."

"You really *want* to?"

Zandra held her gaze. Her pallor had receded, and some of the color had returned to her face. "Yes, Kenzie," she said quietly. "I do."

"There's no shame—"

"Oh, do stop it. Darling, it was only a case of the last-minute jitters. You know. A bride *is* entitled to an anxiety attack, isn't she? I feel better now. Tons better."

"Prenuptial anxiety? You're sure that's all it was?"

"Yes. And I needed a good cry. Thanks for the shoulder. And for being here. For everything, actually."

"Remember, I'll always be there if you need me."

Zandra took Kenzie's hands and squeezed them.

"I know. And I do appreciate it, darling. Really I do."

She smiled tentatively and Kenzie smiled back.

"Now, before we both get misty-eyed, please. Help me get presentable! There's the makeup to do, and—*shit!* I'm not even dressed!"

They both got busy.

Ten minutes later, Zandra was ready to face the world. The transformation that had been wrought was remarkable.

The uncertain woman who had locked herself in the bathroom had been pale and ill and red-eyed. The one who gazed into the full-length mirror at herself was self-assured and ready to do a cover shoot for *Brides* magazine.

"My God," Kenzie whispered. "You look incredible!"

Zandra hugged her.

"Well? What do *you* think, darling? Shall we put Gräfin Fuchswalder and Baroness Fröhlichhasen out of their misery?"

The square in front of the cathedral wore a festive air. Bells pealed from high in the Gothic spires, and sidewalk vendors were doing a brisk business. The crowd which had gathered included many whose own ancestors had, over the centuries, stood here to watch von und zu Engelwiesens arriving in gilded coaches and carriages for their nuptials.

This being the last half of the last decade of the twentieth century, tabloid photographers were out in full force, and video crews from various countries had come to capture the rich, the famous, and the titled for television.

A roar rose from the crowd as a motorcycle escort in green and white *Polizei* uniforms turned the corner, leading the cavalcade to the cathedral. Behind them came a train of stately Daimlers and Mercedes limousines carrying the bride and groom's closest relatives, the best man, the bridesmaids, and the flower girls.

Next came a group of mounted horsemen who rode two abreast in perfect cadence, their nineteenth-century uniforms exquisite, with polished boots trimmed in gold lace and ceremonial swords in filigreed scabbards.

Behind them, inside a gilded horse-drawn carriage emblazoned with the von und zu Engelwiesen coat of arms, rode Karl-Heinz.

The crowd's cheers intensified as he waved from inside.

His carriage was followed by another group of mounted horsemen, and then came a second, even more elaborate horse-drawn coach.

Now the crowd truly roared, for inside sat Aunt Josephine and, across from her, veiled in white lace, the bride everyone had turned out to see. Zandra turned from left to right, waving at the crowds on both sides.

When she emerged from the coach in front of the cathedral, the crowd went wild. The photographers pushed and shoved, and it was all the phalanx of policemen could do to keep the spectators back.

Baroness Frölichhasen, who had been rushed to the cathedral ahead of time, came hurrying down the stone steps.

"Oh, *danke Gott!*" she prattled nervously. "We are late! The guests are all seated and the cardinal is waiting! As you already know, tradition dictates that the bride must remain hidden in the choir loft until the Mass is over."

She hustled Zandra and Aunt Josephine up the front steps and through the arched portals.

Inside the cathedral, the mighty pipe organ drifted ecclesiastic chords over the swell of murmurs and the rustling of guests.

As soon as the bride and her party were settled, the chords segued into a hymn and the boys' choir rose in unearthly song.

Kenzie, seated on Zandra's left, glanced around.

Lady Josephine, on Zandra's right, sat erect as an old-fashioned head-mistress; next to her, Lady Cressida was smiling into the distance.

And Lady Alexandra, bless her octogenarian heart, beamed happily throughout—aided, no doubt, by the silver flask from which she took occasional swigs.

Eight decades of family weddings, each preceded by a lengthy Mass, had obviously taught her to come prepared.

After the wedding ceremony, the eight hundred guests were shuttled to Lake Engelwiesen by a fleet of limousines and chartered tour buses. There, a flotilla of speedboats ferried them out to the island castle.

In the Hall of Mirrors—Schloss Engelwiesen, like so many palaces built in its day was a direct, if somewhat smaller, imitation of Versailles—the newlyweds received their guests, each of whom was formally announced by a footman.

Becky, on the arm of Lord Rosenkrantz, swept from one ornate room to another, admiring the painted ceilings here, giving a critique of the ceramics there.

The children of Zandra's cousins Emily, Elodene, Francesca, Adrian, Timothy, and Christopher, a veritable army of pretty little girls and miniature gentlemen, happily forgot their manners and played tag, screaming and racing around the guests until they switched to less strenuous, and far more suspenseful, games of hide-and-seek.

Princess Sofia, dressed in black mourning, marched around dourly, her stinging glares and rebuking frowns expressing disapproval of this invasion.

Erwein, wisely, had made himself scarce.

Dina floated around in a state of enchantment, wondering how best to approach Robert about buying her a castle, preferably in France, and not too far from Paris. Lady Alexandra fell asleep in a chair, which two footmen lifted and carried upstairs, where they laid her in bed. Kenzie met Zandra's dashing, newly divorced cousin, Adrian, who plied her with champagne in hopes of taking her to bed, efforts she easily resisted.

The receiving line continued for nearly an hour and a half, and Karl-Heinz's hand was sore from congratulatory handshakes. Zandra, as radiant as ever, wondered how much more hand-kissing she would have to endure from the men; how many more women would kiss her flushed cheeks.

At last, the guests were shepherded to the sit-down dinner, for which one hundred round tables, each seating eight, were set up in an enfilade of ten adjoining rooms, each of which had its own string quartet and one footman for every four guests.

Finally, the twelve-tier, fourteen-foot-high fantasy of a wedding cake, decorated with lacy spun sugar and one thousand white sugar roses, was wheeled into the Hall of Mirrors.

The bride and groom cut the first slice, and more magnums of champagne were popped. A dance orchestra played waltzes and fox-trots.

Kenzie, watching the newlyweds dance the first waltz beneath the candlelit chandeliers, tried to discern Zandra's true feelings. Whether her friend was still haunted by doubts, or whether she truly was the happy bride she outwardly appeared to be, was impossible to tell.

Later, a million-dollar fireworks extravaganza drew the guests to the windows, after which the newlyweds made their getaway in a waiting executive helicopter.

All in all, the fairy-tale wedding had done Gräfin Fuchswalder and Baroness Fröhlichhasen proud. The majority of the guests lingered and drank too much. The children dropped from exhaustion. Sofia stalked the premises in search of Erwein.

And Kenzie, who had caught the bridal bouquet of miniature white roses and lilies of the valley, sat in a window seat in one of the empty rooms, dreamily wondering who would walk *her* down the aisle—

—and when.

❧ *46* ❧

*K*enzie flew back to New York the following day. The magic of Zandra's wedding was behind her, and she felt curiously out of sorts. It wasn't at all the way it had been during the flight over to Europe.

She and Zandra had flown together, and they'd made it into a midair party, gulping glassfuls of champagne and vowing eternal friendship, no matter what. They'd reminisced and laughed and cried.

Now, returning by herself, Kenzie was hit by an aching loneliness which was intensified when she let herself into her apartment.

It seemed eerily quiet.

I miss Zandra, dammit! she thought, walking around and opening the windows to air out the stuffy rooms. *She was the sister I never had, the best friend I could tell anything. And now she's up and married.*

There would be no more late-night gab fests. No more waiting turns to use the bathroom. No more sharing of makeup and secrets or of rushing off to work together.

Living by herself again would take getting used to.

She unpacked her suitcase and hung away her maid of honor gown.

"The reason I chose this *particular one,"* Zandra had confided, *"is because it's* absolutely *appropriate for just about any formal occasion. I mean, why just wear it the* once?*"*

The words echoed in Kenzie's head, brought home just how empty and purposeless and devoid of meaning her life really was.

I'm twenty-eight years old and still single. I've devoted seven years to musty old paintings and foxed drawings. And what do I have to show for it? Two boy toys, neither of whom is ready for a real relationship.

She sighed to herself. What it came down to was that she had nobody.

Might as well face it, Kenz, she told herself. *There's no house with a picket fence in* your *future.*

She finished unpacking, put her suitcase away, and went to the kitchen to make herself a cup of Earl Grey tea, another legacy from Zandra. While it steeped, she checked her answering machine.

The LED display indicated six messages. She punched the playback button.

Charley: "Hey-a you hot-a mama! It's-a me—" Fast-forward.

Hannes: "Kenzie, it is me. I was wondering—" Fast-forward.

Mr. Spotts: "Hello, Kenzie. This is A. Dietrich Spotts. I'm soaking up the rays down here in the Sunshine State, and just got through talking to somebody who talked to somebody . . . well, to make a long story short, I heard there's an opening in the department. I know of a young woman named Annalisa Barabino who trained under Fiorentino at the Ambrosiana, and then worked at the Uffizi. I told her to contact you." Beep.

Woman with a thick accent: "Hello? Ms. Turner? This is Annalisa Barabino. I'm sorry to call you at home. Mr. Spotts said he would contact you—" *I'll listen later.* Fast-forward.

Voice from home: "Hi, sweetheart. It's Dad. How's my little girl? Just calling to wish you a happy birthday—"

Kenzie punched the *pause* button and frowned. *What's with this happy birthday—?*

And then she suddenly remembered. He was right.

Today *was* her birthday. She'd turned twenty-nine.

"The answerin' machine. The fuckin' telephone answerin' machine!" Charley steamed, angrily returning from the pay phone at Live Bait, on East Twenty-third Street. "All I get's the fuckin' telephone answerin' machine!"

He threw himself into his chair, took a swig from his beer, slammed the mug down, and glared broodingly at the gaggle of leggy young models clustered in front of the bar.

"You know what I'd like?"

"No," Hannes said, in an attempt to humor him. "What?"

"To go back in time." Charley nodded. "That's right. Just like in *The Time Machine.* Or *Back to the Future.*"

"But why should you want do do that?" Hannes sipped his own beer slowly.

"Because that way I could get my hands on the dipshit who invented that infernal machine! I'd be able to strangle the livin' daylights out of him *before* he can invent it!"

Charley gulped beer and wiped his mouth on his sleeve.

"Come to think of it, same goes for the inventor of the car alarm. Yeah. How many times has their racket kept you awake? Huh?" He didn't wait for a reply. "Justifiable homicide," he growled, "that's what it would be. Isn't a jury in the country wouldn't acquit me!"

He finished off his beer and signaled the waitress for another.

"Why don't we leave," Hannes suggested. "It's late, and we've both had enough to drink."

"Oh, for cryin' out loud, don't start naggin'. I want another one for the road." Charley looked up at the waitress. "Two more. One for my buddy and one for me. With two chasers of—" He looked at Hannes. "What's that stuff you drink in Finland? Acquavit? Or is that Sweden?"

"Charley, we don't need—"

"Neh, neh, neh! *Shit*," Charley brooded. "You're startin' to whine like a goddamn wife!" His eyes narrowed. "Didn't you have a phone call to make?"

"Yes." Hannes got up. "Just a beer for me," he told the waitress.

"Two peppermint schnapps," Charley ordered. *"Two."*

Hannes threaded his way past the tables to the phone. He could feel Charley watching him and ignored the appraising eyes from several extraordinarily beautiful young women and at least two exceedingly handsome young men. He dug in his pocket for a quarter and dropped it into the phone and punched.

There was an explosion of breath behind him, and then a strong hand came around and depressed the cradle. The coin clinked and fell into the return slot.

Hannes turned around in surprise, receiver in hand.

Charley glared angrily. "You fuckin' bastard," he said tightly.

Hannes looked at him blankly. "What's the matter?"

"You wanna step outside?"

Hannes hung up the phone. "Why?"

"Why?" Charley's face twisted with rage. "You know very well why, you fuckin' son of a bitch!"

Hannes stared at him. "Actually, I don't," he said calmly. "Perhaps you'd like to tell me?"

"You were calling *her!*" The words tore from Charley's lips.

"Yes?"

"Who the fuck you think *I* called?" Charley shouted.

All around, conversation in the room suddenly fell silent. Two sturdily built men came slowly from the bar where they had been chatting with some girls.

Hannes could feel the momentary suspension of time as all eyes fixed upon him and Charley.

Not that Charley was aware of the audience. He was raging. His fiery Italian temper and chauvinistic possessiveness had him in its grip.

"Why the hell can't you find your own woman! Unless you get a special charge out of stealin' someone else's? That it? Guess it makes you feel more like a man?"

Hannes stared at him for a moment as everything suddenly fell into place. Then some of the tension went out of him. "Is that who this is about? Kenzie? You have been seeing her also?"

"Yeah," Charley snarled belligerently. "As if *you* didn't know!"

"I didn't," Hannes said quietly. "I thought it was over between the two of you. Why didn't you say something?" And with that, he turned and began to walk away.

But Charley wasn't finished with him quite yet. He spun him around and slammed him up against the wall.

"Listen, you cocksuckin' douche bag!" He had Hannes by the shirt. "You think I'm gonna let you get away with this?"

Hannes stared at him coldly. "I think you'd better get your hands off me."

Charley's right arm arced and his fist blurred, but Hannes intercepted it, grabbing Charley's wrist with his left hand and bringing it to a complete standstill in midair.

Only the quivering of both their arms showed the effort it took to still the blow.

"As you can see," Hannes said softly, "we are not evenly matched. Now, I suggest you settle down and I'll help you sober up. Afterwards, we can discuss this like gentlemen."

"Gentlemen!" Charley spat, eyes ablaze. "What would you know about bein' a gentleman?"

"Don't do it," Hannes warned, sensing that Charley was doubling up his knee to kick upwards. "I do not want you to get hurt."

"Me get hurt? By you? Don't make me laugh!"

The anger abruptly left Charley, and he let go of Hannes and stepped back.

"I'm goin'. But believe me—" He pointed a trembling forefinger at Hannes "—*You* haven't heard the last of *me!*"

Then he turned and stomped out. The crowd at the bar parted silently and let him pass.

There was a communal sigh when he was gone, and the patrons began to murmur. The two bouncers made their way back to the bar. Then somebody laughed, and conversations continued where they'd left off.

Hannes decided to leave also. He stopped at the table, tossed several bills down, then he made his way past the bar.

"Yo. Buddy." It was one of the bouncers.

Hannes looked at him.

"Nice work, blocking that fist. How'd you do it?"

"You don't want to know." Hannes turned away.

"Whoa, there."

Hannes looked back. "Yes?"

"Where's the fire? Whyn't ya give it a minute? You know." The bouncer nodded toward the front door. "Let him cool his heels out there some more?"

"I'll be fine," Hannes said.

But he wasn't fine. His nose was bloody and he had an ugly gash on his forehead when he staggered, doubled-over with pain, up the front steps of Kenzie's building.

He leaned on her doorbell.

"Who is it?" she squawked over the intercom.

"Hans."

"Can't it wait? I just flew in from Europe."

"Please. Something's . . . happened."

There was a pause, and Kenzie buzzed him in. She was upstairs, leaning over the landing, barefoot and in her nightgown, when he stumbled in. The moment she saw the way he was staggering, she ran down to help him.

"My God!" She draped one of his arms over her shoulder and let him lean his weight on her. "What happened?"

"Just . . . get me . . . upstairs," he gasped.

She did as she was told, got him inside, and bolted all the locks. Then she looked at him. "Who did this?"

"You really don—"

"Cut the shit, Hans." She stared at him, gingerly touching his puffy eye. He was going to have quite a mouse. "It was Charley," she said quietly, "wasn't it?"

"Forget it," he muttered thickly.

"Come on. Let me get you into the bathroom and clean you up. You look like shit."

She gave him a level look.

"And then you've got some major explaining to do."

It was seven-thirty in the morning when Kenzie's alarm went off. She groaned and rolled over. She wasn't nearly ready to get up. Her head throbbed, and she was bleary and depressed from being up half the night playing Florence Nightingale.

That on top of jet lag.

I'm getting too old for this shit, she thought.

She was tempted to call in sick, but decided against it. Having taken Thursday and Friday off to attend Zandra's wedding meant that work would be piled up. And, with Zandra gone, the department was short-staffed. Arnold had been holding down the fort alone. *It's not fair to expect him to carry the entire burden.*

Sighing, she crawled reluctantly out from under the covers, took a quick shower, and somehow made it in on time.

Arnold swiveled around on his chair. "Ah so," he greeted. "Insider has finarry arrived with the scoop! I want to hear arr about oh-so honorabbe wedding!" He dropped his routine and said: "And that means dishing the *dirt!*"

"How about over lunch?" Kenzie begged weakly. "I'm only half alive, and there's tons I've got to catch up on."

"Lunch is fine, and *I'll* even buy, so long as *you* promise not to leave anything out!"

"I promise," Kenzie smiled. She washed two aspirin down with her coffee and got busy.

At ten-fifteen, Bambi popped her head into Old Masters.

"Hi guys!"

"Hi," Arnold mumbled, not deigning to look up.

Kenzie turned around. "Hi."

"I'm glad you're back," Bambi told her. "Personnel ran an ad in yesterday's *Times* to find a replacement for Zandra. The applicants are waiting out in reception. I'd interview them myself if I had the time, but I've simply got to get my hair cut. You don't mind, do you?"

"Of course not." Kenzie smiled brightly, which wasn't easy. Time had only intensified her loathing for Bambi.

"Great. I knew I could count on you."

Couldn't you just, Kenzie thought.

"Oh. And one more thing."

Kenzie waited.

"One girl out there looks like a *dog,*" Bambi warned. *"Definitely* not Burghley's material, if you get my drift?" She cast Kenzie a significant look.

Kenzie nodded and smiled until it hurt.

"It's all in your hands," Bambi said severely. "You may use my office."

And she breezed back out.

"It's all in your hands," Arnold mimicked archly as soon as she was gone. "I've simply got to get my hair cut."

Kenzie cracked up. "Arnold, will you *stop,*" she pleaded. "I've got to be serious for this."

"All right, just so long as you don't hire any *dogs,*" he guffawed. "We want Burghley's material!"

Kenzie dug through a stack of color photos and selected a handful.

"Arnold, where did you put the sample canvases?"

"They're down in the vault. I'll go get them."

Kenzie went to Bambi's office, waited until Arnold had brought the canvases, and then called reception. "How many job applicants are there for the Old Masters position?"

"Eight."

There goes lunch, Kenzie thought. *I owe Arnold dinner.*

"Okay," she said. "Send the first one in."

The interviews began.

On the surface, each of the first seven applicants seemed well-groomed, bright, articulate, and qualified. Their ages ranged from the mid-twenties to the late thirties.

The five women were attractive, appropriately dressed, and perfectly made up. The two men were handsome and wore expensive conservative suits. Each had worked at one of the other auction houses or a gallery, and while their résumés were impressive enough, Kenzie knew better than to trust in that alone.

She used the photos and sample canvases to test their expertise. All seven misidentified at least two of what should have been ten easily distinguishable works. That was bad enough. But it was the close-up photos of various artists' brushstrokes and techniques which proved everyone's undoing.

Not one of the seven passed.

Kenzie was aghast. *Good Lord,* she thought. *I wouldn't want to have to rely on any of them! They're all hopeless!*

She ended the seventh interview the same as all the others, with a brisk handshake, a smile, and the words: "Thanks so much for coming in. We'll be in touch."

To let you down easily, she didn't say.

She called reception. "I believe there's an eighth applicant?"

"That's right. Would you like me to send her in now?"

"Please," Kenzie said.

Before long, there was a loud crash outside the door. Kenzie gave a start and got up to investigate. When she opened the door, she found a woman on her hands and knees, retrieving a pile of dropped books.

"I'm sorry," the woman murmured, glancing up nervously.

Kenzie smiled. "That's quite all right. Do you need help?"

"No, no. Please." The woman bit her lip. "You are . . . Ms. Turner?"

Kenzie groaned inwardly. *Oh, no,* she thought. *Don't tell me.* "Yes . . . ?"

"I'm here about the interview."

So this is who Bambi meant. "Well, you'd better come in, then."

The woman tottered inside and put her books down on a chair.

She was, to put it generously, a frumpy plain Jane. She was of average height with a splotchy complexion. Mousey hair pulled back in a bun, little wire-rimmed granny glasses, and no makeup.

Her clothes were drab and two sizes too large. The cuffs of her cardigan were so long they hid all but the tips of her fingers.

The nails were bitten down to the quick.

Kenzie felt a wave of pity. *Dear God, how do I handle this? I mustn't hurt her feelings.*

"Please." She indicated a seat and smiled, she hoped reassuringly. "I take it you've brought a résumé?"

"A . . . résumé? Oh. Yes. I have . . ."

The woman dug through a handbag which had been repaired with duct tape, and the papers she produced were wrinkled and grease-stained. She did her best to smooth them with her hands.

"*Scusi.*" She smiled apologetically as she held them out.

Kenzie took them. "All right, let me just glance over this a mo—"
Her smile froze. "It says your name is . . . ?"

"Annalisa Barabino," the woman supplied.

"Right," Kenzie said weakly, wondering: *Why does this have to be the woman Mr. Spotts called about? Why couldn't it be someone less clumsy and more presentable?*

Yet despite its condition, the résumé was highly impressive.

But then, it would have to be, for Mr. Spotts to recommend her.

At this point, Kenzie was beyond surprise. She simply presumed Annalisa would pass every test with flying colors, which she did. Her eye was superb, and her knowledge encyclopedic.

If only, Kenzie thought despairingly, *she didn't look like a bag lady!*

"Mmm," she murmured, drumming her fingernails on the desktop.

"Please? Is something wrong?"

Yes. Everything.

"Well, er, it has to do with your . . . ah, image," Kenzie said tactfully.

"My—"

"I have an idea," Kenzie said. She snatched up the phone and pressed three digits. "Arnold? SOS."

"What's wrong?"

Kenzie glanced at Annalisa and smiled to put her at ease. "Eliza Doolittle requires Professor Higgins."

"Oh-*oh*. Sounds ominous."

"Well, it *is* a challenge. Tell you what. It's too late for us to have lunch, but if you can swing this, dinner's on me. Le Colonial, Daniel, Petrossian, you choose."

"Dinner! At Petrossian! Kenz, why do I smell snake oil?"

"You don't, but your flawless taste is desperately required. And do hurry, will you? Or *don't* you want to pull a fast one on Bambi?"

"What! Well, why didn't you say so in the first place? Be right there!" he sang.

When Arnold and Annalisa returned three hours later, Kenzie couldn't believe her eyes.

Gone was the frumpy wallflower.

In her place was a chic young woman in a navy blue skirt, blazer, white blouse, and a patterned silk scarf tied loosely around her neck. Her hair had been highlighted and was fashionably slant cut, and her face glowed like a palette. Even her glasses were gone.

"I'll be damned," Kenzie exclaimed softly.

Annalisa looked stricken. "Something is wrong?" she ventured anxiously.

"No, no. Not wrong—*right*. Arnold, how did you do it?"

He smiled hugely. "First, we took care of the essentials."

He indicated the shopping bags from Daffy's.

"As you'll notice, we bargain-hunted. Three suits, three blouses, four scarves, the bag, *and* the shoes. For—would you believe?—three hundred and fifty bucks. *Including* tax."

"Remind me to take you shopping the next time I need something," Kenzie said.

"Next stop was the hairburner," Arnold continued. "An old flame of mine owed me. So that was a freebie. Ditto the makeup, courtesy of waltzing through the first floor of Bloomie's. The perfume's tiny vials of giveaway samples. Add a set of press-on nails and—*voilà!*"

He gestured grandly.

"What you see is what you get!"

"And the granny glasses?"

"Turns out she just uses them to read. However, I insisted upon picking out a tortoiseshelly-looking pair. But what do you think of the low black heels? Nice touch, isn't it? Really makes her *that Burghley's girl*. Hmm?"

Just then Bambi came sailing in. "Hi, guys! What's up?"

"This is Annalisa Barabino," Kenzie said. "Zandra's replacement."

Bambi gave Annalisa a hard once-over and nodded briskly. "You'll do." And to Kenzie: "Thank God. I wouldn't have put it past you to have hired the *dog*."

The voice on the telephone echoed from the soundtracks of countless late and late-late shows. "Mizz Tarna?"

Kenzie felt a tide of goosebumps. That smoky, Eastern European accent was unmistakable. For a moment, she was unable to speak.

"Mizz Tarna?" The woman's tone grew louder. "Can you hear me?"

"Y-yes," Kenzie said faintly. She put a hand over the mouthpiece and quickly cleared her throat. "Yes," she repeated, more authoritatively.

"Good. Do you know who zis eez?"

"I . . . I think so," Kenzie said. "You must be Miss Po—"

"Ah-ah-ah!" The voice cut her off. "Pliss. You are nefer, efer, to refer to me by name. 'Mizz P.' vill do nicely. Also, you must nefer bring up my former career." There was an imperious pause. "Eez zat clear?"

Kenzie swallowed. "Yes, ma'am. Perfectly."

"Good. I haff zome Old Mazterz I vish to have appraized."

"And when would you like to have this done?"

"Tomorrow afternoon. Zree o'clock sharp."

Kenzie began to reach for her Filofax, but then decided: *What the hell.* Lila Pons was the last great legend of the silver screen. *It isn't as if she calls every day.*

She said, "Yes, three o'clock tomorrow will be fine."

"Good! I vill be expecting you."

"I'm looking forward—"

But Lila Pons had already hung up.

"—to see you tomorrow," Kenzie completed softly as she replaced the receiver.

47

*F*antasy Island has a name, and its name is Mustique. An emerald in the turquoise sea, it is situated in the northern Grenadines, that necklace of islands one hundred twenty-two miles west of Barbados and is, at a mere 1,350 square acres, one of its tiniest jewels.

And its most priceless.

For there are, in all, only two small hotels, one bar, and some sixty private houses on the entire island. Tourists are discouraged; ship anchorages difficult to come by.

This is a private playground, and the likes of Princess Margaret and Mick Jagger, Lord Glenconnor, various Guinesses, the Earl of Lichfield, and David Bowie, intend to keep it that way. For privacy is the last frontier; the ultimate luxury in an ever-shrinking world.

And nowhere is luxury more in evidence than in the architectural fantasies hidden amid the rolling hills and white cedars, the frangipani, bougainvillea, and jasmine of Mustique.

It is the oddest assortment of domiciles imaginable: the English fort complete with crenelated battlements, the miniature Japanese village set around Koi ponds, the Indonesian-style complex built from elaborately carved teak housefronts which had been dismantled from a Javanese village, the Moorish palace, the Gingerbread House, and yes, even a Taj Mahal.

The names given to these architectural quirks and follies is in keeping with the Mustique mystique—Oceanus, Serendipity, Fort Shandy, and Blue Waters.

Here, in this enchanted Eden, did the newlyweds honeymoon.

Their Serene Highnesses occupied Villa Neptune, a rambling columned temple built around three sides of an aqua pool. Behind the deep and shady loggias, the coral limestone walls were punctuated with open Palladian arches—in these balmy climes the boundaries between indoors and out were blurred, and doors and windows unnecessary. White jasmine and bougainvillea ran riot, enclosed the house within their fragrant bowers.

Marble statues cavorted around the pool—Neptune, mermaids on dolphins, fauns, centaurs, sphinxes, river gods, and other eighteenth-century fancies. Beyond them, the lushly planted gardens dropped abruptly to the aquamarine sea below.

There, at anchor inside the reef, were a big white motor yacht and a sleek mahogany sloop with a hull like a knifeblade.

On this particular afternoon in mid-March, the trade winds were one constant perfect breeze which blew in from one side of the house and out the other, and the sky was a deep and pellucid blue. The neighboring islands were hazy: distant humps, like whales sunning themselves on the horizon.

Or so opined Zandra, who lay sideways on a cushioned chaise in the cool, shadowy darkness of the loggia.

"What I absolutely love most here," she declared, clad in a diaphanous white djellaba, "is that so long as the roofs extend out far enough there's simply no need of windows! I mean, brilliant! Just shade and ceiling fans *and* tradewinds . . . Oh, this truly is paradise, darling, it truly is . . . What? My move? Really?"

Eyeing the chessboard on the low table between them, Zandra's brows drew prettily together in concentration.

Karl-Heinz, reclining sideways on his chaise, watched her and smiled as he listened to her upbeat chatter, the words twittering like swirling birds around his ears.

I could stare at her forever, and still never tire of it, he thought, realizing it was the corniest of sentiments.

It was, however, the truth. Her mere presence intoxicated him, filled him with a golden glow. She made him so happy, this luminescent lively creature, that he thought he might literally burst apart at the seams. At last he understood what inspired poets to write sonnets, and why love songs he'd once pooh-poohed were the only things which adequately described his feelings.

She lights up my life, he thought. *She's my one and everything.*

"Oh, Heinzie," Zandra said almost despairingly. "I really hate having to do this, but winning *is* what this game is all about . . . I mean, that's the whole point, isn't it? Frightfully sorry."

And she moved her rook, took his queen, and smiled brilliantly.

"Your move," she said blithely, reaching up and snapping a stalk of giant red hibiscus from the big potted plant behind her. Humming softly, she twirled the trumpet-shaped blossom so that the petals tickled her face.

He forgot the chessboard and stared at her, drawing bleary pleasure from just watching her. He had never known anyone who took such sheer delight in the physical sensations of flowers. It seemed she was forever plucking a bloom here or a bud there, just to stroke it sensuously against her skin or dip her nose into fragrant petals.

I wonder when she'll realize that this is more than a mere business deal, that if I didn't love her I wouldn't have married her?

"Now, Heinzie." Zandra was glancing over the hibiscus at him. "You're not concentrating."

"The anthers are going to leave pollen smudges on your nose," he said softly.

"God, it's probably all smudged already." Zandra leaned forward and wrinkled her nose. "Is it? Smudged?"

"Charmingly smudged."

"Then I'll leave it! We'll pretend I'm an urchin!"

She laughed with delight and jumped up, deliberately knocking over the chessboard. The figures scattered on the stone paving, and before he knew it, her hands swooped down, grabbed his, and tugged him to his feet.

"Darling, we don't *have* to play chess, do we? Not on such a lovely day as this. Let's swim."

"All right," he laughed. "Why not? I'll be right back."

He began to go inside, but her hand closed on his arm.

"Heinzie. Where on earth are you going?"

He turned around. "To get a swimsuit."

She rolled her eyes. "Oh, for God's sake, darling. Whatever for? Don't be such a prude! Besides, the servants can't see us from their quarters, and, so long as we don't stand at the very *edge* of the dropoff, the yacht's crew can't see us from down below, either."

She held his gaze.

"As for me," she added huskily, "well, I *am* your wife, you know."

"I know," he said softly.

She let go of his arm. In one smooth movement, she slipped the djellaba up over her head and let it drop. She shook out her hair.

He caught his breath. She was naked underneath. Her strawberry nipples jutted forth from her strong, perfect breasts and her pubis was a curly marmalade-colored triangle.

"Well? Darling, *will* you get undressed? Or must I do it for you?"

Still holding her gaze, he shrugged himself out of his collarless shirt. Then he began to undo the drawstrings of his silk trousers.

She said, "Oh, good," and strode out into the dazzling sun, heading straight to the poolside.

He watched her lift her arms and launch herself into midair, then arc and jackknife so neatly into the water that she barely disturbed its surface.

Karl-Heinz could only shake his head in wonder. *How is it that everything she does is pure perfection? Surely she must have* some *flaws?*

She surfaced at the far end, beneath the big marble statue of Neptune, and sleeked back her hair and waved. "Darling, what *are* you waiting for?" she called. "Do join me! It's super!"

Stepping out of his trousers and briefs, he walked to the pool and dove in neatly, swimming underwater with quick even strokes. He burst

up beside her, shaking his head and spraying a shower of droplets in all
directions.

"Well? Isn't it terrif?"

All around them the water sparkled, as though sunlight was reflecting
off liquid chrome.

"Oh, it's not bad," he allowed.

"Not bad?" She karate-chopped a sheet of water at him. "What do
you mean, not bad?"

He drew his lips across his teeth and grinned. Chopped water right
back at her.

She squealed. Gulped a deep breath and quickly submerged.

He swam around in place, looking for her, thinking: *Where is she?
What's she up to—*

Without warning, she shot up behind him and dunked him under.

A burst of air surfaced, bubbling furiously. Then he came up, spout-
ing a mouthful of water.

He glared at her. "That wasn't nice!"

"So?" She laughed with delight.

Her playfulness was difficult to resist, and he lunged at her.

Pretending terror, she shrieked and swam hell-bent for the other end.
He gave pursuit, but they were evenly matched and she managed to stay
just out of reach.

"Aha! You're scared!" he taunted.

Her laughter rippled above the thrashing of water. "Oh, really? And
what of?"

"Me."

"*You!* And why is that?"

His eyes glinted. "Because you know what will happen if I catch you!"

"What?" she challenged.

He couldn't tell if she'd purposely slowed or not, but he caught her
by one ankle, held on, and pulled her to him.

"This," he said.

And gathering her in his arms, he covered her lips with his and plundered their sweet warmth. Her breasts were flattened against his chest; his
phallus was erect.

Zandra felt a quickening inside her. She twined her legs around his
and trapped his straining manhood against her belly. In this embrace they
submerged, swirling down into the aqueous blue, their mouths locked as
their tongues flicked and probed, explored and feasted.

Despite the pressure of the water she could feel the rapid thuds of his
heartbeat, and the scalding fires of his needs reached out and suffused her
in a radiant glow.

With her entire soul she returned his passion, gripping him as fiercely as he gripped her. Weightlessly they tumbled, somersaulting in slow motion, her hair fanning out and waving like a mermaid's.

All around, squirming reflections of sunlight flashed like rippling quicksilver, turning the pool into an underwater ballroom.

One of his hands moved to the back of her head, keeping her face pressed against his. With the other he cupped a breast, gently brushing her nipple with circular movements of his thumb.

Her breast tingled like a point of fire, and she moaned into his mouth.

Slowly his fingertips drifted lower, lower, inexorably lower, tracing the concave indentation of her belly, caressing the rise of her mound, exploring the tender intimacy between her thighs.

Her legs quivered and a shudder coursed through her.

For what seemed an eternity, they floated in this silent lucent world, his fingers bringing on the first sputters of rapture.

Then, the air in their lungs diminishing, they rose up as one and crashed through the surface.

Zandra's mouth gaped as she gulped deep lungfuls of air.

"God," she gasped, her breasts and abdomen heaving.

There was a strange, untamed light in her eyes. She, who had always thought of her sexuality as subtle and constrained, now found it overpowering. A driving force over which she had no control.

"Come," Karl-Heinz said, and swam her to the edge of the pool.

There was no longer any need for words. The moment her shoulders nudged the smooth aqua tiles, she let go of him, reached behind her, and held onto the coping.

The rigidity of his maleness prodded the petal-like folds between her thighs. She drew a deep breath and looked up at him. Her eyes glowed brightly. In one smooth movement he drove himself inside her.

Tears sprang to her eyes. "Oh, yes," she moaned. "God, yes!"

And filling her completely, he slowly began to thrust.

Zandra threw back her head, turning it from side to side, and she arched her back, pressing her hips against his.

Faster he pummeled, faster and faster, until the water around them thrashed like a boiling cauldron.

She could feel the first tide gathering force, and then the torrent was upon her, carrying her higher, filling her completely.

A scream tore from her throat as the flood of pleasure swept her away and over the edge.

But it was only the beginning.

Princess or no, she fucked like a whore.

≈ 48 ≈

"*Tree o'clock sharp.*" Thus spake Miss P.

Kenzie arrived at First Avenue and Fifty-second Street a full twelve minutes early. She had the eeriest sense of déjà vu, of repeating something she'd done the exact same way before.

Which, of course, she had.

On her last visit.

The doorway on First Avenue into which she ducked to change from her Reeboks into her best heels (now repaired and no longer flats), was the same one where she'd changed shoes the last time. Ditto the shoulder bag into which the Reeboks were relegated.

The sun, beginning its descent behind the Jersey Palisades, sent a tunnel of light straight across Fifty-second Street and on over the East River, where it glinted on the mullioned windows of a thousand factories and warehouses.

As Kenzie approached River House, she was aware of the doorman inspecting her carefully through the thick glass door.

That she passed the first test was apparent when he held it open and let her in, not that she got far. The sign proclaimed that ALL VISITORS MUST BE ANNOUNCED, and it was a house rule which undoubtedly extended to the President of the United States. This was, after all, River House, undeniably one of the premier residences in the entire world.

"May I help you, ma'am?"

The doorman's creaky voice was an instant replay of Kenzie's previous visit, and again, she had that jarring sense of déjà vu. For not only were his words the very same, *but so was he!*

She recognized him at once. The same shuffling geezer who chased her off the last time.

Tossing her head, Kenzie tried to dazzle him with her thousand-watt smile.

He stared back at her: silent, unimpressed, and expressionless.

Breezily she said, "I have an appointment with Miss P.," thinking: *There! At least that's different! The last time, I called her "Miss Pons." Maybe this'll cut the mustard.*

It didn't.

"What makes you think we have a Miss P. living here?" His voice was flat and blank, just like his face.

Kenzie turned up the wattage of her smile.

"Because," she said smugly, "she called me yesterday. I spoke to her personally."

"That so?"

"Yes, that's so." *God, what a doubting Thomas.* "Perhaps you remember me? I was here once before. I represent Burghley's? The auction house? Here's my card . . ."

Her voice trailed off as she began to unbuckle her shoulder bag.

"Not necessary." He waved a hand and picked up the house phone. "Ma'am? What you say your name was?"

"Turner. MacKenzie Turner." She looked around the lobby while he dialed, pretending to inspect the decor. Then: "Yeah. This is Artie downstairs? There's a Ms. Turner here. From Burghley's. Claims to have an appointment with Miss P. Yeah . . . uh-huh . . . right."

Kenzie watched him surreptitiously, but his face gave nothing away.

"Well?" she joked brightly as he hung up. "Am I cleared by the KGB?"

"Nope." He shook his head. "Sorry."

"What?" she demanded, staring at him in disbelief.

He coughed discreetly, but wouldn't meet her eyes. "Housekeeper says Ms. P.'s in Klosters. That's over there in France or somewhere."

"Switzerland," Kenzie corrected automatically. "When did she leave?"

"Dunno, ma'am," he said. "Musta been on someone else's shift."

"But I just spoke to her *yesterday!"*

"I wouldn't know about that, ma'am. Perhaps if you tried some other time—"

"Other time? *What* other time? *I* was summoned here, dammit!"

"Then perhaps if you telephoned ahead—"

"But that's just it! Don't you see? I don't *have* her phone number. *She's* the one who calls *me!"*

"Then I'm afraid I can't help you." Stony-faced, he went to open the front door to show her out. "Ma'am?"

Kenzie refused to budge. "Look, this is important," she stressed. "Maybe . . . maybe there's been a mix-up. What if I used the house phone—"

He looked shocked. "Absolutely not!" he snapped, letting go of the door and striding to the house phone in his determination to intercept her, and guard it with his life, if necessary.

"Then could you *please* call upstairs once more?"

He shook his head regretfully. "No can do, ma'am."

"But why not?" she demanded incredulously, hands poised on her hips.

"Because we have strict orders," he replied. "The resident of that apartment allows only one call per visitor. No exceptions." He paused. "Ever."

"But surely, when there are extenuating circumstances—"

"No such thing, ma'am." He smiled tightly. "I assure you, not with apartment 5C."

5C. Kenzie mentally filed the number. *You never know,* she thought. *It might come in handy sometime.*

"So," she asked broodingly of him, "what do I do *now?*"

"Ya got me," he said.

"Shit," she swore, under her breath.

"Sorry, ma'am. I don't make the rules."

"Damn and blast it all to hell!" Kenzie muttered. "What I won't do for Burghley's!"

Talk about Kafkaesque! she thought. *This is what I'd expect down at Motor Vehicles, not in the most distinguished building in town.*

Whirling around, she pushed on the heavy door and let herself out, so quickly that the doorman didn't stand a chance to jump to. She was out before he knew it.

Marching away from the building, Kenzie tried to contain her frustration when—

—she felt it *again!*

That powerful frisson.

That eerie, spine-tingling sensation of being watched!

Slowing her pace, she felt herself twisting her head, eyes involuntarily drawn to the fifth floor, automatically seeking that same window which had caught her attention the last time.

The breath caught in her throat. *There! Invisible unless you knew where to look, the haunting pale image of—*

—*her!*

"Klosters, my ass . . . !" Kenzie exclaimed softly.

Lila Pons. It had to be. Cinematically posed behind the squares of casement, head in a turban, she stood with one forearm across her stomach, her hand cupping an elbow as she smoked a cigarette.

For a split second, distance contracted and their eyes seemed to meet.

Then, before Kenzie could react, the ethereal figure drew back into the shadows.

The curtain swung shut.

The window went blank.

Show's over, she thought sardonically, and got a move on. She'd wasted too much time already.

"Final fade-out for Ms. Turner," Kenzie muttered darkly. "Cut and . . . *print!*"

❧ 49 ❧

"Whatever happened to good old-fashioned coffee shops?" Charley said mournfully.

It was early Friday evening and Seattle Bean on Second Avenue—one of some eight dozen coffee bars which had mushroomed, seemingly overnight, all over Manhattan—was filled with a young, outdoorsy-looking crowd.

"The coffee happened," Kenzie said. "They served shit."

"Yeah, but *this?* Seattle's revenge, that's what this is."

Kenzie, sitting on a stool opposite him, was slowly working on a slice of dense chocolate cake and sipping cappuccino.

"What this city needs," he growled, "is a proliferation law. For coffee bars."

"And here I always thought you Italians liked good coffee."

"Good coffee," he said, "doesn't have to cost three bucks a cup."

Kenzie used her fork to cut a minute sliver of cake, speared it on the tines, raised it to her mouth, and chewed in slow motion.

"Heaven," she sighed, shutting her eyes in ecstasy.

"For what it cost, it had better be."

"Charley, I'm trying to enjoy my calories. So get off this thrift kick and let's change the subject."

"Okay." He folded his hands on the tiny table. "Why'd you drag me in here? You said you wanted to discuss somethin'."

She put down her fork and dabbed her lips delicately with the paper napkin and took a sip of cappuccino.

"That's right," she said.

"You also said you didn't want to discuss it over the phone. Or over dinner. Or at home."

She nodded. "That is correct also."

"So discuss."

She took a deep breath. "There are women," she said slowly, "who would undoubtedly feel flattered by displays of Cro-Magnon behavior among males. I, as you should know, do not number among them."

He gave her a funny look. "This Swahili you're speakin', or what?"

Kenzie sat forward. "I am speaking about fisticuffs," she said quietly.

"Fights in the schoolyard. 'Wanna step outside, buddy?' That sort of thing."

He rubbed his forehead. "Kenzie," he said wearily. "Fuck are you talkin' about?"

"I am talking about your temper. I am talking about *insane jealousy.* I am talking about your use of *violent physical force.*"

"Run that by me again?"

"You heard me."

"Yeah, I heard you. But I might understand you if you'd stop speaking in goddamn tongues!"

"All right." Kenzie took a moment to collect her thoughts. "I am referring," she said primly, "to Hannes."

"Oh, yeah. Way I understand it, you've been burning the candle at both ends."

"Charley, who I see, and choose not to see, is my business. It does not give you the right to go beating up on that person."

"Excuse me?" He looked genuinely bumfuzzled.

"And you can wipe that look of innocence off your face," she said severely. "We both know what you did."

"Hell I do!" he said heatedly.

"Keep your voice down!" she hissed. "It's bad enough you slugged Hannes—"

"I did *what?*" He stared at her. "Christ, Kenz! What put that idea in your head?"

"Let's just say I have it on good authority," she said stiffly.

"As God is my judge, Kenz, I swear I didn't lay a hand on that son of a bitch!"

She sighed heavily. "And I," she said quietly, "am supposed to believe you?"

"Hell, yeah!" He stared at her. "You do, don't you?"

She did not reply.

"Aw, shit!" He raked a hand through his hair and brooded. "Guess I have Blondie to thank for this."

"Charley, there's really no need to get into name-calling."

"Hell there ain't! Guy I'm on the street with pretends he an' I're buddy-buddy. Meanwhile, he cuckolds me an', to top it all off, runs to you an' starts spreadin' lies. Makes me wish I *had* slugged the shit outta him!"

"He says you did," she said quietly.

Charley couldn't believe his ears. "An' you fell for it?"

Kenzie said, "Put it this way. I don't *dis*believe him."

Charley was incredulous. "Oh, that's just *beautiful!* You've known me for years and along comes Blondie an' *snap!*—you take his word over mine."

Kenzie let out another exasperated sigh. She picked up her cup and sipped a little and put it back down. "Then why is it," she inquired, "that *your* knuckles are all bruised and scraped?"

"This?" Charley held up his hands. "That's from when I fell."

"You fell?"

"Goddamned right I fell! After I found out he was shtuppin' you, I tied one on. Or is that a crime suddenly?"

"Be that as it may," she said, "Hannes is the one with the black eye."

"Well, if I were you, I'd stop seein' the bastard." Charley stared at her. "It ever occur to you he might be dangerous?"

Kenzie was amused. "Come on, Charley. From the physical evidence, it strikes me that you're the one I should be worried about."

"Christ, you don't quit," he said, "do you?"

She was silent.

"That why you dragged me in here? To drink cap-pu-*cci*-no and give me shit?"

"Charley," she said, "I am not giving you shit. I wanted to discuss this like civilized human beings."

"Oh."

"Also, I thought it time I started . . . well, laying down the law."

"Law?" he said suspiciously. "What law?"

"Kenzie's Law."

"Now you've lost me completely."

"Well, the truth is this. I like you, Charley."

She looked at him directly, her tawny eyes reaching down deep.

"In fact," she added softly, "I like you a damn lot."

"Gee, thanks," he said sarcastically. "Makes all the difference."

"But I like Hannes, too."

"No doubt a whole lot also," he observed wryly.

Her expression did not change. "That's right," she nodded.

"Well," Charley sighed, "I won't pretend the truth doesn't hurt."

"At any rate," Kenzie continued, "to uncomplicate matters, I thought it best to keep the two of you separate."

Charley simply stared at her.

"I also thought it fair to give each of you equal time."

"Did you now?" he said bitterly. "Just like opposing opinions on TV?"

"Just until we all know where we stand emotionally," she emphasized. "I have, therefore, decided that Hannes can see me Mondays, Wednesday, and Fridays."

"Yeah?"

"Which means," she said, "that Tuesdays, Thursdays, and Saturdays are yours."

"Gee. An' Sundays? What about Sundays?"

"On Sundays," she said succinctly, "I rest."

"Sounds like you're gonna need it."

She shrugged.

"Also sounds like you wanna have your cake and eat it, too."

"I will not," she said, "dignify that with a response."

"Sure you're not playin' one of us against the other?"

"Charley," she said patiently. "I'm trying to keep the two of you from each other's throats." She sat erect, her hands folded. "So. Are you in agreement?"

He eyed her narrowly. "You float this by Blondie yet?"

"I discussed it with *Hannes,*" she said. "Yes."

"An'?"

"He didn't voice any complaints."

"I bet he didn't!" Charley was silent for a moment. "And if I do?"

"I'm hoping it doesn't come to that," Kenzie said softly.

"That like me hopin' Blondie drops dead?"

"Charley, look," she said. "I'm trying to make this as painless as possible for all three of us." She took a deep breath. "You can either take it or leave it."

He stared at her.

She stared back at him.

"Oh, *great!*" He rubbed a hand over his face. "I get to choose between the devil and the fuckin' deep blue sea!"

"I'm sorry if that's the way you perceive it, Charley."

"Shit." He shook his head. "You really know how to kick a guy where it hurts, don't you?"

"Hurting you is the furthest thing from my mind. I'm only trying to be fair."

"Yeah." He gave a negating snort. "Right."

She waited, her mouth pressed in a thin tight line.

"Well, I don't do my best thinking on an empty stomach," he said. "An' last I heard, ca-pu-*cci*-no doesn't qualify as a meal. Am I correct in surmising that we're *not* leavin' here and goin' someplace for real food?"

"You surmise correctly."

"Then how come you got all doozied up? You ask me, basic black with spaghetti straps ain't exactly a coffee bar getup."

"No," Kenzie said softly, "it's not."

"So. What gives?"

"It's Friday night," she said gently.

"Fri—" He slapped his forehead. "Oh, yeah. How stupid of me. This is *Blondie's* night!"

Kenzie flinched as though she'd been struck.

"So you and him," Charley said, "are gonna go do dinner. And whatever."

She raised her chin. "That's right."

"Well, fuck you!" he shouted angrily. "Fuck you both!"

And jumping up, he knocked over his stool and stormed out.

"I broke the news to Charley," Kenzie told Hannes over dinner at Privé, on East Eightieth Street.

"How did he take it?"

She sighed and sipped her white wine spritzer. "Not well, I'm afraid."

"I'm sorry to hear that, Kenzie."

She nodded. "So am I," she said. Then she smiled. "Do you know, he believes you might be dangerous?"

"*Me!*" Hannes laughed. "What a marvelous absurdity. Look at me, Kenzie! I am still walking around with a bruised face."

"I know." Kenzie smiled.

She ate a bite of grilled vegetable and goat cheese tart.

"It gives you that dashing, heroic air," she added.

He laughed and then abruptly fell silent.

"Kenzie, has it occurred to you," he asked slowly, "that Charley might have a point?"

She gave a start. "What do you mean?" She stared at him.

"Well, he may have every reason for feeling paranoid. What he did to me, for example."

"Yes?"

"He could quite honestly be unaware of having done it."

"Hannes—"

"Please, Kenzie. Listen to me. Charley drinks quite heavily."

"True."

"Perhaps he suffers blackouts. That would explain why he doesn't remember what he did."

"Oh, God. Now you're frightening me!"

"He would never wish you harm, Kenzie. At least, not intentionally."

She tried to draw comfort from what he said, but she felt a chill instead.

Charley may not want to hurt me, she thought. *But who can predict what he might do in a blackout?*

Hannes was watching her. "I'm so sorry, Kenzie. I didn't mean to alarm you."

She pasted on a smile. "You didn't," she lied.

Charley's always been gentle with me, she told herself. *He's never shown violent tendencies. Being scared of him is ridiculous—*

—or isn't it?

Suddenly she really didn't know.

50

"Sweeties!" Dina trilled.

Arms flung wide in welcome, she tossed kisses left and right.

"How *was* the honeymoon? Zandra, I simply must hear all about it. Goodness! Heinzie, you're both tanned as nuts. Well? Do sit down. I apologize for these humble quarters. It's only temporary, but it already feels like *forever* . . ."

While their apartment was being redecorated, the Goldsmiths, their majordomo, Dina's personal maid, and a small selection of their museum-quality paintings were camping out in high style at the Carlyle Hotel. The "humble quarters"—a four-bedroom corner suite which rented for $24,000 a month—was on a high floor, with both north- and west-facing views. The foyer had a marble floor, the enormous living room a grand piano, and each bedroom an *en suite* bath. A separate room on a lower floor had been converted into an office for Gaby.

Julio hovered discreetly.

"Champagne," Dina decreed as they got settled on plump floral chintz sofas. "Cristal. And send downstairs for tea sandwiches."

She beamed at Zandra and Karl-Heinz.

They both looked radiant, exactly like a couple returning from their honeymoon should look. Obviously, marriage agreed with them.

As well it should. They had everything anyone could possibly want. Wealth, power, glamour—you name it.

Well, almost everything, Dina thought. But she had to wait for the right moment before raising that particular subject.

Meanwhile, there was much gossip and news to exchange. It had been two weeks since the wedding, and Dina realized she didn't even know where the happy couple had honeymooned.

"Oh, sweeties, this is fantastic!" she purred. "I couldn't *wait* for the two of you to get back. Without you, this city's been dull, dull, dull!"

Karl-Heinz laughed. "You're not prone to exaggeration, are you?"

"Me?" Dina laughed. "Of course not. Anyway, do tell! Where did you get those magnificent tans?"

"Oh, *these?* Why, Mustique, darling. Where *else?*"

"Mustique!" Dina looked nonplussed. "But . . . it's so *quiet* there."

"Dead, actually," Zandra said cheerfully.

"My point exactly. And you didn't go stir-crazy? Not in two entire weeks? Sweeties, what did you *do* there?"

"Oh, Dina, *really.*"

Zandra exchanged a sly, amused glance with Karl-Heinz.

"Darling, what do you *think* couples do on their honeymoons?"

"I see. Well, we needn't get into *that*. Ah! Saved by Julio and the champagne."

While Julio uncorked the bottle and poured, Dina eyed the newly-weds closely. There was something different about Zandra and Karl-Heinz . . . something she couldn't quite put her finger on.

Then suddenly she knew what it was. They really *were* a couple. And there was something else, too. They were happy. You could tell just by looking into their eyes.

Whether they realize it or not, she thought, *they're in love. Genuinely in love!*

Julio drifted away and Dina raised her glass.

"A toast," she proposed. "Here's to the both of you and the timely arrival of a bundle of joy."

"To a bundle of joy," Zandra repeated softly, and the three of them touched glasses and sipped.

"Delicious," Karl-Heinz said.

"Yes," Dina said. She put her glass on the coffee table. "Now for some news. I hope you won't mind my meddling, but during the past two weeks I took it upon myself to do a little research."

"Research?" said Zandra blankly. "Darling, whatever for?"

"Why, for your little bundle of joy, of course! What else?" Dina smiled like a benevolent fairy godmother. "And there's good news and there's good news! I myself couldn't believe the leaps and bounds obstetrics has made during the past few years. I don't think you will, either."

Zandra had to smile. *Good old Dina,* she thought. *Trust her to have gone sniffing around the halls of science and medicine.*

She said, "Well? We're all ears. Aren't we, Heinzie, darling?"

Dina picked up her glass and took a tiny sip and set it back down.

"It used to be," she said, "that a child's sex was a toss-up. Sort of like pot luck."

"Still is, I should imagine," said Zandra.

"Ah." A faint smile hovered on Dina's lips. "You'd be surprised, sweetie. Dr. Lawrence Rosenbaum has proved otherwise."

Karl-Heinz frowned. "Rosenbaum . . . Rosenbaum . . ." he murmured, crossing his legs and pinching the perfect crease of his trousers. Then he shook his head. "Never heard of the man."

"That's not surprising," Dina said, "because before this, neither had I."

"Darling, you know how I absolutely despise mysteries," Zandra said. "So who is he?"

"Only this city's most famous obstetrician/gynecologist. That's right, sweetie. In fact, he's often referred to as the *top* OB/GYN expert in the world."

Dina folded her hands in her lap. "Lawrence Rosenbaum and I," she said, "had a nice long talk. And guess what?"

Zandra and Karl-Heinz looked at her expectantly.

"Apparently, a new procedure was developed a few years ago which can *help influence the sex of a child*. That's right!"

Dina sat forward on the sofa. She was seized with a barely contained excitement, and her pale eyes shone like faceted aquamarines.

"Heinzie! Zandra! Sweeties! *Did you hear me?* He can help you produce a *male . . . heir!*"

"I wonder how he does that?" Zandra mused thoughtfully. "Last I heard, the sex of a child is determined by nature."

"It seems that nature can be helped along. I forget the exact name of the procedure—" Dina waved a slender hand airily. "—you know I have absolutely no head for medical terminology, sweetie, but I did gather it's done through artificial insemination."

Karl-Heinz shook his head. "I'm not sure I like the idea of Zandra submitting herself to—"

"Darling, it isn't the method of insemination that's important, really it's not!" Zandra told him softly.

"But—"

"We need a male child, darling, and I'm willing to undergo anything within reason so long as there's a chance it'll help. I can live with that . . . if you can."

Karl-Heinz sighed and rubbed his forehead.

Dina pressed onward. "The process is really very simple. What they do is . . . let me see . . . first they take some sperm—in this case yours, Heinzie—and then they spin it or shake it in a laboratory, which causes the female sperm to drop, and the male sperm to come to the top—"

"Did you say . . . *shake* it?" Zandra giggled. "Like a martini?"

"Spinning the sperm," Karl-Heinz uttered in amused incredulity. "And that is supposed to guarantee us a male child?"

"No," Dina conceded. "It doesn't guarantee anything. But it *has* been known to be effective. If you're interested, Dr. Rosenbaum can explain it all far better than I can."

Karl-Heinz exchanged glances with Zandra, who gave an imperceptible nod.

Dina drank some of her champagne.

He sighed. "It just sounds so . . ." He held up his hands . . . "so over the top."

"Sweetie, it is not over the top," Dina objected. "Lawrence Rosen-baum is a highly respected scientist who happens to be practicing medi-cine." She paused and stared at him. "Besides, do you have a better idea?"

He shook his head.

"Look at it this way," Dina's voice gentled. "What have you got to lose?"

Karl-Heinz did not reply, but Zandra thought: *Only about twelve billion dollars.*

She sat up straight and tall, and as she raised her chin she was every inch the princess.

"Darling," she told Dina, "call Dr. Rosenbaum. Ask how soon he can see us."

"Zandra!" Karl-Heinz protested. "Draconian measures like this weren't—"

Part of the bargain, he didn't have to say.

Zandra smiled at him. "You're sweet, but my mind's made up, Heinzie."

"But why not let nature take its course? See what happens?"

"Because, darling, nature may take months—years even!—just to fer-tilize me. I know your father's condition is currently stable, but he is still in a coma. *You* heard his doctors. It's only a matter of time."

"Yes, but—"

"And besides," she said, "how can I let Sofia's munchkin inherit? Any woman who dresses in mourning for my wedding's certainly not go-ing to get the better of me!"

Zandra looked at Dina.

"Make the call, darling," she said huskily, taking Karl-Heinz's hand. "Make it now."

51

"Sure you ain't hungry, Ferraro?" the deputy chief asked. "Best grub on earth's right 'round here."

They were pushing their way through the dense Chinatown crowds, Ditchek's nose on full alert even as he gnawed on a sweet-and-sour rib.

Charley gave a sickly smile. "Thanks, Chief, but I'll pass."

That earned him a scornful look and a shrug.

Deputy Chief Tyler Ditchek was Charley's direct superior. A hefty beer barrel of a man, he was neither muscular nor flabby, had hard, suspicious eyes, a rumble of a voice, and a bullish, pockmarked face. Plus a cast-iron stomach, judging from what he'd already put away—a container of fried dim sum, two fatty whole duck legs, plus the bag of greasy, baby-back ribs he was working on.

Gnawing on the last one, Ditchek stuffed it in the bag, sucked on his fingers, and ditched the bag in a trash bin. He wiped his hands with paper napkins and produced a robust belch.

"All right, Ferraro. I got a tight schedule." He flicked a sideways glance. "Whaddya wanna see me about?"

"This pilot program I'm stuck in," Charley said.

"Whaddabout it?" Ditchek's stony face showed what he personally thought of it, which wasn't much.

Charley said, "Interpol and the Job don't mix. I want out."

Ditchek snorted. "Shit," he said. "You got the cushiest job on the entire force." He eyed a row of crisp whole piglets hanging from hooks. Seemed to have trouble deciding. He said, "They're better on down a ways," and continued on.

Charley looked back at the piglets. "Least there you know what you're eating, Chief."

Ditchek said, "Fun-nee. Gonna hit me with that If-It-Moves-They-Eat-It shit?"

"Actually I wasn't, but now that you mention it—"

"Best grub on earth," Ditchek pronounced, cutting him off. "Couldn't ask for fresher."

"Yeah. Like going to a pet store to buy groceries."

"That's what I mean by fresh."

"Yeah," Charley said. "Around here, fresh means it hops. It crawls.

It swims. It slithers. I should come down here at Easter, buy little chicks and rabbits."

Ditchek laughed. "Don't have to wait for Easter," he said. Then he got serious, his brows drawing together and beetling. "Now, what's this shit about you wanting out? Huh?"

Charley's face tightened. "I've had it, that's all."

"Yeah, but *why've* you had it?"

" 'Cause this NYPD-Interpol shit sucks!"

"Yeah?" Ditchek chuckled. "Tell me something else that's new."

Charley drew a deep breath. "Way things are headed, me and the Finn are going to kill each other."

Ditchek looked at him sharply. "Thought the two a you had a marriage made in heaven."

Charley scowled. "Had's the operative word. It's time we got a divorce, and it had better be a quickie!"

"This all happen overnight?"

Charley shook his head. "Nah. It was a while in coming. Just took me some time to wake up."

"To what?"

"The guy's screwing my girl."

"I hear right?" Ditchek squinted at him. "You both porkin' the same broad?"

Charley thrust his hands into his coat pockets. "Yeah," he scowled. "And *I'm* supposed to trust him to watch *my* back? No way!"

Ditchek shook his head. "Life's a bitch."

"Christ, but I'd like to take that bastard and hang him out to dry!"

"Must be some broad," Ditchek said admiringly, "huh?"

"Listen, Chief," Charley growled.

"All right, all right." Ditchek held up his meaty paws. "Don't be so goddamn touchy! Hell, I'm not porkin' nobody."

Ditchek stopped walking, his eyes on greasy clumps of mystery meat being scooped out of a deep fryer.

Charley waited as Ditchek gestured to the Asian vendor, saying: "Gimme a bag a those."

Money exchanged hands, and Ditchek took the bag and walked on, tossing crispy morsels in the air and catching them in his mouth.

"Now, getting back to serious shit. I want *you* to listen to *me* a moment, Ferraro." Ditchek squinched his eyes. "Hear me out. Okay?"

Charley resigned himself. "Yeah. Sure."

"You know what we have in this here city?" Ditchek asked rhetorically. "Well, I'll tell you. We have a bad case a 'the gots.' "

" 'The gots.' "

"Right. We got everything, see. We got us a crack epidemic. We got us a hundred thousand heroin addicts. We got us a million people on welfare. We got us gun-totin' eight-year-olds shootin' each other dead in the schools. We got us nine-year-olds tossing six-year-olds outta twenty-story windows. We got us hordes a homeless, and as if that's not bad enough, we got kids dousing 'em with gasoline and setting 'em on fire."

Charley waited.

"And you," Ditchek said caustically, *"you* would rather be on the mean streets? That what you're telling me?"

"If that's what it takes," Charley said, "yeah. I would."

"Asshole," the Chief said, without malice. "Okay. Lemme list the reasons why wanting out's too much to ask for."

"Come on, Chief—"

"Unh-unh." Ditchek scowled. *"I got the floor."*

"Christ, Chief, you don't expect me to just sit back and—"

"Ah, shut the fuck up, Ferraro. Lemme say my piece." Ditchek crunched a morsel between his molars. "Now, you're good at what you do. Hell, ain't nobody else on the force can tell a Picasso from chicken scratch. That, my friend, is reason *Numero uno."*

Ditchek tossed another morsel in the air, caught it in his mouth, and chewed.

"Numero dos. You can work both sides a the art scene. You can fit in at an opening without screaming, 'Lookit me, I'm a cop!' *and,* you can go undercover, pass yourself off as one a the bad guys. Not many guys good at that, either."

"Chief," Charley pleaded.

Ditchek tossed and caught another morsel.

"Numero tres. This NYPD-Interpol thing's a pilot program. *You* know—" he pointed a thick index finger at Charley "—and *I* know—" he jabbed it in his own chest "—that it's the mayor *and* the PC's *pet project."*

"Like I give a shit," Charley mumbled.

"Maybe *you* don't," Ditchek growled, "but *I* sure the hell do! Wanna know why?"

Here goes, Charley thought, knowing what was coming. At one time or another, everyone who was answerable to Ditchek had heard the same unvarying routine.

Ditchek said: " 'Cause I'm retiring next year, that's why. 'Cause I don't want to be on the PC's shit list for all that time. 'Cause I don't want *your* dick—or anybody else's—fucking up my retirement!" He vented a noisy breath. "Got that?"

"Yeah, Chief," Charley sighed.

"You're what? Six months into a one-year test program?"

"About that." Charley nodded. "Yeah."

"Well, goddammit, detective! Stop sniveling, get your ass in gear, and toe the line! Six months ain't *nothing."*

"But that cocksuck—"

"Yo, hold it right there." Ditchek held out a hand like a traffic cop stopping traffic. "Personally, and off the record," he said softly, "I can't blame you. I were in your shoes, I'd feel the same way. Okay?"

"Gee, thanks, Chief."

Ditchek's voice hardened. "But professionally, and *on* the record, save me the sob story. Whatever grudges you got, my advice is, clear the air and bury the hatchet. Translation: I don't give diddly squat. And you'd better not make this into a bigger issue than it already is. You do, and I'll have your *ass!*"

The furnishings at the art theft squad office were standard city issue. Gray metal desks. Gray metal swivel chairs. Dented black filing cabinets. The computer, on a workstation shoved against the far wall, would have looked incongruous, save for the familiar, sticky dirt which had coated it gray. Ditto the fax machine. Hardly the most cheerful of surroundings.

But then, Hannes was not exactly conducting very cheerful business. He was, in fact, typing up his letter of resignation.

When he was done, he read it through, signed it, and faxed it to Paris:

03/24/1995 12:36 NYPD ART THEFT DIV PAGE 01
FACSIMILE MESSAGE
TO: M. Christophe Boutillier, Interpol, Paris
FROM: Hannes Hockert

M. Boutillier:
Due to circumstances I would rather not go into, I am sorry to inform you that I am experiencing severe difficulties with the Interpol/NYPD pilot program. I know that we were very excited about it initially, but that enthusiasm has since waned.

Furthermore, I fear my continuance with this project will result in more harm than good. I therefore respectfully ask to be reassigned and replaced immediately.
Respectfully,
Hannes Hockert

After the fax was transmitted, Hannes got his coat and left the building. He took the subway up to Times Square. Walked briskly over to Eighth Avenue, ignoring the peep show shills with all the brusqueness of a born New Yorker. *Amazing,* he thought, *how quickly one adapts.*

His destination, the West Side karate dojo, was on the second floor, above a vacated storefront. No sign advertised its function; it was not even listed in the telephone directory.

Once upstairs, he felt as he always did, that he was crossing a threshold and stepping into another world.

The loft was bright, airy, high-ceilinged, and functional, the city kept at bay by shoji screens covering the windows. The wooden floor was varnished, and gleamed with a mirror finish. Mats covered half the area.

On three of them, pairs of fighters thrust, feinted, and parried, their shouts and expelled breaths mingling with the noise of body slams.

Unlike most dojos in the city, visitors were not welcome, which was what had attracted Hannes here in the first place. To him, the martial arts were not spectator sports, nor were they to be taken lightly. They were solemn rituals requiring a lifetime's commitment, and he honed them with a religious fervor. They demanded the concentration of all one's powers— peak physical condition, a deep, emotional intensity, superb intelligence, razor-sharp alertness, timing, and speed.

The reward was confidence, fearlessness, and caution. Plus the powerful knowledge that one's body was ready to give its ultimate performance, anytime, anywhere.

And while practice made perfect, it did more than keep him in mere fighting shape. The physical and mental workouts cleansed his mind and mended his spirit.

So it was for all who came here. None of them were beginners. None of them showed off unneccesarily. In one way or another, *budō*, the martial path, was a way of life.

"Ah. Mr. Hockert." Hannes was greeted with a polite bow by a slight, white-haired Japanese who was dressed in the traditional loose white cotton pajamas and a black cotton belt.

"Good afternoon, *sensei*," Hannes replied, bowing even lower, to show his respect to the other man.

Yoshihira Fujikawa, the founder of this dojo, did not look dangerous, but he had a seventh degree black belt in karate, and was a master of Jun Fan kickboxing, judo, and jujitsu, as well.

"If you wish, Mr. Hockert, I have time to give you a personal workout."

"I would be much honored, *sensei*," Hannes replied humbly, bowing again. "But today I came to work off my aggression."

The *sensei* locked eyes with him, and nodded. "*Hai*. Then it is best you practice alone."

Hannes went into the locker room and changed into the same white outfit which the *sensei* wore. He, too, was a black belt. Then he walked out into the dojo and selected an empty mat.

First, the warm-up.

He rolled his head from side to side, then stretched his neck and arms frontward, backward, and from side to side. Hunched and unhunched his shoulders. Made certain he missed nothing—legs, spine, ankles, knees. No tendon was unimportant, no part of the body skimped upon.

Finally, twenty minutes later, he launched himself against an imaginary opponent, in today's case, Charley Ferraro. Pummeled him with high kicks—front, back, sideways. Switched to lightning punches, pulverizing the air with blurring hands and fists, putting the power of his hips behind him, always bracing himself against the envisioned impact with the enemy.

Soon he was exercising at peak form, one foot firmly anchored, his torso perfectly balanced. Focusing his muscles, he transmitted an awesome power, his mind and body a superb machine.

Finally he whipped himself up into a devastating fury of smooth kicks and punches, swiveling on one leg, lashing out high with the other.

In his mind he saw Charley stunned, staggering around in a jerking dance of death until he slowly collapsed in a lifeless heap.

Hannes became absolutely still, took a series of deep breaths, and then turned and headed to the locker room.

"Mr. Hockert," Yoshihira Fujikawa called quietly.

Hannes walked over to him. "Yes, *sensei?*"

The Japanese's face was expressionless. "I was watching you. Your form was the best I have yet seen."

Hannes bowed. "Thank you, *sensei.*"

"Tell me," Fujikawa said, "were so many killing strikes truly necessary?"

Hannes looked down. "I let myself get carried away."

"Indeed. You must have battled a true enemy."

"Yes, *sensei,* I have."

"One word of caution, Mr. Hockert. Do not forget what Sun Tzu has written. 'To subdue the enemy without fighting shows the highest level of skill. Thus, what is supreme is to attack the enemy's strategy.' "

"I shall not forget, *sensei,*" Hannes said softly.

When he returned to the office from the dojo, he ignored Charley, who sat with his feet casually up on a desk, taking giant bites out of a shiny red apple.

"Fax came for you," Charley said.

Hannes walked over to his own desk and uncurled the thermal paper. It was from his immediate superior.

The message was short and to the point:

24 Mar '95 18:55 INTERPOL PARIS PAGE 01
FACSIMILE MESSAGE
TO: Hannes Hockert, New York
FROM: Christophe Boutillier
Your letter requesting immediate reassignment was received. The request is denied.
C. Boutillier

Hannes showed no expression. He took the fax over to a filing cabinet and stuck it neatly in the appropriate folder.

Charley was watching him. "Funny, ain't it?" he said. "Seems we both tried to do the same thing on the same day. And we both struck out."

Hannes did not speak.

"Looks like we're stuck with each other."

Hannes shrugged.

"Way I see it," Charley said conversationally, taking another crisp bite out of his apple and talking while he chewed, "we can do either of two things. One, we can step outside and settle this like school kids. Or two, we can be gentlemen about it. Which is it to be?"

Hannes looked at him. "Since we obviously have no choice but to work together, we might as well behave like adults."

"My thoughts exactly."

Hannes smiled slightly. "And may the better man win."

"Good."

Charley swung his feet off the desk, tossed the remainder of the apple across the room, heard the satisfying *clunk* as it landed in the wastebasket, and got up.

"Now let's vamoose. Some Park Avenue princess is raising holy hell. Someone apparently broke in and stole her van Gogh. Might as well put her out of her misery."

𝟧𝟤

The chauffeur opened the door of the Bentley and Karl-Heinz emerged first, turning to help Zandra out. Holding onto his hand, she ducked out and stared at the building. "It doesn't look like a clinic," she said softly.

"No," he agreed, "it doesn't."

She felt him take her by the hand. It was a robust, Belle Epoque mansion built of gray limestone. More than fifty feet wide and six stories high, it was sandwiched between two tall apartment buildings in the East Seventies, right off Fifth Avenue. Amazingly, it was set back behind a tall ornate wrought-iron fence, and there was a small cobbled front yard lined with topiaries.

No brass plaque identified its function as a fertility clinic. Nor even as a doctor's office. Only the house number, a gilded number 9, gleamed from within the wrought-iron scrolls.

Karl-Heinz opened a small gate set into two giant ones, and Zandra stepped inside and waited for him. Together, they crossed the cobbles and climbed the imposing front steps. The carved front door was polished, and flanked by massive coach lamps.

"Ready?" he asked her softly.

She nodded and took a deep breath. "Ready," she said.

He pressed the doorbell.

A tall young woman with blonde hair pulled back into a chignon opened the door. She wore a well-cut, salmon wool suit and expertly applied makeup. "May I help you?"

Karl-Heinz took a card from his pocket and handed it to her.

"Your Serene Highnesses," she said respectfully, and opened the door wide. "We've been expecting you." She smiled politely and gestured. "If you'll follow me, please."

Inside, there was no evidence of a clinic, either. The marble foyer was bare, with a grand staircase sweeping up to the next floor. A huge Brussels tapestry hung on one wall, and a large marble fragment of a Roman frieze, depicting an imperial woman holding the hand of a small child, was mounted against another.

"This way."

Heels clicking, the young woman led them to a concealed jib door, which opened into a small mahogany elevator. She waited for them to enter and followed them inside.

They rode up to the next floor, then walked down a spacious paneled corridor. The woman opened one of the many tall doors.

"If you'll be kind enough to wait in here, doctor will be right with you."

"Thank you."

Zandra and Karl-Heinz went inside and the door closed quietly behind them.

The hushed, lofty room looked as if it belonged in one of the great houses of Paris. The walls were boiserie, there was a fine Heriz palace carpet on the parquet, a huge crystal chandelier overhead, and a fire crackling in the marble fireplace. The furniture was genuine Louis XV, and a huge ormolu-mounted *bureau plat* was angled across one corner.

Zandra took a seat in one of two plumply upholstered *bergères* in front of it.

Hands in his trouser pockets, Karl-Heinz walked around, studying the paintings on the walls. The Mary Cassatt depicted a mother and child, as did the Renoir, the Manet, the Daumier, and the Gainsborough.

"*Mein Gott!*" He whistled softly. "These are all genuine."

"His Serene Highness has a fine eye," commented a deep bass voice, and Karl-Heinz turned around.

Dr. Lawrence Rosenbaum was not Marcus Welby, M.D. He did not wear the traditional white doctor's smock. Nor did he look like your average family doctor. Dressed in a custom-tailored suit from Huntsman and Sons, a Turnbull and Asser shirt, Hermès tie, Cartier cufflinks, and Piaget watch, he could have been taken for a high-powered lawyer, a merchant banker, or a wealthy art collector.

He was six feet two inches tall with the thin, elongated face of an El Greco saint. Salt-and-pepper hair combed back from a slightly receding hairline, intelligent sable eyes, and a pointy Vandyke beard. In his mid-fifties, he was sleekly groomed and had a courtly, European air about him.

After they exchanged greetings, the doctor went behind his *bureau plat* and sat in his chair while Karl-Heinz took a seat in the empty *bergère* next to Zandra's.

"You seem to be doing quite well," Karl-Heinz observed, glancing around.

The doctor smiled. "I hope you don't expect any apologies."

"Of course not. Excellence deserves its rewards. From what I was told, you are the best in your field."

Dr. Rosenbaum permitted himself a modest little smile. "I have had some successes, yes. Babies are priceless, you know. As for the paintings—" He motioned around with a hand "—they are more than mere symbols of motherhood."

"Indeed?"

The doctor nodded. "They were gifts, Your Highness. From grateful childless couples I have managed to help."

Karl-Heinz looked impressed. "Obviously, you have an important clientele. Not to mention a very wealthy one."

The doctor smiled faintly. "Discretion precludes me from mentioning names, but word gets around. One person talks to another, and that one to another. I do not advertise, Your Highness. My patients are all personal referrals. They come to me."

"As we have," Karl-Heinz said.

"Yes." The doctor held his gaze. "I take it you are here because you wish to have children."

It was Zandra who replied. "That's right," she said quietly, and leaned forward. "May I speak frankly, doctor?"

"By all means. Please do."

"I imagine that in your field you've probably heard just about *everything*. I mean, you must get all sorts of strange requests. Well, here's another. My husband needs an *heir*, doctor. Oh, not just any heir, I'm afraid. A *male* heir."

"Hmmm. I see." Dr. Rosenbaum steepled his fingers. "It is a matter of primogeniture?" he guessed.

"Exactly."

"Then we shall see what we can do," he said reassuringly.

He slid open a drawer and took out two folders and two gold pens. "First, I shall require some in-depth personal and medical information."

He slid a folder and pen toward each of them.

"The forms inside," he said, "are self-explanatory. Fill them out as completely and honestly as possible. Also, do not write your names, address, or telephone numbers anywhere. We do not use personal identities here, only numbered codes. If you'll notice, yours are printed on the folders and also on each form they contain."

Karl-Heinz nodded approvingly. "I see that you were not exaggerating. You do run a most discreet operation."

"Unfortunately," Dr. Rosenbaum sighed, "it has become a necessity. Despite state-of-the-art security, doctors' offices are broken into all the time. With clients such as mine, I cannot risk having their confidentiality invaded."

"But surely, you must keep a master list somewhere," Karl-Heinz said. "How else can you keep track of people by numbers?"

The doctor smiled again. "It is all in here." He tapped his head. "I have a remarkable memory when it comes to numbers. Now, then. It should take you approximately half an hour to complete the forms. I shall have returned by then."

He pushed his chair back and rose to his feet.

"Sylvie will drop by to see whether or not you would like some refreshment. Also, if you should need anything, or have any questions, simply press this button to summon her. Now, if you'll excuse me, I have another patient I must attend to."

As soon as he was gone, Zandra and Karl-Heinz got busy, and they were just finishing up when, exactly thirty minutes later, Dr. Rosenbaum returned with Sylvie, the blonde woman who had let them in downstairs.

"Sylvie, please show His Serene Highness to the library. I will see Her Serene Highness first."

Karl-Heinz squeezed Zandra's hand encouragingly, got to his feet, and followed Sylvie out.

Dr. Rosenbaum took a seat behind the *bureau plat*, opened Zandra's folder on the gilded and embossed leather surface, and took a pair of gold-rimmed half glasses out of a case. He looped the earpieces carefully over his ears.

"Now, let's see what we have here," he murmured, flipping through Zandra's file and scanning the information. "I notice you have only recently been married."

"Yes." Zandra twisted her engagement ring with its giant pink diamond nervously around and around her finger.

He looked up over his glasses at her. "Have you tried to conceive yet?"

"My husband and I have made love, yes," she said softly.

"I see." He picked up a pen and made a notation. "And have you ever conceived before? With anyone else?"

Zandra shook her head. "No."

"You put down that you've never undergone an abortion."

"That is correct."

He tilted his head. "But you have taken the Pill."

"Yes. Until two months ago. I stopped taking it when my husband and I were engaged."

"Hmmm." Dr. Rosenbaum glanced over the tops of his glasses again. "I see you have noted that your menstrual cycle is very regular. Every twenty-eight days?"

"Absolutely. It's so regular you could actually set your calendar by it."

He frowned and put down his pen and aligned it precisely with the folder. "I don't want you to get overexcited," he said, "but correct me if I'm wrong. According to what you've written down, I do believe your cycle is twelve days late."

"What?"

Zandra stared at him and frowned and began counting backward. Suddenly her eyes went huge.

"My goodness," she exclaimed softly, "you are right. Gosh. You don't really think—?"

He said, "Experience has taught me to think, but never to assume. As you probably know, the peak times for a woman to conceive are on the fourteenth, fifteenth, and sixteenth days following the onset of menstruation."

Zandra nodded impatiently. "Yes, yes. I know."

"Those, of course," he said, "are only the most likely days, and it doesn't take into account that the human body is constantly full of surprises. Pregnancy has been known to occur anytime."

"But if you actually think there might be a possibility—"

"As I said, Your Highness," he repeated kindly, "I never assume. What I do suggest is that we give you a blood serum test. Who knows?" He smiled. "You may not need my services after all."

He pressed the buzzer on his desk. After a few moments, Sylvie came in.

"Yes, doctor?"

"Show Her Highness down to the laboratory, Sylvie, would you?"

He made a notation on a chart, then closed Zandra's folder and handed it to the young woman.

"Have Queen run a blood serum test."

"Yes, doctor."

Zandra rose to her feet and looked at Dr. Rosenbaum questioningly.

"We have our own laboratory on the premises," he explained. "It won't take long. After that, a gynecological examination may, or may not, be in order." He smiled reassuringly. "Now just relax. This is not the end of the world."

Oh, but it might be, Zandra thought. *For Heinzie it could very well be.*

Unconsciously she touched her belly.

A girl. Oh, God. If I'm carrying a girl, then what do we do?

She tried not to think about it.

Dr. Rosenbaum gestured for the uniformed black nurse with the elaborate Cleopatra cornrows and beads to help Zandra out of the stirrups of the examination table.

"Doctor?" Zandra said, clutching the pale blue examination gown which fell forward as she sat up.

"Later," Dr. Rosenbaum said absently. "Queen will help you get dressed, and Sylvie will bring you back upstairs."

He snapped off his gloves and tossed them in the red trash receptacle. And he was gone.

Zandra looked baffled. "Did I say something wrong?" she asked Queen, who was bringing her her clothes on a wooden hanger.

"Lord no, honey," Queen said warmly. "Doc's just thinkin's all. Here, what d'you say I help you get presentable?"

Fifteen minutes later, Zandra was shown back upstairs to the salonlike office. Sylvie withdrew and closed the door carefully.

Dr. Rosenbaum, glasses perched on the tip of his nose, was behind the *bureau plat* scribbling into Zandra's file.

Zandra looked around. "Where's my husband?" she asked.

"Right now, he's having a blood test. Meanwhile, I need to ask you a few personal questions."

Blood test! Personal questions! "Why?" she asked, in rising alarm. "What's wrong?"

"Why, nothing, Your Highness. Please." He gestured. "Have a seat."

Zandra sat nervously on the edge of the *bergère*. She was wringing her hands.

He took off his glasses, placed them in their case, then shut the folder and clasped his hands atop it.

"You're pregnant," he stated simply.

Her voice was hushed. "Pregnant?"

He nodded gravely.

She felt colliding emotions inside her, as though joy and despair were battling for supremacy. Her voice was quivering. "You're sure?"

"Oh, yes," he nodded. "Quite sure. The blood serum tested positive, and the gynecological examination bears it out. Not that there's much to be seen at such an early stage. However, the tiny, telltale signs inside your cervix are unmistakable."

She soughed a deep breath.

"From all appearances," he said, "you must have become pregnant within the first few days of your wedding."

She was silent for a moment. "May I ask you a question, doctor?"

He smiled. "That's what I'm here for. Fire away."

She hesitated. "How long before an amniocentesis can determine the sex?"

"Unfortunately, not until fourteen to seventeen weeks into the pregnancy."

"That long!"

He nodded. "Anything earlier could result in miscarriage."

"Damn."

"However, there is another method to determine the child's sex. It is called chorionic villus sampling, commonly known as CVS. It can be performed between eight and eleven weeks of pregnancy. In other words, approximately six weeks from now. Say . . . May the fourteenth, to be on the safe side. Then, should you choose to do so, that gives you adequate time to consider a safe termination."

She sat there, deep in thought. "My husband *needs* a male heir," she said slowly, "and yet . . ."

"And yet there is a tiny spark of life growing inside you." He nodded compassionately. "I understand what you are going through."

She looked at him. "Thank you, doctor, for telling me first."

He bowed his head slightly, his face expressionless.

"Now could you summon my husband? This child is his as well as mine. As its father, he has every right to know."

🜚 *53* 🜚

The first two months of the year had been terrific. Burghley's consistently out-performed Sotheby's and Christie's, GoldMart, Inc. stock kept rising, Bambi gave good head and few problems, and GoldGlobe International, the conglomerate Robert was attempting to consolidate, looked like a go.

March 31 brought Black Friday.

At least to Robert A. Goldsmith.

In more ways than one, it was The Day the Shit Hit the Fan.

In the morning, a meeting with institutional investors and mutual fund managers went sour. Representing six billion dollars in outstanding GoldMart and Burghley's stock, they threatened a mass sell-off if Robert went ahead with the GoldGlobe International merger.

Which meant he could kiss that sweet deal good-bye.

At noon, as a direct result of the four-company merger falling through, Standard and Poor's downgraded one of the corporations involved, the Home-on-the-Range fast-food restaurant chain, from Buy to Sell, plunging the NASDAQ-traded stock a full 4⅛.

Which meant he could kiss something else good-bye—fifteen-something million dollars.

And the afternoon . . . well, the afternoon brought troubles of an entirely different nature, and all because he'd forgotten three cardinal rules:

1. You can only juggle things for so long before they eventually come crashing down.

2. That Manhattan, and the Upper East Side in particular, is the smallest town on earth.

3. And that you never, ever shit where you eat.

On this Friday, March 31, the combination of Robert's understandably foul mood, his healthy erection, a sick hairdresser, a cancelled lunch date, and an exhibition of Highly Important Jewelry, proved to be his undoing.

By one o'clock, Robert had had it. He was convinced that the longer he stuck around his office, the more bad news he was likely to receive. *Face it,* he thought, *today just isn't your day.* What he should have done was stayed in bed.

Bed.

Now *there* was an idea whose time had come! Just the thought was enough to bring on a king-size boner. What better way to forget all his troubles, forget all his cares?

What indeed?

Grabbing the phone, he punched the autodial and called Bambi's work number. *'Course, with the crappy kinda day I'm havin', she proba- bly won't be in—*

"Bambi Parker," chirped the teensy voice.

"Good," he rasped, thinking, *miracle of miracles!* "You're in."

"Ro-*bert.* Of course I'm in," she said, feigning whispery affront. "What's up?" She giggled at her double entendre.

"I'm up," he growled. "I got a hard-on's gonna bust a hole through my pants, we don't do somethin' about it!"

"You are *sooooo* gross! I take it this is an obscene phone call?"

"You betcha sweet patootie it is."

"Well, at least that explains why you're bothering a busy work- ing girl."

Working girl! He nearly guffawed. *Who's she kidding? From what I've heard, the only thing she works at is on not working.*

"I wanna see ya," he panted.

"And?" she teased.

"I want ya to go down on me."

"And?"

"I want ya to be wearin' one o' those lacy l'il whatchamacallit outfits I got ya."

"Which one?"

"How about one a them three-piece corset sets with the garters?"

"I don't know, Robert," she sighed reluctantly. "Those wasp-waist corsets have to be laced real tight, and they *hurt."*

"Oh, yeah?"

"Uh-huh. I get all these funny crease marks all over me." She paused, a petulance coming into her voice. "That's what you like, isn't it?"

"What?"

"Hurting me."

"Shit. Whaddya do? Start moonlightin' for one o' them 1-900 numbers?"

"Ro-*bert!"*

"Well, that's what ya startin' to sound like."

"What do you take me for?" she sniffed. "Some cheap hussy?"

"Well, I don't think anybody'd call you *cheap,"* he cracked.

"What's that?"

"Nothin'. I wanna see ya."

"What, *now?"*

"Soon as I can get up there. Yeah."

"Mmm," she said playfully. "Better let me check my calendar . . ."

"Better clear it," he growled. "I'm on my way. *Be there.*"

An elevator ride later, he was in his limo, inching through the Wall Street congestion.

Heading uptown.

Bound for disaster.

One for the record books. All dressed up and nowhere to go.

It had been ages since Dina last had free time on her hands. Now that she did, she felt lost and out of sorts. *I don't know what to do with myself!* she realized with a start.

First, Sergei, her hairdresser had called to say he was sick and had to cancel, and should he send his replacement and the manicurist?

Dina had glanced in the mirror, inspected her nails, and said no, she could wait until Monday.

Then, Guerlained, Cartiered, Chaneled, and Blahniked, she had been sailing out the door when Julio intercepted her.

"You have a call, madame."

"Later," she told him breezily. "I'm off."

She was to meet Suzy, Becky's sister, for lunch at Le Cirque.

"But it is the *Vicomtesse* de Saint-Mallet on the telephone, madame."

Suzy? Dina decided she'd better take the call.

And a good thing she did, too. Her lunch date was in the emergency room at Lenox Hill, having tripped and broken her big toe.

Now two empty hours loomed. Immediate problem: What to do. Dina knew better than to lunch at Le Cirque by herself.

She tried Zandra. Who she'd forgotten had flown to Paris.

Becky. Who was lunching with someone else.

Balls! Dina felt like kicking herself. Why *hadn't* she heeded Becky's advice? Not two weeks earlier, her friend had urged her to find herself a walker.

"You know, *chérie.* Someone *quel attractif.* Or terribly, terribly witty, who is always available to escort a lady."

In short, a bachelor escort—societyspeak for a homosexual, who would never make physical demands or pose any threat to Robert.

Well, it was too late now to pull a walker out of the hat. *I'll have to make it my priority to find one,* Dina decided.

Which still left her in a quandary. What to do in the meantime?

She considered her options.

Perhaps she should check up on how the apartment was progressing?

No. She would get covered with plaster dust or find herself knee-deep in debris.

Perhaps she should get comfortable and relax?

No. She needed to get out of the house.

Then the Burghley's catalogue for Highly Important Jewelry caught her eye and *wham!*—suddenly she remembered that the auction was tomorrow! That today was the *last day* of the exhibition! She'd been meaning to go and check out the merchandise, only she'd never found the time.

Well, she had plenty of time on her hands right now, and Burghley's was just a convenient block away.

What could be more perfect?

Kenzie was puzzled. She couldn't figure Annalisa Barabino out. Now that a few weeks had passed, Old Masters's newest employee still remained a total enigma.

Not that there were any complaints. On the contrary, Kenzie had never seen anyone who worked so hard, or knew so much. Without fail, Annalisa was the first one in at work in the morning and the last one to leave at night.

Her dedication was truly astounding.

And yet . . .

Kenzie found the young woman's lack of personality disturbing. It was as if work was the only thing she lived for. What was missing was a lively core, an essential spark of life.

And when it came to interacting with people on anything other than a business level, Annalisa invariably clammed up:

"Good morning, Annalisa. Did you have a nice weekend?"

"Yes, thank you, Kenzie."

"What did you do?"

"Oh, nothing really. Now, if you'll excuse me, I'd better get back to this . . ."

Or:

"Herro, Annarisa! Why don't you join us for a rovery runch?"

"I'm sorry, Arnold. I can't. I must finish this. I hope you have a nice time."

"It would be nicer if you'd join us."

"Me? Oh, no! You wouldn't want that. I would only bore you."

Yet when Annalisa studied a painting or a drawing, her entire face would light up with joy, and she would launch into an animated discussion about the subject and its artist, touching upon the most complicated and obscure facts during her impassioned art-fueled flight, only to fall silent and retreat into her shell once she was finished.

Kenzie couldn't understand it.

She's like a fragile, wounded bird, she thought. *Someone must have hurt her deeply. I wonder if she'll ever fully recover.*

And so began her obsession with Annalisa. Annalisa, who was shyer and more withdrawn and serious than anyone she had ever known.

Annalisa, who flushed when people spoke to her, who walked around with her head down and her eyes averted.

"Have you ever heard her laugh?" Kenzie asked Arnold.

"Nope. And I've never seen her crack a smile, either."

"Maybe," Kenzie said thoughtfully, "it's because she's got nothing to smile about."

"Maybe."

Kenzie was determined to draw Annalisa out of her shell. She told Arnold she was going to take her under her wing.

"I'd say you've got your work cut out for you," he sighed. "God knows, *I've* tried. And if *I* couldn't get past first base . . ."

"Perhaps it's because you're a man," Kenzie speculated. "It could be she distrusts men. Who knows? She might have been abused."

"And it could be she's just plain weird."

Kenzie shook her head. "I don't think so. She's suffered, Arnold. Somewhere along the way, she's been hurt."

"Saint Kenzie, patron of the wallflowers," he said kindly.

Kenzie decided to invite Annalisa to lunch, which was easier said than done. After being politely declined four days in a row, she finally said, "Today I won't take no for an answer. We'll be discussing business, so you have to come. It's an order."

"Yes, Kenzie," Annalisa said meekly. "All right."

"Good. Do you like Chinese?"

Annalisa frowned. "I like the porcelains," she said slowly, "but the paintings are too stylized for my taste."

"*Food,* Annalisa. I mean Chinese *food.*"

"Oh." Annalisa fidgeted. "I-I really don't know . . ." she murmured.

Kenzie took her to First Wok, where they sat at a table for two and perused their menus. Annalisa put hers down almost immediately.

"You've already decided?" Kenzie inquired in surprise.

Annalisa shook her head. "I'm not used to eating in restaurants. I wouldn't know what to order."

"Then I'll order for you," Kenzie decided.

For herself she chose vegetable dumplings, followed by a vegetable platter with chili sauce, and for Annalisa a spring roll and crispy shrimp. "And make it brown rice," she told the waiter.

While they waited, they sipped tea from little cups without handles. Kenzie couldn't help noticing that Annalisa's fingernails were bitten down to the quick. Obviously, she'd stopped wearing the press-on nails.

A closer inspection revealed something else. Annalisa's appearance was slipping. Her blouse was rumpled and the shoulders of her suit jacket were sprinkled with dandruff.

Soon she'll look like a frump again, Kenzie despaired. *Shit. How do*

I broach the subject of grooming without hurting her feelings? Well, now certainly wasn't the time.

Attempting to jump-start the conversation, she smiled brightly and said, "I know so little about you. I was hoping to take this opportunity to get better acquainted."

Annalisa nodded. "I studied under Professor Fiorentino at the Ambrosiana—"

"—and worked at the Uffizi," Kenzie said, remembering the résumé. "Yes, yes, I know all *that*. What I meant was . . . personal things."

Annalisa looked at her blankly. "Personal things?"

"Yes. You know. Where you came from. What your hobbies are. Whether you have any brothers or sisters—"

Annalisa's face blanched and her body tensed as if preparing to be struck. Then her mouth opened, and her eyes filled with tears. Quickly she looked away.

Kenzie was appalled by the reaction she had provoked.

"I'm sorry, Annalisa," she said guiltily, backing off immediately. "You don't have to talk about it if you don't want. In fact, we don't *have* to discuss anything."

Annalisa nodded, wiping her eyes with the palms of her hands. She looked tiny, frail and forlorn, staring down into her empty teacup as if attempting to divine the leaves.

"It's all right, Kenzie. There are . . . some things I just cannot—"

"I understand."

Kenzie saw the waiter approaching.

"Get ready. Here comes our grub."

Annalisa stared in amazement at the proliferation of plates and bowls and condiments which suddenly appeared on the table.

"There's so much!" she exclaimed. "I can never eat all this."

Kenzie tore the wrapping off her chopsticks and gestured with them. "Well?" she said. "What are you waiting for? Let's dig in and eat."

Annalisa picked up her fork and attacked her food. She ate in silence, seemingly without chewing, as if she hadn't enjoyed a full-course meal in weeks. Kenzie was still working on her appetizer of dumplings when Annalisa put down her fork and sat back.

Her plates and bowls were empty; not so much as a grain of rice remained.

"Should I order you another course?" Kenzie quipped, still attempting to break the ice.

"Oh, no," Annalisa said earnestly. "But thank you for asking."

Kenzie couldn't believe the response. *My God,* she thought. *How humorless can anyone be?*

Annalisa was beginning to fidget self-consciously. "I . . . I really should be getting back to work now, Kenzie," she murmured.

Kenzie stared at her. "But this is our lunch hour."

"Yes, but there is so much to get done."

Kenzie didn't argue. "You run along then," she said, forcing a smile.

Annalisa opened the black leather bag Arnold had picked out for her. "How . . . how much do I owe?"

Kenzie waved a hand airily. "Nothing. I'll put it on the expense account. Burghley's is paying."

"Really?"

"Yes." Kenzie thought it easiest to lie.

"Well, thank you for inviting me." Annalisa scooted her chair back and got up. "Enjoy your lunch."

Then, hunching her body protectively in on itself, and keeping her head down to avoid making eye contact, she darted off.

Kenzie sat there, staring after her. *Arnold's right,* she thought, with a sigh. *The patron saint of the wallflowers certainly has her work cut out for her.*

Robert had been getting increasingly careless of late, a far cry from the beginning, when he'd been overly cautious.

At first, whenever he'd come to visit Bambi, he would order his stretch limo to be driven directly down into the maw of Burghley's underground parking garage. From there, he'd pass a security desk, identify himself, and take the elevator straight up to the twenty-seventh floor of One Auction Towers.

With never a hitch.

After a while, he'd become less panicky and had his limo pull up to the canopied entrance of Auction Towers and let the doorman jump to, while keeping an eye peeled in case the wife was on the sidewalks in the vicinity.

Still never a hitch.

Finally, Robert stopped scanning the sidewalks altogether. After all, was there really any need for subterfuge? As Bambi had pointed out, he had every right to be there.

Damn right, he did! This was one helluva fine piece of real estate and he owned the lion's share. This was *his* turf. *He* was the big cheese around here.

To think he used to skulk in like a pussy-whipped eunuch—what a laugh!

Now, as his limo surged to a halt in front of Auction Towers, he didn't bother to glance either to his left or his right but straight ahead, a careless oversight he would soon deeply regret.

Dina, waiting for the light to change at the corner of Madison and Seventy-fourth, did a double take. Even without checking out the GOLD-

MRT vanity plates, her sharp eyes recognized the customized black stretch
Caddy with the tinted windows, and her antennae went on full alert.

Sure enough. There was Robert, *her* Robert, charging from the car
into Auction Towers as if there were a fire.

On an impulse, she changed her plans and decided to surprise him.
Perhaps she could even corral him into taking her to lunch; she'd forgotten to call Le Cirque and cancel, and Sirio would be holding the table.

Plus, she'd still have plenty of time to check out the jewels afterward.

Lunch with her husband. Why not? It had been forever since they'd
done that. It might even prove a pleasant diversion.

Dina altered her course and made a beeline for the Towers.

"Shit!" Robert glared at the elevator indicators. He was tuned-up, primed,
and ready for lift-off.

Unfortunately, the elevators weren't as obliging. Three of the six cars
of One Auction Towers were being serviced. One was on its way up. Two
on their way down.

"Come on, come *on!*" he muttered, sliding a hand into his trouser
pocket to cop a feel.

No problem down there, thank God! All systems were definitely go.

Now if only a goddamn elevator would come! Christ, but he hated to
be kept waiting—

Bing! A pair of elegant bronze doors slid soundlessly open.

"About time!" he huffed, charging inside and hitting the panel for the
twenty-seventh floor.

Robert's chauffeur was too engrossed (in the personals section of *Screw,*
which he kept under the front seat) to see Dina coming. Likewise Robert,
who was too hell-bent on rushing into the elevator.

Only the liveried doorman, who didn't know her from Adam, took
notice and pushed open one of the heroically scaled bronze-and-
glass doors.

"May I help you, madam?" he asked politely, once she was inside.

"Yes. Mr. Goldsmith just came in. Where can I find him?"

The doorman's face became a mask. "I beg your pardon, madam?"

"Mr. Goldsmith," she said impatiently. "Look, I just *saw* him come
in. And his car is parked right outside. I need to see him."

"I'm sorry, madam. I couldn't say."

"Oh, I think you most certainly could."

He pulled the door open to show her back out. "Madam?"

Dina imperiously stood her ground. "Do you know who I am?"
she demanded.

He gave her a vacant stare. He saw a fine-looking woman hitting thirty and fighting it every inch of the way. But what he did *not* see was someone he should recognize, like Becky V or Ivana Trump or Madonna.

"No, madam, I don't," he said. "Now, if you'll be so kind as to leave—"

"I will not!" Incensed, Dina unsnapped her crocodile bag and produced her wallet. She brandished her driver's license like a weapon.

"As you can see," she declared, "I am Dina Goldsmith." She paused. "Mrs . . . Robert . . . A. . . . Goldsmith," she emphasized.

The doorman was mortified. "I-I'm sorry, Mrs. Goldsmith, but I didn't recognize—"

"That's quite all right. Your apology is accepted. Now. Where can I find my husband?"

The doorman sensed big trouble. He knew exactly where Robert A. Goldsmith could be found—what member on the building staff didn't? Speculation was rife about the entertainment 2714—Ms. Parker—provided, and the consensus was that it wasn't tea and crumpets she was serving.

"Tea and *strumpets*," one staff wag had proclaimed, to much hilarity.

But the doorman wasn't laughing now. The last thing he needed was to be caught in a domestic dispute.

"Well?" Dina tapped a restless foot. "I'm waiting."

He took a deep breath, shifted uncomfortably, swallowed, and refused to meet her gaze.

Dina, reading his body language, didn't need an interpreter.

So, she thought grimly. *Robert obviously isn't here on business. He's seeing somebody—*

—screwing somebody.

"Where?" she asked tightly from between clenched teeth.

"Apartment 2714," he whispered miserably.

"Thank you."

She began to head into the lobby, then had a thought and turned around, lasering him with her ice-blues.

"Oh, and one more thing," she said. "I strongly advise you against calling upstairs and forewarning anyone. Do I make myself clear?"

"Yes, madam," he sighed, seeing unemployment looming.

Dina clickety-clicked across the marble lobby to the elevators. Bronze doors slid obligingly aside as she approached.

One punch of a button and she was on her way up.

Robert leaned on the doorbell.

Hell's keeping the bitch? he groused, wishing Bambi would get a move on.

He didn't like being made to wait out here in the hall. He felt exposed and vulnerable—especially since her apartment was located right next to the bank of elevators.

He leaned on her bell some more.

"I'm coming, I'm *coming,*" he heard from the other side of the door. Then it opened as wide as the security chain would permit.

"What's kept ya?" he rasped.

"I was in the bathroom," Bambi said, with a pout.

"Well? Gonna let me in?"

"Oh." She giggled. "Sure."

She shut the door, removed the security chain, and opened it wide, posing with one hand on a hip and the other on the doorframe.

"Hi, lover." She batted pale lashes. "Wanna play?"

Did he *ever!* Christ. Just the sight of her nearly made him cream. He ate her up with his eyes.

She was wearing a white peek-a-boo bra with strategic cutouts through which luscious nipples, like pointy cherries, thrust temptingly. A wasp-waisted, tightly laced corset. Crotchless white panties which left her curly blond bush open for inspection. Plus white stockings and garters, and black Mary Janes.

"Well?" She licked her lips with slow deliberation. "You likee?"

"Yeah." He was positively slavering. "I likee a *lot.*"

She broke her pose, flung her arms around his neck, and pressed herself tightly against him, right there in the open doorway.

"Tell me you're happy to see me." Her eyes glowed up at him.

"Shit, yeah. Now let's get inside before—"

Bing! The doors of the nearest elevator slid open, and they quickly jumped apart.

Not quickly enough.

Out stepped Dina, the wrath of God.

"Shit!" Robert cursed under his breath, his hard-on and scrotum shriveling.

It was too late to lunge inside and slam the door. Useless to try and explain the situation as anything other than what it appeared to be.

Seeing was believing, and Dina saw plenty. She was a believer, all right.

"Just what the *fuck,*" she demanded, "is going on here?"

Bambi stared at Robert.

Robert stared at Dina.

Dina stared at both of them. Then she pinned Robert with her eyes.

"Really, sweetie," she told him, advancing slowly, "I'm very disappointed in you."

He thrust his hands in his pockets, shuffled guiltily in place, and looked studiously up at the acoustic ceiling and down at the carpet.

Next, Dina focused her attention on Bambi. "And as for you, you little slut—"

"I beg your pardon," retorted Bambi, hands on her hips, "but I am not a slut!"

Dina raked her from head to toe and smiled like a shark. "Then what are you dressed up for? A go-go bar?"

"Well, maybe if *you'd* satisfy your husband, he wouldn't have to come and see me!"

That did it.

Dina's hackles rose, and a surge of red-hot anger shot through her. Making a fist, she swung and caught Bambi flush on the chin. The right hook connected solidly, and she could feel the shock of the punch jolting through her arm.

Bambi spun around once, looking dazed. Then her eyelids fluttered, the whites showed, and her knees buckled as she collapsed.

She was down for the count.

Dina prodded her with a well-shod foot. "Too bad I KOed her. I'd love to do that again."

She fixed Robert with a glare.

"And as for *you,* sweetie," she said quietly, jabbing an ominous finger at him, "you have some major explaining to do."

And with that, she turned on her heel and marched back to the elevators. After a moment, she called, "Robert?"

He was staring down at Bambi, who was struggling up onto her elbows, shaking her head to clear it of cobwebs.

"You can stop worrying about her, *sweetie,*" Dina advised grimly. "If you know what's good for you, she's *history.*"

He quailed inwardly. He wasn't ready to face the music. Not now. Not *ever.*

Still, he might as well get it over with. Knowing Dina, she wouldn't rest until they had it out.

With a sigh of resignation, he followed his wife.

54

_D_ina struggled to keep a lid on her temper. She was enraged, wounded, bitter, humiliated, and boiling mad. How could Robert _do_ this to her? And who the hell was that floozie?

Of course, Dina knew very well that Robert had a wandering eye—what healthy man didn't? But to ogle was one thing; keeping nookie stashed in a love nest was a monster of an entirely different sort.

No way was she going to put up with _that._

"I want you and Darlene out of here," she told Julio in no uncertain terms as she and Robert returned to the Carlyle. "Stay down in your rooms until you are summoned." She raised an imperious eyebrow. "Do I make myself clear?"

"Yes, madame."

"I do _not_ wish to be interrupted."

"No, madame."

Seconds later, Julio and Darlene wisely made tracks.

While Dina ousted the help, Robert made a beeline to the living room and the bar, where he proceeded to top off a much-needed highball with fifty-year-old scotch.

Hearing the clink of crystal, Dina stalked into the living room and stood there, icing him through slitted lashes.

"You might as well bring the decanter," she said frostily. "You're going to need it."

Goddamn it! he thought peevishly. _Trust her to rub it in! Aren't things bad enough as it is?_

He wished he'd never had the bright idea of visiting Bambi. In fact, he wished he'd never taken up with her in the first place. He wished—

It's too late to wish, he told himself grimly. _It's time to face the firing squad._

Dina headed regally for a straight-backed chair, took a seat, and clasped her hands primly in her lap. She waited, armored with heavy metal from Cartier, her spine erect and her chin raised, the ice queen preparing to pronounce sentence.

"I'm ready whenever you are," she told him quietly.

Robert cringed. Quickly he tossed back half the glass and waited for the fireball to sear his belly.

He expelled a scorching breath. Then, putting down the glass, he hunched over the bar, leaning on his hands and shutting his eyes.

Time to face the firing squad . . .

Heaving a sigh, he pulled himself together, grabbed his glass, and trudged reluctantly over and plotzed down opposite her.

Dina looked him straight in the eye.

"I cannot pretend," she said with dignity, "that I'm not disappointed in you, Robert."

Oh, great. Just what I need. A lecture.

Tightening his lips, he shifted uncomfortably and looked away. What unsettled him most was that he'd fully expected her to blow a fuse. He'd been all prepared for rants and raves and identified flying objects.

Instead, she was surprisingly, *alarmingly,* cool and collected.

The quieter the species, he thought, *the deadlier. I've got to watch every word.*

"Do you," she asked, "have anything to say for yourself?"

He was tempted to say, It isn't what you think. He was tempted to say, Couldn't we just forget this and pretend it never happened? He was tempted to say, If you put out more, maybe then I wouldn't have to play around.

No, he thought. *Talk about making a big mistake.*

Besides, he knew it wasn't true. The truth was, he *liked* playing around. He *liked* having a Blow Job at his beck and call.

Was it his fault that he was led by his penis? Maybe it was a sickness. You couldn't be held responsible for your actions if it was a sickness, could you?

Better, he decided, *to say nothing than to lie.*

"Could you at least tell me how *long* this has been going on?" Dina asked, her chilly expression unwavering.

Oh, Christ!

He gulped down half of what remained in his glass, not about to return her gaze. How was he supposed to respond? Did she expect him to spill his guts? Maybe even go groveling around on his knees begging for forgiveness?

Fat chance.

Robert A. Goldsmith might be in the dog house, but he was damned if he was going to act like a fuckin' trained poodle!

"I take your silence to mean it's been going on for a while?"

Shit! Another loaded question. Better leave this one unanswered, too. If she found out, she'd really have a fit.

How long has it been? he wondered. *Seven months? Eight? Something like that.*

In all truth, he hadn't been keeping count.

"Look, Dina, I'm sorry," he whispered miserably, "aw right?"

"You're *sorry?*" Dina widened steely eyes. "You've been keeping a mistress and now you're telling me you're *sorry?*"

He nodded. "Yeah." He was sweating profusely and fumbled a hankie out of his pants pocket, mopping his glistening brow.

"So," she said, "who is she?"

He shrugged. "Just some girl."

"Should I know her?"

He shrugged.

"She looked vaguely familiar. I could swear I've seen her around."

"She . . . works."

Dina smiled icily, her expression saying: *I bet she does.*

"At Burghley's," he sighed.

She frowned, and then it suddenly dawned on her. "You're right," she said, "I have seen her there. And . . . I've seen her elsewhere also, but where . . . *where* . . . ?"

Frowning slightly, she tapped her lips with a finger.

"Ah!" she exclaimed. "Of *course.* At Heinzie's birthday party. *She* was the girl who was all over you!"

He sighed again, not at all pleased by Dina's mnemonic powers. Her memory was like an elephant's, something he kept forgetting and—unless it was too late—it would behoove him to start keeping in mind.

"Now let me see—" She smiled acidly "—that was back in October, and this is March. Good heavens. This must have been going on for at least six months! I would say that makes her more than just *some girl,* Robert."

He thought it prudent to keep mum.

"I think," she murmured, "that I could also use a stiff drink."

Dina stood up, walked to the bar, quietly poured a little cognac into a glass, and returned to her chair. She took a tiny sip and put the glass down on the end table, the faceted crystal catching the light and refracting blue fire. Then once again she folded her hands in her lap.

"There are two questions I need to ask you, Robert. Just two. Please consider them carefully and answer truthfully."

"What are they?" he rasped guardedly.

"Do you love her?" Dina's voice carried a vibrato of unease.

He shook his head.

And shook it some more.

"I'd like to hear you *say* it, Robert. With your *lips.*"

He looked at her, as if drawn by the intensity of her stare.

"No!" he expelled, his voice a strangled growl. "I *don't* love her!"

She held his gaze. "And do you love . . . *me?*"

"Goddamn it, Dina! What kinduva stoopid question is that?"

"It is not stupid in the least," she replied softly. "It is, perhaps, one of the most important questions I've ever posed."

His chin went up pugnaciously and he retained eye contact with her.

"Yeah, Dina," he said, soughing a deep breath. "Yeah, I love ya, for cryin' out loud. God help me, but I do. What I did . . ."

He lifted his hands in a futile gesture and let them drop. "Well, what I did hasn't changed the way I feel about ya. Ya know?"

He shot her an appealing look, which her Teflon armor deflected.

"Look, I made a mistake," he pleaded. "I admit it—okay?"

She pursed her lips and looked down, studying her clasped hands.

"I won't pretend I didn't screw her. I did. But I wasn't emotionally involved with her."

"A fine distinction," Dina murmured dryly.

"Yeah. But it is one. Right?"

"Robert," she sighed, "tell me something. Do the names Michael Kennedy, Raoul Felder, and Marvin Mitchelson ring a bell?"

Ring a bell! Christ almighty, just their names set alarms clanging, sirens screeching, and lights flashing. What wealthy married man *didn't* know Husband Enemy Number One? He felt a chill terror, like a physical stab, reach all the way to the marrow of his bones.

Holy shit! he thought in disbelief. *She's talkin' divorce lawyers! She's talkin' New York's* top three *divorce lawyers—the best carcass pickers a woman could buy.*

"Aw, come on, Dina!" he cajoled. "You're not gonna divorce me over this?"

She raised her eyes slowly. "I very well may. It all depends."

"On what?"

"Robert, Robert," she sighed despairingly. "Will you *stop* pretending to be so dense? You know very well it depends upon you."

"*An'* you," he pointed out.

"And me," she agreed, nodding. "Yes."

He contemplated ways to sweet talk her, ascertained that this was one situation where no amount of words would help. Beneath the ice queen demeanor, she was mad as all hell.

Not that I can blame her, he thought, feeling a wave of guilt.

"Is there any way I can make this up to ya?" he asked.

"No, Robert, I'm afraid there isn't. There are, however, several . . . er, things you might do which could influence my eventual decision."

He went into desperate overdrive: "You name 'em. Jewels, yacht, paintings . . . a new jet? They're all the same to me."

"Truly, Robert. Do you take me to be that mercenary?"

He shrugged. "Just tell me what ya want."

"First of all, I want this young lady . . . she does have a name . . . ?"

"Bambi Parker."

"Bambi? Why, how *sweet.* How *adorable.*" Her face hardened. "I expect *Bambi* to be given the ax at Burghley's—immediately."

"If I see she gets a pink slip," he promised, "she can be outta there Monday mornin'. What else?"

"I want her to be evicted from Auction Towers. Forthwith."

"Okay."

"*And,* I expect you to never, ever, see or speak to her again."

"And if I do that?" he said hopefully. "This mean you *won't* consider a divorce?"

"It means nothing of the kind. I am not promising anything."

Fuck! Just his bad luck to have shit happen the one day Dina wasn't bent on wheedling somethin' out of him.

"This isn't," she continued, "the type of thing one decides lightly. I shall have to sleep on it for a few days first. As soon as I've come to a decision, I'll let you know."

He sighed but nodded.

"In the meantime, I need time to myself. I'd appreciate it if you called downstairs and secured yourself another suite."

Robert's mouth gaped. "You're throwin' me *out?*" he exclaimed.

"Under the circumstances, a short separation is not inappropriate."

"You gotta be kiddin'!"

"On the contrary, Robert," she said coldly. "I am quite serious."

His mouth gaped some more.

Son of a bitch! he thought, wondering whatever happened to a man's home being his castle. *Like I need this!*

"Aw right, aw right," he wheezed. "You want me out, I'm outta here!"

He struggled to his feet and trudged heavily over to the house phone.

One call secured a suite. Another summoned Julio.

Fifteen minutes later, Robert's necessities were wheeled out on a chrome trolley and he was gone.

Dina had the suite to herself.

✍ *55* ✒

On Monday morning Bambi was arriving at Burghley's at her usual late hour when the doorman failed to open the heavy etched-glass door. For a moment she stood there, then looked daggers at him.

"I'm sorry, Ms. Parker," he told her. "I'm afraid you're not permitted inside."

"I beg your pardon?" She drew herself up and stared at him, not sure she'd heard correctly.

He looked away, coughed discreetly into his cupped, white-gloved hand, and cleared his throat uncomfortably. "I've been given orders, you see. You're not allowed in."

"Oh?" Bambi's withering gaze raked him up and down. "And why the hell not?"

"I really wouldn't know, but I was told to give you this."

He produced a sealed envelope.

She snatched it out of his hand, ripped it open, and speed-read the enclosed memorandum. It was short, not sweet, and to the point:

April 3, 1995

TO: Barbara (Bambi) Parker
FROM: Sheldon D. Fairey
A recent review of your performance as director of the Old Masters Paintings and Drawings department has found you seriously lacking in leadership abilities, expertise, and on-time performance.

Subsequently, I regret to inform you that you are dismissed from that position as of immediately.

Naturally, you are entitled to the usual severance package and unemployment benefits. Please contact Ms. Heidi Ross at personnel for details.

It goes without saying that this has no bearing on your becoming a future Burghley's customer, and you will always be welcome as such.
Sheldon D. Fairey

cc: Heidi Ross, personnel

Bambi's first reaction was annoyance.

If this is someone's idea of a joke, she thought angrily, *I'm not having any of it.*

A second read-through, and an inspection of the signature, proved otherwise. It was for real, all right.

She felt a sudden fear clutch at her insides. *I'm fired. I'm really fired!*

"Sheldon D. Fairey regrets!" she huffed. "He'll regret it all right!"

Brandishing the memo and shaking with fury, she pushed past the doorman and yanked open the big heavy door herself.

She found her way barred by two beefy security guards.

"Sorry, ma'am," one of them said. "Our orders are to deny you entry."

She stared at them.

Deny. Me. Entry. It's that bitch of a wife's doing!

"I insist upon speaking with Mr. Fairey," she demanded.

"Sorry, ma'am. He's not available."

"Then where the hell is he?"

"He didn't say."

"I want to use a phone."

"Sorry, ma'am. You'll have to use one outside this building."

It was like finding herself trapped in a nightmare.

"What about my personal belongings?" she wanted to know.

"They'll be messengered to your home."

She glared at both guards, then spun around and stalked back out.

Hurrying down the block to the entrance of Auction Towers, she could feel her face burning with humiliation. She could already hear the girls in The Club dissecting her. Yak-yak-yaking and picking her to pieces while going brush-brush-brush with mascara.

Did you hear about Bambs?

Wonder what the story behind that *is!*

Thank God she hadn't run into one of *them!* She'd as soon have died!

As soon as Bambi was gone, a security guard called Sheldon D. Fairey.

"The doorman served Ms. Parker with the notice, sir."

"Thank you. Was there a problem?"

"No, sir."

"Good. If she returns, you know what to do."

"Yes, sir."

"Hopefully it won't come to that."

"Hopefully not, sir."

"Keep me informed."

Sheldon D. Fairey pressed the intercom button. "Miss Botkin, please call Ms. Turner. Tell her I wish to see her at once."

* * *

For Kenzie, the day had begun like any Monday morning. Her alarm clock had jolted her awake. She had showered, put on makeup, and gotten dressed. Had rushed to work wearing super comfy Mephistos (bye-bye, Reeboks), and along the way picked up a container of takeout coffee.

At Burghley's, she and Arnold exchanged stories about their respective weekends, tried to get Annalisa to join in—a hopeless task—and was soon immersed in work.

Then Ms. Botkin called.

Now, heading to Sheldon D. Fairey's office, she felt a wormlike sense of apprehension twisting in her stomach.

Something had to be amiss. Why else would she have been summoned?

Miss Botkin was her usual unsmiling self.

"Please have a seat, Miss Turner," she sniffed, indicating a chair. "Mr. Fairey will be with you shortly."

Kenzie thanked her and sat down. Five minutes later, the intercom buzzed and Miss Botkin showed her into the inner sanctum.

Sheldon D. Fairey was standing at the window behind his massive uncluttered desk, his back turned, looking out.

"It's a grand day, Ms. Turner, wouldn't you say?" he said in that rich plummy voice of his.

Kenzie, approaching the desk, looked out. The sky was gray and overcast, an April showers kind of day.

"It looks like rain, sir," she said.

He turned around, a distant, slightly chilly smile on his lips. "Grand days," he said, "don't necessarily have to mean nice weather, do they?"

Kenzie frowned, wondering what on earth he was getting at. "No, sir," she said. "Not if you like May flowers."

He waved a long-fingered hand at a chair. "Please, Ms. Turner. Do have a seat."

"Thank you, sir."

She pulled up one of the Anglo-Indian, carved ebony armchairs and he took a seat in the executive swivel chair behind his giant, ivory-inlaid calamander, thuya, and ebony desk. Lacing his hands, he tilted back his chair and regarded the ceiling, the wintry smile still hovering on his lips.

"Tell me, Ms. Turner," he said, "do you believe in miracles?"

"I suppose that would depend upon the definition of a miracle, sir."

He nodded, abruptly tilted his chair forward, and stared intently at her.

"What would you say," he asked gravely, "if I told you we've had our very own miracle right here at Burghley's?"

"Then I'd have to ask you what it is and judge it for myself."

"Ah. Cautious as ever, I see." He looked mildly pleased and flipped the switch on his intercom. "Miss Botkin?"

"Sir?" came the crisp, disembodied reply.

"About the memorandums. They can be distributed now."

"Yes, sir."

He sat back, elbows resting on the arms of his chair, and tapped his fingertips together in slow motion.

"If it were in my power to grant you one wish, Ms. Turner, what would you ask for?"

"I'm afraid you've caught me completely unawares, sir. I'd really have to think on it."

"Come, come, Ms. Turner! You needn't be so tactful. What does anyone here want? Power. Position. Promotions ... meaning a hefty raise, of course."

Kenzie smiled. "I suppose that brings us back to the subject of miracles, doesn't it, sir?"

"Miracles," he said softly, "have been known to happen."

She was silent.

He regarded her thoughtfully for a moment, then pulled open a desk drawer and slid a sheet of paper across to her.

"Even as we speak, copies of this are being distributed throughout the various departments," he said.

She picked up the piece of letterhead with its impressively embossed, intagliolike seal and read:

BURGHLEY'S
FOUNDED 1719

April 3, 1995

TO: All In-House Staff
FROM: Sheldon D. Fairey

Although we regret the sudden resignation of Ms. Barbara (Bambi) Parker from the Old Masters department, we are pleased to announce the promotion of Ms. MacKenzie Turner to the post of director, Old Masters Paintings and Drawings.

This promotion is to take effect immediately.

On behalf of our entire staff, I want to be the first to congratulate Ms. Turner, and know you will all enjoy working closely with her.
Sheldon D. Fairey

Kenzie sat there, stunned. "Well, mercy," she whispered, and glanced over at him. "Has Bambi resigned?"

"Renews one's faith in the human race, eh?" he said, with a rare chuckle.

"Yes, sir. I suppose it does."

"Well, I'm sure you'll have your hands full moving into Mr. Spotts's old office and all."

He rose to his feet, indicating that the meeting was over, and came around from behind his desk.

"Please accept my congratulations, Ms. Turner," he said in diapason tones, shaking her hand warmly and walking her to the door. "You see, miracles do sometimes occur."

"Yes, sir." She held his gaze. "It does seem that way."

It did not escape her that he'd neatly sidestepped the issue of Bambi's "resignation."

No sooner was Bambi in her apartment than she charged straight for the phone and punched Robert's private line.

A recorded message informed her that the number she was calling had been changed. She waited, but no new number was forthcoming.

Wrong number, she thought, and punched again.

Same message.

Frowning uneasily, she called information.

"I'm sorry," the operator told her, "it's an unlisted number."

"But this is an emer—"

The operator hung up.

Frantic, Bambi tried the switchboard at Robert's office.

She got as far as his secretary. "I'm sorry, ma'am, but Mr. Goldsmith is unavailable. If you'd like to leave a message—"

She couldn't believe it.

I've been dumped, she thought, *and without so much as a good-bye.*

"The chickenshit!" Her eyes were hot with tears. "He could have had the decency to tell me in person!"

With that, she flung the phone across the room.

Dina started off with a black-and-white Chanel suit. *Too businesslike.*

Changed to a ruffled pink silk minidress from Valentino. *Too flirty.*

A white silk shantung dress with a snappy Pompeiian red jacket from Saint Laurent. *I'm not going to lunch.*

A lantern-shaped, pleated silk dress in carnival colors from Issey Miyake. *Great for South of the Border.*

An oversize brown velvet top with floppy batik trousers from Lacroix. *Too casual.*

Nothing suited.

Finally, gazing at her Boldinis for inspiration, Dina decided upon the yellow silk morning gown. With its translucent muslin overgown and lavish trim of yellow silk bows, it was a couture fantasy of a fin de siècle housedress. *Perfect.*

She wore a minimum of makeup. *Even more perfect.*

Sweeping into the living room, she struck a Tissot pose on the *duchess brisée:* lounging sideways with one leg up and one down, and only the tips of her slippers peeking out from under two layers of extravagantly ruffled hems. She looked languidly, supremely, confidently at ease, the slim volume of poetry on her lap adding the crowning touch.

Julio cleared his throat. "Mr. Goldsmith is here, madam."

"Thank you, Julio. Please show him in." She picked up the little book of poems and pretended to read.

Two days and three nights had passed since Dina had insisted upon the trial separation, and she'd had plenty of time to take stock of the plusses and minuses of remaining married.

On the plus side were wealth, power, position, and unlimited charge accounts.

On the minus, everything boiled down to basically one thing—an unattractive, uncouth philanderer with peculiar sexual appetites.

Which wasn't exactly a revelation.

And, although in the beginning she had married Robert solely for his money, over time, and despite all his faults, Dina had to admit that she really *had* grown rather fond of him.

Besides which, the fact remained that she'd worked hard—*damn hard!*—to reach her social position. She'd literally invested years—nearly a decade, to get where she was.

Did she want to throw all that away? And for Bambi Parker?

No, she'd decided. *I'd sooner slit my wrists.*

And besides. She and Robert didn't have a prenuptial agreement. That put *him* over a barrel and *her* in the driver's seat.

And he damn well knew it.

"Scram, Tinkerbell! I can find my own goddamn way!" Dina heard from out in the foyer, and then Robert came charging into the living room, puffing tycoonlike on one of his Flor de F. Farach Extras.

"Charming as ever, I see," Dina observed with a glimmer of a smile.

"Goddamn twinkletoes!"

Robert squinted balefully in the direction of the foyer.

"Who's he think he is, keepin' me waitin' out in the hall? The public hall! An' *I* pay the rent on this place."

"But *I*," Dina reminded him sweetly, "happen to live here. Now, why don't you calm down and fix yourself a nice drink?"

"Why?" he asked edgily, although he was already at the bar. "Am I gonna need one?"

"That depends," Dina said vaguely.

He poured himself a drink, downed some, and paced the room impatiently, glass in hand.

"Well?" he scowled. "You wanted me here, an' I'm here."

As if that wasn't obvious.

"So. What's up?"

"Will you sit down? Really, sweetie. You are making me dizzy."

He looked wounded. "This the way I get welcomed home?"

She clarified one point. "I wouldn't exactly call this a homecoming, Robert. I called you so we could discuss matters."

"So? Let's discuss." He sank into the couch across from her. "Whatcha decide?"

"Always to the point," she sighed.

"That's 'cause I'm busy."

"Sweetie, you'll be a lot busier *and* a whole lot poorer if I want a divorce."

That silenced him—as she knew it would—and she took a moment to regard him closely. On the surface he was the same old Robert. Grouchy, demanding, and a pain in the behind. But under the blunt bull-in-a-china-shop bluster, she detected something different about him.

But what?

And then she knew.

There was an undercurrent of wariness and unease she hadn't noticed before.

"I have," she said, "given us a lot of thought. Not only in regard to this particular situation, but to our entire relationship."

"Yeah, yeah." He nodded impatiently and rolled the cigar around in his mouth. "An'?"

"*And,* the old saying goes that a leopard does not change its spots."

He glowered. "Yeah, but leopards ain't *people.*"

"You know very well what I mean, Robert."

"C'mon, Dina." His gruffness abruptly gentled. "We have a good thing goin', don't we?"

"I thought so. Until it was ruined by a certain affair with a certain young lady."

"Yeah, but she's history."

"*She* may be. But what about other young ladies down the road?"

"Aw, Christ!" he blurted. "Gimme a break, Dina, will ya?"

He pushed himself to his feet and clumped back and forth across the room, reminding her of a man dying to take a leak.

"Look, I did everythin' you asked for," he growled. "I got her fired. She'll be outta Auction Towers. *An',* I'm cleanin' up my act."

He churned up humongous, lavish clouds of blue smoke.

"What more d'ya want?"

"Reassurance would be nice," she said.

"Okay. *Okay.*"

He scratched the back of his head as he paced.

"Look. I'm not exactly proud about what I've done," he said miserably. "An' I'm not tryin' to wheedle out of it, either. Believe it or not, I feel guilty as all hell!"

He shot her a pleading look. "That satisfy ya?" he asked.

"Well, it's certainly a step in the right direction."

"A step! Look, I'm tryin' ta tell ya that I missed ya!"

He stopped pacing, took the cigar out of his mouth, and jabbed it in her direction.

"Yeah, *you!* I missed *you!*" His voice abruptly softened. "An' I'm sorry, Dina. Really I am. Last thing I wanna do is hurt ya, 'cause ..."

He sighed heavily, shifted position, and looked down at his feet in obvious embarrassment.

"... 'cause I love ya," he said so quietly she could barely hear.

Dina looked at him in amazement. "I love you." He'd actually said, "I love you!" And now he was blushing and glancing shyly over at her like a schoolchild!

Surprise, surprise! she thought. *Good heavens!*

If memory served her correctly—and it had never failed her yet—this was the first time he'd *ever* uttered those three magic little words. And, however clumsy and inept the delivery, she couldn't help but be touched.

She found her anger and harshness dissipate, and smiled at him slowly.

"Well, perhaps it's quite a large step," she qualified.

"Oh, yeah?" He perked up. "This mean you'll gimme another chance?"

"I'll give *us* another chance," she emphasized.

"Hot damn!" His face lit up like a Christmas tree. "You won't regret it," he promised.

"I certainly hope not."

"That mean I can move back in?"

"As long as you remember you are on probation. But don't forget, sweetie. If I so much as catch you sneaking a *glance* in the wrong direction ..." Her voice trailed off.

"I won't."

"You'd better not," she said darkly.

He glanced at his watch. "Shit. I'm late for a meetin'."

She sighed. "Sweetie, you are so romantic."

He puffed away grandly. "Gotta keep my babe in moolah, right?"

She smiled happily. "Right. And speaking of which, Mr. Mongiardino needs two million dollars to continue on the apartment. You will see that it's paid promptly, won't you, sweetie?"

Another two mil! Robert's cigar nearly fell out of his mouth. "What's the guy do with money," he asked. "Eat it?"

Well, what the hell, he thought. *What's a few mil?*

Pocket change.

A divorce could easily have set him back a quarter of a *bil.* Put into that context, he was getting off cheaply, and knew it.

Bambi heard the chime of the doorbell, and her heart gave a leap.

Robert . . . !

Convinced he had come to tell her it was all a mistake, she rushed to the door and flung it open.

What . . . ?

It was not Robert standing there, but the building manager.

"What do *you* want?" she snapped.

"I'm sorry, Ms. Parker, but we have received complaints. As this is an illegal sublet, I'm afraid you're going to have to vacate the premises."

She couldn't believe this! The nightmare was continuing!

Will it never end? she wondered.

"Just what sort of complaints are you talking about?" she sniffed.

He cleared his throat. "As you know, here at the Towers we pride ourselves on the utmost discretion—"

"Well, stick it up your discreet ass!" she declared, slamming the door.

Then she collapsed against it and shut her eyes.

Oh, God, she thought. *This can't be happening! Where will I* go? *What will I* do?

She was stumped.

But only temporarily. Bambi was, above all, a survivor.

The following morning, she moved in with Lex Bugg.

56

"I have your report in front of me," Karl-Heinz said into the telephone. "Other than ironing out a few minor details, I don't anticipate any problems."

He glanced through the open door. Zandra was pacing restlessly along the tall windows in the next room, every so often gazing out at the rainswept Place Vendôme.

She was agitated. He could see that. And it had been building up over the past few weeks. He knew that, too. No matter what she happened to be doing—eating, dressing, shopping, conversing—before long, she would begin prowling restively. Comforting herself by clasping and unclasping her hands.

Her attention span was down to nothing. Clearly, something was eating at her.

But whatever it was, wild horses couldn't drag it out of her, at least not until she was ready. This too Karl-Heinz knew, for he had tried on countless occasions to do just that.

"You can assure Mr. Yazahari that in essence we both agree to the same terms," he said into the phone. "We can discuss the minor details when we meet in Hawaii."

As the phone conversation wound down, he kept his eye on the next room. Zandra had stopped pacing to peer out a window yet again.

April in Paris, he thought. *The trees are supposed to be in bloom, the skies should be warm and sunny, and lovers ought to be promenading along the Seine and in the Bois de Boulogne and the Jardin de Luxembourg.*

Instead, it had been raining steadily ever since they'd arrived.

A portent?

In the adjoining room, Zandra had resumed her pacing, and was hugging herself, her hands tucked under her armpits.

She needs me, Karl-Heinz thought. *She needs me now.*

"Please convey my best regards to Mr. Yazahari, and tell him I'm looking forward to meeting with him," he said politely, and hung up. In one elegant movement he pushed back his chair, got to his feet, and went into the next room.

"Zandra," he said softly.

She stopped pacing and looked at him.

He advanced toward her and held her gently by the expensive sleeves of her unbuttoned Ungaro jacket. *"Liebchen?"* He looked into her eyes. "What *is* it?"

"It's . . ." she began, then gave a shrug of futility and hugged herself even tighter. "Oh, Heinzie, it's everything. And nothing. That, *too*. Do you suppose it's a phase pregnant women go through?"

He shook his head. "There's more to it than that, *Liebchen,* and I think we both know it."

She looked away suddenly, over his shoulder, her face pinched with anxiety.

"Can't we talk about it?" he asked quietly.

She expelled a sigh and bit her trembling lip.

God, but it pained him to see her like this! What a different Zandra this was from the radiant bride in Augsburg Cathedral, or the carefree honeymooner who insisted upon making love at various times of the day, or the rabid shopper to whom the couture salons were like candy stores, just waiting to be raided.

Where, he wondered, *have all those other Zandras gone?*

Indeed, it was high time for a serious talk.

Wrapping an arm around her, he led her across the room and sat her on a delicately carved settee. Then he went over to the round *bouillotte* table which held stemware and bottles and came back with two full shot glasses.

"Here," he said, holding one out to her.

She glanced at the clear fluid, then up at him. "What is it?"

"A little schnapps," he answered. "To soothe your nerves."

She shook her head. "No. Not while I'm pregnant."

He set both glasses on the coffee table and then perched on the arm of the settee, stroking her hair. She rested her head against his side.

"God," she murmured, "you must think me one hell of a self-centered bitch."

"I don't think that at all." He planted a kiss atop her head and continued brushing her hair with his hand.

"I wouldn't blame you if you did," she said pensively. "I mean, I've been beastly and absolutely no fun at *all."*

"Zandra," he urged gently, *"share* your misery. Please. Nothing is so bad that something can't be done about it."

She smiled wryly. *Sweet Heinzie,* she thought. *He means so well. But how can he begin to understand? Men don't get pregnant. Men don't nurture a spark of life from conception until birth. How could any man understand?*

"It's about the baby, isn't it?" he asked softly.

She twisted her head to look up at him.

"Yes," she whispered, "it's about our baby."

"Don't you want to have it?"

She jerked, as though an invisible fist had slammed into her. *Oh, Heinzie, Heinzie! How can you misread things so badly?*

"That isn't it at all," she said quietly. "I *want* this baby, Heinzie. Oh, God! If only you knew how badly I want it!"

He slid off the arm of the settee and dropped to his knees in front of her, placing his head in her lap, the side of his face touching her belly and the child growing within.

Tears suddenly welled up in her eyes. With her hands, she pressed his head even closer.

She took a deep breath, and with huge reluctance, plunged ahead.

"Oh, Heinzie," she said ruefully, "I know I'm being an absolute shit, and I can't bear to disappoint you. But I just loathe the way we're having this baby. I mean, it's not at all fair to the child."

He raised his head from her lap and looked deep into her eyes. "What isn't?" he asked softly.

"The mercenary way we're going about it. Don't you see? Having a child shouldn't be a sweepstakes you enter for a prize, should it? I know a male child's necessary for you to inherit, I *know* all that. But . . . darling, it's our baby I'm carrying! Our baby! Our own flesh and blood."

"Yes." He smiled tenderly and reached up and gently touched her face. "I know," he whispered.

"And, I already feel connected to it. I realize it's still early, but I am its mother."

He was still smiling.

"I know we made a deal," she said, "but suddenly I don't give a whit whether it's a boy or a girl. And, if it is a girl, what's going to happen to it? I mean, I want us to have a son, I really do, worse than anything. But now that I'm carrying, that's suddenly unimportant. Darling, I love it already—boy *or* girl. Whichever it is."

The tears which had welled up in her eyes started flowing down her face.

"I just want us to have a normal, healthy child!" she blurted. "Is that too much to ask for?"

She paused and sniffed.

"Darling? Won't you *say* something?"

"*Liebchen,* don't you realize? I love the baby, too!"

"You . . . do?" Zandra's voice quavered uncertainly.

"Of course I do. And I want what's best for all three of us."

"Yes, but Heinzie, what I *can't* do . . ."

She stopped and gulped a lungful of air.

". . . I can't allow it to be prodded and poked," Zandra whispered fiercely. "I know it's only been weeks, but suppose it can already *feel* things? And what about the risk? Dr. Rosenbaum put the risk of villus sampling at somewhere between one and two percent, but he did say some doctors put it as high as eight. And even an amniocentesis carries some risk. There's the chance, however slight, of triggering a spontaneous abortion, injuring the fetus, or even introducing an infection!"

She was sobbing noisily now.

"And even if it were a hundred percent safe, which it isn't, and if we find out it's a girl, I . . . I could never bring myself to abort it!"

"No one is asking you to," he said gently.

"I mean, I'll gladly do anything—anything at all—so long as it doesn't endanger the child."

"Liebchen! Haven't you listened to a word I've said?"

She stared at him. "Then you . . . you don't mind? You'll accept it even if it's a girl?"

"How could I not? She would be our child."

"But the inheritance—"

"The hell with the inheritance! I'm rich enough in my own right. My personal fortune's over two hundred million."

"That much!"

He smiled. "Besides making money for the family, you don't think I didn't make some for myself, do you? So stop worrying."

She smiled. "I'll try."

"And promise me one thing, *Liebchen.*"

"What?"

"From now on, if something bothers you, don't keep it bottled up inside. For God's sake, share it. This is my baby, too, you know."

She felt like hugging him to death.

"Oh, Heinzie, *Heinzie!*"

She flung her arms around him.

"I'm so happy!" she cried. "You don't know how happy you've made me!"

Then he had his arms around her, and tears streaked down both their cheeks, and it seemed they stayed that way forever, clinging to each other as though for dear life itself.

When the telephone rang, Karl-Heinz ignored it, and then Josef discreetly cleared his throat at the door. "It's a personal call from Mr. Yazahari, Your Highness," he said in German.

Karl-Heinz didn't even turn around.

"Later, Josef," he said. "And shut the door, would you?"

"But shouldn't you take it?" Zandra asked. "It might be important."

"There are only two really important things in my life," Karl-Heinz told her softly. "I know that now. You and our baby—and that's all."

And for some crazy reason, they both burst out into a fresh round of joyous tears.

57

"*P*reg—!" shrieked Princess Sofia in horror.

She clapped both hands over her mouth to stifle the devastating word in midsyllable. Her eyes bulged in shock.

"—nant," she expelled in a gulping whisper.

She sank down onto a severely plain Biedermeier settee, afraid that if she remained standing for a moment longer her legs would surely give out from under her.

Outside the arched, neo-Gothic windows of the sitting room of Schloss Schweingau, the steamer that regularly plied the lake was passing by. Two little sailboats, tacking into the wind, bobbed in the steamer's wake. Storm clouds were gathering, and the snow-clad Alpine peaks to the south seemed to press closer.

"They've been married . . . *what* now?" Sofia whispered shakily. "Six weeks? Seven? And you tell me she is already pregnant!"

"Z-Zandra?" piped up Erwein, whose presence Sofia had demanded when Herr August Meindl, the senior von und zu Engelwiesen solicitor, and his four solicitor sons, had come calling.

Erwein put his teacup into the saucer he was holding, and his hands were so shaky that cup and saucer rattled.

"It is Z-Z-Zandra you're t-talking about?" he stuttered.

"No. The Duchess of York," Sofia snapped sarcastically. "Who *else's* pregnancy would affect us, you subnormal cretin? You moronic, duncical chain around my neck!"

Erwein cringed, and his cup and saucer rattled even louder.

"And do put your tea *down!*" hissed Sofia irritably. "That infernal racket is driving me up the wall!"

Erwein immediately thrust the offending cup and saucer on a round fruitwood table.

Wearily Sofia rubbed her face with her hands. Only then did she turn to the messenger who had delivered the unwelcome news.

In his youth, a very, very remote youth—that is to say, sometime in the years preceding the First World War—Herr August Meindl had made a hobby of studying the classics, so the traditional fate befalling messengers of bad tidings was not lost on him. He fully expected Sofia's ax to fall, though he did not fear it.

Herr August Meindl was too old, too cunning, and had dealt with Sofia too long to let her unsettle him. And Sofia knew it.

His four sons, full partners in the family's *Rechtsanwalt* firm, were younger carbon copies of their father. Not that they were youthful by any means: the youngest, Franz, was well in his mid-fifties, while the eldest, Anton, was in his early seventies.

Their sons, and their sons' sons, all worked for the Meindl family firm, groomed since childhood to represent but one exalted client—the von und zu Engelwiesens.

Sofia asked, "How long, exactly, has Princess Zandra been pregnant?"

August Meindl shrugged his narrow, bony shoulders. "His Highness did not say," he told her in his thin, warbly voice.

Sofia took a deep, steadying breath.

August Meindl sat there, his ancient, sticklike body jerking and trembling. "I am truly sorry, Princess Sofia. I know that this must come as a terrible blow."

"Blow? Why should it come as a blow? Granted, I was initially *surprised,* gentlemen, but I am thoroughly delighted. Thanks to the news you have brought, the family's uninterrupted line of male succession shall, God willing, be assured."

The Meindls looked as though they couldn't quite believe their ears.

Erwein couldn't believe his, either. He had been expecting a full-scale apocalypse.

Incredibly, Sofia seemed to gain strength and serenity right in front of their very eyes.

"The family and its fortune," she continued, "must always take precedence over any of our individual wants, concerns, and wishes—and that goes for my own, as well."

The five solicitors stared at her.

"This is," she said, "a *happy* occasion. As you well know, this family has been around for nearly six hundred years, and I fully intend for it to be around for another six hundred. I expect each of you to give my brother your full cooperation and unfailing support."

She paused and looked from one of them to the other.

"Do I make myself clear?"

"Very clear, Your Highness," said Franz Meindl.

"Perfectly, Your Highness," echoed Klaus Meindl.

"Indubitably, Your Highness," added Gerhard Meindl.

"Pellucidly, Your Highness," summed up Anton Meindl.

Only ancient August was silent. His cunning legal brain was such that he never rushed into anything.

Sofia looked at him with raised eyebrows. "Herr Meindl?"

August Meindl cleared his throat, multiple dewlaps and wattles quivering. "Am I correct in intuiting that you do not perceive this information to be bad news, Your Highness?" he asked cautiously.

"You intuit correctly." Sofia forced a thin smile.

All five Meindls waited.

"And, much as I admire, love, and respect my brother," Sofia went on, "the family has, in the past, suffered its share of treachery and deception from within its ranks. The temptation of taking the helm of one of the world's mightiest fortunes can seduce even the most honest among us. We must proceed with extreme caution."

"Indeed." August nodded sagely. "We cannot take anything for granted."

"Also," Sofia said, "we cannot *discount* even the most implausible kind of plot. In 1598, Freda von und zu Engelwiesen gave birth to a girl, but attempted to secure the inheritance with a boy not of her womb."

"Not of her womb!" exclaimed Franz Meindl, the youngest of the five.

"She sent a servant out to buy a newborn son to pass off as her own. That is why our family law specifies three solicitors to witness the birth."

Gerhard Meindl plucked at his protruding lower lip. "A wise stipulation."

"Indeed," Sofia said. "Now then. Did my brother happen to mention any tests being done to determine the sex of the child?"

Her sharp gaze met five shaking heads.

"Have you run a check on her doctor?"

"Not yet," said old August.

"Do it."

He nodded.

Sofia took advantage of their silence to bring them even further around.

"A girl, beloved though a daughter might be, would be as tragic for my brother as his wife's not giving birth at all. *Gentlemen.*"

Sofia sat up straighter, her own words and thoughts fortifying her like an impenetrable skin of Kevlar.

"Pregnancies, as we all know, are unpredictable at best. Even if Princess Zandra *is* carrying a boy, she could miscarry. Or the child might be stillborn. Who knows what will happen?"

The air seemed suddenly charged with ozone. The room had grown dark. Then it pulsated with lightning, and a crash of thunder followed.

Erwein all but leapt to his feet in terror.

Sofia waited until the noise subsided.

"Whatever the case may be," she said softly, "we must not jump to conclusions. My brother inherits *if* and *when* his wife gives birth to a male heir, and *only* if this occurs before the death of my father."

"I quite agree, Your Highness," old Herr Meindl concurred in a quaver.

"Good. The inheritance must be procured justly and fairly, and must adhere strictly to the laws of primogeniture."

Sofia paused.

"To the very *letter* of the laws of primogeniture," she added emphatically.

"You have my word," the old man said.

Sofia nodded. "And do I also have the word of your sons?"

August Meindl glanced to the left and right of him. Franz, Klaus, Gerhard, and Anton Meindl all nodded.

"They are agreed, Your Highness. You may rest assured that everything about the birth will be aboveboard and legally binding. Three attorneys shall be present in the delivery room to witness it."

"No, Herr Meindl." Sofia shook her head. "Not just three attorneys. Three of *you.*"

"If that is your wish," the old man said, inclining his head.

"It is."

Sofia looked at him with a pleased expression, much as she might have bestowed upon a shop clerk who had unlocked a cabinet to show her a bijoux she particularly fancied.

"Now then," she said. "Since that is out of the way, I would like to take this opportunity to broach another matter."

"Yes?" the old man asked cautiously.

"I fully realize, Herr Meindl, that your firm represents the interests of this family as a whole. However, I also realize that since my father's illness, you presumed my brother was in charge."

Old Herr Meindl started to say something, but she held up a hand.

"Until Princess Zandra produces an appropriate heir before my father dies—which, unfortunately, could be any day now—*I myself* stand to inherit on behalf of my eldest son."

August Meindl pursed his lips. "Hmm," he murmured noncommittally.

"I have looked it up in the family book of primogeniture," Sofia told him. "Section sixteen pertains specifically to incapacitated heads of family and their childless heirs. It is quite specific. Erwein!"

Erwein jumped up and hurried to fetch a thick, illuminated manuscript of great age. Puffs of dust rose from the priceless leather volume as he placed it on the table in front of August Meindl. The thunderstorm outside raged like an amplified omen.

Herr Meindl got out his reading glasses and managed, despite his palsy, to place them on his beaky nose. Then, carefully, shakily, reverently, he turned the thick pages to where a silk ribbon marked section sixteen.

He read the giant Gothic script slowly, running his bony finger along each line and whispering the words to himself.

Sofia fidgeted impatiently, wishing he would hurry up.

After what seemed an eternity, the old man carefully closed the precious book, put away his glasses, and cleared his throat. "You are quite correct, Your Highness. Section sixteen does indeed spell it out. And quite explicitly."

"Exactly!" trumpeted Sofia smugly. "Therefore, since my father is in a coma, *my* eldest son is, for the time being, the crown prince of this empire. As such, I fully expect you to extend him—and myself— every courtesy."

She glanced around the table.

"Naturally, should my father miraculously improve, or should my brother's wife produce a male heir in time, your allegiance shall automatically switch back to him."

She stared long and hard at old Herr Meindl.

"Well, gentlemen?"

The younger Meindls glanced at their elder for guidance.

"We must do as it is written, Your Highness," the old man said expressionlessly. "You are, for now, the family's regent."

"Good. And as such, I am giving you your first order. By midsummer, Princess Zandra should be in the fifth month of pregnancy. At that point, I want your three most trusted sons to keep her under close observation."

He coughed discreetly. "You mean . . . surveillance?"

"A matter of semantics, but yes. Surveillance. They may hire detectives, but are to follow her personally wherever she may travel. Cost is no object, and they will report directly to me. I want to know everything— whether they think it significant or not."

"We are, as always, at your service, Your Highness."

Sofia positively purred. "That will be all for now, Herr Meindl. Thank you, gentlemen, and *auf Wiedersehen.*"

Thus dismissed, Herr Meindl and his four sons rose, bowed formally, and left.

Once they were gone, Sofia remained seated, too deep in thought to notice Erwein tiptoe out.

TARGET: BURGHLEY'S COUNTDOWN TO TERROR

Somerset, New Jersey, May 11

There were no dogs.

Had there been, they might have made things more difficult. Not impossible, of course. Nothing was impossible. Donough Kildare would simply have dealt with dogs as he dealt with everything else—quietly, ruthlessly, and lethally.

The night was chill, the fleeting clouds his accomplice. Dressed in tight, form-fitting black, rubber-soled shoes, snug leather gloves and night-vision goggles, he was one with the darkness. Everything he needed was in the four padded pouches strapped around his waist.

On he crept, toward the isolated compound and his destination, the Greek Revival mansion.

It's such a beautiful house, he thought. *What a pity it must be destroyed.*

Tonight would be his sixth and last invasion of the mansion. He had been inside on five previous occasions without being detected, and was familiar enough with the security devices that he could have bypassed them in his sleep.

Unless they've changed the alarms, he thought, *it's a piece of cake.*

He took a moment to search his plan for flaws. There were none. He had left nothing to chance. For two months now, he'd rented a nearby farmhouse, and not a day had gone by that he had not reconnoitered the compound from a distance.

He knew everything there was to know.

Because of the horses and wild animals setting them off, no alarms existed on the property itself. *Stupidity!*

The porch was protected by infrared beams, but the doors and windows by an antiquated, easily bypassed alarm system. *Child's play.*

And as for the Secret Service agents, lack of action had lulled them into a false sense of security. *Tonight, you'll pay for it with your lives.*

On he crawled, until he reached the house. There he lay stock-still, looking and listening.

All was quiet in the pastures. All was quiet in the house. The only sounds were the occasional neighs from the horses in the stables and his own steady breathing.

It's time to get a move on, Donough Kildare told himself. *Time to create my "natural disaster" while the target's here.*

From his vantage in the woods, he had watched her arrive yesterday, his ten-by-fifty binoculars making it seem like she was right in front of him. There was no mistaking her.

Blimey! he'd thought. *In person she looks exactly like her effing photographs!*

Not that it made any difference who she was. A job was a job, and the pay was excellent.

Now he switched his night-vision goggles for a pair of infrareds.

Instead of murky green, everything suddenly took on a red hue. Beams of light, invisible to the naked eye, crisscrossed the porch.

He was not deterred. The drainpipes, which he'd climbed on his previous visits, had been completely overlooked. Bad breach of security, that. Almost an insult. *You're making it too easy!*

Checking his watch, he ascertained that he had twenty-three minutes before one of the Secret Service agents made his next round.

Now to bypass the alarm wires.

He stowed the goggles in a pouch, sprinted around to the back of the house, and crawled underneath a spreading yew. Switching on his penlight, he played it over the wires.

They were exactly as he'd left them—temporarily connected.

Holding the penlight between his teeth, he set to work. Produced a six-inch length of wire with alligator clamps on either end. Unwrapped the electrical tape he'd placed around two of the wires the first time he'd stripped them, and clipped one clamp to each. Snipped the alarm wire with a small pair of wire cutters.

He crawled out from under the shrub and took some long, deep breaths. Then, grabbing hold of the nearest drainpipe, he shimmied up it without a sound.

When he reached the roof, he did a slow pull-up, swung one leg up over the edge, then hoisted himself, and stood up. Through force of habit, he took the time for a quick scan of the grounds.

Nothing doing. *Good.*

Next, he checked the dormer window he had left unlocked, but had wedged shut, on his last visit.

He removed the wedge.

The window was still unlocked, and opened as if in welcome.

He climbed inside, careful to distribute his weight evenly on the old floorboards. Then, using his penlight, he wove his way around mountains of discarded furniture, boxes, and trunks. The air was acrid with dust; cobwebs stuck to his face.

A minute later, he reached the door.

Opening it a crack, he peered out.

The coast was clear, the stairway thoughtfully lit.

He switched off the penlight, put on his goggles, and checked for newly installed infrared alarm beams.

There were none.

Walking in a crouch, and avoiding the steps he knew to be creaky, he crept down the narrow stairs to the second-floor landing. There, he flattened himself against the wall, edged along it, and peered around the corner.

He was at the grand staircase which curved down to the oval foyer. Silent as a ghost, he moved toward it, looking up, down, and out past the railing. Eyes everywhere, ears attuned.

It's like the night before bleedin' Christmas, he thought. *Not a creature is stirring, not even a mouse ...*

Swiftly and quietly, he descended the stairs, listened at the door to the service hallway, then opened it and slipped inside. Second door to the left led down to the basement.

This was the door with hinges badly in need of oiling.

No problem. Two squirts of WD-40 and it opened without a whisper. He stepped inside and closed it behind him.

Now he was atop the basement stairs. Switching on the penlight, he shone it down the steep concrete steps and started down.

The basement smelled of moist stone and rotting wood. Old spiderwebs, like dirty angel hair, spanned the bare beams overhead, trapping the dried carapaces of long-dead flies. He could hear a sump pump kick in, the furnace going *fa-lump!,* the steady plops of water from a leaky pipe.

He headed straight for the furnace, shut it off, and extinguished the pilot light. Then he turned it on full blast.

He smiled to himself as he heard the snakelike hiss of escaping gas. Lovely.

Now for the two boilers.

He turned them both off, blew out their pilot lights, and switched them back on also.

Time for the main event: the gas line feeding into the house.

When he reached it, he clipped the penlight to his jacket, took a gas mask out of a pouch, and slipped it over his head. Next, he took a small, carefully sealed, heavy glass bottle from its snug, foam-padded nest in one of the pouches.

Inside was acid: corrosive, nonflammable, quick-acting.

He broke the seal cautiously. *Don't want to get this stuff on me,* he thought. With utmost care he began to dribble it on the gas line.

The metal pipe instantly began to blister and disintegrate. Within a minute, it was thoroughly eaten through.

Gas, silent and deadly, started pouring into the basement.

Carefully he stoppered the empty bottle, placed it back in its pouch, unclipped the penlight, and went back upstairs.

He left all the doors open so the gas could fill the house. Sprinted up the grand staircase. Headed down a second-floor corridor to the east wing, where the master bedroom was located.

Every bomb needs a fuse . . .

He switched off the corridor lights. Popped the penlight in his mouth and unscrewed the switchplate. Carefully uncapped the wires and joined them together, making sure they touched metal.

One spark is all it takes . . .

He screwed the switchplate back on and grinned to himself. *I'm glad I won't be around when that light's turned on,* he thought sardonically.

He was on the roof, wedging the dormer window shut when he spied a Secret Service agent coming out of the guest house, flashlight in hand. *Much good a check of the grounds will do,* he thought.

Fifteen minutes later, the agent was back inside. *Now!*

Donough Kildare scuttled down the drainpipe. Crawled under the yew to reconnect the alarm system. Then disappeared across the meadow, a lithe, barely visible shadow.

He stopped a hundred yards from the house and dropped to the ground, taking up position under a paddock fence. Got out that most ancient of all weapons—a slingshot and a stone.

After the Big Bang, investigators could sift through the rubble all they liked. They'd never find the telltale residue of matches, timers, fuses, explosives, or bullets. All he'd have to do was launch a single stone at a window.

The lady will do the rest.

He settled down, deciding to give it two-and-a-half hours. By then the house would be a bomb waiting to go off.

Ingenious.

Becky V was jolted awake by the deafening, shattering bedlam of the alarms. *What the devil—*

She sat up in bed and looked around wildly.

The outdoor floods had automatically clicked on, bathing the perimeter of the house, and she could see the stark, glaring white light through chinks in the drawn curtains.

Tilting her head, she listened for the shouts of her Secret Service detail, but it was impossible. Everything was drowned out by the ear-splitting din.

Why don't they shut the infernal thing off? she wondered.

Then she relaxed.

It's probably just a false alarm. It certainly wouldn't be the first time.

She decided to go and switch it off herself.

Turning on her bedside lamp, she got up, shrugged herself into a blue silk nightgown, and tied the sash as she crossed the room. Opening her door carefully, she peered out.

The corridor was dark; the dimmed sconces were off. *That's strange. They're always left on.* Suddenly she felt sick to her stomach. *What's that stench?* she wondered. *It smells like gas.*

Hurrying now, and trying not to breathe, she stumbled down the corridor to the light switch.

The fumes were overwhelming. *Good Lord! It is gas! I'd better turn on the lights so I can see where I'm going.* She reached for the switch and flipped it.

There was a blinding flash and a tremendous roar, and the entire mansion exploded in a fireball.

At seven-thirty that evening, Donough Kildare was at a Toms River, New Jersey, marina. *Another job well done,* he thought. *This one was certainly my crowning achievement. Maybe it's a good time to retire . . .*

As prearranged, he boarded a forty-one-foot Hatteras double-cabin motor yacht, slid open the door, and stepped down into the compact salon.

"Close the door," the man seated in the club chair said softly.

Kildare slid it shut and froze as he heard the familiar click of a gun hammer. Slowly, he turned around.

He was looking at the silencer of a .44-caliber Magnum revolver. "What the bleedin' fuck? I only came to collect my—"

"Did you ever hear my Arnold Schwarzenegger routine?" the man with the gun asked softly.

Kildare stared at him. "Huh—?"

The man said, *"Hasta la vista,* baby," and pulled the trigger.

Donough Kildare's head burst like a ripe watermelon.

The man blew on the smoking barrel and smiled. *Now all we have to do is wait,* he thought. *When Becky's things come on the auction block, we'll have the world's richest collectors and celebrities under one roof.*

Sitting ducks, the lot of them. Just waiting to be plucked . . .

He could hardly wait.

Book Five

THE AUCTION TO END ALL

**Becky V Death Ruled a Tragic Accident.
Legend's Collections to Go on the Block**

SOMERSET, N.J., June 26 (AP)—A gas leak coupled with faulty wiring was the probable cause of the explosion which killed six people here, including former First Lady Rebecca Cornille Wakefield Lantzouni de la Vila, federal investigators and local fire officials said today.

But investigators admitted they were baffled by how a gas leak could account for an explosion of such magnitude, according to Dwight Kramer, a federal official.

When the fire department arrived on the scene, all that was left of the mansion was a giant smoldering crater.

"It looked like a bomb had been dropped," said Chief Fred Czubik of the local fire department.

The victims, which in addition to the Duchess de la Vila included three servants and two Secret Service agents, occurred about 4:15 A.M. on Saturday, May 11. All were identified through dental remains.

Lord Rosenkrantz, the investment banker, who had been staying in the nearby guest house, escaped with minor injuries and was treated and released from the local hospital.

The team of investigators worked around the clock for six weeks before reaching their verdict. According to Mr. Kramer, they ruled out the possibility of arson early on because of the lack of an incendiary device.

"It's an act of God," Chief Czubik said. "We've never seen this before, and hope we'll never see it again."

Local gas company officials were not available for comment.

November Auction Planned

Beginning on November 11 in New York, Burghley's will kick off a series of auctions of art, antique furnishings, decorative objects, and important jewels owned by what the auction house calls "one of the most famous and fascinating women of our century."

Born Rebecca Cornille, the woman who came to be known as Becky V was married to, and widowed by, President William Winterton Wakefield III, Leonidas Danaus Lantzouni, the shipping magnate, and *Gran Duque* Joaquín de la Vila, and maintained various residences around the world.

According to Burghley's, thirty-two experts from eight departments will catalogue the various collections.

Over eight hundred of the world's finest Old Masters, including works by Velasquez, El Greco, Rubens, Titian, Veronese, and Goya will be sold, as well as furnishings by Roentgen, Jacob, and Boulle.

"It's a pity to see the collections broken up," the *Gran Duquesa*'s sister, the *Vicomtesse* Suzy de Saint-Mallet said, "but as Becky would say, 'We're just temporary custodians.' "

All proceeds from the sales will go to charity.

❦ *58* ❧

The mayor charged into his office twenty minutes late, personality and charisma creating a cyclonelike burst of energy, a fluttery aide at his heels.

"Sorry I'm late, gentlemen," he apologized, flashing a mouthful of bright teeth. "Couldn't be helped."

The seated men had risen to their feet. Each received a brisk, campaign-trail handclasp, a sincere look straight in the eye, and heard the mayor say his name: "Mr. Goldsmith. Mr. Fairey. Detective Ferraro. Mr. Hockert."

Hizzoner had obviously been briefed in advance. Not that it mattered. He liked giving that personal touch, and knew from experience that people fell for it.

He didn't shake hands with the police commissioner, but acknowledged him with friendly familiarity. "Ed," he said, "Thelma and the kids okay?"

"They're just fine, Mr. Mayor," beamed the tall black man in uniform.

"Good. Be sure and give them my regards. Gentlemen, please. Have a seat."

Greetings over, the mayor was suddenly all business. He strode behind his desk, sat down in his red tufted-leather executive swivel chair, and leaned forward. Behind him were two flagpoles, one with the Stars and Stripes, the other with the state flag.

"You're here to discuss security at the auction on—?" He clicked his fingers.

"November eleventh, Mr. Mayor," supplied his hovering aide.

"Right. At Burghley's." He eyeballed the PC. "Have you been filled in, Ed?"

"Yes, Mr. Mayor."

"And?"

"In my opinion, police presence is a definite must. Mr. Fairey gave me a partial list of people who'll probably attend. There's a copy of it on your desk."

The mayor picked up the sheet of paper and quickly scanned it. He looked up sharply, his voice incredulous. *"These* are some of the people you expect at the auction?"

"Yes, Mr. Mayor," Sheldon D. Fairey replied. "Those and many other notables."

"Good God! This looks more like an international summit than an art sale!"

"That's why we're being so security-conscious," Fairey said.

"I take it you have your own security staff?"

"Naturally, and we plan to augment it. But with two heads of state, some former ones, major celebrities, movie stars, and hundreds of the richest people in the world—" Fairey gestured eloquently. "Their safety has to be our foremost concern."

Frowning thoughtfully, the mayor swiveled on his big chair and stared out the window, where a light rain was falling. After a moment, he swiveled back around. He looked at the PC. "Your call, Ed."

"My advice is we pull out all the stops, Mr. Mayor. Treat this as if the President were coming to town."

"You're talking expensive." The mayor was only too aware of the city's budget deficit.

"Can't be helped. We'll need heavy security around Burghley's and wherever the most politically sensitive VIPs are staying. Also, we should consider providing police escorts to a select few. And we should definitely close off a section of Madison before and during the auction."

The mayor pinched the bridge of his nose. "You know what this means, Ed. Don't you?"

"Yes, Mr. Mayor. A lot of overtime."

"Which the city can't afford."

"Yes, but there's something the city can afford even less."

"Which is?"

"There are people on that list who've survived several failed assassination attempts. How would it look if someone succeeded at it here?"

He didn't have to spell out the ramifications of such a scenario. The mayor knew them well.

The press would have a field day, he thought grimly. *The city would suffer an onslaught of adverse publicity. Tourism would plunge. And I can kiss reelection good-bye.*

"And to think they're all coming here because of the Becky V auction," he marveled softly, shaking his head. "Unbelievable."

"Not if you bear in mind who Becky V was, Mr. Mayor," Fairey said quietly. "Besides being a national icon, she was inarguably the most famous woman in the world."

"True." The mayor nodded. "Tragic, what happened to her."

There were murmurs of agreement.

Robert decided it was time to chip in his two cents. "Somethin' else to keep in mind," he said, changing the subject. "Becky V's art treasures."

"Yes?" the mayor said.

"Well, outside a few museums, so many masterpieces've never been in any one place at one given time. Our insurance company's bustin' its gut tryin' to get other companies to help underwrite the policy. Four to six billion's a lot a simoleons."

The mayor leaned forward and stared. "Did you say . . . *billion?* With a 'B'?"

Robert returned his stare. "That's right."

"Holy cow." The mayor leaned back in his chair and whistled softly. "I see that this is going to mean more than just a day or two of extra police presence."

"I'd say it's justified," Robert said.

"Yes, but we're talking a major tab here. And the city's stretched thin as it is."

The mayor rolled back his chair, got to his feet, and moved over to the windows. He looked out thoughtfully, silhouetted by rain-squiggled glass. "Also," he said, rubbing a hand over his face, "the taxpayers are going to scream bloody murder. They'll want to know *why* their hard-earned money's being spent protecting a very small segment of very rich people who've gathered for a very exclusive, private event."

"You might," Robert said serenely, having come armed with figures, "remind them that Burghley's paid over *ten mil* in city taxes last year. An', that doesn't include another *eight point seven* mil we collected in sales tax. You want, I can reel off the fed and state figures, too."

The mayor turned around, walked back to his desk, and lowered himself into his chair. "I don't believe that'll be necessary."

"You ask me," Robert glowered, "we're entitled to some protection."

The PC spoke up. "If I may suggest something, Mr. Mayor."

"Suggest away, Ed." The mayor smiled bleakly. "Heck, I'm open to any ideas."

"Well, you know the old saying about an ounce of prevention."

"What about it?"

"For starters, Detective Ferraro and Mr. Hockert can do a study of Burghley's security system, see what flaws can be ironed out. The same goes for whatever transport system is used to move the art. That'll take care of the first line of defense, if Mr. Fairey's amenable to putting their findings into effect."

"I certainly would be," Fairey said.

"Then I'm in favor of it." The mayor looked at Hannes and Charley. "Take all the time you need, gentlemen."

"Thank you, Mr. Mayor," Fairey said.

"However," Hizzoner pointed out, "it still doesn't solve the cost dilemma of providing extra police protection."

There was a moment's silence, then Robert spoke. "Seems to me, the city'd try harder to keep its tax base here."

The mayor blinked. "I'm not sure I follow you, Mr. Goldsmith."

"Oh, I think ya follow, aw right. But let me spell it out. I *could,* for instance," Robert said, putting the screws on the mayor, "move our warehouse from Long Island City over to Jersey, and use Jersey truckin' firms. Hell of a lot cheaper than what it costs us here."

The mayor frowned.

"For that matter, I can move GoldMart's headquarters *and* my investment office across the river, too. Everything's computerized, so it doesn't matter where we are. But the city'd lose out on an annual tax base of sixty to seventy mil—minimum. More, if we move some a our employees, too."

"I . . . see," said the mayor slowly.

"Guess you do. This is one a those times the city's got to divvy up an' do its duty."

The mayor did not look happy. "It seems you have us over a barrel," he sighed. "I'll see to it you get the extra police protection."

Robert rose to his feet. "Good. Glad we could see eye-to-eye."

59

"A pizza, a large, double cheese, fried eggplant and onion pizza," sighed Kenzie ecstatically as she dropped two nylon carry-ons and three shopping bags to the floor while Charley struggled her suitcase into her bedroom.

Kenzie felt both electrified and exhausted—a pardonable condition, considering she had just returned from a two-month European sojourn, in which every waking hour had been devoted to cataloging the paintings in Becky V's various *palazzi, palacios,* villas, elegant apartments, and townhouses. She had, in fact, studied so *many* masterpieces that they still tumbled, helter-skelter, around in her sassy little head like clothes in some cosmic dryer.

"But please, Charley, *please* tell them to hold the olives," she called out beseechingly. "Between Madrid, Seville, and Athens, I swear I was *olived* to death."

"And Monte Carlo?" asked Charley, coming back out into the living room.

"A sunny place for shady people. Why, it made me feel positively prepubescent! Really, Charley, I've never in my life seen so many pickled old farts. Wall-to-wall elephant skin—no amount of diamonds could help *those* pachyderms! I vowed never to lie out in the sun again. Oh," she exclaimed happily, flopping down on her cut-velvet, Napoleon III sofa, "but it does these bones good to be home! Even if this place seems to have shrunk in my absence."

"A result, no doubt, of all those palaces you stayed in."

"You can crack all the jokes you want. But between you and me, I've never seen anything like it. I mean, every one of those places was a *museum.* A girl could get used to living that way, Charley," she said, stretching luxuriantly. "Uh-huh, she easily could."

"Earth to Turner, Earth to Turner. Come in, Turner—"

Kenzie tossed a cushion at him, which he easily deflected.

"Well?" she asked. "Gonna order that pizza? Or you'd rather I starve?"

"What's the matter? Airlines suddenly stopped serving food?"

"Food?" Her amber eyes slid him a pitying glance. "Since when," she demanded, "have inflight meals been considered *edibles?* Food indeed! I fasted in anticipation of my eggplant pizza, thank you very much!"

He approached her in a bowlegged, Howdy ma'am, cowpoke kind of walk.

"This mean," he drawled, hooking a thumb in his belt, "you're really hungry?"

Kenzie squinted narrowly up at him. "Didn't I say I was?"

"Yeah, but I just wanted to get things straight. You know. Make sure it's pizza you're *really* after."

"Why? Would you rather I be hungering for something else?"

He thrust out his pelvis and grinned. "Thought you might like to take a bite out of life."

"Same old Charley," she sighed, feigning boredom. "Same juvenile, one-track mind." She pretended a mighty yawn and tapped her mouth with her hand. "Which are you today? Beavis? or Butt-head?"

He assumed a hurt expression. "You rather I didn't miss your bod?"

The corners of her mouth twitched with a tiny smile. "Why? Did you? Miss it?"

"Do bears—"

"Puh-*leeze!*"

"Well, seeing as how I'm a man of few words, I'll have to let my deeds speak for themselves."

"Oh, yeah?"

"Yeah," he said.

And three fly buttons later, he did.

Ah, would wonders never cease? And how could she have so completely forgotten the velvety softness of his mouth, the strength behind the muscle-corded arms which tightened around her, the good, fresh masculine fragrance of his skin?

At his entry, she gasped and felt as though she was floating sumptuously. Wondrous, this melting desire, the delicious weight of him as their two bodies fused into one!

"Oh, Charley," she moaned, "Charley . . ."

Then he began to thrust, and she loosened his belt, pulled his trousers farther down, gripped his small firm buttocks in order to press him closer.

"It's been so long!" she gasped. "Oh, God! It's so good! So *damned* good—"

And in her mounting passion, she kissed him deliriously: lips, cheeks, chin, neck, shoulders, chest.

"All the way, Charley!" she pleaded. "All the fuckin' way!"

Harder and harder he drove into her, faster and faster, and she squirmed and arched beneath him, tightening herself around him, matching his rhythm, thrust by thrust.

Then the first wave crashed over her, caught her in its vortex, and swooped her down into its trough before lifting her higher and higher. Great spasms of ecstasy bucked uncontrollably through her body. She cried out, and a fierce growl rose from Charley's throat as he could no longer hold back, and together they let themselves be lashed by the orgasmic storms.

Slowly, the raging fires and tempests abated. He was atop her, his weight heavy but not crushing, and they were both gasping for breath.

"Welcome home, babe," Charley said, after their shudders subsided and they lay there panting, face-to-face and eye-to-eye.

"Did you?" asked Kenzie. Her pupils were dilated, and she was still clutching his moist, perspiration-sheened buttocks. "Did you really?"

"Did I really what?"

"Miss me *that* much?"

He kissed the tip of her nose. "That much, babe," he said, "and a whole lot more."

Her eyes sparkled mischievously. "Then I take it there's second helpings where that came from?"

"Seconds," he assured her, with a lopsided grin. "Thirds."

"Wow!"

"But the pizza—"

"Charley?"

"Huh?"

Her voice was husky. "Fuck the pizza."

It was the following day. A glorious, snappy October afternoon. Kenzie and Zandra were in a rowboat in the Central Park lake.

"The seventh month?" Kenzie was exclaiming in astonishment. "You're going into the seventh month! It can't be! It's just not possible!"

The sky overhead was silvery blue, the leaves on the trees just beginning to turn, and everyone was out taking advantage of the weather. Tourists in horse-drawn carriages, children with Mylar balloons bouncing happily in the air, marathon hopefuls doing some serious jogging, dogs catching Frisbees. Like superior beings, the exclusive apartment buildings lining Fifth Avenue showed their dignified facades from above the tree line.

Zandra swallowed the last of her giant pretzel and washed it down with a mouthful of chocolate milkshake from a giant paper cup.

"Oh, for heaven's sake, Kenzie," she said. " 'Course it's possible. Do arithmetic, darling. You'll see. I was married last March. Right?"

"Right," Kenzie said, dipping the oars slowly.

"And, this is the beginning of October. Right, darling?"

"I know it's October. I just want to know where all the *time* has gone!"

"Darling, you tell me. I was already *pregnant* in April. And, poor lovely sweetie, unfortunate dear Becky. She died in *May*. That's only five months ago. Is it any wonder that Lord Rosenkrantz is still inconsolable? Thank God for Dina. He'd be lost without her."

"Is it true she's adopted him?"

"Not adopted, darling. He's her *walker.*" Zandra eyed the remainders of Kenzie's deli lunch on the seat. "Are you going to eat your pickle, by any chance?"

"No. Be my guest."

"Oh, *good.*" Zandra sat forward, swooped it up, and bit off a crunchy end. She chewed with ecstatic enjoyment. "Lovely." Leaning back in the transom, she let her other hand trail lazily in the water.

Kenzie made a face and shuddered. "Chili, pretzel, milkshake, *and* pickles? *Oy vey*. And that doesn't include the lox and bagel you ate on the way here, or that cheese Danish."

"Well, I *am* eating for two."

Kenzie locked the oars and took another bite of her own lunch. A BLT—actually, a triple-decker BLT without the B, but with sliced hard-boiled eggs and dressing.

"Yum, yum," she said, talking with her mouth full. "Oh, but isn't this splendid? Do you realize, after all the years I've spent living in New York, this is the very first time I ever did this?"

"Rowing, you mean?" Zandra looked appalled. "Darling, you can't be serious! Whatever else are parks for?"

"Your common urban ills?" Kenzie suggested. "Muggers? Rapists? Robbers? Addicts?"

"Goodness, you are jaded. I mean, look how marvelous this is!"

"Yes, but that's only because *you're* here." Kenzie unlocked the oars and resumed rowing.

"Still, with two boyfriends, surely you could get one of them to take you rowing?" Zandra withdrew her hand from the lake, flicked water from her fingertips. "You still have the both, don't you? Charley and Hannes?"

Kenzie sighed. "I've given myself until after the auction." She dipped the oars, pulled, lifted, and dipped. "Then I'll have to decide upon one or the other."

"Do either of them know that?"

"I told Charley last night."

"Oh?" Zandra popped the last of the pickle into her mouth. "And how did he take it?"

"Remarkably well, all things considered."

"And Hannes?"

"I'm telling him tonight."

Zandra shook her head in disbelief. "You really are Kurt Weill's

Jenny. You know—poor Jenny? The one who couldn't make up her mind?"

"Oh, let's change the subject," Kenzie pleaded, "please?"

"If you like. Anyway, I was wanting to ask you something. Now, honestly. What would you say to being a godmother?"

Kenzie stared, her jaw dropping. "Can you fly that by me again?"

"I'm asking you to be godmother to my very own little serene bundle of joy."

"Why, I . . . I'd be delighted! And honored!"

"Oh, I'm so glad. That's taken care of, then. Now, about the rest of your sandwich . . . ?"

"Have it."

"You're sure?"

" 'Course I'm sure." Kenzie laughed. "After all, I have a vested interest. Got to make certain my godchild grows up strong and healthy!"

"You're a darling! Really, I'll love you for absolutely ever and ever." Zandra attacked the remains of the sandwich. "As will little Ernst-Albrecht," she added.

"Ernst . . . Albrecht?"

"Mmm . . . hmm." Zandra patted her belly. "Ernst-Albrecht Rudger Gregorious Baldur Engelbert Burchard Georg Lorenzo Rainer-Maria von und zu Engelwiesen. That is," she added, "if he's a boy."

"And a godmother has to remember all *that?* And in order?"

"I should hope so!"

"Holy shit! You'd better write it down so I can start memorizing it. But I don't have to call him that tongue-twisting mouthful all the time, do I? I mean, a simple Ernie or Al will do? Won't it?"

"Not Al." Zandra shook a finger back and forth. "Never Al. But Albie . . . perhaps."

"After the auction? Of course that's fine with me," Hannes said. "But why specifically then, Kenzie?"

They were taking time out to savor the lulling, satiated feeling of postcoital bliss.

"Oh, I don't know."

Kenzie freed herself of the tangle of rumpled bed linens, took a sip of Veuve Clicquot, set the glass on the nightstand, and cuddled against him, the back of her head resting on his chest.

"I suppose," she said thoughtfully, gazing up at the dim ceiling, "it's a time point. You know. A landmark of sorts? Like New Year's or something? The end of one juncture, the beginning of another? Don't ask me why, but in some strange sort of way, it just seems to make sense."

He kissed the top of her head and wrapped his warm arms around her.

"Hannes . . ."

"Yes, Kenzie?"

"If I should decide upon Charley, you ... you wouldn't hurt him, would you?"

"Really, Kenzie," he chuckled. "What makes you think I would do something like that?"

"Nothing. I'm being silly, that's all. Forget it."

She twisted around and changed position, lying on her side so she could see his profile.

"I mean, I'm hardly the femme-fatale type." She laughed softly at the notion.

He rolled his head sideways on the pillow to look at her. "Then what type are you, my love?"

She shrugged. "I've never really thought about it." Her eyes seemed fastened to his. "Just your garden variety, all-American girl next door, I suppose."

"No, Kenzie." He shook his head and smiled. "I don't think you are that ordinary at all."

"Then what do you think I am?"

"The right woman for me," Hannes said softly.

🌹 *60* 🌺

One thousand invitations, engraved on the heaviest, pure cotton stock and affixed with an oxblood silk bow, were mailed out on the fifteenth of October.

Hand-addressed in beautiful calligraphy, the addresses had been culled by computer and included the cream of the world's richest, most powerful, and socially prominent citizens (500 of them), the most highly recognized celebrities (50), Burghley's top spenders (390), the world's leading authorities on Old Masters (15), and the directors of the world's leading museums (45).

Naturally, a few macabre glitches were bound to develop—and did. For instance, Becky V was mailed an invitation, since she had yet to be deleted from the computer files. And Karl-Heinz's father, the old prince, received one, too—despite languishing in an irreversible coma.

But no matter. Around the world, the invitations were being delivered to the powerful, the privileged, and the chosen few:

The sultan of an oil-rich emirate was brought his on a solid gold salver along with his Coca-Cola, which was specially bottled for him in silvered glass.

"Oh, my pet, my pet," he told his favorite young boy of the moment. "I am going to show you New York . . ."

* * *

In Beverly Hills, the world's most famous screen actress squealed with delight when she opened hers in the swimming pool.

She smiled at her sweetie pies—her sixth husband, lounging on the chaise, and her six Lhasa Apsos, which ran around yapping up a storm.

"See whose private jet we can borrow," she said to her secretary. "And let's see, we'll need enough suites at the Waldorf Towers for the usual entourage . . ."

In Boca Raton, A. Dietrich Spotts ran his hand over the coveted invitation and smiled.

I wondered when it would come, he thought, making a mental note to call the airlines for reservations, and Burghley's to RSVP. *This is one occasion I wouldn't miss for anything.*

Dina Goldsmith couldn't help herself. Sitting on the sidelines never had been her style, nor would it ever be. To the chagrin of everyone at Burghley's—and Sheldon D. Fairey in particular—she threw herself into the midst of the whirlwind. And with a vengeance.

Before anyone realized what had happened, she was in charge. Orchestrating every phase of the Becky V auction.

If the atmosphere at Burghley's was tense before Dina's involvement, it now became as deadly as the inside of a pressure cooker. There were a thousand and one things to be done, and a limited amount of time in which to accomplish it all.

And Dina was damned if she would permit anything to slide.

She encouraged and cajoled, threatened and gave ultimatums.

It was she who made all the final decisions. She who rewrote the press releases. She who fielded a hundred calls a day, attended the sales conferences, came up with suggestions, and approved the advertisements. And it was she, also, who demanded changes in the catalogue proofs. She, who when there were problems shipping Becky's paintings out of France, saw to it that the necessary documents were rushed through. She, who when a lost crate from Palm Beach needed tracking down, or damaged canvases required quick restoration, made certain immediate results would be forthcoming.

Somehow, she seemed to be everywhere at once, and employees began looking over their shoulders before grumbling among themselves.

Not surprisingly, Dina managed to step on more than a few toes. When complaints reached Robert, he decided to have a talk with her.

"I don't know why ya had to get involved with this shit," he grumped. "Ain't ya got enough to keep ya busy?"

"Of course I do, sweetie," she cooed, throwing her arms around his neck. "But I have to make certain this auction goes purr-fectly. Who else has Daddy's best interests at heart?"

Who indeed?

Overnight Dina had become an awesome force to be reckoned with. Naturally, she had the final say regarding those coveted last-minute invitations.

As soon as word of that leaked out, "friends" she never knew suddenly popped out of the woodwork.

People tried to wine and dine her. They offered to put private jets and yachts at her disposal. They showered her with expensive gifts.

Several big name fashion designers went so far as to promise her free, unlimited wardrobes in exchange for an invitation.

To Dina's credit, she returned each gift and graciously refused every offer. It was easy. Because, for once in her life she did not *want* presents. She did not *need* bribes. The only thing that really mattered was that she was *courted;* that the offers were made so that she could reject them.

Dina soon proved that she had a genuine aptitude for organization. True, she still had her share of detractors, but she was also a powerhouse who knew how to get things done. Employees quickly learned that the surest way to cut through red tape was by going to her.

Slowly but surely, Dina was gaining respect among the various echelons.

Robert still received complaints, but they slowed to a trickle. One thing, however, did not escape his notice—the lack of bills. Unbelievable as it seemed, his wife was suddenly too busy to go shopping, a fact which delighted him.

If this would only keep up, he thought wistfully. And then it hit him. There was a way.

No fool, he knew better than to approach Dina with his suggestions. She'd sniff a rat instantly. Wisely, he put a bug into Gaby's ear instead.

"You know what you should be doing?" Gaby suggested to Dina the following day.

"What, sweetie?"

"Putting all this energy of yours into charitable projects."

"What do you think I'm doing?" Dina retorted. "I'm not on the payroll, and the entire proceeds of the sale go to charity!"

"I meant after this is all over."

"Hmm," Dina said slowly.

Gaby might be onto something, she thought. *It could prove to be fun. And at least it wouldn't be boring.*

"Perhaps I shall," she said. "I'll have to think it over carefully."

Meanwhile, the date of the sale loomed ever closer, and an overwhelming amount of things still needed to be done.

Dina saw to it that they were.

On time.
And to her own discriminating standards.
For when Dina Goldsmith spoke, people listened—and jumped.
Or else!

Gerhard Meindl was waiting on the other side of customs in the International Arrivals terminal at Kennedy Airport. When he saw them coming, he adjusted his somber gray tie. Then he took a deep breath and strode toward them.

"Welcome to America, Your Highnesses," he said in German. "I trust your flight was pleasant?"

"It was dreadful," sniffed Princess Sofia. "Nowadays they let anyone aboard a commercial plane! Even in first class you find yourself seated next to the most horrid people. The most hideous young couple was across the aisle. Both with rings through their lips and noses and eyebrows. Disgusting!" She threw up her hands. "It really does make one yearn for the good old days. Isn't that right, Erwein?"

"*Ja,* Sofia," he said, with weary resignation. He was just behind her, carrying her jewelry and cosmetics cases. Behind him, three porters were wheeling mountains of vintage Vuitton luggage.

"Next time," Sofia added, "we're taking the family jet."

Gerhard Meindl nodded sympathetically; he knew why they hadn't this time—Sofia didn't wish to forewarn her brother of her arrival.

"The car is this way," he said smoothly, and gesturing with one hand, led the entourage toward the automatic glass doors and out into the sunshine. "Ah, there it is."

Sofia eyed the silver gray stretch limousine with disgust. What an abomination! she thought, comparing it to her own stately old Daimler. It was like everything else here in America. The few times she had visited this country, the sheer crassness of everything had simply overwhelmed her. Now it was overwhelming her again—and she hadn't even left the airport!

She glared at the porters who were depositing her luggage none-too-gently in the trunk.

"Tip them, Erwein," she snapped. "But not too much?" She raised her eyebrows.

"*Nein,* Sofia."

She ducked into the car and waited for it to be loaded up. Extracted a gold compact from her handbag and dusted her face with powder.

"You made our reservations?" she asked, once they were rolling.

Gerhard Meindl, seated on the jump seat, nodded his head. "Yes, Your Highness," he assured her. "A two-bedroom suite at the Carlyle, just as you requested. I inspected it personally. I think you will find it quite satisfactory."

"If I do not, you *and* the management will hear of it."

I'm sure we will, he thought.

She eyed Erwein, who was seated beside her, with mounting irritation. He had both of her cases on his lap, as though clutching them from invisible thieves.

"Oh, do put them down!" she snapped.

He did; at once.

"Did you decide how long you would be staying in New York, Your Highness?" Gerhard Meindl asked solicitously.

"We came for the auction," Sofia said, "but we will stay until the child is born. That way, I can rest assured that nothing about the birth is shady or contrary to family law."

It was a direct insult to the Meindls, a deliberate slap in the face, but Gerhard kept his emotions carefully in check. "And the old prince? How is His Highness, if I may ask?"

"You may, and he is not at all well," Sofia said, her lips settling into a satisfied expression. "He had another stroke last week."

"I'm sorry to hear that."

"Yes," said Sofia slowly, "I don't doubt that you are."

Dina marched to the entrance of Burghley's, Gaby half a step behind. All that was missing were drums and trumpets to announce their arrival—to Gaby, it would have sounded like the lead-in accompanying a Twentieth Century Fox film logo.

"Morning, Mrs. Goldsmith." The doorman.

"Good morning, Raoul."

"Lovely day, isn't it?"

"Why . . ." Dina stopped in the doorway and turned around, looking up at the sky in surprise. "Why, yes, Raoul. I suppose it is!"

And in she swept, Gaby in tow.

"Damn brownnoser," Gaby mumbled under her breath, spiking him with a glare.

Raoul grinned and touched his visor. "And a nice day to you, too, Ms. Morton."

Gaby scowled. "That and two quarters buys you a cuppa coffee."

"Good morning, Mrs. Goldsmith," the security guard greeted.

"Good morning, Carmine. I see you're looking sharp."

Passing him, Gaby pointed at his shoes. When he looked down, she quickly tweaked his cheek.

On they marched, to the sound of Gaby's silent drum and trumpet flourishes.

First on Dina's agenda: The showroom galleries, where the last exhibit before the Becky V auction—Impressionist and Modern Paintings, Drawings, Watercolors and Sculpture—was being taken down.

Next stop: The auction gallery proper, where the theaterlike red velvet seats, which she had insisted upon last October *(A year? Can it really have been that long?)* curved in elegant amphitheater-type rows.

A vast improvement over those cheap metal folding chairs, Dina thought, *even if I say so myself.*

Suddenly she stopped walking and stood there, frozen. "What the hell?" she said softly.

Then, charging up and down the center aisle, she pointed an accusing finger left and right in outrage. There and there and there . . . there, there *there* . . . The upholstery of fifteen red velvet fold-down seats had been slashed open, exposing the white stuffing and springs.

"Vandals!" Dina exclaimed. "My God! Vandals in *Burghley's!* What is the world coming to?"

She marched furiously back out, her face grim, and sought out the nearest security guard.

"Ma'am?"

"Who permitted someone to vandalize the seats in the auction gallery?" Dina snapped.

"Beg your pardon, ma'am?"

"Call the head of Security. Tell him to meet me in Sheldon D. Fairey's office. *Now.*"

"Yes, ma'am!"

"Gaby?"

"Right here."

"See that the damaged seats are removed and reupholstered. At once."

"Will do."

"Make sure the fabric matches!"

"Right."

"And call those two detectives. You know the ones. I want this reported at once."

He watched the slashed seats being loaded into the panel truck. CHANTILLY & CIE CUSTOM UPHOLSTERERS *was emblazoned on the sides of the vehicle, along with a Long Island City address and a 718 phone number. He memorized both.*

It was so ludicrously simple. Child's play, really. Just one of many security gaps, and not even a highly original one at that.

People would do well to remember the classics, he thought. It was the story of the Trojan Horse all over again, but with a slight variation. When the seats returned, they would be stuffed with goodies. Explosives, semi-automatics, handguns, ammo.

    So simple.

    So ancient.

    So beautiful.

    So deadly.

    He could hardly wait.

TARGET: BURGHLEY'S COUNTDOWN TO TERROR

Near Wilmington, Delaware,
November 7

"Ninety-four hours and eighteen minutes until zero hour."

The hooded figure's electronically distorted voice echoed eerily in cavernous space.

The old pesticide packaging plant on the banks of the stagnant, polluted canal—like the idle buildings surrounding it—was a relic of a reckless past, and thus ideal. This was the fourth industrial space they had occupied since Long Island City.

There was survival in unpredictability, safety in staying on the move.

As usual, all the lights save one had been doused for his arrival. The single naked bulb glared, swinging in an arc from its overhead wire, and threw shadow monsters against pitted cinderblock walls.

From between the slit in his convex lenses, he eyed his handpicked crew. With Kildare out of the way, that left eight men and one woman.

"Everything is in readiness?"

"Everything." *The former Israeli commando.*

"Weapons? Explosives?"

"Already in place." *The ex-navy SEAL.* "Piece of cake."

"Getaway?"

"All prepared." *The French daredevil.*

"Appropriate attire?"

"Black tie for the men." *The woman.* "No labels to trace the purchases."

"Invitations?"

"In hand." *The Japanese.* "Hacking into their computer was child's play. All I had to do was put our false names on the list. The invitations were waiting in the various post office boxes."

"Everyone familiar with the layout?"

"Familiar enough to find our way around that place in the dark." *The Libyan.*

"Let's hope it doesn't come to that."

The hooded man's breathing was amplified, like a horror movie's soundtrack.

"Any last-minute qualms?"

Laughter. *The Colombian brothers.*

"Remember! I want no senseless killing! Only take out whoever's necessary. Is that understood?"

"Sure, *amigo.*" *The shorter of the two Colombians.* "We comprende."

His sibling chuckled.

"You better *comprende!*"

The Colombian's laugh died in his throat.

"This has taken over a year of planning! Any of you fuck up—you're dead! You *comprende* that?"

There was silence. Nine heads nodded somberly.

"Last chance for questions. Anyone have any?"

No one did.

"Don't worry." *The German.* "They'll never know what hit them."

"They'd better not!"

On that note, the hooded figure moved balletically, seemingly without weight or substance, a mere shadow melting into the dark. A minute later, there was the sound of a car door slamming. Then a souped-up engine roared to life.

The German pressed a remote control device. It activated a hidden video camera, fitted with an infrared lens, over in the loading dock.

They waited until the car had driven off. Then the German went to collect the tape. Upon his return, he fed it into the VCR, switched on the monitor, and hit the *play* button.

On the screen, a New York license plate was barely visible—but visible all the same.

He hit *freeze frame.*

"You have it?"

"Got it."

The Japanese already had his computer booted up; within half a minute, he'd hacked his way into the New York State Department of Motor Vehicles.

"Now we'll find out who our boss is," he said.

The other eight crowded closely around, eyes on the glowing monitor as his fingers tapped the license number on the keyboard.

Within seconds, the information jumped onto the screen:

```
FERRARO, CHARLES, G
7 JONES STREET
NEW YORK NY 10014
```

⚛ *62* ⚛

*T*he months-long whirlwind was over.

Three days before the auction, Burghley's sparkled with spit and polish. The traveling exhibition of highlights from the Becky V collection had returned, none the worse for wear, after having attracted record crowds in Tokyo, Hong Kong, London, Geneva, and Dubai.

Now it was New York's turn, and Burghley's was ready.

Armed security had been tripled.

Airport-style metal detectors were installed just inside the front doors.

Fifty extra video cameras tracked the public areas and corridors.

Each employee, from Sheldon D. Fairey down to the last janitor, had been issued new credit-cardlike identification cards, complete with holograms and photographs.

Every door, from the loading dock to the fire escapes, was under twenty-four-hour guard, and no one was permitted to use any but the main entrance.

At night, newly installed floodlights washed the exterior of the building in bright, garish light.

Outside, patrolmen walked the beat, a high-visibility police presence augmented by slowly cruising blue-and-whites.

For security reasons, the paintings carried no estimated prices, neither in the catalogues nor on the descriptive three-by-five cards affixed to the walls beside them. Three telling words said it all: *Estimate Upon Request.*

And small wonder.

Never before had such a wealth of treasures filled a single auction house, and in the climate-controlled galleries, the hundreds of spotlit paintings hung in hushed splendor:

Veronese, Bellini, Titian, Rubens, della Francesca. *Treasures for the richest of the rich, for those two or three thousand people who could afford them.*

Raphael, Leonardo, di Cosimo, Caravaggio, Poussin. *Treasures for the handful of museums with deep pockets, and for others which would have to deaccession—sell off lesser works in order to purchase a true masterpiece.*

Rembrandt, Dürer, Tintoretto, Pontormo, Boucher. *Treasures for investor groups and pension funds, corporate raiders, and crime lords.*

Van Dyck, Gainsborough, Reynolds, Ingres, Turner. *Treasures for walls in Monaco and Brunei, Riyadh and Belgravia, Sutton Place and Beverly Hills.*

The paintings went on display at ten o'clock on the morning of November fourth. Despite the steady cold drizzle, a queue of hundreds—unheard of for auction exhibitions—had already been waiting for hours, and the line outside Burghley's stretched halfway around the block.

For security purposes, only a hundred people at any one time were permitted inside; as soon as one came out, another was allowed in.

The line grew. And grew.

By noon, wooden police barriers had to be erected, closing off one entire lane of Madison Avenue. By afternoon, Port-a-Potties were trucked in.

At five o'clock, the galleries were closed to the general public. For the next four hours, entry was by invitation and special appointment only.

That first day alone, awed thousands traipsed through the showrooms in wonder-struck silence.

On the following day, the crowd waiting to see the exhibition had doubled. The catalogues sold out, and thousands more had to be printed and shipped overnight.

According to news reports, attendance at the Metropolitan Museum had dropped to a trickle. Everyone wanted to see Becky V's treasures.

"Shit!" Robert A. Goldsmith was overheard muttering. "We shoulda charged admission!"

"Dina!" Robert bawled from his bedroom. "Fix my goddamn tie, will ya?"

Par for the course: the Wall Street tycoon was getting dressed.

"Coming, sweetie," Dina called, taking one last, long look at herself in the mirror.

A runway model looked back at her, which was exactly the effect she'd sought. Lips reddish-pink, cheekbones emphasized with five tones of blusher, eyes accentuated with amethyst shadow and dark mascara.

She was wearing drop-dead Ungaro—a pink lace bustier with red and black beads blatantly outlining every seam. A floor-length skirt in burgundy cut-velvet. And a matching, long-sleeved jacket lined in pink silk.

Plus canary diamonds the size of pocket change, and black mesh gloves with little black polka dots.

Delectable.

Sweeping into Robert's room, she found him seated on his bed, cigar clamped between his teeth.

"I hate black tie!" he complained. "Shoulda nixed it while I had the chance."

"Now, now, sweetie," she soothed, taking matters into her capable hands and expertly flipping the two ends into a bow. "You know how handsome you look in black tie."

"Yeah?" He squinted a leer through the cloud of smoke.

"Yes." She patted his cheek. "Now do come, sweetie. You know there's champagne before the auction. How would it look if you aren't there to greet people?"

"I'm coming," he grumbled, heaving himself to his feet.

She adjusted his off-center cumberbund. "Oh, sweetie," she cooed, "I'm *sooooo* excited!"

"As long as ya don't get carried away. Last thing I need's for ya to start biddin' like crazy!"

"Really, sweetie." She gave him a reproving look. "You'd better not let anyone at Burghley's hear you talk that way." She helped him into his jacket. "There. You're all set. Now button it, and off we go!"

"Your Highness!"

Karl-Heinz and Zandra were about to step into the elevator when Josef caught up with them, remote phone in hand.

"Yes, Josef? What is it?" Karl-Heinz asked.

"It's Dr. Rantzau."

The director of the clinic outside Augsburg.

Karl-Heinz felt his stomach contract. *Please God,* he prayed. *Don't let it be bad news.*

Somehow he kept his face expressionless. "Thank you, Josef."

Karl-Heinz let the elevator go and took the phone. Josef discreetly withdrew.

"Dr. Rantzau?" Karl-Heinz switched to German. "What can I do for you?"

The doctor answered in the same language. "It's about your father, Your Highness." His voice was apologetic.

"Yes?"

"His heart stopped twenty minutes ago."

For a moment Karl-Heinz felt his own heart stop, too. Then it kicked in again, pounding so furiously it seemed intent upon escaping his rib cage.

Zandra was frowning and looking at him. "Heinzie?" she mouthed. "What is it?"

He covered the mouthpiece with his hand. "My father," he said quickly.

"Fortunately," Dr. Rantzau was saying, "we were able to revive him. However, he has become so frail and brittle that any further such attempts could well do him more harm than good."

Karl-Heinz took a deep breath. "I understand, Doctor," he said tightly. "From now on, we let nature take its course."

"Oh, Heinzie!" Zandra moaned, clutching his arm.

"Are you certain, Your Highness?" the doctor asked.

"Absolutely. It is not fair to put my father through this. I'm certain he would prefer to die with dignity. I know I would."

"Yes, Your Highness. I quite agree."

"Perhaps I should be there," Karl-Heinz said softly.

"Of course you are welcome to come," Dr. Rantzau said. "But why don't you give it twenty-four hours? He will either pull through, or he won't."

What he's really saying, Karl-Heinz thought, *is I'll either be too late, or else he'll continue to hang on.*

"You will keep me informed, Doctor?"

"Of course, Your Highness."

"I can be reached at my cellular number." Karl-Heinz hung up.

Zandra was staring up at him, her green eyes wide. "I'm so sorry, Heinzie," she said softly.

"I know," he said quietly. "Not that this should come as any surprise. Still, the shock—"

"I can imagine. Come on, darling." She took his arm and started to lead him back to the apartment.

"No." He shook his head. "It won't matter where I'll be. I'll take the Concorde in the morning." He raised his voice. "Josef?" he called.

His valet hurried out of the apartment. "Yes, Your Highness?"

"Take this," he said, handing him the phone. "Bring me the cellular."

Zandra looked stunned. "You mean . . . we're still going to the auction?"

"Why not?" Karl-Heinz smiled grimly. "Perhaps it will be a momentary diversion."

In her suite at the Carlyle, Sofia had old August Meindl on the telephone.

"I want you and your son Klaus to go to that clinic immediately," she was saying. "I don't trust the staff. Should my father pass away tonight, you are to witness the exact time of his death."

"Yes, Your Highness."

"And you are to call me at once. I will have the telephone with me."

"Yes, Your Highness."

"And Herr Meindl?"

"Highness?"

Sofia's voice was quiet with menace. "Do not fail me."

"No, Your Highness."

Sofia broke the connection and stuffed her cellular phone into her beaded bag. *With luck,* she thought, *with just a little bit of luck . . .*

"Erwein!"

"Ja, Sofia?" He was sitting right behind her on the sofa.

She turned around in a swirl of celadon chiffon and ostrich feathers. "Are you ready? We are leaving for Burghley's."

"I'm ready," he said, getting to his feet.

"You have our invitations?"

"*Ja*. Right here." He patted his breast pocket.

She cocked her arm to link it through his and smiled. "Who knows? Perhaps I shall even buy a painting. Tonight, I feel like celebrating!"

"Can you *believe* this turnout?" Kenzie whispered to Arnold from the sidelines. Her eyes were continuously roving the second-floor gallery like an alert hostess's.

"You should see outside," he said. "There are more spectators than at a Hollywood premiere. The only thing missing's the searchlights. Oh-oh. Annalisa's motioning to me. Be right back." He slipped into the crowd of champagne-sipping tycoons, celebrities, film stars, and their spouses and companions.

"Kenzie?" warbled a thin familiar voice.

Kenzie looked around, and there he was: tall, cadaverous, and stooped, with warm topaz eyes regarding her over the tops of his half lenses.

"Mr. Spotts!" she cried. "Oh, but it's good to see you!" She flung her arms around him in a welcoming hug.

"Now, now," he chided. "If you're going to continue calling me Mr. Spotts, I shall have to revert to calling you Ms. Turner."

"Just a slip of the tongue, Dietrich," she said happily, "just a slip of the old tongue. God, Arnold's going to flip when he sees you! Oh, I'm so *glad* you could make it!"

"How could I possibly stay away?" He gestured around with a palsied hand and smiled. "This is, after all, the auction of a lifetime."

Out front on Madison Avenue, Lord Rosenkrantz was helping Suzy de Saint-Mallet out of his vintage Rolls-Royce.

Next to his Pickwickian proportions, Becky's twin sister looked particularly wraithlike and fragile. She was wearing a black Valentino toga which left one skeletal arm and shoulder bare, and the other completely draped.

"I wish you weren't putting yourself through this, my dear," he murmured, eyeing the crowds of photographers and celebrity-watchers with distaste. "You know you don't have to be here."

Her chin went up. "Nonsense, *chéri!* Of course I must. This occasion needs that old Cornille–Saint-Mallet–de la Vila magic. People are expecting me to be here. Besides, it's probably good for me. Perhaps this will help give the entire nightmare a sense of closure."

He shook his head. "Anyone else in your shoes would gladly stay away from this circus."

"Perhaps." She took his arm. "But what about yourself?"

He looked at her. "What about me?"

"This cannot be easy for you, either," she said huskily. "I know what Becky meant to you."

He smiled sadly. "Perhaps I am hoping for a sense of closure also."

She patted his hand. "You're a good man," she told him. "You brought Becky so much happiness."

He shrugged. "It was mutual. She made me very happy, too."

"Suzy! Darling!" a female voice called out.

For one split second Suzy's face froze; then she turned up the dazzling public smile she had long ago perfected.

"Charley?"

The word seemed to be snatched from thin air by the mini-receiver in his ear. The transmitted background noise of chatter and billowing laughter was a hivelike buzz. Charley let his roving, trouble-shooting gaze sweep the auction gallery proper, where a few scattered, red plush seats had already been taken. He wiggled a finger inside his constricting shirt collar, obviously uncomfortable in his rented tux.

"Charley?" he heard repeated.

He turned toward the wall to conceal his movements and lifted his right arm to his mouth. "I read you, Hannes," he said into his wrist transmitter.

"There are no problems here in the lobby, Charley. Only people setting off the metal detectors. Twelve were carrying guns, but they had permits. The police chief persuaded them to check their weapons."

"Good. Everything's cool up here, too. I'm going to check out the temporary painting storeroom once more. Over."

He turned around to find a few more seats filled. All men, he noticed now. All in choice—

—*strategic?*—

—aisle seats.

Why? the suspicious cop in him wondered.

Probably because they don't want to be hemmed in, he answered himself, suppressing a niggling sense of uneasiness. *Not that I blame them. I'd want the most legroom, too.*

Such an innocent explanation. And how like him to overreact. But then, letting his imagination get the better of him was an occupational hazard, and one not helped any by the heightened security measures.

They were enough to make anyone paranoid.

Better check on the paintings, he told himself.

* * *

The seven men in their predetermined aisle seats waited patiently, studiously ignoring each other. Pressure applied in two spots under their seats would release the spring-loaded bottoms. The weapons clipped there could be grabbed in an instant.

All were loaded.

And ready to fire.

Watching the seats fill up with the world's richest and most powerful people, he felt a supercharged rush of adrenaline. They were coming in like lambs to the slaughter—smug and insular, like superior beings who thought they owned the planet. But that feeling would not persist for long, he knew. Soon they would be terrified and cowed. Soon more than a few would soil themselves. And soon, at least a few of them would die.

ᘐ *63* ᘑ

The auction was underway.

In the rows of plush seats, the secure, satisfied faces of the rich and powerful had given way to bright-eyed tension and excitement.

On the block was Lot 17, *The Infanta, Margarita, in Red,* by Velázquez. Displayed on the easel of the revolving platform, as well as projected onto the back wall, it had hung above the mantel in Becky V's Fifth Avenue living room, and bidding was hot.

From behind his lectern, Sheldon D. Fairey orchestrated his audience like a veteran symphony conductor, coaxing them to bid higher, higher, ever higher.

"Twenty-two million, one hundred thousand dollars," he announced.

Kenzie, Arnold, and Annalisa whispered hurriedly into their telephones, listened to their absentee bidders, and lifted their pencils like wands.

Fairey acknowledged them with a nod, his eyes everywhere at once. "Twenty-two million, two hundred thousand . . . twenty-two million, three hundred thousand—"

Kenzie's bidder dropped out. She hung up the phone and glanced around.

On the far side of the gallery, Hannes was patrolling the aisle, and on this side, Charley was doing likewise. In front of each of the three sets of double doors stood a pair of armed, uniformed guards, hands clasped behind their backs.

Her eyes skimmed over Zandra and Karl-Heinz, Dina and Robert Goldsmith. In the back row, she caught sight of her old nemesis, Bambi Parker.

"Thirty million dollars."

Kenzie realized that during the minute she'd permitted her mind to wander, the bids had shot through the roof, and the atmosphere had reached that supercharged moment during which no one dared breathe.

"Thirty million, one hundred thousand . . . thirty million, two hundred thousand . . ."

A handful of numbered paddles went up and down, up and down; discreet signals were semaphored: the Middle Eastern sultan rubbing his chin, the Hong Kong banker tapping the side of his nose.

And still Fairey kept the bids coming, playing to his audience and cajoling, exhorting, inciting them on, the astronomical numbers swirling hypnotically, spiraling up like some magical genie. . . . This was auction at its finest—equal parts shopping, high-stakes gambling, and theatrical drama.

"Forty million dollars!"

Forty—?

Kenzie snapped her head toward the lectern, where Sheldon D. Fairey surveyed the electrified room.

Surely there's some mistake! she thought. *I couldn't*—could not!—*have heard right!*

The hushed silence was broken when Arnold, telephone to his ear, gave a signal.

"Forty-two million."

Kenzie's involuntary gasp of shock joined the others which rolled, like an ocean swell, along the rows of seats.

Forty-two million dollars? Appalled, fascinated . . . then feeling a burgeoning sense of triumph, she glanced at the easel on which the target of this bidding was displayed.

The gilt-framed portrait of the infanta stared out of the canvas with a child's seventeenth-century hauteur while, overhead, like a departures and arrivals board at a busy airport, the bright LED numbers rippled, instantly converting the latest bid from dollars to six other currencies:

BURGHLEY'S

FOUNDED 1719

LOT 17	US $	42000000
	BR POUND	24990000
	FR FRANC	268443000
	D MARK	79422000
	LIRA '000'	58096500
	SW FRANC	70896000
	YEN '000'	5628000

All conversions approximate

The expectant hush grew, the tension now a living entity, so real one could almost see it stretching the room like elastic. Kenzie had to consciously will herself to breathe.

God in heaven, she wondered. *How much higher can the bids go?*

But even she, veteran of countless auctions, had no idea. Quality, scarcity, and market value aside, one overriding wild card made conjecture impossible. It had been owned by Becky V.

What that's worth is anybody's guess. We'll just have to wait and see.

* * *

Charley turned to the wall and spoke quietly into his wrist transmitter. "Hannes? You read me?"

Static crackled, then Hannes's murmur burst in his ear. "Yes, Charley."

"I'm going to check out the security-control room. Keep your eye on things, will you?"

"No problem."

"Over and out." Charley turned around, adjusted his cuff, and glanced across the sea of heads to the far side of the gallery. He exchanged nods with Hannes, then glanced up at the dais.

For the moment, at least, he might as well have been invisible. Kenzie's attention, like everyone else's, was riveted on the skyrocketing bids. He felt a pluck of resentment, then shook his head with irritation.

"Forty-four million," Fairey was saying. "Do I have a bid for forty-four million, one hundred thousand?"

The outrageous sums seduced, cast a hypnotic spell.

Jesus H. Christ! Charley thought. *You'd think these people would be inured to these numbers. But they're as entranced as any audience watching a game show.*

Abruptly disgusted, he strode rapidly toward the nearest exit, bestowing glares at the two overweight security guards who were following the bidding as avidly as anyone else. "Look alive!" he snapped, forcing them aside to push on the heavy steel swinging doors.

Walking swiftly down the corridor, he shook his head in exasperation. The guards' inattention nagged at his sense of well-being. Dumb, dim-witted simpletons! Didn't they realize they were supposed to offer protection?

He had a good mind to beef up security by pulling some seasoned cops in off the street . . . but their job was outside, patrolling the perimeter of Burghley's. That was where their presence was really required. If worse came to worst, danger would come from without, not from within.

Even so, once he got to the security control room, it wouldn't hurt to rattle the cage. Raise a little hell.

"Fifty million dollars," Sheldon D. Fairey called out. "I have a bid for fifty million dollars."

A murmur, like a tidal wave, surged through the auction room while, quick as a flash, the overhead LED numbers converted the amount.

"Do I have a bid for fifty million, one hundred thousand?"

On the left side of the gallery, the Italian tycoon's paddle went up.

Arnold's bidder had dropped out; Annalisa, still on the phone, raised her pencil.

"I have two bids for fifty million, one hundred thousand. Do I have a bid for fifty million, two hundred thousand?"

Again, the tycoon's paddle was raised, and again, Annalisa signaled with her pencil.

There was a gasp of thunderstruck awe. Even Kenzie found herself openmouthed with disbelief. *Over fifty million? OVER FIFTY MILLION DOLLARS?* It was not to be believed! Never before in history had an Old Master brought such a mind-boggling bid. The highest ever paid was when the Getty Museum shelled out 35.2 million at Christie's for Jacopo da Pontormo's portrait of Cosimo de' Medici.

But fifty million, two hundred thousand—?

Kenzie sat there in shock. The entire room was frozen, and it seemed the infanta's gaze was tauntingly amused by the silence.

"Fifty-one million," a regal, balding gentleman in a Savile Row dinner suit called out calmly, raising the ante by $800,000.

Everyone started, as though an electric jolt had shot through their plush red seats; heads swiveled to eye the new bidder. Annalisa spoke rapidly into her telephone, then hung up.

"Do I hear fifty-one million, one hundred thousand?"

Utter silence. Excitement had reached a crescendo. Noses twitched, scenting the air for the next exorbitant bid.

"Going for fifty-one million dollars," Fairey announced. "Going once, going twice—"

He raised his gavel, but before he could bang it down, everything suddenly became a kaleidoscope of confusion and death.

Eight men, in eight of the corner seats, bent down and released their spring-loaded seat bottoms. When they jumped to their feet, each brandished an Uzi .45 semi-automatic assault pistol in each hand.

What in bloody hell—? thought Kenzie. *Where had those come from? And then she knew. The seats! The vandalized seats which had been sent out to be recovered!*

But things were happening too fast for her to grasp. She caught horrifying split-second images, as though nightmarish scenes were momentarily frozen in the strobelike glare of flashbulbs.

One of the guards, realizing what was going down, yelled, "Freeze!" and valiantly reached for his revolver.

He was too late; they were all too late. The ex-navy SEAL and the Colombian brothers whirled around, each firing two pistols apiece.

Staccato bursts of semiautomatic gunfire exploded—*rat-tat-tat-tat-tat!*—and the guards twitched like puppets, their chests, arms, and legs erupting in clouds of blood. Bullets ricocheted off the steel doors; zinged in all directions.

A terrified chorus of screams rent the air, and the well-dressed crowd ducked down in their seats or dove to the floor.

When the firing finally stopped, the gallery was eerily silent.

No one dared move.

No one dared make a sound.

The smell of cordite, and the stench of fear and death, were strong in the air.

On the dais, Kenzie, Arnold, and Annalisa sat frozen, too shocked to have moved or dived for cover. Sheldon D. Fairey was gripping the lectern, his face ashen, his knuckles white.

Below, the Japanese, the German, and the Libyan sprang into action. Each raced to one of the exits, kicked the dead guards out of the way, and slammed two connected, magnetic explosives devices on each of the swinging doors.

A movement in the aisle caught Kenzie's eye. The former Israeli commando had Hannes covered.

The sight was like a physical pain. She stifled a gasp and willed Hannes to be docile. *Please, God,* she beseeched, *don't let Hannes do anything stupid.*

He didn't. Slowly, carefully, he raised his arms in surrender, and she felt a rush of dizzying, sickening relief. He was frisked and relieved of his revolver, transmitter, and earphone. The latter two were tossed to the ex-SEAL, who proceeded to don them. Then Hannes was shoved brutally toward the rows of seats.

He lost his footing and fell, but he was alive, thank God. They *hadn't* killed him!

Kenzie offered up a silent prayer of thanks . . .

. . . and realized that in the sudden commotion she'd completely lost track of Charley.

Charley!

Where is he? she wondered frantically. *And who are these murdering bastards, and what do they want?*

She had the nasty feeling she'd soon find out.

"The fuck is goin' on?" Charley shouted, bursting into the security-control room. "My earpiece just went berserk—"

The ten operators monitoring the built-in banks of black-and-white video screens, which were augmented by dozens more in neat rows on shelves against the other two walls, jumped in alarm. Ignoring them, he headed straight to the monitors, which showed bird's-eye views of the auction gallery.

He was silent, leaning his weight on the counter, his knuckles white, his face suddenly weary. "Aw, shit," he said softly.

"You right about that." One of the operators, a black man in his forties, scooted back his chair and looked up. "You might say the, ah, effluvia has hit the fan."

Charley kept his eyes on the monitors. "You notify the PC?"

"Just got off the horn with him. He pissed as all hell."

"He's not the only one," Charley said grimly. He tapped one of the screens. "The guards. Wounded or dead?"

"They dead. Gotta be, considering what they took."

"Semiautomatics?"

"That's right. All multiple direct hits. I watched the whole thing."

"Damn!"

Charley took deep and regular breaths to calm his churning stomach and racing heart. *We fucked up,* he thought bleakly, trying to subdue his angry frustration. *But where did we go wrong? How—?*

He turned to the black man. "Any other casualties?" he asked tightly.

"Too early to tell."

Charley nodded. He pulled back his cuff, raised his wrist to his mouth, and said: "Hannes. Come in, Hannes. You read me?"

The airwaves were silent, save for the rushing of static.

"Hannes. Do you copy?"

"Yo!" a stranger blurted in his ear. "Who're *you?*" The voice was taut and edgy and held the faintest trace of a drawl.

"I might ask you the same thing."

"Except you're in no position to ask for anything."

"Where's Hannes?"

"He the guy wore this contraption?"

"That's right."

"He's neutralized, but fine. 'Less he decides to be a hero, that is."

"Maybe you'd like to tell me what's going on down there."

"You watching? On video?"

"That's right."

"Then I'll give you the advantage of putting a face to the voice."

Charley saw the formally clad gunman saunter toward a camera and raise his face. A moment later, he brought up both revolvers and fired.

The picture on the monitor turned to snow.

"Shit," Charley muttered, moving to another screen.

Seeing Kenzie seated onstage, he felt a massive surge of relief. He raised his wrist again. "If you're holding those people hostage, you obviously want something. What is it?"

But his question went unanswered.

"One word of warning," came the voice in his ear. "All entrances are wired with Semtec. That's just in case somebody gets the bright idea to come storming in. Anyone touches a door and breaks the connection— *pow!* It's *adiós* for you guys *and* half the people in here. You *capiche?*"

Charley gnashed his teeth. "Yeah," he said quietly, fighting to keep the frustration out of his voice. "I *capiche.*"

He didn't know when he'd felt so helpless.

I should be down there, he thought, staring at a monitor. *If I had been, maybe I could have headed this off.*

Suddenly it occurred to him that it was just as well he wasn't. *Chances are, I'd be dead already. Then I'd really be useless. At least this way I can do something.*

If only he knew what.

A telephone rang and the black man snatched up the receiver. "Security control. Yes, sir, he's right here. I'll tell him. Yes, sir. At once." He hung up.

Charley looked at him questioningly. "Who was that?"

"The PC. He's in the lobby assembling a strike force. He, ah, wants to end this situation before it gets any stickier."

"Call him back." Charley was already halfway to the door. "Tell him he can't."

"He'll want to know why."

"They've wired all the entries with explosives," Charley told him grimly, "that's why. If he sends in the cavalry, he'll blow everyone to kingdom come. I'm on my way down to the lobby to see him now."

"What do you want me to do?"

"Watch TV. I want to be kept informed of any new developments."

"Oh-oh," the operator said. "There go our eyes."

He and Charley watched as, one by one, all the monitors hooked up to the auction gallery went blank.

❧ *64* ❧

*I*n the auction gallery, the ex-navy SEAL hopped up on the dais, elbowed Fairey aside, and stood behind the lectern, surveying his audience. The auction-goers were still huddled between the rows of seats, and his seven cohorts patrolled the three aisles, semiautomatics at the ready.

"Ladies and gentlemen," he called out, "if I might have your attention, please. You'll be quite safe as long as you do as you're told. First, I want you all to get back in your seats."

No one moved, and his automatic weapon stuttered briefly, spitting warning shots into the ceiling.

"I don't want to have to tell you twice."

There was a lot of rustling as the billionaires and museum curators, art dealers, and socialites slowly raised their heads and peered around. Then, cautiously, they got up from the floor and took their seats. Their confident air of superiority had vanished. For many, it was the first time in their lives that they had been totally powerless, and their helplessness and fear were apparent.

"You're probably wondering what the hell's going on, so I might as well tell you." His hard eyes didn't match his grin, and he spoke without inflection. "We're going to have ourselves a little auction. Also, in case any of you try to make a run for it, I should tell you that the doors are wired with enough explosives to blow half this room to kingdom come. I suppose that makes you a, er, captive audience."

People were moving restlessly in their seats, looking at each other nervously, and seeking mutual comfort by holding hands.

"Now then, please allow me to introduce myself. For all practical purposes, my name is Mr. Jones, and I am the auctioneer for the rest of this auction. Unfortunately, I am not licensed by the Department of Consumer Affairs, but I don't believe that'll present a problem, do you?"

No one spoke.

"I should also mention that the lots and their numbers have changed. One of my associates—we'll call him Mr. Smith—is going to pass out a number to each of you. Those are your lot numbers."

There was dead silence.

"You see, ladies and gentlemen, we are going to hold the ultimate auction. One in which far more precious commodities than mere paintings will be sold. The lots are *you*."

There was a visible reaction of shock. Everyone stared at him in disbelief.

"That's right," he continued, "you heard correctly. Each of you is an individual lot. Your reserve prices have already been predetermined. Payment is to be made in negotiable bearer bonds, and delivered here by noon tomorrow. As soon as your payment is received, you will be released. You may bid on behalf of yourself, your spouse, and friends."

His cold obsidian eyes roamed the room.

"If anybody cannot make their reserve, or payment is not delivered in time—" he shrugged "—tough titty. You will be shot. However, you can rest assured that death will be mercifully quick. We are not sadists."

He gestured for Sheldon D. Fairey to step down off the dais.

Fairey stood there possessively. "This . . . this is outrageous!" he sputtered, drawing himself up to his full height. "Auction indeed! This . . . this *travesty* amounts to nothing more than pure ransom."

"Mr. Jones's" voice was a whiplash. "Either step down or face the consequences."

Fairey looked into his eyes. Seeing no mercy, his confidence and assertiveness evaporated, and he wisely did as he was told.

"Thank you, sir. Now then. I would like the two telephone operators at the end—" "Mr. Jones" gestured to Kenzie and Arnold "—to step down also. The other young lady shall remain."

Kenzie and Arnold squeezed Annalisa's arm and quickly followed Fairey. They stood against the side wall, next to the four green-aproned young men from the temporary painting storeroom.

"Mr. Smith? If you will kindly pass out the lot numbers now. In the meantime, as long as no one leaves their seats, you may confer quietly among yourselves."

"Mr. Jones" glanced at his wristwatch.

"The auction," he said, "shall begin in exactly ten minutes."

The lobby of Burghley's had taken on the look of a police command center. The metal detectors had been moved out of the way, and uniformed patrolmen and detectives in civilian clothes were everywhere. Outside, Madison Avenue began to look like a precinct parking lot.

"Chief, EMS is sending ten ambulances," someone reported.

"Three SWAT teams are on their way, Chief," someone else shouted.

Charley fought to keep his voice even. "Chief, you've got to listen to me! If you're gonna send in SWAT teams, you might as well forget the ambulances. You'll need a fleet of meat wagons. I keep telling you, this is a one-man job."

The PC rolled his eyes. "Officer Ferraro, you're on the art theft squad. What makes you think you're suddenly Rambo?"

"Sir, my partner's in there. So's my girl. Long as I can sneak in, I can enlist their help. That makes three of us."

"You told me yourself all the ways in are wired."

"Yes, sir. But I can crawl through the ducts. Before the videocams were shot out, I caught sight of an overhead heating vent."

"Yeah?"

"And it wasn't wired," Charley said, thinking: *God help me if it is. I didn't see jack shit. But I'm willing to risk it. I have to risk it. Kenzie's in there.*

For the first time, the PC began to look interested. He stood there looking thoughtfully at Charley. "Give me one good reason why I should stick my neck out and send you in."

"Because I have everything to lose, sir."

"Shit." The PC heaved a deep sigh. "Personal motives scare the living daylights out of me. How do I know you won't put everyone at risk just to save two people?"

"Sir, with all due respect, I think *your* way would put everyone at risk. The SWAT teams might work, sure. But how many people would end up getting killed in the process?"

"Chief," someone shouted. "The Eyewitness News van just pulled up."

"Goddammit!" the PC swore. "And we purposely used phones, not police band. Some fuck at EMS must have tipped them off. I find out who, his ass is grass!"

"Chief?" Charley said urgently.

The PC said, "All right, listen to me carefully, Ferraro. I don't want you to do anything that'll jeopardize the lives of those people. We both know there's strict SOP for dealing with hostage crises. I'm sticking my neck out by letting you go in. Got that?"

"Loud and clear, sir. And I really appreciate it. But I need you to do a couple of things."

"What are they?"

"Leave the heat on, but turn it way down. I don't want to roast."

"You fuck up, you *will* roast. I'll personally see to that. What else?"

"They've got Hannes's transmitter and earphones, so don't try to communicate with me. Think you can scare up an old-fashioned walkie-talkie?"

"You got it."

"And, if you could cover me by tossing out some fake info over the microtransmitters every now and then—"

"Done." The PC drilled Charley with hit-man eyes. "I just hope I'm not going to regret this, Ferraro."

"I hope I won't either, sir." Charley flashed him his most engaging, hard-to-resist grin. "But look at it this way, sir. What've you got to lose?"

"Just the mayor, the governor, two ex-presidents, and practically everybody on the Forbes 400. And that's just for starters."

"Right." Charley frowned. "We got any semiautomatics on hand?"

"Only a Wilkinson Linda we're holding for some tycoon's bodyguard."

"Good. I'll borrow it."

The PC didn't look pleased. He handed Charley a walkie-talkie. "Just don't disappoint me, Ferraro."

"I won't, sir. I really apprec—"

"Save it. Now get going before the Feds show up and nix this half-assed plan of yours."

"Yes, sir."

The PC went with him to okay the appropriation of the pistol.

"I lost count of how many laws we've already broken, Ferraro, so I don't want to know about any others. You're on your own now. I'll try to buy you as much time as I can. But that's all I can do. And I might not even be able to do much of that."

"I understand, sir. And thanks." Charley stuck the pistol in his belt and the walkie-talkie in his pants pocket. Then sketching a wave, he sprinted back up the stairs.

Two minutes later, he had stripped off his jacket, tie, and shirt and was standing on a chair unscrewing an overhead heating vent.

Talk is cheap, he thought, tossing the grille to the floor. *Now I've got to deliver.*

Reaching up into the duct, he put his hands flat on the sheet metal and did a neat pull-up.

The metal buckled under his weight and made a loud popping noise. Once he squeezed inside and released his weight, the metal popped back into shape with a peal like thunder.

He cringed and made a mental note to make less noise. *Sound travels,* he reminded himself. *Especially through a metal tube.*

But he was in and stretched out flat, his weight evenly distributed. Lifting his head two inches, he peered ahead into the gloom.

Every fifteen feet or so, little lattices of light leaked up through the grilled vents. Otherwise, the duct was dark, cramped, and stifling.

Now I know what being in a coffin is like, he thought. *If I get through this, I'll rewrite my will; specify cremation.* He changed his mind almost instantly. *If this heat's any indication, I don't want that, either. Hell, last thing I need to think about right now is death. There are living people who need my help.*

And using his palms, elbows, knees, and feet for traction, he began to crawl.

* * *

In the auction gallery, the ten minutes were nearly up.

From the sidelines, Kenzie could sense the growing air of dread. In the front row, Robert was holding Dina's hand, trying his best to console her. Next to them, Karl-Heinz had his arm around Zandra's shoulder, while whispering something.

All over the vast auditorium, nearly identical scenes were endlessly replicated.

On the dais, the Velázquez infanta seemed disdainfully superior to the dramas of mere mortals, and Kenzie wondered how many other horrors and tragedies she'd been mute witness to over the centuries.

Certainly none like this, she thought. *This has got to be a first.*

The ten minutes were up. "Mr. Jones" was back on the dais after conferring with his "associates" in the aisles.

With his reappearance, the temperature seemed to have plunged several degrees—at least, that was the way it felt to the defenseless captives in the plush red seats. Their fear was an almost palpable entity, like a giant turbulent cloud churning madly above their heads.

"Mr. Jones" was addressing them.

"Ladies and gentlemen. I have with me—" he unfolded a sheaf of paper he had in his breast pocket and placed it on the lectern "—a list of each of your individual estimated net worths. I must say it is highly impressive."

He scanned the rows of seats as dispassionately as a poultry farmer surveying a brood of fat hens.

"In the past, that wealth has bought you many luxuries, but this evening, it can buy you the most precious necessity of all—*your lives.* When I call your lot number, you will come forward and stand over there, beside that painting."

He paused and looked down at the lectern. Then he raised his rugged, lean face.

"Lot number one," he called out. "Will you please come forward."

The auction had begun.

For Charley, the going was slow. The cramped duct hindered his modified crab crawl and restricted his movements.

If only he could speed up!

But it was impossible. There was not enough height to get on his hands and knees, and his scrabbling low crawl depended upon using his elbows and legs for traction. It was all he could do to manuever forward a few inches at a time.

Worse, the furnacelike heat was rapidly weakening him, sapping him of energy. He was already drenched in sweat, and his arms and legs were numb and starting to cramp.

The temptation to just lie there and rest a while was overwhelming.

Can't, he told himself, letting out a sigh, the exhalation like a loud blast of hot air in the stifling, metal confines. *Mustn't stop. The hostages are counting on me. Kenzie's counting on me—*

—Kenzie!

He had to keep moving. Rest was a luxury he couldn't afford—and the hostages could afford even less.

Runnels of sweat trickled down his forehead, burned saltily in his eyes.

On he crawled. On . . .

"Lot number one. This is your last chance."

"Oh, hold your horses!" called a feisty, elderly voice.

People twisted around in their seats and craned their necks, curious to see who it was.

Near the center on the left, an imperious lady in her eighties with fluffy white hair like cotton candy was getting to her feet. She wore an old-fashioned gown shot through with jet beads, and diamonds to die for.

Leaning on her cane, she made a progress of apologies as she brushed against people who sat sideways or half rose to let her by.

Once in the aisle, she came forward at her own stately pace, her bearing proud and erect, her face unafraid. One of the Colombians approached to help her onto the dais.

"I neither want nor need help," she snapped, wielding her cane threateningly. "Especially not from the likes of you!"

Chagrined, the Colombian gave her a wide berth and she slowly ascended the three steps. Standing beside the Velázquez, she raised her chin, her forthright, denim-blue eyes flashing.

"Mr. Jones" said, "Mildred Davies?"

"That's *Mrs.* Davies to you," she clarified acerbically.

His features fluttered with a muscular tic, and he lifted one, then two sheets of paper; ran an index finger down the third.

"Here we are. Davies, Mrs. Edgar. Age, eighty-two. Widowed. Resident of Washington, Connecticut. Fortune derived from Yankee Corrugated Cardboard. Net worth eight hundred fifty million dollars."

"So you read *Forbes,*" she sniffed. "Am I supposed to be impressed?"

The eyes of everyone in the gallery were riveted on her.

"Your reserve price has been set at fifty million dollars. Who would you like to call to arrange payment?"

"No one," she said succinctly.

There was a communal gasp.

"Sorry?"

"If you didn't hear me, young man, I advise you to have your ears checked. I said, you're getting nothing for me."

"You do realize the alternative?"

"Death?" She laughed. "You young fool! I'm not afraid of dying. The doctors only give me eight more months, anyway. So go ahead. Shoot. You'll be doing me a favor."

"Mr. Jones" motioned to one of the Colombians, who came trotting.

"You're sure, Mrs. Davies? This is your last chance."

"I'm positive, may your soul be damned to eternal hell!"

The Colombian raised one Uzi lazily and, amid horrified screams of protests, pressed the trigger.

Semiautomatic gunfire chattered—*rat-tat-tat!*—and the old lady seemed to dance like an amphetamine-crazed marionette before collapsing, as though her strings had been cut, abruptly to the floor.

The screams of the multitude suddenly stopped, as if a circuit had been switched off. Everyone sat there in frozen shock.

"Mr. Jones" banged the gavel. "Bought in," he called out.

He paused and looked around.

"You'd all better start taking this seriously," he advised grimly. "Unless, of course, you want to join Mrs. Davies, there?"

No one responded.

"All right, then," he continued, "lot number two—"

At that instant a cry of agony rent the air.

andra's face had gone chalk white. Her eyes bulged, and with one hand she clutched Karl-Heinz, her fingers digging painfully into his thigh; with the other, she gripped Dina's arm as though to crush it. Then her body convulsed, and it was all she could do to hold on tight as she doubled over.

"The baby!" she gasped. "Oh, bugger it! Something's happening. Oh, Heinzie—!"

She raised her perspiration-slick face and stared at him in fear and pain.

"Hush," he said gently, starting to get up.

She grabbed his arm. "No!" There was a pleading note of desperation in her voice. "Please don't leave me!"

"I won't," he said gently. "I promise." He got to his feet.

"Sit down!" "Mr. Jones's" voice cut the air like a knife.

Karl-Heinz stood his ground. "My wife is going into premature labor," he said calmly. "She requires immediate hospitalization."

"Mr. Jones" shook his head. "No one leaves here."

"For God's sake—"

"Sit down!" "Jones" thundered. "Or do you want to join Mrs. Davies?"

Karl-Heinz's face narrowed. He refused to be cowed and remained standing. Everything about this situation—the armed criminals strutting about, the dead woman lying on the dais, Zandra in torment—filled him with rage.

"I don't have *time* to argue with an underling!" Karl-Heinz snapped coldly. He raised his hand and pointed an accusatory finger at the lectern. *"You're* not in charge. You don't have the brains to be. I suggest you consult whoever's *really* running this fiasco. Or hasn't it occurred to you that we're not worth anything to you dead?"

"Jones's" face reddened with fury, but Zandra's sharp cry robbed him of a response.

Karl-Heinz bent down to soothe her. "It's all right," he told her softly. "Everything will be fine."

She looked up at him and shook her head. "No, Heinzie." Her eyes filled with tears. "It isn't—"

Suddenly she shuddered and blood began staining the lap of her loose white gown. Something was obviously very, very wrong. She was hemorrhaging badly.

Karl-Heinz glanced around, his face filled with alarm.

Even Dina, who had never given birth, could tell that Zandra's heaving body was trying to expel the child. Quickly she rose to her feet.

"*What the hell—?*" "Jones" roared, glowering at her.

You stupid idiot bastard, Dina thought, and said: "Unless you let us do something, she's going to bleed to death. Is that what you want?"

He glared at her in silence.

Dina continued to laser him with her eyes. *Why do things in halves?* she thought. *Once you're on a limb, you might as well climb all the way out.*

"If she dies because of you," she went on, "you can kiss her ransom good-bye. As well as Prince Karl-Heinz's, I would imagine. And the same goes for the Goldsmiths. My husband *and* I."

Her words had a galvanizing effect: a mutinous rumble of angry murmurs rose from the crowd.

"It seems to me," Dina added, with stinging scorn, "that you're intent upon shrinking your imaginary coffers by the minute."

For a moment "Jones" seemed confused. This volley of verbal arrows was the last thing he'd anticipated.

These people aren't easily cowed, he thought. *And as to whether or not this woman's bluffing, that's not my decision to make.*

Dina saw him glancing around, his eyes searching the gallery as though seeking advice—no! *Not advice,* she realized. *Permission!* She followed his gaze, but nothing caught her attention.

"Are you thinking what I'm thinking?" she whispered to Karl-Heinz.

He nodded. "Yes. Besides the eight of them, there's a ninth. Whoever the ringleader is, he's seated among *us.*"

"Jones's" pager emitted three short beeps.

"All right," he barked. "Move her to an aisle. But she can't leave. No one can."

An aisle? Kenzie thought, with outrage. *They're going to lay Zandra down in one of the aisles?* She was shocked. This was no way for anybody to have to give birth—least of all someone suffering serious complications. *Zandra won't have to,* she decided. *Not if I have anything to say about it!*

Kenzie stepped forward. Her throat felt constricted, and her heart was ka-booming. For an instant she wondered if she might not be making a terrible mistake. But there was no time to consider the consequences. Zandra's life was at stake.

"What about taking her into the painting storeroom?" she called out.

"That way, it won't interfere with . . ." Her voice trailed off. *With whatever,* she thought grimly.

"Right," "Jones" decided, and grinned. "Since you thought of it, you can help carry her in there."

Gladly, Kenzie thought, hurrying around to the front.

"The prince and I will help also," Dina decided imperiously. "My husband has our lot numbers."

Without waiting for a reply, Dina tossed her purse into Robert's lap and tore off her black mesh gloves. Then she and Karl-Heinz reached down, placed one of Zandra's arms around each of their shoulders, and lifted her upright. As gently as possible, they held her up between them and did a slow sideways shuffle to the aisle.

Kenzie was waiting. She grabbed Zandra's feet and lifted her legs.

Together, the three of them carried her, like a fragile, priceless heirloom, to the dais, up the steps, and around the easel and through the double-width doorway behind it.

Once inside, they lowered her slowly to the floor between racks of paintings. Zandra's stomach was heaving again, and Karl-Heinz took the cellular phone and his wallet out of his breast pocket and tossed them to the floor. Then, swiftly shedding his jacket, he rolled it up and placed it under her head.

"You'll be fine," he kept telling her softly. "Do not be afraid."

Zandra stared up into his face, her eyes darkened by shadows. She shook her head. "I'm going to lose the baby."

"Hush. Don't talk like a fool." He put his hand over hers and covered it. She gripped his fingers tightly.

Dina and Kenzie, kneeling on either side of her, pushed the bloodied white gown up to Zandra's waist.

Kenzie drew a deep breath. *Oh, shit,* she thought.

The hemorrhaging had not abated. If anything, it was even worse.

Dina met her gaze levelly. "We need a doctor," she said firmly, getting to her feet.

"Where are you going?" Kenzie asked.

"Why, to fetch one, sweetie," Dina said, surprised that she should ask. "Where else would I be off to?"

Kenzie stared at her in amazement.

Sofia slid her cellular phone out of her purse and punched the automatic speed dial for the clinic outside Augsburg. Lifting the phone to her ear, she spoke softly into it. "Dr. Rantzau, please. Tell him it's Princess von und zu Engelwiesen."

Then she waited, ignoring the Lebanese who was cursing her from the aisle and gesturing that she put the phone away.

Dr. Rantzau came on the line. "Your Highness? I was about to call

you. I'm sorry. Your father is slipping away. The priest has just been here
to give him his last rites."

The priest! Sofia thought. *Who gives a damn about the priest?* "Are
Herr Meindl and his son there?" *That's what's important!*

"Yes, Your Highness."

"They are to remain there to time and witness what happens."

"Yes, Your High—"

Sofia punched off the phone and slid it back inside her purse.

She thought: *If Zandra should give birth now, it's doubtful the child
will live. Not that it matters, anyway. There's not one, let alone the* three
requisite lawyers present to confirm the birth.

She was smiling.

Things really couldn't be working out any better . . .

Outside Burghley's, the floodlit Venetian facade throbbed with colors from
the flashing blue, red, and orange light bars atop the various emergency
vehicles. Inside the police barricades, the number of squad cars had tripled, joined now by FBI sedans, a total of twenty EMS vehicles, six fire
engines, and two bomb squad vans.

Overhead, news helicopters circled the twin campaniles of Auction Towers like predatory birds, feeding live aerial footage back to
the networks.

The number of spectators on the scene had multiplied, obviously a result of the breaking news headlines.

All over the country, people were glued to their TV sets.

This was television at its best. Not only was a real-life hostage drama
unreeling, but the victims were among the richest, most powerful, and
protected people on earth, the privileged few who waltzed through life inhabiting a seemingly more elegant and brighter parallel universe.

Now the sordid horrors of the real world had caught up with them.

And millions watched. Fascinated.

"The fuck is going on?" Charley muttered silently to himself. He was
above the auction gallery, peering down through a ventilation grille. At
first glance, everything *looked* normal, like an auction was in session.

Then a man with a semiautomatic Uzi revolver in each hand passed
directly below him.

Definitely not normal, Charlie thought. *Just about as far from normal
as you can get.*

Now that he was on the lookout, other gunmen caught his eye, eight
if you counted the one behind the lectern. Beside him stood a well-known,
elegant white-haired man in his seventies. Charley turned his head sideways, putting his ear to the grille to listen.

"Lot number two. Veroni, Maurizio Paolo. Age, seventy-three. Married. Resident of Bareggio, Como, Rome, Pantelleria, New York, Paris, and London. Industrialist. Fortune derived from Fido automobiles. Net worth six billion dollars. Your reserve price has been set at five hundred million . . ."

Holy shit! Charley raised his head. *They're auctioning off people!*

He quickly crawled on, trying to move faster. Hoping to God that the painting storeroom wasn't guarded. That he could crawl out and hop down in there.

I've got to radio for help, he thought. *There are too many of them.* Trying to take them out single-handedly would be suicide. *And I'm not ready to die just yet.*

The police commissioner was taking the heat from the Feds. *"You* have done *your* part, now *you* stay out of this," the head of the local FBI office was telling him, punctuating each "you" and "your" with a jab of his finger. "From here on in, it's our call. You got that?"

As usual, the Suits had come barging in, trampling over everyone and leaving a trail of bruised egos in their wake.

Except this isn't a matter of bruised egos, the PC thought. *It's a matter of life and death.*

"Back off, buddy," he retorted, showing starch and backbone. "First off, I've put a man in there. No one jeopardizes him or does anything until we hear from him."

"And how long's that going to take?"

"Till I say so. Second, unless I personally hear differently from your director, we do this my way. You don't know diddly about what's going on in there. Third, you want to know how many of the hostages are personal friends of the President's? I'll gladly show you the list. You get trigger-happy, I'll go right over your head and call the White House. You'll be lucky if they send you to a field office in Alaska or North Dakota!"

"Fifteen minutes," the Fed snapped. "After that, it's our show. Fifteen minutes is all I'll give you." Again, he jabbed his index finger on the word "you."

Quick as a flash, the PC grabbed the digit and held tight.

"Hey—!"

"And fourth," the PC growled quietly, "next time you point your fuckin' finger at me, I'm gonna fuckin' break it off, buddy! *You* got that?"

Then the PC let go of him and strode toward the waiting SWAT teams to brief them on the heating ducts. *I must be crazy,* he thought. *I've got more faith in Ferraro than all the Suits combined.*

He wondered if maybe it wasn't time to get his head checked.

"Lady, you're becoming one hell of a pain in the ass. Give me one good reason why I shouldn't shoot you right now."

Dina was undaunted. "Because," she informed him calmly, "my friends and I are much too valuable to shoot. Or perhaps you'd like to use your beeper and ask permission from your superior?"

The blood blossomed under the skin of "Jones's" face, coloring it crimson. "*I'm* in charge," he snarled. "Maybe killing you will prove it." He raised one of his revolvers and aimed it at her.

Dina froze. For one horrible, drawn-out split second, she wondered whether she had actually gone too far.

Then his beeper emitted a single burst of sound.

He kept the revolver trained on her a moment longer before slowly lowering it.

So Heinzie and I guessed correctly! Dina thought. The mastermind really was out there somewhere. *Somehow, we'll have to find a way to flush him out.*

But that could wait.

She addressed the assemblage in a loud, clear voice: "I believe I recognized Dr. Irving Landau, the heart surgeon, when we first came in. Dr. Landau? If it is you, *please*. We need help desperately."

The handsome, gray-haired surgeon rose from the eleventh row on the right.

"I can't thank you enough, doctor. We shall cover your . . . er, reserve price." Carefully avoiding Robert, who was no doubt keeping a mental tally and ready to go ballistic, Dina's eyes swept the rows of seats. "Also, to witness the birth, we need three practicing attorneys—"

"*No!*" Sofia screamed, jumping to her feet. "You *can't* let her—"

"*Silence!*" thundered the Lebanese on her side of the aisle, who raised his Uzi. "Sit *down!*"

"Erwein!" she whined. "*Do* something!"

Erwein did. He grabbed her by the wrist and yanked her down into her seat.

She shook off his hand and turned on him. "I told you to *do* something!" she hissed.

"I did. I was saving your life."

"Humpf!" she sniffed, turning away. *Erwein saving me!* she thought. *What a joke!*

"For legal reasons," Dina continued, "this child's birth must be witnessed by three attorneys. So please. If there are three of you, we'll be happy to pay for your reserves also."

Now she could distinctly hear Robert choke.

"Any three of you," Dina added urgently as five men rose from their seats. "But please! *Hurry!*"

Dr. Landau had reached the dais and Dina swiftly took him by the arm, guided him around the Velázquez, and into the painting storeroom. He took one look at Zandra and stripped off his jacket.

"Cover her with this." He tossed it at Karl-Heinz. "We don't want her to go into shock."

Unasked, Kenzie unbuttoned her suit jacket and gave it to Karl-Heinz, and Dina slid out of her burgundy cut-velvet silk jacket and did the same.

"We need to keep her covered," Dina told the three attorneys as they came in. "Please, gentlemen. If you could lend us your jackets?"

Kenzie stared at the attorneys as they shed their coats. Each was famous, a star in his own field.

One was the top divorce lawyer in the country.

Another was the infamous *consigliere* of a Mafia crime syndicate.

And the third was a well-known entertainment lawyer.

Only Dina could have come up with that selection, Kenzie thought admiringly.

"Water," Dr. Landau ordered, plucking the gold cufflinks off his white shirt, rolling up his sleeves, and kneeling between Zandra's parted legs.

Kenzie said, "There isn't any, I'm afraid."

He shook his head in despair and sighed. "Well, then we'll just have to make do. Perfume?"

"Zandra was still clutching her purse when we brought her in," Kenzie said. "Let me see."

She looked around, spied it, and snapped it open. "Will a spray bottle of Panthère de Cartier do?"

"In a pinch, yes." Dr. Landau held up his hands. "And be quick about it."

Kenzie liberally squirted both sides of his hands and half his forearms.

"Now, here's what's required, sweeties," Dina was telling the attorneys. "If the child is a boy, we shall need an affidavit confirming its sex, the exact time of birth, and the fact that you each witnessed it, and that it came from the womb of Princess Zandra. That's all. Here. My watch keeps perfect time."

She unclasped her diamond-encrusted gold timepiece and handed it to the *consigliere.*

The three attorneys compared the time on Dina's watch with their own wristwatches, and looked at one another and frowned.

Meanwhile, Dr. Landau was putting his hand up inside Zandra to dilate her cervix. He felt around carefully.

Zandra clenched her teeth against the pain.

"I can't feel the child's head," Dr. Landau said. "The womb is blocked by the afterbirth. This won't be pretty, but—" Swiftly he began pulling out the bloodied tissue. When the obstruction was cleared, he broke the waterbag, and the amniotic fluid flowed forth. Then, gently but firmly, he guided the tiny, sixteen-inch child down the channel and out of Zandra's body.

"Eight-seventeen," the entertainment lawyer announced, consulting Dina's watch. The others looked at it and murmured their concurrence.

"Look!" Kenzie exclaimed. "The bleeding! It's stopped!"

"Thank God," Karl-Heinz offered up softly.

Dr. Landau placed the child on Zandra's abdomen.

"Is it . . ." Kenzie began uneasily. "It doesn't seem to be breathing."

"Give it a second." The doctor gently rubbed the infant's back to stimulate its breathing.

Nothing.

Quickly he turned the child around, put his mouth around its tiny nose and mouth, and sucked to clear the passages.

Then it came. A feeble cry, but a cry all the same.

The child *was* alive! And breathing!

"Look!" Dina clapped her hands together in delight. "It *is* a boy! Oh, Zandra! Sweetie, it's a son! You have a *son!*"

"Truly?" Zandra whispered, looking up at Karl-Heinz.

He grinned. "You'll see for yourself in a moment."

"Scissors," Dr. Landau said.

"My Swiss Army knife has a tiny pair." Karl-Heinz dug it out of his trouser pocket.

"If anyone has a lighter, please sterilize it."

The divorce lawyer flicked his gold lighter and Karl-Heinz held the tiny folding scissors into the flame. Then the doctor took them, cut the umbilical cord, and tied it.

"Clean handkerchiefs."

Several were forthcoming, and Dr. Landau dried the tiny, skinny red infant. It let out a thin but indignant bleat and clenched and unclenched its tiny hands.

"It's very important you keep him warm," Dr. Landau cautioned. "I don't know whether it's my imagination or not, but it seems to have gotten decidedly chilly in here."

Carefully he placed the baby in Zandra's arms. "Here you go."

"Oh, gosh. But, he's so tiny and frail!" she exclaimed. "He feels frightfully light." She stared at Dr. Landau. "He can't weigh more than three or four pounds!"

"I know. Keep him under the covers, but don't smother him. He needs all the oxygen he can get. His lungs won't be fully developed yet."

Zandra nodded.

"Also, in order to survive, he'll require incubation. And soon."

Just then the heating vent on the overhead duct at the back of the storeroom popped open and Charley's head poked out, upside down. He was holding a finger to his lips and grinning from ear to ear.

Kenzie looked back and forth from him to the baby. It was hard to assimilate everything. Too much was happening all at once.

Then she felt a surge of joy the likes of which she had never known.

"It won't be long before he's incubated," she assured Zandra confidently. "See? My Charley is radioing for help already. Now let's quiet down and not give away what's happening. But first, will some of you men *please* help Charley down? That's quite a drop, and I don't want my hero to get hurt."

⚐ *66* ❧

*I*n the lobby, the police commissioner listened to the squawks coming from the walkie-talkie, and his face lit up like a Christmas tree. He flashed the Fed a grin.

"Your guy?"

"That's right," the PC said. "SWAT team!"

The waiting special forces jumped to attention.

"Listen up good!"

He relayed Charley's information.

"Any questions?"

There were none.

"*Go!*"

The assembled squad rushed the stairs with a clatter, heading toward the open vent on the floor above.

The cavalry was on its way.

In the painting storeroom, time was passing with excruciating slowness. For everyone, the wait for the SWAT team seemed the longest and most difficult of their lives.

Out in the gallery, the obscene mockery of an auction had resumed. The air of mutiny had given way to resignation, and "lots" two through eleven had capitulated. The high and mighty, reduced to fear and powerlessness, were on the telephones, arranging for the delivery of bearer bonds.

No one wanted to join Mildred Davies.

Lot number twelve was being called.

In the storage room, time seemed to have come to a complete standstill.

Behind one of the rolling racks laden with sideways stacked paintings, Kenzie was keeping Charley company, the two of them sitting on the floor.

"You risked your life being the first one through!" she marveled. "What made you do it, you lovable fool?"

"Keep your voice down," he whispered, raising his revolver and chancing a moment's glance around the corner before ducking back out of sight. "Last thing we need's for one of those thugs to come investigate."

"Is that any way to answer a question?"

"If you must know, I have a personal stake in this," he said.

"Oh?" Her eyebrows, raised in amusement, disappeared up under her bangs. "And what might that be?"

"What do you think, you amoral, heartless, infuriating, two-timing, prick-teasing pain in the ass?"

"Why, Charles Gabriel Ferraro!" she said huskily, staring at him in pleased, wide-eyed wonder. "I do believe that's your way of saying you love me!"

"Maybe," he said, holding his revolver with both hands and keeping it pointed ceilingward in readiness.

"And to think," she murmured, "how much misery I put you through. All because I was unable to decide."

He squinted at her. "This mean you finally made up your mind?"

"Oh, I think so."

"And?"

She held his gaze. "First, why don't we see about getting out of this alive."

"This your way of saying yes?"

"Could be."

"Still afraid to commit," he said in exasperation. "That it?"

She shook her head. "You're my number one hero," she said.

"What does that mean?"

"Oh, really, Charley! Don't you ever pay attention to the movies? The hero *always* gets the girl in the end."

"Takes a tough man," he cracked, "to win a tender woman."

Intuition told Dina not to press her luck by interrupting the "auction" yet again. "We have pens, sweeties," she informed the attorneys, "but no paper. In order to be legal, the affidavit doesn't *have* to be written on paper, does it?"

The divorce lawyer shook his head. "So long as the wording's correct, and it's properly signed and witnessed, it can be written on most any surface."

"Splendid!"

Dina looked around, spied a small gilt-framed painting in the nearest rack, and appropriated it without giving it a glance. She placed it upside-down atop the rack, the back of the aged, stretched brown canvas facing up.

"Here you go, sweeties," she purred. "You can write up the appropriate legalese on this."

The three men looked at one another and shrugged.

"Why not?" said the *consigliere*. He gave Dina a solemn look. "Just so long as the prince buys the painting. If anyone else winds up with it, he's out of luck."

"Oh, he'll buy it, sweetie," Dina assured him. "Don't you worry about that."

The men huddled around the canvas, deep in whispered conversation about the precise wording of the document.

Zandra, holding her newborn under the warmth of the jackets which covered her, lay with her head cradled in Karl-Heinz's lap.

"You see?" he whispered, smiling down at her. "Did I not tell you everything would be fine?"

She stared up at him. "Yes," she said softly, "you did." Then her voice took on an anxious edge. "But, darling, what about an incubator? He needs one in order to survive!"

"You heard Kenzie," he said. "Help is on the way. Give it a few min—"

He was interrupted by the chirrup of his cellular phone. Reaching out to where he'd dropped it, he picked it up, and took the call.

"Yes?"

"Your Highness? It's Dr. Rantzau."

Karl-Heinz instinctively tensed, bracing himself for bad news. "Yes, doctor?"

"If I might extend my most sincere condolences," the director of the clinic said gravely. "His Highness, Prince Leopold, passed away several minutes ago."

Karl-Heinz lowered the phone and momentarily shut his eyes tightly. The news should hardly have come as a shock, and yet it left him stunned.

He thought: *I wonder. Are we ever prepared for the death of a loved one?*

"Heinzie?" Zandra was asking. "Darling, what *is* it?"

"My father." His voice was choked. "He's dead."

"Oh, no!" She reached up and touched his face. "Oh, darling, I am sorry."

He drew a deep breath and let it out slowly.

The Lord giveth, he thought, *and the Lord taketh away. Truer words were never written . . .*

"Ironic, is it not," he said softly, "that our son should be born within minutes of my father's death? How is it that such joy and tragic loss can come so closely together?"

Dina gently took the telephone from his hand and moved a few steps away.

"Hello? Who is this? I see. The prince needs some moments to himself, Dr. Rantzau. Tell me, could you give me the exact time of his father's death?"

"It occurred precisely at thirteen minutes past two, Central European Time."

Dina's heart sank like a stone. *The baby was born at seventeen past eight, Eastern Standard Time.*

"You're certain?" she asked.

"Absolutely. Two attorneys were at his bedside to confirm the time of death."

"I see," Dina said dully. "No, there's nothing else. Thank you, Dr. Rantzau. His . . . his Serene Highness will be in touch."

She jabbed off the phone, tempted to hurl it against the wall.

"Four minutes!" she said tightly. "The child was born four minutes too late!"

The *consigliere,* scratching away on the back of the canvas with his fountain pen, abruptly stopped writing. He turned to look at her. "What do you mean?" he asked.

Dina filled him in on the death of the old prince and the timing of the birth. "You see, sweeties?" she said bitterly. "He died *before* the birth. Four minutes before. Now Heinzie cannot possibly inherit."

The *consigliere* frowned thoughtfully. "Perhaps he can," he told her. "Why don't you call up 976-6000 for the correct time?"

"But I don't see what—"

"Please. Just do it."

Dina shrugged, pressed seven buttons, and listened.

"It's eight twenty-three," she said.

"Could we?" The entertainment lawyer held out his hand for the telephone and raised it to his ear to verify. The two others put their heads close enough to listen in. Then all three of them glanced at their watches and smiled.

The entertainment lawyer handed the phone back to Dina.

"It's just as I suspected," the *consigliere* said.

Dina looked bewildered. "What is?"

It was the divorce lawyer who replied. "Look at your watch and tell us what time it says."

Dina lifted her wrist and consulted her diamond-studded timepiece. "It shows eight thirty-three," she said. "So?"

And then her mouth fell open as she suddenly understood.

"*Thirty*-three! Oh, my God!" she whispered, slapping the side of her head. "How could I have forgotten? I *always* set my clocks and watches ten minutes ahead!"

The *consigliere* smiled. "I must admit you had us a bit confused. All our watches were within a minute of each other's, but since you assured us that yours kept perfect time—"

"—you obviously thought yours were running too slow," Dina completed for him, with a sudden smile. "Well, sweeties? What are you all waiting for? Proceed with the document! And whatever you do, for God's sake, *please*. Do put down the correct time!"

Dina was consulted twice, each time to provide the father and mother's full names:

"... His Serene Highness, Prince Karl-Heinz Fernando de Carlos Jean Joachim Alejandor Ignacio Hieronymous Eustace von und zu Engelwiesen ..."

and "Her Serene Highness, Princess Anna Zandra Elisabeth Theresia Charlotte von und zu Engelwiesen."

Five minutes later, the lawyers were done. They brought Dina the painting, and she took it, her lips murmuring as she quickly read what they'd drafted:

"On this eleventh day of November in the Year of our Lord ... et cetera ... whereas we, the undersigned practicing attorneys ... et cetera ... inasmuch as having duly witnessed, at the eighth hour and seventh minute of this evening ..."

Dina was impressed. There was no doubt as to the document's validity.

Ceremoniously, she carried the fait accompli over to Zandra and Karl-Heinz. "*Voilà*, sweeties!" she said brightly. "Proof of the birth."

"Goodness, Dina," Zandra said. "But, darling, it's written on canvas. On the back of a painting. Will it stand up legally, do you think?"

"Of course it will. All you have to do is buy the painting. I'll see to it that it's withdrawn from the auction, and arrange for a private sale."

"Well?" Karl-Heinz asked. "Do we get to see what's on the other side?"

"Who cares?" Dina said, turning it over.

Zandra stared at the portrait. "*Dina!* Darling, couldn't you possibly have found us something, well, something a little cheaper?"

"I chose it specifically because it's small," Dina sniffed.

"Small in size, perhaps. Dina! That's a bloody Rembrandt!"

"It is? Well then, it looks like you've bought yourselves a Rembrandt, doesn't it?"

Then Karl-Heinz and Zandra began to laugh. Dina would have joined in also, but at that moment, she caught a movement out of the corner of one eye.

She turned and watched, her heart leaping, as the first member of the SWAT team dropped soundlessly out of the vent, landed lithely on the carpeted concrete, and rolled a perfect somersault before leaping to his feet, the weapon he held never once scraping the floor.

In short order, three other men followed, none in the usual protective gear, which would have rendered them too bulky for the duct.

The leader of the four gestured toward the open double door. Two of them nodded and slipped behind the painting racks, using them for cover to reach the far side, where they melted silently against the wall, their weapons raised and ready.

The other two took up identically stealthy positions at the near side.

Dina watched them, impressed by their catlike agility. They were undeniably pros. For some strange reason, she no longer felt frightened, and was certain she and the others would come out of this alive. But a niggling thought bothered her, as if there was something she should tell the men.

She couldn't recall what it was, and then it was too late, anyway.

Simultaneously, and without warning, they sprang into action and leapt out onto the dais, semiautomatics stuttering.

"Jones," hit repeatedly, spun around under the impact of the bullets and then collapsed. One of the Colombians and the Lebanese raised their weapons, but too late. Bullets hit them squarely in the center of the chest, and the impact hurled them backward and off their feet. Before the terrified, screaming auction-goers could dive for cover, the ceiling seemed to spit bullets, and death rained selectively down out of the heating vents.

Within twenty seconds, the shooting stopped. There was an awed silence. All five of the remaining terrorists had either been killed or entirely disabled.

The gallery had been secured.

"Ladies and gentlemen," the leader of the SWAT team announced through a miniature microphone. "Everything is under control. Please remain in your seats while we remove the explosives from the doors. I repeat: do not try to leave until the explosives are removed."

The atmosphere in the gallery had changed. Now it was that of an airliner which had crash-landed safely, and whose passengers sat there, relieved, confused, stunned, *dazed*. Unable to comprehend that it was over. That they had gotten through this alive.

A pair of men sprinted to each of the three sets of doors, where they began the meticulous process of removing the magnetized Semtec, careful to keep the connecting wires intact.

Kenzie and Dina went out onto the dais, avoiding the bodies of Mildred Davies and "Mr. Jones." Standing side by side, they looked around in amazement.

"Can you believe it, sweetie?" Dina was saying. "The only casualties other than poor Mrs. Davies are the terrorists!"

But Kenzie wasn't listening. Hannes had hopped onto the dais and had taken her in his arms, saying, "Oh, Kenzie, my darling. Thank God nothing happened to you!"

She stared into his eyes and listened to his voice, soft and full of concern, and loved him for it. But she wasn't *in love* with him, she knew that now. It was Charley to whom she would yield her soul, with whom she wanted to spend the rest of her life. And she knew that Hannes could somehow read that in her eyes.

"You're shivering," he said, taking off his jacket and draping it around her shoulders.

She nodded. "I think they turned the heat down so the SWAT team wouldn't roast. I wish they'd turn it back up."

"I have to go see the SWAT team commander." He placed one hand on each of her shoulders and held her gaze. "You're sure you're okay, Kenzie?"

She nodded and smiled. "Yes, I'm fine."

He kissed her forehead chastely. "We'll talk later?"

"Yes," she said softly, "we'll talk later." She watched him hurry off. *There's really nothing to talk about*, she thought. *I had my fling. I was in lust with Hannes, but that's all. It's Charley I love.*

Slipping her arms into the sleeves of Hannes's jacket, she looked around and saw Arnold sitting there, looking dazed; Annalisa was pushing her chair back from the desk and getting to her feet. Both had come through the ordeal miraculously unharmed.

And then she saw Mr. Spotts coming forward from where he'd been sitting.

Kenzie's heart soared. *Thank God he's okay!* she thought warmly. *This can't have been good for his heart.* And then he was on the dais and she threw her arms around him. "Oh, Dietrich!" she cried. "I was so afraid something might have happened to you!"

He smiled. "Didn't you know I have nine lives?" he said.

And he pressed the barrel of a handgun against her forehead—

—while Annalisa thrust a revolver under Dina's chin.

"You see, my dear?" Mr. Spotts said. "It isn't over until it's over."

❧ 67 ❧

*I*n the painting storeroom, the first of the sharpshooters from up in the ducts dropped down through the open vent.

"First thing I want in here's EMS," Charley snapped into his walkie-talkie. "We got us a newborn preemie and its mother. Front of the gallery, storeroom behind the dais. This kid has priority. Got that?"

"Roger."

"Over and out."

Zandra, head still nestled on Karl-Heinz's lap, smiled up at Charley with misty-eyed pleasure. "Oh, Charley. That's frightfully sweet of you."

"You're talkin' about Kenzie's godchild," Charley said. "Anybody tries to mess with the little guy, they gotta answer to *me.*"

Suddenly he cocked his head and frowned.

"The fuck—?" he whispered, reaching for his weapon.

"What's the matter?" Karl-Heinz asked.

"Can't you hear it?"

Karl-Heinz listened and shook his head. "I can't hear anything."

"That's what I mean. All of a sudden it's *too* damn quiet out there."

Charley gestured at the sharpshooter to stay back, then moved, seemingly like a liquid shadow, to the edge of the doorway. Pressing himself flat against the wall, he inched his head around the doorjamb—

—then just as quickly whipped it back out of sight.

He slumped against the wall, feeling nausea and a dry, aching scream well up inside him.

Aw, shit! he thought. *That palsied, crazed old coot Kenzie used to work for's holding a gun to her head! And that bitch she hired's jamming a revolver up Dina Goldsmith's chin!*

Now what?

"Now," Charley told himself soundlessly, "you do what you gotta do."

He signaled at the sharpshooter to gauge the situation from his side of the doorway, then watched the man flatten himself next to it, inch his head around, and just as swiftly duck back.

A look of understanding passed between them.

Charley raised the Wilkinson Linda, and with his left hand, mimed masturbation. Then he pointed at himself.

Man. Mine.

The sharpshooter nodded.

Next Charley mimed voluptuous, imaginary breasts. He pointed at the sharpshooter.

Woman. Yours.

The sharpshooter nodded again.

Then they took up position, each a mirror image of the other, each prepared to whirl around, aim, and fire.

But they had to wait for the right moment, for all they would get was one shot each.

Neither of us can afford to miss, Charley thought grimly. *Dina's life is in his hands. And Kenzie's is in mine.*

On the dais, Dina stood stock-still, not daring to move anything except her eyes. The muzzle of the revolver dug painfully into the soft flesh beneath her chin, forcing her to keep her head raised at an unnatural angle.

Then a thought flashed through her mind and she suddenly remembered what it was that she had forgotten, but had wanted to warn the SWAT team about.

The ninth man—the one in the audience with the gadget which activated "Mr. Jones's" beeper.

Only I was wrong, Dina thought. *Dead wrong.*

There wasn't just a ninth man.

There had also been a tenth person. *This woman.*

Standing beside Dina, Kenzie remained equally still, but her eyes snapped around in desperation, beseeching someone—*anyone!*—to please try to help them. She had already used her eyes and words to plead with Mr. Spotts, but he wasn't buying. Nor was he in the least concerned for her. He kept glancing at Velázquez's infanta, his eyes aflame with a maniacal kind of greed.

"Can you imagine what it was like, my dear," he was saying, "devoting my entire life to providing rich collectors with the paintings *I* loved, which *I* cherished, and which *I* needed to possess? No, of course you can't. You are far too young and still an idealist. But wait a few decades, and maybe then you'll understand. Oh, yes! You'll come to *loathe* those *nouveau-riche* culture vultures who can't tell a Rembrandt from a Rubens!"

Kenzie shut her ears to the warbly diatribe. She kept thinking, *This can't be happening. If I pinch myself, I'll wake up and discover it's only a nightmare.*

For this was not the kindly A. Dietrich Spotts she'd once worked with, that gallant, polite gentleman of the old school.

This A. Dietrich Spotts was clearly unbalanced, and had to have been one of the masterminds behind this terror-ridden night.

"You played your part well, Kenzie," he told her. "If you hadn't hired Annalisa, we would never have managed to smuggle the weapons in."

Kenzie said sharply, *"No!* You are *not* going to hang any of this on *me."*

And the SWAT commander called out, "Drop your weapons and let the ladies go. It's over. You're surrounded."

Mr. Spotts cackled. "Oh, no. It *isn't* over. Not by a long shot."

Charley and the sharpshooter peered around the corner, then swiftly slammed back out of sight.

Goddammit! Charley growled to himself. *Why can't they move? We need to get clear shots!*

Mr. Spotts raised his quavery, thin voice. "We want our choice of ten paintings. Also, twenty million dollars in cash, transportation to the airport, and a waiting jet. You have one hour to arrange it, or . . ." His voice trailed off.

Kenzie stared at him. "You're crazy! You'll never get away with this!"

"But we *are* getting away with it, my dear, we *are!*" he crowed, leaning his face right into hers and spraying spittle.

Kenzie's reflex was automatic—she winced and jerked her head aside.

Charley and the sharpshooter, sneaking another quick glance, mouthed, "Now!" And raising their weapons, they simultaneously pulled the triggers.

The bullets hit Mr. Spotts and Annalisa squarely in the forehead, killing them instantly. They both let their weapons drop and then fell, their heads striking the wooden dais with sickening thuds.

"Charley!" Kenzie screamed. *"Charley!"*

But he was already rushing forward, sweeping her up in his arms and twirling her around in midair.

"It's over, babe," he murmured softly when he set her back down. "God, but I love you!" He cupped her face in his hands. "I didn't even realize how much until I thought I might lose you!" He kissed her passionately, then enveloped her in his strong arms and held her close.

The three doors of the gallery were suddenly thrown open and EMS personnel trotted in with collapsible gurneys. The ones in the lead headed straight for the painting storeroom.

"Ladies and gentlemen," the SWAT commander announced, "you can leave now. If you'll take it slowly—"

He could have saved his breath. There was a mad rush for the doors.

Only Charley, Kenzie, and Dina remained where they were.

Dina, weak-kneed and wobbly, sat down on the edge of the dais.

Robert lumbered forward. "You aw right?" he asked, showing uncharacteristic concern.

"I-I think so, sweetie. But I could use some Xanax. It's in my purse."
He lumbered back to their seats to fetch it.

"Well?" Charley was asking Kenzie. "Does the hero still get the girl?"

She sighed with exasperation. "Charley, how many times do I have to tell you? The hero *always* gets the girl. Hasn't tonight taught you anything?"

"Like what?"

"Like, the only thing that matters are happily ever afters?"

She took off Hannes's jacket, and a thin, square plastic object with push buttons fell out of a pocket. The moment it hit the dais, the beeper in "Jones's" belt emitted a bleat.

Dina jumped to her feet. "What the—?" She stared around in terror.

Kenzie slowly bent down to retrieve the object. She pressed one of the buttons.

"Jones's" beeper sounded again.

"My God," she exclaimed softly. "This is Hannes's jacket! He lent it to me. Charley?"

"I have to go find him." He turned to go.

She took hold of his arm. "I don't think you need to hurry."

"Why?"

"Because something tells me you'll never catch him. I bet you anything he slipped the gadget into this pocket on purpose."

"But why would he—"

"To tell us. Not to thumb his nose, just to let us know. Like leaving a calling card."

"I'm still gonna have to put out an APB on him."

"If that's what you have to do, fine." She wrapped her arms around him. "But not before you give me one more nice big kiss."

They were too wrapped up in each other to notice the EMS gurney with Zandra and the baby rolling past. Karl-Heinz was hurrying alongside it, and Sofia and Erwein were trying to keep up.

"But . . . but that's *impossible!*" Sofia was screaming. "You're *lying!*" She was tugging on the tail of Karl-Heinz's jacket. "It's a *plot!* You're all conspiring against me!"

Robert, bringing Dina her purse, stared at Sofia. "What in all hell—?"

"Oh, that," Dina said dismissively. "It's proof, sweetie. That's all."

"Proof?" His bushy eyebrows drew together. "Proof a what?"

And Dina, deciding against her tranquilizers and getting out her compact instead, said: "That all's well that ends even better!"

EPILOGUE

*L*ate morning the following day was crisp and cool. The cerulean sky was dabbed with feathers of clouds, and a brisk ocean breeze had scrubbed the air crystal clear.

Hurrying purposely down Madison Avenue to Burghley's, Kenzie looked up at the sky. *Of all the clouds, there's one only I can see,* she thought with elation. *And that's the cloud I'm on.*

She was on cloud nine.

Yesterday's nightmare was far from forgotten, and she knew it would haunt her for days, weeks, and months to come. Years, even. A hostage crisis wasn't the kind of thing one got over quickly. But good news negated the bad.

Before leaving the apartment, she'd called Lenox Hill. Zandra and the baby—*my godchild!*—were doing splendidly.

Moreover, the hours she and Charley had spent tumbling between the sheets last night, affirming life after staring death in the face, had been the first step in the healing process.

The second would be their appointment at City Hall this afternoon. They weren't exactly going to the chapel, but they *were* getting married.

"We'll meet at City Hall at one," Charley had told her. "Count on it, babe."

Oh, you can, Kenzie thought happily, *you bet your sweet patootie you can!*

And she loved the way he'd put it: "I'm gonna make an honest woman outta you, Kenz."

So trite and old-fashioned, and yet so . . . *so Charley.*

She thought of the things he'd promised her. *A rose garden.* "How's a house in the 'burbs sound? White picket fence? Rug rats? PTA meetings?"

And she could still hear her own laughter. "Well, I don't think I'm ready for the 'burbs and the picket fence, but roses on a *terrace* . . . oh, I might be able to live with that."

One o'clock. City Hall.

Kenzie tried out variations of her new name, saying them softly as she walked: "Mrs. MacKenzie Ferraro . . . Mrs. Charles Ferraro . . . Charles and Kenzie . . . Charley and Kenz."

She sailed into Burghley's and headed straight for her office, shutting the door so she wouldn't be disturbed.

For a moment, she just stood there and stared. Smack dab on the center of her desk was the most massive flower arrangement she'd ever seen. She wondered from whom it could be.

She unpinned the little envelope and slipped the card out of it and read:

I'm far from the reach of the long arm, but I expect you have already guessed that.

We won't be meeting again, Kenzie, but what we shared was special.

You added sparkle.

I wish you and Charley the best. Don't get sidetracked, you won't find a better man. Take the plunge, no matter what.

Oh, if Charley is wondering why his car has 240 extra miles on the odometer, I borrowed it a few nights ago.

Hannes

Kenzie smiled and slipped the card into her shoulder bag and began cleaning out her desk. She glanced at her watch and ascertained that it was almost noon.

She'd have to get a move on if she was to meet Charley on time. Meanwhile, she still had her letter of resignation to write.

There was a tentative knock on her door.

"Come in," she called.

Kenzie didn't care who it was. Nothing would deter her from the path she had chosen. No amount of raises or perks could make her stay. She had her own agenda to think about.

I won't end up like poor Mr. Spotts, so obsessed with paintings that nothing else exists. I'm packing up and getting myself a life!

She glanced up as the door opened hesitantly.

A thin old woman in a trench coat with a slouch hat pulled low and big sunglasses over her eyes was standing there.

"Can I help you?" Kenzie asked politely.

"Miss Tarna?"

That voice! Kenzie was momentarily struck speechless, and it was all she could do to nod dumbly.

"Vell? Do you, or do you not vant to come and appraise my collection?" asked Lila Pons.

GOLDMART OWNER TO SHED BURGHLEY'S STOCK

Three Months After Hostage Drama, Goldsmith Packs It In

Special to the New York *Times*

NEW YORK, Feb. 8—Robert A. Goldsmith announced his intention to sell his majority stake in Burghley's, the auction house. The plain-talking, tough-dealing tycoon, best known for GoldMart, Inc., the discount giant, owns 32.5 million shares of Burghley's.

"Retailing is dog-eat-dog, but the auction business is a real killer," he said at a news conference today, wryly referring to last year's hostage drama during the Rebecca de la Vila auction.

He cited various factors having helped influence his decision, including the start-up of Dina's Corner, a new chain of women's apparel shops named after his wife, and a foray into television shopping.

"It's exciting," he said. "I love building something from scratch. It's like giving birth and then watching your baby grow."

And as for Burghley's?

"I'm a discounter at heart," he conceded bluntly. "Burghley's is too rich for my blood. Just too damn rich!"

A NOTE ON THE TEXT

The typeface used in this book is a version of Sabon, originally designed in the 1960s by Jan Tschichold (1902–1974) at the behest of a consortium of manufacturers of metal type. As one who began as an outspoken design revolutionary—calling for the elimination of serifs, scorning revivals of historic typefaces—Tschichold seemed an odd choice, but he met the challenge brilliantly: The typeface was to be based on the fonts of the sixteenth-century French typefounder Claude Garamond but five percent narrower; it had to be identical for three different processes, working around the quirks of each, such as linotype's inability to "kern" (allow one character into the space of another, the way the top of a lowercase f overhangs other letters). Aside from Sabon, named for a sixteenth-century French punch cutter to avoid problems of attribution to Garamond, Tschichold is best remembered as the designer of the Penguin paperbacks of the late 1940s.